Pauline Bentley
as a legal secret
she dreamed of being a writer and indulging her
passion for historical drama. Her first novel was
published in 1987. As a dedicated author she is
meticulous in her research and enjoys visiting historical sites and houses. She now writes full time,
and lives with her husband and two teenage children
in Sussex.

was born in Thurrock. She trained
ny and worked in London, where

Rogues and Players

Pauline Bentley

HEADLINE

Copyright © 1992 Pauline Bentley

The right of Pauline Bentley to be identified as the Author of
the Work has been asserted by her in accordance with the
Copyright, Designs and Patents Act 1988.

First published in 1992
by HEADLINE BOOK PUBLISHING PLC

First published in paperback in 1992
by HEADLINE BOOK PUBLISHING PLC

10   9   8   7   6   5   4   3   2   1

All rights reserved. No part of this publication may be
reproduced, stored in a retrieval system, or transmitted,
in any form or by any means without the prior written
permission of the publisher, nor be otherwise circulated
in any form of binding or cover other than that in which
it is published and without a similar condition being
imposed on the subsequent purchaser.

All characters in this publication are fictitious
and any resemblance to real persons, living or dead,
is purely coincidental.

ISBN 0 7472 3979 7

Phototypeset by Intype, London

Printed and bound in Great Britain by
HarperCollins Manufacturing, Glasgow

HEADLINE BOOK PUBLISHING PLC
Headline House
79 Great Titchfield Street
London W1P 7FN

Dedicated to the memories of John Frost, my father, and John Frost, my brother.

And to Chris, with love.

Chapter One

Chichester, 1588

The sun broke through pewter clouds to gild the octagonal cupola of the market cross. The meeting point of the four streets was choked with a mass of revellers eager for the awaited diversion. Suddenly a cry went up.

'The players are coming. Lord Barpham's Men are coming!'

The announcement was accompanied by a fanfare from a trumpet. Over the crowd's heads two riders dominated the street. One was resplendent in a doublet of cloth of gold and a scarlet cloak, his gold hair lifting from his shoulders in the breeze as graciously he bowed to his audience. This was Cornelius Hope, the leading actor, but it was not upon him the young woman's stare was fixed. It was upon his companion. Older by ten years, his thick hair now receding and greying at the temples, the man's commanding figure filled Gabriellen Angel's heart with pride.

Her adoration was clear in her expression for all to see. When the riders drew level with her, the acclaimed playwright held Gabriellen's rapt gaze. Then, with a flamboyant gesture, he tossed the nosegay of spring flowers he was carrying into her hands. Favouring her with a bold wink, he rode on.

Gabriellen lifted the flowers to her face and inhaled their sweet fragrance as she followed the progress of her father, Esmond Angel.

Ahead of the two riders the rest of the troupe paraded on foot. Poggs the clown danced a jig as he played his pipes. Behind came the two Florentine musicians accompanying him on tabour and guitar, followed by the other actors. There were no more than ten in all, but their presence filled the street. All were dressed in their finest

1

clothes, laughing and waving as they acknowledged the cheers from the crowd.

Throughout the street excitement and expectancy were tangible. It was not just the coming of the players. Today was 23 April, St George's Day. A Fair Day in Chichester, and the townspeople seemed determined to cast aside their fears of the threatened invasion by the Spanish Armada and enjoy themselves.

They began to disperse. The play would not begin until the afternoon and there were other entertainments until then. Gabriellen turned towards Pallant Street and the glover's shop where she lived with her aunt and uncle. It had been two months since her father last visited Chichester. The troupe had only returned for this fair because tomorrow Poggs was marrying her aunt's maid, Agnes.

Gabriellen smothered a twinge of guilt. There was still much work to be done for the wedding feast and she had stolen out of the house to watch the parade. Unintimidated by the rowdy element in the crush, Gabriellen shouldered her way along East Street. At the corner of Pallant Street a cluster of the town's matrons barred the pavement.

'Your pardon, goodwives.' Smiling, she waited for them to move aside. A narrow-faced matriarch tipped back her head to peer at Gabriellen's flushed face. The woman sniffed her disapproval as she glared along her hooked nose, her thin lips compressed into a sneer.

'The Angel wench!' she addressed her companions. 'Out in the street without a chaperon. But then, what else can one expect from that family?'

Gabriellen stiffened and with difficulty checked her rising temper. At sixteen she was a half-head taller than any woman present. 'I would like to pass, goodwives,' she said firmly. 'Would you kindly step aside?'

The woman who had spoken drew aside her stiff brown skirts as though she feared contamination.

Gabriellen's green eyes took on a dangerous light as she held the woman's contemptuous stare. 'Have you something to say, Mistress Reed?'

The matron lowered her gaze from Gabriellen's forthright stare and moved aside. As she crossed the cobbled street to her uncle's house she heard Mistress Reed's high piping voice proclaim: 'Bad blood, the Angels. Did you see the brazenness of her stare? What else can you expect from

2

that devil's brood? There's only one of them received the justice they deserved, and that was Wildboar Tom Angel. They hanged him for the outlaw and rogue he was. The blood is tainted. There's not one of them died respectably in their beds.'

All the pleasure of witnessing her father's parade ebbed from Gabriellen's face. She went white to her lips. Since her father's last visit to Chichester at Christmas, she had begun to be the butt of the matrons' vicious tongues whenever she ventured out of the house unaccompanied by Aunt Dorothy or Uncle Ezekiel Otwell. In their company, no one would dare malign the young woman whom the Otwells had reared for the last twelve years, after Gabriellen's mother had died. Ezekiel Otwell was respected as an Alderman of the town, and in the last few months Gabriellen had been made aware just how great a protection her ties to him were.

Often the name of Wildboar Tom Angel had been hurled in contempt at her. Was he an ancestor? Whenever she broached the subject of her family, her aunt changed the subject.

Gabriellen lifted her chin in a gesture of defiance and her step lengthened purposefully as she approached the timber-framed, double-gabled house and its adjoining shop. If there was an unsavoury stain upon her family's name, she was determined to discover its source.

She paused with her hand on the door latch as she saw her aunt's short, plump figure walking along the street. She carried a wicker basket filled with fish from the market. Gabriellen smiled in greeting and waited until they had entered the house before saying abruptly, 'Who was Wildboar Tom Angel?'

'Not now, my dear,' Aunt Dorothy began. 'I must see how Agnes and Cissy are coping with the cooking. There's so much to do for the feast tomorrow.'

'Was he an outlaw? A rogue as the people say?' Gabriellen persisted. There had been something sinister in Mistress Reed's scorn which went deeper than spite. 'Was Wildboar related to us?'

There was no doubt that her questions had flustered her aunt. Dorothy Otwell was in her late forties, and despite her diminutive height and plumpness, an authoritative figure. But now her expression was wary. For a moment

3

there was silence in the dim, unlit hallway. A mouse squeaked behind the wainscot, and beneath Gabriellen's scrutiny her aunt ran a finger along the inside of her starched ruff.

'Really, Gabby my dear, this is no time for idle chatter.' Dorothy refused to meet her niece's challenging stare. That young face which was more striking than beautiful was strong-willed. Nothing would gainsay her. If Gabriellen Angel exerted herself, she could enchant anyone. Confidences and indiscretions were drawn as easily from the unwitting, as was the fascination won by her dimpled smile. Those who knew Gabriellen well, adored her. They also respected the tell-tale glitter in her eyes which warned of an approaching broadside should her temper be roused – a temper inherited from her notorious forefathers.

Dorothy fidgeted with her gloves, equally determined not to answer her niece's question. It always upset her to hear the old rumours about her family revived, as they always were when her brother Esmond was in town. Violent deaths seemed to be the family legacy, caused by a wildness in their blood. Such wildness could blight a life. Her niece's headstrong ways must be curbed.

Clearing her throat, Dorothy evaded the issue. 'I'm all overset, my dear. Some vagabond tried to cut my purse. When I beat him off, the knave knocked me to the ground.'

'Were you hurt?' Gabriellen asked, contrite that she had been insensitive to her aunt's distress, for she loved her dearly.

'I was just shaken.' Then Dorothy continued at a rapid pace, forestalling any interruption, 'As if that was not enough, you cannot imagine the trouble I had getting fresh herring for Mr Otwell, or the insolence I suffered whilst haggling with the fishwife. Her prices were nothing short of robbery. I threatened to summon the constable and have her put in the stocks.'

Gabriellen checked her impatience. She knew Dorothy could not be halted once in full tongue.

'And why should we pay such prices?' her aunt declared. 'I tell you, the Spaniards have frightened those fool fishermen witless. All winter and spring there's been talk of this so-called Armada preparing to invade England. Yet where are they after two years amassing their fleet? Holed up in some port across the water, while we grow more fearful

4

by the day. There's nights I cannot sleep for feeling the Inquisition's fires licking my feet.'

Gabriellen resigned herself to her aunt's evasion as she followed her through a door leading to the inner courtyard. At their approach a sparrow bathing in the shallow pool of the fountain flew up on to the new golden thatch of an outbuilding. Gabriellen kept pace with her aunt, her curiosity as to the mystery surrounding Wildboar still burning like a red hot ember in her mind. She would allow her aunt's tongue to run its course. Her own time would come – when they were alone. Then she would insist on the truth.

'It's the storms that have kept the fishermen at home and the Spanish trapped in Lisbon,' Gabriellen reasoned with deceptive sweetness.

Dorothy Otwell snapped back, 'And by what right does King Philip seek to invade our shores? England never accepted him as more than Queen Mary's consort. It was a sorry day when young King Edward died,' she expounded, her ruff quivering with the force of her mounting anger. 'When I think of the suffering that She-devil . . . that heretic-burning Catholic, Mary Tudor brought to England.' Dorothy shuddered. 'Her reign was five years of terror. And it stirred up a nest bed of vipers. Daily, I give thanks for the day Elizabeth succeeded her.'

Dorothy moved on towards the kitchen. Would her aunt never stop this diatribe? A look at Dorothy's flushed face warned her that she was far from finished upon the subject.

'Not that Elizabeth's reign has been without its storms,' Dorothy continued. 'There's been many plots on our Queen's life.' In her agitation she inadvertently began to cross herself. She stopped with a snort of disgust. 'I've my stepmother to thank for these plaguey Papist gestures. Even after all these years, I catch myself genuflecting. Much good her piety did us!'

Her mouth hardened with bitter memories. It had always irked Gabriellen that Dorothy would never speak of her childhood. Any reminder of it brought a look of pain and misery to her kindly aunt's eyes. It was back now.

Compassion won over resolution and Gabriellen changed the subject. 'Did you see Father while you were out?' At her aunt's guarded look, she could not resist teasing, 'He's not in trouble with the city authorities, is he? Or perhaps

5

he's been fighting again? His troupe were parading through the streets to attract customers to the play.'

They had entered the kitchen where the two servants, Agnes and Cissy, were busy at work.

'Gabriellen!' Dorothy glared from her niece to the servants, defying them to spread such outrageous gossip. 'My brother does not brawl! What put such a notion in your head?'

Gabriellen checked a grin. How stoutly Dorothy defended Esmond Angel. Yet he must be the bane of her prim and orderly life. Only last winter Uncle Ezekiel had been called out to intercede with the constable when Esmond had been arrested in a tavern fight. From the hushed conversations she had overheard between her aunt and uncle, she had learned this was not the first such occurrence. But then, Esmond was a man of fire and vision. He did not act as other men. In Gabriellen's eyes her father could do no wrong. He was her hero. There was no one to match Esmond for wit, personality or sheer presence.

'Dear Aunt Dotty,' she said with a smile, a dimple appearing by her mouth. If she could get her aunt alone she could broach the subject of Wildboar Tom Angel again. 'You're exhausted from haggling with the fishwives. Your brush with the cut-purse has upset you. Let me take your basket and put away the shopping. Shall I bring you some mulled wine while you rest in the parlour?'

'Rest in the parlour! Upon my word, niece, what time have I to sit in the parlour?' She nodded across the kitchen to the tall woman whose long thin body was doubled over as she plucked a goose for the feast. 'Tomorrow is Agnes's wedding. There is still much to be done.'

Gabriellen could have screamed with vexation. It would be some while before she could be alone with her aunt to question her, but nothing of her scalding curiosity showed in Gabriellen's face as Dorothy disappeared into the adjoining buttery. Years of training by her aunt, served her well as she mastered her impatience. Outwardly, she acted and spoke as a gentlewoman, but there were times – when her temper or impatience ran high – that her willpower was tested to its limits.

Her aunt's favourite rejoinder ran through her head. 'You are an Angel, Gabriellen. Never be ashamed of it. You have the right to hold your head as high as anyone.'

Gabriellen was proud enough to believe in those sentiments, but she was not one to stand upon airs and graces – if she saw herself the equal of any woman, or man, she certainly never considered herself better than her fellows. She masked her impatience with a serene expression. Whatever her mood, she could master it, and give a performance as superb as any one of her father's company of players.

Gabriellen turned her attention to Agnes. Since Poggs, the jester of her father's troupe, had proposed to the servant during his visit here at Christmas, Agnes had shed her customary shyness, happiness softening her gaunt face.

'Not long before you'll be doing that round your own campfire, Agnes. How do you feel about the months you will spend travelling the country?'

'I don' mind the hardship. Not with Poggs at my side,' the maid answered without breaking her rhythm.

The servant shifted the weight of the goose from her lame leg which was beginning to ache. Although she was a dozen years older than her young mistress, she would miss Gabriellen when she left here. She frowned and pushed a lock of brown hair back under her plain linen cap. 'But once I'm gone, who'll watch over thy headstrong ways, Miss Gabby? I fear Mistress Otwell is too soft-hearted.'

'Have I been a trial to you, Agnes?' Gabriellen teased.

'Truth to tell, Miss Gabby, at times thee have.' Agnes regarded her solemnly, her straight brows drawn together. She knew she was speaking out of turn for a servant, but she cared for Gabriellen. Nay, loved her with all the possessiveness of a woman who, once abused by her masters, had been denied friendship by others of her sex. 'But I wouldn't change it, though I fear for thee – when that wilful streak takes hold. Thee don't always guard against it as thee should. Though many men will find such spirit irresistible. As they will thy proud beauty.'

Gabriellen laughed aside the compliment. 'One thing I am not and that is a beauty. My eyes are too large and my mouth too wide. Besides, I'm too tall.'

Agnes shook her head. Modesty was part of Gabriellen's charm and no one could accuse her of vanity. From Agnes's height of almost six foot, Gabriellen at a handspan shorter was graceful and lithe, even if she was as tall as the average man. And although her young mistress did not have the ample curves of a voluptuous beauty, there was an arresting quality about her face, an inner light shining through, showing not only a passion for life but a deep sensitivity which drew people's eyes to her time and again.

It was that sensitivity which disturbed Agnes and made her fear for Gabriellen. Yet the young mistress was no fool. She had a strong mind and knew how to use it. Perhaps she was being over-protective? Agnes pushed aside her misgivings, saying meaningfully, 'I dare say it will be thy wedding I'll be dancing at within a year.'

'I doubt it. There's no one in Chichester I would set my cap at.' Gabriellen laughed, unconcerned at her unmarried state. No man had stirred her heart. Yet she often dreamt of her ideal suitor. A man who was handsome, bold and dashing, who was quick-witted and had carved his own destiny, a man very much his own master – a man like her father. She smiled at the servant and smothered a pang of sadness. 'I'll miss you, Agnes. And I envy you the freedom to travel the country as part of my father's troupe.'

A derisive snort from Cissy Tanfield, the cook, greeted her remark. 'Bain't no better than vagabonds, they strolling players be, I says.' Cissy slapped down two hares on the table with such force it set the flabby flesh on her arms shaking. 'I don't know what Mistress Otwell will say to such nonsense.'

Agnes stopped her plucking to look anxiously at Gabriellen. 'Don't thee let the mistress hear thee talk so. 'Twould grieve her sorely. 'Tis a hard life. Thy father wants better for thee.'

'I know, and Aunt Dotty deserves better after all her years of kindness. But it must be an exciting life.' Gabriellen failed to check her yearning. Her face showed the demure smile of a gently reared merchant's daughter, but her heart rebelled, craving another life. None of her aunt's teachings could stifle her longing to travel. She wanted to see the cities her father had spoken of. More than that, she wanted to be a part of the world created by the players.

'A life of shame!' said Cissy, spitefully. 'But then, what else should one expect from an Angel? Devil's brood, the lot of 'em. Once tainted with an outlaw's blood, I says, always tainted. Why, I could tell you . . .'

'Cissy!' Aunt Dorothy, her plump face white with fury, emerged from the buttery. 'You talk too much. There's work to be done.'

8

Gabriellen followed her aunt back into the buttery. 'What did Cissy mean? Did she speak of Wildboar Tom Angel?'

'Pay no heed to Cissy. She's a born gossip.'

Before Gabriellen could ask the questions leaping to her mind, Dorothy held out her hands which were shaking. 'Look at my nerves – all overset. It's all this talk in the market of the Spanish.'

She walked past the girl into the kitchen to unlock the spice chest. Gabriellen knew it was a deliberate ploy to evade further questions.

'A murrain on King Philip and his scaremongering!' Dorothy continued her invective against the Spanish. 'Now that the head is off the Scottish Queen, I thought England free of Catholic Plots.'

'Don' Philip know we don' want the likes of him ruling us?' Cissy snorted, throwing the hares' intestines into a bucket and wiping her bloody hands on her apron.

Agnes stopped her plucking, and frowned. 'Myself, I never understood the half of it. Didn't thee tell me, Miss Gabby, that the execution of the Queen of Scots would end the hopes of Spain and France to see England restored to the Catholic faith?'

'Yes, Agnes. But King Philip now sees himself as God's instrument to stamp out heresy.' Gabriellen took a moment to explain, knowing that the servant liked to understand these things.'That's why the King of Spain will strike.'

'To behead a queen was no light matter.' Dorothy sounded relieved that the subject was safely away from any family outlaw.

Gabriellen sighed. Her aunt would not be stopped now that she had warmed to her favourite subject.

'That foolish queen had only herself to blame.' Dorothy's lips compressed in prim warning as she looked up at her niece. 'I heard you talk of joining Esmond's players. It's out of the question. There's a lesson to be learned from Mary of Scots.'

'I know the story, Aunt.'

'Then heed it, Gabriellen. When Mary Stuart returned a widow to Scotland,' Dorothy pursued, ignoring the interruption, 'she received a chill reception from her Protestant lords. No wonder she turned her eyes upon England. She met her match in Elizabeth Tudor. Cousin or not to our queen, Mary Stuart never forgot she was also the granddaughter of Henry VII. And the vain, foolish creature, encouraged by her Catholic followers, saw herself as the true heir – and Elizabeth a bastard. We were well spared the woman.'

'Amen to that, I says,' Cissy sneered, her hands ripping one hare's skin from its flesh. 'Mary Stuart couldna govern her own life, let alone England. And she were a harlot. After her marriage to Darnley, she took up with that rogue Bothwell.'

Dorothy silenced the servant with a chilling look for presuming to interrupt her. 'It is said that Mary and Bothwell planned Darnley's murder at Kirk-o'-Field where he was ill with the pox. If these crimes were not great enough, within three months Mary had married Bothwell and alienated every Scottish lord.'

'The poor lady had an ill-fated life,' Gabriellen countered. 'It was true she loved unwisely, but who can govern the will of their own heart?'

Dorothy shut the spice chest with a bang, saying, 'Mary Stuart was a wilful, headstrong woman – and she came to a tragic end.'

Gabriellen's patience wore thin. All this talk of the Scottish Queen had been her aunt's way of warning her against her own headstrong nature. What had she done now? She could think of no misdemeanour which would have put her aunt in such a taking.

Clearly out of countenance, Dorothy raised her voice at Agnes. 'Is that goose ready for trussing?'

'I'm just finishing,' Agnes answered apologetically as Dorothy disappeared back into the buttery.

Cissy Tanfield whined, 'As if we don' have enough work to do normal days. An' now all this extra cooking because 'ee be getting married. 'Twill be the death of me, I says. An' 'ee, lazy slut, jus' sit there jabbering an' doin' naught.'

'I'm sorry, Cissy.' Agnes bent her head, a cloud of white feathers wafting around her head as her fingers worked frantically upon the half-plucked bird.

Gabriellen, even though she had been working since first light, looked round for more to do. Through the doorway of the buttery she saw Dorothy checking the pastry dishes which were prepared but awaited baking. Again she curbed her curiosity.

Dorothy turned to regard her niece and felt the familiar

10

tug of love for the girl, even as her gaze ran critically over her slender figure. The determined set of Gabriellen's chin alerted her that she was but biding her time before once more broaching the subject of Wildboar Tom Angel. Perhaps it was time she learned the truth about her infamous ancestors.

Clearing her throat, Dorothy pushed her niece towards the stairs, her voice sharp. 'Why have you not changed? The play will start in an hour. What will your father say if we arrive late and miss his prologue? You know he sets store by your opinion of his work. Though such nonsense it all is! What life is it, wandering the countryside with a band of strolling players? At two and forty he should know better. 'Tis no life for a gentleman. For what Esmond Angel forgets is, he was born a gentleman!'

Gabriellen paused at the foot of the stairs, instantly defensive at any slur upon her father's character, even if it was by his own sister. 'Father loves his life. Would you change him? Especially now that his plays are so well received. He's beginning to make a name for himself. I'm proud of him.'

'You know what they say about pride, Gabriellen – it usually goes before a fall. Upstairs with you. I'll help you change your gown since Agnes cannot be spared from the kitchen.'

Behind her, the wooden stairs creaked under her aunt's weight and the gentle swish of long skirts accompanied their path along the oak-beamed passage. Once in her chamber Gabriellen emptied the ewer into a pewter basin standing on a coffer, slipped the plain linen day gown from her shoulders and washed her face and arms, the cold water refreshing after the heat of the kitchen.

She did not want to upset her aunt with questions, for she owed her so much. From the age of four, after her mother died giving birth to a stillborn son, this had been her home. Aunt Dorothy had raised her: lavished love upon her; grown angry when she got into mischief, which was often; wept when her wilfulness must be punished; and had seen that her father's wishes were obeyed, and that she was attended by a tutor daily. Everything she had accomplished had been through her aunt's and uncle's endeavours. Her life had lacked for nothing – except the adventure she craved.

After drying herself, she swung round to face Dorothy, her voice resolute. 'Now we are alone, will you please tell me of Wildboar? Why is it you never speak of our family?'

Dorothy sighed. 'You're sixteen now and a woman grown. Perhaps you should know. Let their misfortunes be a warning to you.' Her face became drawn as she took her niece's discarded gown and, crossing to the clothes press, lifted a bell-shaped cane farthingale from its hook. 'Angels by name – devils by nature. That was the reputation of our kinfolk. Even the women were not spared the wildness in their blood. It brought many to their downfall. People kindly disposed to us called our kin adventurers. Others, less charitable, named them rogues, outlaws, philanderers – even murderers.'

'Father is none of those!' Gabriellen loyally protested.

There was sadness in Dorothy's answering smile. 'Esmond has his own devil riding him. He was a high-spirited youth. When our stepmother remarried after your grandfather's death, she sent Esmond to London as clerk to a lawyer. It was the worst thing that could have happened to him.' She appeared to be talking to herself as she handed Gabriellen the farthingale and added, 'All the heartache and suffering that caused . . .'

She cut off her words abruptly, the drooping of her shoulders warning Gabriellen that some ghost from the past troubled her.

The pain and frustration in her aunt's voice upset Gabriellen, who was always considerate of others' feelings. But she sensed this was too important to let sentiment stand in her way. 'And Wildboar?' she prompted. 'I'm sorry if it pains you to speak of it, but do I not have a right to know?'

Dorothy pressed a shaking hand to her brow, refusing to meet Gabriellen's stare. 'I will tell you,' she said heavily. 'But you must dress, else we shall be late for the play.'

Once the farthingale was in place over her hips, Gabriellen curbed her curiosity whilst a roll of bombast, which would shape the heavy folds of her gown, was tied over it. It was impossible to speak whilst the six layers of petticoats cascaded over her head, the last of which was an embroidered scarlet brocade. Breathing heavily from her exertions, Dorothy handed Gabriellen the fawn, slit-fronted overskirt, as she forced out,'May our family history be a warning to you. For you can be headstrong.'

Dorothy paused for effect, fixing Gabriellen with an anxious stare. She saw all too clearly beneath the demure countenance of her niece to the volatile, self-willed woman Gabriellen tried hard to suppress. There was loyalty, honesty, and a great capacity for loving in those expressive green eyes. And were not the Angel family renowned for their ill-fated love affairs? May the Good Lord spare Gabriellen from the caprices of the heart.

During her aunt's pause Gabriellen slid her arms into the bodice of her gown and suppressed a shiver of foreboding.

Aunt Dorothy said, 'Many have called us demons' seed. Do they not say that bad blood breeds bad blood and it will always out in the end? Be warned, and guard against your destiny. There are those who say we are damned by the blood of our ancestor – the outlaw Wildboar Tom Angel. He lived in the Weald not far from here. He was the bastard son of a knight and the wife of a yeoman. Little is known of his early years. Rumour has it he was raised by the church. From a young man he was often in trouble with the law. He earned the name Wildboar with cause. A head taller than most men, and so strong he could bend an iron bar as thick as a man's wrist, he used to wrestle wildboars for the devil of it. Killed four of them with his bare hands,' Dorothy went on. 'But the temper of Lucifer and arrogance to match were his undoing. In his mid-twenties Wildboar fell in love with a young nun. By then he considered that he was a law unto himself. He abducted the nun and seduced her.'

At the astonishment on Gabriellen's face, Aunt Dorothy gave a bitter smile. Taking a starched ruff from a coffer she tied it around her niece's neck and added, 'It sounds like something Esmond could have written, but it's the truth.'

'What happened to the nun?' Gabriellen urged, impatient to learn everything.

'She died in childbirth whilst Wildboar was away raiding a farm of its cattle. The child lived. If Wildboar had been a scoundrel before, the death of the nun drove him to unspeakable crimes. In his grief, for he truly loved the woman, he became uncontrollable. He terrorised the neighbourhood with his stealing and wild, drunken ways. They say he killed two men for calling the nun a whore. He was eventually caught and hanged at Lewes.'

13

The ruff felt like a noose tightening about her neck, and Gabriellen unwittingly gagged as the ties bit into her throat.

Instantly it was loosened to a comfortable fit, and Dorothy continued: 'And that was just the beginning. The bastard child of that union was my grandfather who for many years was fostered by woodcutters. He took up a life of soldiering. Despite his scars, he could charm any wench to his bed. When he got a mercer's daughter with child, he married her. Her dowry brought him a grand house in the centre of Portsmouth. He spent much of his time in London where he had business interests. He was killed in a sword-fight over another man's doxy. After his death it was discovered that he had left a fortune in gold and some property in London.'

Gabriellen widened her eyes in astonishment. 'I had not realised my ancestors were such rake-hells. Were they all scoundrels?'

'They have Wildboar's blood in them. Even my father. Some would say he was a wastrel – always drinking and gambling. Somehow, Father kept the creditors at bay, but I suspect many of his dealings had little to do with honest business. His body was found in the Thames one morning with a knife in its back. The London property was inherited by Esmond.' Dorothy's eyes grew wary as she added, 'Does your father never talk to you about that side of his life?'

Gabriellen shook her head, but at once made excuses for her father. 'I had no idea he had property in London. He speaks only of his life with the players. Although he has told me of the great St Bartholomew's Fair held at Smithfield each year and, of course, of last year when he was summoned to Court to present his play to the Queen.' She frowned. 'Perhaps he feels that nothing else is important, but the life he has chosen with the players?'

'Just wishing to forget that which is unpleasant does not make it go away.' Dorothy looked at her fiercely. 'Be forewarned about your blood, my dear, and you may yet spare yourself grief and pain. Especially take care you do not love unwisely. You are very like my sister Sophia.'

Gabriellen started in surprise. 'I thought you and my father were my only relatives.'

'Sophia died twenty years ago, aged eighteen. She ran off with a gypsy lover who later abandoned her. To support her child, she first sold her hair, then her body. Esmond found her in London, so badly beaten by one of her clients that she was dying. The child had not survived the first winter.'

The shocking tale made Gabriellen reel and she bowed her head against the horror of Sophia's fate. 'A tragic story,' she said, hoarsely. 'But every family has its black sheep. Ours seem to have paid dearly for their folly.

'I know Father has had his share of suffering,' she continued, recalling what she already knew. 'He grieved sorely when my mother died so young, but he has found happiness with his plays. Though he is overfond of his wine . . .' she forced a tremulous smile, 'surely his wild days are behind him?'

'In truth, I fear for Esmond,' Dorothy said heavily. 'There is a side of his life of which he never speaks and it troubles me. He has his own ghosts to lay, shows little of what he feels to others. For all I love him dearly, he still has the Angel wildness in him. He was born with the silver tongue of a rogue, and few women can resist him.' She folded Gabriellen's discarded gown. 'At least this playwrighting nonsense seems to have tempered him somewhat. But where will it end, all this consorting with vagabonds and the like? I shudder to think.'

'It's the life Father loves. And sometimes I envy him the freedom of the road.'

'Heavens, child!' Dorothy threw up her arms in alarm. 'Don't ever say that. It is not the place for a respectable woman. Look to what an end life on the road brought Sophia. It's a hard, sometimes violent living. Esmond does not tell you of the squalor of flea-ridden inns where he has to sleep, or the number of times his troupe has been stoned out of a town on the suspicion of theft or some other misdemeanour.'

'Agnes has no misgivings about taking up the life when she marries Poggs tomorrow. He has been the clown of Father's troupe for years and will never leave.'

'Agnes is no innocent girl,' Aunt Dorothy cut in sharply. 'The poor creature had a terrible life before Mr Otwell found her half-dead in some village stocks. She has a deal of common sense. At least with her in the company, Esmond will have a decent meal in his belly. As for Poggs, he may be a strange sort of creature, always playing the fool – but he has a heart of gold. He'll treat Agnes like a princess. And if ever a woman deserved to be loved, it's that one. Mr Otwell has a way of taking in waifs and strays. Agnes's story is a sad one, but that would be for her to tell you, not I. It's my reason, albeit against my better judgement, for saying nothing to keep her here. But such a life is not for you.'

Dorothy stood back from settling the heart-shaped French cap over Gabriellen's dusky gold hair. She studied her niece's oval face, with its light dusting of freckles across a nose which tipped up impishly at the end. The high cheekbones and pointed chin were more arresting than beautiful. Those large green eyes, slanted and provocative, were the legacy of Wildboar Tom. Her throat worked to dislodge a lump of fear. Would Gabriellen be spared her family's fate? It would take an exceptional man to curb her wilfulness. A man who loved her, but could not be swayed by the false promise of a dimpled smile.

'With this wedding in the offing, it makes me realise that a husband must be found for you.' Dorothy was resolved. 'I will speak to Esmond. Master Goodwyn's son, Simon, has shown an interest in you. The son of our lawyer would be a suitable match.'

'I've no interest in Simon,' Gabriellen protested. 'He's stoop-shouldered and as sallow-skinned as a boiled rabbit. And, worse, he hasn't a grain of humour. It would be like being wedded to a corpse.'

Dorothy felt her lips twitch with amusement, and somehow managed to keep her voice serious. The girl was right. 'Simon Goodwyn may not be the ideal choice, but I will speak to Esmond. It is time your future was settled. You spend too long woolgathering when you think I'm not watching. And don't think I didn't know you were up at first light riding Esmond's stallion, when any decent woman would still have been abed.'

'Father accompanied me on Sable. He said I could ride Socrates.'

Dorothy sniffed her disapproval. 'Gentlewomen do not ride stallions. It is . . . immodest.'

'Then they are very foolish and must lead incredibly boring lives.'

Those impulsive words showed Dorothy how little effect her teachings had upon her headstrong niece. Always, just below the serene grace, was a soul craving excitement and adventure. It boded ill, Dorothy was certain.

Seeing her aunt's plucked brows draw together, Gabriellen suspected a lecture was forthcoming. There was her father's play and Agnes's wedding to look forward to. As the notes of a horn carried to them from a nearby inn, she snatched at the chance of the escape offered her.

'That's Poggs announcing that the play is soon to begin. Make haste, Aunt Dotty, we must not miss the start.'

17

Chapter Two

Dorothy Otwell gave the kitchen one last check before leaving for the play. The bread was set out to cool on the table and covered with a cloth, its warm yeasty smell mingling with that of the bunches of dried herbs hanging by the window. The fire in the grate had been allowed to die down to a dull glow and the heat had drained from the high-ceilinged brick room. Where Agnes had just finished scrubbing the smooth flagstones, one or two pools of water remained.

Satisfied, she moved towards the parlour. The household keys, which hung from a gilt chain at her waist, jangled together against her grey velvet skirt as she walked. The sound was as reassuring as it was familiar. Their house, with Mr Otwell's adjoining glover's shop, was one of the finest in Chichester, and Dorothy was proud of her status as the wife of a town Alderman.

The parlour did her justice. Everything was in its place, the silver, oak chests and settle polished so that she could see her face in them. A fresh layer of herb-scented rushes covered the floor and there was not a cobweb in sight amongst the low timber beams of the ceiling. Not that any room in her house was allowed to be other than spotless. Organising the endless household tasks kept her restless moods at bay. If at times she felt stifled by the routine of her life and envied Esmond the freedom and adventure he had found, no one ever guessed. Long ago she had learned to control the waywardness of those desires. On the day of her marriage she had vowed to be a good wife to Mr Otwell, for she loved the gentle glovemaker. It was part of the decorum she adopted that made her address him with such formality, even during the intimacies shared within the marriage bed. Mr Otwell had given her security and love.

It was disloyal to crave the excitement her Angel blood occasionally demanded.

Through the plaster wall which backed on to the work-room of the shop came the sound of muffled laughter from the apprentices. The ringing of the shop bell had taken Gabriellen next door to serve a customer. Her niece jested too freely with the boys, encouraging them to slackness. Dorothy frowned. Where was her husband? Mr Otwell should have returned from the hiring fair two hours past. If he did not arrive soon they would miss the play.

At that moment the latch rattled on the front door. Doro-thy hurried into the hall to greet her husband. Her relief was short-lived, but she hid her disappointment as she regarded the stick-thin girl standing at Mr Otwell's side. The new servant could not be more than thirteen. Here was yet another of Mr Otwell's 'Unfortunates', as he called them. The girl looked half-starved, her clothes filthy rags which would have to be burned at once. And her hair was a fright, all matted and dirty. When the girl absently scratched at her scalp, Dorothy suppressed a shiver of dis-taste. She was probably alive with lice!

'This is Mary Fisher. She will take over Agnes's duties,' Mr Otwell announced. He drew the girl forward and Doro-thy caught the stench of unwashed flesh and rank clothing. Even from here she could see that the thin dirty wrists were reddened by flea bites. Then she saw the pallor beneath the dirt, the eyes wide with uncertainty and fear, and her maternal instincts took over.

'Come with me, Mary. We must find you more suitable clothes. Have you eaten today?'

A nervous shake of the head broke down the last of Dorothy's reservations. 'You poor lamb. You will eat in the courtyard whilst the water is heated for a bath. And something must be done with your hair.'

The girl swayed and clutched hold of the wall for support.

'Are you ill, Mary?' Dorothy asked, all concern.

Mr Otwell removed his hat, his high-domed bald head dented from its tight brim. He was fifty-four and apart from the loss of hair, had the smooth-faced appearance of a man a dozen years younger. 'The poor child is worn out. She's walked fifty miles to the hiring fair. She wanted to

19

get far away from her last master. The man was a brute.'
He turned the girl's head to one side to reveal a large purple
bruise down one cheek. 'She's covered in marks like that.
After a few good meals and a day or so's rest, she will be
the hardest working servant we could wish for. Or so the
lass tells me.'

'I don' mind hard work,' Mary cried. 'Please don' 'ee
send me away. I'm stronger than I look.'

'Why should I send you away?' Dorothy smiled across
at her husband, who was looking guilty. On his departure
she had insisted he employ a strong woman for the work.
She should have realised he would take pity on the weakest
and most vulnerable he encountered. He was a kind-hearted
man and now he suffered, fearing he had displeased her.
Her loving glance took in his wiry figure dressed in its sober
brown and a narrow plain ruff. She would not change him.

'This is your home, Mary,' she went on. 'Do your work
well and you will not find us hard taskmasters. But I do
insist upon cleanliness in your appearance. I shall help you
bathe and see you are settled in your room before I go out.'

'But the play, my dear?' Mr Otwell was apologetic. 'You
were looking forward to seeing it. Mary can eat and then
wait in her room until you return.'

'Not in that condition, she cannot.' Dorothy unbuttoned
her lace-edged cuffs and began to turn back her padded
sleeves. 'Do you want the entire household infested with
fleas and lice? I shall be in time for the last act. That will
pacify Esmond. It's Gabriellen's advice he takes note of,
not mine. You will accompany your niece, Mr Otwell.'

Gabriellen leaned forward on her stool, her hand gripping
the rail of the inn gallery as she watched the players on the
stage. The wooden segments of the raised platform were
supported on sturdy trestles at one end of the inn yard.
They had taken all morning to be erected by the troupe's
carpenter. An undyed linen curtain hung across it as a
backdrop where the players made their entrances and exits.
The only props were a faded day bed and a carved wooden
chest. It was the magic of the words which displayed the
passion and torment of the characters, together with a brilli-
antly staged fight scene, that had captivated Gabriellen and
the audience.

When her father staggered to the front of the platform,

one hand clutching at the dagger apparently embedded in his chest, the tension in the crowded open-air courtyard was palpable. Gabriellen's breath caught in her throat, her eyes wide and spellbound as the play reached its climax.

Esmond sank to the floor, his free hand outstretched to the woman's corpse crumpled at his side as he delivered his death speech. Silence fell over the audience. Then a well-aimed cabbage hit Cornelius Hope, the leading actor, on the arm, to a cry of: 'Take that, you murderin' villain!'

The silence erupted into a thunderous roar of shouts and whistles as the groundlings demanded the death of the villain, so caught up were they in the tragedy they had witnessed.

Gabriellen blinked away tears of pride as the three leading actors came forward to take their bow. At the same time she saw the carpenter, a boy actor apprentice, and the two musicians moving amongst the rowdy audience seated on benches or standing against the sides of the stage. When they played at inns like this which were filled with travellers, there was no way of charging the usual penny for admission as the audience arrived. The actors were dependent on collecting what they could whilst their audience still revelled in the spectacle they had just seen.

Several scuffles broke out below as Cornelius was taking his bow. Amongst the audience, the merchants, farmers and rougher soldiers and apprentices were game for the cut-purses and whores who plied their own trades amongst the crowd.

Then, above the sound of their squabbling, rose the jaunty notes of a flute. The curtain was swept back to reveal a bandy-legged man scarcely five foot high, dressed in purple and gold. Under cover of this diversion, the players left the stage. With the flute to his mouth and the tune quickening its rhythm, Poggs leapt and whirled around the stage, his steps a mixture of the galliard, jig and morris dance. Leaping higher and higher, and spinning ever faster, he drove the audience to a frenzy, their clapping almost drowning out the lively tune.

With the show about to finish Gabriellen stood up, eager to seek out her father.

'Don't let Esmond be too long,' Dorothy shouted above the noise. 'We eat in an hour.'

Gabriellen squeezed her way along the crowded wooden

gallery and down the packed staircase. A bawdy proposition spoken to her by an obese, slovenly traveller earned him a withering glare as she hurried on. Another time such an insult would have roused her to a fury of indignation which she would have hurled upon the man's head. Now her mind was too full of the play to bother with the lecherous sot. Lifting the partitioning curtain at the side of the stage, she ran into her father's arms as the players parted around him. 'It's your best play ever. Just listen how the people loved it.'

'But did you like it, sweeting?' Esmond held her at arm's length, his eyes scanning her face.

Her throat tightened with emotion as she held his gaze. Sweat pearled his brow, the dark curling wig making him look younger than his two and forty years. How handsome he was. Was there ever a man his like? she wondered. And now, this man whom she revered like a god, was hanging expectantly upon her opinion. 'How could I not?' she enthused. 'You had us both laughing and crying in our seats.'

She turned to Robin Flowerdew who played the female leads. He had removed his lady's wig, but still wore the cloth of gold gown which was more expensive than anything Gabriellen owned. No doubt Esmond had persuaded a noblewoman to donate it to the troupe, for he insisted the players' wardrobe was of the finest materials. Robin, at fifteen, was as tall as Esmond. From the bold manner in which he was eyeing the tavern wench serving them with small beer, he had obviously long since shed his innocence. With a smile, she continued her praise. 'Robin was a wonderful heroine. The crowd loved him.'

A deprecating snort from behind her warned Gabriellen that Cornelius Hope did not relish praise given to another. She turned to the leading actor, knowing how jealously he guarded his reputation. 'Mr Hope was superb – as always. I fear, Father, he far outshone you. His final soliloquy was masterly done. When he struck Robin down in a jealous rage, so convincing was he, I thought several young blades from the front rows were about to storm the stage.'

'One does one's humble best.' The middle-aged actor preened his beard, which served to cover his protruding chin, in a way which made nonsense of his show of modesty. His conceit did not impress Gabriellen. He may act the grand nobleman, she thought, but he has the short stubby fingers of a peasant.

Her antagonism flared anew on seeing the sneer twisting the actor's prim mouth as his glance rested on Robin. 'Twice you stole the centre stage from me. And what does Esmond think of the way you mumbled through your lines in the love scene?'

Robin's face reddened with anger. 'Because you robbed me of half my lines, damn you! And added some ten lines from another play to pad out your part.'

'But the audience loved it, dear boy.' Cornelius stood, haughty and imperious. 'I told Esmond that scene needed more bite to it. The crowd went wild. What do you say, Esmond?'

'As always, Cornelius, you judged the mood of the audience and played to it to perfection,' Esmond placated, though his tone carried a warning note. 'However, you were wrong to cut the lead into Robin's impassioned plea for mercy. He did well to salvage what he could from your butchery.'

Cornelius looked down his long thin nose at Esmond Angel, his tone disdainful. 'You speak now as a disgruntled playwright, not as manager and shareholder in this company. I have an eye to my own profits as one-fifth sharer. When have I failed to elicit the last shred of emotion from an audience?'

Esmond turned a stern eye on the leading actor. His role of manager was not easy. A misguided word or reprimand could throw Cornelius into a sulk for days. At such times every member of the troupe would suffer the sting of the actor's spite. But it was not in Esmond's nature to allow Cornelius to undermine his authority, whatever the consequences. 'There was no need to cut Robin's speech,' he said with quiet authority. 'Surely, Cornelius, you did not think that the boy would outshine you?'

The actor puffed out his barrel chest with self-importance. 'Need I fear that whining fop?' Ignoring the youth, Cornelius smiled at the serving maid who had paused to flirt with Robin. Pulling in his paunch and striking an impressive pose, he bowed to the servant with an extravagant flourish of his hand.

'Did ever a more beauteous maid carry forth the sweet nectar of the gods? Such eyes she has, that a man could drown in, and lips . . .' he sighed dramatically. 'Red as the most perfect rose.'

The girl left Robin's side to hold out a tankard to Cornelius. His arm slid about her waist and he bent to whisper in her ear. Blushing poppy-red, she trilled with laughter and, with an inviting toss of her curls, beckoned Cornelius to follow her.

He waved an apologetic hand in Robin's direction, his voice overloud. 'The wench has a discerning eye. She prefers a real man to the fumblings of a hermaphrodite youth.'

As the actor and servant sauntered from the courtyard to a secluded quarter of the inn, Gabriellen caught Robin's furious glare. For an instant hatred burned through the glittering brightness of his eyes. 'Pox rot you, you horny old goat! May your pizzle wither and drop off along with your nose!' He swung up his arm in an obscene gesture, then tugging at the laces which fastened the stomacher of his gown, marched to the stables which the players were using as a tiring room.

Gabriellen sighed. 'Poor boy. Hope becomes more objectionable and conceited each year. He deliberately goaded Robin. Why do you tolerate him in your troupe?'

'Because he's the best actor I can afford and he draws a huge crowd. Pay no heed to Robin's histrionics. His pride is ruffled, that's all. It's part of learning to be a man.'

The stoop-shouldered figure of the company's carpenter, Francis Crofton, ambled towards them. Esmond hailed him. 'The playbills for our next performance are on the seat of my wagon. Will you see they are posted throughout the town and the nearby villages.'

Another man beckoned to Esmond. He excused himself to Gabriellen and hurried over to him. It was always like this – constant interruptions as Esmond was needed to supervise the running of the troupe. All the organisation fell upon his capable shoulders. But since the company needed to be kept small to be profitable, there was no one to whom her father could delegate. Besides, Esmond seemed to thrive on the work.

He returned to her side with an apology just as Poggs danced through the gap in the curtain, still playing the flute. With a final blast he took the instrument from his lips and wiped his sweating, freckled face on his sleeve. Following him, carrying their guitar and tabour, were the two dark-haired, swarthy Florentine cousins, Umberto and Cesare. They were dressed flamboyantly in bold colours, today of azure and scarlet. In his free hand each carried a wooden box which he rattled appreciatively.

''Tis good, maestro. *Bellissima!*' Seeing Gabriellen they grinned and raised their fingers to their lips in Latin approval. They were both in their thirties and rarely separate from each other. When first she met them, they were so alike: both of medium height with wiry bodies, their dark eyes, hair, and small trimmed beards identical, that she had thought them to be brothers. *'Bellissima. Mucha bella,'* they chorused in unison. 'Your little girl, she is mucha grown, maestro.'

Esmond beamed fondly at his daughter. 'Mucha grown,' he mimicked. *'La madre de Dios!* A woman already and I scarce even knew the child.'

''Tis no good, maestro,' said Cesare. 'She is your daughter, no? A stranger she should not be to you.'

They handed the takings to Esmond and strolled towards the taproom, talking excitedly in their own language. As they did so their hands gestured wildly and occasionally their heads came together, more like lovers than cousins.

Gabriellen laughed. 'What an excitable pair they are. But sincere. You cannot help but like them.'

'They keep themselves very much to themselves,' Esmond said. 'As long as they do not interfere with the apprentice players, their preferences are their concern.'

Seeing her puzzled frown, Poggs laughed. 'Talking of preferences, where's my Sussex giantess? Not having second thoughts about the wedding, I trust!'

'Never that,' Gabriellen answered. 'Agnes went home with Aunt Dorothy. She still has the favours to sew on her wedding gown. I should go and help her.'

'Nay, my dear,' Esmond put an arm around her shoulders to detain her. 'Stay awhile. Cesare is right. We have too little time together. And once back at the house, Dotty will be fussing and smothering me with her good intentions.' Regret shadowed his eyes as his gaze deepened. 'How quickly the years speed by. Sadly, I'll not be back in Chichester until November. After the wedding we move to Midhurst, Petersfield and Winchester, before taking the road north to York.'

'Then we must make the most of our time now, Father.'

Affectionately, she leant her head against his shoulder. As they crossed to his covered wagon in front of the stables, he hugged her closer to him and his lips brushed her temple in a rare show of tenderness. Why couldn't there be more moments together like this? Turning within the circle of his arms, she looked up at him, love shining in her eyes. 'I wish you did not have to leave so soon.'

Esmond was surprised to see that her eyes were almost on a level with his own. His little girl was a woman now. It came as a shock to admit it. How could he have let the years slip by and allow her to become a stranger? But life was never simple. It would not have been wise for him to settle in one place for long, and there had been the need to protect her. She was safe in Chichester where he believed she was regarded as Dotty's and Ezekiel's daughter, not his.

'Dearest Gabby, I fear I have been a poor father. Have you been happy with Dotty and old sober-sides Ez?'

'They have brought me up as though I was their own. I love them both.'

A spasm of pain crinkled his wide brow and although he averted his gaze, she saw the lines about his mouth deepen. Did he truly regret their long months apart? There was a subtle change in his manner since their last meeting. He looked tired and laughed less readily. From their few meetings in recent years she had considered him invincible. True, he was ebullient and volatile. If he got into fights, it was because he was bold and daring, unlike other men who led staid lives. When his stare returned to hold hers, the laughter was back in his eyes and she wondered if she had been mistaken. The years of frustrated love for him flooded forth, and on impulse she flung her arms around his neck.

'Father, I love you more than anyone. I miss you when you're on the road. I wish I could travel at your side.'

He gave a deep laugh, drawing the attention of several of the inn customers. 'Life on the road is not for a gently reared young woman, much as I would enjoy your companionship.' He kissed her cheek. Then, embarrassed by his public show of affection, quickened his stride across the yard.

'But I long to travel where each town or fair is a fresh adventure – especially to London,' she pressed. Suddenly the settled future Aunt Dorothy would plan for her filled her with dread. She did not want to spend her life buried in the country. 'How I would love to visit London! There I would see the Queen, the water pageants, and stately processions of the courtiers through the city.'

He looked at her sideways, his eyes glinting with a teasing light. 'To what tales have you been listening that you think London is a playground?'

'Why, they were yours, Father!' Her eyes widened as she feigned innocence.

He coughed into his hand. 'It could be that I exaggerated,' he admitted reluctantly. 'Just a little, you understand, to add some colour to a story I was telling you.'

Gabriellen leant against his shoulder, hiding the devilment in her eyes. She felt light-headed at the change in their relationship. He had risen to her baiting. The knowledge exhilarated her. He was treating her like an adult, not a child, and it was more potent than the strongest wine. 'You mean that London's streets are not lined with gold?' she returned with mock dismay. She could not resist teasing him further. 'That I should no longer believe in dragons, fairies and hobgoblins? Or, the greatest disillusion of all, decide that King Arthur was just a warlord, and Camelot no more than a simple motte and bailey enclosed by a wooden stockade?'

'I would not go as far as that,' Esmond began.

Gabriellen's shoulders began to shake with the effort it cost her to contain her laughter.

'Minx! Have you no respect for my venerable years? I see not!' He put his arm around her shoulders and laughed. 'Having you near me is better than a physic.'

A tall man detached himself from leaning against the side of her father's wagon.

'God's greetings, Esmond.' The deep voice contained only the faintest trace of a Sussex burr. Gabriellen tensed, suspecting this precious hour with her father was about to be curtailed as he continued, 'Have you forgotten our meeting?'

'Indeed not, Stoneham,' Esmond answered curtly. 'But not now.' He patted Gabriellen's arm. 'Shall we say in an hour – in the taproom?'

'Very well.' The stranger's grey eyes roamed admiringly over Gabriellen. For a moment their glances met; his bolder than any man's who had dared to look at her. A stinging heat crept over her skin and her heart seemed to somersault. She judged him to be in his late twenties and something of a coxcomb from his immaculate outfit of grey velvet, doublet and sleeves edged with gold piping and slashed to display a silk shirt. The sunlight brightened his thick, short hair to a rich hazelnut brown, and a narrow clipped beard emphasised the strength of his jaw. Above the delicate lace of his ruff his tanned skin was smooth, the only imperfection a thin scar which curved down into his beard. Yet even the scar could not mar his handsome face. But it was his eyes which held her gaze – their smouldering, smoky grey depths seductive and enticing.

Startled, she realised she was staring at him with a brazenness which was immodest, and quickly lowered her gaze.

'I would not deprive you of such delightful company, Angel,' the stranger continued smoothly. 'You are a fortunate man. But then, you always did have the luck of the devil.'

Before either of them could reply he strode off into the inn. Looking back at him, unable to drag her gaze from his tall, broad-shouldered figure, Gabriellen stumbled against a wooden box holding stage props.

'I see Jack Stoneham has the same effect on you as he has on all women.' Her father's voice was heavy with warning. 'Take care to stay away from him, Gabby. I've yet to meet a greater rogue.'

She followed him into the stables where a cloth had been thrown across one of the stalls to give the players privacy to change. A table set up in the light of the open door held the wooden heads to accommodate the wigs, and various boxes containing false noses, chins, beards and moustaches. Esmond sat on an upturned barrel, peered into the polished metal looking glass, then removed his wig and began to wipe the makeup from his face with a linen towel.

'Next we are putting on *The Spanish Deliverance*,' he said. 'It may not be my best play but, with the fear of the threatened Armada, a tale of Spanish defeat fills our purses.'

So he went on. Leaning against the wall, Gabriellen watched him, but his words were only half attended to, as her temper simmered. His reprimand concerning the stranger rankled. How could he think her so addle-brained as to be taken in by a handsome face? And what was Esmond's business with that bold rogue – for there was an air about

Jack Stoneham which made her suspect that he was an adventurer? Against her will she noted he had the same easy charm possessed by her father. The same predatory, catlike stride and cool assurance that he was master of his destiny. Rare qualities. She stopped her thoughts, angry with herself that his image should linger in her mind.

'Tell me more of your new play, Father.'

Heedless of the dust and straw upon the stable floor, she sat at his feet, enthralled by her father's wit and presence. This time Jack Stoneham was forgotten as Esmond wove his tales.

Chapter Three

Esmond peered at his blurred image in the polished metal and threw down the cloth streaked with burnt cork from his painted eyes and brows. Rubbing his hand across his eyes, he swivelled round to regard his daughter still sitting at his feet. The hazy lace pattern which bordered his vision remained. It shut out the corners of the stable and distorted the light from the door, so that an aureole formed about Gabriellen's head but her features were hidden from him. Everything he saw was shrouded by a mist which was denser than it had been during the winter.

How much longer could he keep it from the players? They relied on him, and in many ways were closer than a family. More alarming, for how much longer would he be able to see to write his plays? Once blind, he would be of no use to anyone.

The actor in him rose to the fore. No one, least of all Gabriellen, must guess that his sight was failing. He studied his daughter. In temperament they were very alike. Not a good sign. He alone knew the trouble he had brought upon his own head, by his thirst for adventure. He had seen the way Jack Stoneham had looked at Gabriellen and it troubled him.

For the first time he saw his daughter not through the eyes of a doting father, but as the world saw her. Her figure, though tall and slender, moved with a grace which drew all eyes to her progress. Pride mixed with dread as he noted the sensuous curve of her lips and the tell-tale brightness in her eyes, which betokened passion. They were the signs he looked for on any chance acquaintance with a woman, but they were not what he wished to see in his daughter.

'It is not easy for a father to accept his little girl has become a woman.' He shifted uncomfortably on the barrel.

The duties of fatherhood sat uneasily on him. 'Have you a swain who has found favour in your eyes?'

'In Chichester?' She made it sound as if the principal county town was no more than a simple hamlet. 'No, there is no one here to steal my heart.'

'The prosperity and stability of Chichester are not to be mocked.' His concern grew. 'My visits here have given me the only peace I have known.'

Her eyes widened in disbelief. 'How can you say that? What of your love for Mother? She travelled with you across England. You loved her. Were you not content then?'

'Love. Happiness. Contentment. True, I had those in my short years with your mother.' Unable to meet Gabriellen's stare, he lowered his eyes and ran a hand across his close-cut beard. The rush of memories was still too painful to bear. 'When you experience love, you will know it rarely brings peace of mind.'

He stood up and abruptly changed the subject. 'Perhaps next year I shall take you to London. But you will forget these foolish thoughts of roaming the countryside. Do you think I will allow you to throw away your position and education?' He gestured accusingly at her. 'The education you asked for, let me remind you! Dotty told me I was a fool to give in to your demand. Tutors such as Seb Ruttens are rare.' He began to pace the cramped space. 'Before he died last winter, he had given you an education many men would envy, let alone women! He was scribe to Lord Barpham and visited all the Courts of Europe in his youth. Then he was struck down with the palsy and came to Chichester to be nursed by his daughter. Do you realise how fortunate you were?'

'I do, Father. And I am grateful.' She rose to face him, her dimpled smile almost disarming him. 'But it is that education which has shown me there is more to life than marriage, rearing children, and living in a provincial town such as Chichester.'

'Your words displease me.' He hardened his heart against the coercion of her smile. If unchecked, such sentiments spelt her ruin. 'You cannot tell me that you have no wish for marriage, or children?'

'Of course not.' Her lower lip jutted mutinously. 'But when I marry it will be to a man I both love and respect.

31

The merchants of Chichester are dull.'

Esmond refused to admit that he knew exactly what she meant. The years he had spent as a lawyer's clerk had stifled him. He had yearned for his freedom. But for him it was different, he reasoned. Gabriellen was a woman – not a man. Women were expected to lead conventional lives, or pay the price with dishonour. Clearing his throat, he said, 'It is time you were wed. I'd not bind you to a man who would make you miserable but it's not the Jack Stonehams of this world who will bring you happiness, if that is what you are thinking.'

'What has Jack Stoneham to do with my future?' Her hands rested on her hips, a gesture he knew meant she was preparing for verbal battle. 'I do not know the man, or wish to.'

The flush staining her cheeks contradicted her words. He had seen the effect Jack Stoneham had upon women. 'Enough of your insolence,' he barked. 'I'll not let you waste your life. Too often, daughter, you act without thought. Such impulsiveness can destroy your future – your chance to find happiness.'

'Aunt Dotty is always saying that my temper is too quick for my own good. I do try to bridle it.' She grimaced. 'It has a way of slipping its leash.'

''Tis a family fault,' Esmond admitted with a grin.

There was the swish of long skirts over the stable straw and the dividing curtain was pulled aside. They turned to see the approach of Nan Woodruff, the company's seamstress. She was carrying the gown Robin had earlier been wearing.

'Pardon my intrusion,' she said, lisping through a gap caused by a missing tooth. Her glance softened as she looked at Esmond. 'Would you speak to Robin about his temper? Look, the lad's torn this bodice in his impatience to cast it off. It will take me hours to mend and it's the finest we possess.'

As she spoke she held out the garment. Nan was wearing a plain buff gown over which a large white apron hid most of her figure. The expanse of bright yellow kirtle shown beneath the loose lacings of the bodice caught Gabriellen's sharp gaze. Nan was some months gone with child. Too surprised to feel shocked, Gabriellen glanced significantly at her father. For the last year she had suspected the two

32

were lovers. The wary light in Esmond's eyes confirmed her suspicion.

'Isn't there some news you should be telling me, Father?'

'Your eyes are too keen for your own good,' he began, then seeing her smile, shrugged. 'I won't have Nan spoken ill of. She's a good woman.'

'I am happy for you both,' Gabriellen said, and meant it. She liked Nan. Even though the seamstress had passed her thirtieth year, she was still pretty. If her jokes were ribald on occasion, she was always neat and clean in appearance. Fastidious about such things herself, Gabriellen appreciated similar efforts made by others. Sadly, few of her acquaintances were so particular in their habits. Many considered that bathing invited sickness. There was no false coyness about Nan nor any brazenness, although her body possessed the plump ripeness most men found irresistible. Her happy disposition brought frequent laughter to her lips. It was easy to understand why Esmond was attracted to her.

'If it's Nan's good name you wish to protect, Father, why do you not marry her?'

'You forget to whom you speak!' His stentorian voice boomed and the laughter drained from his eyes. 'Nan knows I will not abandon her – let that suffice. I'll hear no sermon from any chit, daughter or not.'

Her idealistic image of him crashed down around Gabriellen. She had believed her father a man of honour. How could he play Nan false? She backed further from him. 'Whatever Aunt Dorothy says, you are no gentleman.'

She whirled and ran into the yard, feeling her father had betrayed her far more than he had Nan. How could he condemn her half-brother or sister, to be base-born?

'Gabriellen!'

Ignoring Esmond's angry shout, she plunged through the curtain at the side of the stage.

'Gabriellen! Will you stop, woman!'

Esmond was close behind, but she did not want to face him. Hurt and angry, she had no wish to say something she would later regret, so she ran on through the archway into the street.

Pausing, she glanced to left and right. The pedlars were pressing the last of their wares on the few townspeople still abroad. The high gabled houses cast the street into grey shadow, but along one side the overhanging, glazed windows reflected tiny golden triangles of sunlight. At the far end of the street the haggling merchants had deserted the market cross. Now, beneath its eight pinnacled arches and soaring cupola, a group of young townsmen jeered at three farm labourers who were stumbling drunkenly across the square. At any moment a fight would start. She would be running into trouble by taking that route home.

Instead, she turned away from the cross and darted through the grounds of the high-spired cathedral. If she dodged through the close with its jumble of outbuildings, Esmond would not find her. She hid behind a buttress at the side of the cathedral to be sure that no one was following her. Peering round its wide curve, she saw her father staring in the opposite direction. If he came this way he would see her, so she risked speeding across the open patch of grass to the far side where an alleyway led back on to a side street in the direction of Uncle Ezekiel's house. Her foot twisted on the uneven cobbles as she ran down it, the pain making her hop the last few yards to where the side of one of the houses jutted out. Hiding behind it, she absently massaged the throb in her ankle and listened. As she expected there was no sound of pursuit.

The ache in her foot easing, she straightened to lean her head against the timber corner post of the house. The skyline above her head was dominated by the tall cathedral spire with its gilded weathercock shining in the bright sunlight. Closing her eyes, she tried to shut out her inner pain. She did not want to accept that her father was less than perfect.

The late afternoon sunlight was trapped in the recess, its warmth playing over her upturned face and neck. Somewhere in a room above her a man was scolding a servant, and the muffled sound of carts rumbling along the street carried to her. Close by in a garden, a goldfinch proclaimed its territory, the pure notes a balm to the turmoil raging through Gabriellen. Putting one hand to her temple, she inwardly reproached herself. She was acting like a child. Why did she never stop to think before leaping to conclusions? If Nan and her father were happy with each other, what right had she to interfere? What did she know of the circumstances? Perhaps Nan had a husband somewhere and could not marry?

The man stopped shouting at the servant but the gold-finch continued its song. Gabriellen listened, her eyes closed, intent upon its melody. Her breathing slowed whilst the sun caressed her face. Within moments she felt calmer. What a fool she had been to run from the inn. The absurdity of it now made her laugh, ridiculing herself. As her laughter faded a shadow passed across the sun. Instantly alert to danger, her eyes opened, her body tensed ready to flee.

She was no longer alone. Opposite her, lounging against a garden wall, was Jack Stoneham. He moved quickly. Closing the gap between them, he placed his hand against the corner timber to block her escape.

He had been returning to the inn after seeking out the fishermen who had been to sea today. None had sighted his ship *The Swift* which had been due in the port on the morning tide. Only last week there had been reports of Spanish spy ships off the Cornish coast. It would not be the first time an English vessel had been captured and the crew tortured to reveal the strength of the coastal garrison and fleets. Not that he feared for his men. Each of his three ships had captured their share of Spanish gold. He himself had captained *The Swift* when he had sailed with Drake last spring, in '87, and they had scorched King Philip's beard with their raid on Cadiz.

A short distance from the inn, he had heard Esmond Angel's angry shout. When the woman who had earlier been with the actor ran into the street and hid herself behind a buttress of the cathedral, his suspicions were aroused. They increased when, moments later, Angel emerged from the inn. The actor looked furious as he ran in the opposite direction.

Jack summed up the situation at a glance. In his mind there was only one reason why the actor should be so eager to detain his companion. Since it would benefit him to have Angel in his debt, and seeing the woman run across the green, Jack followed her into the alleyway. He had seen how her type worked too often to feel sympathy for his victim. To his surprise, she had not fled the vicinity. His challenge checked as he studied her. Her eyes were closed, her head thrown back, lips slightly parted, and the curves of her breasts rose above her bodice as she recovered her breath. Her face was too thin to be of outstanding beauty but there was an unconscious sensuality in her pose which held his attention. As she leaned back against the house, she laughed out loud. You laugh too soon my pretty thief, he thought.

Then her eyes opened. They shone with vivacity. Fire and ice was his first impression. From that moment he was intrigued. Instinct told him she was no seasoned cut-purse, but she must be taught a lesson. The pleasure would be all his in the teaching.

'Well now, my pretty,' he drawled. 'Gabriellen, isn't it? You must be new to the game, to run to such poor cover after robbing a cove of his takings.' He leaned closer, again astonished by the fresh scent of lemons rising from her skin. She was uncommonly clean for a whore and a thief. His curiosity matched his growing ardour. Nothing of these thoughts was apparent in his voice, which sharply demanded: 'Hand over the purse. I will return it to its rightful owner. Esmond Angel is an acquaintance of mine.'

'Aye, that I know. He warned me you were a rogue,' she returned with an audacity which surprised him.

His eyes narrowed. She was a cool one. Did she dare mock him? She would learn the folly of that. His hand slid down the timber post to grip her shoulder and he felt her stiffen.

'Release me, sir.' Her chin lifted, her tone indignant. 'Or I shall scream for the Watch.'

He laughed down at her. That act of innocence and outrage would put a seasoned actor to shame. 'I should have thought it is I who should summon the constable. Esmond Angel is lighter of a purse. Return it to me or it will go ill with you.'

'Have your wits gone begging?' The green eyes close to his sparked defiance. 'I am no thief.'

The show of spirit transformed her face, he noted with growing admiration. It gave her a proud grace, an untamed beauty, which was unforgettable. 'No innocent maid runs as if the devil is on her tail,' he mocked. 'I heard Mr Angel shout at you to stop. Yet, I am a reasonable man.'

There was unbridled passion in her level stare which sent the blood coursing through his veins. ''Twould be a shame to pay for your crime amongst the vermin in a bridlewell, then afterwards be whipped through the streets.' He ran a gloved finger along the slim column of her neck. 'Were you to persuade me I am mistaken . . .'

At her gasp, the corner of his mouth lifted knowingly. She knew what was expected of her, but was going to put up a fight. Good. He was bored with easy conquests.

'Perhaps you are no thief!' he conceded, warming to a new explanation for her conduct. 'Was it Mistress Woodruff who came upon you? I thought Angel had more sense than to take his pleasure with another under her nose.'

Jack smiled, knowing its effect had won many a conquest. 'I'm not as Esmond Angel. Nor will you find me ungenerous.'

Her lips parted as she drew in a sharp breath, the most entrancing dimple appearing in her cheek. It bespoke compliance and was all the invitation he needed. He bent his head to kiss her. There was a brief encounter with warm scented skin; then, the wire of her French cap grated against his teeth as she wrenched away from his mouth.

He smothered an oath, impatient but not averse to her provocative tricks. Gripping her chin, he turned her face towards him, still more amused than angry.

'First you accuse me of theft,' her low voice quivered with the force of her emotion, her words the token resistance he expected, 'then you dare . . . you dare name me whore!'

The pain firing down his shin through the silk of his hose caught him unawares. His hand shot out to capture her but she shrugged off his hold and ducked beneath his arm.

No longer amused by her antics, Jack ran after her. 'Not so fast, my pretty,' he said as he caught her round the waist and pushed her back against a flintstone wall.

Gabriellen winced as the edge of a flint jabbed into her shoulder.'Get your hands off me!' She struck his chest. The easy way he captured her hands and forced her arms down to her sides, caused the first chill of fear to grip her body. Her wrists felt as if manacled by steel. Clenching her fists with impotent fury, she recalled some advice once given her by Agnes. When she tried to draw up her knee, the pressure of his thigh against her own prevented her movement.

'Certes, but you're a firebrand!' Anger sharpened his voice.'You and I have a score to settle.'

'You'll pay for this outrage,' she began, but the heat of his body pressed against hers choked her words. Even through the thickness of her clothes she could feel the rigid muscles of his thighs. She glared scornfully up at him.

As their gazes clashed, she felt herself caught like a hare transfixed by the light of a lanthorn. One moment his eyes bored into hers, dark pewter orbs as menacing as storm clouds; the next they sparkled with enticement, their threat the greater for the temptation they promised. For a long moment they stood motionless. His breathing quickened, matched by a strange breathlessness of her own and the erratic beat of her pulse. Beneath that stare, her anger dissolved. Every pore in her body became attuned to his nearness, to the attraction of his handsome face so close to hers and, most dangerous of all, his virility, and the inner certainty that what this man wanted from life rarely escaped him.

He pulled her closer. She should be shocked, but instead an insidious warmth spread through her body. Expectantly, she waited for his kiss.

'Gabriellen!'

The furious voice crashed over her head like cannon fire. Instantly, she was released. Turning, she met her father's incensed glare. He stood legs apart, hands planted on his hips, in a pose which reminded her of the portrait she had seen of Henry VIII. With sinking heart she knew the likeness did not end there. When roused her father had a temper which, given tongue, could cut like a birch rod.

'What devilry is this?'

'That's gratitude, Angel,' Jack countered smoothly. 'I heard you order the wench to stop. When I saw her run this way, I followed to detain her. We were about to return to the inn.'

'If you've laid a finger on her . . .' Esmond accused.

Jack Stoneham's hand closed over his sword hilt, and aware of Esmond's explosive temper, Gabriellen hastily intervened.

'It's not what you think. Mr Stoneham believed I had stolen your purse.'

'A likely tale,' Esmond scoffed, his eyes squinting against the glare of the setting sun. 'Pray tell me why my daughter should steal my purse, Stoneham?'

'*Your daughter!*' Jack strode forward, too astonished to conceal his limp where his leg still throbbed. 'I've heard no mention you had a daughter. I thought she was your . . .' He stopped abruptly, a flush spreading over his cheeks.

Esmond stared at the dusty stain along the shin of Stoneham's grey hose. Unexpectedly, he laughed. 'You know, I taught Gabby that trick when she was thirteen. Not many women have refused your favours – but then, my daughter is not as other women. She's too much sense to have her head turned by the first handsome rogue she meets.'

Gabriellen saw Stoneham's hand tighten over his sword hilt. For a horrifying moment she thought he meant to draw it. 'Father, Mr Stoneham thought he was doing you a service. It was my fault. I should have told him who I was.' She could not resist a taunt at Jack. 'And I was never in any danger.'

'You have a daughter to be proud of, Angel.' Jack bowed to Gabriellen, and taking her hand raised it to his lips. The light in his eyes changed to a blatant challenge as he whispered, 'I look forward to our next meeting, Miss Angel – for I vow, we shall meet again.'

'I think not,' she answered coolly, although her temper was simmering at his impudence. 'Save your gallantry for those more gullible than I. It is not every day that I'm taken for a cut-purse . . . or have my virtue so questioned.'

'I can never resist a wager, Miss Angel. Or a challenge. We *shall* become better acquainted.'

He smiled, revealing a slightly chipped front tooth. Why should even that imperfection be so attractive? It added to the image of rake and scoundrel. He was being deliberately provocative and, despite her antagonism, her heart beat faster. This was not a man to cross, common sense warned, but his challenge could not be ignored. That was not her way. 'You presume much upon a chance and unfavourable meeting, sir.'

'Then I must redeem myself in your eyes, dear lady,' he whispered, before stepping back to face Esmond. 'It grows dark. You will wish to escort your daughter home. I shall await you at the inn to discuss our business.'

A scathing comment burned on Gabriellen's lips but she bit it back. The tension within her remained. Her sentiments were conveyed to Jack Stoneham by the blazing of her eyes. He acknowledged them with an amused twist of his lips as he placed his hand over his heart and bowed to her. Through narrowed eyes she watched him stroll away. The man's self-assurance was infuriating. Why then did he fascinate her? He had an air of command she had never encountered before, even in her father. Everything about his manner warned her he was an adventurer. But after her sheltered life in Chichester, it was an exciting combination.

Once they had gone their separate ways, her curiosity got the better of her. 'Father, if that man is the scoundrel you proclaim, what is your business with him?'

'I have met him only twice. He spent most of the last years at sea, earning himself both a fortune and a reputation as a bold privateer. Other than that, I know little of him except that he has influential friends at Court. My business with Stoneham is not your concern.'

The finality of her father's tone warned her he would not be questioned further. She looked at him archly and smiled. 'I begin to suspect that you have a disreputable past, Father – if you number Jack Stoneham among your acquaintances.'

She expected a bluff denial. Instead his lips clamped shut and he did not speak during their walk home.

From the moment Esmond entered the darkened inn he was on his guard. He looked around the taproom where all the faces were a blur to him. In one corner a group of men were arguing heatedly. The serving maid who had been with Cornelius Hope earlier pushed past him, carrying three foaming tankards of ale in each hand. After the fresh night air, the musty smell of dirty rushes, burning tallow and the woman's stale sweat caught in his throat. There was a scream from the serving maid as she was pulled down on to the lap of a fat merchant, the ale slopping over the large breasts displayed above the low neck of her bodice. Greedily, the merchant lapped at the droplets glistening on her flesh, cheered on by his companions. Putting down one fistful of tankards, the woman cuffed him on the ear and laughter rose around them.

Esmond moved further into the room. He returned a wave of greeting from Umberto and Cesare, their azure and scarlet-clad figures a bright splash of colour against the sombre garb of the towns' inhabitants. Then in the light of a table candle he saw Stoneham. There was no mistaking the proud set of that head or the richness of his fine clothes. The sea captain sat with his back to the wall, next to the rear exit. From there he faced the occupants of the room and the main entrance. It told Esmond much about the man. Had he not used the same ploy on countless occasions to prevent anyone coming upon him unawares – the door by his shoulder a quick retreat. No honest man needed such precautions.

In the gloomy light of the taproom Esmond knew himself at a disadvantage. Carefully he made his way through the carousers, lest an unseen stool or a sprawling foot bring him to the floor. As he approached the table Stoneham beckoned to a serving woman to bring more ale. When she would have loitered, offering him a silent invitation as she deliberately rubbed her hip against his shoulder, he smiled and flipped her a silver coin. With a slap on her buttocks, he sent her away.

'You've made a conquest there,' Esmond remarked, seeking to bring a light note to their meeting.

'I have no taste for any tavern slattern, but the wench had a pretty smile. From the bruises on her arm there's little kindness in her life.'

Such consideration was a twist of character Esmond had not expected from a hardened rogue, but he was too shrewd to interpret it as weakness. To a wealthy man a silver coin was no loss, and a smile cost nothing. It would ensure though that the sheets on his bed were clean and aired and he had the choicest food served for his meals.

A packet was pushed across the table towards him. Esmond covered it with his hand as he sat down. Turning it over, he studied the wax seal. The imprint of it was smudged.

'Damn you for a blackguard!' His hand moved to the dagger at his belt. 'What means this infamy? You've opened this.'

'You'll find the hundred pounds intact.' Jack kept both his hands on the table as his gaze dropped to the knife hilt clasped in Esmond's fingers. 'Your poniard will serve you ill against my sword, should you be rash enough to draw it. Your dealings with One-eyed Ned are your own affair – if they are purely monetary. I agreed to be his messenger, but it does not pay to be too trusting. Ned was involved in smuggling letters from the captive Queen of Scots across the country. Her beheading at Fotheringhay may have seen an end to her plans to rule England, but there's many a

Catholic who still plots to see our Bess deposed.'

Esmond controlled his anger. Now the rogue dared imply he was a traitor, damn him! He glared at his antagonist, seeing only a hazy outline of the arrogant features. The effort made his head throb and his temper eased. 'One-eyed Ned provides a service. His web of accomplices guarantees to get anything, anywhere – no questions asked. Those who break his rules usually meet an unpleasant end.'

'Ned knows how I work.' The voice from the shadows was without fear or repentance. 'This package had to reach Chichester within the week and I was on my way here. I also wanted to meet you. We are not so very different, you and I, and we have another acquaintance in common – Lord Barpham.'

Esmond said nothing. Why should he? It was Stoneham who was after something. But what? An uncomfortable feeling settled in his stomach. Let Stoneham make the first move. He was too experienced to be drawn by this trick of the expectant pause. Whilst Esmond supped his ale, the silence between them was allowed to stretch on, until to continue it would be to lose any advantage which had been sought.

Jack Stoneham leaned forward into the ring of candle-light. 'Lord Barpham is your patron, I believe?'

Still Esmond did not rise to the bait. Each assessed the other, with an unwavering stare. Reluctantly, respect stirred in Esmond. That steady gaze took an iron nerve. It was the measure of a man confident of his own worth. From his fine clothes, he had taken Stoneham for a fop. Not so. It took either a very brave man or a foolhardy one to risk One-eyed Ned's wrath. Stoneham was no fool. Few men had that courage, fewer still lived to speak of it. He knew the type well – an ambitious opportunist. Nothing and no one would prevent him carving out his own destiny. Twenty years ago it might have been himself seated across the table, with the same hard eyes and resolution. If Stoneham had deliberately sought him out, it was with reason. And the ends served would be his own rather than Esmond's.

'What is your connection with Lord Barpham?' Esmond asked.

'I met him in London at Nell Lovegood's establishment.' Stoneham paused, alerting Esmond to an unspoken threat. 'Perhaps you know the place, Angel?'

42

'What man with fire in his pizzle does not? Nell Lovegood prides herself that her whores are free of clap.' The actor in Esmond allowed him to appear relaxed, even as he braced himself against an expected attack. This was no idle gossip.

Stoneham leaned back, appearing too at ease for Esmond's peace of mind. His misgivings were proved correct as the sea captain went on to: 'In such congenial surroundings, especially when a bottle or two of wine has been shared, bargains are easily struck. Lord Barpham owns an iron foundry here in Sussex. With our navy so short of ships, he has agreed to supply extra cannon for all mine, providing he can captain one of them against the Armada when it sails.'

Esmond topped up their tankards from the pitcher on the table. Was he being too suspicious of Stoneham's motives?

'You still have not stated your business with me.' Esmond sat forward, irritated by the prevarication. A hot meal was waiting for him back at Dotty's and it was rare he could relax in the company of his family. Impatient to be gone, he added sharply, 'How can I serve you?'

Jack Stoneham tipped his stool on to two legs and leant his shoulders against the wall. At last he had Esmond Angel on the defensive – that was where he wanted him. A little flattery, a touch of pressure, and Angel could not refuse his offer.

'Her Majesty was much taken with your last play – but I hear that the cost of presenting it at Court near bankrupted you.' He began to bait his trap. 'You have several gambling debts, not to mention a dozen or more creditors howling for payment. It is but a matter of time before one of them issues a warrant for your arrest.'

Esmond leapt up, slamming his tankard down on the table, its contents splashing over his fingers. 'What villainy is this? You insult me, sir, and will answer for it.'

'Sit down, man,' Jack ordered, his voice quiet, but with the edge of one who expects to be obeyed. 'I did not come here to insult you, but to help. The property you own in London offers many possibilities for an improved income.'

'That's my affair.' Esmond remained standing. In another moment he would lash out and bloody Stoneham's face. He took a deep breath. He had promised his sister that he would not brawl whilst in Chichester. It had taken all Ezekiel's influence with the City Aldermen to allow his troupe to perform here. During his stay at Christmas he had spent a night in gaol after some real, or imagined, slight upon his name. He forgot how that particular fight had started – there had been many such instances. He glowered at Stoneham, resenting any man's interference in his affairs.

'What if I say I am willing to invest in the property?' Stoneham continued. 'I could increase your present income six – nay, seven – times over. If we were partners.'

Esmond swung round, his tone scathing. 'By God, I'll give you your due, Stoneham. You've got the devil's gall to suggest such a thing.'

Jack refilled the two tankards and smiled. 'Twenty years ago would you not have made the same offer – given the same circumstances? Age is mellowing you. I would make us both rich. Is there any harm in that? You've little interest in that property, except for the income it brings. Last year the house next door was gutted in a fire. The landlord is willing to sell it cheap. We could extend the present property – add to the facilities.'

'I want no partner,' Esmond dismissed the venture. 'The property has been in my family for generations. Its income saved my father and I from a debtor's prison many times.'

Jack refused to give up. 'But it is falling into disrepair. Money needs to be spent on refurbishing it. Why, part of the new structure could be turned into a playhouse. Think how that would improve the profits.'

He allowed his words time to tempt Angel. The actor sat down on his stool, his expression wary. He rubbed a hand across his brow as though it pained him, and in the candle-light Jack saw the gossamer web growing across his pupils. How much longer before he went blind? Five years? His proposal would support Angel in comfort long after his sight failed.

'Well, man, do you agree?'

'The overheads of a playhouse are high.' Esmond remained suspicious. 'The Theatre opened in Shoreditch nine years ago, followed by The Curtain a year later, and there's now The Rose on Bankside. I doubt even London will sustain four playhouses, unless the Queen herself is our patron.' For a moment he almost wavered. To possess his own playhouse – what an achievement that would be!

'I had heard Esmond Angel was a man of fire and foresight. What is life if it has no challenge? Think on it, man. I am in Chichester until the end of the week.'

'I have no need of a partner.' Angel remained wary. 'My debts will be settled out of the remainder of this.' He touched the package containing a money pouch from One-eyed Ned.

'And what will you do when the interest is due on that loan?' Jack correctly guessed it had come from a moneylender.

'That's my affair.' Esmond stood up, his figure stiff with affronted pride. 'I bid you goodnight, Mr Stoneham.'

Jack raised his tankard in salute. 'Think well on my words. Your own playhouse: The Angel. It has a fine ring to it. If we were partners, within a year the increased profits would be such that you would have no further need of moneylenders. In five years you would be a wealthy man.'

'Your offer is tempting – as it was meant to be.' Esmond eyed him coolly. 'But only a fool enters into a partnership with a man he does not know. I like well enough my life on the road. London has no lure for me.'

As he watched Esmond Angel weave his way through the crowded taproom, Jack put his fingers together and touched them to his chin. He knew Angel would not accept his first offer, but he could wait. If the playhouse was not the key to gaining a hold on that property, there were other ways to win his end. Before approaching Angel he had learned all he could of the man. The actor was more cunning than any fox and had hidden his past well. There was more than one skeleton in his family priest-hole.

The daughter, however, had been a surprise. His interest deepened. The Angels were no saints, if rumours were true.

Jack propped up his long legs on the table and ran a hand thoughtfully over his moustache. He would not make the same mistakes as Esmond Angel, for strangely there were similarities in their lives. Their backgrounds might be different, but their souls fed on the same spirit of adventure – driven by the need to be one's own man and to succeed.

It was a good life, one that was fashioned by your own hands. Jack had long since made strategic plans to win advancement and fortune. He had come a long way from his childhood in a rickety hut on Hastings beach. His father had been a fisherman owning a one-third share in a leaky boat who had drowned at sea. Jack, the youngest of four sons, had left home the following winter at the age of ten – the day after his mother's funeral.

London drew him like a lodestone. Once there he discovered that the only life open to him was one of squalor, where to survive he would have to beg or steal. For a year he had lived on his wits amongst the hardened villains of Alsatia, a district stretching south of Fleet Street to the river. Life endured in the filth and poverty of the labyrinth of those twisting lanes, the heart of the London Underworld, had given him an edge which still served him well. In the end it had been the squalor and filth, as much as the prospect of ending his days by swinging from Tyburn's gallows, which had turned him once more to the sea. For seven years he had served the same master, starting as a cabin boy, then later, after acquiring a rudimentary knowledge of figures and letters, learning how to navigate. A further two years of roaming the Spanish Main had put a silk lining in his pockets and taught him much of the handling of men.

Leadership came easily to him. Those who disputed it soon learned he could hold his own in any fight, whether it was with knife, sword or bare knuckles. Since then he had not looked back. He had taken pains to erase the roughness from his speech and dressed the equal to any gentleman. By twenty he owned his first ship and now, five years on, two further vessels sailed under his command, captured from the Spanish.

Yet in the last year the lure of adventure offered by the sea was waning. He missed London: the constant excitement, the deals and intrigue. He wanted that property owned by Esmond Angel – even a partnership would do to begin with.

He cursed the man's stubbornness. But Angel would not hold out against him for long. Once in the hands of the moneylenders, few men escaped. Angel was too old to curb his extravagant ways or his love of gambling. Jack knew he had but to wait and the property would be his.

Chapter Four

Agnes moved away from the well-wishers in the crowded parlour. It was stuffy and she opened the lattice window. The sky was ominously dark against the square of golden thatched roofs surrounding the inner courtyard.

'Looks like rain,' Poggs said as he joined her. 'A pity there'll be no dancing for our guests.'

She gazed lovingly down at his short figure. 'It'll spare thee having to lead me out. I'm no dancer. My lame leg makes me ungainly. But I would have liked to see thee, and Gabriellen too, enjoying the country dances.'

'You're never ungainly.' Poggs smiled up at her, his freckled face creased with happiness. 'I'll be proud to dance with you. Let's hope the rain spares us.'

He put his arm around her waist and stood on his toes to plant a kiss upon the side of her neck.

'Poggs!' A good-natured shout from Esmond drew them apart. 'Stop making love to your bride. Time enough for that later.'

Agnes blushed. She was no innocent virgin, but had been abused from the age of twelve by the two teenage sons of her last master. Her lameness made her an easy victim and she was too frightened by their threats to speak out. At fourteen she became pregnant and as soon as her figure showed her condition, she had been turned from the house. It was midwinter. She was an orphan, and with nowhere to go had turned to the Parish for help. They put her in the stocks for wantonness and depravity, and left her there for two days in freezing weather. She was pelted with filth and even stones by the villagers. After a night of snow, she had gone into premature labour. She would have died had not Ezekiel Otwell ridden through the village that morning. Appalled at her treatment, he insisted upon her release and paid for a midwife to attend her. The woman was a drunken slattern and inept at her duties. The child died and since that time Agnes's monthly flux had been erratic and visited her only twice a year. It was unlikely she would ever have children.

She looked across at her benefactor and felt a surge of gratitude. It was typical of Ezekiel that he had stayed in the village for two days until she had been well enough to travel. Then he had hired a cart to bring her to Chichester as a servant. When Poggs proposed to her, she had confessed her past to him before accepting. She had expected him to recoil from her in horror. Instead he had brushed her tale aside, and his words still echoed in her mind. 'You were not to blame for another's depravity. Forget your past. Think only of the future. *Our* future.' From that moment she had lost her heart to the little man. To her, Poggs soared head and shoulders above all present. She was not clever like him. She could not always find the words to express her love, but now it shone in her eyes so brightly his smiled widened. With a characteristic whoop of joy, he gave her another resounding kiss to the delight of the wedding guests.

Irrepressibly he winked up at her and, still grinning, looked out of the window. Nodding towards Gabriellen who stood in the courtyard, he said, 'She'll be the next of us to wed.'

Agnes followed his gaze, her eyes softening with pleasure. Gabriellen was beautiful in her finery. The hundred lace points of a fan-shaped ruff framed her face, and her pale gold hair was curled and adorned with the rope of pearls given to her by Esmond on her sixteenth birthday. Gabriellen was one of the few women tall enough to wear with such elegance the latest French farthingale, shaped like a wheel. The square-necked bodice, with its cloth of silver stomacher which dipped to a point over the front of the flounced hips of a sapphire blue gown, emphasised the slimness of her waist. As Agnes watched, Gabriellen lifted her hand palm upwards. From the eaves of the storehouse opposite a sparrow flew down, alighting on her wrist.

'Look at her with those birds – they have no fear of her.' Agnes spoke her thoughts aloud. 'It never ceases to amaze me. 'Tis the same with all dumb creatures. For them she has unlimited patience. A pity that's not more evident when she deals with human folk. I fear her headstrong ways will lead her into trouble. When she weds, it'll not be a day too soon.'

'I'm surprised some man has not already asked for her hand.' Poggs shook his head, mystified.

Agnes shifted her weight from her lame leg, her gaze held by the scene. What did the future hold for her mistress? 'There be plenty who've tried to court her. She'll have none of them. 'Tis my thinking that none matches up to her father. The lass dotes on Esmond. She can't see that his kind make the worst possible husbands.'

'Aye, likely so,' Poggs said drily. 'But no dour, penny-counting merchant will ever win her love, that's for sure.'

Agnes sighed. 'I hope she finds happiness. I'll miss Gabri-ellen. She's been the only friend I've known – 'ceptin' thyself, dear Poggs. And despite being mistress and servant, we've been close.' She dabbed a tear from her eye with a kerchief. 'We both came to this house in the same year. Just a week apart. Poor little lass, she were lost without her parents.'

'Knowing your story, Agnes love, it's no wonder you're so fond of Miss Gabby. She was an adorable child. A golden-haired imp forever getting into scrapes and mischief.'

'She was that.' Agnes nodded. 'An imp she truly were in those days – wild and undisciplined, and far from angelic when thwarted. But through it all she was kind-hearted. Never once making fun of my lameness, nor mocking my beanpole height. Aye, I shall miss her. And worry for her too. She's too like her father for her own good.'

'Don't you fret over the girl.' Poggs patted her hand. 'Miss Gabriellen never shows that wildness now – she's a proper gentlewoman.'

Agnes wished it were so, but she knew better than anyone that the wildness always lurked beneath the surface – leashed but not tamed.

Poggs turned at the sound of his name. 'Our guests grow impatient for our company, my love, and I have not yet thanked Mr Otwell for all he has done. Especially for the fine gloves he made for all the wedding guests. He would accept no payment for them, though it is the custom for the groom to give such gifts to his bride and guests.'

He moved away and was immediately hidden amongst the taller players. Agnes was seized by a laughing Cesare.

'It is our turn to kiss the bride.' He kissed her on both cheeks before being slapped on the back by a grinning Umberto who took his place. '*Bellissima*, I am much happy for you.'

'Th-thank y-you,' Agnes stammered, flustered by their friendliness.

They laughed appreciatively, and to her relief withdrew. A silver wine flagon filled with malmsey was thrust into Agnes's hand and, wedding or not, she found herself subjected to Cissy Tanfield's scolding tone. 'Mr Otwell has an empty goblet. Do 'ee think I can manage all the serving on my own? That new girl, Mary Fisher, has disappeared. Another of Mr Otwell's waifs, I says. An idle baggage she's turned out. The good Lord alone knows where she's come from. The poorhouse likely, from the state of the rags she arrived in.'

'Mary is an orphan and still little more than a child,' said Agnes. 'Did thee see those bruises on her arms and face? Poor mite. Last I saw her she was looking poorly.'

'Plain idle, I says,' Cissy grumbled. The heat from the kitchen had turned her fat face red. 'I'll box the lazy chit's ears when I catch 'er. And just look at the young mistress!' Cissy jerked her head towards the window, setting her chins wobbling. Gabriellen was still in the courtyard where a half-dozen birds were now eating from her hand. The crumbs gone, she watched the birds fly away, her expression becoming dreamy. 'Just look at 'er, I says, woolgathering as usual.'

'I've always enjoyed the tales the mistress weaves,' Agnes defended. 'Though who'd have thought that such a fireball of mischief would take so readily to her lessons?'

'Filling her head wi' nonsense, I says,' Cissy snapped. 'Wonder she kept her wits. Such reading, and the scribblings she were always doing, weren't healthy. Indeed, 'twas unnatural. I wouldn't be surprised if it hadn't addled her brains. And where will that leave her? With her wits agone begging and chained up in a madhouse – that's where!'

Cissy stomped back to the kitchen, leaving Agnes to refill the guests' goblets. A final glance out of the window showed her that Gabriellen had disappeared. The first drops of rain were striking the panes. Agnes didn't care what Cissy said – Gabriellen might be spirited, but there was no harm in her woolgathering. No, it was not lack of wits which now made Gabriellen Angel different from other women, for her green eyes sparkled with a lively intelligence. But for all that, Agnes could not help wondering if the rumours she had heard about the family were true. How could Wildboar Tom Angel's descendant escape the legacy of that devil's blood?

Another full flagon was thrust at her and Cissy dug her in the ribs, whining, 'Am I to be left to do everything? The guests want cinnamon cakes with their wine. Esmond Angel and his damned players are worse than scavaging kites.'

'Thee forgets thyself, Cissy,' Agnes defended. 'Mistress Otwell has been good to me. Thee have no right to speak so of her brother. 'Tis a wicked tongue thee has. And from the way thee take on so, I think thee be jealous and begrudge me a chance of happiness.'

'Happiness!' Cissy scoffed. 'There's little of that ahead for 'ee, 'ee poor lame fool. What did 'ee want to marry that Poggs fellow for? The man's a strutting buffoon – a clown. Why, he's no more than a dwarf . . . a maypole and a dwarf. In all my born days I've never seen such a comical, mismatched pair.'

'Thee keep such opinions under thy cap.' Years of resentment at bearing the brunt of Cissy's sharp tongue flowed from her. Agnes had never liked the cook who was a lazy slut when the mistress was not watching her. No longer would she suffer her scolding. She was leaving tomorrow and it was time Mistress Tanfield had a dose of her own poison. 'Thee's mean and jealous. Poggs loves me, and I him. He's a good man – a kind man . . . a better man than I deserve. Lame I may be, but I'm no fool. Why, now that Lord Barpham is patron to Esmond Angel's players, they'm have a licence to travel the countryside as respectable folk. They'm Lord Barpham's Men on the playbills now.'

The cook expelled her breath in disgust. 'And when, pray, have strolling players been respectable? I says they'm rogues and vagabonds to a man. This is where 'ee belong. Master Otwell saved 'ee from a life of sin and shame. I says 'tis a cruel way to treat folk, leaving him with a useless half-wit girl to replace 'ee.'

Tears prickled Agnes's eyes and her lips trembled with hurt. Before she could reply, Cissy was pulled round to face an incensed Gabriellen.

'I can scarce believe my ears at your cruelty, Cissy Tanfield.' Her eyes flashed with outrage as she poured out her scorn. 'This is Agnes's wedding day. Why must you spoil it?'

The cook had the grace to look repentant. 'If it weren't for that lazy chit, Mary, who's gone missing, leaving me to do all the serving, I'd never have spoken so hasty. But what use to me is another of Mr Otwell's "Unfortunates", I says? It'll take me months to train her – as if I didn't have more than my share of work to do.'

Agnes snorted. 'To hear thee talk, Cissy, thee'd think thee were Madam Innocent. Were thee not also one of those "Unfortunates"? And a convicted thief in the bargain! Mr Otwell took thee in when no one else would give thee work.'

'I was innocent. I never stole no brooch from my mistress. She lost it, I says. She were always losing things. And when her husband got angry, she says I'd stole them.'

'They were never found though, were they? And there was more than a brooch went missing. There were a ring and a rope of pearls too. The magistrate thought thee guilty. That's why thee spent a day in the pillory. And thee would've been whipped from the town, 'ceptin' Mr Otwell took pity on thee.'

'Why, 'ee foul-mouthed shrew . . .' Cissy began, her hand reaching up to snatch at Agnes's ruff.

Gabriellen caught the cook's hand before it met its target, her voice low with controlled anger. 'That is quite enough from both of you. You should be ashamed of yourselves. This is a day for rejoicing.'

The two women hung their heads and shifted uncomfortably. Agnes cleared her throat. 'I dare say I spoke out of turn. But she had it coming.'

'That's enough, Agnes. You've worked with Cissy too long to part bad friends. She's spent hours toiling in the kitchen to give you a wedding feast to remember with pride.'

'Aye, I'm sorry.'

'So am I, Miss Gabriellen.' The cook apologised, but did not meet her mistress's gaze. It was rare she did. However much Gabriellen tried, she had never really liked this servant. She sensed a slyness about her manner which left her uneasy. But as far as she knew her aunt had no complaints about her work. It was probably just her imagination, for

Cissy was a born complainer, and as such, inspired no confidences or friendship as Agnes had done.

She turned to a more practical matter. 'Have either of you seen Mary?'

Cissy shrugged and Agnes shook her head.

'In that case I will look for her,' said Gabriellen. 'Then I'll ask Umberto and Cesare to play for us. Now that it's raining, it looks like there'll be no dancing outside.'

Clutching a wine flagon tightly in her hands, Agnes moved amongst the guests. When the bell to the front door sounded above the noise of the wedding party, she glanced round the crowded parlour. The players were laughing heartily at an anecdote of Esmond's, and the two glover's apprentices were sitting in a corner gulping down a stolen tankard of strong ale between them. Mrs Otwell would tan their hides if she found out. Of Mary Fisher there was no sign. Agnes smothered a pang of guilt that Mary was such a poor replacement for herself. But to be fair to the girl, she'd looked very pale when last she'd seen her. The bell rang a second time and Agnes hurried to answer it.

Outside the violence of the rain had turned the gutters into small rivers. A flotilla of discarded rushes, a soleless shoe, a decomposing rat along with various household rubbish which was carelessly tossed into the street, sailed past the door. The tall stranger standing in the narrow porch glowered at her when she prevented him from entering the house.

'Can I be of service, sir?'

'I have business with Mr Esmond Angel.' He paused at a burst of laughter from the players in the parlour. 'It appears I have come at a time when the family are entertaining. I would not intrude.' He removed his jewelled velvet bonnet, the curling plumes beginning to droop in the rain, and smiled at her.

Agnes felt that potent pull. How many hearts had that careless smile already broken? she wondered. Even she felt her normal reserve crumble.

'Thee had better come in out of the rain, sir. Who shall I say is calling?'

'Jack Stoneham.'

So this was the man who had put her young mistress in such a taking when she returned from the play yesterday. This was the unprincipled knave, the pompous, conceited lecher, she had raged about. Self-assured and handsome enough to turn any woman's head he might be, but surely Gabriellen had exaggerated? Such a man had no need to force his attentions upon an unwilling woman. Or perhaps her mistress had not been as unwilling as she had protested?

'Agnes, what are you doing away from your guests?' Gabriellen called from the end of the passageway. 'This is your celebration. Mary should have answered the door.'

'This gentleman has business with Mr Angel.'

The dimness of the passage showed Gabriellen the dark silhouette of a tall figure outlined against the oak panelling. 'Then do not leave him standing in the doorway,' she remonstrated. 'It is pouring with rain. Bring him into the parlour.'

Gabriellen watched the visitor remove his short cloak and hand it to the servant. Those languid movements were uncomfortably familiar. When Agnes moved past her into the parlour and the guest made to follow, she encountered an amused grey stare. Her initial surprise was quickly followed by irritation. After the way he had treated her yesterday, how dare he have the audacity to show his face in her home?

'I am surprised it is you, Mr Stoneham,' she said coldly.

'I have no wish to intrude if Mr Otwell is entertaining. Perhaps I could call tomorrow to see your father?'

'Poggs and Agnes were married today. Father will be leaving Chichester in the morning. Since you have business with him, it would be churlish to turn you out in the rain.'

He moved closer, his tall, broad-shouldered figure seeming to fill the narrow, low-ceilinged passage. As in the alley yesterday, his nearness was disturbing.

'From your tone you are still angry with me, Miss Angel. How can I make amends? Your censure casts me into despair.'

She saw a raindrop roll from his thick brown hair and course down his cheek into the neatly trimmed beard. Perversely, she wanted to follow its path with her finger, to feel the texture of his bronzed skin and the roughness of his beard. The impulse shocked her. The threat he presented was in the tumult he caused to her senses, with that grey, penetrating gaze. If her pulse quickened it stemmed from anger at his boldness. Since it was her way to face danger squarely in the eyes, she lifted her chin. Did he think her so naive a maid? It was time he learnt otherwise.

'Your words are those of an accomplished courtier. I doubt any woman, saving Her Majesty, could bring you to despair.'

He laughed. 'You have a ready tongue, Miss Angel.'

'I speak as I find.'

'Is that another challenge?'

There was no reasoning with this conceited knave. She gave him a withering glare. To her annoyance he seemed to be enjoying her discomfort. Devil take him! Turning on her heel, her back stiff and eyes still snapping fire, she said over her shoulder, 'I'll send my father to you.'

'Godsdeath!' Esmond raged. 'What's brought him here?'

From the angry colour suffusing his face as he strode away, she expected Jack Stoneham to be sent from the house without delay. When her father's temper was at its height, tact and diplomacy deserted him. His three crooked fingers and bent nose were testimony to the bones broken in tavern fights when someone had roused his wrath.

The noise in the crowded parlour drowned out any sounds from the passage. Since neither Poggs nor Agnes had any family, the players formed a vivid group around them with the reds, azure, golds and greens of their clothing bright as popinjays against the dark panelling on the walls, their faces rosy-hued from the effect of the strong sack or malmsey.

In a corner, bemused by the loud voices and extravagant manners of the actors, were the two apprentices from her uncle's shop. They sat looking flushed and ill at ease in their sober dun-coloured Sunday clothes, their hair slicked down with oil after Aunt Dorothy had trimmed it to the lobes of their ears this morning.

From the centre of the room came an indignant squeal from Agnes. Cornelius Hope, under cover of snatching for good luck one of the white ribbon favours sewn on her wedding gown, had pinched the bride's bottom. A retort from Poggs drew hoots of laughter from the guests at Cornelius's expense.

Even as Gabriellen kept an amused eye on the antics of the guests, her glance kept returning to the door. She was curious that her father had not returned. With a cough, she gestured for Daniel Luffe, the eldest of the apprentices, to pass her the hidden tankard of strong ale and replaced

55

it with two horn cups of weak wine.

'There's a whole day of merrymaking ahead of you,' she said with a smile. 'If you are wise, you will stick to weak wine. You'll be merry enough, I promise. The ale will only make you sick. Enjoy yourselves. The actors will not bite.'

Dan Luffe grinned self-consciously. He was fifteen and ill at ease in the players' company.

'That's fine for thee to say, Miss Gabriellen.' The colour deepened over his pimply complexion. 'I spilt some wine over Mr Hope's hose last year and my ears are still ringing from the tongue-lashing he gave me.'

'Mr Hope will not remember. Heed well that an actor cannot resist flattery. Tell him he's the finest actor you've seen. That will win him over.'

Umberto was beckoning to her from the window seat and she joined him in the embrasure. The Florentine cousins stood up, their swarthy faces breaking into smiles.

'Such a happy day. Our friend Poggs is a lucky man,' Umberto said. 'Agnes – she is a good woman, yes?'

'A good woman and much tall.' Cesare laughed and jostled Umberto with his arm as though they shared a secret joke. His dark Latin features were mobile with restrained laughter and his brown eyes shone with devilry. 'She will keep the little fellow in his place, no?'

'Have you something planned for them?' she asked.

Cesare grinned. 'Just a little jest we will play on them. It is the custom.'

Gabriellen looked across to where Poggs and Agnes stood talking to Uncle Ezekiel. Her uncle was beaming with pride that they were celebrating their wedding in his home. There was even a tear glistening in the corner of his eye as he gave the couple his blessing. Poggs and Agnes did make an incongruous pair. With Agnes standing nearly two yards high, there was nearly half a yard's difference in their height. But just to see the happiness in both their faces was proof that love was more important than shape or size.

A movement by the door caught her attention, and to her astonishment her father led Jack Stoneham into the room. More puzzling still, his hand was on Stoneham's shoulder as though they were friends. What trickery had the knave used to worm an invitation to the feast? Still smarting from the humiliation of yesterday's meeting, she turned her back and continued her conversation with the two musicians. Yet all the time she was aware of him moving through the crowd of people behind her. She laughed at something Umberto said, though she had not heard his words. At the same time she was conscious of the scent of sandalwood, which Jack Stoneham favoured, close by. When a hand briefly touched her waist, lingering longer than was necessary as someone squeezed by, her flesh tingled from the touch. It had to be him. No one else would be so forward. She kept her face averted.

The stinging reprimand she had meant to utter dried on her tongue. He had not stopped to speak with her, but had moved on. Her chagrin rose. Under cover of repinning a curl of hair which had fallen over the lace of her half-moon ruff, she looked through her lashes at his progress across the room. Her father was introducing him to Uncle Ezekiel and the bride and groom. She might not have existed for all the notice that Jack Stoneham gave her. Unaccountably, that pricked her pride.

'The newcomer interests you?' Cesare asked.

'Not at all,' she replied.

The two cousins raised their brows, then nodded and smiled at each other.

'A fine figure this man presents,' Umberto commented. 'See how he bows over Agnes's hand. Very graceful, he is.'

'Ah, he treats a servant like a Contessa,' Cesare added. '*Madre Maria*, he has a way with the signorinas, no?'

Gabriellen voiced her irritation. 'He flatters and cajoles, if he thinks it will get him what he wants.'

She watched Jack Stoneham speak to Poggs and Uncle Ezekiel. They threw back their heads, laughing uproariously. The knave was ingratiating himself with everyone. He turned, and catching her stare upon him, his mouth tilted with amusement. Furious at herself, she scowled. Let him charm all present in the room, he would not beguile her.

'That man, you no like him?' Umberto asked.

'Mayhap, dear cousin, she likes him too well,' Cesare said with a wink.

'I am just surprised Father saw fit to invite the likes of him to our table,' she retorted, and moved to the far side of the room away from Jack Stoneham.

With the meal about to be served, Gabriellen scanned the parlour for sight of her aunt. Ah, there she was! Cornelius Hope had her boxed in while his loud voice boasted of the way the Queen had praised his acting. It was obvious that Dorothy was finding it impossible to get away. More worrying still was the continued absence of Mary Fisher. The servant was needed in the hall to serve the meal.

She beckoned Dan Luffe. 'Mary is needed. Will you see if she's in the garden?'

Gabriellen checked the kitchen herself. It was deserted, as was the old hall. In this the oldest part of the house, the room rose two storeys high. The blackened timbers above her head still bore traces of soot from the fires of a century earlier when this had been the main room of the house. Often Aunt Dorothy spoke of having a low ceiling put in, which would make another room above. But Uncle Ezekiel liked it as it was, and since it was only used on special occasions, the oak-beamed roof remained in all its four-teenth-century splendour. The floor was spread with fresh rushes which were scented with dried flowers and herbs. A tapestry of a hunting scene covered one wall: the others were whitewashed and painted in a red and blue leaf design. Over these, in honour of the celebration, were hung green garlands woven with wildflowers.

Everything was in readiness for the meal to begin. The long table was laden with platters of cold spiced capons, geese, snipe and woodcock. Several pieces of table silver decorated its length, and the Venetian glass goblets were set at the places of the guests of honour. Others would use the transparently fine horn cups banded in pewter. It was Aunt Dorothy's pride that the table could be extended to sit comfortably ten people along each side. Even though Agnes was a servant, the best dishes and finest linen table cover had been laid out. With everything prepared, all that was missing was Mary Fisher.

Resuming her search, Gabriellen finally found the servant curled in a miserable heap on her truckle bed in the tiny attic room given to her. From the two spots of colour on her cheeks it was obvious she was ill.

'What's wrong, Mary?'

''Tis my head. It aches so.' She sat up and sniffed back her tears. 'Mistress Otwell gave me a tisane of meadow-sweet, but it pains me still.'

The girl loosened the front lacings of her bodice and through the linen kirtle, yellowing bruises could be seen.

'Your last master mistreated you cruelly. Sometimes a fever comes after a severe beating.' Gabriellen's voice was gentle with compassion. 'And didn't you say you were drenched in a storm two days ago? Rest now. We can manage without you. I'll bring you some delicacies from the table later.'

'Don' 'ee trouble wi' me, Miss Gabriellen. I couldn't eat a bite. There's lemon water I can drink.'

'Then try and sleep, Mary. It's the best cure.'

'Yes, Miss Gabriellen,' she said, flopping back on the straw pallet. 'I don' deserve such kindness. Master Hinchley always beat me when I was sick.'

'There's no beatings in this house, Mary. Sleep now.'

Gabriellen returned to the parlour as everyone was going through to the old hall to eat. When she took her place on the bench, between her father and Robin Flowerdew, she found herself staring across the table into Jack Stoneham's taunting gaze. As she passed a dish of steamed fish cooked with almonds and apples to her father, she whispered fiercely: 'What possessed you to ask him to dine with us?'

'Mr Stoneham leaves for Plymouth on the morrow. He asked me to deliver a packet to a friend whom he was supposed to meet in Chichester later this week. A man I did not know Stoneham was acquainted with. I may have misjudged Mr Stoneham. Besides, it would be inhospitable to turn him out in the rain.'

Intrigued that her father had been so easily won over, she asked, 'This friend of Mr Stoneham seems to have made an impression upon you?'

'Who – Mark Rowan?' A guarded look came over her father's face. He shrugged as he handed Gabriellen a bowl of salad which included violet buds. 'He travels the fairs with his stallion. We've met from time to time – shared a drink or two. I told Stoneham that it was unlikely I would meet Rowan for some weeks. We do not travel the same routes to the fairs. Like myself, when someone is willing to pay him for his services, he does not refuse extra custom. Rowan can spend several days at a manor should his stallion be needed at stud. Which is often. Glendower is the finest chestnut roan I've ever set eyes on. A pity I could not oblige Stoneham.'

'Why can you not take the package with you?'

Esmond frowned. 'You ask too many questions. It's

enough that its contents must be dealt with without delay.'

'Why then can it not be left at the inn for Mr Rowan to collect?'

'Because . . .' He faltered, his voice impatient as he jabbed his knife into a slice of plover pie. 'Because it is not something to fall into the wrong hands.'

'Father!' She remembered in time to keep her voice low, aware that Jack Stoneham was watching her. 'You say the man is a rogue, then you invite him to sit at our table. What devious scheme would he now embroil you in?'

'You mistake the matter.' Esmond's lips thinned at her censure. 'Even rogues have their own code of loyalty.'

He turned away to answer a question from Cornelius. Gabriellen refused to look across the table, knowing that she would be subjected to that too assured grey stare. She leaned towards Robin, favouring him with a dimpled smile.

'Yesterday you played the part of Wendella superbly. How long have you been with Lord Barpham's Men now?'

'Three years.' Robin pouted, his round cherubic face turning sullen. 'I should be playing the male second leads by now, only Hope refuses to permit it. And as a sharer in the company, he always gets his way.'

'But surely my father plays the second leads?'

'He does, but he prefers writing to acting. He always did.' His tone was confidential, warming to her interest. 'But the costs of the troupe must be kept down. Mr Angel agrees I am ready for the roles but Hope won't hear of it. A murrain on him! I hate the conceited popinjay. What makes him think he's so damned important?'

Gabriellen sympathised with Robin for she knew how spiteful Cornelius could be, especially when guarding his own position within the troupe. Even so, her loyalty to Esmond made her try to smooth Robin's ire. 'Cornelius is a great actor. One of the best.'

'And doesn't he just glory in it! He lets no one forget.'

'Your time will come, Robin. You have talent – real talent. Shall I speak with my father?'

He looked suddenly shamefaced, a blush spreading over his smooth cheeks. 'No, Miss Gabriellen. You must think me disloyal. I'm proud to serve your father, and he has his own worries. I'll not add to them by feuding with Hope.'

'What worries?' She felt the beginnings of alarm. She had noticed the deeper lines about her father's mouth which had not been there during his Christmas visit.

Robin shrugged. 'Nothing for you to concern yourself with. Mr Angel takes his responsibility to the troupe seriously – rather like a feudal baron. The bad weather has meant poor takings for some weeks. When we played before the Queen, a fortune was spent on new costumes. Following that, one of the wagons had to be replaced. It had not been secured properly when we camped on the Downs for the night. It rolled down the slope into a tree and was smashed beyond repair. Life on the road is always like that. There's always something one hasn't prepared for. We accept it as part of the trials we endure. There's not one of us who would change what we are.'

Feminine laughter from across the table drew her attention. Stoneham was talking to Nan Woodruff. From the heightening of the woman's colour, he was flirting outrageously. He turned his head and, catching Gabriellen's gaze upon him, smiled.

'It is long since I have enjoyed such pleasant company,' he said, raising his goblet in salute to her.

Nan leant sideways, touching his arm to regain his attention. 'But surely, Mr Stoneham, you spend much of your time in London.'

'I've been at sea for most of the last two years.'

'Were you with Drake when he raided Cadiz?' Nan asked, her eyes widening with wonder.

'I had the honour to be present on that occasion.'

'Then you're a hero, Mr Stoneham.'

Nan positively glowed with admiration. Until then Gabriellen had thought the seamstress a level-headed woman. Yet, despite her resolution to ignore Jack Stoneham, she found herself waiting for his reply. She began to think of an appropriate setdown should he boast of his exploits.

'No hero, madam.' He laughed and shook his head. 'I am just a sea captain.' Although he answered Nan, he turned his admiring stare upon Gabriellen.

That he made no secret where his real interest lay caused a ripple of excitement to speed through her veins. It sparked the impulse to goad him and lead him into a trap of his own conceit. 'Will you not tell us of your adventures? I do so enjoy tales of valour.'

'Would you make of me a braggart, Miss Angel?' He fired a warning shot across her bows. 'The glory is all Sir

Francis Drake's, not mine. I but obeyed orders.'

So, he would not be baited. Their verbal jousting was exhilarating. She inclined her head in silent acknowledgement, responding against her will to his disarming smile.

Laughter and voices raised to make themselves heard above the general drone of conversation, the steady strumming of a guitar and beat of a tabour – all these rose from the house to penetrate the tiny attic room high in the roof. Mary Fisher clamped her hands against the sides of her head. Would the pain never stop? The throbbing increased, forming a red haze across her eyes. She was alternately hot and cold, and once she thought she heard her mother call her. How could that be? Her mother was dead. If only the music and laughter would end. They hurt her head. Hurt it so bad.

The room was growing dark. She had to get up. She daren't risk Mistress Otwell thinking her lazy. Apart from the enforced bath, she had been treated with a kindness she had never before known. Her nose wrinkled with distaste as she recalled the long hot soaking – the first in her thirteen years, and she hadn't liked it one bit. The mistress had scrubbed her skin until it changed from its usual dull grey to a pink and white which reminded her of the flowers of the bindweed which curled round the hedgerows. If the Otwells had strange ways in their unnatural bathing, it was little enough to suffer to ensure good food in her belly and a kind word, instead of being half-starved and constantly beaten.

Why wouldn't her legs and arms obey her? She sobbed as she tried to rise and failed. She lay on the bed, trembling, a sudden chill replacing the burning heat. The pain in her head seemed to be spreading throughout her body until she ached all over – not just where the bruises covered her flesh. Her throat was parched, her tongue sticking to the roof of her mouth. When her arm flopped uselessly as she tried to reach the pottery cup, her misery became too much to bear and tears coursed down her sunken cheeks.

She lay in a daze of torment. A fly buzzed around her head. Skimming the low ceiling, it would suddenly whizz down across her face and then up again to thud against an oak timber. Sometimes it felt as if she was that fly, diving and climbing, a prisoner in a swaying room. And, in a frenzy to escape, her head was continually battered against the wattle and daub wall.

So hot. Now she felt she was being roasted on a kitchen spit. She plucked at her clammy garments, managing to loosen the front lacing of her bodice. Still her flesh was on fire. She scratched at the persistent itch across her stomach and chest. Damned fleas and lice! But no, not fleas. The bath and fierce scrubbing had rid her of those.

Her body ceased its restless thrashing, her mind locked upon a dawning horror. She cried out, 'No! It couldn't be!'

The feverish haze was stripped from her mind. Easing herself up, she lifted her skirts with shaking hands until they reached her waist. Her eyes rounded with horror.

'Holy Mother, *no*! Please let it not be.' Her prayer dried on her cracked lips as she saw the crop of rose-red spots which covered her stomach. Thrusting her skirt down, she screamed. The thin wavering sound died in her throat, lost amongst the music and laughter below.

Some days ago on her way to the hiring fair she had taken shelter from a thunderstorm in a barn. She was not the only occupant. A woman reeking of stale beer screamed abuse at her from a dark corner. More frightened of the violent storm than of a woman's drunken ravings, she had huddled on the far side of the barn. All night above the boom of thunder the woman had continued her shouting until at last, in the early hours of the morning, she had grown quiet, and Mary fell asleep.

When she awoke the barn stank of vomit. As she shook the straw from her skirt, she cast a curious glance at the sleeping woman. The sight disgusted her. Not only had she been sick but from the smell and dark stain on her worn, dishevelled skirt, the filthy old crone had wet and fouled herself. Turning away, nauseated, something struck Mary as odd about the unnatural position of the woman's limbs. She edged closer, almost gagging on the stench rising from the still figure whose face was turned away from her.

The woman's homespun skirt had been hoist above her knees. Through the holes in the wrinkled yellow hose which covered her skinny legs, scabs and running sores vied for space amongst the teeth marks of rats. Cautiously, Mary stepped over the sprawled limbs. Tufts of grey hair stuck out of a dirty linen cap which had fallen down over the woman's brow. Mary leaned closer to peer beneath the frayed linen of the cap. The eyes were open and staring, the vomit dried where it had spilled from her mouth on to her cheek and chin. Holy Mother, the woman was dead! Choked to death on her own drunken vomit. Shuddering, Mary stepped back and thrust her knuckles against her mouth to combat her horror.

It was then she saw the corner of a money pouch tucked into the bodice of the woman's gown. Desperation overcame her fear. What use had the old crone for money when she, Mary, had not eaten for two days? She pounced on the body, tearing the fabric as she tugged the purse from its hiding place. The ripped bodice revealed a bony chest and sagging breasts covered in livid red flea bites. When her hand touched the cold body, her flesh seemed to shrink on her bones. The moment her fingers closed over the leather pouch, which held the promise of coins within, Mary scrambled away, her thoughts turning to the hot pies the few meagre coins would buy her.

On the pallet bed Mary continued to sob and scream. The image of that hideous twisted body filled her mind. The red marks – the flea bites as she'd thought – she now realised had been too large. They were the same as those on her own body. If they were not flea bites, what were they?

Terror brought a rush of vomit to her throat and she retched over the side of the pallet on to the floor. The old crone had not been drunk. Dear God, have mercy on her! Again, her body ran with icy sweat and she began to shake uncontrollably. She was doomed. The old woman had died of the pestilence.

Chapter Five

It was an unforgettable day. The wedding guests were boisterous from the effects of wine, and their laughter was unrestrained. Even Christmas had never been like this. To have the family and players together, for once in harmony and enjoying each other's company, was wonderful.

The players had always fascinated Gabriellen. They were an incongruous medley of characters, with diverse temperaments and assorted backgrounds. Brilliant, butterfly people, often blustering and bickering, but always sensitive to the hierarchy of their positions in the troupe. Her father ruled them. He fussed over them when they were ill, was the diplomat who settled quarrels and fits of injured pride, and had the brawn to separate them when they came to blows. But let anyone outside that troupe verbally or physically attack one of their number, and all united to defend their own.

Today in their company it seemed to Gabriellen that the music was merrier, the food more succulent – even the weather had been kind. After the cloudburst, the sun had come out to spread a golden glow over the festivities. By the time the feast was eaten the flagstones in the courtyard had dried enough for the dancing to begin.

The rhythm of the music grew wilder in the country reels and jigs. Gabriellen danced on, enjoying herself too much to feel tired as partner followed partner. Some like her father and Poggs had claimed her several times. Since Robin Flowerdew still smarted from the humiliation that Cornelius had subjected him to yesterday, Gabriellen paid him special attention, hoping to soothe his wounded pride. But always she was aware of the one guest who had not danced with her – who was surrounded by players hanging on his every word.

How was it that the more she tried to ignore Jack Stoneham's presence, the more she was conscious of his gaze upon her? At such times her body seemed to take on a life of its own, causing sensations that both tantalised and excited her. She resolved not to look in his direction again.

After another three dances, a touch on her elbow spun her round. Thinking it to be Robin, she laughed, her hand half-raised to take his. To her consternation she saw that it was Jack Stoneham. Inclining her head in stiff acknowledgement, she laid her hand on his arm.

'You move with a grace and lightness which would make you the toast of Her Majesty's Court,' he said as their bodies slowly responded to the sensuous rhythm of the music.

She refused to be drawn by his compliments. Undaunted by her silence, he smiled deep into her eyes. It softened the haughty lines of his face and lit his grey eyes in a way that sent a quiver through her limbs. He was devastatingly handsome, and being flesh and blood, she could not remain unmoved. How much simpler it would be to ignore him as he deserved. And how was it possible that the warmth of his hand supporting hers burned into her flesh? Why should her skin tingle wherever his bold glance rested on her body?

As the dance steps moved them forward and back, his eyes sparkled with a teasing light. 'All afternoon I have heard nothing but praise for you,' he continued. 'Your beauty, grace and elegance I have witnessed for myself. But this sweetness they speak of – the charitable heart, the soul of gentleness. Why, for a moment I thought they spoke of someone else! Where was all this virtue and sweetness when I was faced with a raging termagant yesterday?'

'It was no less than you deserved.' She struggled to keep her voice cool, annoyed that the impact of his charm was burrowing through her reserve.

'My dear Miss Angel, surely my misunderstanding of the incident was not unreasonable? Did I not act as any law-abiding citizen would have done? Ludicrous as it now seems, at the time I believed you had run off with Esmond's purse. How can I make amends?'

Had he continued with his flattery she would have quashed him with a stinging retort. That he had both complimented and rebuked her, whilst at the same time appearing contrite, was her undoing. Of course that was his intent.

66

Yet in all honesty, he was right. Her actions must have looked suspicious.

'That may be so,' she parried, unwilling to concede too easily. 'However, that did not excuse your later conduct.'

Instantly, his expression changed. As the dance took her beneath his upraised arm, he looked almost – but not quite – repentant.

'I scarcely slept knowing how shamefully I had misjudged you.'

Though that was too preposterous to be true, the admiration in his eyes made her catch her breath.

'I saw only what I wanted to see,' he continued. 'A beautiful woman upon whom Esmond Angel doted. Even suspecting you to be a thief, I admired the spirit with which you challenged me. It is that fire and courage which make such men as Drake and Raleigh the great leaders they are. But I have never met them before in a woman, except in our Queen.'

'Mr Stoneham, you are an outrageous flatterer!' She could no longer stop her lips curving in amusement. 'You make me sound like a cross between the fearsome Catherine d'Medici and Queen Boudicca of the Iceni.'

'The Iceni wench I know nothing of.' He dismissed the warrior queen with a shrug. 'I had hoped for your forgiveness. It certainly was not my intent to compare you with that Florentine witch who rules France and had good Protestants massacred in her country.'

She was startled that his education was not the equal of hers, but his sentiments concerning the St Bartholomew's Day Massacre were commendable, especially since so many of her French mother's family had died in it. Her antagonism mellowed. It was her turn to smile mockingly. 'Whilst I am prepared to suffer a lapse of memory concerning a misunderstanding, it does not mean I can forgive your forwardness on that occasion.'

'I would not expect otherwise, now that I know you better, Miss Angel. But will you not permit me to redeem myself in your eyes?'

A tremor of excitement started low in her stomach and spread up to her breast with suffocating intensity. It was just more of his shallow flattery, she told herself. Better to heed her father's warning that this man was a rogue to be avoided. But then, had not Esmond welcomed him into their home – apparently changed his opinion of him? There was much which intrigued her about Stoneham. His life at sea. His part in the firing of Cadiz. How well he knew Sir Francis Drake. Was he one of the Queen's favourites? She could not believe that Her Majesty, who loved to surround herself with witty, handsome men, would exclude Jack Stoneham from that circle.

At the end of the dance he bowed over her hand. She saw Cornelius Hope strutting in their direction with the obvious intention of asking her to dance. She resented the actor's intrusion. She had already danced twice with him. Each time Hope's conversation had been about himself and the praises lavished upon his acting.

'You look pale, Miss Angel,' Jack Stoneham said. 'Perhaps some wine would revive you?'

'Yes, I am a little tired,' she replied, loud enough to reach Cornelius. 'I think I shall rest awhile.'

There was a hardening of Hope's features as he heard her remark. With a curt bow, he asked, 'May I fetch you some wine, Miss Gabriellen?'

'How considerate of you, Mr Hope, but Mr Stoneham has already offered.'

She found her arm taken by the sea captain and pressed to his side as he led her to the table set with wine flagons.

'Thank you for rescuing me from Cornelius. He may be a great actor, but the man is an insufferable boor.' She took the goblet he handed her and allowed herself to be guided to a bench set away from the other guests. A prick of conscience warned her it was unwise to encourage him, but the seat was still in view of the dancers and she could not resist the opportunity to learn more of his life and adventures.

'I am delighted to have been of service to you,' he said as they sat down.

He did not immediately release her arm. Instead he took her hand and squeezed it gently. A delicious warmth spread through her veins and it took a conscious effort for her to draw her hand away.

'Gabriellen . . . an unusual name for an unusual woman.'

'My father was writing his first play when I was born. It was the name he gave his heroine.'

'I have seen the play. Gabriellen was the enchantress sent

to King Arthur's Court to seduce Merlin. For a time she stripped the magician of his powers. When she fell in love with Arthur, she killed herself to save her lover and Merlin's powers were restored.'

He smiled and gazed deep into her eyes. 'Gabriellen – the enchantress. How well the name suits you. I may call you Gabriellen?' It was a command more than a request.

'We hardly know each other, sir.'

'That is a matter soon remedied. I must have been blind to have wronged you so. There is honesty in your face, and more. Your eyes are beautiful. They remind me of the colour of the Mediterranean on a hot, tranquil day, and are just as compelling – beckoning me to drown in their seductive depths.'

Suspicious of his flattery, she laughed it aside, though a traitorous part of her had responded to the caress of his voice. 'A pretty speech, sir. But all nonsense! And now I must see to our guests.'

She made to leave and found her hand gripped as he gently pulled her back on to the bench.

'I speak only the truth.' He leaned closer. 'Can you ever forgive me for the wrong I did you, dear lady?'

His voice was low and husky, and Gabriellen needed all her willpower to dispel the assault upon her defences. That slow, lazy smile destroyed her calm. A part of her was sane enough to know that to encourage his attentions was courting danger. He was too handsome, too assured, and irresistibly exciting. She hesitated to go as she knew she must. He had fought with Drake, sailed the seas and seen places she could only dream of. The temptation was too great. What harm in a few stolen moments of conversation?

'If you promise never to refer to the incident again.' She withdrew her hand and eased away from him, belatedly aware of the demands of propriety. 'I shall forget it ever happened.'

'But I would *not* forget it. How can I, when the memory of you has been with me every waking and sleeping moment?'

She drew back, fighting to rekindle her outrage at his boldness. His nearness was having a suffocating effect on her breathing and it was impossible to keep her voice stern. 'You must not speak that way. If you continue, I will join the other guests.'

'You could not be so cruel as to leave me bereft. How could I not be moved by your beauty and that indomitable spirit? I never thought any woman would affect me so profoundly. Indeed, I fear I am losing my heart.'

It was the most outrageous speech she had ever heard, but treacherously her pulse responded with a wild beat which would not be stilled. Had not Agnes warned her to beware the smooth tongues of accomplished rakes? And she had been fool enough to listen to him!

'Sir, you forget you are a guest in this house!' She spoke sharply and stood up. 'It would be better if you left.'

'You doubt my word?' He was on his feet, barring her escape, his voice clipped. 'Do you doubt my honour! I have crossed swords with many men for less.'

'I would have thought it was my dishonour which was in question,' she snapped back, her eyes glittering dangerously. 'How many foolish women's hearts have you stolen by such honeyed sentiments?'

'The devil!' He looked at her in astonishment. Then to her surprise he grinned. 'There's none to match you. Most women would think such scandalous thoughts, but they would never utter them.'

Gabriellen felt the blood rush to her face. She had forgotten Aunt Dorothy's strict teachings. How could she have lost her temper and spoken so immodestly? Her lips compressed mutinously. She would not let him see he had discomposed her. As she glared up into his eyes she saw the laughter lurking in their depths. Now he was mocking her. She closed her fist to strike him, then remembering that they were surrounded by wedding guests, forced out between clenched teeth: 'You are insufferable and conceited. First you insult me, now you . . .'

His laughter drowned her words. 'My dearest Gabriellen, you are adorable. I meant no insult. That you are unaware of the potency of your charms makes you even more precious.'

She stood up, disturbed by the frantic pounding of her heart. For once she found herself tongue-tied, and dragging her gaze away, saw her father watching them, his brow creased into a frown. He did not approve of the attention Jack Stoneham was paying her. Her conscience stirred. She was inexperienced in the ways of love, and was being drawn against her better judgement into a situation she could not control. She had to get away, to escape the intoxicating madness Jack Stoneham was plunging her into.

'There are guests I must attend to.' She left before he could stop her.

As she threaded her way through the dancers, the torch-light from the flambeaux now lighting the courtyard caused shadows to leap over their laughing, sweating faces. Cornelius Hope caught her arm, giving her no chance to object as he whirled her once round the square.

'Where have you been hiding?' His voice was slurred from the wine. 'I have not told you how Her Majesty praised my role of King Arthur.'

'You have told me several times, Cornelius.' She disengaged her arm. A call from Uncle Ezekiel gave her the escape she needed, and she hurried to his side.

He whispered conspiratorially, 'Poggs and Agnes are about to slip away to the inn where he has taken a room. They want to escape the ribaldry the players have in store for them.'

As he recalled the antics he had overheard the actors planning his eyes crinkled with humour, but for Agnes's sake he was glad Poggs had had the foresight to outwit them. Once the bride and groom had left, he supposed he would have to tackle the cupshot players who would feel they had been deprived of their bawdy horseplay. He nodded in the direction of the kitchen as his attention returned to Gabriellen. 'They are in the kitchen taking leave of your aunt, if you want to see them before they go.'

'Of course I must wish them well. Thank you for reminding me.' Impulsively, she kissed his cheek. 'You have done Agnes and Poggs proud, Uncle. It's been a wonderful day.'

'That handsome sea captain you've been talking to has nothing to do with your happiness, has he?' There was no censure in his tone, only curiosity and love. 'You seem to have made an impression on him. He looks a man of some standing.'

'Uncle, I know that tone,' she cautioned. 'I am not looking for a husband.'

'Then it is time you were.'

She shook her head and kissed him a second time, her voice teasing. 'Am I such a burden to you, you cannot wait to see the last of me?'

'No, my dear, indeed not.' He looked so shocked she regretted teasing him.

'Then do not try to marry me off to every personable

man you meet,' she rebuked him gently, with laughter in her eyes. 'It may be Father has a different opinion of Jack Stoneham than either of us. Though I own, he's a fascinating rascal.'

She moved on before he could reply. She really should not tease Uncle Ezekiel as she did, but he was such a soft old soul she couldn't resist it. In the kitchen she found Poggs and Agnes on the point of departing. She hugged them both, her eyes shining with pleasure.

'There's no need to wish you joy of each other – that much is obvious in this match. But I do wish you good health and success. Look after Agnes, Poggs. She's been a good friend and I will miss her sorely.'

'Think of the tales she'll have to tell you when we return with Esmond for the winter,' Poggs replied brightly.

Gabriellen gave Agnes a last hug and stepped back. 'You have a good man. I'm happy for you both. Now unless you want the guests beating a noisy escort to your inn, I would leave before you're missed.'

As she watched the couple hurry giggling from the kitchen, her smile faded. She would miss Agnes as she would any friend but, more than that, she wished it was herself who was leaving to travel with the players. But that was selfish, and small reward for her aunt's and uncle's kindness over the years.

She smothered her wayward desire. Her mind was in a turmoil from the day's events. Music beckoned from the courtyard where the dancing continued. But that way lay Jack Stoneham. It was a potent lure – yet was it wise? The feelings he roused in her were unsettling and outside her experience.

Troubled, she went into the garden, her steps taking her to her favourite spot in the orchard. It was getting late, for the moonlight was forcing its way through the flower-laden branches, turning the blossom to silver stars and casting delicate lace patterns of shadow across her face and gown. She caught her breath at the ethereal splendour of the moonlit orchard and inhaled the sweet fragrance which filled the air. It was a romantic setting – too romantic for her disturbed thoughts. Leaning back against a tree, she stared up at the vagrant moon.

How was it that after so short a time away from Jack Stoneham, she was craving his company once more?

Already she missed the warmth of his smile and the racing of her pulse whenever their hands touched. Was it just a temporary madness? Yet no one before had made her feel as he did. Could it be possible that she was more than halfway in love with that incomparable rogue?

The realisation left her shaken. From the bough by her head, a furry head rubbed itself against her cheek. Turning, she petted the white cat purring for attention, and spoke softly to it of her uncertainty. 'Oh, Tristan, you wise old friend, how can I be falling in love with a man I barely know?'

'Perhaps because he feels the same about you.'

She started violently as Jack Stoneham materialised before her, conjured like a devil from her mind. Tristan hissed, arching his back at the newcomer before he leapt to the ground and disappeared.

'Did I startle you?' he said, blocking her path of escape. His hand took her shoulder and drew her closer. 'Is it so strange that two people should feel an instant attraction?'

'I had thought myself alone,' she accused, refusing to allow the frantic leaping of her heart to betray her sense of propriety. 'I must return to my uncle's guests.'

'Not before we talk. Do you deny your words?'

'They were not meant for your ears, sir. If you were a gentleman you would forget them.'

'That I could never do, for they are what I desire most to hear.'

'Let me go.' Her voice shook as she fought to master the effect he was having upon her. She pushed away from him. 'Be still!'

Subdued by the quiet authority in his tone, she stopped struggling. His face, silvered by moonlight, was inches from her own and the bold gleam in his eyes halted her breath in anticipation. His roguish smile, with the fascination of his chipped tooth, held her captive. Tenderly, he touched her cheek, his fingers moving slowly down to trace the outline of her lips. She should pull away now, she thought, but found herself helpless, unable to move, wantonly expectant for the mastery of his kiss.

His mouth claimed hers, warm, demanding, exploring the taste of her lips as it moved with growing insistence over them. His beard brushed against her skin, its perfumed silkiness pleasant, adding to the intensity of his kiss.

With deepening pressure he parted her lips and she tasted the sweetness of his breath. A delicious heat flowed through her veins, turning her limbs weak and causing her blood to pound with a beat as ancient as the earth itself. When her fingers curled against the slashed velvet of his doublet to steady herself, she felt the quickening rhythm of his heartbeat – a beat which echoed the wild drum-roll of her own.

She pulled away for a brief moment, unaware that a soft moan rose from low in her throat. His breathing changed. It was harder now and the sound filled her ears. Urgency kindled a hunger deep within her as his mouth again sought hers. Their arms tightened around each other. The implosion of sensations left her near to swooning with pleasure, her body quivering from head to foot. Unconsciously, she had waited all her life for this moment.

'My darling Gabriellen, how beautiful you are!' he groaned. 'How sweet and wondrously innocent.'

Passionately, he sought her mouth again and pulled her deeper into the darkness of the orchard. She could not resist, yearning for his kisses with a hunger that matched his own. His hands moved down her spine, spreading ripples of fire along its length, binding her closer to his hard figure as his fingers searched out the mysteries of her young supple body. She heard his groan of frustration through clenched teeth when he encountered the canvas-stiffened stomacher which denied the feel of her breasts to him. His hand moved to the neck of her bodice, thrusting inside.

'No!' She pushed away from him with sudden fright at his boldness.

Jack cursed roundly beneath his breath. The pain of wanting her was almost unbearable. The girl was a virgin. He'd broken his first rule of conquest: Always keep to married women. But her proud spirit had pierced his cool reserve. That she refused him served only to inflame his desire. Common sense warned him to leave and forget her, but the surging of his blood would not be stilled. At whatever cost, he had to make her his. She deserved better than a hurried coupling in an orchard. For her, he was prepared to exercise a patience he had not known he possessed.

'Forgive me, my darling. I will be patient. But you have the power to make a man lose control of his reason.'

He kissed her again, her response assuring him that his

wait would not be a long one.

'Gabriellen! Gabriellen!' a call shattered the stillness of the orchard. 'Are you out there?'

'Heavens! My father!'

Brusquely summoned to her senses, Gabriellen freed herself from his embrace. 'I must go. Father is calling me. The music has stopped. The guests must be leaving.'

'Don't go.' Jack drew her back into his arms.

'I must.'

He did not loosen his hold. His eyes willed her to stay, his handsome face taut with his need for her as his hands caressed her shoulders. Somehow she found the will to shake her head in denial, her voice hoarse with the effort it cost her. 'I have to go . . . please.'

Unexpectedly, he laughed softly and released her. 'Duty may take you from me now, but not for long, darling Gabriellen. Regrettably my time in Chichester is short. We must steal what moments we can together.'

'You have mistaken me, sir.' She was suddenly appalled at her behaviour. How could she have acted so wantonly? 'I want no clandestine affair. Foolishly, for a moment, I lost my head. You must forget what has happened.'

'Forget I held an enchantress in my arms? Forget the sweet taste of your lips or the feel of your heartbeat against mine? How can I banish the vision of your loveliness – or the memory of your eyes? Eyes that smouldered with passion. I would have to be cold and mouldering in my grave to forget that! I lost more than my head tonight – my heart is yours. I can never forget the only woman who could have any meaning in my life. The only woman I want.'

Obedience to her father's command pulled her one way; desire to stay with Jack, to savour his kisses and words of love, pulled her another. She hesitated. Then duty won and she moved away.

'Go then, since you must,' he called softly after her. 'But I shall call on you tomorrow.'

'Where have you been?' Esmond bore down upon her, looking strained and worried, as she entered the old hall. 'Stoneham's missing too. Were you with him?' his distracted voice continued. 'The players have returned to their lodgings at the inn. Dotty was looking so worn out from all her work I've sent her off to bed. I said you'd help Cissy tidy the mess.'

'Of course.' Gabriellen began to collect the discarded wine goblets. 'I was in the orchard. I needed time to myself after saying goodbye to Agnes.'

She hated the need for evasion, but did not want a lecture from her father to spoil the moment of ecstasy she had experienced in Jack Stoneham's arms. She could feel her father watching her suspiciously and concentrated on her task. The evening's entertainment had gone well judging by the few remains of food on the table and the heap of discarded platters and goblets, though she thought that the garlands of wildflowers and greenery were now a sorry sight, many drooping from the heat of the candles, others hanging down forlornly where the guests had knocked against them. It was as well Aunt Dorothy was abed, the mess in the old hall would have distressed her. Everything must be cleared and put straight before her aunt came down in the morning.

'Ah, there's Stoneham,' Esmond said from behind her.

She turned with a laden tray in her hands. Esmond was staring through the unshuttered window to the torchlit courtyard. Jack was lounging against the wall, laughing heartily at something her uncle had said. The relief on Esmond's face was obvious, adding to her sense of guilt.

Pride smothered it. To allow Jack Stoneham one kiss was not a sin, especially since he felt as she did. As she worked, she hummed the tune Poggs had danced to at the end of the play. She was in love – and was loved in return. After his impassioned speech in the orchard, Jack's intentions could not be other than honourable. A life shared with him would hold all the excitement and adventure she craved.

The smile she gave her father was dazzling, her thoughts still upon Jack as she said, 'It's been a wonderful day. I shall never forget it.'

Chapter Six

'Praise God, 'tis not the plague! They may yet live.'

Ezekiel, his eyes reddened by tears, stared down at the sweating figure of his wife. Her face, fiery with fever, was scarlet against the creamy lace nightcap.

'The pestilence is its own grim reaper,' Steven Merdon advised him soberly as he removed the last of the bloated leeches from Dorothy's chest and put them back into a jar.

Sweat glistened on the barber-surgeon's upper lip and his long thin face was drawn with fear. He pressed a pomander to his nose to safeguard himself from the corrupt and contagious air. Merdon glanced across at Mary Fisher on the pallet bed which had been in the room the last two days, both patients isolated from the rest of the household. The girl was out of her wits with fever. Incomprehensible croaking wrenched from her tortured throat sapped the last of her strength.

'I can do nothing more for the young girl. As to your wife, I've bled her. Make sure she takes the physic with the herbs I have given you.'

Ezekiel was certain he would not return to the house again, but had to concede that Merdon, with a family of six children, could not risk contagion.

'I brought my wife to this,' Ezekiel groaned, his hand shaking as he rubbed his temple. 'It is all my fault.'

'You were not to know that the servant was sick when you brought her to your home, Mr Otwell. God willing, the girl's fever will break today. If not . . .' Steven Merdon shrugged, packing his leeches and powdered herbs into a leather bag. 'I've seen fevers such as this wipe out entire households. Let no one near the sick, unless they have to be.'

'At the first sign of Mary's fever, I shut the shop and sent the apprentices away. I told them not to return until

I summoned them. They had not been in contact with the girl. I pray they are not infected. I pray also that none of our wedding guests has taken this fever.'

Merdon was edging to the door, clearly impatient to be gone. 'If, as you say, the girl had kept to her room most of that day, your guests may have been spared.'

Ezekiel bowed his head, his shoulders slumping. He felt he had aged fifteen years in as many hours since Dorothy had been stricken.

'I shall tend them both,' he said, and added to himself, 'I'll not endanger Gabriellen.'

'God be with you, Master Otwell.' Merdon left without a backward glance, his heavy footsteps stumbling on the polished stairs in his haste to leave the doomed household.

'Mr Otwell!' The weak voice from the bed drew him instantly to his wife's side.

'Hush, my love. You must rest.'

'But you . . . you must not get sick.'

'Nor shall I. I've never had a day's illness in my life.'

She took his hand, her sunken eyes glistening with tears. 'Mr Otwell – Ezekiel – I love you.' Her voice grew weaker. 'I love you so very much.'

He kissed her hand and laid it back on the cover. Bowing his head he prayed, desperately, as he had never prayed before. 'If it is your will to take one of us, Lord, take me. Not Dorothy. And the little one is so young. Spare her, Lord, I beseech you.'

That night Mary Fisher died. An hour later Ezekiel, a victim of the fever himself, collapsed over his wife's unconscious form.

The next ten days passed in a daze for Gabriellen. She alone tended her aunt and uncle as they clung precariously to life. It was impossible to rid the room of the stench of vomit, excrement and urine. On the barber-surgeon's advice she had kept the windows shut and the stifling heat added to her discomfort. To bring some ease to the fetid air in the chamber, she swung the brass plague pan backwards and forwards. Shaped like a warming pan, its lid was punctuated by dozens of holes and the hot coals within wafted a herb-scented smoke about the room, in something like the way of an incense burner. It helped to ease her aunt's and uncle's laboured breathing, but only temporarily.

Placing the smoking pan on the polished floorboards, she wrung out cloths from the cool water she had recently drawn from the well, and replaced the drying ones on the patients' burning brows. Wearily, she sank down on her pallet under the lattice window. Tonight had been the worst she had known; their fevers had risen and both raved in delirium.

At least for the moment they were quiet, but Gabriellen was exhausted past sleep. To take her mind from the frightening sickness which had invaded the house, she conjured up memories of Jack to comfort her. She had seen him only once since Agnes's wedding – a short, wonderfully happy hour.

'God knows I don't want to leave you,' he had passionately declared. 'But one of my ships has been damaged in a storm and has put into Plymouth for repairs. Then I must supervise the installation of Lord Barpham's cannon on all my vessels. The crews must be trained in their use, for they are used to firing lighter guns.' He had kissed her fiercely, before adding, 'God and the Spanish willing, I shall return to Chichester within a month.'

How handsome and elegant he had looked in his burgundy doublet and hose, a heavy gold chain across his chest. 'Your cause is a noble one. I shall think of you, and pray for you daily,' she promised.

'I could ask no more. Were it not for the cursed Spanish, ready to wage war, nothing could take me from your side. To be parted from you will be a torture.' He kissed her again with such ardour she no longer doubted his devotion. When at last he released her he handed her a packet, his voice serious. 'I have no one to trust with this but you. Do not let it out of your sight. A man will call for it – Mark Rowan. He is dark-haired and has a Welsh accent. Remember, my love, it is for his eyes, and his alone.'

'I will not fail you.'

They kissed again and when he finally drew away he pressed a jewel into her hands. 'Wear this always. The emerald is the stone of love – and I do love you, never doubt it, my dear.'

'And I love you, Jack.'

79

Those words had sustained her through the gruelling days to follow and now she lovingly touched the pendant hanging round her neck. The thumb-sized emerald set in a gold heart was surrounded by pearls and from its point hunt a large tear-shaped pearl. On its back was inscribed 'Love conquers all.'

Now she had only the pendant and her memories to cling to. She never doubted that their brief meetings had been long enough to fall in love. Jack was all she had ever dreamed a suitor would be. A smile played over her lips at the thought. In many ways Jack, with his recklessness and his bold grasp at life, was very like the father whom she idolised. She did not know when she would see Jack again and his packet was hidden under her pillow where she had put it for safety.

A cry from her aunt took Gabriellen to the bed and it needed all her strength to hold the struggling woman still. The fever had stripped the rounded flesh from Dorothy's bones, but the delirium gave her the strength of a man. At her side Ezekiel also began to thrash about. They were both dying. Dragging up her last reserves of strength, Gabriellen tended them, her face wet with tears.

Outside a cart rumbled over the cobbles, the sound bringing a deepening dread. In the last ten days she had received no visitors. Afraid of spreading the sickness, she had told Cissy to stay indoors so no news had reached them. How far had the pestilence spread? What if it reached plague proportions? Her body went cold at the thought. There would be no public burials. The image of her aunt and uncle being dragged unshrouded from the house to be piled on to the death-cart at the cry of 'Bring out your dead' filled her with revulsion.

Please God, spare them that, she prayed. It was the ultimate indignity, a horror which filled every living soul with terror.

By morning both were dead. She had held each one in turn in her arms to comfort their last moments, her aunt the first one to succumb.

Few attended the funeral. Thank God a proper burial had been permitted. There were no other cases of pestilence in the city. Even so, fear of the sickness kept the Otwells' friends away. The morning mist still clung to the treetops and a constant drizzle accompanied the small procession to the graveyard. Long after the bodies had been lowered into the ground, Gabriellen watched the gravedigger shovel the earth over the coffins. She was numbed, her mind dazed with shock. With her head bowed against the rain, she tried to find the words for a prayer and failed.

'Come home, Miss Gabriellen,' Cissy Tanfield urged, her small eyes in her fat face devoid of tears. 'They'm at peace now. They's them that says 'ee be a wealthy woman – once 'ee come of age – since the master left everything to 'ee.'

'Gossip has it wrong,' she corrected tonelessly, her grief raw and aching. 'The property goes to my father, as is right.'

Cissy sniffed disdainfully. 'Well, 'ee got the freedom 'ee wanted. Will 'ee be off now to join the players?'

'I suppose I will.' The longed-for dream tasted bitter as aloes. The shackles of her aunt and uncle's love had been gossamer fine. She had always known that if she had really sought to leave them to join her father, they might have tried to dissuade her but in the end would not have stood in her way. 'Chichester holds too many memories for me to stay. But I'll not turn you out, Cissy, if that's what you fear. The house will need looking after until my father returns.'

'That's as maybe if'n I were willing to stay.' The cook folded her hands over her vast waist and sniffed. 'I've had offers, don' think I haven't. Happen I might move on, I says. I've folk down Portsmouth way if I've a mind to seek them out. But are 'ee so certain Esmond Angel will welcome 'ee? He hasn't wanted 'ee to live wi' 'im these last years.'

'Of course Father will welcome me,' she answered quickly, more to allay her own doubts than the servant's. But would he? He'd always shied away from her joining him. But that was when she had the security of a loving home in Chichester. Now she had just empty walls. The pain of her loss returned to override everything else.

'Go back to the house, Cissy. I shall stay by the grave for a while.'

She stared at the earth mound dotted with sharp flint stones which now covered the double grave. The persistent cold drizzle soaking through her woollen cloak went unheeded. 'Why them?' she sobbed. 'Dear God, why them?'

'It is not for us to question the ways of the Lord,' a stern voice answered. It was Father William who had returned from changing his vestments. He looked at her with disapproval. Two inches shorter than herself, he had the purple-veined, bulbous nose and balding head of a man many years over his true age of fifty.

'They are in God's hands now, my child. What of your own plans? Surely you are not going back to an empty house?'

'No. There is Cissy Tanfield, our cook.'

'That is not fitting. You are without a suitable chaperon.' The priest thrust out his hand, his manner changing to one of prim censure. 'One of the goodwives of the town will give you a room and safeguard your reputation.'

Heaven forfend! She had no intention of being foisted upon one of the town's worthy matrons. Not one of them had a good word to say for her father's way of life. She kept her opinion to herself, but her head lifted with stubborn pride. She was not alone in the world. Now her father would have to accept her place was with him. And there was Jack . . .

'I shall close the house here. My place is with my father.'

'That is not a godly life.' The priest was outraged. His hands came up as though to fend off the wickedness of her suggestion. 'Do you think Master Otwell would have approved?'

'Yes. He would have been the first to agree that families should be together.'

She faced the outraged priest calmly. She had little liking for the sour-faced Father William who had toadied up to Uncle Ezekiel. It was well known that her uncle was quick to part with his hard-earned silver for any charitable cause. From the number of times Gabriellen had seen the priest, walking with an uncertain tread through the town, she had often wondered how frequently that money benefited the wine-merchant more than the parish's widows and orphans.

Father William sniffed his disdain. 'How can you say that? That devil's advocate, Esmond Angel, did not trouble to attend his own sister's funeral! I was shocked to learn you were not Ezekiel's daughter but spawned by that devil.'

'It was impossible to contact my father in so short a time.' She had not slept for more than an odd hour snatched intermittently during the last eleven days and nights. Her head ached and she was bone-weary. Even so, she would not allow her father to be slighted. 'Your words discredit your calling, Father William.'

Not trusting herself to remain polite, she turned on her heel and hurried through the churchyard into the street.

'Those are the words I would expect from a descendant of Thomas Angel – whom all the world knows to have been a blackguard!' Father William shouted as he followed her. 'Decent folk still hold up their hands in horror should they hear that demon's name mentioned. He was feared and hated in these parts. We want none of his kind here.'

She refused to give way to the rage which scoured her. It gave her the strength to drag her weary body, in its heavy black velvet mourning robes, through the town. As soon as she had delivered Jack's package to Mark Rowan, she would leave Chichester. Nevertheless, she was shaken at the venom of the priest's tone.

Once the door of her uncle's house closed behind her, she sank against it, exhausted.

'Cissy!'

Shocked at the weakness of her voice, she wiped a hand across her hot face. Beneath the weight of her petticoats and the padded sleeves of her gown, sweat dampened her armpits and stuck her bodice to her back and beneath her breasts.

The cook ambled into the passage from the kitchen. Taking one look at Gabriellen's flushed face and bright sunken eyes, she kept her distance.

'I'm so tired, Cissy,' she croaked. 'I think I will lie down. Would you bring me something light to eat later?'

The gloomy passage seemed to sway around Gabriellen. Her stomach contracted and a wave of sickness robbed her of breath.

'Cissy, help me!'

She staggered forward and fell to her knees. Her hand reached out towards the plump servant, who backed away, her face white with terror. It was the last thing Gabriellen saw as darkness claimed her.

Mark Rowan pulled the doorbell a third time, using greater

force. A frown drew together his black brows, the hollows of his angular face tightening with irritation when no one answered his ring. It was dark, but not so late that the Otwells would have retired for the night. Though it was hard to tell, since no chink of candlelight was visible through the closed shutters. His hand paused over the iron lever of the bell, then hesitated. Instead, he rapped hard on the door with his fist. To his surprise it swung open. He waited, expecting a servant to appear. No one came. Then he heard a faint groan – the sound of someone in pain.

Pushing the door further open, he discovered that the house was in darkness. Puzzled, he stood for a moment, listening. Something was very wrong. Instinctively, he tossed the corner of his short cloak over his shoulder, his hand resting on his sword hilt which hung from a narrow belt over the soft leather of his trunk hose.

The soft cry came again. Shoving aside his scruples at entering a house uninvited, he went in.

'Good sir,' he called as he picked his way carefully along the dark passage, 'can I be of aid?'

There was no answer but as he reached the first room the acrid odours of sickness clawed at his nose and throat. His eyes now accustomed to the gloom, he saw the dark wood of a staircase outlined against the white plaster wall. Again, the agonised groan was heard. This time it came from above. Delaying no longer, he took the stairs two at a time. A small unshuttered window on the landing let in enough moonlight to show him four doors leading off a narrow passage. The first two rooms yielded nothing. At the third a white cat meowed and ran out and down the stairs. The stench from within made Mark gag as he pushed open the door. A figure lay groaning by the bed. What churl could have left this poor wretch to lie in its own filth? Where were the servants? The smell of death clung to this house. Had it claimed the master, and the servants had deserted? What tragedy had he stumbled upon?

The questions chased one another through his mind as he strode to the shutters, opening them and throwing the window wide. He had no superstitions that the night air was noxious to the human body. What this poor wretch needed was fresh air. Moonlight illuminated the room. Turning back to the figure partly obscured by the hangings of the four-poster, he was moved by compassion. A woman lay slumped up against the bed, her arms and head resting on the mattress. Her legs, buckled beneath her, told their own story of her frantic attempts to reach the comfort of the mattress before she had collapsed.

'Good God, you poor wretch!' he said, torn between anger at her pitiful state and sympathy. 'How could anyone have left you to suffer so?'

During his travels he had learned much of sickness and its cures. There were few emergencies he could not cope with. Besides, this was not the first time he had encountered the pestilence. Had he not survived it himself, three years ago? And there were some fevers that never struck twice. 'Dear God, let it be so,' he breathed as he stared down at the helpless woman. 'I can't leave her to die.'

Common decency warred with the reluctance to court danger. If he fell ill then a cause greater than his own could be jeopardised.

Throwing aside his cloak and scuffed leather doublet, he rolled his sleeves up his brown arms. 'There's no time to waste if you're to be saved.' He continued to speak softly to the woman all the time he worked.

'Cissy, help me!' she groaned as he settled her on the floor with a pillow beneath her head.

'Rest easy. You're in safe hands,' he soothed. It was doubtful in her condition that she could understand him, but at the gentle tone of his voice she quietened.

'Aunt Dotty . . . Uncle Ez . . . don't die, please.'

The tormented cry thrust thoughts of his own safety aside. Stripping the soiled sheets from the bed, he bundled them up and threw them down the stairs to be burnt later. Beneath one of the pillows he found the package he had come for. He put it aside and went in search of clean linen. Once the bed was fresh and sweet-smelling, he turned his attention to the woman. As he lifted her, her eyes opened, their green depths staring unseeing into his face. 'Jack . . . my love. You came back. They're dead . . . dead!'

'Hush, my lovely. You're safe now.'

She slumped unconscious once more as Mark laid her on the bed. Suppressing his revulsion, he began to strip her of her vomit-stained garments, one by one.

An hour later he was downstairs burning the last of the soiled linen and clothing. He had poured away the buckets of water used for washing the woman's body, satisfied that though she was still gravely ill, he had done all he could to make her comfortable. A search had revealed the herbs left by the barber-surgeon and some of these were now infusing in hot water for a posset. The others were in the plague pan, smoking in a corner of the sick room to sweeten the air.

Once more upstairs he sat on the bed and held the posset to her lips. 'Drink, my lovely. Come now, drink. It will make you well. Give you the strength you need to fight the fever.' He forced a small measure down her throat. The cold compress he placed on her brow quietened her feverish ramblings. Experience warned him that the fever was approaching its height. If he could prevent it from soaring dangerously high, and she was able to keep the posset down, she would stand a fighting chance.

Her unbound hip-length hair spread like a silken web across the pillow and his fingers tightened on the scissors with regret. To save her life it would have to be cut as short as a man's. Her face was delicate and intelligent, the features even in repose speaking of a quiet but determined courage. She would need all her hidden resources to survive the night.

'You will live, my lovely. You can't die now. Fight it.'

Gabriellen was aware of sound first. A pigeon cooed from the garden and there were footsteps and the creak of the loose floorboard by her window. Then the bed moved as someone sat down on it. The effort needed to open her eyes was too great and her head felt muzzy. The fire which had consumed her body was replaced by languor as she became aware of the soft stroking movements across her shoulders and neck moving up to her face. So light was the touch it barely disturbed her, only the refreshing coolness of the cloth dragging her dulled senses back to reality.

She lay absolutely still, trying to fathom what had happened. Her mind refused to work. There was only the touch of linen sheets against her body and a growing discomfort which gnawed at her stomach. She was hungry. Then the caress of the damp, fragrant cloth upon her brow drew a soft sigh of pleasure from her, followed by a catch in her breath as the pain in her parched throat intensified.

'Drink, my lovely,' a deep sonorous voice commanded –

a voice which had broken through her unconsciousness – a kind soothing voice, but one she could not place.

A cup was pressed to her mouth and a few drops of soothing honeyed water trickled past her lips. Feeling stronger, she opened her eyes. A man's cleanshaven face, tanned from a life in the open, hovered above her. She blinked stupidly, her mind refusing to function as she stared at the stranger. Should she know him? No, it was a face one would certainly remember. His short black curly hair fell over his high forehead. His face was rugged, the nose sharply pointed, and his chin square. His ebony eyes were hard and assessing as they regarded her with a serious expression.

'Who are you?' she croaked, her eyes widening in alarm. 'What . . .'

'Please, Miss Angel, rest easy.' His voice carried the melody of Wales in its accent. 'I mean you no harm. You've been grievously ill and I fear your servants have fled the house. I am Mark Rowan.'

'Jack's friend.' She relaxed, then realising that he was in her bedchamber, immediately tensed.

'I found you near to death and alone,' he explained. 'I have been here for two days.'

Memory flooded back. She, too, had succumbed to the fever. But she had survived. Not so Aunt Dotty and Uncle Ez. They were buried. She squeezed her eyes shut to combat the agony of grief. After several moments she found the strength to ask, 'Where's Cissy? She would not have left me. Is she dead?'

'She's gone, that's all I know.' His quiet, lilting voice washed over her, its calm authority soothing and reassuring. It was the tone one used to an ailing child or a sick animal. 'Rest now. You are not strong enough to talk.'

The tiredness was returning but she fought against it to enquire, 'Why are you doing this?'

'Someone had to look after you, and I was here.' He shrugged aside her words.

'Jack said you could be trusted,' she murmured sleepily as she settled more comfortably on the mattress. The cool sheet against her bare skin made her gasp in alarm. Her hand sliding across her stomach confirmed her fears. She was naked beneath the covers and from the smell of lavender soap, her body had been freshly bathed. How long had

Cissy been gone? Hadn't he said two days?

'Were you the only one to tend me?'

The dark eyes were unapologetic. 'I know of only one way to halt a fever: a regular infusion of prepared herbs, and the patient's temperature lowered by cool compresses and baths.'

Her flesh burned so fiercely with embarrassment, she thought the fever was returning.

'I would have spared your blushes if I could. But to preserve your modesty would have cost you your life.'

There was no salacious gleam in his eyes, only concern. Common sense told her he could not have done otherwise. It was unlikely that any of the townswomen would have risked contracting the pestilence to save her. She looked into his face, and saw only kindness and concern.

Holding the sheet to her chin, she tried to sit up and failed. Her gaze could not meet his as she said, 'In the coffer in the corner is a clean shift. Would you kindly pass it to me.'

When he placed it in her hands, she looked down at the lace edging the cuffs. He'd been kind to try and reassure her, and kinder still to have taken the time and risk to nurse a stranger. Not an enviable task, she knew. Had she not cleaned up after her aunt and uncle? Her blush deepened, her voice becoming a self-conscious whisper. 'You saved my life, for that I thank you. But now that the fever has gone, I shall need a maid to tend me. Just for a day or so, until I can get up.'

'No one will come to this house. I've tried.' There was a questioning edge to his voice which hardened his tone. 'And it's not just the contagion they fear. One called you an outlaw's spawn.'

Her green eyes widened with shock and then clouded over. 'Sweet Jesu, how I despise those sanctimonious crones. I had not realised the extent of Uncle Ezekiel's protection.'

Mark checked his words of sympathy. She did not need them. There was nothing self-pitying in the anger which returned the colour to her cheeks and set her eyes afire.

Gabriellen heaved herself on to her elbow, her voice impatient. 'When I am strong, I shall leave this place. But first I must send word to Jack.'

'To Jack?' A wary note entered into his voice. 'What is Jack Stoneham to you?'

'I love him.' The simple words were out before she realised she had been indiscreet. She slumped back on to the pillow, suddenly tired. Why had she found it so easy to tell this comparative stranger the truth? Mark Rowan had a way with him which drew confidences. She looked at the bedside table, her glance softening as she saw the emerald and pearl pendant safely placed there.

'That necklace was a gift from Jack, I'll warrant,' he said, his expression thoughtful.

'Yes. It was his parting gift.'

He smiled. 'Sleep if you can. It is the best healer. I shall prepare some soup for you to eat. You must be hungry.'

'I am.'

'That's a good sign.'

He left the room so she could rest. In the kitchen he prodded the fire to life and stirred the cooking pot hanging over its flames. A frown puckered his brow as he reflected on the woman's words. During her delirium she had called out often to Jack. Her love for him was obvious. But Jack always had that effect on women – even after the briefest encounter. He had not realised the pendant had been Jack's gift. He had read the inscription and it troubled him. Jack was usually more circumspect.

Clearly, the woman upstairs was no ordinary light of love to his friend. She had a strength of character and courage which set her apart from others of her sex. Jack would have found the combination irresistible.

It had shown in her acceptance of his presence in her sickroom. Thank God there had been no maidenly hysterics. But despite her calm upon learning that he had tended her, there was no brazenness in her manner. At two and twenty he had experience enough to know innocence when he met it.

Mark took the packet of papers his friend had left for him from his doublet and sat on a kitchen stool to read them again. Once he had memorised the names and dates they contained, he tossed them into the fire. As the parchment turned brown at the edges, then curled into a blackened mass, he stared into the flames. He brought his mind back to his immediate plans. As soon as the wench was strong enough, he must leave this house. He had delayed his work and it was time he obeyed the instructions in the packet and journeyed to Bosham and Pagham.

Suddenly restless, he went out into the garden. The day was warm but overcast. He went to the stables where the two horses whinnied a welcome. Taking a honeyed confection from the pouch at his waist, he held his palm out to the black gelding and rubbed its nose before moving on to his own horse two stalls away.

'Hey, old fellow, are you getting restless too? Not long now. There'll be a mare for you to service at Bosham – that will cool your blood.'

He stroked Glendower's neck as he spoke. The stallion flexed his muscles as Mark's hand moved over them, but remained calm under his experienced touch. Though should a stranger try such familiarity, Glendower would become a rearing, snorting beast, his shod hooves deadly as they lashed out. Mark alone could handle him. He had bred and trained the horse himself. Wherever he went, the stallion gained him the entry he needed. Glendower was the finest of his kind. In beauty, speed and stamina he was unparalleled. His rich chestnut coat and striking white blaze were the envy of every horse-owner Mark met. Few could resist the chance to have Glendower cover their mares.

Roving the countryside with the stallion had become a way of life to Mark. The income from it was steadily rebuilding his family's fortune and the home he loved. Every groat he could save went into improving the breeding mares he owned in partnership with Saul Bywood, who was married to his youngest sister. Mark was justifiably proud of his achievements. His father's death after a decade of ill-health had left their family almost penniless. To survive and keep their house and land, Mark, then seventeen, had decided on a new venture.

At first the family were against him. But with Saul's help and shared enthusiasm, they had been won over. When his invalid mother went to live with his eldest sister Faith, Saul and Aphra had moved into the house with him. A keen horsewoman herself, Aphra at five years his senior had not scrupled to put on her oldest gown and muck out the stables when their meagre savings would not stretch to more than one hired groom. Success had now brought the means to hire three grooms, and this allowed her to divide her time between running the house, bringing up four children, and training the yearlings. It took years to establish a stud farm but slowly their reputation had built up. Mark was determined that his horses, already known as the Rowan strain, would be the most sought after in England.

'And we will succeed, won't we, my handsome boy?' he said as he began to brush Glendower's chestnut coat. 'God willing, this winter will see an end of my need to travel the countryside. I grow weary of this constant life on the road. Five years it's been. I miss the old place and the hills of home. But the threat of a Spanish invasion cannot be ignored. England has its trials to face before its future can be settled. And like all true subjects of our Queen, I'd die rather than see the Inquisition bring its reign of terror to these shores.'

Chapter Seven

Gabriellen held Tristan over her shoulder, stroking the cat as she sat in the parlour. She looked up as Mark Rowan entered the room carrying a posset for her to drink. It was her third day after rising from her sick-bed and ten since she had woken to discover the Welshman in her chamber. Whilst he had been away visiting Bosham, a servant had been grudgingly loaned by a neighbour to attend her.

Her lips set stubbornly as she looked at the posset he held out to her. She held Tristan defensively against her and wrinkled her nose at its pungent smell. She had forgotten how persistent he could be when it came to making her take the foul-tasting brews. 'I do not need that. I'm much stronger.'

'If stubbornness is a sign of returning strength, then you progress rapidly by the hour!' He stood over her, his hand extended. 'Drink it. It will do you good.'

'I did not suffer these foul brews when Jane tended me.' She pushed his hand away. Tristan meowed in protest and jumped out of her arms to stalk off. 'I do not need another posset. I am strong. Strong enough to travel.'

'We have discussed this already. You know my views. Now drink this!'

She knew better than to argue with him when he used that tone. She drank it down and pulled a face at him.

'The wind will change and you will stay like that,' he said with a dry laugh. 'Now you have drunk your medicine you should rest.'

'I do not need to. And don't treat me like a child.'

'Then do not act like one.'

She glowered at him, searching for a suitable reply. Seeing the amusement in his eyes, she shrugged. How was it he always got the better of her? Well, he would not on this occasion. 'Tomorrow I intend to leave here to find my father.'

Mark put down the bowl and pushed back a lock of black hair from his brow, his voice sharp with exasperation. 'You cannot travel the highways alone. Be patient. I've sent word to Jack at Plymouth, and to your father. Esmond will make the necessary arrangements for you to join him.'

She owed Mark her life. But indebted or not, she now found her will locked against his in their first quarrel. He could be as stubborn as herself. It was irritating to discover that beneath his concern and persuasiveness, there was a will of iron.

Her temper began to rise and her eyes flashed green fire. 'Jack's first duty is to his country. The English navy is now gathering at Plymouth. How can he leave? He must remain with his ship, ready to sail should the Armada be sighted. And contacting my father could take weeks.'

She glared at him mutinously. As usual he wore the same battered green leather doublet, breeches and tan high boots. He dressed for practicality and comfort not fashion. It was that cool practicality she was at odds with. She did not doubt for a moment that Jack would have taken her with him, if he had been here instead. But then, from the first Jack had made no secret of his designs upon her virtue. Not so Mark. It was why she felt secure in his company. His voice and manner were at all times those of a gentleman and he treated her accordingly. Not once had he tried to press his attentions upon her. Irrationally, she now felt he was treating her like a wilful younger sister and she resented it.

She said, 'Why can't I ride my uncle's gelding? I know Father's route to Winchester.'

Mark again brushed his fingers through his hair, a sign she recognised that his patience was wearing thin. He sat down on the wooden settle by the hearth and crossed his legs. 'You know as well as I that the players go where they are in demand. Your father could be anywhere. The safest place for you is here, until Esmond can send a servant for you.'

Against that stoic reason, a show of temper would get her nowhere. Breathing deeply, she calmed herself and looked round the familiar walls of the parlour. A large cobweb had formed high in a corner and the wooden furniture had dulled. She had never seen the house so neglected. The familiar ache of grief returned and her throat worked against the pain of her loss.

'Can't you see, I cannot stay here? Everywhere I look are memories of Dotty and Ezekiel. My place is with my father. The apprentices have been released from their indentures. There are no servants I am responsible for . . .'

He uncrossed his legs and sat forward, anger sparking in his black eyes. 'That cook of yours should be found and punished. Not only for what she stole from this house – but for leaving you to die from neglect. God knows I've tried to trace her, but it appears she's left the district.'

'Cissy had seen three people die from the pestilence in this house, and was frightened.' Gabriellen found it hard to condemn the woman for running away. 'That I can understand and forgive. But not the theft of the silver and Aunt Dotty's jewellery.' Her voice shook as grief took hold of her once more. 'Not for its value, but because her stealing was a wicked ingratitude to Uncle Ezekiel's memory – to all he believed in. He gave her a second chance to live a respectable life, and she repaid him with treachery.'

A tear rolled down her cheek and she wiped it away. Mark crossed to the window and lightly squeezed her shoulder as he sat at her side. 'Don't upset yourself over that woman.'

How often he found the right words to comfort her. She managed a weak smile and her chin came up. 'I've no right to ask more of you, Mark. You've done so much. You have neglected your business because of me. It must have cost you dear.' Her voice softened. She needed to speak, but was uncertain of his reaction. 'Please let me repay some of your losses.'

'Would you now insult me?'

She shook her head and smiled fondly. 'Of course not. Nevertheless, I'm in your debt. Jack is fortunate to have you as his friend.'

Mark held up his hands to stop her, and laughed. 'I know that tone, Gabriellen. You're a scheming wench. Flattery will not change my mind. The roads are not safe for a woman to travel. Besides, have you considered the harm to your reputation if I am your only companion?'

She looked up at him, a dimple appearing at her mischievous smile. 'My reputation is in shreds. Have you not stayed here alone with me for ten days?' The banter died from her eyes as she added witheringly, 'The gossips of the town are not known for their charitable tongues. While I care nothing for their malicious censure, I'd not relish their persecution. Once you leave I will be at their mercy. A day in the stocks for immoral behaviour would be the likely punishment.'

He regarded her through the screen of his black lashes. His voice was bland when at last he spoke.'Undoubtedly they think I should offer you marriage.'

She rolled her eyes heavenwards in mock horror. 'Heaven spare us from virtuous matrons with minds like middens! It's unjust. You saved my life. I despise those sanctimonious crones. You have treated me with courtesy, honour, and brotherly respect.'

He sat back and recrossed his legs. 'You are very like my sister Aphra. Not in looks – she is all Welsh with her dark eyes and hair. She thumbs her nose at convention to get her own way. Saul married her when she was fifteen and curbed her headstrong ways. They adore each other. Fortunately, he is man enough to tame her wild spirits, without breaking her will.' Mark looked her squarely in the eye. 'But I am not your brother, Gabriellen, remember that.'

There was nothing in his expression or voice, which allowed her to read the thoughts behind his warning. 'Jack is my friend. Because of his affection for you, I stayed to ensure your recovery. He'll not thank me if I put you in danger.'

She met his stare, equally resolute. 'My place is with my father. If you will not allow me to travel with you when you leave tomorrow, I shall send word to Dan Luffe. I doubt he has as yet apprenticed himself to another master. I will pay him to escort me.'

'Good heavens, woman! An apprentice is but a boy. He cannot protect you.' He stood up and glared down at her, the taut set of his face warning her of the control he was keeping upon his temper. 'How can I convince you that the highway is no place for a woman? I've been set upon more than once by outlaws.'

'Than I shall not travel as a woman, but a lad. I'm tall, and since the fever, slender enough, to carry off the disguise.'

'It is madness.'

'No, it will work.' Her voice warmed with enthusiasm. 'As a surprise to my father at Christmas, I acted the role of Prince Richard from his play *The Warrior King*. Father said it was a pity that women had no place on the professional stage for I was a natural actor.'

'This is no Christmas revel,' he warned. 'The subject is closed.' He strode to the door.

Gabriellen overtook him and although the sudden exertion left her pale, her grin was impish as she looked over her shoulder, her foot on the first stair. 'Then I must convince you I am no faint-heart.'

Despite his exasperation at her stubbornness, Mark noted the lightness in her step as she ascended the stairs. He shook his head. What was she up to now? Gabriellen had recovered with remarkable speed from the ravages of the pestilence. Still his misgivings remained. His friendship with Jack had governed his actions in tending her, and to his surprise he had found her company enjoyable. That she was Jack's woman put all thoughts of physical attraction from his mind. The one thing he and Jack never shared was a woman. But having saved Gabriellen's life, he now found himself feeling protective of her. Couldn't she see the difficulties, not to speak of the dangers, involved if they travelled together? If she did, he suspected, she would dismiss them. She was brave to the point of foolhardiness. Short of locking the headstrong minx in her room and employing a gaoler, there would be no stopping her carrying out her threat to join her father.

Going to the stables, he took off his doublet and picked up the pitchfork to clear out the soiled straw. As he worked, he cursed Jack's message which had brought him to this house. He did not regret saving Gabriellen's life, but his work had its commitments. The woman's presence on the road would be an added complication. Tossing the straw into the wooden barrow with a will, he almost choked on the particles of dust that rose into the air. He swore heatedly in Welsh. How could he allow Gabriellen to make the journey alone? The adamant light in her green eyes had told him she was set upon the course. Reluctantly, he admired her courage. Leaning on the pitchfork he ran his hand through his hair. What choice had he? He would never desert a friend who needed him.

The thought brought a frown to his brow. It was inconceivable but true, he did regard her as a friend. Acquaintances he had beyond number. He was never short of a drinking partner, and having natural, healthy appetites, there was always a wench willing to serve his comfort. But the tie of friendship he had been sparing of, even amongst his mistresses of long standing. It was a bond he did not forge easily. To him it was sacrosanct, severed only by death or betrayal. Until now he had never accorded it to a woman. Not even to Meredith . . . A shutter closed over his mind before cruel grief at his sweetheart's death broke his composure. Four years had not eased his pain. A week before their wedding, Meredith had been thrown from her horse and killed.

He pushed his thoughts back to the present problem and Gabriellen. Jack Stoneham held her in high regard, the pendant proved that. He owed it to Jack to protect her. It was little enough against the greater service Jack had done him which had begun their incongruous friendship.

The sound of footsteps outside on the flagstoned yard took him to the stable door. His mouth opened in astonishment. He caught his lower lip between his teeth to hide his amusement.

Dressed in a russet padded doublet and venetian knee breeches, short black cloak swirling about swaggering shoulders, and plumed cap tipped rakishly on a slant, was what appeared to be a handsome young gallant. Gabriellen strutted towards him. She even managed to avoid tripping over the sword hanging from her side. One gloved hand rested negligently on the sword hilt, her mouth twisting in a disdainful sneer as she studied her audience. It was a stance she had copied from Cornelius Hope when he paraded across the stage and wished to steal the scene. Her shorn hair had been brushed back from her forehead in a masculine style and the narrow ruff hid the feminine curve of her throat. She cut an impressive figure, he'd give her that.

Placing one foot before the other, Gabriellen swept the cap from her head with an elegant flourish and bowed to him. 'What say you now, my disbelieving Celt? Is not my

97

reputation safe?' Even her voice had deepened, and the baggage had the audacity to copy his own lilting tones. 'I travel incognito. Master Gabriel Angel, at your service.'

Mark raised a dark eyebrow quizzically, his eyes crinkling with amusement. 'Incognito! With the name Gabriel Angel you will be remembered from here to the Scottish border! Master Angel Gabriel – where is your halo?'

'I take your point.' She joined in his laughter. 'It shall be Master Gabriel . . .'

'Rowan.' Mark conceded defeat. 'Master Gabriel Rowan – my cousin from Pembrokeshire. A young coxcomb to be sure in his fine velvet, which puts my battered leather doublet to shame.'

She bowed again. 'Master Gabriel Rowan. Your servant, sir.'

Delighted that he had agreed to accompany her, she ran to his side and impulsively kissed his cheek. 'You'll not regret it, Mark. I'll be no trouble.'

'Never forget your role.' His voice was stern. 'From this moment you are Gabriel Rowan. Many would misconstrue such a show of affection. There are men enough who have a yearning for pretty boys, but I am not such a one. Nor do I wish to duel with every knave who suggests it.'

Her shocked expression made him soften his words. The girl was an innocent, and as such, would need vigilant protection. He did not relish the role of knight errant now forced upon him. God willing, they would meet up with Esmond Angel before too long.

He returned to mucking out the gelding's stall, his voice deliberately impersonal. 'If you are to wear a sword, you will need some idea of how to handle it. And also the dagger at your belt. Time is short. We will begin our first lesson in the courtyard as soon as the horses have been tended to.'

From the day Lord Barpham's players left Chichester they were plagued by ill luck. Both Cornelius Hope and Robin Flowerdew developed a throat infection and lost their voices. At Midhurst only two performances instead of four were played. The audience, disappointed that Hope was not to act, were restless, and even Esmond as his replacement, was poorly received. At the second performance Will Appleshot, the apprentice who stepped into Robin's part, was so nervous he forgot half his lines, and even Poggs could not save the day. After settling the inn bill, they left Midhurst having made a loss of two pounds instead of a profit. Two other village shows could not be played because of a week of rain.

Esmond Angel stared down into his empty tankard oblivious to the noise of the taproom around him. Why does ill fortune dog my life? he wondered wearily, passing a hand across his reddened, bleary eyes. In a vain attempt to recoup his losses, he had just gambled away the last of the troupe's reserve money. Now he could not even meet the bill of this rat-infested hovel which passed as an inn. Removing his hands from his face, he clenched his fists and banged them on the table. What was he to do? The next quarter day's profit from the London property was already accounted for to pay off the interest from the last moneylender. Even the money left him by Ezekiel would be swallowed up by his debts. He could not sell the house in Chichester, which was left in trust to Gabriellen. It was too much to contemplate. Not that he wanted to profit from their deaths. Thank God, Rowan had found Gabriellen in time. But now the girl wanted to join him. How could she? He did not want his daughter to see him like this. She was better off in Chichester. An hour ago the messenger had left with his reply to her request.

He drained his goblet and signalled for the dowdy servant to refill it. He scowled at the watery brew, his thoughts growing more gloomy. As if his personal problems were not great enough, Cornelius Hope – who spent as extravagantly as Esmond – was threatening to leave the troupe because his share of the profits was so small. Without him Lord Barpham would withdraw his patronage. And without Lord Barpham's support, the troupe would lose its licence – a serious matter since they would then be regarded as vagrants, thereby forced to take their chances whilst scraping a living and avoiding arrest whenever they played. Cornelius had given him a week to resolve their financial problems. God's nightgown! This was Petersfield not London. Where was he going to find a moneylender here?

Victor Prew's bony face set into a satisfied smile as he continued to study Esmond Angel. He had followed the actor here after he had seen him lose a small fortune at cards two hours earlier. Prew patted the bulging money pouch concealed inside his doublet. He knew a man in need of money when he saw one. This was the chance he had been waiting for.

During the three years since, at the age of twenty-seven, he had inherited his father's money, he had doubled his fortune. Prew chewed the corner of his wispy mouse-coloured moustache. He had been keeping an eye on the progress of Lord Barpham's players since their performance before the Queen had been so well received. They might be a small troupe but they were a rising one.

Or would be, if Esmond Angel curbed his gambling. But, then, that very weakness was his entrée into their circle. And with it, he would gain the admittance he needed to Elizabeth's Court.

As he watched, Angel shoved his tankard aside and swayed to his feet. Prew stepped forward, smiling ingratiatingly as he blocked the actor's path.

'If my eyes do not deceive me, it is Esmond Angel, is it not? I have seen several of your plays – all excellent. I must congratulate your troupe on their expertise, their wit and sense of drama. I was cast down that I arrived here today to discover I had missed your performance.'

Esmond stared down at a man a head shorter than himself. The candlelight fell full on the stranger's face. What he could discern of his thin features and hooked nose did nothing to impress him. Neither did the man's short, puny legs in red hose which were reed thin and looked ridiculous beneath the padded peascod belly of his velvet doublet and stiffened trunk hose. Upon noting the ruby buttons on the man's doublet and the wide band of sable edging his cloak, however, Esmond halted his sharp rebuff. He allowed the man's flattery to act as balm to his wounded pride and lift his flagging spirits.

'Will you join me in a tankard of sack, Mr . . . ?' Esmond invited. If the man was that interested in the troupe, he might be gulled into providing the badly needed loan.

'Prew. Victor Prew. Merchant of London. Your servant, sir. I would be honoured to take a drink with you. I insist that I pay for the privilege of toasting your health. I've a passion for the play, sir. Sadly I've no memory for lines and would make a shoddy actor. I indulge my passion whenever I can by watching the masters of the craft. Lord

Barpham's players are the equal, if not the superior, of the Admiral's.'

'You are very kind, Mr Prew.' Esmond warmed to the man. The fatness of Prew's purse was encouraging. Give him an hour and he would have this skinny runt begging to part with his money. Yes, indeed, Esmond mused with satisfaction, when had his able tongue ever failed to gull an innocent cove? Within the hour his financial worries would be over. Or at least drastically deferred. 'You are a man of sound sensibility, Mr Prew. I admire that. Let us drink to the wonders of the stage and to the magic it weaves.'

Jack Stoneham stood on the quarter-deck of *The Swift* watching the first of Lord Barpham's cannon being hauled up from the quayside by a creaking pulley. His face was drawn with concentration as he saw it rise higher. All around him was ordered confusion. Men pulled on the ropes and shouted instructions as they manoeuvred the cannon into position through the hatch in the ship's side. It was a dull misty morning. A stiffening wind blowing off the sea caused the ship to rock against its moorings, making the task dangerous and difficult. Timing was all important. If the heavy gun slipped it could kill or maim a sailor, or even seriously damage the ship. The carpenters had been at work for a week to accommodate the larger guns upon the strengthened floor of a lower deck. Unlike the six smaller guns mounted on the forecastle and half deck, these had to be placed low in the ship for greater stability, and fired through newly cut gunports.

'Well, Jack, what do you think of my guns?' Lord Barpham demanded, his Sussex burr much stronger than Jack's own. 'There's nothing like Wealden iron for forging a solid cannon. They'll smash the Spaniards to pieces.'

Jack turned to Lord Barpham, whose round face was reddened by the wind and sun. His lordship wore a sleeveless jerkin with shirt-sleeves rolled to the elbows. He was bare-headed and his straggling blond hair blew untidily across his bushy cinnamon beard. There were times, as now, when Barpham looked more like a seaman or iron-master than a peer of the realm.

'Had I those guns two years ago when I sailed the Spanish Main,' Jack admitted with a grin, 'I could have tripled the treasure brought home to fill England's coffers.'

'Not forgetting your own.' Lord Barpham chuckled. 'I envy you those years. Though it's a narrow line drawn between privateering and buccaneering these days. But what a life! The freedom and excitement of the sea – the freedom from a wife's nagging tongue.'

Jack tensed, suspicious of his lordship's insinuation.

Lord Barpham shook his head as he regarded Jack's stiff figure and added without rancour, 'No offence intended.'

Jack relaxed. 'None taken, my lord. Am I to understand from your words that Lady Barpham wishes you to return to Court?'

'Sadly so. I've no patience with all the intrigue that life entails. I'm a man who likes to say what I think – not coat it with honey, so that no one knows what I'm thinking or scheming. Our Queen knows my loyalty.' He nodded towards the other cannon waiting on the quay. 'That's what's important. Good Wealden ore to make the best shot and cannon money can buy. If I can't have the sea, I can make the arms which will make England the master of it. Give me the satisfaction of that – and my horses – and I'll die a happy man.'

Jack despised Lord Barpham's lack of ambition. He could understand the frustration of Lady Barpham, who spent all her time at Court trying to marry her two sons and five daughters into the most prominent families in the land. For her pains she received little help from her husband. But Jack could not fault Lord Barpham's generosity. It was agreed that the cannon would remain on his ships after the Spanish were defeated, providing Lord Barpham captained one of them. Since it would be an experienced second-in-command who actually gave the orders, Jack had no qualms as to the safety of the ship. He was happy to let Lord Barpham have his moment of glory.

The first gun safely on board, Jack turned his attention to the ship's supplies also being loaded. The quay at Plymouth was crowded with stacks of barrels, ropes, cannonballs, spare anchors and chains – the stores needed for the growing number of ships provisioning in readiness to fight the Spaniards. Everywhere he looked men were busy. Even the narrow sloping streets of the town were packed with carts and wagons bringing goods from the surrounding countryside and towns.

His gaze moved seaward to where the mist distorted into

ghostly spectres the vessels riding at anchor. Here stately galleons, smaller pinnaces and armed merchantmen jostled for anchorage and, weaving through these, scores of row-boats ferried provisions from land to ship. All his three ships were here, their masts part of the forest of rigging blocking out the sight of the sea beyond.

At least on *The Swift* the provisioning was almost complete. The cannonballs were stored below decks, together with the new sails which replaced those shredded by the storm. Two planks were placed against the ship's side and along these men rolled the barrels of dried peas, oatmeal and casks of vinegar – the latter used to disguise the taste of stale food and also for cleaning the ship's timbers. Last of all to be brought aboard would be the livestock: pigs, chickens, and possibly a goat or two.

He raised his gaze to the leaden sky where a watery shaft of sunlight scythed through the thinning clouds to brighten the church spires and towers of the port. Directly above him, a flock of seagulls screeched. Fights broke out among them as they searched for scraps of food, their raucous cries adding a further din to the shouts of the sailors working on the quay. With each passing day tempers became more frayed. The ships' captains, impatient and argumentative, fretted at the delays and shortages of supplies. The number of ships was so vast it seemed they would never be properly provisioned. The town was overcrowded. Many of the more respectable inhabitants found themselves virtual prisoners in their own homes for fear of being accosted by drunken, brawling sailors.

A cormorant landed on the ornately carved stern of *The Swift*'s after-castle. Black neck arched and wide wings spread, its dark shape stood sober sentinel upon the red, blue and gilded paintwork. The noise and the scenery had become so familiar to Jack he scarcely noticed them. All he felt was the grinding frustration of a man used to action, who suddenly found himself cooped up in port.

What he would not give to break the monotony and spend a pleasant hour or two with Gabriellen! A tightness formed in his chest. Several days ago he had received Mark's letter. He had been stricken to learn that Gabriellen had been so near to death when his friend had discovered her. He was indebted to Mark for saving her life, but how was Gabriellen now? He was stuck in Plymouth and forced to obey Lord Effingham's orders now that the English navy was amassing here.

A footfall at his side jerked him from his reverie.

'That's the second cannon loaded,' said Lord Barpham. 'I'll check below they are properly secured on to their carriages. With luck we shall also get *The Bonaventure Elizabeth* armed before nightfall. That will leave just *The Golden Lady* for tomorrow. Wasn't she your first ship?'

'Without the *Lady* I would never have captured the other two from the Spanish and would still be an impoverished second-master.' Jack kept his voice quiet but impersonal. The acquisition of the *Lady* was a part of his life he did not wish to dwell upon. He deliberately changed the subject. 'With your guns, there's no reason our names should not be as famous as Effingham, Hawkins or Drake.'

'Aye, that should please Lady Barpham – and it will do you no harm at Court, Jack.'

He made no comment. The feel of the deck beneath his feet no longer gave him the thrill it once had. When the Armada was defeated he would have done with the sea-roving life. Ambition burned strong in him and he was involved in several ventures he hoped would make him his fortune. He had already bought the land he needed. It was a short step from that to visualise the manor he would build there. No longer was it an impossible dream. Within five years he was determined it would become a reality. The once penniless fisherman's son would become a country gentleman. Even a knighthood might be his. There was no place in his plans for false modesty. Every aim he had so far aspired to, he had achieved, and he intended it would remain so.

However, that was in the future. Now he was impatient for the work to be finished. Then he would sail to Chichester where a muster of Sussex recruits would be trained in seamanship and fighting. It was the lack of trained mariners which concerned him most, as systematically the coastal shires were being stripped of able-bodied men for service by the muster-masters. And in Chichester, Gabriellen awaited him.

'Cap'n Stoneham! Is Cap'n Stoneham aboard ship?' A puny lad in a battered brown felt cap, dusty sleeveless jerkin and long loose breeches hollered from the quay.

'Cap'n's aboard,' a surly, bearded midshipman answered.

'What's yer business wi' 'im?'

'I've to deliver this.' The lad waved a letter in the air, its red seal like a coin of blood on the creamy parchment.

Jack signalled to the midshipman to let the lad come aboard. 'Have you travelled far?' he asked when the messenger stood before him.

'From Chichester, cap'n. I'd have got here yesterday but me horse went lame – miles from anywhere it were. I've walked best part of twenty miles on foot.'

Jack tossed him a silver coin. 'That's for your trouble.'

Turning the parchment over in his hand, he studied the writing on the front. To his disappointment it was in Mark's hand. Until now he had not realised how eagerly he had been awaiting Gabriellen's reply to his letter. He paused before breaking the seal and looked at Lord Barpham.

'Don't mind me – read your letter,' his lordship responded affably. 'Tis not bad news, I trust?'

'It's from Mark Rowan. Since it was through Mark that we were introduced, it may interest you that recently I met another of your protégés. Esmond Angel was in Chichester. One of his players was getting married.'

'A charming man, Angel. But there's a bit of the rogue about him. Of course it was Lady Barpham who insisted I give my patronage to his players, especially since the Queen was so delighted with their play last winter. Truth to tell, I enjoy a good play with lots of action – just the type Angel favours – so I willingly agreed. Come to think of it, the troupe are not far from here in Dorset, if my memory serves me right. If we're to be holed up here for some weeks, waiting on those damned Spaniards, I may send word to Angel. He can put on a play or two for our entertainment.'

Seeing Jack impatiently finger the seal, he added considerately, 'But I'll leave you to read your letter.'

As Lord Barpham disappeared down the stairs to the lower deck, Jack broke the seal. Mark's missive was short.

My friend,
To ease your mind, I would inform you that Gabriellen has fully recovered. She speaks of you constantly but is unhappy here after the death of her relatives. She is determined to join her father. Would that I had received word from you to know your mind upon the matter. Having

failed to dissuade her, I have agreed to escort her to Win-
chester. Believing your affections for her are genuine, I
will guard her reputation as I would my own sister's.
   Your servant and friend,
      Mark Rowan

He crushed the letter in his hand and swore loudly. Clearly
his letter had not arrived at Chichester, and now Gabriellen
was to set out with only Mark for company. A stab of
jealousy pricked him at the thought of her and Mark alone
on the road for some days. He checked his thoughts. Gabriellen had proved her innocence and virtue, and Mark, perhaps alone of all men, would never betray a friend.

Still the thought of them alone tore into him. The intensity with which he had missed Gabriellen, and the constant
way that she filled his thoughts, had surprised him. No
woman had ever affected him so deeply. The glib words of
seduction had rolled with accomplished ease from his
tongue when he had courted her. They had never yet failed
him. But it was not just the anticipation of bedding her
which fired his blood. He wanted her completely and irrevocably as he had never wanted any other woman. For the
first time in his life he was in love – truly in love.

The knowledge both exhilarated and exasperated him.
Love was a complication in his life he could ill afford,
especially when the woman concerned was no more than a
playwright's daughter. Ambition had been his master for
so long, he could not curb it now – not when all he had
worked for was so close at hand. But he wanted Gabriellen
with a need which defied reason. Whatever sacrifices would
have to be made, she would not be one of them.

Chapter Eight

It was the first day of June. A new month and a new beginning, Gabriellen thought, as she guided her horse out of the stableyard and into step alongside Mark's stallion. At last she was leaving Chichester. Tristan had been found a home on a farm. Since Ezekiel had no relatives of his own, the house had been left to Esmond in her uncle's will, which had been drawn up several years earlier when Gabriellen had been a child. It had been like sealing a tomb when Mark had helped Gabriellen secure the shutters and lock the outhouses. Now the keys Aunt Dorothy had worn so proudly at her waist were hidden amongst her saddlebags.

Even at this early hour people were gathering at the gates of the city, waiting for them to open.

'Better pull your hat lower over your face,' Mark cautioned as they joined the queue as the gates were hauled apart. 'There's no point in adding to the gossip about you. One day you may wish to return to Chichester.'

Gabriellen obeyed. Mark kept Glendower on a tight rein, but the stallion strained forward, refusing to ride on a level with Sable, Gabriellen's mount. Wisely he permitted Glendower to keep his head in front, whilst preventing the horse from gaining a greater lead. An accomplished horsewoman herself, Gabriellen admired Mark's skill. He rode the prancing stallion as though they were one. Horse and rider made an impressive pair. Glendower held his tail in a proud arch, the sunshine turning his coat a glorious reddish-ginger. Even in his battered leather doublet, Mark attracted women's glances. His dark Welsh looks were a mixture of the sardonic and the sensual and the female attention he attracted amused Gabriellen.

Yet he was an enigma to her. She was sure the kindness he had shown her when she was ill was the same he would have shown to anyone in need. Yet his concern for others did not detract from his strength of character. He was not gullible like Uncle Ezekiel, and there was a steely streak in him which reminded her of Jack.

'No regrets?' Mark eyed her warily as they passed through the stone gateway and on to the Sussex Plain. 'It's not too late to change your mind.'

She shook her head emphatically. 'Once I set my mind upon a course, I stick to it.'

'I've come to learn that.' He lifted a brow as he taunted: 'Only you would make stubbornness a virtue.'

Once outside the city walls they crossed the level pasture used as practice butts since Plantagenet times. Here they skirted the contingent of men of all ages which was assembling. All were armed – albeit with a strange mixture of weapons. Whatever they happened to possess they held with pride. A few owned firearms, but the majority were poorly equipped. Merchants and craftsmen pitted their ancient swords against lawyers and churchwardens; shepherds and butchers competed with the long bow against fishermen and farmers; while the grooms and apprentices from the town and nearby villages launched into the affray with pitchforks, knives and staves. They were the local militia, some of the two thousand men raised by Sussex to be trained in readiness to fight should the Spanish try to invade.

The air resounded with the sounds of matchlocks firing, the clash of crossed steel, and of loud voices raised in battlecries as they charged straw effigies of Spanish soldiers. Enthusiasm outweighed discipline. From the occasional bursts of temper it was evident that the arms practice was being used to settle old scores. Nevertheless, it was a sight to stir her pride and patriotism, though running parallel with this was a sense of shock that so few local men were present.

'Where are they all?' she said indignantly. 'Two years ago when the call was first raised, Uncle Ezekiel was amongst the first to join. Their numbers then were much greater. How can it be that now the threat of invasion is upon us, their numbers have dwindled?'

'I doubt not that should the beacon fires be lit there will be men enough to guard our shores,' Mark replied. 'The farmers must tend their crops and livestock and the fishermen sail when the tide dictates. We need all the fish they can catch to be salted down to provision the English fleet gathering at Plymouth. Who knows how long they will be at sea!'

'Is Plymouth far from Winchester?'

'Far enough.' Mark turned to regard her, his voice terse. 'So don't get any ideas of visiting Jack. Plymouth will be filled with sailors, men preparing to face death in battle. They will all be drinking and carousing. It will be no place for a gently reared woman.'

The faint hope of persuading him died in her breast. 'Did I say I would go to Plymouth?' she retorted hotly.

'You did not have to. I have come to know you too well, Master Gabriel Rowan.'

Gabriellen checked a heated response, tempted though she was to pursue the matter. A quarrel might provoke Mark to drag her back to Chichester. She would not put it past him. She'd go mad trapped in Chichester. One day of encountering the glares of the townswomen had been enough. They saw her as a wanton for allowing Mark to remain in her house. Hypocrites! Not one of them had offered to help her. They would have let her die. Only pride had kept her from declaring publicly that she was innocent and still a maid.

The sounds from the training militia faded as they climbed the grassy slopes of the South Downs and passed a beacon, one of many in a chain across the high ground of southern England. On top of its high pole a brazier was stacked with logs and faggots ready to light at the first warning that the Armada was in the English Channel. It was a stark reminder of the uncertainty of the weeks ahead.

They rode for a league in companionable silence, both absorbed by their own thoughts. It was often like that between them. They would talk for hours upon interests they shared, then lapse into silence as they read, played chess, or worked upon some task together. Frequently they would exchange glances, a smile of understanding passing between them, until quite naturally the teasing conversation would resume. Even their arguments were resolved without any aftermath of ill-will. She felt at ease with Mark. It was a rare kind of friendship and she had come to regard him as the brother she'd never had.

Their route took them along the South Downs Way

which followed the ridge of hills from Buriton in the west to Beachy Head in the east. Gabriellen did not gaze back at the city with its cathedral mantled in golden sunlight. Chichester might have been her home since she was four, now she resolutely looked to the west and the future.

Beneath her black velvet bonnet the wind lifted her shorn tawny-gold mane. Enjoying her newfound freedom, she shook her head and delighted in the touch of the light breeze.

She laughed. 'You men don't realise how lucky you are. We spend our lives trapped by the foolish dictates of fashion which encases us in wire cages and dozens of petticoats. Our hair is confined by pins, padded and wired into styles which make our heads throb with pain.'

'There's always a price to pay for vanity. I prefer comfort to fashion.'

She looked at his leather doublet which had seen better days. His attire was far removed from the fashionable clothes that Jack wore. Yet until now she had scarcely noticed how Mark dressed. Despite his scruffiness he possessed several shirts, which although they too showed wear, were always freshly laundered and regularly changed. The way he carried himself, with self-possession and confidence, made what he wore seem unimportant.

Gabriellen lifted her head, breathing in the tangy scent of grass still covered in morning dew. Even with the light breeze, the day would be hot. The sultry June sun, still low in the sky, was already gathering heat, making the dew glitter like diamonds before the remaining droplets evaporated. By noon, that breeze would feel as if it was escaping from a furnace as it became trapped in the valleys between the Downs. Overhead, high out of sight, a skylark poured out its song, while from a distance the bleating of the sheep which populated the Downs carried to them.

Although the green arm of hills looked uninhabited, below them across the flat, darkly wooded Weald the rhythmic chopping and sawing of woodcutters could be heard. Interspersed between the great patches of trees, thistledown clouds of smoke rose from the charcoal burners' fires. The peace and tranquillity of the scene were an illusion. Over everything, like a great heartbeat, vibrated the deep, resonating thud of the heavy hammers worked by waterwheels as they beat out the iron ore in the furnaces. Even here

110

there was no escaping the industry and activity brought on by the approaching war with Spain.

With a sigh, Gabriellen turned in the saddle to look out to sea. From the top of the Downs the water looked like cloth of silver, with trailing pennants where the river inlets covered the flat marshland to the south. The cliffs of the Isle of Wight were visible and the flat Sussex coastal plain stretched far west into Hampshire – to Portsmouth, Southampton and beyond. Beyond, far beyond, to the high cliffs of Dorset and Devon, and further yet to Plymouth. Plymouth and Jack!

'You're quiet, Master Gabriel.' Mark broke into her thoughts. 'Are you tired?'

'We've scarcely travelled five leagues,' she dismissed his concern. Although her legs and arms had begun to ache, she would never admit it. 'I said I would not delay our travelling and I meant it.'

'I don't need a stubborn martyr on my hands,' Mark countered. 'If you're tired we will stop. If not we will ride for another hour before eating. In this growing heat the horses will need to rest in the shade, even if you do not.'

He began to hum a popular ballad and then, softly at first, to sing the words, until his baritone voice rose, delighting Gabriellen with the richness of its sound. She was entranced with the haunting song, and with his voice so full of Celtic feeling. As the last of the words trailed away, she clapped her hands and laughed.

'That was lovely, Mark. You have a magnificent voice.'

He shook his head in denial. 'No. My uncle is the singer in our family. But the Welsh part of me cannot resist giving voice on a day such as this.'

'And your English part makes you unduly modest. Although,' she added, 'I can see that you obviously regard yourself as more Welsh than English.'

'My mother is Welsh and she is a strong-minded, fiercely patriotic woman. All my sisters except Aphra married our countrymen. I suppose with such maternal influence my heart is inevitably Welsh.' He gave a twisted smile. 'That's as it should be since my home is there.'

'Mark Rowan is a very English name.' Her curiosity flowed as strongly as the playful urge to taunt him.

Glendower pranced sideways, taking advantage of his master's slackening the reins. Instantly he was brought under control. Mark slid a gloved hand along the chestnut's neck as his attention returned to Gabriellen. 'Mark is really Marcus, after my English father. My full name is Emrys Marcus Llewelyn Rowan.' His black eyes sparkled as he matched her teasing tone. 'Is Emrys Llewelyn Welsh enough for you?'

'Quite enough,' she answered with a laugh. 'Yet you spend much of your time roving the countryside. Is that not your chosen life?'

'It serves its purpose. Glendower is one of the best stallions of his kind. But his son, Cadwallader, a two year old, shows signs of surpassing him. It's upon Cadwallader that I build my hopes for the future. Through him the Rowan strain will be the most sought after in England – and Wales, of course.'

His voice warmed with passion and the conviction of success when he spoke of his home and future. But she sensed it was his home and family which were the most important. Ambition was not the force that drove Mark. How different he was to Jack. Even in their brief meetings she had sensed Jack was ruthlessly ambitious, perhaps too mercenary. She dismissed this thought as disloyal. She loved Jack with a fierce and abiding passion. He could do nothing wrong in her eyes. But despite her own yearnings to travel, her family would always come first in her life. The years of missing her father when he was absent for months at a time, of never truly knowing her mother, or having no brothers and sisters had always left an empty space in her life – for all Uncle Ezekiel and Aunt Dorothy had been unstinting in their love.

She crushed her fleeting envy of the stability that gave Mark his assurance and resumed their banter, mimicking his accent. 'Of course also Wales. With your horses named Glendower and Cadwallader after the great Princes of Wales, I would not dispute it, Emrys Llewelyn.'

He raised a questioning brow but before he could answer she went on, 'I cannot imagine a finer horse than Glendower. You will succeed, I know.' Talk of his home made her realise how little she knew of him. 'You have said you share your home with your sister Aphra and her husband Saul. You did not mention a wife or children. Are you married? And where is your home? What part of Wales? What is it like?'

He held up a hand in mock horror to ward off her barrage of questions. 'Whoa! This is an inquisition. Did you bombard Jack with so many questions? 'Tis small wonder he ran off to Plymouth.'

'I had not meant it to sound so,' she answered with a laugh. 'Jack and I had little time together. I learnt little of his life. I have no wish to pry into yours. Forgive me. I was interested – as a friend.'

'An inquisitive friend. As to your questions, no, I am not married.' His voice was gruff and a shadow crossed his face. Then it was gone, his grin strained as he added wickedly, 'Neither to my knowledge do I have any children. And my home is in the Vale of Clwyd, where the grass is the greenest I have ever seen. As for the mountains . . . there's beautiful they are. Proud cloud-capped sentries, who in winter guard our homeland from all but the most intrepid travellers. The house is old and rather rambling and often the roof leaks. I would not change it, but it is in dire need of restoration.'

Again the fierce pride in his voice struck her. 'You make it sound very special and beautiful.'

'To me it is. But you would probably not think so.' He turned away from her to scan the track ahead, his eyes crinkling against the bright sunlight. 'I'm sure you would regard life on a Welsh estate miles from anywhere to be boring. You cannot wait to start a new adventure – either with your father's players or Jack. And whatever life Jack may give you, it will never be dull.'

'Surely it is not the lifestyle you lead but the person you lead it with,' she found herself defending the dream she had yearned for over so many years. 'I cannot deny that there are places I have heard of which I would dearly love to see. And my father's life sounds exciting. But I am no different from other women. At some time in the future I want a home and children.'

'And in the meantime, why not a little excitement and adventure?'

Her chin tilted as she suspected he mocked her. 'Most certainly, why not?'

She found herself subjected to an unreadable ebony stare. 'That is what makes you very different from most other women.'

Unsure whether he was teasing her or not, she checked

113

a sharp retort. Without Mark she could not have under-taken this journey and, besides, it was a lovely summer's day – too lovely to allow her pride to spoil it. Her lips lifted in a smile of devilment and she flicked the russet doublet she was wearing. 'Surely it is more to the point that at this moment in time I *am* very different from most other young men.'

'Touché, Master Gabriel. Just remember that – should we reach Winchester and discover that your father is not there.'

Esmond Angel left Winchester a happier man. His purse was again full after they had played three performances to capacity crowds at one of the larger inns, Cornelius Hope was no longer threatening to leave the troupe and his own debts were cleared – all except the last account from Prew – but that was not pressing. Nor would be for another month.

Esmond looked across at Cornelius Hope who had urged his horse level with him.

'I've no idea how you do it, Esmond. Every time the company looks about to break up from lack of funds you find the means to keep us going. And most handsomely too.' He tapped the money pouch at his belt.

'I cannot have my best actor reduced to penury. I told you the depletion of our funds was but a temporary one.'

'Certes, you gulled that cove Prew right enough. Serve the runt right. I didn't like his eyes – too close together. And did you notice how they never smiled?' Cornelius dismissed their benefactor summarily. 'Who did the poxy cur think he was, demanding to become a sharer for so trifling a loan? Not that you were taken in, Esmond. Once a rogue always a rogue. What say you, dear fellow?'

'It is just another loan and I have faith in our company.'

Esmond hid his misgivings behind a bland smile. He neither liked nor trusted Victor Prew. Had there been another way he would have avoided dealing with the man. The interest on the loan was extortionately high.

Cornelius tossed back his head, his expression haughty and assured. 'Indeed, are we not the finest players in all England? Of late I have given much thought to our position. We would be better served if another experienced actor joined our troupe and you devoted more time to writing for us. It is time we concentrated on cultivating an audience amongst the nobility. We must put on more plays in London. Your meeting Sir Gilbert Wirley so fortuitously could be the start of grander things to come. An old acquaintance, was he?'

'No. Our reputation has begun to precede us. He especially requested *The Spanish Deliverance* when we entertain his son's wedding guests. Fortunately for us, he wants a different play performed every night for a week.'

Esmond had no intention of telling Hope that Sir Gilbert was the grandson of the Sir Henry Wirley who had hired his own grandfather as a mercenary. Apparently Thomas Angel, son of Wildboar, had lived up to his father's reputation and Sir Henry had related every wild escapade of his notorious retainer to his family – not least that Thomas Angel, unprincipled and undisciplined as he was, had risked his life to save Sir Henry's. That was something Esmond had not known, which did not surprise him, considering that since the days of Wildboar, people recounted all that was dissolute in members of his family, and not their saving graces.

'Esmond, dear fellow!' Cornelius preened his fair moustache, his head tilted grandly to one side. 'There will be nobles amongst Sir Gilbert's wedding guests. I trust you will use our week there to good purpose. I begin to weary of this constant travelling. Have you considered we could have our own playhouse in London? With the right patrons . . .'

He let the unfinished sentence hang in the air. Was it another hint that Hope no longer considered Lord Barpham's players grand enough? Esmond speculated. Without Hope the company would founder. Was there no end to the problems he must resolve? Suddenly, Jack Stoneham's proposition of a partnership was tempting.

'A playhouse of our own is not inconceivable,' he said. Noting the glow which ambition brought to the actor's face, he hastened to amend, 'Of course, such plans take time. Be assured they are in hand and will be further considered upon my return to London.'

'So, Master Playwright and Manager,' Cornelius pronounced in pompous tones, 'in the meantime, from the obscure depths of Wirley Manor we must drag ourselves wearily up to York, playing the larger towns on our way?'

115

Esmond relaxed. Here was safer ground upon which to pacify Cornelius and no prevarication was needed.

'Those plans are changed,' Esmond informed him. 'I received word from Lord Barpham today. At our first convenience we are to attend him at Plymouth. We are to entertain his guests. Since they are likely to include Lord Effingham, the Queen's Admiral, I shall depend upon you to show we are the match of any company in England – including the Admiral's own.'

'There shall be no doubt.' Cornelius puffed out his barrel chest. 'Of course we must put on *The Triumph of King Alfred*. It is my finest role. A revision or two to the new play would not go amiss. It lacks strength in places. In my opinion it would be improved if in the second act we were to include King Richard's address to the troops from *The Warrior King*. The final act needs more drama. Would not Merlin's speech of prophecy from *The Enchantress* be most suitable?'

'I will not have my plays cobbled together,' Esmond flared. 'Damn you, Hope, I've promised I shall extend your part in the new play, but not at the expense of other works. Besides, I intend we shall perform *The Enchantress*. The role of Merlin is always popular, and never more so than here in the West Country where we are close to the legendary Camelot. How can you fail to steal their hearts?' He looked accusingly at Hope. 'Do you have reservations that young Robin will outshine you? He is exceptional as the enchantress Gabriellen.'

'That poxy apprentice outshine me! When hell freezes over maybe, but not before. I'll have that audience eating from my hand. My Merlin is acclaimed. Even Edward Alleyn in his most renowned role of Tamburlaine cannot match it. Why, the Earl of Leicester has said that I am . . .'

Esmond let the actor run his course. Hope was becoming more unbearable and self-opinionated with every success they met. They had covered a half league before Esmond interceded.

'That the audience adore you, I do not dispute,' he said. 'But give Robin his due – he's an excellent player. Can you not see that his accomplishment but adds to the superior quality of your own? Without a worthy protagonist there can be no foil for your wit and expertise. I will give you the lines you want, but I will not have any of Robin's cut.

The week at Wirley Manor will give us time to rehearse the new scenes. I have a mind to extend the swordplay in some of them. You are getting lazy in your sword practice, Cornelius. There is nothing the audience loves more than a good fight.'

Hope snorted deprecatingly. 'As you grow lax in writing another play. It's three months since the last. We must have an extensive repertoire if we are to survive.'

'The play is almost completed,' Esmond evaded. It would not do for Cornelius to suspect that only a rough draft of the first act was written down. It was impossible now for him to write by candlelight, which always made his head ache, and too many daylight hours were swallowed up in sorting out the problems of the troupe. 'Besides,' he added, 'a new play cannot be performed until it has been licensed by the Master of Revels office in London. We do not return there until the autumn.'

'Then send someone to London with it.' Cornelius's voice, loud with frustration, resonated along the narrow, treeless coombe they were travelling. He struck his chest dramatically with his hand. 'As I live and breathe, I am an actor. I need new plays. I cannot wait upon the vagaries of the worthy Master of Revels, to say yea or nay.'

'Wait you will.' Esmond barely managed to keep his slipping temper in check. 'There will be no plays performed without authority. I have no wish to languish in gaol by pandering to your ego. If needs must, I shall send a messenger to London with it. In this I will not flout the law. Too many livelihoods are at stake.'

'As clearly will be mine if I remain with this clutchfisted band,' Cornelius scowled.

'How can you say that?' Esmond paused, needing a moment to control his anger. He was heartily sick of Hope's threats and histrionics. Unfortunately, he knew that he could not afford to sack the actor. 'We esteem you highly, Cornelius. Would you desert your friends? You shall have your speeches for the plays at Plymouth, never fear.'

The sullen pout of the actor's lips dissipated. 'How many lines do I get, my dear fellow?'

'Thirty.'

'A trifle, and not worth the writing of. Sixty, I say.'

'Fifty, providing there are no cuts to Robin's speeches.'

'Fifty and not a word less.' As they rode Cornelius

extended his arm to encompass the pasture before them filled with cattle, his eyes glazed with reflected glory. 'Fifty lines where the King addresses his army. His words will swell the hearts of every Englishman alive. That's all I ask, dear fellow. A paltry fifty lines. Then that mewling Robin can keep his speeches.'

Esmond nodded, though his heart sank at the project Hope demanded. He had no false illusions; he wrote adequately and could thrill an audience. But he was no Christopher Marlowe or Robert Greene. He wondered if he even matched the impassioned scribblings of his friend Will Shakespeare whom he had first met when they played in Stratford-upon-Avon. Recently they had renewed their acquaintanceship when Shakespeare had come to London. Last time they met, Shakespeare had read to Esmond the beginning of a play he had started to write about a Prince of Denmark – Hamlet, he thought Will had called him – and Esmond had begun to doubt his own capabilities. Shakespeare's writing had such fire, wit and drama, one day companies would be clamouring to put on his plays. Esmond dismissed his self-doubts. Until now his troupe had survived and Gabriellen had given him several good ideas to use in his latest play.

Cornelius slowed his pace to ride beside the wagon where Nan sat, and Esmond heard him describe to the seamstress the improvements he wanted made to Merlin's robes. The actor's self-interest was irrepressible. Esmond rubbed a hand across his throbbing temple. The bright sunlight hurt his eyes and further impaired his vision. A year ago he had thought himself able to conquer the world if he so chose. He had thought himself invincible. Brutally, his encroaching blindness had shown him that he was not.

The week at Wirley Manor looked to be a long and tiring one, and Plymouth would be equally as arduous. Not that he was complaining. From those performances he would have the means to pay off the debt owed to Victor Prew. An unsettling cold touched his spine and he suppressed a shiver. There had been a malevolent twist to Prew's lips when he learned that Esmond had tricked him into giving the loan, yet had withheld the share he wanted in the company.

'Make good use of that loan, Angel,' Prew warned. 'I'm not a patient man. If the loan and interest are not paid on time, you'll rue the day you thought to play me for a fool.'

It was too late now to regret taking the loan. He must be getting old if he paid a second thought to any threat from a puny cur the likes of Prew. In his time hadn't he outwitted some of England's greatest rogues? Was he not respected and deferred to by the Upright Men, the leaders of the London underworld of miscreants? The life of a playwright and player manager was respectable compared to some of his earlier escapades. No man had yet bested him and he was no dotard to lose any battle of wits.

Another horse rode alongside and he turned to it irritably. Poggs was watching him with concern. 'You look tired, Esmond. What did Cornelius want?'

He forced a lightness to his voice. 'You know Cornelius. He asks for a soliloquy to rival all soliloquys – words which will be unforgettable, and make his name as the most memorable actor who ever lived.'

'He thinks of no one but himself,' Poggs said fiercely. 'You work too hard.'

He looked anxiously at Esmond and a frown puckered his freckled face. Esmond was pale – too pale – and his eyes bloodshot and lined with pain. 'Those headaches of yours grow more frequent. Have you seen a physician?'

'Too much writing in poor light is their opinion. I cannot argue with that.' Esmond dismissed the subject. 'Besides, I indulged too freely in a most excellent brandy last evening. A sign of old age, my friend, when a man cannot take such pleasure without suffering for it the next day.'

Poggs was not convinced Esmond spoke the truth, and said so when he rode back to Agnes, who was sitting on the back of the cart which transported the stage props. He tethered his horse to its rail and climbed up beside her.

Agnes took one look at his face and asked, 'Are thee still worried about Master Angel?'

'Aye. Why will he not own his health is failing? His face is pale and drawn, and I swear the sunlight hurts his eyes.'

'Of all the players, thee've known him the longest. Does he not confide in thee?'

Poggs took off his cap and scratched the bald patch on the top of his freckled head. 'Esmond Angel confides in no one. Twenty years I've known him, ever since he saw me acting the fool at St Bartholomew's Fair. I were a 'prentice then to a boot-maker and hated it. I was mimicking our master, a fat pompous clod of a man, and the other 'prentices were cheering me on.' He grinned, showing yellowing teeth. 'You know me, old girl, I can't resist a crowd. So I does a little jig for 'em. Some even threw pennies to me. When I'd done and was scrambling on the floor for the coins, I sees Esmond watching me. We got to talking. He told me he had a small band of strolling players – asked were I interested.' He slapped his thigh with his hand and laughed. 'I were interested all right. I couldn't get away from that miserly boot-maker quick enough. Four of us there were in that troupe and a sorry lot we were too. But I loved every minute of it. Aye, we've come a long ways since then. Twenty years . . . who'd have thought it?'

He shook his head, his sandy brows drawing together, his hazel eyes sobering as he went on, 'Twenty years I've known him . . . yet I don't know him at all. Occasionally on the road he ups and disappears for odd days. And when we're in London he's frequently away from his lodgings. Wherever he goes, he goes in the thick of night and never speaks of it.'

'There's times I fear for Master Esmond,' Agnes said. 'He drinks and gambles too much. And he took his sister's death hard though he never speaks of it. Dear God, Poggs!' She gripped her husband's stubby fingers in her anguish. 'What will happen to Gabriellen? Why wouldn't he let me go to her like I asked?'

''Tweren't possible. I'd not let you travel alone and I can't leave the troupe. She'll bide just fine. She's a sound head on her shoulders, that one.'

Esmond was also worried about his daughter. For the next month at least he could see no way of returning to her. His letter to Mark Rowan suggested that Gabriellen might, for a month or so, live with one of Rowan's sisters. He hardened his heart against the urge to have her near him and ease her grief. Gabriellen had a habit of asking too many questions. And questions were the one thing he had spent his life avoiding.

Chapter Nine

'We've made good time.' Mark smiled across at Gabriellen. 'There's an hour before curfew. Once we top this rise you'll see Winchester.'

'I'll sleep soundly in my bed this night.' With a laugh she rolled her shoulders to ease their stiffness, for the first time permitting him to see any sign of her tiredness.

'You've done well and pushed yourself hard.' He unhooked the leather wine flask which hung from his saddle and, uncorking it, offered it to her.

She took a mouthful and handed it back, shrugging off his praise. 'You entertained me all afternoon with your singing to help me forget my tiredness. I'm grateful.'

They had reached the top of the hill and she caught sight of Winchester lying in a fold of the Hampshire Downs. The crimson sunset mellowed the formidable stonework of the defensive walls surrounding the city to a circlet of pink and gold. Behind them, the church spires paraded as proudly as the noblewomen who had worn the tall steeple headdresses of a century earlier. In contrast to these, the large squat cathedral presided amongst them like an imposing queen bee. On the city's highest mound, dominating everything, stood Winchester's sprawling castle.

Gabriellen no longer felt tired. Her sense of history was stirred, revitalising her weary body. This city had once been the ancient capital of England. 'Along this road have ridden the monarchs who live on in my father's plays.' She spoke her thoughts aloud, unable to contain her wonderment. 'All the legendary characters of romance and chivalry. King Alfred the Great, Henry the first of the Plantagenets and his queen, Eleanor, who was a prisoner here for many years of their turbulent marriage. Also their sons, Richard the Lionheart and the much maligned King John.'

'To name but a few,' Mark responded.

He looked at her with deepening interest. Her knowledge of history and politics surprised him. He had attended a grammar school, but upon his father's death left university to take charge of the estate. He had been fortunate, for his father had a substantial library which had continued his education. 'You have a knowledge unequalled by most women.'

'My father indulged me, though my Greek, Latin and French were the despair of my tutor. But I persevered and in the end was grateful for his patience.'

'Was it perseverance or a stubborn refusal to allow a subject to defeat you?' he taunted.

She threw back her head and laughed. 'Stubbornness, I suspect.'

As they neared the city Gabriellen fell silent.

Reining in Glendower, Mark flung out his arm towards Winchester, his expression one of amazement. 'Master Gabriel, if Winchester can so effectively silence you, be prepared when you see the splendours of York, Canterbury or London. They will strike you dumb for a week. Should you journey to Wales, I should be afeared for your sanity if you set eyes upon our finest jewel – Caernarvon.'

'Mock me, I care not.' She turned a radiant face upon him. 'You have seen these places. Did you then feel the presence of our greatest heroes?'

A dark brow curved up into his tousled dark hair. 'I am but a humble horse breeder, and not a playwright's daughter. You have the soul of an adventuress.'

'I have not!' She squared her shoulders, her eyes narrowing. For all she had come to regard Mark with sisterly affection, he had the irritating habit of nettling her in a way which sparked her temper. 'You insult me, sir. Know you well, Mark Rowan, I hold honour high.'

'Sheathe your claws, little vixen. I but warn you. Even for a man, adventure and honour are uneasy bedfellows.' His black stare regarded her sternly. 'The dangers are greater for a woman. Should your reputation be lost, you will be prey to every prejudice and lecher.'

'Why should women be considered inferior to men?' She rounded on him, her eyes fierce with rebellion. 'Because men decree so, that's why! In a world where the rules are made by men – for their convenience – women are expected to conform. Heaven help them if they don't! We must then suffer the false hypocrisy heaped upon us should we dare to break those rules.'

'Whoa!' He raised a hand in feigned horror. 'I note your point.'

She was too angry to be side-tracked. 'This is no jesting matter. I will never be so constrained. I will act as befits my beliefs and conscience.' Her clenched fist struck her knee and she saw that he was no longer mocking her, but was studying her intently. 'Those men soon grovel when they pay homage to our Queen. Has not Elizabeth brought England to prosperity? She does not tremble in her petti-coats at the thought of war with Spain. Rather she urges it, so that we may be free to worship as we please. Her Majesty is an example to all women that we should not be overshadowed by men. Jack understands how I feel.'

Drained of energy by her outburst, she looked at Mark, and gathered her strength to combat the argument she expected.

'Jack would appreciate those qualities of independence in the woman he loved.' Mark startled her by the solemnity of his tone. But ever a man of unfathomable moods, the Welshman then grinned, adding wryly, 'Be true to yourself, Gabriellen. Else you will never find happiness.'

'How can I be other than happy with Jack?' Her face flushed with the assurance of her love. 'I care not what others think of me. But your respect is important, Mark – as is Jack's.'

Mark ran a hand along Glendower's ginger neck, his face serious. 'We are all as we are. A friend should not stand as judge, but try and help should they be called upon. As for Jack . . .' He shrugged. 'Jack lives by his own code. He's my friend and I'll not speak ill of him. But by the same token I would not see you hurt. Don't let love blind you, Gabriellen. Jack is a man of many parts and his ambition is limitless.'

'If by that remark you believe that Jack thinks a play-wright's daughter beneath him, it's not so. He loves me.'

'And is that enough?'

'It is everything.' She smiled confidently.

'God willing, it will remain so.'

Within the city the cathedral bells began to chime for mass. Nearer, from the hovels built against the walls, the whine of beggars drifted to them. And close by the muted clang of a leper's bell, the bedraggled figure hunched by the roadside as it rendered its pitiful cry, 'Have mercy. Have mercy on God's afflicted.'

The coin Mark tossed rang dully as it landed in the leper's wooden bowl and Gabriellen urged Sable closer to Glendower as they passed by. Further on, he halted by a beech tree severed in two by lightning. Leaning over his saddle, he snatched a torn playbill from its blackened trunk. With a frown he handed it to Gabriellen.

She read it quickly, her throat cramping with momentary panic. 'It says the last performance by Lord Barpham's players was two days ago. Where do we go now? The players will have moved on.' She squared her shoulders undeterred by the setback. 'They cannot be far off. Father spoke of travelling north to York for the summer, but I've no idea of his route.'

'First we need somewhere to spend the night.' Mark's jaw tightened grimly. Moving forward they joined the line of travellers entering the city before the gates were closed at curfew. 'That done, I shall make what enquiries I can.'

As they drew closer to the walls the cathedral bells stopped ringing, while the cries of the beggars intensified. Two hooded figures detached themselves from their companions, thrusting stumps and ulcerous limbs at Gabriellen.

'Alms, good sir. Alms!'

Pity and horror mingling in her breast, she reached for her purse concealed by her doublet. The cripple nearest to her grabbed Sable's stirrup. As he did so, his hood fell back to reveal a noseless face, rotted by the pox.

'Get away!' Mark ordered, backing Glendower to jostle the beggar out of Gabriellen's sight. He threw several copper coins into the road for the beggars to scramble for, whilst his concerned stare remained upon Gabriellen who had begun to tremble. 'Stay close to me.'

She needed no second reminder. The hideous mutilations of the cripples had shaken her.

As they moved away Mark warned, 'Never take out your purse to give alms to a beggar. Keep a few coins loose in your pocket. Every cut-purse amongst this rabble will have noted where you keep your money and will be assessing his chance of relieving you of it.'

The rebuke was justified and brought with it a moment

of doubt. Had she acted too rashly by leaving Chichester? It could be weeks before she found her father. Pride sustained her and she thrust her misgivings aside. As they picked their way through the streets, she said, 'I should not have involved you in my troubles. You have your own work to pursue.' Her chin tilted resolutely. 'I cannot give up my search for my father.'

'Nor will I waste my breath by arguing with you.' A quirk of his eyebrow signalled his exasperation at her stubbornness. 'I warned you this could happen. Even knowing the risks, did I not agree to help you? The next days will be harder. It will be safer for you to continue in the disguise as my cousin. But that in itself will bring its own complications and I fear moments of embarrassment for you.'

'You mean we might be forced to share a room together?'

'We may be forced to share it with other male travellers.' He looked at her sharply. 'But I would avoid that at all costs. I will ensure you have the privacy you need.'

The setting sun had cast long shadows between the gabled houses and robbed the evening of its warmth. Hordes of flies and an occasional rat ran over the piles of rubbish filling the gutters, the stench of rotting vegetation catching in their throats after the freshness of the countryside. As they passed the market cross a commotion broke out ahead of them. The crowd spilled across the road forcing them to ride in single file and making further conversation impossible.

From her vantage point in the saddle, Gabriellen stared over the heads of the crowd jeering at a hunchback. The man was beating a bear with a cudgel for refusing to perform. The bear remained stoically on all fours. Its head swayed backwards and forwards in the fretful way a child will rock to and fro when emotionally disturbed. There was blood streaking its russet chest. The abused animal wore a red and gold ruff which was torn in several places where it had caught upon a cruel spiked collar. Gabriellen was appalled at the wretched state of the creature. Pink froth oozed from the side of its muzzled mouth and its dull coat was bald with mange in several places. When a vicious blow landed on its nose, the bear hung its head, and she saw that one eye was closed from a running sore which was covered in flies.

'A pox on it. What kind of dancing bear is that?' a

spectator scoffed. 'Now if we was to 'ave a bit of baiting, that might be worth us parting with a groat or two.'

A terrier barked hysterically and strained at its lead to get at the bear. His master laughed. 'Perhaps once 'e feels the nip of ol' Patch's teeth, 'e'll dance right enough.'

Gabriellen glowered at the bandy-legged hunchback. Urged on by the derisive hoots of the crowd, the twisted, ragged figure continued to beat the bear.

'That horrid brute!' she gasped. 'Look at the poor animal. It's sick and in pain.'

The bear no longer moved. It remained with head dropped down, looking utterly dejected. The hunchback screeched with fury, his pock-marked face twisting cruelly. Throwing down the cudgel, he picked up a lead-tipped flail, lashing the bear as he screamed. 'Up, you lazy whoreson. Up and dance, you scurvy turd, or I'll let the dogs on you.'

'That's enough, man!' Mark rapped out, the cool authority of his voice clear above the rowdy din. His expression forbidding, he guided Glendower through the crowd. The sound of the horse's hooves striking the uneven cobbles enhanced his authority. Inches from the hunchback Mark halted and Gabriellen found herself holding her breath.

'I said, put aside that whip!' Mark ordered.

Scuffling broke out as the shouting mob fell back, leaving the hunchback to stand alone before the man and horse. The men at the back of the crowd strained forward hoping for a fresh diversion. Glendower snorted and pawed the ground. Those at the front, eager to escape contact with the big stallion, pushed back their companions. A tense hush fell over the crowd, the only sound the splashing of water on to the cobbles from a leaking conduit.

As all eyes turned upon Mark, the air was charged with menace. The stunned silence was replaced by hostile murmurs as the crowd realised they were being robbed of their sport. Gabriellen swallowed against the sudden dryness of her throat, her palms growing moist inside her leather gauntlets.

Again Mark's clipped voice rang out, 'Put down that whip. Lest you find it turned upon yourself. The bear is sick.'

'Who the 'ell are you to tell me what to do?' The hunchback who had stopped beating the bear raised the whip threateningly at Mark.

'Go on, humpy – you give it to 'im,' someone shouted.

'Yeah, we're just having a bit of harmless fun,' another man joined in. Four of his companions closed ranks to turn on Mark, their ruddy, drink-bleared faces antagonistic at being denied their sport. 'It's just a bear anyways.'

The bear was temporarily forgotten as Gabriellen's fears now centred upon Mark. She could feel the danger sparking in the air, but he remained calm, his expression unyielding. Just in time she remembered to deepen her voice. 'Come away. There's nothing you can do. Much as I pity the poor creature.'

A thick-set man with a huge wart on his hooked nose shoved forward to shake his fist at Mark. The sudden movement caused Glendower to snort and sidestep, his eyes rolling dangerously.

'Steady, boy!' Mark commanded and increased the pressure of his knees to bring the stallion under control. He knew the likes of these ruffians. Men who were intent only on their own mindless sport. He could feel their hostility surrounding him. But he would not stand by and see the bear suffer.

From the corner of his eye he saw Gabriellen edge her gelding closer, her hand gripping her riding whip. He almost balked. He did not want Gabriellen involved in a fight. From the set of her chin he knew she would not hesitate to use that whip upon anyone attacking him. Her courage apart, he was aware of the danger to them both.

He turned his contemptuous glare upon the crowd. 'Have you nothing better to do than watch a sick animal abused?'

'Tha' pretty boy speaks sense.' The man with the warts eyed Mark belligerently. 'Be off with 'ee and leave us to our fun.'

Four men converged upon Mark. They were all large and unkempt and used to throwing the weight of their heavy bodies around to get their own way. The malicious glitter in their eyes warned him they were ready to tear him from Glendower's back and beat him bloody. They could try. He remained impassive though the blood began to pound through his body. As the nearest made a grab for Glendower's bridle, Mark touched his heels to the stallion's side. The horse reared, his forelegs pawing the air, and the men stumbled back. Expertly, Mark brought Glendower down on all fours, drew his sword, and leaning over his saddle touched its point against the chest of the ruffian who had challenged him.

The man's eyes rolled with fear as he fell to his knees. 'Mercy, sir. I meant no offence. Don't kill me. 'Twas only a bit of fun.'

'What fun is there in baiting a sick beast?' Mark snapped.

''Tis poor sport, 'ee be right.' The man turned a sickly grey, his gaze fixed upon the point of Mark's sword still pressed against his chest. Sweat trickled down from his temples and his voice shook as he blustered, 'What say 'ee, friends? Let's away. The cockfight's about to start in the pit.'

'Spare Tom,' two others cried, trying to distract Mark as the fourth edged towards Gabriellen.

'Get away from my companion, or your friend will find himself a cripple,' Mark pronounced. 'You three get back over there.' He indicated a wall several yards away on the far side of the square. Instinctively his hands checked Glendower who, nervous of the tension, began to paw the ground and snort, the evening air causing his hot breath to steam like a dragon's from his nostrils.

'For the love of God! Do as he says,' Tom croaked, his body shaking in a convulsion of fear as he strained away from the stallion's hooves.

When the other three scuttled to the wall, Mark withdrew the pressure of his sword, but kept it pointed at Tom who grovelled before him. With a jerk of his wrist he gestured for the labourer to rise. The crowd, sensing the matter was at an end, finally began to disperse. Still keeping one eye on Tom, Mark addressed the hunchback who was spitting and jumping up and down with rage. 'If I see you mistreating that bear again, it will be your turn to feel the edge of my sword.'

'Plague take yer!' the hunchback screamed, his voice a high whistle through his black and broken teeth. He picked up his battered cap from the ground which was empty of coins. 'I hope yer rot in 'ell fer this. Bastard! Yer cost me. An' I don't take kindly to that.'

Mark ignored the threats as one would ignore an irritating

128

fly. From somewhere above him a well-aimed turnip struck the hunchback on the head, followed by a juvenile chorus.

'Grumpy, lumpy. Lost yer money, humpy.'

Mark looked up to see two young apprentices squatting on a low jutting roof of a saddler's shop.

'Piss off, yer little sods.' The hunchback waved his fist at them and was pelted with a fresh barrage of turnips.

Mark lowered his sword and nodded for Tom to join his companions. Wheeling Glendower around, Mark returned to Gabriellen and the remainder of the crowd parted, making no attempt to detain their passage.

'That was brave of you. But was it wise?' Gabriellen's voice trembled with the fear she had been controlling.

He smiled unabashed, lifting a brow as he teased. 'If I always acted wisely, you would still be in Chichester.' He turned sharply at the sight of a woman hurrying along beside them. She was waving to attract his attention. Her bright blonde hair was unbound and fell in tangled curls to her waist. Saucily, she blew him a kiss.

'"Twere wonderful what ye did back in the square. So brave, ye were. So magnificent and handsome. But when I saw they'm bullies turn on ye – why, poor Rosie's heart fair burst wi' fear.' Her eyes gleamed with admiration and her pretty oval face was becomingly flushed from her exertion. She looked up at him provocatively through her lashes. 'Ye'll be staying at The Sun, will ye not?'

Mark winked at her, his stare lingering appreciatively on her voluptuous figure as Rosie slowed her pace.

'Oh, Mark, how can you encourage such brazenness?' Gabriellen said, shocked.

'You forget your role, Master Gabriel.' He grinned wickedly. 'Besides, I have known Rosie for three years.'

From the look which Rosie gave Mark it was obvious the two were lovers. Gabriellen stared ahead feeling foolish. It had been naive of her not to have realised that a single man who travelled the roads would be acquainted with women such as Rosie. They rode in silence past several inns where every courtyard was crammed with horses and baggage carts. Finally, they turned into the yard of The Sun Inn, and Gabriellen felt a twinge of chagrin that whilst here she would lose Mark's companionship as he would undoubtedly seek out his mistress. She had expected to be reunited with her father this night and enjoy the warmth and friendship of the players. Now it looked as though she would spend it alone.

The courtyard was cluttered with wagons and carts. Dusk was fast turning to night. An ostler was lighting the wall torches which cast dark shadows over whitewashed timber-framed walls. The three-storeyed building with its thatched roof leaned tipsily towards them. The inn looked respectable and the landlord, who was hurrying to greet them, had an open, friendly face.

He nodded to Gabriellen. 'Goodday, sir.' Then, turning to Mark, his smile broadened. ''Tis good to see ye, Mr Rowan. I've a last room free. Such fine gentlemen as ye can't do with sleeping in the taproom. Such a week it's been! And now the Earl of Tregellon arrived not an hour past with a large party of noblemen. The city be packed wi' 'em. But seeing as ye be travelling together, sharing a room will be no hardship, I warrant.'

'In the circumstances, we are fortunate that you have a room to spare, Ben,' Mark replied. 'My cousin is recovering from an illness and is tired. We will eat in our room.'

He dismounted and Gabriellen also leapt to the ground. In her role of a young man she could expect no assistance. She was shocked at how shaky her legs felt and paused for a moment to hold on to the saddle for support.

Mark waved an advancing groom aside. 'I shall attend to my horse. He does not take easily to strangers. But see to my cousin's.' He turned back to Ben. 'I hear the players have just left the city.'

'Aye, a right fine show they gave. But it stirred up trouble, and the Aldermen were glad to see 'em leave. Stayed in this very inn they'm did. Set up their stage on this very spot.' A note of pride crept into his voice. 'The place were packed. Though the actors took some getting used to – one of them thought he were some sort of God the way he strutted and posed. And the arguments . . .' Ben shook his head. 'I've never heard the like as when their leader lost a small fortune at dice. Can't say I was sorry to see 'em go.'

'Where were they heading?' Mark asked. 'Was it north?'

''Tweren't north. They rode to the west gate this forenoon. Why, do ye know 'em, Mr Rowan?'

Mark glanced across at Gabriellen, who looked pale and

near exhaustion. This was the news he had feared. It could be weeks before Esmond Angel was found. The protectiveness Gabriellen roused in him was becoming a millstone around his neck. He could not desert her when she needed him. Aware that the landlord was awaiting an answer, he shrugged as though the news were unimportant, and said, 'Mr Angel, their manager, is an acquaintance of mine. I'd hoped to meet up with him here. Since my business will keep me in the district for some time, I wondered if a meeting could still be possible.'

'Could be they headed Plymouth way. There was a messenger from Lord Barpham asking for them. He rode in from Plymouth.'

Several shouts rose from inside the inn demanding wine for Lord Tregellon. Ben backed away, anxious to return to his duties. He pointed to the first-floor gallery. 'Your room is at the end of the balcony there.'

As Sable was led away, Mark saw Gabriellen pick up the saddle baggage the groom had dropped at her feet. When she stumbled over the uneven flagstones, he managed to check in time his instinct to help her. A mistake like that would have given the lie to her disguise.

'You look exhausted. Go and lie down.' There was concern in his voice and he added in an undertone, 'There's nothing I can do about the room. I warned you that your disguise was not without its pitfalls.'

'I'm not worried about that. It will not be the first time we have spent the night alone.'

Her calm practicality unaccountably annoyed Mark. She was actress enough to fool the casual observer when she strutted about in her man's clothing, but there were times when her naivety and innocence exasperated him.

'Mark, are you listening to me?' She broke through his thoughts. 'What do you think? Could Father be at Plymouth?'

Despite the dark circles beneath them Gabriellen's eyes glowed with an excited light. It was not just Esmond she was eager to meet at Plymouth, Mark thought. The softening of her mouth and eyes spoke volumes of her love for Jack.

'I shall make enquiries,' he answered as he turned to run his hand over Glendower's neck. The stallion was becoming restless and he nimbly avoided Glendower's teeth when the horse tried to nip his shoulder. Rubbing the horse's muzzle he spoke over his shoulder. 'We will travel nowhere unless we learn your father's route. More importantly, in ten days Glendower is to service a mare near Dorchester. My word was given in March and I'll not break it.'

He looked long and hard at Gabriellen. The enforced intimacies which their travelling together would arouse was a complication he did not need. 'I'll not abandon you. Someone must know in which direction the players travelled.' His voice showed none of his misgivings. 'I'll ask around. Go and rest. And, remember, you are supposed to be my cousin.'

'I'll not forget.'

He led Glendower into the stable, his mood darkening. Now Gabriellen was well again he could no longer look upon her as a patient. She was a desirable woman. Yet his friendship with Jack barred any dalliance between them. Not so with Rosie. They had been lovers on the numerous occasions he visited Winchester, and many times her charms had turned a two-night stay here into a week. Rosie was the diversion he needed. It would also give Gabriellen the privacy she was entitled to.

An hour later they had finished their meal in their room and Mark saw Gabriellen's lids begin to droop. He excused himself, telling her to rest as he went down into the taproom. He called for a tankard of ale and smiled up at Rosie when she sauntered over to serve him. She placed a hand upon his shoulder, her mouth curving with invitation.

''Tisn't fitting a brave man such as ye should drink alone.'

Rosie was an attractive woman. Her blonde hair tumbled over her shoulders and her oval face was unblemished by disease or excesses. Although he knew her to be a widow in her early thirties, the dim light of the taproom softened the lines about her eyes and mouth, making her look much younger. She had a warm-hearted nature and it surprised him that she had remained a widow for seven years without remarrying.

'I'm not alone now that you're here.' He pulled her down on to his lap. 'Who else do you think I've been waiting upon, but the lovely Rosie with the beguiling eyes?'

She gave a low husky laugh and ran one hand through his hair. 'And it would be inhospitable for me to disappoint you. Though that Welsh tongue is too smooth with its flattery.'

''Tis not flattery, but admiration. You grow more beautiful each time I see you.' He kissed her shoulder and hearing her soft catch of breath, stood up and drew her against his body. 'I could talk all night of your charms, my lovely. But would you not rather I showed my appreciation?'

'As only ye know how. But there must be a woman in every town tells ye that.'

'Now you flatter me, Rosie.' He laughed as he followed her out of the taproom and towards the stables. Rosie shared a room with two other servants and the only privacy they would find this night was in the hayloft. 'Did you not travel the West Country with me for two months last summer? There was only you then. I thought you were to stop working at The Sun and marry some farmer.'

She shrugged. 'Can ye see me isolated on a windswept farm on some bleak moor? But I'm to wed another come summer's end.' She pulled him behind the stable door as they entered the long building. Wrapping her arms tight around him, she kissed him with deepening passion. When they broke apart she leaned back against the wall and sighed. 'This must be our last night together, my darling Mark. Clem, whom I'm to wed, is a good man. Once I'm wed, I'll not deceive him. I knew ye'd come this way afore then.' Her voice broke. 'I wanted one more night wi' ye.'

Rosie closed her eyes against the pain. She had loved Mark for three years, ever since he first came to Winchester with Glendower. He was the first man she had lain with since her husband's death and, although she had occasionally since then taken a lover, none had given her the pleasure Mark could. She had hoped that during the weeks she spent with him last summer, he would have proposed. She had tried to force his hand by telling him she meant to wed another. Which was a lie. The way he had kissed her and wished her well showed her that Mark was not yet ready to settle down with one woman. He was content with his freedom, and who could blame him when there must be others such as herself, eager to dispel the loneliness of the months he spent upon the road?

The sweet earthy smell of the animals and straw from the stables assailed their nostrils as they climbed into the hayloft. Below, Glendower stamped restlessly as he caught

Mark's scent and Sable whinnied a welcome then grew quiet. Tangles of straw hung down from the rafters above making an intimate curtain, shutting out the dark wood of the walls. Taking Rosie in his arms, Mark pulled her down into the fragrant straw. A shaft of moonlight through the dusty window caught the tear-bright glitter in her brown eyes.

With sudden clarity Mark knew that Rosie loved him. How could he not have guessed? She was not the kind of woman to give her favours freely. He was very fond of the widow, but did not love her. He had loved only Meredith and since then his heart had been locked against other women, the pain of Meredith's death still raw within him.

Touched by remorse at the hurt he had unwittingly caused Rosie, he kissed her tenderly. He drew back, gazing down at her, hoping his words would bring her ease.

'What we had was special to me, Rosie. I wish you happy with Clem. He's a lucky man.'

Sensing that for Rosie their farewell was important, he would not disappoint her tonight. He kissed her bare shoulder and as he drew the loose blouse from her breasts, he felt her body quiver with delight. As the layers of clothes slid from her eager body, his lips and hands moved sensuously over her breasts and hips. There was a frenzied impatience in her fingers as she tore at the buttons of his doublet and the rest of his clothing.

When a long time later he lay listening to her breathing deepen with sleep, he knew there would be nights of regret that Rosie was another's wife. But despite the pleasure she gave him, the regret would not be strong enough for him to offer her marriage. The life of a horse breeder which he had chosen was not an easy one. And there was his work for the Queen's Secretary of State. That was too filled with danger to consider marriage for several years to come.

Chapter Ten

The brusque persistence of the cathedral bells ringing out Prime brought Gabriellen awake with a start. She opened her eyes to a room shrouded in gloom and the sound of rain hammering against the window. Retreating beneath the pillow, she hugged it close over her head to deaden the clangour of church bells. The movement tore at her stiff muscles, reminding her that Mark had planned an early start to make enquiries about the players. She dragged the pillow from her face.

'Mark, it's past Prime! Come, slug-a-bed, rouse yourself.'

With a fond smile curving her mouth, she levered herself on to her elbow and looked across at his pallet. The smile faded. It was empty, and from the neatly made covers it had not been slept in. He must have spent the night with Rosie. Where he slept was his affair, she thought grimly as she threw back the covers with a violence which left her gasping in pain. Every muscle in her body seemed to cry out its protest. Swinging her legs over the side of the bed, the pains shooting through her thighs made her slump forward and hold her head in her hands. She felt weak, vulnerable, and unaccountably angry at Mark for deserting her.

'Confounded men!' she seethed, condemning all of their kind in a spate of ill humour. Why couldn't her father have been in Winchester? Her annoyance intensified as she realised she was indulging in self-pity.

Pushing her hand through her shorn hair, she stared down at her breeches and hose. Oh Lord, what a fright she must look dressed as a man and with her hair cut short. No wonder Mark preferred Rosie's company. Idly, her fingers continued to comb through her hair. What if Jack now thought her unfeminine and undesirable?

The thought devastated her. Her hand traced her jutting

cheekbones and down over her slender body. The fever had stripped most of the flesh from her and she was only just regaining it. She was like a scarecrow compared to the voluptuous curves of Rosie.

She stared resentfully at the saddle baggage propped in a corner. It contained two clean shirts and two of her plainer dresses and a petticoat. The beautiful gown she had worn for Agnes's wedding was packed in a trunk with her other clothes, awaiting the time she could send a carrier to collect them. Would Jack, who was so meticulous in his dress, think her ugly in her simple gowns without her farthingales or ruffs? She stood up to pace the floor. Mark had warned her she would have these misgivings and at the time she had laughed his advice aside. All she had wanted was to get away from Chichester, join Esmond, and eventually be reunited with Jack.

She scowled down at her garments. The bizarre figure she presented now bore little resemblance to the woman Jack had fallen in love with. What if he did turn from her in horror?

Angrily, she answered her own question. 'Heavens, Gabriellen Angel, what's the matter with you?' She swung round and snatching up her boots, pulled them on. 'You've more hair than wit to doubt Jack.' She grimaced at the unfortunate choice of phrase. 'You love someone for who they are, not what they wear.' Pouring cold water from the pitcher into the pottery washbasin, she splashed her face. The fever had taken more out of her than she would admit. Only a fool wasted time in useless worry.

The empty room intensified her feeling of loneliness. Looking out of the window she saw that the rain was easing, and decided to visit the stables and check on Sable. Two cloaked serving girls hurried past weighed down by the buckets of water they had drawn from the well. They paid her no heed, their heads bent against the drizzle. Gabriellen quickened her step across the yard. Somewhere beyond the ostlery she heard a man whistling, but otherwise the inn was deserted at this early hour.

Inside the stable door she paused. To her left were several stalls and she could see Glendower's head with its white blaze at the far end. A sound drew her eye to the hayloft ladder directly behind her. Looking up she saw a flash of white petticoats, then the foot of a woman about to descend.

Upon catching sight of Rosie's bright blonde hair, Gabriellen drew back into the shadows.

Rosie halted at the foot of the ladder to stare up at the hayloft, her face naked with yearning.

Gabriellen held her breath, unwilling to be discovered. When the servant turned to leave she saw the tears glistening on her cheek. Gabriellen frowned. Mark had proved himself the perfect friend. Handsome and carefree as he was, she could believe that many women would be susceptible to his masculine charm. Until today she had accepted her easy comradeship with him without question. It struck her now that their friendship was an unusual one.

As she emerged from the shadows she became aware of a pungent odour which mingled with the scent of straw and horses. There was a sound behind her, a wheezing hiss of breath as unnatural as it must be painful. Turning to investigate she saw a heavy chain secured to a ring on the wall. Attached to it lay a pitiful mound of reddish fur. It was the bear which the hunchback had been tormenting in the square yesterday. She moved cautiously closer.

'Steady, old one. I'll not hurt you,' she reassured the animal, noticing with horror the amount of dried blood on its coat where it had been beaten. Still wary she knelt a few feet from it and put out her hand. The bear raised its rust-coloured muzzled head to study Gabriellen with one dull eye, then flopped back on to the straw. 'Be still,' she continued in a soothing voice. 'I'm a friend, let me look at you.'

When she lightly stroked its coat the bear flinched, but allowed her to continue. The bones were clearly discernible beneath its ragged fur and in several places the ribs were bruised from its beating. Starvation had further weakened the animal and from its laboured breathing it was close to dying from its injuries. On its back leg, an old festering wound from what looked like a dog bite, was crawling with maggots. She gulped back her rising nausea, her fury centred upon the man who had reduced a once proud creature to this pitiful state.

''Ere, wot yer doin' near Soulful?' the whining voice of the hunchback demanded from the doorway. A bony hand gripped her shoulder and, with a strength which surprised her in one so deformed, he pushed her aside. 'Clear off afore I take my whip to yer.'

137

Gabriellen scrambled to her feet, and pointed angrily at the man as rage overran her. 'You're not fit to own the fleas on that bear's back. The poor beast is dying from hunger and abuse.'

'Says who?' The hunchback's mouth twisted menacingly. 'She's just lazy. When she don't do 'er act, she don't eat.'

'Why, you snivelling little toad!' Gabriellen's voice rose. 'How can she perform when you have beaten her so that she's too sick to move?'

'Yer poxy whoreson, I know yer now.' He drew a dagger from his belt. 'Yer were with that interfering bastard, Rowan. I lost me takings yesterday, coz of 'im. Piss off – or I'll stick yer with this.'

Too outraged by his inhumanity to feel fear, Gabriellen drew her own dagger. 'I'll not go until I know Soulful will be properly cared for.'

'Oh, she'll be cared for all right! At least so she can stand.' The hunchback sniggered. He poked his dagger at Gabriellen's chest and she leapt aside to avoid its blade. His unwashed body stank worse than the bear's. 'She's to take on three dogs this afternoon. 'Tis all she's fit for is baiting. She'll last long enough to earn me a groat or two.'

'That's barbarous!' Gabriellen cried, avoiding another lunge of his dagger. 'Soulful will be killed.'

The hunchback circled, his arms outstretched, ready to renew his attack. Gabriellen side-stepped, keeping opposite him.

'I own 'er. There's nothing yer can do to stop me using 'er 'ow I please.' He eyed her dagger and jeered. 'Unless yer know 'ow to use that, pretty boy.'

'I'll buy her from you,' she declared, prepared to do anything to spare Soulful being savaged by the dogs.

He stopped circling. ''ow much?'

'Two gold angels. That's more than you'll make at the baiting.'

'Aye, but who's to know she won't survive?' A calculating grin twisted his pitted face. 'Soulful is a fighter. She could last three, maybe four, sessions. Six gold angels.'

'Three, and that's my last offer.' Gabriellen brought up her dagger, praying that the hunchback would not call her bluff. 'Or we could fight for her?'

'Be warned, Gubbett,' Mark's voice called from the foot of the loft ladder. 'My cousin is an adept hand with that

138

weapon. Three angels is more than a fair price. I'd take it and think myself fortunate, if I were you.'

Cecil Gubbett hopped from one foot to the other, his face turning from scarlet to white, then back to scarlet again. He knew Rowan from the fairs. The horse breeder was respected among the officials at those events. More than once Rowan had ensured that an entertainer who mistreated his animals found himself banned from a particular city or town. He had a voice many in authority heeded.

Gubbett lowered his dagger. He'd not risk being banned from the cities. Even without the bear he could earn a good living as a cut-purse or sneak-thief. He also knew many a trick to gull an innocent cove of his money. The hunchback eyed Rowan with hatred. He'd not forget this day. He didn't take kindly to being bested. There were men who owed Cecil Gubbett. One dark night Mark Rowan would find himself alone in an alleyway. Then Gubbett would have his revenge.

He scowled at Rowan's cousin. 'Three gold angels, and the bear is yours.'

Gabriellen drew her money pouch from inside her shirt and counted out the coins. That left her with two angels out of the five Uncle Ezekiel's lawyer had given her. They would suffice until she met her father, if she was careful.

She handed the money to the hunchback who spat on the coins before putting them inside his boot.

'Little good Soulful will do yer. She'll be dead within the week.' Laughing maliciously, he shuffled away.

'Gubbett is a mean beggar,' said Mark, standing at her side. 'He'd have stuck you with that dagger as soon as look at you. Noble though your actions were, have you considered how we are going to manage with a bear?'

'I bought her to save her from the dogs,' Gabriellen began. She stopped with a start as she saw that Mark was only half dressed. Clad in his leather breeches, his chest with its smudge of dark hair was bare, as were his feet. A blue line of stubble accentuated his sardonic looks and a lock of black hair fell over his brow. Her argument with the hunchback must have woken him and brought him down to investigate. Without cause, she resented his intrusion and criticism.

'I'm sorry if I woke you. I could have dealt with that objectionable man on my own.'

'Could you, cousin?' He seemed amused by her antagonism which flicked at her pride and brought her head up. 'Since Soulful is now your property, we had better see what can be done to ease her suffering.'

Mark knelt beside the bear, speaking softly while he ran his hands over her injured body. Gabriellen had never seen a man without his shirt and doublet and her gaze watched the play of muscles over Mark's shoulders and back. A scar across his taut ribs was unmistakably that of a sword or knife cut and a knot of flesh upon his shoulder showed where once a bullet had entered. These were not the wounds one would expect a horse breeder to carry.

'Soulful's in a bad way,' Mark looked up at her.

Aware that she had been staring at him, she blushed and averted her gaze. 'Will she live?'

Mark continued to examine the bear and Gabriellen, discomfited by his half-nakedness, looked down at his feet. They were dusty from the straw, and she saw that his fifth toe was the same length as the fourth. Then a long groaning breath from Soulful drew her full attention to the bear and she forgot everything but the creature's misery.

Mark raised Soulful's scarred eyelid to look into her eye before sitting back on his haunches. 'Gubbett spoke the truth. The bear is dying. She's old and has lost the will to live.'

'Is there nothing we can do?'

'She's in great pain. We can spare her several days' unnecessary suffering. Nothing more.' He stood up and rubbed a hand across his stubbled jaw. 'If I were back home, perhaps, with vigilant nursing and kindness, she could be persuaded to eat and would eventually recover. That would take weeks. Here she has no chance. And before you ask, she would not survive the journey to Wales.'

Gabriellen bit her lip to combat the pain caused by his words. She had guessed that Soulful was dying, but now that her fear was put into words, she felt crushed. Her shoulders sagged in despair. 'I suppose you think I was a fool to buy her. But I couldn't stand by and see her savaged by dogs.' She blinked rapidly against the sting of tears, her hand covering her mouth as she visualised the horrific scene. 'No creature deserves that death.'

'I would have done the same.'

He clasped her shoulder, his eyes sombre. Their gaze

held, words unnecessary in this affinity between them. All her life Aunt Dorothy had chided her for bringing home injured creatures and trying to heal them. Mark understood her oneness with animals – not only understood, but felt the same.

'I'll fetch my pistol,' he said heavily.

Gabriellen knelt on the straw, her heart aching with sorrow. Soulful drew another agonised breath, the muscles along her back contracting in pain. Tears blinded Gabriellen's eyes. She swallowed against the ache closing her throat. She did not want Soulful to die, but to hear the bear's tortured breathing tore at her caring heart. Mark was right. All they could do was to shorten Soulful's suffering.

'Turn away,' Mark commanded when he returned to her side.

She obeyed, steeling herself against the inevitable. At the sound of the pistol being cocked, she covered her ears. Holding her breath, she shut her eyes, tears running down her cheeks. The shot rang through the stables, making the horses at the far end stamp nervously then grow still. The silence which followed was awesome. A tremor ran through Gabriellen's body, then another, until she was shaking so violently her knees threatened to give way beneath her.

'It's over,' Mark said, his hand on her shoulder drawing her away from the carcass. A groom entered the stable. Mark turned to him saying abruptly, 'The bear is dead. Tell the landlord to dispose of its remains.'

Suddenly she could not stop the sobs which wracked her body. She wept for the untimely death of her aunt and uncle. And she wept for the sickness of cruelty that pervaded the countryside, where men's love of sport took precedence over the suffering of so many animals.

'Cry all you need, Ellen.' She was gathered against his chest as he comforted her. 'You've kept too much hurt casked inside for too long. We did what was right.'

As his sonorous voice murmured against her ear, her sobs gradually ebbed. Lifting her head, she asked in anguish, 'Why didn't I listen to you, Mark? I should have stayed at Chichester.' She poured out her doubts. 'Look at me! I'm a freak in these clothes. Jack will turn from me in disgust when he sees me with my hair short like a man's.'

He raised one dark brow, the amusement in his eyes shredding the last of her courage.

'Don't mock me, Mark. I can't bear it.'

She struck his chest with her fist and found her wrist caught and gently lowered to her side. 'I'm not mocking you, Ellen. Far from it. Have you no idea of the ravishing figure you present? Jack will not turn from you. Rather, he will do this.'

Her face was taken in his hands. Then his lips were upon hers, warm, caressing and infinitely tender, so that for a long moment she was too stunned to resist. Their touch brought heat to her body as his arms slid around her, binding her to him. Dazed, she clung to him, the touch of his bare skin burning against her palms. A tremulous glow spread through her veins and still his kiss deepened.

Dear God, what was happening to her? A warning chimed in her mind. The few swains she had allowed to kiss her before she had met Jack had never stirred her blood. Her attraction to Jack had been instantaneous. But Mark had tricked her, had played upon her vulnerability. She loved Jack, yet like a wanton her blood had betrayed her. Appalled at her reaction, she pushed away from him. Breathing unsteadily she glared at him, furious that he had overstepped the bounds of friendship.

'You had no right to do that!' she fed her outrage. 'Let me go!'

Although he loosened his hold, he did not release her. The light from the door was behind him, dark shadow hiding the expression in his eyes. 'You were beginning to doubt your womanhood, Ellen. I but proved you are still a very desirable woman. And I wanted to stop the hurt you were feeling at Soulful's death.'

'You had no right,' she repeated stubbornly. 'I trusted you. It's impossible for us to continue to travel together.'

'Good God, Ellen!' The sudden flaring of his anger startled her by its vehemence. 'It was a kiss, nothing more! Do you think I've turned into an ogre overnight?' He took a step forward, the light falling across his face revealing the sardonic twist of his lips. 'If my intent was seduction I had opportunity enough at Chichester. Jack is my friend. I do not betray those who have given me their trust.'

He spun on his heel and climbed the ladder back into the loft. Stunned by the violence of his anger Gabriellen remained where she was, until moments later he descended, now fully dressed. The deep furrow between his brows warned her his anger had not receded.

'I said I would escort you until we find your father and I will do so. If you think I'm such a hardened lecher, how do you think you will fare with a stranger? After I've seen to Glendower and eaten, I'll ask at other inns and at the city gates for news of Esmond. Someone may know his destination.'

In spite of her confusion she knew he was speaking the truth. She had over-reacted to his kiss – felt he had betrayed her trust when merely he meant to comfort her. Men viewed these things more lightly than women, she supposed. Nevertheless she remained guarded, her temper ruffled as she faced him. 'I must have your word it will not happen again.'

'Now you insult me! Think well on this morning, Ellen. Should I have left you racked by doubts? If you're confident of your love for Jack, and his for you, where is the problem?'

He walked away from her without a backward glance. She watched him stroke Glendower who nuzzled his shoulder with his chestnut head. Mark's words rocked her. How dare he take that tone with her? Had he not taken advantage of her? Furious with him she ran out of the door and, ducking her head to avoid the heavy drizzle, she collided with a groom.

The man shoved her roughly aside, his puffy eyes still bloodshot from a night of heavy drinking. 'Plague take you! Look where you're going,' he mumbled, and hurried on into the stable to get out of the rain.

Gabriellen fled to her room. Banging the door behind her, she leaned against it. Arrogant swine! Jackanapes! Conceited oaf! The list of invectives against Mark grew. When she began to repeat herself she felt better and her head cooled.

She crossed to the window and frowned down into the puddle-filled courtyard. Mark emerged from the stables with the groom she had collided with. Only he wasn't a groom, she now saw, but a liveried servant. Gabriellen shrugged, but on the point of turning away, her sharp eyes noticed something vaguely familiar about the badge on the sleeve of the man's doublet. From this distance she could not be sure, but it looked very like Lord Barpham's scarlet oak on a silver background. Could this be the messenger his lordship had sent from Plymouth who had spoken to her father?

Chapter Eleven

It was five days since they had left Winchester. Gabriellen's senses were assailed by the colour and noise of Plymouth. The hot June sun shone in an azure sky, gilding the white-washed houses. Wealthy townsfolk paraded in rich brocades and silks, their scarlets, blues and emeralds flaunted against the brown and grey worsted of more sober citizens. Disorder reigned, but to Gabriellen it was exciting. It was here the English fleet was gathering. She was breathing in the air of history in the making and it set her blood racing.

She noticed with astonishment that such patriotism was lacking in the faces around her. Normally serene, black-garbed housewives became harridans as they battled their way past shouting piemen, pedlars and seamen who barred their passage. Harassed merchants muttered oaths as they side-stepped out of the way of carousing sailors. In the porch of his church a priest called upon the Almighty to save England from the terror of a Spanish invasion, whilst wide-eyed children peered timorously from behind their mothers' skirts.

For over an hour Gabriellen and Mark had been surrounded by the multitude of supply carts crowding into the port. Even that slow passage had left her unprepared for the press of people and wagons which packed the narrow streets at the town centre.

Ahead of them two carts tried to push past each other, both refusing to give way. The drivers shouted abuse as the carts rammed together with a splintering of shafts. One tipped back at a dangerous angle, spilling cages filled with poultry on to the hard ground. The freed horse bolted. A father cried out as he grabbed for his young son playing with a hoop, scooping him clear of the plunging hooves. There was the crash of breaking cages. Hens and ducks, clucking and squawking, fluttered up into the air, adding to the chaos. Several landed in the snatching arms of pass-ersby who fled with their plunder. Others, when they swooped to the ground, ran dementedly through the feet of the pedestrians, tripping several into the filth of the gutter.

Gabriellen did not know whether to laugh or cry. There was an amusing side to the scene, but her laughter was swiftly stifled as alarm took over. The two carters were now rolling on the ground, fists smashing into each other's bodies. Within moments the street erupted into a dozen fights.

Mark turned Glendower from the crush of the people into a side street. 'Down here – it's safer.'

At that moment a terrified goose darted through Glen-dower's legs, startling the stallion. Mark's swift reaction calmed his nervous mount before he could kick out and injure someone in the crowd. But the goose suffered for its rashness and was squashed beneath Glendower's stamping hooves.

'We'll have to find stabling for the horses,' Mark shouted, keeping the stallion on a tight rein. 'After that we can look for the players, or Jack, on foot. From the looks of it, we'll have a problem finding rooms.'

Gabriellen stared with dismay at the number of men filling every alley and doorway, mostly sailors lounging outside the inns as they swilled tankards of ale. A crackle of tension overlaid the bravado in their voices. At any moment the beacons' fires could be lit and these men would sail away to fight the Spanish. How many would return? It was a harrowing thought. Worse was the image of failure . . . of England aflame from Cornwall to Northum-berland as the Inquisition's fires consumed the flesh of heretics. Drake, Hawkins and Jack would not fail them. Be they outnumbered, one Englishman was worth ten Spaniards.

'There are no playbills posted. It would seem the players have not yet arrived.' She shaded her eyes to stare down an alleyway which led to the harbour. Her heart lifted at the sight of the hundreds of masts which forested the bay. It was a stirring spectacle, the might of England's fleet. More than that, it set her pulses racing. Somewhere out there was Jack.

146

Mark grimaced. 'God knows where we shall lodge this night.'

Aboard *The Swift* Jack sat with his long legs up on his desk as he frowned over the letter from York. It looked as if once the Spanish were defeated he would have to go there to sort out his business interests. He had planned to spend that time with Gabriellen.

When he heard the thud of a longboat coming alongside he stood up and reached for his doublet. Any diversion was welcome to break the boredom of being stuck in port. At dusk he had been invited to dine with Drake, and Lord Effingham would be in attendance. Who knew what favours a meeting with the Queen's Lord Admiral might bring his way?

He looked up as his cabin door opened and Seth Bridges entered. 'Master Rowan and his cousin have come aboard, cap'n.'

'Rowan, here?' He grinned with pleasure. 'Bring him down, Bridges. And fetch a bottle of my best brandy.'

'You'll be wanting to finish dressing.' Seth ignored his order and opened the leatherbound coffer containing the captain's ruffs. To his surprise it was waved aside.

'Later, man. Fetch Rowan.'

'You've not forgotten you're to dine with Drake?'

'Indeed not, but with Rowan I need no formality.'

Seth left the cabin thinking Jack looked a grand figure – ruff or no ruff – in his cambric shirt open at the neck. It was an appearance more in keeping with the buccaneer the capn'n was at heart, than the immaculate gallant he presented to the world. Though who could blame Jack for his pride in his fashionable clothes? They proclaimed how far he had risen.

If the cap'n dressed in a grand manner, so that no man would remember his humble origin, that was fine by him . . . In Seth's eyes Jack could do no wrong. They had come a long way, he and the cap'n, from the London gutters. He had risen high on Jack's rising star and would go higher. Life as a man-servant, tending those Jack-a-dandy trappings, beat begging in the filth of the gutter any day. Not that he always cared for the swaggering companions Jack surrounded himself with. Noblemen or not, they were conceited buffoons who would barter their friendship as cheaply as any whore. Drake was an exception – and, of course, Rowan. Out of all the cap'n's acquaintances, Rowan alone was a man you could truly count on when the cards were stacked against you.

'Cap'n Stoneham will see ye now, sir.' Seth allowed a rare warmth to enter his gruff voice. ''Tis good to see ye again, may I say.'

'You're looking well, Seth,' Rowan replied with a welcoming smile. 'This life agrees with you. Why, you're even putting on weight.'

'That I am, sir,' Seth chuckled. 'And in my pocket too. 'Tis a tidy nest-egg I've now put by, thanks to the cap'n. Many a man would have cast me aside after my face became so raddled by the small-pox last year. Not he. I were never handsome, but now even whores find me so hideous they charge me double. 'Tis thanks to the cap'n that I can afford them.'

'Captain Stoneham knows the value of loyalty,' Mark answered. He glanced at Gabriellen but was not surprised that she showed no revulsion at Seth's disfigurement.

Jack was at the door waiting for them. 'Never was a friend so welcome,' he greeted, his hand upon Mark's shoulder to draw him further into the room. He gave no more than a cursory glance at the cousin who hesitated in the shadows. 'You cannot guess at the boredom of life in port. But you have news . . .'

He paused as Bridges entered carrying the bottle of brandy on a silver tray and three Venetian glass goblets. Once these were filled and Bridges had retired, he pursued his questioning. 'Do you have news, my friend? Come, put me out of my misery. How is Gabriellen? Have you a letter from her?'

Mark sipped his brandy, his expression unreadable when he finally drawled: 'She sent no word.'

'No word!' Jack rasped, his eyes growing dark with shock. 'Certes, I never could have believed her faithless!' He turned away and tossed back the contents of his goblet, a muscle pumping along his jaw.

'Jack, I have been remiss in introducing you to my cousin.'

He swung round and Mark raised a brow as his friend cast an impatient glance towards the door. There was no

148

recognition in his eyes. How could there be when he
scarcely saw her? The pinched whiteness about his nostrils
showed his pain. He believed Gabriellen had forsaken him.
So it was true. Jack loved her. For reasons of her own the
minx was keeping well into the shadows.

He cleared his throat. 'May I present Gabriel Rowan?'

'Your servant, Master Rowan,' Jack responded
abstractedly.

'That is a chill greeting, good sir,' Gabriellen returned,
her voice continuing its disguise. She bowed, and as she
straightened swept her bonnet from her hair. With a shake
of her head, which was as sensual as it was defiant, her
tawny-gold hair fell into curls above her shoulders. 'I had
hoped for a warmer welcome. Perhaps I should not have
come.'

Mark watched Jack's proud hauteur drain from his face
as his eyes softened with recognition. Then they blazed
with a fierce light.

'It is you!' Thrusting his goblet into Mark's hands, he
embraced her, kissing her with passion.

Mark saw it was time to leave. He put the goblets on the
desk and was at the door before his discreet cough broke
them apart.

'I shall leave you to your reunion. Perhaps another time
we can have that drink, Jack!'

'You cannot just leave,' Gabriellen said from the shelter
of Jack's arms. 'You and Jack must have much to talk
over.'

Mark shook his head, his voice teasing. 'I'll play no third
in a lover's tryst. Take care of her, Jack.'

'Mark!' Gabriellen wrenched herself free to go to her
friend. 'Is this goodbye? Will I see you again?'

'You have Jack to look after you now.' He raised a dark
brow in taunting reminder. 'I travel to Dorchester. If you
join your father's players, our paths will cross again.'

When he drew back to leave, she put a hand on his arm
to stop him. 'I owe you so much. Take care, Mark.' She
reached up on tiptoe and kissed his cheek.

As she stepped back, Jack was at Mark's side. 'I will
accompany you to the deck.' Holding up his hand, he
gestured for Gabriellen to stay. 'Your pardon, my dear. I
shall be but a moment.'

Once by the ship's rail Jack gripped Mark's arm and

spun him round, his face stiff with anger. 'That was a very touching scene. Rather tender, was it not – for a friend? What passed between you and Gabriellen?'

Mark shook his arm free of Jack's hold, his expression bland. 'Careful how you choose your words, Jack. Insult neither Gabriellen's virtue, nor my honour, unless . . .' His hand rested on the rapier at his hip. 'Gabriellen loves you. I am honoured by her friendship.'

'Forgive me.' Jack relaxed. 'I should not have doubted you. Nor her.' He rubbed a hand across his brow. 'I've been in torment these last weeks. Knowing she was ill – wanting to be at her side. But all the while trapped here. I was wrong to insult you.'

'I have shared many things with you, Jack, but never a woman. But I tell you this – as a friend to you both – should Gabriellen have need of me, I shall be there. If you love her, Jack, then keep her faith in you inviolate. Should you break that faith . . .'

They eyed each other for a long moment.

'Were I to break faith with her,' Jack said, 'I would deserve your contempt.'

Recognising the sincerity in his voice, Mark nodded. 'Be true to her, Jack. I wish you both happy, my friend.'

Gabriellen paced the cabin, nervous at finding herself without Mark's reassuring presence. Not that she doubted Jack's feelings. His reaction to Mark's words and his ardent kiss had proved he still loved her. But rather it was her own reaction, the fierce scouring of the blood through her veins at his slightest touch, that was the deeper threat. Her glance fell upon the wolfskin covers flung over the bed which suddenly seemed to dominate the cabin. She looked quickly away. Had it been madness to come here? No, she defended her motives. Where else could she have gone until her father arrived in Plymouth? There had been no rooms available in the port.

To calm herself she picked up the goblet and swallowed a mouthful of brandy. Its liquid fire burned her throat and stomach, making her eyes smart. As the heat subsided the warmth it created eased the tension from her muscles. Another swallow and she was confident she had made the right decision.

The click of the door latch swung her round to face Jack.

He filled the portal, and in the fading light of the setting sun his presence seemed to invade the whole cabin.

'Dear heart, I've longed for this moment.' He took her into his arms, his words muffled as his mouth played over her throat. 'I was so worried when I learned that you had taken the fever. And I could do nothing!'

'Your love sustained me.' She leaned back in his arms. 'I was so wretched when Aunt Dotty and Uncle Ez died, and so frightened. Through those terrible days of nursing them, memories of our meetings were my only respite.'

'And now we are together, you'll find your memories pale in comparison to the joy of our loving.'

He laughed deep in his throat. Then his lips claimed hers, warm, passionate, demanding, his beard lightly grazing her chin. An iron embrace bound her to his hard body with an ardour that set her heart pounding. The warmth of his mouth moving over hers parted her lips with masterly insistence and their breaths mingled. His hand caressed her throat, his thumb tracing lazy circles over her skin, sending delicious shivers through her body which spread lower and lower. Not until he drew back did she realise, with a shock, that her doublet and shirt were unfastened and Jack's lips were moving over the upper curves of her breasts. She pulled back, alarmed. In the fading light from the window she caught the flash of steel in his eyes.

'No, Jack.' Her hand gripped the edges of her doublet together. 'I came here not for dishonour but for . . .' She halted, her gaze lowering, uncertain as to why she was here. Except that she yearned for his touch. But that was wrong. 'I should not be here alone with you, but I . . .' Her eyes wide with confusion, she met his gaze. 'This is wrong, Jack.'

He took her head in his hands, his voice smooth and persuasive as he stared down into her face. 'It is I who am in the wrong. You are innocent. You cannot know the torment of wanting you as I do. I love you, Gabriellen. And though I will suffer the torture of Hades, I shall never force you against your will.'

'Is it such torture, my love?' She felt guilty that he should suffer because of her.

'How could it be otherwise? To hold such beauty in my arms . . . to feel you respond to my kisses . . . I want you.' His amorous smile almost destroyed her resolve. 'I'll be patient. There is no shame in loving. To love is to share. To give, not just to take.'

He kissed her briefly and released her. Turning his back he moved away. Immediately she wished herself again in his arms. More confused than ever, she watched him through lowered lashes as he picked up a silver tinder box, struck a flame and lit the two candles in the double candlestick. As its light flickered over her, his sidelong glance travelled over her man's attire.

'What possessed you to travel in that outlandish mode?'

'You do not approve?' She was stung by his censure. 'How else was I to travel with Mark and keep my reputation safe? He introduced me as his cousin, Gabriel Rowan. Are you ashamed to see me in these clothes?'

He laughed. 'You mistake me, my love. It is a fetching disguise, if rather too provocative for my peace of mind.'

'Until I can join my father, it is a disguise I must maintain. How else can I remain on *The Swift* without becoming the subject of scandal?'

'My dearest, I applaud such practicality.' His eyes lit with pleasure. Lifting the two goblets, he was about to pass one to her, then paused. 'Perhaps Master Gabriel Rowan would prefer something less manly? A glass of canary, maybe?'

Gabriellen took the brandy from him. 'When I play a role, I play it to the end.' She drank the contents with a defiant gulp. But as she turned to place the empty goblet on the desk, the ship seemed to rock more noticeably in the water.

Chuckling softly, Jack drew her into his arms. The cabin revolved before her eyes. 'I love you, Jack. I don't want you to suffer.' Her voice slurred and her head dipped forward to rest on his shoulder. Suddenly the long hours of travelling left her weary and her eyelids felt leaden.

Jack lifted her in his arms and moved towards the bed. Immediately, she began to struggle. 'Jack, no. What trickery is this? Put me down!'

'Hush, my love. Have I not said I will take nothing you do not freely offer? I meant that. You are worn out from your travels. It is but days since you rose from your sickbed, and you drank that brandy too quickly.' He laid her on the mattress. 'Regrettably, I have an engagement with Drake and Lord Effingham which I cannot ignore. Sleep, my love.

Only Bridges and I shall know your secret.'

'But you, Jack?' She fought against the fuzziness blurring her brain. 'Where will you sleep?'

'I shall not be far away.'

She turned her head, suddenly suspicious. 'It was wrong of me to come. I cannot stay here, I see that now.'

'Do you not trust me?' Jack came over and took her hand in his. 'That says little of your faith in my love.'

She was torn. How could she doubt him? She had trusted Mark and come to no harm. But Jack was not Mark. Jack had never hidden his desire for her. Her distrust must have shown on her face; she felt Jack grow tense, his manner showing he was affronted.

'I see you doubt me. Do you think me less noble than Rowan? You did not hesitate to spend weeks alone with him. I love you, Gabriellen.'

All she could hear was the pain in his voice. She sat up, determined to reassure him. 'It is not the same. I do not love Mark. There was no temptation.'

He released her hand and clasped her shoulders as he looked down at her. 'When I leave, I want you to lock that door. Does that reassure you?'

What a fool she had been to doubt him. Contrite, she rested her hands on his chest and slid them up around his neck, saying softly as she offered him her lips, 'I wronged you. If I cannot trust you, then I can trust no one.'

He laid her down on the bed, his kiss light and restrained before he drew back to move about the room. Tiredness and the effects of the brandy in the warm cabin made her sigh sleepily as she watched him select a ruff from its coffer and a cloak and hat from a chest at the foot of the bed. Before he left he said quietly, 'Bridges will leave some food on the table should you waken before I return. No harm will come to you while you are aboard my ship.'

The touch of his lips against her mouth brought a soft sigh to her throat. Then the brandy and hours of riding at last overpowered her and she drifted into sleep.

An unidentified sound brought her awake to find the cabin bathed in the guttering light of a single candle. As the ship rose and fell in the water, the timbers and rigging creaked, the waves slapping the sides – soft, soothing, and not a little seductive. Stretching languidly, she gazed around the cabin, familiarising herself with her surroundings.

The golden glow from the candle mellowed the light oak panelling covering the walls. There was little furniture: two coffers, a chest, a desk on top of which charts were neatly stacked, a clothes-closet, and a walnut chair. All were richly carved and ornamented with brass. When she saw the tray of food and flagon of wine laid in readiness, her stomach protested with hunger. Once the cold rabbit pie, slices of powdered beef and mustard were eaten and washed down with the sweet canary wine, she felt better.

She moved restlessly around the cabin, her hands trailing over the surface of the desk where Jack worked and along the carved back of the chair he sat in. A velvet cloak edged with sable hung with three others on a peg on the wall. She could not resist touching it, then lifting its hem to her cheek, savouring the sweet fragrance of sandalwood which mingled with the muskiness of Jack's own scent. Her heart ached with longing and she moved to the small window to look out. The moon was a wedge of silver, a lazy crescent dozing in an ebony sky.

It was a beautiful night – a night for romantic trysts. Somewhere on a nearby ship a sailor played a gittern. Its haunting melody was taken up by two singers – a song of seas crossed and of parted lovers reunited. She scanned the dark outlines of ships with their winking lights. How long before Jack returned? It was cruel that duty had taken him from her this night. She hugged her arms about her body to crush the fierce need growing within her, for was not her country's need greater than hers? Impatient with herself, she pulled off her boots and removed her doublet, trunks and hose, leaving only the full shirt which covered her to mid-thigh.

At the sound of a footfall outside in the passage, she checked the door. It was still locked. Uneasy nevertheless she got into bed and pulled the covers to her chin. How had Seth brought her food if the door was locked? She heard the sound of a latch being lifted. It came from near the desk. As a portion of the panelling slid open, her heart thumped against her breastbone. 'Who's there?'

There was no answer. Her alarm mounted. She snatched up a boot from the floor, wielding it above her head as an improvised weapon. The candle stub spluttered out in the draught. All she could discern in the moonlight was a dark

154

shadow moving silently across the room.

'Jack, is that you?'

His deep chuckle drifted to her. 'Who else? I thought you asleep and had not meant to disturb you.' He moved closer and the moonlight fell across his tall figure. With a start she saw he was dressed only in a black damask robe. 'I could not sleep and came to collect some papers I was working on earlier. Are you feeling better?'

He looked at the boot still clutched in her hand above her head, his teeth flashing pearl-bright as he grinned. 'Is that how you would defend yourself against a man who intended to ravish – by attacking him with a boot?'

The mattress moved beneath his weight as he sat on its edge. 'Have I not said you are safe here? No sailor would dare enter my cabin without permission.' With a laugh, he removed the boot from her grasp and tossed it aside.

'I'm much better,' she said at last, wishing she did not feel so excited by his nearness. For protection she held the covers to her breast as the scent of sandalwood hovered like a seductive whisper between them.

The ship dipped in a sudden swell and Jack's hand on her shoulder steadied her swaying body. She stole a glance at him, the moonlight showing nothing more intimidating than a concentrated and thoughtful frown. It also cast silver reflections over the cosy, intimate cabin, a setting made for lovers. She shivered, no longer apprehensive but expectant. She had been denied Jack's presence too long not to enjoy this stolen moment.

Moving her head so that it rested in the crook of his elbow, she looked up at him through half-closed eyes. Her breathing slowed when his face lowered towards hers. He paused a finger's breadth from her lips, watching her closely. His long fingers touched her cheek, slowly turning her face to his. When his eyes darkened with desire she felt no fear, only anticipation. Then his lips were upon hers, moving with expert thoroughness, kindling a fire she had not even guessed lay dormant. Her hand crept up to touch his narrow beard and on to nestle in the thick locks of his hair.

His kiss was a masterpiece of passion and subtle restraint. In the art of love, he knew every nuance to bring a woman to submission. Beneath such mastery, her innocence would be sacrificed like a moth drawn by the irresistible lure of the flame. The heat of his body burned through the thin covering of the sheet. So potent was the magic he wove, she had not noticed how skilfully he had removed the fur covers.

A semblance of sanity returned. She pushed against his chest, summoning the strength to deny him.

'If you want me to leave,' Jack murmured, 'you must say now, my love.'

She hesitated. She was torn between right and wrong, honour and dishonour. The blood of Wildboar Angel taunted her. Where was the dishonour in loving Jack?

He felt the hesitancy in the slightest yielding of the hand against his chest. He saw it illuminated in her beautiful face, her green eyes shimmering with passion. His blood clamoured for her. He was surrounded by the warmth and scent of her. The sweet fragrance of her hair and body rinsed in the scent of jasmine intoxicated him. She moved very slightly. The sinuous caress of her body and the pressure of her uptilted breasts against his chest, primed his need for her. His restraint waned before the turbulence of his passion.

Gabriellen shivered as he lifted her tawny hair aside, his mouth tracing a molten path across her shoulder. The sheet was cast aside and his hand moved down across her breast.

His mouth closed over hers. What began low in her throat as a protest was transformed into a moan of ecstatic pleasure. It was received by his ravening kiss, parting her lips with passionate ferocity. She gasped as he took hold of her shirt and forced it from her shoulders down to her waist.

'Nay, Jack.' Her hand flew to hide her breasts from his gaze, her cheeks flaming. 'Would you dishonour me?'

'Do you doubt me still, my love?' he asked passionately. 'You are mine, Gabriellen. A love such as ours is destined. I'll never forsake you, my darling.' Her hand was pushed aside and taken to his lips where he kissed its palm. She looked up at him, propped on his elbows, smiling at her. 'Tonight is ours.'

He began to kiss her again, his voice soft and coercing. 'You are the most exciting woman I've known. My love, you drive me to the brink of madness. I forget you are so innocent. But deny me, my darling, and you gainsay our love. Is that not greater than the ties of convention?'

His unwavering grey stare defied her to rebuff him as his dark head lowered and he repossessed her lips, his mouth firm upon hers, its demand voracious but infinitely persuasive. She sighed beneath its masterly onslaught, insisting, arousing, demanding her surrender. Every touch ignited fires like sparks from a heath fire and destroyed conscious thought and reason. The caress of his beard, slightly rough but shamefully exciting, heightened the sensations now raging through her body. The endearments he breathed against her fevered flesh as he pressed a ferment of kisses along her throat, roused her to an ungovernable passion.

His lips never leaving hers, he removed his robe. Then the shirt was pulled down over her hips and they lay flesh to flesh. Her pearly skin contrasted with the bronzed darkness of his. The hair-roughened contours of his thighs tantalised the satin smoothness of her skin. Shyly, her gaze moved over his lean muscular body. A delicious quiver sped through her limbs and centred upon a point low in her stomach. To deny him would give the lie to her very existence. Her blood flamed. And God help her, the same blood as Wildboar Tom Angel flowed no less hotly in her veins.

Soft feminine curves subservient to the lean hardness of sculptured muscle, Gabriellen gave herself up to the wildfire sweetness of Jack's lovemaking. She returned his kisses with unrestrained pleasure. As his hands feathered across her breasts, waist and stomach, her body burned with a restless longing that caused her to writhe with indefinable need. Then, as his fingers travelled lower, she tensed, suddenly fearful of the unknown.

His hand stilled. 'Gabriellen, my love, there's nothing to fear.' His voice against her ear was hoarse with passion.

He gave her no opportunity for words. Covering her lips with his, he ensured her senses centred solely upon each new response to his caress as he stroked her breasts and moved over her stomach and thighs. This time the rhythm of his fingers as he found the most feminine place of her body drew soft moans from deep in her throat, and she arched against him.

Of its own volition her body began to move, the tumult of her senses craving release from the inexorable promise building within her. A promise of pleasures untold . . . of an ecstasy unequalled. Half wild with the frenzy which carried her in its wake, her inhibitions were forgotten, fading into insignificance under the onslaught of Jack's passion. She yielded. Her pliable, eager body was guided by expert hands, and she closed her eyes, lost in a storm of overwhelming desire. Jack lowered his weight upon her. Hungrily, his lips sought her breasts, his tongue teasing them to a vibrant aching fullness, instilling a luscious craving which demanded release. Their bodies blended and became one.

Gabriellen gasped, its sound captured by Jack's mouth, moulding her lips. The exquisite pulsating hardness filled her, and instinctively she responded to the primeval force which possessed her. She was initiated into a world of budding sensuality, its blossoms ripening and swelling until they were scattered in a storm of such magnitude, she felt she could bear it no longer. Her ardour matched his. Desire, all-consuming, throbbed through her in an explosion of passion.

Cocooned in a lethargy of contentment she floated slowly back to earth. Satiated, replete, her body pulsated in the after-glow of their lovemaking. When at last she found the strength to open her eyes she saw Jack leaning on his elbows above her, and at the tenderness in his expression she reached up to draw his head down upon her breast, joyful and at peace beyond her wildest dreams.

'Gabriellen, my enchantress, you are well named,' he murmured as he pressed a kiss upon the pulse at her throat.

'As are you, my handsome Jack-o'-lantern, my elusive will-o'-the-wisp, to allure and mislead me from the path of virtue.'

The grey eyes regarded her with love. 'You've no regrets?'

She shook her head, her heart too full of love to speak. The next instant she was held within a fierce embrace as his lips found hers and played upon them, his tongue lightly teasing them, his teeth gently tugging.

With a soft laugh she snuggled back into the crook of his arm. 'Nay, my love, I have no regrets. With a love as true as ours, it cannot be wrong to forestall our vows.'

Did she imagine it or did Jack imperceptibly draw back from her? She went cold. Pushing him away she sat up, her knees drawn to her chin. 'You do mean to marry me, Jack?'

'You are the only woman I have ever loved. There's no one else I want to spend my life with,' he reasoned smoothly. 'But with the English fleet about to do battle, it's not a time to think of marriage. That does not mean I love you less.'

She hid her disappointment. 'I'm being foolish. It is our love that matters. Only . . .'

'Only, like all women, your conscience would rest easier with the promise of marriage?' His cynical tone cut her.

She lashed out in pain and anger, her palm stinging as it struck his jaw. 'Damn you, Jack! Damn you and your false tongue! You speak of love, then would make me a whore.'

He caught her wrists and pushed her down into the pillow. 'Listen to me, Gabriellen, I love you. I've never said those words to another woman. But marriage is not possible at the moment.' His voice was low, urgent and persuasive. 'If you love me, let that suffice for now. Does not tonight prove that you are my woman?'

'I do love you, Jack.' She smothered her misgivings. What had Aunt Dotty said about their family often loving unwisely? No, it was not like that between Jack and herself. She had given herself freely. She would not regret it. The blood of her ancestors was too strong in her veins. The suddenness of her aunt's and uncle's deaths had shown her how fleeting was this life. How many people in these troubled times could have experienced the happiness she had found in Jack's arms this night? She was his woman. Nothing short of death or betrayal would ever change that.

'I did not tell you the news from Lord Barpham,' Jack said as his kisses again began to stir her blood. 'Your father's players are due to arrive in Plymouth in three days. So, my love, we have three days and nights for you to learn to love me better and trust me more. For myself, I know my heart and mind. Eternally, I am yours.'

Poggs looked anxiously towards the closed door of the covered travelling wagon. The raised voices of Cornelius and Esmond could be heard quite distinctly beyond it.

'Damn Hope!' he said to Agnes who was looking equally concerned as she sat at his side by the campfire on Plymouth Hoe. 'He's bullying for those damned lines of his. Can't he see that Esmond is far from well? All Hope thinks of is himself. I've had enough. I'm going to give him a piece of my mind.'

'Don't interfere, Poggs,' she counselled. 'Esmond will not thank thee. He knows how to pacify Hope. Hasn't he been doing it ever since the man joined the troupe? They have these rows every week. It will all blow over, just thee see.'

'It's Esmond I'm afeared for. He doesn't say, but his headaches are getting worse. That's why Hope's lines aren't written down. He should send for Gabby. Wasn't it she who copied down his last play for him at Christmas?'

A door slammed and Hope stormed across the campsite, cuffing Will Appleshot about the ears when the actor apprentice got in his way.

Poggs stood up. 'I'm going to talk to Esmond.'

'Then take him this bowl of potage. He's eaten nothing all day.' Agnes scooped out two ladles of the thick soup simmering in the cauldron over the campfire. She reached for a jug holding the liquid from the meadowsweet she had earlier boiled and poured a measure into a horn cup, mixing it with wine. Adding a sprinkling of herbs from the pouch at her waist, she then took an iron poker from the flames and plunged it into the cup. It sizzled, filling the morning air with a sweet pungent scent. 'Make sure he drinks the mulled wine. The meadowsweet will ease his aching head.'

'However did we manage without you?' Poggs grinned. 'A proper mother you've become to us all with your cosseting.'

'I do no more than Nan would were she able. Poor dear, her pregnancy seems to be draining all the strength from her. She's not over young to be having her first. She needs all the rest she can get.' Agnes drew herself up to her considerable height and smiled down at her husband. ''Sides, I like to fuss. Much as I miss dear Gabby, the players have become a second family to me.'

Poggs rapped on the wagon door and entered at Esmond's command. The troupe leader sat in the direct light of the single window, his head bent low over a sheet of parchment as he wrote. Looking up, Esmond squinted as he peered at the wooden bowl in Poggs's hand. 'I'm not hungry, Poggs. But if that's a cup of Agnes's mulled wine, leave it on the table.'

'You can't work without eating.' Poggs put the cup and

bowl on the table and pushed the parchment aside. 'You do too much, Esmond. Let Hope wait for his lines, damn him.'

'They were promised and are long overdue,' Esmond said heavily. 'Since we are to act *The Warrior King*, the lines Hope demands for King Richard to rally his troops in the Holy Land are fitting for an audience about to fight the Spanish. With patriotism fierce in everyone's heart, such stirring words will bring new life to the play and make us our fortune.'

'If it's at the cost of your health, it's not worth it. You can't do everything, Esmond. Your sharp wits have saved this company from disbandment time and again. I know you fob Hope off with promises. This is the first time in weeks I've seen you with a pen in your hand.' He frowned as he looked down at the few scrawled lines. 'It's your eyes, isn't it, Esmond? From the way you were stooping over this, I guess they're not as sharp as they were.'

'There is nothing wrong with my sight.'

Poggs detected the trace of fear in Esmond's voice and his heart went out to his friend. Esmond was a proud man who would never own to weakness. 'Of course not. But you do too much.' He set about persuading his friend to see reason. 'Why don't you let Gabby join us? It's what she wants. She can't be happy alone in Chichester. Let her come, and copy out the players' scripts to your dictation.'

'I will not have Gabby here. That's an end of the matter.'

He turned away and as he reached for his quill, knocked the horn cup over, spilling the wine over the script. The ink ran into an illegible blur. 'God damn you, Poggs! Now look what you've made me do. Get out! And send Agnes with some more of that wine. I've fifty lines to produce before nightfall or the play will never be ready in time.'

Poggs retreated at speed. He was used to Esmond's volatile moods, but there was more behind this one than a spilt cup of wine. Each day Esmond became more melancholy. The deaths of his sister and her husband had struck him hard. He scarcely noticed poor Nan Woodruff who had blown up like an inflated pig's bladder during the last few weeks. What Poggs would not give for sight of Gabby's cheerful face! She was the physic Esmond needed, only the proud fool was too stubborn to admit it.

As he jumped down the last step of the wagon a movement on the edge of the campsite caught his eye. The young man approaching looked vaguely familiar, a rare cock-a-dandy with his curled dark blond hair and fine russet doublet.

'Gabriellen!'

He was startled by the whoop of delight from Agnes and watched in astonishment as his wife picked up her skirts and fairly flew across the ground to fling herself into the young gallant's arms.

Chapter Twelve

Gabriellen tossed aside her quill with a satisfied sigh. Since her arrival two weeks ago, she had copied out all the parts for the troupe's actors. Following her father's dictation, she had produced the extra speeches for Cornelius and Robin to pacify their feuding. When she looked across at Esmond, she was relieved to see that the lines around his eyes no longer seemed so tight and painful.

'That's the first act of the new play completed. Tomorrow we can start on the poison scene. Or have you decided to use garrotting as I suggested?'

'Garrotting, I think.' Esmond stood up, stretching his arms above his head to ease their stiffness. 'I like well your idea. I had no idea you were so bloodthirsty.'

She laughed, unable to contain her happiness. These moments were the most precious of her day, healing the rift which had opened between them when she first arrived. 'It just seemed right for the plot. Besides, poisoning has been done before.'

'And one must not repeat what has been done before.' Esmond grinned as he pulled at a gold band in his ear.

'Not if you want your name remembered as a great and original playwright,' she answered, earnestly.

'You are a jewel, my dear,' he chuckled as he collected the papers together. Gradually his smile disappeared and his mood became abstracted. Gabriellen did not notice, she was too excited that her idea would be used in the new play.

'There'll be no writing tomorrow,' he announced, dispelling her elation. 'We shall be moving on.'

He turned away to gaze out of the window across the field to where the stage was erected and the actors rehearsing their final play.

'Moving on!' she repeated beneath her breath. 'When will I see Jack again?'

'Did you speak?' Esmond said without turning.

'No, Father.' She hid her fears. To keep the truce between them, Jack's name was never mentioned.

Tomorrow they would leave Plymouth. It would be weeks before she saw Jack again. Today's play, *The Warrior King*, was expected to instil fire and patriotism into every man who watched, to aid in the vanquishing of the Spanish.

Gabriellen glanced at Esmond who continued to watch the rehearsal. Camp life was now so familiar to her, she did not have to look outside to know what he was seeing. Cornelius Hope would be strutting across the stage, each eloquent gesture matched by an equally grand one from Robin Flowerdew. Their rivalry intensified with each play. Robin was gaining confidence. He no longer crumpled under Hope's abuse, and never lost an opportunity to steal a scene from the leading actor. Will Appleshot, if not needed as a messenger, would be sitting in a quiet corner poring over his few lines. Umberto and Cesare would either be tuning their instruments, or sitting under the oak tree, talking animatedly. The constant hammering told its own story of Francis Crofton's industry.

The carpenter's latest work was another triumph for Gabriellen. At her suggestion, he had erected two square wooden turrets, joined by battlements, with steps leading to a second platform above the stage. On this some of the most dramatic scenes would be enacted. At first both Esmond and Cornelius had objected, calling her notion insane.

'No strolling players use, or need, scenery. It's unheard of,' Esmond protested.

Crofton, though, had been excited by the idea, and against Esmond's wishes followed Gabriellen's instructions.

The finished work added more spectacle to the play. When Esmond saw it, he shook his head, still sceptical of the need for such elaborate props.

'Father, if we are to be the best players in England, we must elaborate. We must give the playgoers something different and better than any other troupe. Then they will flock to see our performances.'

Esmond regarded her thoughtfully. 'You take this very seriously. So you would make of us the best players in

England, would you? You are ambitious, daughter.'

'Is that not your wish? To be the best.'

Francis Crofton stood between them, twisting his cap in his hand as his handiwork was studied.

Esmond pursed his lips. 'I grant you its effect is spectacular. But is it practical?'

'It's made in segments,' Francis explained, his thin face animated. 'It takes only an hour to erect, less to dismantle, and can be transported without difficulty.'

'You do not object to the extra work?' Esmond asked. 'I would not have your acting suffer.'

'No, sir.'

'Then we shall use it.' Esmond clapped him on the shoulder. 'Well done.'

Gabriellen had felt a twinge of guilt that Francis would have more work to do. He already worked hard, although it was expected that every man with the troupe was capable of being an actor or stage hand when called upon – with the exception of Cornelius Hope, who refused to soil his hands. Though even he, upon occasion, could be coerced by Esmond to parade through the streets dressed in his finery and riding Socrates. There he would pass out handbills whilst permitting his admirers to proclaim him the greatest actor of the age. Hope could be exasperating, but he knew how to draw the crowds.

Aware that the silence in the wagon had stretched on, her thoughts returned to Esmond. She was saddened to see him frowning. Money had been pouring into the troupe's coffers from the collections made at each performance. Yet she sensed that he was troubled. Why?

It was more than the usual tantrums and problems which were part of everyday life with the troupe. Whenever she questioned him, he avoided giving her a straight answer. She knew the signs of evasion well enough. Hadn't she refused to speak of her relations with Jack?

Why had her father gone into town twice this week and returned drunk? Could the company be in debt? There was a melancholy droop to Esmond's mouth these days. She looked at the padlocked chest where the ledgers were locked away. Usually he was pleased for her to keep the accounts for him.

'Are you still angry with me for coming here?' She moved to his side. When he remained silent, she kissed his cheek.

165

He took a moment to drag himself back from his reverie. Then, patting her hand, he said, 'Nay, I've forgiven you that. You were unhappy in Chichester. Besides, minx that you are, have you not made yourself indispensable?' But his frown remained as he looked over his shoulder at her. 'This is not the life I would have chosen for you, though.' With no warning his mood veered, his voice rising. 'And as for your conduct with Jack Stoneham – staying on his ship . . .'

Unwilling to resurrect that quarrel, she drew back from him and smoothed the folds of her split skirt. Her voice was sad as she replied, 'Father, will you not let the matter rest.'

'No, by God, I will not! I gave Rowan more sense than to leave you in Stoneham's clutches. Rowan will pay for this. As for Stoneham, when I get my hands on him . . .'

'Father, please,' she interrupted. 'Mark was not to blame. Jack and I mean to marry.'

Esmond thumped the table and glowered across at her. 'Has he asked you? I doubt it! Seduction was his aim!' His face suffused with angry colour. 'My daughter is dishonoured, and that rogue . . . that arch-scoundrel . . . is nowhere to be seen.'

'Jack sailed to Chichester to take aboard the mustered recruits. They have to be trained in seamanship before he returns.'

'How convenient for him, sailing on the day I arrived!' His sarcasm lashed her. 'He's taken you for a fool, girl.'

Gabriellen shook her head. 'We love each other.'

'Love!' he scoffed. 'What can you possibly know of love? What do you even know of life? Or of a daughter's place? A place that calls for obedience to her father.'

'I know that a daughter's place is with her father.' She turned Esmond's words to her advantage, away from the danger of discussing Jack. 'I want to be part of your life, and of this troupe's. You must concede, Father, that a playwright and sharer is a far cry from the respectability of a lawyer's life. Was that not the profession Grandfather planned for you?'

Esmond's face took on a bitter smile. 'It appears Dotty raked up the family skeletons before she died. What else did she make it her duty to tell you?'

'Very little. She said being clerk to the London lawyer

was the worst thing that could have happened to you because of the heartache and suffering it caused. She never said what suffering.' She paused, waiting for him to speak. When he remained silent, his expression closed against her, she continued. 'She told me of Wildboar and the wildness she feared in our blood. But she said little of your life, Father.'

She observed the tense set of his body, the corded muscles in his neck, lips clamped shut as he maintained his silence. That hurt her more deeply than any physical wound. What was there in his past that he was guarding from her? Was it so terrible? Didn't he know that nothing he could have done would change her love for him? She didn't want to pry. She just wanted to understand . . . to help to ease the melancholy which was never far below the laughter.

'I'm not a child any longer, Father. I want to help, and I can't when you shut me out like this. Do you realise that you have never once spoken to me of my mother?'

The lines about his mouth were etched deeper. He threw the papers he was holding down on to the table with such violence that several sheets floated to the floor. 'One day I shall tell you of Sabine. I've been my own counsellor for too long to shed the habit easily.'

At the harshness of his voice she bent and picked up the papers. 'I will try to be patient, Father. But surely you can understand how much I need to know what she was like?'

He swept a hand across his broad brow and through his greying hair. For a long moment he studied Gabriellen's taut expression. Then with a sigh he continued, 'I'm selfish not to talk of her. She was French. A Huguenot. After the Paris massacre of Huguenots on St Bartholomew's Eve, your mother and her wounded brother, the only survivor of their family, escaped to England. They landed in Rye. Within a week Sabine's brother was dead from his wound. We were playing at Rye and I found your mother wandering the streets in a daze. She was always highly strung – excitable as only the French can be. But she was beautiful and so trusting . . .' His voice broke, the pain in his eyes striking at Gabriellen's heart. 'She did not deserve so short and tragic a life.'

He turned away to look out of the window and although a stream of questions leapt to Gabriellen's mind, she withheld them. Talk of Sabine obviously disturbed Esmond. It had shown her the weakness in her father's armour.

He said softly, 'I loved Sabine as I have no other woman.' He bowed his head, and once he had mastered his pain, added hoarsely, 'Sabine did not die in childbirth. She drowned herself a month after our stillborn child was born.'

Gabriellen stared at him, shocked. 'Why?'

The look Esmond turned on her was so agonised, she hoped never to witness it upon anyone's face again. 'Because I failed her.'

He turned away. The stiff set of his shoulders warned her he would say no more. Stunned by the news, Gabriellen sank on to her stool. She put a hand to her head, still not understanding the whole story. How could Esmond have failed her mother? By his own admission he loved her. He looked so haggard she could not bring herself to ask him. Most of his life was a mystery to her.

Unaccountably, she felt betrayed that she had never been told the truth of her mother's death. What could have driven her to suicide?

The shock stayed with Gabriellen as she watched Esmond lean against the window, his thoughts far away and troubled. Instinct warned her that it was not just the memory of Sabine which disturbed him. He had been in a strange mood all day, ever since Victor Prew had been closeted with him. Concern for her father overrode everything else. Her mother's death, terrible though it was, had happened long ago. It was Esmond who needed her now. Why did Prew keep pestering him? Three times this week the merchant had come to their campsite. On each occasion Esmond had been in a foul mood for hours afterwards. It had been after Prew's earlier visits that her father had got drunk. Somehow, Prew was at the root of his worry, she was sure.

A commotion outside made her go to Esmond's side at the window.

'God's nightgown!' he groaned in exasperation. 'Hope and Flowerdew are at odds again. If I don't calm them down, they'll come to blows.' He spun round quickly, his foot tangling with the stool Gabriellen had been sitting on. As he pitched forward, he managed to keep his balance by throwing out an arm against the wall. 'What possessed you to leave that where anyone could fall over it?' He scowled at her. The door slammed behind him, warning the players of his approach.

She put the stool under the table. Something really was amiss. Clearly worry had caused him to fly into a rage like that. Whatever it was she meant to find out. Could it be his eyesight? Poggs had confided in her that Esmond suffered from headaches. Her heart clenched with pity. That would explain his ill temper. Esmond would never admit to any physical failing.

Gabriellen looked out of the window. Her father was standing before the stage, hands on hips, legs straddled. The sky overhead was heavy, the black clouds as threatening as his mood. He was shouting up at the players. Francis Crofton, who was hammering a board into place, stopped his work. She could hear her father's angry voice but not the words. Robin hung his head, Cornelius threw up his arms and stamped to the back of the stage. This time her father had failed to pacify Hope, another sign that all was not well with him. Usually he did not allow his own ill-humour to affect his judgement when making peace amongst his players. To her relief she saw Poggs take Cornelius aside, and after a moment lead him forward to where her father was now agitatedly pacing.

Nearer at hand there was the creaking of wood from the wagon steps, followed by a gasp as Nan Woodruff hauled herself inside. The seamstress looked ready to collapse, her face drained of all colour. She was clutching a bunch of coloured ribbons and some streamers of gold and silver lace.

Gabriellen turned from the window and looked at her in dismay. 'You've not walked into the town for those?' Worried at the breathlessness of the pregnant woman, Gabriellen took her arm and led her to the bed. Nan's voluptuous figure had swollen out of all proportion to the length of her pregnancy.

'The gold lace is for Esmond's new doublet. They say Lord Effingham will be at today's performance.' As she spoke, Nan swayed and put a hand to the small of her back.

'You've been told to rest,' Gabriellen admonished, throwing aside the petticoats and shirts Nan had earlier been mending. She pressed the seamstress down on to the covers, and lifted her swollen legs on to the mattress. 'I'd have gone into town for you if the errand was so important.'

'I'll not be a burden on the troupe. I'm the seamstress, Miss Gabby.' Nan wiped a shaky hand across her flushed brow, her puffy eyelids shadowed with fatigue. 'It would not be right to ask you to run my errands.'

'I will hear no more talk of you being a burden to the troupe.' She took Nan's hand and squeezed it. 'You're not a workhorse. Please, in future allow me to do what is needed. We're a family. For the sake of the babe, you should rest.'

Nan turned her head away, her voice strained. 'You've work enough helping Esmond. I can't sit about doing nothing.'

'You can sew whilst you sit with your feet up,' Gabriellen smiled wryly. 'I've no skill with the needle. You're an artist, Nan. Merlin's cloak and the King's ceremonial robes you made are the finest possessed by any acting troupe. The audience demand magnificent costumes for the heroes of the play. Without your skill we would be no better than vagrants performing at the market cross for our living.'

'You're very kind, Miss Gabby.' Nan managed a tired smile.

Gabriellen was frightened by the weariness in the woman's voice. 'Tell me what needs doing to Father's doublet and I will ask Agnes to start work on it.'

'No, I must sew it.' There was no moving her.

'There you are, Nan!' Esmond said as he returned to the wagon. 'Good God, woman, you look like death!'

'She's been to town for gold lace for your doublet,' Gabriellen explained. 'Father, can't you make her listen to reason. She must rest more.'

Esmond stooped over the bed and took Nan's hand in his. 'You wouldn't want to lose the child now, would you?'

'No.' Nan clutched at her swollen belly, her voice rising in fear. 'That won't happen, will it? Tell me it won't happen.'

'Not if you take care of yourself,' Esmond murmured. Gabriellen was touched by the gentleness in his voice as he spoke to his mistress. 'You're no longer young, Nan. This is your first.'

To Gabriellen's consternation, Nan burst into tears. 'I'm so fat. I've no energy. 'Tis no wonder you prefer the pot-girl at the Golden Goose.'

'Where did you get that notion?' Esmond exploded with indignation.

Aware that the turn of the argument was none of her concern, Gabriellen departed, seeking out Agnes to help with preparing the next meal.

Inside the wagon, Nan forced out between broken sobs, 'Cornelius told me. That's where you've been spending your evenings, isn't it?'

'Hope? Curse the man! I might have known his poisonous tongue would be behind this.' Esmond controlled his anger. He looked down at the bloated body which only weeks ago had been desirable. There was something wrong with Nan to make her swell up like that. She was only five months gone and looked nearer eight. She had been large from the start. He felt a moment's guilt. The pot-girl – he could not even remember her name – had been a passing fancy. Until now Nan had understood and forgiven his occasional lapses. They'd been together long enough for her to know they meant nothing.

Theirs was a comfortable union. He didn't love her. How could he when he still mourned Sabine? The familiar ache of loss returned. After twelve years the longing had not eased. He passed a hand across his jaw. He was fond of Nan. Too fond to see her upset, especially in her condition.

He sat on the edge of the bed and tenderly pushed a damp curl back from her forehead. 'You're not upset over a pot-girl, are you? You're worth a score of her kind.'

Nan sniffed and wiped the tears from her eyes. 'I don't blame you. Look at me! I'm like a stranded whale.'

'Nan dear, you're still your sweet, lovable self. What is it now, four months before the child is born?'

'An eternity,' she wailed. 'I started to blow up like a rotting carcass from the start.'

'You're too hard on yourself.' Her anguish touched him. He kissed her to dispel her fears and when he drew back, saw that her eyes searched his with uncertainty.

Resting her hands on his shoulders, she said softly, 'There was a gypsy woman in the town selling heather.' She shifted her weight and fumbled in her pocket to produce the squashed stalks. 'She said I was so big because I'm carrying twins. Boys, she said. And indeed, Esmond, there be times when it feels I've a giant spider kicking out with all its legs.'

She gasped and at the same moment he felt the child move within her to push against his side. Not just a single kick but three separate movements.

'Twins!' The actor in him feigned delight as he hid his misgivings. Twins meant a difficult birth. 'That's wonderful! And boys, you say?' He laughed and took her into his arms. 'You know, if it were possible for us to wed, I'd be asking you, don't you, Nan?'

'Well, it isn't possible as well you know!' Her face brightened at his reassurance and a glimmer of her former beauty shone though the bloated face. 'I've longed for a child for years. Let's be content with what we have.'

Rolling on to her side, she held him tight, her body pressing against his as she placed his hand on her full breast.

'Make love to me, Esmond. Let me think I'm still young and desirable.'

'You are, my dear,' he said thickly, his hands on the front lacing of her bodice. His passion was unfeigned. Nan had spent three years in the stews of Southwark and knew every whore's trick to drive a man to madness. A more able bedfellow he had not met. Despite her bulk she still had the power to rouse him. The twins which distorted her luscious body had been conceived on a night of wild abandon. The memory alone could bring a fire to his loins.

He drew the bodice and shift from her shoulders and buried his head in her swollen breasts, his mouth teasing their dark erect peaks until she writhed with pleasure. Eagerly her hands reached for the points fastening his breeches, and their skilful play left him panting with his need for her.

'There'll be no more pot-girls, Nan. Not if it grieves you.'

She put a finger on his lips. 'No false promises, Esmond. I warrant there'll always be the occasional pot-girl, serving maid, even a grand lady when the chance is offered. I know you'll never love me. That you'll never love any woman but Sabine. But what we have will endure.'

'So it will, my dear.' He rolled over on his back and pulled her on top of him, so that his weight did not press against her.

'You always were a wicked one, Esmond Angel,' she chuckled. Her lethargy vanished at the ardour in his eyes.

She dipped her head, her mouth closing over his straining manhood, her tongue and fingers stroking and caressing until he moaned in ecstatic torment.

'Nan – my sweet Nan,' he panted as he raised his head and kissed her, his fingers sliding up into the heat of her, rousing her to ecstasy. None of her former clients in the stews had thought it necessary that she take pleasure in their coupling, but Esmond always considered her needs as much as his own. When she could stand the building torrent no longer she reared up to impale herself upon him, their cries of fulfilment muffled by the passion of their kisses.

When at last they lay quiet and their breathing had returned to normal, Nan risked Esmond's displeasure by repaying Gabriellen's kindness to her.

Softly she said, 'Poggs told me that you and Gabriellen were quarrelling again.' His scowl almost deterred her, but she pressed on. 'She's your daughter, Esmond. Perhaps she's too like you in some ways. Obviously she's in love with Jack Stoneham. Like as not, she has your hot, passionate blood. Could you expect a daughter of yours to live like a nun?'

Mark Rowan ran a calming hand over the white blaze on Glendower's head as he led the stallion across the stableyard of Wynwood Grange. A breeze swirled wisps of straw across the cobbles, and lifted the edges of a milkmaid's apron as she leaned against the flaking daub of an outbuilding. The flapping apron caused Glendower to sidestep nervously, and Mark silently cursed the gathering spectators.

'Whoa, boy. Steady,' he soothed. Mark nodded a greeting to Sir Philip Templeton, master of the Grange. The giggling serving wenches, and grooms and gardeners with their loud bawdy jests, always unsettled the stallion. The servants regarded the arrival of a stallion man as an entertainment, welcoming any break from the monotony of their daily routine.

Mark accepted their jokes with good humour. During the tense moments before the mating, he parried their jests adroitly. It was what they expected, but all the while his attention was upon Glendower. Now, with caution, Mark approached the mare tethered at the rail. Glendower raised his head, pulling his top lip back over his teeth as he tasted the air which carried the scent of the mare in season. At

such a time the stallion could be unpredictable and dangerous. The mare's nostrils flared as she in turn scented the
stallion. Showing the whites of her eyes, she pulled back
on her rope, her back leg lashing out. Mark kept Glendower
at a distance until the mare became used to the stallion's
presence. He was too experienced a handler to rush the
mating, especially if the mare was skittish. Anticipating
Glendower's excited sidestepping, Mark braced his body
against the animal's strength, the muscles of his arms straining as he tightened his hold on the leading rein.

'Patience, my proud beauty,' he spoke softly. 'Patience.
Your lady is going nowhere.' Mark rubbed the stallion's
muzzle. The big horse quietened, but his agitation showed
in the muscular spasms bunching his haunches and the way
his chestnut head strained back against his halter. 'Steady,
boy.'

Mark walked the stallion slowly around the courtyard to
calm him, ignoring the ribald comments from the spectators. The mare was accepting Glendower's presence.

In the three weeks since Mark had left Gabriellen in Jack
Stoneham's care, he had resumed the old pattern of his
life. Wherever he went, Glendower's magnificent looks had
gained his owner the entry he needed to pursue his secret
work. Mark had ridden to Dorchester as planned, and while
there had overheard a casual comment by a guest at the
manor. It was enough to take him on the road to Cerne
Abbas. There he had spent an uncomfortable night in a
wood overlooking the hillside where the chalk outline of a
giant strode across its meadow. That had been a false trail.
They happened sometimes; each must be investigated. On
that particular night the only other person to endure the
cold drizzle on the hillside was a woman who had arrived
on foot. Mark saw her approach and prostrate herself face
down in the centre of the pagan chalk figure. She stayed
like that for a long time. It was a sad and desperate ritual
which barren women had performed for centuries in the
belief that they would then conceive.

For him that night on the Dorset hillside had been fruit-
less and he had wished the woman better served. Yet the
detour to Cerne Abbas had led him onwards to Wynwood
Grange, three miles from Sherborne. Its owner, Sir Philip
Templeton, was a known Catholic who once before had
been under suspicion of treason. On that occasion nothing

174

had been proved. In the two days Mark had been in the district, his suspicions about the man had again been aroused. To obtain the evidence he needed, he would have to visit the manor. In this Glendower had not failed him. Mark stayed overnight at the village inn. By the next morning word had reached Sir Philip of Glendower's looks and reputation. A groom arrived to ask Mark whether the stallion would cover one of Sir Philip's mares.

The village was not as peaceful as it seemed. He'd wager the stud fees that this manor had its secrets. He knew the signs – eyes which never quite met his steady gaze, a conversation hastily stifled. This morning as he crossed the innyard on his way to Glendower's stall, he had glimpsed a furtive figure skulking in the shadows. The last time he had seen that emaciated face was at Bosham. Then the man was being ferried ashore from a ship moored in the harbour. There was a certain look about him which Mark had long ago learned to recognise. He was a Jesuit priest. The trail which had vanished a month ago at Arundel in Sussex, emerged unexpectedly here in Dorset. The priest's presence confirmed Mark's suspicions of another Catholic plot against the Queen.

Mark glanced over his shoulder at the mare who was still too restless to accept the stallion. Murmuring soothing words to Glendower, his thoughts returned to his real reason for being here. For the last five years Mark had been in Lord Walsingham's pay. The Queen's minister alone was privy to his double identity. He had lost count of the plots he had rooted out and defused. It was he who had first discovered the Babington Plot in 1586 which planned a Catholic rising in favour of Mary Queen of Scots, and the murder of Elizabeth. After he had intercepted an early communication from Anthony Babington, the leader of the assassins, he had passed the information to Walsingham. He had had no part in the later investigations and the arrest of the conspirators.

A faraway look came into his eyes as he recalled those turbulent days. Although his work had undoubtedly saved Elizabeth's life, it had led to the implication of the Scottish Queen, who was later found guilty by a special court and then beheaded at Fotheringhay. He shifted uneasily. The knowledge that even in a small way he had been involved in Mary's downfall still troubled him. But an England governed by the Scottish Queen would be an England crushed under the yoke of the Inquisition, of persecution and torture for all Protestants. He told himself, not for the first time, that his conscience dictated his first loyalty should be to Elizabeth – no matter what the consequences.

He felt no such qualms about the other fanatics he had helped bring to justice. High treason was no light matter. Elizabeth had been a more tolerant monarch than her Catholic sister, Mary, who had roasted hundreds of heretics at the stake. Elizabeth's reign had been a time of compromise. In the early years, even the recusants who adhered to their Catholic opinions were tolerated – providing they paid their fines and attended a monthly communion at their parish church. The change had come with the infiltration of the Jesuit priests into England. With the support of Philip of Spain, they sought Elizabeth's death. Their influence must be crushed to safeguard the Queen and ensure her subjects remained free from the persecution of Rome.

Over the years Mark had become adept at his task, a sixth sense warning him when he had touched upon the beginnings of such plots. That frisson of anticipation was with him now.

'Hey, Rowan!' The head groom reclaimed his attention. 'The mare's quietened. Let's see if your stallion performs as well as he looks.'

While two grooms continued to hold the mare's head and a third lifted her tail, Mark led Glendower to the rail. Emitting a high whinny, the mare bucked once, then stood still. Her red coat was flecked with sweat and muscles twitched along her sleek back. Glendower was positioned directly behind her. Mark braced his legs, extending the leading rein as the stallion reared up on his hindlegs, his forelegs curving in the air before anchoring over the mare's back. His first attempt failed and with a snort Glendower clattered down on all fours.

As the stallion pranced, Mark took care to keep his feet from being crushed by the stamping hooves and felt his arm almost jerked from its socket. He circled Glendower, then led him forward again. This time the stallion successfully came down upon the mare's back. Slackening the rein, Mark moved swiftly, expertly guiding the stallion into the mare. The sweat broke out on his own body as he again took up the leading rein, tense lest at any moment the mare twist away and Glendower topple disastrously, risking a broken leg or back. Above him the stallion snorted and shuddered, then reared away from the mare to stand with head tossed high, his mane and tail lifting proudly in the breeze.

'Well done, my beauty,' Mark crooned as he backed Glendower away. He turned to the waiting groom who held a bucket of cold water. 'Quickly, douse the mare's quarters. It'll make her tense her muscles and seal in his seed.'

'You are a true master, Rowan,' Sir Philip Templeton declared as he followed Mark to the water trough where Glendower was to drink. 'I count it my good fortune you were in the district just as Ruby Lady was in season. She's the best of my mares. There'll be a fine foal from his siring.'

'She's a good horse,' Mark answered. Taking a cloth from the pouch at his waist, he began to wash the mare's scent from Glendower's nostrils and chest.

'You never said what brought you this way?' Templeton queried.

'Just following the road.' Mark shrugged and smiled amiably. If Templeton was involved in a Catholic plot there was no point in rousing his suspicions. Besides, he was too experienced at this intrigue to destroy his cover. 'There's St James's Fair at Bristol at the end of the month. I'm bound for there – and grateful for any stud fees I can earn on the way.'

'So you'll be moving on now?' Templeton asked, keeping in step with Mark as he led the horse from the stableyard.

He raised his brow in surprise. 'Not for two days. The stud fee includes another visit. That's how Glendower has won his reputation of never failing to produce a foal.'

Templeton looked less sure. 'I thought it would be but the once he covered my mare, since you were travelling through.'

'No,' Mark returned emphatically. 'It would be more than our reputation was worth. Glendower is no ordinary stud. He is the Rowan Strain. Apart from covering my own mares in Wales, he never services more than another twenty in a year. That's what makes the Rowan Strain so prized.'

'So that's your excuse for the exorbitant fee you charge,' Templeton grunted. 'Still, you say he's never failed to sire yet? I had Ruby Lady covered last autumn and nothing came of it. Perhaps your method is right. So you'll return in two days?'

'Yes. I'm staying at the inn until then. I prize Glendower too well to overtax his strength. A rest and good pasture are his reward.'

'Wise words,' Templeton agreed as he walked with Mark to the drive which led to the Lodgehouse. 'I've seen many a good stud broken afore his time by misuse. If you are this way next year, come see the foal. I'd like your opinion of its worth.'

'It would be my pleasure.'

Templeton held out his hand and jangled some coins. 'That's half your fee against your return.'

Mark took it and raised a brow at the shortfall.

''Tis as agreed.' Templeton coughed pompously. 'Less the price of the bread, meat and ale the cook gave you. I know a proud man like yourself, Rowan, would not accept charity.'

Mark walked on without a word. Charity he would never accept, but hospitality was the mark of any man who regarded himself a gentleman. Well, Templeton could keep the few groats for the watery ale and tough meat Mark had been given, though he himself would have been ashamed to give a passing beggar such mean fare. Mean of purse meant mean of nature. If Templeton was involved with the Jesuit priest, then his miserly carcass should fare well upon the thin gruel of Her Majesty's gaol.

Later that night Mark crouched in the shrubbery of Wynwood Grange watching the house. He had been there since Templeton returned from visiting a neighbour two hours ago. The moon was veiled by a thin layer of cloud, but enough light illuminated the greystone manor and grounds to show anyone arriving or leaving.

The evening mist rose round his legs and he wrapped his dark woollen cloak tighter about his chilled body. He'd give much for a warming cup of brandy and the comfort of his own home at this moment. He dismissed his fancies. It was more than patriotism which made him keep such cold vigil. He had his own personal vendetta against any who would bring the Spanish Inquisition to England.

The old anger and hatred returned to heat his blood.

What was his cramped discomfort this night, compared to the torture his father had endured? Mark's jaw clamped with the pain of his memories. For five years his father had been a prisoner of the Spanish. He had been a passenger on a ship bound for La Rochelle to visit his dying brother who was a merchant there. A storm which had lasted for seven days had blown the ship far off course and it had been wrecked off the Spanish coast. For six months Marcus Rowan had mouldered in a Spanish prison, frequently tortured for his Protestant faith. The fate of such prisoners was usually burning at the stake, but his father had been spared that. Instead they made him a galley-slave. For four and a half years he had lived that particular hell. The ship was eventually rammed by an English buccaneer and during the fighting both Marcus's legs had been fractured. The English took the ship and, discovering his father to be English, rescued him. But his legs had turned gangrenous, and to save his life they were amputated.

The years as a galley-slave had reduced the strong laughing man Mark remembered to a shrunken cripple. For ten years his father had lived, confined to a chair and facing the indignity of being carried everywhere. To avenge him Mark had taken up the cause to bring down any who would introduce those injustices and horrors to his country.

From the house a yellow glow briefly lit the entrance porch and a cloaked figure was outlined against the candle-light. Then the door was shut and the man cut across the grass towards the shrubbery where Mark was hiding.

He sank lower, recognising Sir Philip Templeton when he passed a few feet in front of him. He followed, keeping to the shadows as his quarry moved towards the parish church next to the Grange's land. Whilst skirting the manor pond, Templeton startled a pair of mallard out of the rushes. Clearly the man's nerves were betraying him, for he stopped to look over his shoulder. Mark pressed his body against a beech trunk until a twig snapped some distance ahead. Edging forward, he saw Templeton weaving through the gravestones. At the churchyard wall, Mark paused, his eyes and ears straining for evidence of other conspirators. Silently climbing over it, he moved like a dark spectre across the churchyard. A jangle of harness from the direction of the two yew trees ahead made him drop to his knees behind a stone angel on a family tomb.

The conspirators had chosen their place well. There was no cover for him to move in closer. To his frustration only an occasional word reached his hiding place. But from the voices another man was present, apart from Templeton and the Jesuit.

'We will rid England of the Protestant bastard!'

The stranger's high voice carried to Mark. Then the wind stirred through the trees, taking their words away from him, and he caught only snatches of their conversation.

'. . . I meet them again at Bristol. The fair is the perfect cover . . . Then, my friends, to London – even unto the Court itself.'

The rest was lost to Mark as the wind stiffened. Moments later a heavy footfall warned him that Templeton returned. He flattened himself against the ground until the man had passed by. Lifting his head, Mark saw two riders head away from the yew trees. The moonlight shone upon the ascetic countenance of the Jesuit. It also lit the pale narrow face, thin moustache and small but dissolute eyes of his companion. Even cloaked the man looked small and puny. Mark would recognise him should they meet again at the fair.

Chapter Thirteen

The stage had been erected on Plymouth Hoe for the entertainment of Lord Barpham and his special guest the Queen's Lord Admiral. Gabriellen stood at the side of the stage and closed the leatherbound prompt book with a snap. The sound was lost amongst the cheers from the groundlings in the audience, and the applause from the platform where the guests of honour were seated on benches.

She blinked aside tears of pride as the acclaim rose to a crescendo. The cheering from the sailors – whose blood was roused with determination to trounce the Spaniards – would not allow the actors to leave the stage. Cornelius Hope, with a gesture which was meant to elicit the last shred of emotion from the audience, took Robin's hand and led him forward. Robin was dressed in a bright auburn wig and an elaborate court gown. He was Gloriana personified. There was not a man present who did not feel that to fight for England and Elizabeth would be the greatest honour of his life.

Listening to the deafening roar from the crowd, Gabriellen felt elated. It had been her suggestion that an epilogue be written to follow on from the story of King Richard. The Lionheart's ghost appeared to Elizabeth Tudor, likening the forthcoming battle with the Spaniards to his own Holy Crusade. He had damned the Inquisition and the might of Spain as oppressors. England had risen to greatness upon the valour of its soldiers. To rousing acclaim, King Richard had cried out: 'Remember the Infidels' defeat at Acre! Remember Crécy! Remember Agincourt! The morrow is your hour of glory in a battle as yet unnamed.'

How that speech had driven the groundlings to a frenzy. Only she knew that she had fed those lines to Esmond, who had seized on them, changed a word or two, and now

181

believed them to be completely his own.

She watched the players make their exit on the far side of the stage. Immediately her father was surrounded by Lord Effingham and his entourage. When he disappeared from sight, taken away to dine as the Lord Admiral's guest, she was overcome with pride.

'See how they love us!' Poggs cried, catching her around the waist and swinging her round in an impromptu dance.

'*Bellissima!*' Cesare cheered as he beat his tabour in time with their steps.

They were joined by Umberto, his face still blackened by cork for his part as the vanquished Moor. Clapping his hands to the rhythm, he grinned. 'We are a success – no?'

'We are a success – yes!' Gabriellen laughed.

'What a week!' Poggs declared, his laughter joining theirs. 'Nay, two weeks! Have we not done our part for England? And we owe much to you, Gabby. Because you were at Esmond's side encouraging him, he has written some of his finest lines this week. You've spent hours copying the actors' parts. Some of that acclaim is yours.'

Gabriellen spun to a halt, breathless and exultant. 'Now I know why you're all driven to this life. It's in the blood.'

'Aye, there's little to match it,' Poggs said with a chuckle. 'It's times like these which keep us going through the rough days.'

Cesare bowed to Gabriellen, saying, 'Bad days we no more have. Gabriellen, she is our good luck – yes?'

Over Cesare's head she saw Will Appleshot and Francis Crofton, in their Crusaders' chain mail and tunics with the red cross, walking towards them.

'That was a grand performance, Will,' she called out, knowing how nervous he had been before the play began. 'Four costume changes you had, and you never missed a cue. Well done! You, too, Francis. The stage set was wonderful.'

Young Will smiled shyly, his eyes glittering with the same elation she knew must be in hers. A laugh from Umberto drew her attention to the two musicians standing below the stage.

'Ah, this fever, it has taken you.' Umberto's dark eyes sparkled as he held out a hand to help her down the steps to the ground. '*Madre a dios!* The cheers, the praise – there is nothing like it, yes?'

She echoed his laughter as Poggs leapt from the stage and moved away to take Agnes into his arms. 'You're right, Umberto. There is nothing like the sound of applause. I can understand why Cornelius thinks himself one of God's most favoured creatures. He held the audience in his hand today.'

She glanced across at Poggs and Agnes walking arm in arm to their wagon, and through her elation felt the ache of loss. Only one thing marred this day: Jack was not here to share it.

'The cheering is good.' Umberto cut across her thoughts. 'Only one thing stirs the heart more.' He put his fingers to his lips in a Latin gesture of appreciation. 'It is love. *Si*, I am right?'

'Life without love is no good,' Cesare added. 'The capitano of the sea . . . you miss him, yes?'

'Is it so very obvious?'

'Why you wish to hide it?' Umberto regarded her solemnly. 'Love is good. You no be ashamed.' He looked at Cesare, his brown eyes soft as a woman's caressing her lover. She realised then that it was more than cousinly affection which the two musicians shared. She should be shocked, yet she was not. There was nothing effeminate or offensive in the manner of either of them. They lived very private lives. They were cousins – friends – lovers – an association as strong as any marriage. During the six years she had known them she had always liked the two musicians. She felt no differently now.

'My father does not approve of Captain Stoneham.' She shrugged.

Cesare tapped his long nose with his forefinger. 'Angel by name no mean Angel by nature, with the maestro. You understand? Nan is not his only woman.'

Umberto said, 'Men such as the maestro – who make love to many women – they not so understand for their daughters. It is so in Italia. Here the same, I think.'

She nodded. 'I fear it is. Father has the devil's own temper. I could not bear it if he picked a fight with Jack. What is worse is that Father will insist that Jack weds me.' She fidgeted with the pendant at her neck.

'Your capitano, he no wish to marry you?' Cesare asked. 'For you, that is bad.'

'The captain's duty for the moment lies with his ships.'

Her head stayed high as she held his gaze. She refused to be ashamed of her love for Jack. 'Until the Spanish are beaten, it is not fitting we think of marriage.'

'These are his words?' Cesare's dark stare was accusing.

Her green eyes snapped with defiance. 'I agree with him.'

'Such words will bring you heartache,' Cesare answered. 'You are a proud woman. Too good for dishonour and shame. You want for people to spit on you in the street?'

The look of surprised innocence on Gabriellen's face showed Cesare that she had no idea how cruel people could be. It saddened him. She should be warned. His English was not good enough to explain what he felt. He looked at the emerald pendant she always wore, recalling the inscription which she had once shown him. He rubbed his narrow beard. Love does not conquer all. He should know.

Had he not been disowned by his father for loving Umberto? His beloved City of Florence was lost to him. His father had vowed to kill him if he should return. Until then he had been the pampered son of a wealthy goldsmith. That was fifteen years ago. A long time to be parted from the family he loved. He looked across at Umberto and saw the understanding in his eyes. It had not been so hard for him to leave Florence. He was four years older, his father an artist who was rarely at home as most of his commissions were in Rome. At sixteen, Umberto was married to the woman he had been contracted to since he was three. She was a shrew and slovenly. She hated Umberto's friends and despised his talents as a musician. Umberto had been his lover for two years when Cesare's father discovered their relationship.

The memory brought a resurgence of pain and anger at his father's treatment of him. One day he would return to Florence. His brothers and sisters were grown now, his father an old man. Yes, soon he would return. No matter how fiercely he loved Umberto, the ties of his family went deep. He had lost much. But he looked at Umberto and knew if he had to make the choice again, he would act the same way.

Cesare realised Gabriellen had not understood his warning. How could she? All her life she had been surrounded by love. He hoped she would not have to face prejudice for loving unwisely. He looked at her with concern and added,

'I no give you sermon. I your friend. I no wish to see you hurt.'

Gabriellen was moved by his solicitude. 'Do not worry about me. I have faith in Jack.'

A white plume waving some inches above the dispersing crowd's head caught her attention. It was moving towards them. At the sight of a dark beard, she held her breath. How many times in the past week had she seen every tall dark figure as her love, only to be disappointed? Her hand tightened over the emerald pendant. This time, the determined way the man cut a path through the throng was unmistakable.

Tactfully, Cesare and Umberto melted from her side. Jack broke through the edge of the crowd and swept her into his arms. With a jubilant laugh he pulled her behind the corner of the stage, seeking privacy for them.

'My love, at last we are together.' His voice was muffled against her hair, her cheeks, her eyes, until his mouth claimed her lips.

He tasted of salt from the sea, but to Gabriellen it was as sweet as nectar. 'Have you missed me, Jack?' She pulled back to gaze into his handsome face, her heart aching with the force of her love.

'Never have two weeks seemed such an eternity.' As he spoke his lips moved over her face and neck, his words disjointed as they stood locked together, both barely controlling the desire which had flamed into life. 'I came as soon as we moored. For two days the wind has been against us. I feared I would never get here. Now I find the players leave tomorrow.'

The sound of approaching voices drew them apart as Cornelius appeared, surrounded by admiring women. Surprise widened Hope's eyes as he looked from Jack to Gabriellen, then they narrowed in speculation. Gabriellen inclined her head in polite acknowledgement. One of the women, dressed in silk and laden with jewels, tapped Hope's arm.

'Mr Hope, such an honour it is to meet you. I've seen every play these last two weeks. I declare, you have quite stolen my heart.'

The woman's praise continued as they moved on. Cornelius preened his moustache, his swagger more pronounced as he lapped up her admiration.

Jack still held Gabriellen, but before he could speak Francis Crofton and Will, already changed from their costumes, came into sight. Smothering an oath Jack released her, his face drawn with impatience.

'There's no privacy here. Neither will there be on *The Swift*. She's reprovisioning at the quay. Besides, I'll not have you leered at by my men.' His grey eyes reflected the blue of the sky as they stared into hers. 'But privacy we shall have. I've hired a room above an apothecary's.'

He kissed her hungrily. 'Go and fetch a cloak. Though the afternoon is warm, for the sake of your reputation I would not have you recognised.'

She ran to the wagon to collect her cloak, resenting every second they were apart. When she returned to him, he paused to pull the hood further over her face. Then, her arm tucked in his, they walked down from the Hoe to the port below, oblivious to the people and noise around them. At each step their bodies touched, the warmth and intimacy fuelling the need to be alone – to forget everything but their own love and desire.

In their haste she scarcely noticed that they had entered the poorer streets of the port, close to the quay. The apothecary's shop smelt of pungent herbs and damp, and was dingy after the bright afternoon sun. It was a fleeting impression. Jack was taking the stairs two at a time, urging her to hurry. Then the door of their chamber was closed behind them, the drone of voices and carts outside hushed as he took her into his arms.

'Gabriellen.' He spoke her name like a caress. 'My sweet Gabriellen. My love.' He took her face in his hands and stared down at her, his eyes smoke-grey and heavy-lidded with passion. Jack's fingers moved to the fastening of her cloak, drawing it from her shoulders, before moving to lift the small heart-shaped hood from her hair. Impatiently, he tossed it on to a nearby coffer. Loosening the pins from her hair, he shook down her thick tresses to lie on her shoulders.

Conscious of their shorn length, she put up her hand to cover them. He pushed it aside. 'Already it is growing. Once it must have been truly glorious, and it will be so again.'

His words made her suddenly conscious of the simple

closebodied gown she was wearing with not even a fashionable ruff to redeem it, only a high-standing collar. Neither was she wearing a farthingale to hold out her skirts. Against the rich brocade of his sapphire doublet and the wide gold chain about his shoulders she felt ill-at-ease and dowdy. 'Had I known of our meeting, I would have dressed to please you.'

'There is a place for finery, my darling. This is not it. I would have you undressed to please me.'

To her consternation a blush heated her cheeks.

Jack laughed softly. 'When I see your eyes glowing with passion, I'm bewitched. I forget how innocent you still are. Kiss me, Gabriellen.'

Her lips parted in a wordless moan as his arms tightened around her, binding her within his embrace. She touched her mouth to his tentatively, savouring the taste of him, then growing bolder at the firm warmth of his response, her tongue teasing his as she kissed him with deeper intensity.

'I've missed you, my love,' Jack said as he lifted her into his arms and strode to the bed. Still clasping her to him he sank on to the mattress and with a twist of his body rolled on to his back, holding her captive above him. Gabriellen laughed down at him and shifted her weight as his sword hilt dug into her hip through her layers of petticoats. 'You're a man of few words and little patience.'

Easing back on to her elbows she unbuckled his sword belt, casting it aside to fall to the floor with a clatter. Her eyes holding his gaze, she began to unfasten the pearl buttons of his doublet. She smiled as she studied his straight nose and finely arched brows. His cheekbones were delicately moulded above the line of his beard, with the fascinating and rather wicked-looking scar disappearing into the close-cut contours. A brown curl had fallen across his wide brow, softening the imperious lines of his face. But it was to the wide sensuous mouth her gaze was inevitably drawn. The corners had lifted with amusement, revealing his chipped tooth which she found so attractive. There was no laughter in his eyes, only a smouldering promise of pleasure to come.

'Heartless jade, to accuse me of impatience.' He forced her head closer to his and pressed his lips against the pulse at her neck.

''Tis two weeks since I held you in my arms.'

187

Staring into his grey eyes she could not doubt both his desire and his love for her. His fingers sure upon the lacings at her back, he eased her gown and chemise from her shoulders. At the touch of his hands upon her spine, she gasped, arching back in pleasure at the sensations it evoked. A quiver of longing rolled her shoulders sensuously, the movement sliding her loosened gown down to her waist. She bent forward, shaking her hair so that it cascaded in a tawny canopy over their faces. With a smothered groan Jack twisted her beneath him, his kisses searing like liquid fire as they travelled over her flesh.

Emboldened by the nights she had spent aboard *The Swift* she undressed him, wanting to learn all the secrets of his body as he had discovered hers. She matched him kiss for kiss, touch for touch, until both naked they lay entwined, the sunset illuminating the room through the narrow window and lighting their bodies with a pale golden glow. His broad chest was covered with fine dark hairs which teased her breasts to an aching fullness as she moved beneath him. He took her hand and guided it to him. The burning vibrancy of his hardness, its power leashed beneath the gathering tempest of his desire, drew a gasp from deep within her. At the touch of his thigh nudging her legs apart, conscious thought fled. With savage abandon he possessed her, carrying her with him to breathless, spiralling ecstasy.

Jack lay on his side watching Gabriellen as she lay curled against him, her eyes still closed as her breathing returned to normal. Her soft warmth and perfume wrapped him in a sensual mantle. Even now, moments after their passion had reached its heights, he wanted her again. No woman had ever woven this spell upon him. The memory of her beckoned as remorselessly as a siren, tempting him with her sensuality and the hidden promise of a born seductress. From their first meeting she had beguiled him, filled him with a yearning which only she could appease. He wanted her beside him always, and God alone knew the damnation that could bring him.

She sighed and moved, curving her body against his. The effect was immediate, his need to repossess her more intense than he had thought possible. He kissed each eyelid until her eyes opened to gaze up into his, lips swollen from his kisses parting in a playful smile. His mouth sought her breast, teasing its pink crest, and he felt her nails kneading his back in her passion, her hips moving rhythmically against his flesh. The wildness of his earlier desire was tempered now to a new sweetness. He kissed her lingeringly. Their murmured endearments were unintelligible, smothered by the fervour of their kisses. Her moan of pleasure as her legs wrapped around him was the most satisfying accolade he had ever won. Oblivious of everything but the rapturous pleasure each gave and received, their passion transcended even the heights it had climbed before.

'I could not bear to lose you,' he rasped against her ear. 'My life would have no meaning without your love.'

She turned to look at him but his face was shadowed by the darkened room. Only a few amber rays of the dying sun filtered through the dusty window panes. Her heart contracted. It was almost dark. Soon they must leave. Their time together was brutally short when tomorrow they must part.

'I love you, Jack. When the Armada is crushed, nothing need keep us apart.'

He leaned above her and she felt the tensing of his muscles. 'Nothing could, could it? Not destroy what we have!'

'Distance is a physical thing,' she answered. 'Love overcomes distance and time. If duty makes you sail the seven seas, I may hate every moment we are apart, but I'll always be waiting for you, my love. As long as you are true to me.'

He kissed her shoulder but his voice sounded oddly strained in the encroaching darkness. 'You know I would never willingly cause you hurt, my darling.' He stood up and began to dress. 'Now the hour has forsaken us. We have overstayed our time as it is.'

Gabriellen stretched languidly and nestled deeper into the pillow. It was then she smelt the cheap perfume clinging to the linen pillowcase. She sat up with a start, clutching the cover to her breasts. 'What room is this?'

He looked up from fastening the points of his hose. 'A room for trysts such as ours. This is a sea-port, my love. There are many rooms available to lovers.'

She sprang from the bed, appalled at his words. 'It is nothing short of a bordello! You made love to me on a whore's bed.' Shame crimsoned her cheeks as she began to

189

struggle into her clothing. 'How could you bring me here, Jack? Is that what our love is to you? A quick tumble on a whore's bed?'

'Trust a woman to take affront.' Jack spun her round to face him, his anger matching hers. 'Where in all Plymouth was I to get a room? Every decent place is taken. We've had our privacy, a rare commodity and not easily come by. Five angels I paid for this room. If I'd wanted a whore I could have got one for a few groats.'

She held herself rigid in his arms, her eyes flashing with shame and contempt. 'How could you, Jack?'

'Because I love you, and this is the only time we have.' He ignored her unyielding body and drew her closer. 'To me it was the woman I was with who was important, not the place. If I could have offered you a palace, I would have done.'

Slowly his words penetrated her hurt. 'I love you, Jack. But I hate this secrecy. I dare not mention your name to my father lest he flies into a rage. He does not believe you mean to marry me. I have that faith, Jack. It's what sustains me. If you love me you would never dishonour me, would you?'

'I do love you,' he sighed.

'Then you will speak to Father?'

'When it is possible for us to marry, I will speak with him.' There was an impatient edge to his voice. 'Now I have to prepare for battle.'

Her hand flew to her throat. She was filled with an aching void as the meaning of his words struck home. 'Oh, Jack, my love! How could I doubt you when your life is so filled with danger?' She stared up at him, relieved that the tension had left his body, but the fading light cast a shadow across his eyes. 'Forgive me. I scold you cruelly when in truth I yearn to stay with you.'

'I will miss you the moment you leave my arms.'

For a long moment his mouth searched the sweetness of hers. Then abruptly he released her, giving her a playful pat. 'Dress, wench, before we are thrown half-naked into the street. You tempt me to bind and gag the landlord and keep you captive here until sunrise.'

Cornelius Hope flicked his scarlet cloak over his shoulder the better to display the gold brocade finery of his new doublet and trunk hose. His mood was bleak. After the euphoria of the acclaim at the end of the play, the wealthy merchant's wife he had chosen for company had been a sad disappointment. She had been an unimaginative bedfellow and now he sought livelier sport in one of the bordellos near the quay. Carefully avoiding the rubbish which filled the gutters, he rounded a corner. A couple emerging from the apothecary's shop ahead caught his eye. In the gloom something about the man was familiar, and not wishing to be seen in that district, he ducked into a doorway.

The woman's laugh stirred his curiosity as they hurried towards him. He scrutinised the couple. The woman was covered in a long cloak, the hood well down over her face, but the man he recognised as Jack Stoneham. Curious, he drew further into the doorway as they approached. The woman laughed again and looked up as Stoneham whispered in her ear. Her face was clearly revealed to Cornelius in the light of an overhead window. By God, it was Gabriellen Angel! His lips twisted into a knowing grin. If she was with Stoneham and had come from the apothecary's, he knew their business there. And her face wore the misty look of a woman who had not only been most thoroughly made love to, but had enjoyed every moment of it. Not so angelic was the prim Miss Angel it would seem.

His own frustration and disappointment remained and he rubbed his groin. Although he liked variety, it was often wearisome to seek a new bedfellow at each town. What better than to have a ripe piece waiting for him in his own wagon? With Stoneham stuck in Plymouth, a lusty baggage such as Gabriellen would welcome the attention of the troupe's most admired and accomplished actor. What woman would not?

191

Chapter Fourteen

The taproom in Taunton was noisy and crowded, like all the taprooms Gabriellen had seen on their travels. She leant on the table, resting her chin on her knuckles as she listened to Esmond read the latest scene of the new play to the players. As he approached the final lines, she stared round at their faces. Poggs lolled back, his arm around Agnes's shoulders. Nan was smiling, her head bent over the torn hose she was darning. Cesare and Umberto nodded in approval, whilst Robin leaned forward, eager to catch every word. But it was the glitter in Cornelius's eyes which told her the play would be a success. He had not interrupted once since Esmond began to recite.

Several of the inn's customers had stopped their chatter, their figures hunched over their tankards as they too listened to the words. The occupants of the room were ringed by a haze of tobacco smoke, their bodies casting wavering shadows on the limewashed walls, their faces yellowed and cadaverous from the dim candlelight. It was now apparent to Gabriellen that life upon the road was hard and unglamorous. But moments like this, when the players were united by enthusiasm, were worth all the discomfort and petty squabbles.

It was ten days since they had left Plymouth. Most nights had found them camped by the roadside. They had been caught in a thunderstorm near Okehampton and given shelter in a manor house, their performance of *The Spanish Deliverance* earning them no more than their meal and a bed amongst the servants in the draughty hall. At Exeter two performances in the Guildhall had revived their spirits. But two days later they were fleeing for safety from a puritan village, whose preacher had roused his congregation to wrath, hurling abuse and stones at the ungodly vagrants, as he had publicly named them.

All this was far removed from the comfortable life Gabriellen had taken for granted in Chichester. Yet despite the deprivations, it still retained its magic for her. Here at Taunton three performances were to be staged. One in the Guildhall for the town's dignitaries, and two in this innyard.

'Bravo, maestro,' Cesare enthused as Esmond fell silent. 'It will be a masterpiece, this new play.'

'A rousing piece indeed, Esmond.' Cornelius twirled the ends of his moustache. 'But if I may suggest . . .'

Gabriellen glared at him and, catching the anger in her eyes, the actor stopped in mid-sentence. Flicking a speck of dirt from the ruff at his wrist, he continued magnanimously, 'May I suggest it be finished with all speed?'

He smiled across at Gabriellen who suppressed a shiver. In the last few days Cornelius had begun to show an unwelcome interest in her. Until now she had avoided confrontation with him. She had no intention of encouraging him, but neither did she wish unduly to antagonise their leading actor. Cornelius had an unpleasant way of adding to her father's worries when he found his wishes thwarted.

Esmond put up his hand for silence. 'I plan to open with it when we return to London in September for St Bartholomew's Fair. There are still three more acts to be written.' He turned to Gabriellen. In the dim light his face looked free from worry. 'My daughter has been my inspiration.'

Gabriellen swallowed against the emotion which closed her throat and put her hand on her father's. Since they had left Plymouth the tension between them had faded and they had grown closer. It saddened her to admit that much of the change in his manner was due to the absence of Jack Stoneham from her life.

Cornelius called for more wine and as their horn cups were filled, raised his in salute to Esmond. 'Sadly, we do not always appreciate the great talent of our playwright and chief sharer. A toast to Esmond and, of course, to his lovely daughter, who has been an inspiration to us all.'

'As long as she remains just an inspiration to you, Hope,' Esmond joked, but there was a warning glint in his green eyes before their heavy lids shielded their expression.

A fresh wave of anguish smote Gabriellen. She could handle Cornelius's unwanted attentions. She looked at both men and felt the antagonism deepen between them.

'Beauty is always an inspiration.' Cornelius preened his moustache as he allowed his gaze to slide appreciatively over Gabriellen's figure. He was deliberately provoking Esmond.

'I warn you, Hope!' Esmond banged his cup on to the scoured table and stood up. 'Keep away from Gabriellen or . . .'

'Mr Angel, do I interrupt?' A thin ingratiating voice came from behind Gabriellen to cut through her father's words.

Esmond squinted over her head into the shadows beyond. 'Prew!' he exclaimed. 'I'd no idea you were to visit Taunton.'

Gabriellen was relieved by the diversion. The short man moved forward to join them and at once she felt her relief evaporate. There was a coldness in Prew's pale eyes which made her apprehensive.

'One would think you were not expecting me, Esmond,' he said. 'It is a month since . . .'

'Yes. Yes, of course,' Esmond blustered. To Gabriellen's annoyance she saw that his bluff welcome was a part he was acting. ''Tis just that since you mentioned you would be in Bristol for the St James's Day Fair, I thought we would not meet again until then.' Esmond beamed with false bonhomie. 'But well met, Prew. I think you know everyone present? Except my daughter, Gabriellen. You have not been introduced to her.'

When he touched her shoulder, Gabriellen felt her father's hand shaking and she saw the lines of worry again furrow his brow. What hold could Prew have over Esmond?

Victor Prew bowed to Gabriellen and took her hand, his touch cool as a lizard's skin. She supposed he was about thirty, and before he straightened she noticed that his scalp shone pinkly through his elaborately curled hair.

'Your servant, Miss Angel.' He raised her hand to his lips. As his damp moustache touched her warm flesh, she suppressed a shiver of distaste. He was four inches shorter than herself, his padded doublet and trunks doing little to enhance his skinny figure. His stick-thin legs with their protruding knees in orange-tawny hose made him look like a startled heron. As he took a seat next to the commanding figure of Esmond, she dismissed her fears. It was impossible to believe that this ineffectual cock-a-dandy could cause any distress to the bluff, self-assured figure of her father.

'You seem to travel a great deal, Mr Prew,' she commented as much out of politeness as curiosity as to why this man kept seeking out Esmond.

'My business takes me to various ports to oversee the work of my agents. I import exotic spices, perfumes and fabrics for my warehouse in London. I also have several business ventures on the continent.' As he spoke, his thin voice rose. 'A man who puts too much faith in his agents or stewards may soon find his coffers have emptied. Without my constant vigilance they grow slack and the unpaid debts soon rise.'

Esmond coughed. 'Now you are here, there's a matter I would discuss with you, Prew.' He stood up and led the merchant to another table.

Nan Woodruff rose and swayed tipsily. 'I'm to my bed.'

'I'll come with you,' said Gabriellen, taking the seamstress's arm. She wished Nan would not drink so much. From the quantity she imbibed each evening, it was obviously a regular habit, and one that Esmond frequently joined her in. Gabriellen was beginning to see a wilder side to her father which had been curbed during his short visits to Chichester.

Nan leaned heavily on Gabriellen's arm as they crossed the taproom and mounted the steps to her room on the first gallery. 'You're a good lass,' she slurred. 'Not many a daughter would take such care of her father's whore.'

'You and Father care for each other. And you're carrying his child. Twins, no less. They'll be my half-brothers or - sisters.'

Nan staggered. Gabriellen braced herself against the streamstress's weight to keep her upright until they reached her room. Once inside, she began to help her undress.

'Good man, is Esmond,' Nan mumbled into the folds of her petticoats as Gabriellen pulled them over her head. 'Fine man. Bit of a rogue when the mood takes him, but that's what attracted me to him.' She tottered uncertainly to the bed and flopped down. As Gabriellen pulled the covers over her, she yawned and peered blearily up. 'He'd marry me, you know, if it were possible.'

'Of course he would. I'm sure he feels it strongly that you're wed to another at such a time. Now, sleep.'

Slurred laughter followed Gabriellen to the door. 'You worship your father, don't you, child? Remember, once a rogue, always a rogue. But he were always honest wi' me. Just mind your Cap'n Stoneham don't play you for an innocent. Him and Esmond are alike – too alike.'

Gabriellen ignored Nan's drunken mumblings and closed the chamber door. The flambeaux lighting the gallery had gone out and the shadows were deep and black. She hurried the three doors along to her own room. As her hand reached out to lift the latch, it was grasped from the side and she was pulled roughly against a man's chest.

'Well met, dearheart,' Cornelius chuckled. He breathed like a blown horse and his thick-set body was trembling.

'Let me go,' she demanded.

'Now is that any way to speak to Lord Barpham's most prized actor? Women flock to win my attention. Tonight, I am yours.'

The sheer audacity of the actor stunned her. Before she could deliver a scathing reply, his moist, slack lips clamped over hers. He held her pinned against him with one arm around her waist, while his other seized the shoulder of her gown. The jonquil damask ripped like lace, exposing her arm and one breast. He crushed her against him, the semi-precious gems sewn on to his doublet grinding into her flesh. As he fumbled with the door latch, she struggled for breath. Fighting him with outraged anger, she beat his chest and head with her fists, her nails clawing at his face.

He snapped his head back. 'Don't play the innocent with me,' he panted, his grip bruising her shoulders. 'I saw you in Plymouth with Stoneham. I want you. I shall have you.'

'Never!' Gabriellen choked out as she continued to hit him, and managed a blow to his right eye. When she grazed her shoe down the length of his shin, he trumpeted with rage.

'Bitch!' With a twist of his body, he forced her against the chamber door.

It opened under their weight. Caught off balance, Gabriellen screamed as she toppled backwards. They crashed to the floor. The breath was knocked from her lungs and her head hurt from the force with which it had hit the floor. She lay for a moment, too dazed to move.

'That's where you belong – on your back,' Cornelius grunted. 'With your heels kicking up to the ceiling.'

The touch of his fingers on her naked breast brought Gabriellen back to life. 'Get off me, you horny goat! Go rut somewhere else.' She fought like a tigress, wriggling, biting, scratching. A rush of cool air met her thigh as her skirts rode up in her struggles. The blood was hammering in her ears and still she fought on. When her hand touched the large gold ring in his ear, she yanked it hard. With a howl Hope reared back and put his hand to his torn, bleeding lobe. She struck then without mercy, bringing up her knee to ram it into his groin. He doubled over and lay groaning on the floor.

Gabriellen scrambled to her feet. The caul which covered her head had been lost in the fight and her hair tumbled on to her shoulders in disarray. Breathing heavily, she thrust the tawny mane out of her eyes and drawing the dagger from the sheath at her waist, waved it menacingly at the groaning figure on the floor.

'Get out of here!'

A movement by the door brought her head round. Wild-eyed, she stared at the insignificant figure standing there. Someone had relit the flambeaux on the gallery wall and it threw its wavering light over Victor Prew.

'Miss Angel, I heard a scream and ran to help. Did this carrion harm you?'

'I am unhurt.' Gabriellen controlled the tremor which had entered her voice. She did not like the way Prew was watching her. Her hand tightened over the dagger hilt while the other held the torn pieces of her gown over her breast which was imprinted with bloody flecks from Hope's jewelled doublet. Controlling her dislike of Prew, she stared across at him.

'Would you remove this creature from my room?'

Cornelius swayed to his feet, his face scratched and his right eye already blackening. 'I won't forget this insult.'

'Neither will I.' Gabriellen lifted her chin and raised the dagger. 'Save your histrionics for the stage, Mr Hope.'

Staggering to the door, Cornelius angrily shrugged off Prew's hand.

The merchant paused before leaving. The woman had turned from him, apparently forgetting his existence. She put a shaking hand to her head, then straightened her spine. Her pose showed almost noble breeding although she came of yeoman stock. Or did she? He remembered some story about her forebear Wildboar Angel. Wasn't he the bastard son of a knight? And that fiery spirit with which she had fought Hope had been exciting to witness. She turned and looked surprised to discover him still there.

'I'll bid you good night, Miss Angel. I'll tell Esmond of this incident. He will wish to reprimand Hope most severely.'

'No, please say nothing, Mr Prew.'

He looked askance. Her face was animated with alarm, the force of her beauty striking him for the first time. The defiance in her eyes roused his interest.

'It is better for the troupe if the incident is forgotten. Father will be furious. Should Cornelius leave the players we could lose Lord Barpham's patronage, and with it our licence to perform.'

'He should not go unpunished.'

'His pride is wounded. For Cornelius that is punishment enough. He's too vain to press his attentions where they're not wanted. Please say nothing of this to my father.'

'It will be our little secret, Miss Angel.'

Gabriellen remained silent. She did not like the idea of sharing any secret with this man. There was something about him which left her cold. When he left she began to tremble from reaction to her ordeal. Despite her air of easy assurance with Prew, she knew Hope was a vindictive man when crossed. The burden of yet another worry pressed down on her. There was an underlying current of tension within the troupe. All was far from well.

Through the intricate network of spies run by Lord Walsingham, the Queen's Secretary of State, Mark had been ordered to return to London. He had used the three days he had stayed at the inn near Templeton's estate to learn much of the affairs at the manor. A week after he had left, the coded information sent by special messenger to Walsingham had resulted in the arrest of Templeton and the priest.

During all Mark's incognito visits to London, Glendower was stabled at the Cross Keys Inn in Gracechurch Street. Once the stallion was settled Mark went to the attic room he rented amongst the warren of backstreets near the Tower. Here he changed into one of the disguises he often adopted. Tonight, because he was to meet Walsingham at The Clink prison, he dressed in the rusty black robes of an impoverished chaplain, his dark hair covered by a grey wig

198

and his features changed with a false nose and long straggly grey beard.

Leaving his rooms he hired a link boy to light him across London Bridge to the liberty of The Clink in Southwark. No street in London was safe after dark without some hired protection, and Bankside with its brothels, low taverns, beargardens and new theatre was the haunt of every type of thief and scoundrel.

He lengthened his stride as he crossed the Thames between the rows of houses and shops which lined the bridge. From a darkened doorway the laboured breathing and words of encouragement from a cheap harlot accommodating a customer could be heard. Out of an alleyway a beggar called for alms. Figures emerged from shadows to gauge the worth of Mark's apparel, and seeing the shabbiness of his robes slunk back into obscurity.

Mark walked with his hand on his dagger and his sharp eyes alert for any sign of attack. But the guise of an impoverished cleric served him well, and his passage was unmolested. The Clink was adjacent to the Bishop of Winchester's Palace which ran for two hundred yards along the riverbank. As soon as he set foot on Bankside, Mark heard the cries of the inmates of the prison. Even the jangle and clank of chains and fetters, which shackled the prisoners, carried to him on the night breeze. It was said that the prison first got its name as far back as Saxon times from the sound of those clinking manacles. Above the sounds of revelry coming from the nearby brothels could be heard the deeper drone of the suffering of the political prisoners incarcerated within the gaol. Even at night there was no halt to the wailing of inmates pressed against the ground-level grating, their hands thrust through the bars as they begged for food or clothing. The poor unfortunates, once destitute, relied on the charity of the populace to survive.

It was not a place Mark liked to visit even in the call of duty. The suffering of the wretches within appalled him. The gaolers were corrupt, selling rotten food and drink at double the market price. Everything there had its price. The mouldering straw they lay upon; a bribe for the bone-crushing iron collars, which restrained so many of the prisoners, to be replaced by lightweight manacles. Some of the prisoners were naked after being forced to sell their clothes for food to keep themselves alive. To get confessions from priests or recusants, stocks and barbarous iron instruments twisted men's bodies, immobilising them in excruciating agony, often leading to slow and painful death.

In the shadow of the gate Mark felt the hairs at his nape prickle with revulsion. He gave the password and was admitted to the Great Hall of the Bishop's Palace with its rose window at the centre of the elongated chamber. Even here he could feel the atmosphere of hopelessness and fear which pervaded the prison cells.

At the door he stood aside as two guards dragged out an unconscious bloodied figure. One of the man's bare feet was mangled from the crushing application of the boot. As they passed Mark the prisoner's head rolled sideways on to his outstretched arm and Mark felt a rush of bile to his throat. It was the priest from Templeton's manor. Mastering his nausea at the sight of the man's suffering, he hardened himself by recalling the suffering of his own father at the hands of the Spanish torturers. If the Jesuits had their way, every heretic in England would be roasted at the stake unless they recanted to take up the Catholic faith.

His face was devoid of all emotion as he entered the chamber. The room was dimly lit by four tall iron candlesticks. At the far end Lord Walsingham's impressive, well-built figure paced the floor as he dictated to a scribe hunched over his work. At the sound of Mark's footsteps on the flagstones, Walsingham halted his speech, and with a curt nod dismissed the scribe. Glacial eyes flickered over Mark's figure and Walsingham nodded approval.

'You are a master of disguise, Rowan. No doubt it accounts for your successes.'

Mark bowed his acknowledgement and waited for Walsingham to continue. He held Walsingham's stern stare, noting the grey which threaded through the Secretary of State's short cropped hair. A wide ruff accentuated the pallor of his long face and wide forehead, and made the deep-set eyes appear even more uncompromising and menacing. Walsingham was dressed in black, and in these sinister surroundings Mark was reminded of a raven about to gorge itself upon carrion entrails. He suppressed a shiver. Walsingham was the Queen's protector. His ways might be ruthless but more than once an attempt to assassinate Elizabeth had been prevented because of the confessions wrung out by her secretary and his henchmen.

'Well done, Rowan. Your work in Dorset uncovered another plot,' Walsingham announced. 'Templeton was arrested but admits nothing, though he is now in the Tower. He will undergo further examinations before his execution next week. The priest was less stoic. He condemned Templeton and has named several others in his confession tonight. Tomorrow he will be burned at the stake.'

Walsingham picked up a piece of parchment and held it out to Mark. 'This is a list of the places the Jesuit stayed, and of the people he met. Memorise it before you leave. Unfortunately, the name I want most is missing . . . that of King Philip's paymaster. Discover who he is, Rowan. He's at the root of these recent conspiracies in England. Whilst he lives, the Queen's life remains in danger.'

'I shall not rest until he is found,' Mark vowed.

Walsingham nodded. 'You're our best agent. This man is most cunning, and takes pains to keep his identity hidden.'

Mark studied the list of names and places on the parchment. Several were known to him and the districts were covered by the fairs he would visit with Glendower. The list memorised, he handed the document back to Walsingham who held it over a candle. As the paper burst into flames, Walsingham dropped it into a metal dish and watched it blacken and curl until it was no more than a heap of red-edged ashes.

'I need more time to repay your loan, Mr Prew.' Esmond sat alone with the merchant in a quiet corner of the taproom. 'At least until after our visit to Bristol.'

He hated to play the supplicant, but Prew had to be pacified. The threat of a debtor's prison hung over Esmond. He was no stranger to the horrors of Marshalsea or The Clink. His brief imprisonments there during those dark years of his early manhood were still vivid in his mind. Recalling the pitiful wails of souls whose only hope of escape was death, he shuddered, remembering the stench, the degradation and squalor. Squaring his shoulders, he threw off the unpalatable memories. He was not beaten yet. This had been a bad year. They had never recovered from the heavy cost of performing at Court. Added to the mounting debts was the worry of Nan's pregnancy, the shock of Dotty's death, and his fear of blindness.

He peered at Prew, trying to judge his mood. The merchant gnawed the edge of his straggling moustache, his small eyes cold and remorseless. Esmond knew he should have paid Prew what takings they had left and renegotiated terms for the balance due. Instead his gambler's instincts had incited him to recoup his losses at cards. Those three travellers had looked to be easy pickings. That was where his failing sight had duped him. He had used every sleight of hand he knew. Too late he realised that they were as accomplished tricksters as himself. Three against one, he had not stood a chance.

Prew rubbed his hooked nose and continued to consider the matter. 'I have been talking to the players. Naturally I did not mention our arrangement. That is between us. As I said at Winchester, I have a love for the stage. I'm a wealthy man. Your plays are fast winning acclaim, and you are hailed as a rival to Marlowe. Such greatness should not go unrewarded.'

Prew paused but Esmond was too shrewd to be drawn by flattery. He bided his time in silence, forcing Prew to reveal his motives.

'I am prepared to offer you financial support for the honour of becoming a sharer in your company,' said Prew. 'Cornelius Hope was most agreeable.'

'Once your loan is repaid, there is no reason why the company should not support itself.' Esmond was poised, wary.

'Should I become a sharer, naturally that loan would be waived. In the interest of the troupe.'

Esmond was tempted. To be free of debt would ease his problems. Even so, he did not trust Prew. He needed to play for time – thus avoiding arrest for debt or giving Prew a partnership in the troupe. He felt invigorated. When could he ever resist parting a willing cove from his money?

Smiling, he put a hand upon the merchant's bony shoulder. 'You understand I can agree to nothing without Lord Barpham's approval? That could take some weeks since he is involved with the English fleet.'

'Your word is good enough.'

They were hailed from across the room by Hope. Esmond watched the actor approach, noting his black velvet cloak, lavishly embroidered with gold and trimmed with miniver.

'That's a new cloak, is it not, Cornelius?'

'Indeed. Mr Prew most generously purchased it. He believes an actor of my standing should be dressed as befits his station.' 'Most generous.' Esmond felt a hollowness invade the pit of his stomach. Prew could prove more wily than he suspected. And Hope? Cornelius, for all his grand airs, was by birth the son of a defrocked priest and a tavern wench. It showed in his grasping ways. He would always put his own interests first and would not let the rich booty from Prew slip out of his clutches. Esmond resisted the need to rub his aching brow. He had lived by his wits too long to ignore the first warnings of danger. He had to appear unconcerned and in control. Why had Hope been avoiding him during the last three days, his manner more surly than usual? Then there was Prew. The man was too eager to become a sharer in the company for his peace of mind. Hope was too conceited and grasping to see Prew's gift for the bribe it was.

He looked closer at the actor, surprised to see his discoloured eye and scratched cheek. It was not like Hope to get into a fight. He was too vain of his looks for that. 'Cornelius, what happened to your face?'

The actor snorted and walked away. Hope was a lecher and a fortune hunter. He had probably been pursuing a rich widow and been brought to account by a kinsman.

Loud shouts from the innyard turned his attention to the door. Poggs burst into the taproom, his crinkled cap of red hair damp from running, his freckled face working with excitement. 'The beacons are lit. The Spanish are sighted. God bless England and her brave sailors. They're giving chase along the English Channel.'

Jack stood on the quarterdeck of *The Swift*, watching the widening pennant of light brighten the horizon. The water seemed to heave and roll beneath the slow-moving sea mist and the day was devoid of warmth. In the silver glow of morning, both sea and sky met in a creamy haze. As on previous days, during the week since the Armada had been sighted and the English fleet had sailed out of Plymouth Sound, there was no more than the lightest wind. Jack stared into the mist. Unless the wind stiffened it looked like another day of petty skirmishes. They had set sail determined to rout the Spaniards. In that week they had done little more than prevent the Dons landing upon English soil.

He turned as Seth Bridges appeared at his side. The servant held out a steel breastplate. Sliding his arm through the opening, Jack held it in place over his black leather doublet as Seth fastened the buckles.

'Do yer think we'll be at 'em today, cap'n?' Seth asked.

'God willing,' Jack rapped out. 'But we will need the devil's luck to break the Spanish formation.' He stared in the direction of the Armada, the dark outline of the ships just visible in the thinning mist. 'Until now they have proved formidable. Much as I hate the Duke of Medina Sidonia and all he stands for, I have to admit he's trained his men well.' He fingered the large pearl drop in his ear, his tone showing his frustration. 'I have never seen the like before. One hundred and thirty ships and all sailing in disciplined formation. Nothing we do has broken them, but we'll crush them. Give us a strong wind and they'll feel the roar of the English lion devouring their might.'

Jack looked up at his topmen scurrying along the topsail yards to unfurl the sails. Then his gaze travelled to the men assembling on deck. Their faces were as set as his. Faces of young men eager to win glory in battle, of leathery seamen who stoically did their duty. They were all faces he had learned to recognise. He believed that if a man was prepared to die, following his orders, it was a small courtesy to know his name. This belief was repaid by the crew's unswerving loyalty.

A herald's trumpet pierced the mist and Jack moved to the ship's rail. The traditional gestures of chivalry were about to be exchanged before battle. Medina Sidonia hoisted his banner to his maintop, and Lord Effingham aboard the English flagship *The Ark Royal* sent a pinnace to bear his challenge to the Spanish Admiral.

'What I would not give for a wind to hound the Spanish from our waters,' Jack said by way of greeting to Harry Dobson, his second in command. Seth Bridges whistled as he made his way to the orlop where he would spend the battle aiding the ship's surgeon to tend any wounded. 'We can scarcely manage two knots. After a week at sea, we're still off the Sussex coast.' Jack looked up at the English flag with the red cross of St George which barely moved in the light breeze. 'Our ammunition is running low, yet our constant cannonading and harrying achieves little against that damned formation.'

'Drake captured *The Rosario* after it was damaged in a collision.' Harry Dobson grinned. 'There was a king's ransom in its money chest, so they say.'

'Drake gets his hour of glory.' Jack scowled. 'Yet when our shot demasted that Spanish galley and splintered its oars, we were ordered not to board her.'

'The risk was too great, captain.'

'The prize was worth it.' Jack paced the deck. 'Certes, we do no more than snap like terriers at the Spaniards' heels.'

'We are preventing them from landing, is that not enough?'

Jack inclined his head and sighed. 'I would have more. I would see them crushed – broken for their impudence.'

'And Spanish gold lining your coffers.'

Jack ran a hand across his beard and laughed wickedly. 'Aye, I would have their gold in my coffers. The mantle of respectable sea captain sits lightly upon my shoulders. The years as a privateer are not easily shaken off. It was the same with Drake when he took *The Rosario*.'

Dobson grinned. 'There's many who name Drake a pirate.'

The distant beat of a drummer boy aboard the *The Ark Royal* ordered the English to prepare for action. Jack scanned the sky. Spears of weak sunshine probed through the mist down into the milky water between the two fleets. Then off the leeward bow, he saw the prize he craved. A Spanish straggler was begging to be taken. He turned to survey the deck of *The Bonaventure Elizabeth* which sailed alongside *The Swift*. Lord Barpham, his steel helmet and breastplate shining in the sun's rays, raised his arm in salute. Jack drew his sword and indicated the lone Spaniard. Barpham made no response and Jack realised *The Swift* was shielding the Spanish vessel from him. Then a sailor called down to Barpham from high in the ratlines and his lordship raised his own blade in understanding and acknowledgement.

'Weigh anchor,' Jack commanded.

A dozen hands already in position began to turn the capstan, singing a shanty to keep their rhythm as they worked. Other seamen ran to their posts, their bare feet slapping on the sanded deck.

'Anchor's aweigh,' the boatswain shouted. The great ship jerked as the wind began to fill her sails and she was put under way. With *The Bonaventure* keeping pace, *The Swift* closed on the Spanish ship, the *Gran Griffon*.

'Stand by!' Harry Dobson shouted as he ran down to the half-deck.

Jack looked down upon the three guns. The gunners crouched behind each breech, their torches trailing ribbons of smoke across their pale faces. Harry Dobson moved along the half-deck, pausing at each gun to peer along its muzzle. Satisfied, he raised a hand, signalling to Jack they were ready.

Jack held his sword aloft, judging the distance. Before they came in range of the crossbowmen mounted on the *Gran Griffon*'s forecastle, he brought down his arm.

'Fire!'

He tensed as the broadside erupted in a burst of orange flames and sent a shudder the length of the ship. The gun carriages hurled themselves backwards over the planking, their muzzles smoking. Dobson grasped the mizzen mast for support, rubbing his eyes which were blinded by the smoke blown back across the deck. The gunners were coughing and swearing in the choking fumes, but their training served them well. At a sharp command they continued to sponge out the muzzles and ram home fresh charges in readiness for another broadside.

Whilst Jack's ears rang from the deafening bang of the cannon he saw several Spanish galleons coming to the aid of the *Gran Griffon*. An answering crack echoed across the water and a white fountain of spray splashed up some yards off the starboard bow. A chorus of jeers from his men greeted the wide miss. Every face showed intensity of feeling: pride, anger, bloodlust, a twitching muscle betraying fear held in check.

A second shot from the Spaniard crashed through the foremast topsail and three men lay writhing on the deck, pierced by flying splinters. As the battle raged a pall of smoke hung over *The Swift*, clawing at Jack's throat and stinging his eyes. The *Gran Griffon* was hit several times, but as the Spanish galleons came to her defence Jack was forced to tack leeward to prevent their broadsides destroying his ship.

Shocked, he saw the *The Bonaventure Elizabeth* had not followed. He watched the smoke belch from the *Bonaventure*'s ports and roll over the sea, where it hung suspended in a trailing cloud. A gun spouted in reply and Jack felt the wooden deck leap under his feet as a cannonball smashed into its side. Then, as the smoke cleared, he saw a Spanish galleon, a dozen or more gun ports flaring, as she bore down on *The Bonaventure Elizabeth*. Cursing Barpham for a fool, he gripped the ship's rail. 'You should have gone about sooner,' he groaned. 'You're in the path of the Spanish guns.' He spun round and shouted: 'Man the braces. Steer nor' nor' west.' Even as he gave the order he knew it was too late to save the *Bonaventure*. He could only watch.

As he paced the sterncastle he saw the cannon balls plough through her sails and rigging, tearing them to shreds. A brown canopy of smoke rose above her deck as again and again the merciless broadsides thundered into her. The cries of the dying and wounded carried above the boom of guns and splintering of wood. The block and tackle from the severed main braces catapulted through the air as the spar from the mizzen sail crashed down over the side, torn and blackened canvas dragged behind. Corpses with missing limbs were tangled in its ratlines. Their wide-eyed faces locked in a silent scream, they plunged down into the churning water and were carried away, the creamy foam growing pink with their blood.

He went cold as he watched the grisly flotsam bob past the stern. Behind him the steady tattoo of the drummer boy beating the battle orders was cut short. Whirling around Jack saw the young lad fall to the deck in a faint, dangerously close to a hole ripped in the ship's rail. Grabbing him by the collar, Jack hauled him to his feet. 'Stand up, boy. If you go over the side you'll drown.'

Ashen-faced, the boy stared dumbly back at him.

'Beat the attack,' Jack shouted, his anger directed at the Spanish not the drummer boy. 'By Christ's bones, we'll make those Spanish whoresons pay for the English lives they've taken today.'

He surveyed the carnage, his face marble white. A head

separated from its body was borne towards him on the crest of a surging wave. For a moment he found himself staring into Lord Barpham's sightless eyes. Hardened though he was to the gruesome sights of battle at sea, nausea rose to his throat. He fought it down. As the horror which was once his friend was swallowed by the reddening water bound for its unhallowed grave, he turned away. Later he would grieve. Now all his concentration was needed to ensure those aboard *The Swift* did not meet the same fate.

Jack continued to shout his orders. The English fleet had surrounded the Spanish ships and the battle blazed hotly for some hours. In the afternoon the wind dropped, bringing a halt to the fighting. Frustration ground through Jack at the lack of wind. Yet another indecisive battle and no Spanish ship had been sunk. He surveyed the damage to his vessel. The carpenters were already aloft repairing broken spars, the decks were being swabbed and the damaged sail lowered for mending. His visit to the orlop had shown him several seamen wounded, but none mortally, thank God. Back on deck he received a summons to attend a council of war. Before ordering the long boat lowered, Jack cast a critical eye upon *The Bonaventure Elizabeth*. Sailors were climbing the mizzen ratlines and repairing the broken rigging. From the reports he had received only five men had died. Lord Barpham had been decapitated by a swinging tackle block.

It was however much later that the full impact of Lord Barpham's death struck him. Much as he would miss his fellow captain and companion, his lordship's death could mean the ruin of Gabriellen's father. Without a patron, the players had no licence to perform.

Chapter Fifteen

'Behold the greatest sights in all England!' a bearded man proclaimed. Dressed in a long purple robe and an oriental turban, he was standing on a stool before a cherry-striped pavilion. 'Gentlemen and fair maids, feast your eyes upon the two-headed calf. See the wonder of the shrunken head from the far shores of Africa.'

'Ribbons, pretty lady!' another voice boomed. 'Come forth, you lusty swains. Buy here! A ribbon or a trinket to win the favours of your love.'

'This way, good people! See the bearded lady!'

'Roast suckling pig! None tastier! Come buy!'

On this morning of St James's Day, 25 July, the fair at Bristol had opened. The cries of the stall-holders, pedlars, freak shows and troubadours bombarded Gabriellen's ears as she strolled along the aisle of booths. Everywhere bright coloured flags and pennants, strung around the stalls, tents and wagons, showed vividly against the iron-grey sky.

There was still an hour before their second play of the day was performed. Eager as Gabriellen was to see all the sights, she felt restless as her gaze roamed over the throng. The air was smoky from cooking fires and heavy with the pungent aroma of roast meats, hot pies and spiced cakes.

Poggs spread his arm, indicating the rows of stalls. 'How different these are from last night. Then it was the thieves' market, a place for selling on stolen goods.' He chuckled. 'There'll be no sign of any stolen horses, gold and silverware or jewels today. Those illicit goods will be hidden away, replaced by the gaudy trinkets you see now.' He gave Gabriellen a gentle nudge in the ribs as he nodded towards a man in a threadbare jerkin and hose. 'Though I doubt that scrivener is so innocent. For a price, he'll forge a passport for any vagabond who wishes to travel through this county, unhindered by the law.'

'I'd never realised these fairs were frequented by so many rogues and villains,' Gabriellen voiced her astonishment. 'The stallholders all look so honourable by day.'

Poggs gave a twisted grin. 'This is nothing compared to what goes on at St Bartholomew's Fair in London. Us strolling players, like all the people of the road, have a strong link with the Underworld.' He shrugged fatalistically. 'We draw the crowds whom those rascals rob and cheat.'

'Surely, we're not a part of such roguery?' she countered. Her assurance ebbed when Poggs avoided her gaze. In the weeks since leaving Plymouth her sharp eyes had missed little. She had come to recognise faces which were always amongst the crowd. Women who sold more than gilded gingerbread to a fawning male audience. Other faces, glimpsed briefly, but all too often darting into the throng accompanied by a shout of 'Stop Thief'. Most disquieting of all was that twice she had seen her father approached by these bawdy-baskets or cut-purses. Not as a customer, or a victim, but with respect. When she confronted him, Esmond denied that such meetings had been anything but chance, but the unease stayed with her. It disconcerted her to admit that there were many shades to Esmond's character, and some of them were suspiciously dark.

'You cannot live on the road without some links with the fraternity.' There was a tightness about Poggs's mobile mouth that warned her he would not be drawn further.

They had halted by the hiring platform. Gabriellen looked up at the despondent figures seeking new masters. The strongest had long ago been hired. Those who remained were old, infirm, or in the case of a youth whose eyes were dull and vacant, could qualify only as the village idiot. They all looked as though they had spent the summer begging for their bread. It was impossible not to pity them. Struck by the sudden memory of Uncle Ezekiel and his 'Unfortunates', Gabriellen's shoulders sagged beneath a fresh wave of grief.

Through misty eyes she watched the morris dancers performing in their hobby-horse costumes. Behind her a minstrel strummed his guitar and sang out, 'Gather round. Listen to my tale. I've seen the Armada.'

Gabriellen moved closer.

'I've seen our glorious fleet.' His fingers quickened over

the lute strings and his hand banged its side in a rousing beat as his voice rose vigorously. 'Hear how the English guns belched fire like dragons as they chased the Spanish dogs. Draw near, I'll tell you of that battle.'

In the last few days rumours of the Armada were on everyone's lips. At first she had hung upon every word. Farmers would swear they had heard the distant boom of cannon as they reaped their hay. The troubadours, pedlars and mountebanks she soon suspected used the tales of an impending battle as a ruse to draw a crowd to their wares. Everywhere there was speculation. The atmosphere was tense with anticipation that they would hear of the trouncing of the Spaniards; or of the unthinkable – the chilling news of defeat.

Every performance of *The Spanish Deliverance* and *The Warrior King* had played to vast audiences in the towns on the road to Bristol. Their takings had exceeded all expectations. Why then did Esmond look more haggard by the day? And why was he was drinking more heavily?

'Keep your hand tight upon your purse,' Poggs warned as they skirted yet another crowd jostling to watch a troupe of tumblers. 'There'll be cut-purses and pickpockets amongst this gathering.'

She nodded absently. Her gaze had been caught by the sight of Cornelius Hope and Victor Prew together. They were talking in front of a brazier whose owner sold mulled wine. Her lips set into a tight line. In recent days these two had become inseparable. Clearly Prew had bought Hope's friendship. Prew turned and saw her watching them. Doffing his high domed hat, he bowed. Cornelius, however, ignored her as he had at every meeting since his attack in her chamber.

'Those two are thicker than thieves,' Poggs snorted. 'It will bring trouble. That Prew ain't one to part with his money without reason.'

'I don't trust either of them.' She stared worriedly at Poggs. 'Does Father make a habit of drinking as heavily as he has these last days?'

Poggs lowered his gaze and shuffled his feet. 'Esmond has always liked his ale. What man doesn't?'

'Is Father in debt to Prew? Is that why he's drinking?'

Poggs grunted. 'Prew is a louse Esmond could crack between his fingers. In years past I've seen your father best the most arrant of rogues.' He shook his head and grinned. 'There was an incident when he was at Nell Lovegood's place and . . .' He stopped and grinned sheepishly. 'Nay, that's not a tale for your tender ears. But suffice to say, Esmond is as Umberto would say "the maestro". There's not an Upright Man could outwit him.' At her puzzled frown he explained: 'An Upright Man is a leader, or rather head, of the Underworld hierarchy. In Esmond's prime there was none could best him.'

'Isn't that the problem, Poggs? He's not as young as he was. The wild life he's led has taken its toll.' She put a hand on his shoulder, her voice low with distress. 'This is no jesting matter. I'm worried about Father.'

Poggs stared down at the ground then with a sigh looked up at her, his freckled face crimped with worry. 'Aye, so am I. Esmond has been acting strangely these last months. He's been gambling more than usual – and losing. There wasn't a coney-catcher – sorry, I forget you don't know the cant – a trickster at cards to match his skill. I don't want to add to your fears, but I suspect that Esmond's sight is not what it was.'

'I think you're right, and it worries me. But there is more to his troubles than failing sight.' She linked her fingers together and pressed them to her mouth, her fears intensified. 'I love Father and would do anything to help him, but he never speaks of his worries. What could hound a man like him so cruelly? Is the troupe in debt, Poggs?'

'Only Esmond would know that.'

Gabriellen considered his words for a moment. 'I cannot shake the notion that Prew has a hold over him. It must be rooted in money. Rarely a day goes by when I do not see more of Prew's money spent. One day the reckoning must be made.'

'I think your fears ill-founded. There's not yet a man born who can outwit Esmond Angel where money's concerned.' The irrepressible humour returned to Poggs's eyes. With a grin, he linked her arm through his to lead her towards the arena where the trials of strength were held.

As they passed the livestock pens her gaze roamed over the cattle, sheep and horses. The sight of a large chestnut horse drew her gaze.

'Is that Glendower?' She searched the crowd, suddenly excited. Then, disappointed, she saw that the chestnut had

212

no white blaze on its nose and its coat was a dull reddish-brown and not the fine coppery hue of Glendower at all.

'Did you say something?' said Poggs, his attention on two men stripped to their breeches and wrestling.

'I thought Mark Rowan might be at this fair.'

'The stallion man?' Poggs looked up at her from under bushy red brows. 'You'll not be the only wench to wish that! He has a way with the women, has Rowan, which draws them like wasps to a honey pot,' he added slyly. 'I thought you only had eyes for Jack Stoneham?'

'Mark is my friend!' she defended with unwarranted heat. 'I love Jack.'

'So you say. Though, to my mind, Rowan is the better man.'

'Oh, not you too, Poggs!' Gabriellen bristled, quickening her pace as she walked back to where the stage was erected.

Poggs ran to her side, his tone amused. 'You don't like that captain of yours criticised, do you?'

She clenched her hands, striking them against her sides in exasperation as she rounded on him. 'Why is everyone against Jack? Because he calls no man master, or because he made his fortune on the Spanish Main? Drake has done no less and you claim him to be a hero.'

He scratched his crinkled cap of hair, his expression serious. 'Sir Francis Drake is not paying court to you. Stoneham's a wild one – feckless and ambitious.'

'That's enough, Poggs.' Her eyes flashed dangerously. 'In future, keep your opinions to yourself,' she snapped. 'No one has a good word for Jack. It isn't fair! He does not deserve their criticism. He's brave, courageous and kind.' Still angry, she lengthened her stride and Poggs was forced to trot to keep up with her.

He snorted. 'I admit "kind" is not a word which springs to mind when I think of Jack Stoneham.'

The sarcasm in the clown's voice goaded Gabriellen to retaliate. Hands on hips, she turned on Poggs with such violence he took an involuntary step back. 'I will hear no word against Jack. At this moment he faces death fighting to uphold England's freedom.'

Poggs grinned, unabashed. 'Stoneham may be a rogue, but 'tis possible that in you he's met his redeeming Angel.'

Gabriellen hurried on, too incensed to be appeased by Poggs's witty apology. By the time she reached the tiring-tent, which the actors used to change costumes in, her temper had cooled. Lifting the flap she was alarmed to find Robin Flowerdew bent double, gripping his stomach and groaning. When he raised his head to look at her, she saw his face was bloodied and both eyes were blackening.

'What happened to you, Robin?' She knelt at his side, putting a comforting arm around his shoulder.

He answered with a groan and then began to retch on to the grass at his feet.

'We were attacked by the 'prentices from the other troupe of players,' Will Appleshot answered her from a darkened corner. He had a cut lip and held up a fist, showing her his torn knuckles. 'They said they'd make sure we put on no more plays. They're just strolling players with no licence or patron like us. They're mountebanks, unable to act.'

Robin rolled back with an agonised groan and, holding him in her arms, Gabriellen opened his doublet and eased his shirt from his breeches. A vicious bruise was darkening across his ribs and stomach. She ran a hand lightly over his torso. 'No bones are broken,' she said with relief. 'You will be sore for some days. Go to your bed, Robin. Agnes will bring you a tisane to ease the pain.'

'What talk is this of taking to your bed?' Esmond declared as he entered the tent, followed by Umberto and Cesare. 'The play starts in less than an hour. What's this Cesare tells me? Have you been fighting, Robin?'

Gabriellen intervened, 'It wasn't his fault. But Robin is not fit to perform. Young Will must take the female lead in *The Enchantress*.'

Will's round boyish face drained of all colour. At thirteen the responsibility of the lead clearly terrified him. 'But I don't know all the lines. Can't we do one of the shorter pieces?'

'The playbills are out!' Esmond rounded on the stricken apprentice. 'We cannot disappoint our audience.'

'Even Robin says the enchantress is his most challenging role,' Will quailed, his voice squeaking with fear. 'I haven't his skill. I'd be a laughingstock, playing a seductress. I couldn't face those 'prentices. They'll be jeering and hooting . . . And if I falter, I'll be pelted with garbage. I doubt Hope will thank me for having us both pilloried like that. I couldn't do it, Mr Angel.'

'You have to do it, Will,' Esmond insisted as he paced back and forth across the tent. 'Would you have those 'prentices best you? Take a grip on yourself, lad.'

'And who will play Will's parts?' Gabriellen broke in.

'They'll have to be cut.' The irritation in Esmond's voice showed the strain he was under. He always put the welfare of the players first. 'Crofton can double on some of the lines and Hope must improvise.'

'It will be a disaster,' Gabriellen declared.

'You forget your place, daughter!'

'Father, you know I speak the truth.'

'There's no choice.' Esmond cast a stern eye upon each of them. 'We have overcome worse odds. A performance has been announced and it will be given. Though I would give much for another experienced actor to join our company.'

Poggs stood in front of Esmond to halt his pacing. 'Can one performance mean so much? Will has been with us only a few months. You ask too much of him.'

'Aye, you're right, Poggs.' Esmond rubbed his hand across his brow, his voice suddenly old and tired. 'There'll be no performance. I cannot risk the loss of our reputation.'

'Father, a word.' Gabriellen moved to his side and drew him out of earshot. She was convinced now that the company was seriously in debt. Why else should a lost performance make Esmond look so haggard? 'There is a way.' She dropped her voice to a whisper. 'Let me take Robin's place.'

Esmond swung round in amazement. 'Out of the question! No woman has ever acted upon the stage.' His voice began to rise and he checked it. 'You will be ridiculed. Worse, your name will be spat upon by decent folks.'

'Who is to know? I'll wear the golden mask. Robin and I are of a height. No one will guess I'm not him. I know the play by heart and I can act as well as any man – you told me so at Christmas when I entertained the family. No one suspected that I was a woman when I rode with Mark Rowan. I've watched how Robin moves on stage.' Her eyes widened with pleading. 'Let me dress the part and I will act for you Robin's final speech. Then you can decide.'

'It is out of the question,' he repeated.

'Can we afford to lose the takings from this performance? I think not.' She smiled in a way which had never failed to coerce him. 'Why should men have all the glory? Just once, Father, I would know what it is like to act before so many.'

'No!'

'I couldn't help overhearing, Mr Angel,' Robin said from where he was crouched on the floor. 'I'd hate to think those 'prentices got the better of us. Miss Gabriellen could do it. No one need know. It's only the once.'

'Hope will not agree,' Esmond said with asperity.

'He need not be told,' Robin suggested. 'Not until the play is underway. He's bound to have heard I was set upon. Tell him the mask is to hide my battered face. I'll stay hidden until the performance.'

Esmond returned to his pacing. After a pause he said less sharply, 'I like it not.'

Gabriellen sensed he was weakening and seized the advantage. 'Please, Father. Just this once. What harm can possibly come of it? This play has proved the most popular in recent weeks. It will draw a vast crowd and our takings will be rich indeed. Isn't it worth the risk?'

'A challenge, daughter?' Esmond's straight brows lifted.

'It is, Father. When does an Angel ignore the gauntlet once it has been thrown down?'

'When indeed?' He laughed bitterly, standing before her, his expression resigned. 'You have a persuasive tongue.' He rubbed his chin. 'I confess, I like not the thought of some ruffian 'prentices stopping a performance of my company . . .'

An hour later Gabriellen stood behind the backdrop curtain. Esmond had spoken the prologue and Cornelius began his opening speech. She mouthed the words along with him, awaiting her cue. Without warning, her throat dried and her knees began to shake. Panic gripped her. Everyone would see behind her disguise. The play would be a failure. She could not do it. Beyond the curtain she could hear the jeers from the 'prentices. In answer to them, Cornelius raised his thunderous voice and strutted with greater assurance. From behind the stiff golden mask, which hid the upper part of her face showing only her carmined lips and her chin, she turned her anguished gaze upon her father.

'Perhaps we should have told Cornelius that I am to act?'

216

'It is better this way,' Esmond assured her, once more in command of the situation. He smiled. 'Are you nervous?'

She nodded.

'It will pass as soon as you speak your first lines. Don't worry about Cornelius. Listen to him.' Her father paused as they heard Hope answer the 'prentices, twisting their words back upon them and drawing a laugh from the crowd. 'Hope is a professional. No audience will defeat him. With his wit and skill, he will extemporise. And though I often wince to hear some of my best lines cobbled together from several plays at once, Cornelius never fails to enthral the groundlings. You have a natural talent, my dear. Once he sees that you are talented, he will be placated.'

'What of his pride?' Gabriellen queried. 'If he should believe himself demeaned by acting with a woman, what then? His cutting wit is merciless upon any who ridicule him.'

'You are his match.' Esmond was confident. 'Besides, he will do nothing to ruin a performance. Did you not convince me you could play this role and get away with your disguise? You have a talent for mimicry and with words. The crowd will love you. But . . .' He eyed her stonily, his tone adamant. 'There will be no repeat of this day, Gabriellen.'

From the stage Cornelius in the role of Merlin roared out the prophecy that Arthur would unite England against all enemies and invaders. It was almost time for her to go on. Her straining ears caught the distant sounds of fighting amongst the audience as the jeering voices lessened. Cornelius had won by the sheer force of his stage magnetism, the ability to capture and hold an audience so uniquely his.

' "Who dares invade my mystical domain?" ' he thundered.

There was her cue! Offering up a swift prayer, she inhaled deeply and glided through the gap in the curtain. In a voice which imitated Robin's she started to speak, her words carrying over the 'prentices' sneers. Wrapped from head to toe in a scarlet cloak, she threw back its hood to reveal a golden wig which tumbled down her back to her thighs. A chorus of bawdry rose from the groundlings. She ignored them. From the first moment of her entrance as the enchantress she had to capture Merlin's heart. She must be all woman – all seduction. Hardest of all she must never forget that, beneath the sweeping velvet skirts, she was supposed to be a man.

If only Cornelius did not now fill her with revulsion it would be easier. She looked out over the crowd. To overcome her repugnance she would pretend Jack was out there. Her gaze moved quickly over the rows of faces and was drawn inexorably to a dark-haired man leaning against a tree to one side of the crowd. The self-possessed tilt of his curly head and that battered green jerkin were unmistakable. How much easier it must be to play this role to the very real presence of Mark Rowan rather than to an imaginary Jack.

Slowly unfastening the cloak's ties at her throat, she moved forward, confident of her ability.

' "Who is this before me?" ' she began and found her nervousness dispelling. ' "A noble presence. No mere mortal, that I vow. I have travelled far from my land which is guarded by emerald hills to seek the wizard Merlin." '

' "Then speak, for I am Merlin." ' Cornelius strode towards her.

Coquettishly she moved some steps away. Raising her hand to her breast, she cast a languishing look over her shoulder. ' "I had expected a much older man – a stooped grey-beard. Your fame and wisdom are renowned throughout our land." ' She curtsied low and, upon rising, allowed the cloak to slide over her shoulders to reveal a white gown with long trailing sleeves which had been fashionable two centuries earlier. ' "I bring gifts from my master. He reveres you above all men. They say no man has more sway with King Arthur than the great Merlin. It is you who hold the key to Arthur's greatness." '

As she spoke she sauntered slowly across the stage. The long train of the brocade kirtle rustled over the boards. She walked slowly around Merlin, swaying her hips provocatively. By the time she had completed the circle, the scarlet cloak was draped behind her like a sloughed skin. Although her female form was tightly bandaged, she was conscious that the slender-fitting kirtle and surcoat revealed the line of her long legs as she walked. As yet she had not dared to look at Cornelius, but now she must face him.

His expression showed the rapt entrancement his role demanded, but the shadow behind his eyes was puzzled.

There was something sinister to the twist in his lips. It reminded her of his attack upon her and her palms broke out in a cold sweat. For a frightening moment the next lines evaded her. Drawing a steadying breath, she looked towards Mark for reassurance, transposing his image over that of Merlin. It worked. Her fears subsided. A hush had fallen over the audience which told her she had won their attention. It was more heady than any accolade. She forgot everything but the part she played. With an enticing laugh she raised her arm to beckon Merlin closer. It was then she found herself staring into Cornelius's eyes, and saw they were glittering with outrage. He had recognised her. His lips curled back in a malicious snarl.

Time and again he stole the front stage and tried to block her from the crowd's sight. Twice he improvised new lines to cut her speeches. Each action she countered with graceful dignity, leaving him at a disadvantage, whilst her nimble mind parried his verbosity with a wit which set the crowd cheering.

When Esmond made his entrance as King Arthur, the brightness in his eyes showed his pride and approval. Only the rigid set of Cornelius's shoulders warned her of his mounting fury. It challenged her sense of power and elation which so befitted her role. She was no longer Gabriellen Angel but Gabriellen the enchantress, the temptress who had cost Merlin his powers. Neither did she have to blot the image of Cornelius from her mind for he *was* Merlin. She teased, tantalised and cajoled, her wickedness holding the crowd enthralled. So enmeshed in the part had she become, that she performed the role of the seductress with the subtlety only a woman could bring to the part. And the crowd loved it. Without meaning to, she had stolen every scene from Cornelius. From the choleric colour rising beneath his powder, he knew it. She did not care. This was her moment, her only chance to sup from the sweet chalice of success.

In her role no man could resist her. But as the third act began Hope's antagonism cut the air like a rapier. His pale eyes were venomous as they approached the seduction scene where a kiss from the enchantress strips the magician of his powers. Only when Hope captured Gabriellen in his embrace did she experience the first moment of fear. It brought her crashing back to reality. The febrile gleam in his eyes told her he meant to avenge himself upon her, not only for duping him today, but for rejecting his advances in her chamber. Her flesh cringed at his touch. She was powerless to retaliate, the play dictated they kiss. Yet what could Hope do before an audience of so many? Indeed, with Robin, Cornelius turned his back on the audience as he swept the player over his arm in a flamboyant romantic gesture and their lips never touched. An alluring smile remained fixed on Gabriellen's lips, but behind the half-mask her eyes revealed distaste.

' "Fairest of women, thou art mine," ' Merlin proclaimed as he tightened his hold. In an undertone Cornelius grated, 'Bitch! Strumpet! Would you make a fool of me?' His arms held her in a tight grip as his mouth clamped over hers. She all but gagged when his tongue thrust into her mouth. The mockery of passion disgusted her.

When his fingers kneaded her breast, outrage seared her. Her hand closed over his, her nails digging deep into his flesh. A chorus of lewd shouts rose from the groundlings. When his other hand squeezed her buttocks she refused to endure more of this humiliation. Hidden from the audience by her full skirts, she ground her heel on to his foot with all her strength. The hand supposedly caressing his hair pinched his ripped and barely healed earlobe.

With a strangled oath Cornelius thrust her from him and cried out: ' "What seed of Satan sent you to me?" ' His voice was ragged, as much from the pain she had inflicted as from the anguish of his role. ' "My powers – they are gone! You are the devil's daughter!" '

Freed from him, Gabriellen recovered her composure. She forced herself to remember that this was a role and must be played through to the end. When her father, as King Arthur, stormed on to the boards, his anger at the humbled Merlin was all too real. Only those on stage knew the true life drama that was being enacted. The crowd loved every stormy moment of the final scene as it ran its course. Not until Gabriellen had fallen to the floor after her death speech did it become apparent to her that a lethal tension was building between Hope and Esmond. She had thought to save the company from its growing debts by her appearance. Instead, she could not shake the foreboding that she had brought about its ruin.

At the first strains of Poggs's pipe and the shudder of

the boards as he leapt through the curtain, she rose to her feet and ran from the stage. Behind, the full blast of her father's anger carried to her.

'You're finished with us, Hope. I'll stand no more of your lecherous ways.'

'I'll go, and glad to,' the actor raged back. 'Do you think I'll perform with a troupe that puts a woman on the stage?'

Inside the tiring tent, Gabriellen ignored Agnes's and Nan's worried glances. Ripping off the gold mask, she snatched up a plain woollen cloak, wrapped it around her and pulled the hood low over her face before she disappeared again. Tears stung her eyes and blurred her vision. She was angry at Hope for treating her like a whore, but she was furious at herself for believing she could help the troupe. The acclaim she had won from the groundlings rang now like a death knell in her mind. She should have known that Hope would not hesitate to take revenge upon her for rejecting him. Without him, the troupe was doomed.

Gabriellen ran blindly through the crowd. She tripped over an unseen tussock and the pain which shot through her ankle made her pause. It was then she realised she was very close to the tree where Mark had been watching the play. She glanced around expectantly. He was nowhere to be seen.

'Mark, where are you?' Her cry was despondent. Her footsteps slowed. Upset, she had turned instinctively to him for advice and comfort. He was the one person who never condemned her relationship with Jack. He was the one friend who truly understood her.

Without Mark to confide in, she decided to return to the tiring-tent. It had been her idea to take Robin's place. The troupe could not afford to lose Cornelius Hope. Somehow she must make the peace. If it meant swallowing her pride, she would do so for her father's sake.

There was a chill bite to the air and sulky black clouds bruised the sky. As she retraced her steps the first drops began to fall. Several people jostled her as they hurried to take shelter from the rain. One, rougher than the others, knocked back her hood, and the tresses of the long blonde wig she was still wearing tumbled down her back.

'Look 'ere, friends. If it bain't the enchantress come amongst us.' Cruel fingers bit into her arm as she was pulled round to face three apprentices, their faces ugly with malice.

'And there was us thinking we'd warned the arse-licking whoreson not to perform,' jeered the tallest, in a woollen cap and a greasy jerkin. 'Now you've really got it coming to yer.'

'But that bain't the one,' snarled his companion. The speaker's head jutted forward, as antagonistic as a bull terrier's. ''E bain't got a mark on 'im.'

'Let me go!' Gabriellen struggled to pull free. Her heart thumped with fear at the sight of their burly figures around her. Her glance darted to the passersby. All were too intent upon reaching shelter from the downpour to heed her.

'A pretty boy too,' the fattest of the three sniggered.

'And from the horny performance old Hope gave, 'e must be 'is regular bedwarmer.'

'When we finish wi' 'im,' the first apprentice laughed, propelling her roughly forward, 'it'll be weeks before 'e shares anyone's bed.'

Panic filled Gabriellen. Two of them grabbed her arms, dragging her away from the crowd. To stop them, she dug her heels into the ground, but her soft leather shoes skidded on the wet grass. 'Help!' she screamed. 'Someone, help me!'

She kicked out, and with her teeth as her only weapon, bit one of the apprentice's hands. In her struggles the hood and the heavy wig slipped back on to her shoulders. Her assailants gasped. Then one sniggered. 'Well now, if it bain't a bawdy-basket. Merry sport for us. She must be one of Angel's whores. Take 'er to our wagon.' His cry ended in a grunt.

A familiar, softly spoken voice came from behind Gabriellen. 'If you value this knave's life, release the woman.'

The rough hands released Gabriellen. Gripping the edges of her cloak together, to still her shaking fingers, she faced Mark. He stood with his dagger pressed against the heart of the 'prentice leader. The other two backed away, their bravado stripped from them as their mouths slackened with fear.

'We meant no 'arm, sir.'

''Twas merry sport . . .'

Mark eyed them stonily. 'Get out of my sight before I haul you before the Pie-Powder Court. The justice at the

222

fairs is summary, and judgement swift.' Mark shoved the leader contemptuously away from him. 'I have great influence with the Fair officials. Take care you do not cross my path again.'

They disappeared into the crowd as though the devil himself snapped at their ankles.

Gabriellen took a step towards Mark. Her words of gratitude caught in her throat as he turned that condemning gaze upon her. He took hold of her and gave her a shake.

'In heaven's name, woman, have your wits gone begging?' Her green eyes stared up at him with shock. He stopped shaking her, but his anger remained. 'I'd never have brought you to your father if I'd guessed you meant to flaunt yourself on the stage. Even a whore has more pride.'

Her hand blurred upwards and he caught it inches before it met his jaw. 'Hell-cat! The truth rankles, does it?' His voice was cutting. Abruptly he released her and turned to go.

'Mark, wait! It's not what you think.'

The desperate plea in her voice halted him. He turned round. When she held out her hands in supplication, he ignored them. 'My eyes do not deceive me.'

To see the contempt on his face and his dark eyes blazing with scorn was more than Gabriellen could bear. They stood without speaking, both ignoring the rain which splashed their faces. His anger wounded her. She wanted to beg his forgiveness, but that shuttered look prevented her.

'Mark, you once said friends do not stand in judgement upon each other. Please don't hate me!'

'I do not hate you, Ellen. I thought merely that the wildness in you was from a more noble spirit than wantonness.'

She recoiled as though he had struck her. 'I did not see it as wanton – but necessity. Robin was beaten so badly he could not act, I thought only to help the troupe. Father is deeply in debt. We could not afford to lose the takings from that performance. Cornelius was not told of my substitution.' Her voice broke and she covered her face with her hands. 'It all went horribly wrong. He recognised me, and took advantage of the moment to settle an old score. No one was supposed to guess I was a woman – that's why I wore the mask.'

Mark touched her shoulder and felt her trembling. Taking her chin in his hand he turned her to face him, but her gaze remained lowered – shamed. He had never seen her so distraught. The shock he had felt at recognising her on the stage had long since receded. He had been caught by the spell she had woven as the enchantress. Only when Hope had kissed her with such passion had his anger rekindled.

'Your acting was superb. Too good, in fact.' He looked up at the weeping sky and with a terse laugh drew her beneath the sheltering canopy of a birch tree. 'You were all seductress.'

She gave him a low, sweeping curtsey, brushed the rain-drops from her cloak, and tossed back her hair. 'It was but a part.'

Mark drew a sharp breath. The minx was playing that part again now. 'A part too well suited to your ample charms,' he chided. 'Have you no more wit than a titmouse? It was folly!'

As he spoke, her cheeks flared, scarlet with mortification. She stared at him, her green eyes dew bright behind the dampness of her thick dark lashes. 'You must think me shameless.' The contempt in her voice was all for herself. He felt guilty he had been so harsh with her. 'Why, then, did you trouble to rescue me from those 'prentices?'

'No woman deserves to be raped.' He crushed down anger that she should think him so heartless. There was more to her wild flight through the crowd than the humiliation of Cornelius Hope's kiss on the stage. 'You talk as though all is not well with the troupe? Yet wherever I go, I have heard nothing but praise for Lord Barpham's players.'

She did not answer. The stiff way she held her body, her hands tightly holding the cloak to her throat, told him she was troubled. The rain hissed through the leaves above them and a squirrel chittered.

Mark frowned. 'You say the troupe is in debt. How so?' He took her hands in his. They were like ice. He squeezed them gently. 'Esmond's too shrewd. If he needs money, there are always the cards or dice . . . or other means. He's won many a fortune that way.'

She shook her head. 'No longer. Now when he gambles he loses more than he wins. He's become embroiled with a moneylender.' Her voice quivered. 'Though he refuses to admit it. Also, I think he's going blind.'

'I'm so very sorry, Ellen. I misjudged you badly. Is there anything I can do?'

A wan smile touched her lips. 'How are you as a mediator, Mark? Father has just thrown Cornelius out of the troupe.'

'After the way he treated you, I'm surprised Esmond did not run him through.' The anger was back in his voice. 'What score was it that Hope wished to settle with you? If that lecher has forced his attentions upon you, I'll . . .'

'He did not succeed,' she assured him hastily. The dangerous gleam in Mark's eyes stopped her elaborating further. The incident was in the past and best forgotten. That Mark was so ready to defend her honour must mean he had forgiven her. Her spirits lifted. She saw now she had been unwise to perform on the stage. Though the elation she had felt at holding the audience in her power stayed with her. She would never forget it. How unjust it was that women were barred from acting. Hypocritical also since they had always performed in the Court masques.

'Miss Gabby, I've bin searchin' all over for you.'

Gabriellen looked up to see Nan Woodruff heaving her swollen body towards them, her face ruddy from the exertion. The sudden downpour had stopped and the merry-makers were returning to the stalls, the tumblers and minstrels continuing their entertainment.

'Come quickly,' Nan urged. 'Your father's in a rare taking. Hope said such wicked things, I fear this argument will end in a sword fight. Make haste!'

'Nan, you should not be rushing about.' Gabriellen looked worriedly at the seamstress. 'You'll make yourself ill.'

'I'm fine, my dear. No need to fuss.' She gulped for air but already the high colour was fading from her round cheeks. 'Go to Esmond. Thank God Mr Rowan is with you! If anyone can stop those two killing each other, Mr Rowan can. They're in the tiring-tent.'

Gabriellen lifted her long skirts as Mark took her free hand and shouldered a way through the crowd. When they entered the tiring-tent Cornelius was nowhere in sight. Umberto stood over Esmond's slumped figure whilst Cesare knelt at his side, pressing a cloth to his shoulder. To Gabriellen's horror the bandage was rapidly turning scarlet.

'Everyone go look for you, Miss Gabby,' Umberto said, his usually swarthy face sallow. 'You come. You tend your father. That bastard Hope, he draw his sword. He run Esmond through.'

''Tis but a scratch,' Esmond protested faintly.

'You should know better than to duel, Father,' Gabriellen scolded as she rushed to his side. When she lifted the bandage she saw the wound was jagged but not deep. But he had lost a great deal of blood. She looked back at Umberto. 'Fetch the herb chest from our wagon.'

'I go. Quick.'

As the musician left the tent, Gabriellen studied the wound again. 'I'll make a poultice to stop the bleeding. Then you must rest.' She shook her head at Esmond. 'You're too old for such nonsense.'

'Old!' He choked on his ire. 'Insolent chit! I'm but two and forty and in my prime. It will be many a year before a posturing lecher like Hope will be a better swordsman than I. I slipped, or he would never have bloodied me.'

Before answering Esmond she looked across at Cesare still kneeling at her side. She did not wish to talk in front of one of the players. 'Would you bring Father some brandy?' Once he left she whispered, 'Did you slip, Father? Or did you simply not see his blade? I know your sight is failing.'

'The devil it is!' he blustered.

'Father, I am right,' she insisted gently. 'Poggs suspects but no one else. There's no need for them to know – is there?'

The sea green of his eyes shadowed. For the first time in her life Gabriellen saw that he was vulnerable. 'What use is a blind man to the players?' he said. ''It is my life!'

'The players need not know.' She pressed his hand. 'Nan and I will look after you. It could be years before you lose your sight. It will be our secret. But there must be no more gambling or fighting.'

Esmond touched her hair, his eyes clouding with love. 'You sound like your mother used to. It's too late, though. A leopard does not change his spots.'

'But a leopard is a prince among his fellow cats. He has strength and cunning others do not possess.'

Esmond gave a laugh which ended in a grimace of pain

as he put his hand over his wound. 'Daughter, you have a silken tongue.' Looking past Gabriellen's head to where Mark had remained by the tent opening, he raised his voice. 'I've not thanked you, Rowan, for saving my daughter's life in Chichester. Or for bringing her to me. She has been a great comfort.'

'I did little enough.'

'You did a great deal. I'm grateful.' He paused, regarding Mark for a long moment, his mouth narrowing into a censorious line. 'I thought better of you, though, than to deliver Gabriellen into Stoneham's hands.'

Mark's head jerked up. 'I was not her guardian.'

'Father, please,' she intervened. 'When will you accept that Jack and I love each other?'

'If he loved you, he would not have dishonoured you.'

Gabriellen stood up. With her hands on her hips she towered over him, her voice condemning. 'Are you so innocent?'

A flush darkened Esmond's face beneath the powder of his stage makeup. Mark coughed but before any of them could speak, Poggs, Agnes, Nan, and Victor Prew burst into the tent.

'Esmond!' Nan screeched. 'Oh, Esmond.'

He held up his hand for silence. ''Tis but a scratch.'

'My dear Esmond – ' Victor Prew stepped forward. 'I've just seen Cornelius in the most foul taking. He said he has left the troupe.' He paused as he saw Esmond's blood-stained doublet. 'Blessed Mary! So you did duel. I thought Hope was elaborating upon the truth, as he so often does. This is monstrous. A tragedy. Your troupe has no leading actor.'

'You need not fear, Mr Prew,' Gabriellen spoke out. 'It's all a misunderstanding. I will speak with Cornelius.'

'No, daughter!' The strength had returned to Esmond's voice. 'That lecher will never work for my troupe again.'

'I beg you to reconsider, Esmond.' There was an unmistakable threat in Prew's tone. 'You're in no position to lose your leading actor. I shall speak with Cornelius.'

Prew turned to Gabriellen. 'It was very courageous of you to take Flowerdew's place today. I admire that courage. Perhaps together, Miss Gabriellen, we can resolve the difference between your father and Cornelius?'

There was something in the way Prew looked at her

227

which turned her blood cold. If her father was in this man's debt, Prew would show no mercy were the payments not met.

'Ellen, a moment if you please.' Mark's low voice was urgent. She looked round in time to see him leaving the tent. His strange manner troubled her. The command in his voice was obvious. Why had he not spoken in the tent?

'I have a matter to attend to, Mr Prew. Then I shall come with you to speak to Cornelius.' She went out to find Mark.

He was waiting by the stage. Taking her arm he led her behind a wagon. He looked over his shoulder to ensure they were not followed. When he turned back to her, his face was taut with anger. 'What has that man to do with your troupe?'

'What man?'

'The short bird-faced one who just entered the tent.'

She frowned. 'That was Victor Prew. Why do you ask?'

'No matter why,' he rapped out. 'Just answer me. It is important. What do you know of him?'

Gabriellen scanned his face. What she saw there added to her fears. 'He's a merchant. He met Father in Winchester. I cannot understand why Father abides him. Or perhaps he has no choice.' Gabriellen felt the weight of her fear heavy upon her shoulders. She could trust Mark. 'It's to Prew that I believe he is in debt.'

'Then it is worse than I feared.' He pushed a hand through his black hair, his voice taut. 'Have nothing to do with Prew. Get that debt paid and warn Esmond to stay away from him.'

'Without an actor of Hope's skill, what chance has Father of paying off any debt?' Gabriellen sighed. 'It is likely we will sink deeper into Prew's clutches. I don't like the man or trust him, but what makes you so against him?'

'I suspect that he would use the troupe for his own foul means. If you value the safety of your friends, tell Esmond to have no more to do with the man. I cannot say more.'

'Miss Gabriellen,' called Victor Prew. He strutted towards them, the red feather in his hat and his skinny legs encased in yellow hose reminding her of a foraging hen. 'If we are to detain Cornelius, there is no time to waste.'

'Heed my words,' Mark warned.

Before Gabriellen could introduce the two men, he had disappeared into the crowd.

Chapter Sixteen

A menacing silence descended over the two protagonists. Gabriellen glared at Cornelius Hope, her body tense with fury, her hands clenched at her sides. Against the wall of the travelling wagon Victor Prew stood silent throughout. Not that Gabriellen had noticed. All her energies had been concentrated on Hope's pompous figure. They had caught him packing his chests in the wagon he shared with Robin and Will.

She had reasoned. She had apologised. She had flattered and coerced. Hope had been unmoved.

Now Gabriellen lost all patience. 'Have you no sense of loyalty?' she flared.

'I have been shamed!' Cornelius adopted a pontifical self-righteousness. 'Held up to ridicule by your wanton actions.'

In the cramped quarters, their raised voices rebounded off the wooden walls.

'So now you would sulk like a spoiled, wilful child?'

'Harpy! Satan's-spawn!' A tic tugged at the corner of a heavy-lidded eye. Raising a fist, Cornelius shook it at her whilst he swore, foully and profanely. He was trying to shock her to silence, but Gabriellen refused to rise to the bait. When she eyed him with disdain, he turned to mockery. He reviled. He harassed. He hurled abuse which would have rendered a lesser woman cowed and broken.

Gabriellen matched him, her retaliation a blast of pure rage. Finally, it was her vehemence which stunned him to silence, a feat never before known. The advantage won, she swallowed her pride to placate, to plead, to promise a new play which would be his greatest part ever. When even these tactics failed, she bullied and finally threatened.

His florid face turned brutish. He laughed at her. Nothing would sway him. Cornelius was once again at his most affected. He postured like an omnipotent god, his lantern jaw tilted and implacable.

'How will you answer to Lord Barpham for this childish tantrum?' she railed in a voice which could have frozen the Thames. 'Have you no allegiance to Lord Barpham's players?'

'*I am* Lord Barpham's players. Without me the rest of you are nothing.'

'You conceited jackanapes!' The words exploded from her. The violence of her rage swamped all reason. Tossing back her head, her eyes took on a green luminosity. 'For the son of a defrocked priest and a tavern wench, you give yourself airs.'

Momentarily astonished that she knew his parentage, Hope retreated a pace. He forgot to pose and his thickened paunch hung like a sagging pillow about his waist. Beneath his beard, his flabby jowls were prominent.

'No actor is irreplaceable,' she continued scathingly. 'You, sir, are merely as good as the lines written for you. And for your information, Mr Hope, it becomes increasingly difficult to write parts for you as a dashing young hero. At five and forty, you are not as young as once you were.'

'I'm not a day over eight and thirty!' he blustered, pulling in his stomach and preening his upturned moustache.

'So you would have your admirers believe. I shall ask once more – will you stay with Lord Barpham's Men?'

'I'll dance in hell first!' He recovered his composure, and affected a majestic stance. 'You high-flown bitch, I'll teach you to threaten me! I've still a score to settle with you.'

He lurched towards her. Gabriellen darted nimbly to one side and thrust out her leg to trip him. Cornelius yelped. Arms flailing uselessly in the air, he toppled sideways. The wagon shook and dust bounced up off the boards as his weight slammed down upon them.

Gabriellen grabbed at a heavy broadsword used as a stage-prop, which rested against the wall, and held it before her. 'Don't try and get up.'

Prew snickered. 'The wench is more than a match for you.'

Hope's dignity was bruised, as were his buttocks where he had hit the floor. As he tried to heave himself to his feet, blood speckled his eyes and his face turned crimson. He was wedged between a table and the bed.

'You hell-spawned vixen! You damned shrew!' he bellowed. 'You fight like the strumpet you are. I'll not forget this. One day you'll pay!'

Gabriellen jabbed the sword under his nose and Cornelius wriggled backwards as far as he was able. Her face was flushed and her eyes glittered with the force of her rage. 'I'm not frightened of you, or any man.'

So dismissing him, she looked at the chest he had been packing. Partially hidden under the velvet cloak Victor Prew had bought for the actor was the embroidered sleeve of Merlin's purple robe. Snatching it up, she brandished it aloft. 'This is the troupe's property. It would do little for your reputation should you be arrested for theft. I bid you good day, Mr Hope.'

She turned, flinging down the broadsword, and departed. 'Let me help you, Cornelius,' she heard Prew offer. 'Was your outburst wise? Will you not reconsider?'

Cornelius's answering profanity buffeted the air. There were sounds like an enraged bull on the rampage. A stool was kicked, a table thumped, and there was the dull metallic ring of a warming pan striking someone's breeches. She could only suppose they were Prew's. Her mind conjured up a vision of the two men inside the wagon. Despite her anger she smiled grimly. There was an indignant squeak behind her and she turned to see Prew dash down the wagon steps. He was carrying the cloak he had bought for Hope. A bellow emerged from the wagon and Hope was at the door, holding a chamber pot. With a snarl, he flung the contents towards Prew. Fortunately temper had impaired his aim.

The merchant went white as linen. 'The audacity of that man,' he gasped as he caught up with Gabriellen. 'The ingratitude. The arrogance. Miss Angel, I am all admiration for the way you withstood his bullying.' He put a restraining hand on her arm. His short legs could not match her stride. 'You were magnificent. Your loyalty to your father is commendable.'

'You flatter me, sir.' She pulled her arm away, still too angry at Cornelius to have the patience to listen to his witless flattery.

'Indeed not, Miss Gabriellen. To appear on the stage was somewhat hasty, I confess, but you did it for the most noble of reasons. I find you incomparable. Quite incomparable. I am your devoted servant.' He straightened his ruff which Cornelius had crumpled.

Gabriellen walked on. Her mind raced at the implications of Hope deserting the troupe. It would ruin them. Who would draw the crowds? She needed to be alone to think and here was Prew gibbering like a monkey, distracting her thoughts.

'I do not need a servant, Mr Prew,' she responded tersely. Stopping suddenly, she rounded on him. 'I need an actor the equal of Cornelius Hope. Now, if you will forgive me, I have to change and see that my father is settled comfortably.'

'Dear lady, after the way you stood up to Hope, I could deny you nothing. I know the very man.' Seeing that at last he had caught her attention, he placed a hand over his heart and bowed. 'It may take a week to contact him, but he's a great actor. The equal, if not the superior, of Cornelius Hope.'

'If he is so exceptional, why should he wish to join our players?' Gabriellen looked at him with some suspicion.

'Because your father is a great playwright. Those new speeches he produced at Plymouth were memorable. They are the equal to anything Kit Marlowe could write. Lord Barpham's players are destined for greatness. What actor would not wish to rise with them?'

Victor Prew saw the caution shadowing her eyes. She was a sharp one. Until now she had not spared him more than a cursory glance. That he intended to change. Twice now he had witnessed her splendid anger. It changed her into a magnificent virago in a way that captivated his interest.

'His name is Anthony Culpepper.'

'But he is . . .' She could not contain her astonishment. 'He's one of our finest actors. Until two or so years ago he was with the Lord Admiral's players.' She frowned 'Was not a young apprentice-actor killed, and suspicion fell upon Culpepper?'

'A misunderstanding. Nothing was proved. Culpepper was quite devastated. He vowed never to act again. He was stricken by the melancholy and his health declined. To recuperate, he retired to the country.' Prew waved his hand in a vague direction. 'Not far from here, as fortune has it. I believe he would consider returning to the boards if the right company were to approach him.'

'That would be for Father to decide,' Gabriellen announced.

Prew was not deceived by her demure tone. As he watched her walk towards her wagon his gaze was thoughtful. He had his own reasons for wanting Culpepper in the troupe. Since the death of the young apprentice, who was Culpepper's catamite, the actor had become a zealous Catholic. He might prove an ally in Prew's conspiracy. The seed was planted. Gabriellen was the guiding force behind Angel. That force must be harnessed, played to his advantage. Having seen her attack upon Cornelius, he suspected there was nothing she would not do to save her father. Smoothing his elaborately curled hair to conceal his bald patch, he permitted himself a smile of anticipation.

After changing out of her costume it took Gabriellen nearly an hour to pacify her father who continued to deride Hope for his treachery. Anger was draining him of strength. He sat propped up by pillows in his bed, his eyes darkly circled and cheeks pinched with pain. Worried by his paleness, she sought to calm him by speaking of the merchant's proposition. 'Father, Mr Prew has suggested we approach Anthony Culpepper.'

'The man's trouble.' Esmond shook his head.

'But he's a great actor.'

'There's no denying it.'

'Then should we not give him a chance? We need someone immediately. Robin is good, but not good enough to take Cornelius's place.' She added as a mischievous afterthought: 'Unless you wish to play the lead, Father?'

'No, not I.' Esmond was emphatic. 'I know my limitations. But Culpepper . . .' He rubbed his chin. 'He's a degenerate. No vice is beyond him. Every company he has joined becomes a hive of dissent. He thrives upon festering jealousy and takes a savage delight in causing dissension. Though I did hear that after the lad's death, he changed, became almost a recluse.'

'And if any man can keep such a reprobate in line, that man would be Esmond Angel,' she reasoned. 'Have we any choice? Whoever we find must know all the plays by St

Bartholomew's Fair. That is in six weeks. With an actor as famous, not to say infamous, as Anthony Culpepper, the crowds will flock to us. The money earned between now and the end of the fair must see us over the winter months and pay our outstanding debts.'

Although some of the colour was beginning to return to Esmond's cheeks, his eyes took on a guarded look. So they were in debt? The thought of Victor Prew having such a hold over her father was disquieting. She despised the man. But he had handed her the very tool which would enable them to free themselves from this stranglehold. 'Mr Prew is eager that Culpepper join us. Might that not be used in our favour?'

'You have a devious mind, daughter.' Esmond grinned with a return to good humour. 'I may well use Anthony Culpepper . . . for a limited time. Prew is a fool with too much money. This could be to our advantage.'

'Why is he so eager to help us?' she voiced her concern.

Esmond snorted. 'Because he sees us as a means of gaining royal favour – why else? He seeks to become a sharer in the troupe, so that when next we are summoned to Court he would be there to bask in our glory. He's a wealthy merchant who would increase his fortune by supplying the needs of the Court.'

Esmond winked at his daughter. 'I know well how to pander to the vanity of toadying tradesmen, and how to cream their generosity for all its worth.'

'Have a care, Father,' Gabriellen cautioned. 'Prew is an obnoxious rat. I don't trust him.'

She looked down at Esmond's reclining figure. The bandages beneath his open doublet were flecked with blood. Her heart went out to him and she kissed his brow. Whatever Esmond said, Prew was no fool. Not where money was concerned. She was troubled as she left the wagon. It was too dark to risk moving far from the safety of the actors' camp. She could hear Umberto playing his guitar accompanied by Poggs on the pipes as they sat round the campfire.

When a rich baritone voice began to sing, she was drawn to the periphery of light from the fire. Mark sat on the ground, his hand resting upon one bent knee as he sang. The exquisite richness of his voice sent a shiver of delight through her. It was a fierce, passionate song of a woman

235

abducted from her lover's home by brigands and of the lover's feats to reclaim his beloved. The emotion in Mark's voice brought a constriction to her throat. His song encompassed the pain and ecstasy of all lovers.

Gabriellen sighed, consumed by her own yearning for Jack. The few weeks they had been apart seemed like long arid months. She looked accusingly up at the moon. The clouds of the afternoon had disappeared and the crystal brightness mocked her loneliness. The poignancy of the song held her in its thrall. It resurrected her memories of Jack – the warmth of his lips upon hers, the excitement of his touch, the whispered endearments.

'Where are you, Jack?' she whispered. 'I miss you.' She hugged her arms about her, closing her eyes, allowing the melody and words to engulf her.

The song ended and Umberto began the opening chords of the inevitable 'Greensleeves'. Again the sentimental melody in Mark's voice was heartrending. Her gaze sought his recumbent figure. The flames bathed his face in an amber glow, softening the rugged planes. Sensing her stare upon him, he looked across at her, his dark eyes reflecting the warmth of the flames. She smiled fondly, proud that this man was her friend. During the days of her illness she had become used to Mark's Celtic looks, but after the weeks of absence she was struck afresh by the dark brows which curved upwards, the sharply pointed nose and wide mouth. The rugged line of his jaw showed strength and vitality in its commanding lines.

Gabriellen was not the only one drawn to the campfire by Mark's singing; a score of people now ringed the fire. The last notes of 'Greensleeves' had died and Umberto struck up the lively beat of a popular ditty. As Cesare, Robin and Will joined Mark in the song, a disturbance attracted Gabriellen's gaze to the edge of the camp. From out of the circle of onlookers a beautiful woman, her black hair covered with a length of blue gauze, moved into the centre of the firelight.

Clapping her hands, the newcomer swayed her hips in time to the rhythm. Then her feet began to move. She made an exotic figure in a skirt of bold coloured stripes and a scarlet low-cut bodice. As the beat of the music quickened, so her dancing became more abandoned. She spun

236

faster, her skirts whirling higher to reveal her slender legs. Robin's and Will's voices trailed away as they watched the dancer.

'Bravo! Dance on, my beauty!' shouted Francis Crofton in appreciation. His encouragement was taken up by several other men who clapped the rhythm and stamped their feet.

The dancer ignored them. Her bold dark eyes never left Mark. That the Welshman was enjoying her antics was obvious by the greater resonance of his voice. Cesare played with greater gusto as a potent alchemy sparked between singer and dancer.

Agnes limped to Gabriellen's side. 'How I wish I could dance like that,' she said with a sigh. 'She's so graceful and beautiful. She's also a passionate one.'

'She is certainly that,' Gabriellen said caustically as she saw the way Mark caressed the dancer with his gaze. 'And her brazen dance makes no secret of her interest in Mark.'

'And his interest in her is plain for all to see,' Agnes chuckled.

Mark had risen to his feet as he sang. The dancer responded. Pulling the concealing veil from her black waist-length hair, she ran it through her fingers, stroking it as though it were a lover. She spun and swayed around Mark, drawing the veil across the lower part of her face while her eyes spoke their sultry promise.

Gabriellen watched, intrigued at the blatant invitation. The dance was wanton, sultry, deliberately seductive, as the woman's hips undulated to the rhythm of the song. When the dancer lifted her arms above her head, the thin red bodice stretched tightly across her small, pointed breasts and hardened nipples. Mark reached out to pull her closer so that their bodies touched. In a gesture of abandon the woman lifted her long hair from her shoulders, and as she held it high, arched her slim neck. Her smile was bold and inviting as she held his gaze.

Gabriellen drew in a sharp breath. 'I've never witnessed such brazenness. I thought better of Mark than to make a cod's head of himself over such a creature.'

Agnes looked at her and frowned. 'My dear, are thee not taking this too seriously? The Welshman and the dancer are clearly attracted to each other. Such relationships form easily amongst those who live upon the road.'

Blistering words jumped to Gabriellen's lips, but she checked them. Agnes was right. She was being foolish. Mark was free to choose his own companions. It was because she missed Jack that she was so out of countenance.

'They do make a striking couple,' she conceded. 'I felt that instant spark of attraction the first time I met Jack. Truth to tell, Agnes, I envy all lovers who are together this night. Jack is so far away.'

She looked away from the two figures in the circle of light. Tonight was perfect for lovers. Other lovers! Only Jack could ease the ache of longing which tore her apart. As the song ended, the dancer sank to the ground at Mark's feet, her skirts billowing around her. Her dark eyes blazed as she threw back her head to stare up at the Welshman. She was a provocative sight with her breasts rising and falling, exposed almost in their entirety as she fought to recover her breath. Mark took her hands and raised her up to the applause of the crowd. He drew her close, his black eyes glowing with admiration as he kissed her hand. The dancer's smile was pure enticement. With a short laugh, Mark slid his arms around her. He kissed her parted lips lingeringly and very thoroughly, to the shouts of approval from the male players.

'You are bold, sir,' the dancer said. 'I like that in a man.'

As Mark released her, Gabriellen saw that she had kept her hand possessively on his chest, her voice low and husky as she added, 'From your voice you are Welsh. The Welsh are a race of magnificent singers . . . and virile lovers.' There was a chorus of giggles from the woman's companions. 'I am Jesmaine, astrologer, palmist and reader of fortunes.'

Mark was smiling as he bent to whisper in Jesmaine's ear. The fortune-teller answered with a husky laugh. Lifting an arm weighted with wide silver bracelets, she touched his cheek before moving away and calling back over her shoulder, 'I will hold you to that promise.'

Hearing Gabriellen click her tongue against her teeth, Agnes sighed. 'I know thee miss thy sea captain. There'll be many long absences if thee continue to love that wild rogue. Thee deserve better.'

There was a stubborn tilt to Gabriellen's chin which warned her not to pursue the matter. She looked away from that resilient green stare. 'I'm off to my bed, Miss Gabby.

I'll look in on Nan and Esmond to see if they need anything.'

'When I left them a short while ago, they were both sleeping from the posset you brewed for them,' Gabriellen said as she turned away from the servant. 'Goodnight, Agnes. I'll stay awhile by the campfire. I'm too restless to sleep.'

Worry over Esmond and Nan's condition and her constant fear for Jack gave her no rest. So little news reached them of the events at sea. Was Jack safe? Her hand closed on the emerald and pearl pendant at her throat. It was hollow comfort, so great was her need to be held in his arms. The lively conversation and laughter from the players seated round the campfire was too carefree for her mood. It was not like her to give in to melancholy. Even so, she needed to be alone with her thoughts. Moving into the shadows, she sat on the empty shafts of the prop wagon. Her mind revolved in widening circles. Over the last weeks she had assumed more and more responsibility for the troupe. Often now the players came to her before speaking to Esmond. These responsibilities she took on willingly. But there were times, as now, when she herself needed to confide in someone. It seemed so natural for that person to be Mark. Or had been until tonight. Now that he had shown his interest to be in Jesmaine, he would not want to be burdened with her troubles.

'Don't waste no time do you, Rowan?' Poggs quipped, his voice breaking through Gabriellen's thoughts. Her attention was caught. Mark had been walking with Poggs towards her, but they had halted on the edge of the firelight. Poggs's ruddy face was creased with mischief as he craned his head to look up at Mark. 'The lovely Jesmaine is choosy as to who shares 'er favours. 'Er last lover, Augustus the strongman, fell dead two months ago as 'e tried to lift an ox on to 'is shoulders. Since then she's spent 'er nights alone. That'll be changing now, I reckon.'

'You do the lady a disservice.' Mark lifted a dark brow. 'We Welsh are a mystical race. Is it not natural I would wish to consult the secrets of the heavens to secure my future?'

'It won't be the mysteries of any stars you'll be exploring,' Poggs returned, slapping his knee with merriment. 'Lucky devil!'

'Shame on you, Poggs,' Mark mocked good-humouredly. 'And I thought you happily bound in wedlock.'

'Oh, I am,' Poggs hastily agreed. 'There's no other woman for me than my Sussex giantess. 'Tis different for a single man like yourself, Mr Rowan.'

A damp branch cracked, shooting out sparks from the fire. Mark came towards her. Outlined against the fire, she saw how slim and broad-shouldered he was. Those powerful muscles so clearly silhouetted owed nothing to bombast or padding. The moonlight fell across his face as he neared.

'It was a pleasure to hear you sing again, Mark.'

He shrugged aside her praise. 'My greeting this morning was a poor one. How are you, Ellen?'

At the warmth in his voice her chagrin melted. His friendship meant too much to her to spoil it by a fit of pique. 'I'm well, and content with my life.' She nodded towards the players sitting around the fire. 'They have all accepted me. Even Umberto and Cesare treat me as an adopted sister. I would miss any one of them should they leave.'

Mark stepped nearer, his voice low and serious. 'I hear your meeting with Hope did not go well. He's left the fair.'

'I failed lamentably.'

'He's not worth becoming upset over.'

'Oh, I've consigned Hope to the devil.' Standing up, she looked across the expanse of booths, tents and covered wagons. Dozens of campfires, ringed by rosy faces, speckled the field. She needed to confide in someone. Unlike any of the players, Mark did not condemn her for loving Jack. 'I miss Jack so much,' she said simply. 'We spent so short a time together, and every day he faces danger.'

'Jack is an experienced sea captain. And this is not the first time he has fought the Spaniards.'

'There are so many rumours. Some say we have sent the Spanish home like whipped curs. Others that they have landed and have pillaged the whole of Cornwall.' Her glance sought his, praying for reassurance.

'Neither is true. If it were, there would be no fair held this day. If the Spanish had landed, the beacons would have been lit and the militia called out. Every man here would be armed and sleeping amongst the patchwork of defensive trenches which stretch inland from the coast. There has been a sea battle. No more than three Spanish ships were taken and we sustained some casualties.'

Mark watched Gabriellen as she gazed longingly south towards the sea. She sighed. 'Jack and I arranged to meet at the St Bartholomew's Fair. It seems an eternity away.'

'Has he treated you well? You have no regrets?' he could not stop himself asking. He still felt responsible for Gabriellen and did not want to see her hurt.

She did not answer at once. A mistiness turned her green eyes to luminous opal in the moonlight and her face took on the translucent softness of a woman thinking of her lover.

'At this moment,' her voice was impassioned, 'I would rather be aboard *The Swift* facing the Spanish guns at Jack's side, than feel the awful desolation of being parted from him. I love him so very much. He is my life.'

'I am happy for you, Ellen.' Tonight Jesmaine awaited him, an invitation no man could resist. Yet as he stared into Gabriellen's spirited face which held a beauty uniquely her own, he found himself in no hurry to leave. He was troubled by Prew's involvement with the troupe. He had to be certain that the danger he knew to be hanging over the players could be averted.

'I tried to question Esmond about Prew,' he abruptly introduced the subject. 'Unfortunately, I learned nothing. Esmond is not one to confide in another man.' Mark took her hands, his tone growing urgent. 'Prew is not to be trusted, but I can prove nothing. Believe me, Ellen, on no account must he become more involved with the players.'

Gabriellen stared up at him, her heart contracting. 'I fear it could be too late. Already he has suggested that Anthony Culpepper replace Cornelius.'

'Surely Esmond will not agree to so depraved an actor joining the troupe?' Mark said with heat. He disliked the thought of Culpepper anywhere near Ellen. The feeling of danger intensified. He was certain that the third man in the churchyard adjoining Wynwood Grange with the priest and Sir Philip Templeton had been Victor Prew. It would explain the merchant's interest in the players, and Culpepper was a Catholic. What better way for Prew and his accomplices to get closer to the Queen? A troupe such as Lord Barpham's players was rising quickly and Queen Elizabeth would be the first to appreciate the drama and wit of Esmond's plays. It would not be long before they were again summoned to Court. He must not delay in discovering more about the merchant.

The days sped on inexorably for Mark. At the Bristol Fair he had carefully laid his plans. Fate had decreed otherwise. Glendower had been servicing a mare when she twisted sideways and kicked out. Her hoof caught the stallion on the knee, gashing it badly. As he reared away, he had slipped on the mossy cobbles and sprained a tendon. The only cure was rest. Fortunately, a nearby manor was owned by a friend of Mark's late father. Glendower would be looked after there, whilst Mark continued his investigations. It was agreed that he would return for the stallion after the Bartholomew Fair.

That had been four weeks ago. Without Glendower it would have been impossible to maintain his cover as Lord Walsingham's spy at the fairs, or keep watch over Lord Barpham's players. Lucky for him, that night he had met Jesmaine. The fortune-teller had been insistent he journey with her. As his lover, Jesmaine had given him the cover he needed. It had also been a tumultuous affair. Jesmaine was a passionate and exciting mistress and each day Mark's affection for her deepened.

Now it was Lammas. Mark sat in a darkened corner of a taproom in a small wayside inn with his battered hat pulled low over his face. To all intents he looked asleep, but beneath the brim of his hat, his half-closed eyes surveyed his companions. Only four other travellers occupied the fetid room. Three of them were already slumped unconscious over their ale. The fourth – Mark's quarry – was at last beginning to show signs of drowsiness.

He had been pursuing the messenger all day, ever since he had seen Prew sidle up to him behind a booth at a country fair and hand over a sealed document. Recognising the second man as a groom from a nearby Catholic manor, Mark followed him after quickly changing his recognisable leather doublet for a brown homespun jerkin. He also pulled on a reddish-brown wig to add to his disguise. Two miles along the road he saw the groom ahead. On his rented mare Mark followed at a discreet distance until they reached the inn at nightfall.

From beneath his hat, Mark saw the messenger's head begin to nod. Moments later the man's eyes closed, his head falling upon his arms which rested on the table. A short while later all four men were snoring loudly. Mark judged it time to make his move. Stealthily, he rose and crossed the room, his hand sliding as expertly as any sneak-thief's into the man's greasy jerkin. He drew out Prew's letter and went outside to read it in the moonlight. Sliding the point of his dagger carefully beneath the seal so as not to deface it, he opened the parchment. It contained a list of names. Two knights headed the list, a Sir G— and a Sir K—. The initials meant little to Mark. Out of the six other names, which were written in full, there was only one he recognised. That man was known to be a Spanish spy who had so far evaded capture.

Mark memorised the names. Later they would be included in the coded report he sent to Lord Walsingham. He checked his impatience to see Prew imprisoned and safely out of any further involvement with the players. It was not to be – yet. There was larger game to trap. His duty was plain. He had to discover the identity of the two knights on this list. If it then became obvious they were implicated in a plot against the Queen's life, action would be taken to end their conspiracy. Since Prew was the only link he had, he must remain free.

Taking his tinder box from the pouch at his waist, Mark kindled a flame and carefully reheated the sealing wax. The missive resealed, he returned to the taproom, replacing the document in the groom's jerkin without the man even stirring.

Jesmaine sat in her travelling wagon staring down at the astrological figures and symbols on the chart before her. To be certain her calculations were correct, she took a fresh sheet of paper and redrew the twelve zodiac houses. Taking up the astrolabe, she went to the window and studied the night sky, aligning the position of the planets and stars. When she returned to the chart, she worked quickly from long practice. Her calculations were checked against the almanac and finally from the ephemeris, which showed the changing position of the planets since the beginning of the century. The prediction was the same.

She crushed the chart into a ball, her emotions both elated and fearful. She could not determine the exact length of her relationship with Mark, but it would not be a brief affair. That knowledge delighted her. But something else she had seen frightened her. There was a time of danger ahead for Mark. Great danger. Her predictions were rarely wrong. She had lived with the forewarning of Augustus's death for some months before the event. She had known the day but not the manner. That fateful morning he had been so full of vigour that when she had tried to warn him, he had scoffed at her fears. In sheer exuberance he had hoisted the ox on to his shoulders – a feat he had done many times before.

Her skills were not to be mocked. She was no charlatan. She had learned the mysteries of the stars from her father and he had taught her well. He had been a travelling cunning man, wise in the ways of healing herbs and potions. He drew up horoscopes for those who could afford them. Seven years ago, when she was fifteen, her father had died. Her mother had run off with a horse-thief years earlier. Both had been hanged at Tyburn a year later. After her father's death, Jesmaine had drifted from one protector to another. She used them to survive, loving none and tiring of them quickly. Until she met Augustus. It was during her years with the strongman that she took up astrology and palmistry to supplement their income. In London she was beginning to win a name for herself with many wealthy clients seeking her advice. But Augustus's life was on the road and she had forsaken her chance of fame to follow him. Come winter, she would make her home in London.

It did not surprise her that Mark would remain her lover for some years. After their first passionate night of love she had known Mark would always be special to her.

Jesmaine paced the wagon. The danger she had seen hanging over Mark's future worried her. There was much she did not know about her new lover. Such as where he went when he sometimes disappeared for whole days at a time. Confident in her power over men, she knew it was not to visit another mistress. But he would never speak of his absences and she accepted his silence. Looking out of the window to where the stars lit the heavens, she sighed. 'Will you return soon, my Celtic lover?' she murmured. 'Two nights without you is two nights too long.'

If Mark were here now they would make love. Her breasts tingled against the thin linen of her scarlet bodice and there was an ache of desire in her loins. She drew a steadying breath, and catching sight of the crumpled chart on the table, smoothed out its creases.

For a long time she studied it. The danger was there, plain to see. It was influenced by Venus and the baleful Saturn. Two forces – two people who were close to Mark. Biting her lower lip in concentration she referred to the almanac and scribbled further signs and figures. She threw down her quill and rubbed a hand across her eyes. The signs were bad. Saturn – the man – was a dark shadow holding sway over Venus. Venus – the woman – was a creature of many shades, both light and dark. Whoever they were, these people would endanger Mark's life. He must be warned against them.

Chapter Seventeen

Mark Rowan shouldered his way through the noise and confusion of Cheapside. It was the widest street in London and was jammed with people shopping in its market. He strode on past Goldsmith's Row. The impressive timber-framed block of ten houses and fourteen shops decorated with the goldsmith's arms could have been a shabby tavern for all he noticed. The news he had just learned boded ill for Lord Barpham's Men.

'Who'll buy me pies?' a loud voice bellowed. 'Brought fresh from Pimlico.'

A higher voice shrilled, 'Stratford bread! Best in London.'

'Turnips! Hackney turnips. Yer'll not find better.'

'Stop thief! The little bastard stole me purse!'

The cries echoed unheeded by him, as were the exotic sights around him. Close by a peacock emitted its mournful cry from its cramped cage. A monkey chittered as it fought to be free of its chain.

Mark pressed on. He cut through St Paul's churchyard which was filled with booksellers. At any other time he would have stopped to browse, for he rarely came away without a purchase. Today he did not even glance at the trestle tables set outside every shop, over which hung brightly painted signs depicting a mermaid, green dragon, blazing stars or the like. His pace quickened with urgency.

Keeping his hand tight upon his purse, he passed by the shadow of the great church, knowing St Paul's was as much a den of thieves as a prayer house. Within the immense building the south aisle was the home of usury and intrigue, which even in that holy place did not stop short of conspiracy or even murder. Servants seeking work would scan the notices of vacancies posted on the 'Si quis' door. Only the unwary or first-time visitors allowed themselves to be borne by the crowd to the middle aisle – known as Paul's Walk. This was notorious as the haunt of rogues, thieves, and soldiers of fortune. It was a place Mark knew well. Many a time he had been thankful of the anonymity of that crowded aisle. There he exchanged information with others who worked secretly to safeguard the Queen from her enemies.

His stride lengthened as he approached Ludgate Hill, though now he was forced to pick his way along a path of trodden, rutted soil, noxious with the accumulated filth of centuries. Apart from the paved thoroughfares of Cheapside and the Strand, all other streets were little more than narrow tracks. In wet weather they became channels of churned-up mud, stinking from the garbage thrown from doors and windows.

He halted outside the Bel Savage Inn and his worst fears were realised. The notice announcing that Lord Barpham's Men were to perform *The Warrior King* had been torn down. In its place was one announcing that Lord Mincham's players were to perform instead.

He went inside and in the low-beamed taproom saw Poggs, Umberto and Cesare staring gloomily into their tankards. Without preamble he demanded, 'Where is Esmond?'

Poggs looked up, his usually animated face drained of colour, the laughter lines replaced by worried creases. 'Gone with Gabriellen to Lord Barpham's house in the Strand. We arrived here to find Lord Mincham's players booked in our stead, and a note summoning Esmond to attend Lady Barpham.'

A blond, clean-shaven man struck the table with his fist in tragic mode. Mark looked across at him, noting the smooth prominent cheekbones and Roman nose. Although he had never met Anthony Culpepper before, he recognised him from a description, that of a decadent man whose handsome features had been likened to a Greek god. The actor tossed back his flowing hair with a disdainful jerk of his head. 'How dare this scurvy landlord accept another troupe in our place? Who are Lord Mincham's players? Nothing but a motley band of amateurs, of whom no one has heard!'

'Something bad has happened,' Cesare groaned.

Mark was surprised to see that the two musicians sat

apart, the full length of the table between them.

'*Si,*' Umberto nodded. But although in agreement with Cesare, he turned a cold shoulder towards his countryman as he spoke. 'Is no good.'

It was so unlike the two musicians to be at odds, the atmosphere between them noticeably cool. Mark dismissed the strangeness of it. That was a minor problem compared to the one which hung over the players. He turned to leave. 'I will go to Esmond at Barpham House.'

'Mr Rowan!' Poggs crossed to join him. He drew Mark out of hearing of the other players. 'From your face you expected something like this. What's wrong?'

'It is best if Mr Angel explains.' He put his hand on the clown's shoulder. 'But tell me, how have things been with the troupe these last weeks?'

'Never better. Takings are high. Culpepper certainly draws the crowd.'

'He fits in well with the company, I trust?'

Poggs knew evasion of unpleasant news when he heard it. For Mark Rowan to look pale and intense matters must be grave indeed. No amount of badgering or pleading would draw information from the Welshman if he meant to keep it to himself. Knowing Rowan had the welfare of the troupe at heart, he bore no grudge and answered, 'Culpepper has proved his worth better than any of us hoped – considering his reputation. I were in a tavern in Southwark two years ago. He near wrecked the place when a rage took him. He's a changed man, I reckon. He surprised us all by his retiring manner when he joined us. After the first performance he was less so. He's getting worse by the week – puffed up with conceit. Last night he were the cause of a row between Umberto and Cesare. Umberto thought Culpepper was taking too much interest in Cesare. It took all Miss Gabriellen's time to pacify the two musicians, and they're still not talking! Dare say it'll blow over. Excitable lot, the Italians. 'Specially those two. And Culpepper's no better nor worse than Hope – yet.'

Poggs rubbed the russet stubble on his unshaven chin. 'Until we arrived in London to find our booking cancelled, fortune had taken a turn for the better. It's been months since I saw Esmond looking so at ease. Not so now. He had a shouting match with that weasel Prew last night.

That sent the man off in a rare taking. Good riddance to him!'

'That at least is good news.'

'You don't think Prew had anything to do with our losing our performance here?'

'No,' Mark answered. 'It's more serious than that, I'm afraid.' He paused a moment, considering Poggs's worry-creased face. He could trust the clown to keep the news to himself. 'Esmond will need all the support you can give him,' he said at last. 'Say nothing until he returns. There's news of the Armada, which I can vouch is true. It would appear that even as Queen Elizabeth was giving her rousing speech to the army at Tilbury last week, the Spanish had already been beaten. Our fleet chased them the length of the eastern coastline as far as the Scottish border. Then we turned back to reprovision. The Spanish knew they were defeated. Not by a glorious battle won, but by the storms which this last month have scattered their forces. We sustained few losses.' He paused for a moment before announcing the gravest news. 'Unfortunately amongst our dead was Lord Barpham.'

'Then we're without a patron,' Poggs gasped. 'We've been reduced to vagabonds. We could even be thrown into prison should we attempt to earn a living.'

Mark nodded. 'That is unless the new Lord Barpham continues his father's patronage.'

'Do you think that likely?' Poggs eyed him hopefully.

'I do not know the man, so I cannot say. I did hear that his betrothed is a Puritan. That does not bode well. Lord Barpham is a convert to their teachings. You know Puritans – they abhor frivolity in any form. Plays they see as instruments of the devil, luring sinners into lewdness and licentiousness. It is the Puritan zealots who harangue the City dignitaries to close the playhouses.'

'Then we're doomed, Mr Rowan. Doomed!'

'Nay, take heart, Poggs,' Mark encouraged. 'This troupe is one of the best, and Esmond's plays are highly regarded. It will not be long before a new patron is found.'

'Aye, you're right.' Poggs forced a false cheerfulness into his voice. As he walked away his feet dragged in the sawdust on the taproom floor.

Mark hoped that Esmond's argument with Prew meant

an end to their association. In the last weeks he had learned the names of the two knights Prew had sent a message to from the Bristol Fair. They were Sir John Garfield and Sir Henry Kettering, both fervent Catholics. As yet he had been unable to discover anything to implicate the three in a plot against the Queen, but his instincts told him that one was in the hatching.

On the Eve of St Bartholomew's Day, Gabriellen stood at Mark's side by the Great Gate at the west facade of St Bartholomew's Church, watching the opening ceremony of the fair. Tumblers and musicians led the Mayor's procession through the city towards Smithfield. Next, on horseback, came the Mayor in his scarlet gown and gold chain of office, accompanied by twelve Aldermen in their robes. Jugglers followed them; mummers in huge beasts' heads capered whilst the morris men and hobby horses danced. The procession came to a halt opposite Mark and Gabriellen. There was a fanfare of trumpets and the proclamation to open the revels was read.

Despite the gaiety all around her, Gabriellen's mood was bleak. All the pleasure had gone from her visit to London. She could not banish recent events from her mind. The summons to Barpham House had pitched the lives of the players into uncertainty. Her greatest fear now was that they would begin to drift apart. She still could not believe that Lord Barpham was dead. Decapitated. She shuddered with horror. Gabriellen had met his lordship only once, but had instantly liked the unaffected country nobleman. She had not formed the same impression of his son. The memory of that black-gowned bigot roused her anger.

Her lips pursed with returning fury. How dare that sanctimonious carrion castigate her father for encouraging bawdry and idolatry! How dare he proclaim Esmond's genius with words to be profanity, blasphemy, and rooted in depravity! He had the impudence to call the players the disciples of Satan. She hated him. Hated him with a strength which had almost overpowered her reason. Somehow she had held back her wrath until he had ordered them from the house. He had spoken to them as though they were no better than beggars. At that point her restraint had snapped. Rounding on him, she forgot the deference due his rank.

'You're an unnatural son,' she fumed, disgust burning in her eyes. 'By every word with which you condemn our profession, you heap ridicule upon the memory of your father! Devil's disciples indeed! Shame on you, my lord. Your father deserves better.' She drew herself to her full height which topped his reedy frame by an inch or more. 'We were *his* men, under *his* protection. Every one of us respected and held your father in great affection. We were proud to be hailed as Lord Barpham's Men.'

'It is you who are without shame.' The young lord's thin lips drew back over yellowing teeth. His pious stare took in her emerald velvet riding-gown and matching hat which was tilted at a jaunty angle. A golden net sewn with seed pearls held her hair in place. He sniffed with abhorrence. Compared with his unadorned black garb, her attire was sumptuous and decadent. Gabriellen threw back her head. Let him sneer, she was not ashamed of her beautiful clothes. It had been a wonderful surprise upon arrival at the Bel Savage Inn to find that her father had sent for her clothes chest from Chichester. Today she had dressed with care, as befitted attendance upon a nobleman.

'Jezebel!' he spat. 'Beelzebub's handmaiden! Get out of my house before I call the constable.'

'Come away, daughter,' Esmond urged, taking her arm. From the weakness of his voice, Gabriellen saw Barpham's death had severely shaken him. His eyes were darkly circled, nostrils and mouth pinched with pain and weariness.

The rough hands of Lord Barpham's servants had shoved them out of the door and hurled them into the rutted mire. Picking herself up, Gabriellen shook out the muddied finery of her gown to derisive laughter. When she stooped over her father to help him rise, her hand was pushed gently away by Mark Rowan.

'Are you hurt, Ellen?' he asked as he raised Esmond up and began to dust him down.

She shook her head, too furious to speak.

'I'm sorry it has come to this pass,' he said heavily. 'Our present Lord Barpham is not the man his father was.'

'He is not a man at all,' Gabriellen cried, struggling against the humiliation of Mark seeing her being thrown into the street like a common vagrant. Outrage won. 'He is a sanctimonious toad! A bigotted viper! A – a . . .'

'I gather you did not like the man,' he cut her short. In

spite of the seriousness of the situation, a smile hovered around his lips.

'Like him! I could kill him for the way he insulted us.'

'That temper of yours will land you in trouble one day.'

She could have sworn Mark smothered a laugh as he turned solicitously to Esmond. She opened her mouth to challenge him, but it was never uttered. There was blood on Esmond's doublet. The wound from the sword fight with Cornelius, which had been slow to heal, had reopened.

'Father!' she cried anxiously.

Esmond made no sign he had heard her. He continued to gaze unseeing into the distance.

'Take a grip on yourself, man,' Mark remonstrated. 'Barpham's death is a great blow. Are you able to ride? If not, I'll hire a cart to take you back to the Bel Savage.'

Esmond Angel looked at Mark. The glazed expression which had settled over his eyes since he had learned of Lord Barpham's death lifted. He rubbed a hand across his brow. 'Of course I can ride.' He pulled back his slumped shoulders and knocked some clinging debris from his padded trunk hose. Straightening his doublet, he said with returning strength in his voice, 'Barpham would turn in his grave to learn he had bred a mewling Puritan. I have lost a good friend. 'Tis a sad day.'

Esmond permitted Mark to help him into the saddle but, once there, picked up the reins and sat straight and proud on the gelding's back. 'May I count on you, Rowan, to escort Gabby back to the Bel Savage? I must go to Court. Until I can find another patron, our troupe is unable to perform. There is no time to lose.'

'But, Father, your shoulder!' Gabriellen protested. 'It needs attention.'

'Time enough for that later. I have a troupe to manage.' He fidgeted with the reins, impatient to leave.

'I'll escort Ellen to the inn,' Mark answered. 'Good luck at Court.'

Gabriellen was jolted from reviewing these events as a peal of bells rang out. The fair was open and the Mayor's procession moved forward.

Mark touched her arm. 'Ellen, for this afternoon at least, put aside your worries for the players. Esmond said you were to enjoy yourself.'

'Father's spent three days at Court and still we have no

patron. I suggested that we wrote to several prominent courtiers, and though these letters have been despatched, there has been no reply. Without Father knowing, I even wrote to Lord Mincham. I've seen his troupe perform. They are a poor band compared to the skills of Culpepper, Robin and Poggs. But I am not hopeful. Father is proud. He would remain the leader of our men.'

'I believe Mincham is away from Court,' Mark said. 'Did not the Lord Admiral's Men ask Esmond to write them a play?'

'Naturally, Father refused. He does not want to see the troupe disbanded. He feels responsible for his players.' Her eyes widened with fear. 'They are like family. A split is too awful to contemplate. Don't even think of it.'

'Beware that you may be substituting friendship with these people for the family you long for,' he said, understanding her need. She could be wild, impulsive and ruthless in using her wiles to gain her own ends. She could also use her faults and turn them to strengths. It was her driving force. But there was a time to be loyal and a time to be practical. He regarded her solemnly. 'For how long can Esmond afford to keep the company together without the weekly takings? What of his debt to Prew?'

She refused to hold his stare, her gloved hands toying with the nosegay hanging from a chain at her waist. 'Father says it was paid and will talk no further on the subject.'

Mark's eyes gleamed. Gabriellen was worried. Rightly so. Prew, sly and malevolent as he was, had maintained his hold over Esmond. The Esmond Angel he knew of old would never have allowed any man to gain advantage of him. It was becoming apparent that Esmond was losing his edge – that which once had set him above the common rogue. Not so long ago he could charm gold from a miser, and the victim think himself the winner in the deal. Now Esmond looked tired and drawn, the vitality drained from him.

To reassure Gabriellen, Mark smiled with false optimism. 'When has he ever failed the troupe? Look, the procession is moving into the fairground. It's time to enjoy the fair. Have faith in your father. A patron will be found.'

He took Gabriellen's elbow to guide her through the crowd. They walked between the rows of booths to halt by a clearing where the Mayor's entourage had stopped to watch a wrestling display. As they watched the entertainment, Mark stood behind Gabriellen, his hands on her shoulders, protecting her from the jostling of the crowd. The match over, the winners were presented with prizes. For the amusement of the spectators, a parcel of live rabbits was turned loose among the crowd. Young boys and apprentices whooped and shrieked as they flung themselves into the mêlée to catch the animals. The crowd roared with laughter at their endeavours. When two boys ran headlong into each other, both diving for the same rabbit, Gabriellen turned to laugh up at Mark.

'What shall we see first?' he asked. 'The freak shows? The performing animals?' Again taking her elbow, he led her through the press of people.

'Are you hungry?' he enquired as they paused by a vendor selling gilt gingerbread. Buying two, he handed one to her. 'These are known as Bartholomew's babies.'

She bit into it with pleasure. 'They are delicious.'

Mark laughed and brushed a crumb from her cheek. Impulsively she took his hand and squeezed it. 'You've made me feel like a young girl again. It's good to forget one's troubles with so dear a friend. I thought I had seen all there was to see at a fair, but this is so much larger than any we have ever played at.'

'It is the oldest and largest fair in England, dating from the twelfth century.' Seeing he had caught her interest, he continued, 'A monk named Rahere founded St Bartholomew's hospital adjacent to the Priory. Within a few years the cures performed were numerous – many believed miraculous. The priory became a place of pilgrimage and the small annual fair a source of income for the monks. Until the dissolution of the monasteries, all tolls from the traders went to the priory. Each year the fair has grown until it has reached today's proportions. Originally it was the commercial side and not the diversions which was important. Cloth and wool were the main commodities. Now the entertainments dominate.'

'And we were to be part of those entertainments.' Anxiety had returned to her voice. 'The money earned here was to see us through the winter at Chichester.' Realising it was unfair to be downcast when Mark had tried so hard to lift her spirits, she looked up at him. 'But let's not dwell upon that. Besides, you have troubles of your own. I was sorry to hear Glendower was injured. Not badly, I trust?'

'I shall collect him next week and take him home for the winter. I have three horses ready to bring south and will visit London again before I return to Wales, for a few months.'

Gabriellen laughed, unable to resist teasing him. 'Is it the charm of Jesmaine that keeps you in London?'

'What else!' He grinned broadly. It was near enough the truth. Apart from the fact that their relations were good cover for his work, his interest in her had not waned. With winter approaching, Jesmaine had begun looking for a permanent residence to accommodate clients who came to her for their horoscopes. During the last interview with Lord Walsingham, Mark had been instructed to continue his investigations of Prew, Sir John Garfield and Sir Henry Kettering. Whilst Prew remained in London, so would Mark. Besides, his feelings for Jesmaine were strong and he would be loath as yet to leave her and return to Wales for good.

Since they were nearing the fortune-teller's striped tent, Mark suggested with a grin: 'Why don't you let Jesmaine cast your horoscope? She's very good.'

To his surprise Gabriellen shook her head. 'I don't want to know my future.' Her chin lifted defiantly. 'I will shape my own destiny.'

'Lord Barpham's death has upset you.' Mark took her shoulders and turned her to face him. He saw her almond eyes saddened by pain. Lifting one brow, he teased, 'And you are missing that scoundrel Jack. Perhaps Jesmaine will tell you when you will see him again.'

'I was to meet him here . . .' Her voice trailed off as her gaze slid past him. Suddenly her face was lit with a radiance which transformed her completely.

'Jack! Oh, Jack, my love, at last you are here!'

Mark's existence was forgotten as Gabriellen ran into the arms of her lover. Mark watched as his friend wrapped her in a tight embrace. When he turned away he discovered himself being studied by Jesmaine.

'Mark, darling, why did you not introduce me to your friend? You have spoken much of this Ellen. Am I not to meet her?' Jesmaine sauntered towards him and put her arms around his neck. 'You have spent much time these last days in the company of Lord Barpham's players. Or is it this Ellen who takes you so often from my side?'

'Comments like that are unworthy of you, Jesmaine.'

Her dark eyes glittered as she watched Gabriellen and Jack disappear into the crowd. 'I know what is in the stars, Mark. This Ellen holds sway over you.'

He laughed at the absurdity of her words. 'We are friends, nothing more.'

'Perhaps you would be lovers?' she accused. 'I saw the way you looked at her.'

'You have been staring at the stars for too long and have lost touch with reality.' Mark laughed aside the jealousy which sparkled in her eyes. 'I am but an ordinary man, Jesmaine. You are more than enough woman for me. Did I not prove to you last night how great was my need for you?'

'I have no complaints, my handsome lover. And you are no ordinary man.'

She smiled and drew him into the privacy of her tent. The air was sweet with the musky scent of Jesmaine's perfume. The interior was a profusion of colour, yet all blended in a way which was not garish or vulgar. The rich furnishings were used to create an atmosphere of mystery. Green and red painted lanthorns lit the tent, colouring it with a rich exotic glow. A gold and emerald silk hanging adorned one wall. Along another was a painted screen showing the twelve signs of the zodiac. On a chest covered with cloth of gold were the instruments of her work, and elsewhere were various silver figures and candlesticks. All were gifts from her lovers. Jesmaine made no secret of past attachments.

She laughed softly, drawing him past the circular table, spread with a chart of the heavens, towards a day bed covered in silk cushions. Winding her arms about him, she kissed him with passion. The musky scent of the perfume she wore reminded him of last night. It had taken a hot bath to remove its fragrance from his body after her scent had branded him her lover. The memory roused his desire, and as he pressed her hip against his hardening body, she gasped with delight. But to his exasperation Jesmaine evaded his lips when his mouth sought hers.

At his immediate response she drew back with a satisfied laugh. 'I *know* it will be a long time before we part. But I know also that this Ellen is foreshadowed by a portent of

256

tragedy. It will touch you, if you do not end this friendship.'

Believing her words stemmed from jealousy, he kissed her throat to reassure her. When still she withheld herself from him, he voiced his frustration. 'Ellen is not your rival, my lovely. I'm fond of her because I saved her life. It forms a strange bond which is never broken. I should know. I was set upon by cut-throats on Hampstead Heath. Jack Stoneham came to my aid and saved my life. It forged an affinity between us. I think of Ellen as a sister.'

'They bring danger to you, Mark. Forget these people, lest they destroy you.'

He stopped her words with a kiss, refusing to listen. Jesmaine swayed against him, her body pliant to his touch. He eased back, bending his head so that their brows and noses touched, his voice low, allowing for no further argument. ''Tis you I want, Jesmaine. Jack and Ellen are lovers. I will listen to no more of this nonsense. While Jack was away at sea he asked me to watch over her. Now he has returned, Ellen is his responsibility, not mine.'

Jesmaine shook her head, her dark eyes widening with fear. 'Heed me! This man I've seen in the stars – he's the dark shadow at your shoulder.' Her eyes glazed as she looked through him in the way she affected to impress clients who wanted their fortunes told. 'The woman will be touched by tragedy. You must forget her. She will destroy you.'

Mark swore in Welsh, his eyes narrowing as he stared down at his mistress. 'It's you I care for, Jesmaine. Don't spoil what we have with an unreasonable jealousy. I'll not have my friends maligned without cause, or my honour discredited.'

He turned to leave but her cry stopped him. She was shaking as he took her back into his arms. ''Tis not jealousy which makes me speak so,' she said brokenly. 'I know what we have and will treasure it while it lasts. I but warn you. Forewarned, I would try and save you.'

She clung to him, crying softly. Mark's anger died. Jesmaine was a strange creature with strange moods. But the touch of her body pressed against his ignited fires which at this moment only she could appease.

'Let us not quarrel, Jesmaine.'

Mark smiled and Jesmaine felt her blood quicken. She threw back her head and pressed her hips harder against him. The response she sought was immediate and she moved a step back, loosening the ties of her bodice. As she watched his dark stare roam freely over her olive-skinned flesh, she gave a practised roll of her shoulders, her sleeves and bodice slipping to her waist. His ardent gaze alone was sufficient to excite her to a fever of longing for his touch.

She could hardly contain her impatience when he left her to go to the tent opening. A fat merchant was about to lumber inside. 'I fear, good sir, the lovely and talented Jesmaine is temporarily indisposed.'

He prevented the merchant from entering, and as he laced the opening she slid out of her skirt and petticoats. Taking up a length of diaphanous scarlet gauze, she draped it around her naked body and lay on her side upon the day bed. With her dark hair flowing across her shoulders, she propped her head on her palm, her breathing low and uneven as Mark approached.

'You are beautiful, Jesmaine,' he said, his admiring gaze smouldering with passion.

She laughed provocatively and sank down on to the cushions, her body curving sensuously, beckoning to him.

Mark snatched the flimsy veiling from her, his lips parting in a wicked smile. 'Now I shall prove that you are the only woman for me.'

'Love me, my darling.' Her laugh became husky as his hands and mouth moved expertly over her body. They elicited so wild a response, that in her all-consuming passion she forgot to pursue her warning. She was voracious, and Mark gave a delighted laugh at the appetite of her demands. The wildness in her answered a fierce need in him to banish the echo of her words from his mind.

The sounds of revelry outside were drowned by the clamour of their blood. With gathering abandon Jesmaine moved her body against him, feeling the burning heat of his flesh moulded upon hers. It was as though she could not get enough of the touch and taste of him, and he responded with increasing sensuality to the intimate boldness of her lips upon his body. His restraint was immense as he remained apart from her, allowing his fingers to fulfil the urgency of her need. Even then, as she gasped out her pleasure, he continued to fondle and kiss her. His mouth feathered across her taut stomach and thighs, his tongue seeking her inner warmth, prolonging the exquisite sensations which cascaded in a torrent of heat through her loins. When finally they merged as one, incredibly again he roused the scintillating thrills which sped through her body like wildfire. Lost in the ephemeral fever of desire, her nails raked Mark's back. Her slender legs locked about his waist, her long hair tangled about them, Jesmaine held him bound to her, refusing to allow their passion to die.

Satiated, Mark stared down into her beautiful face. Her dark eyes were sleepy with a surfeit of passion. Tenderly he parted the silken curtain of her hair which hid the splendours of her breasts from him, his lips moving down to caress their delicate crests. She sighed, stretching sinuously like a sleek, contented cat.

'Come with me to Wales, dearheart,' he asked softly.

'Nay, my darling. My life is in London. I would pine away with boredom in a remote Welsh valley. I will always be here awaiting you in London.'

She kissed him with returning hunger, but as his lips travelled the smooth line of her jaw he tasted the saltiness of her tears.

The noise of the fair made normal speech impossible, but Gabriellen's voice had risen in anger as she stared up at Jack. 'What do you mean, you have to leave at once for Court?'

She forgot her weeks of longing. How could he, moments after their reunion, speak of leaving? She took a deep breath to steady her temper, her eyes growing large and luminous as she stared up at him. 'I have not seen you for three months. Now, after a few minutes, you would desert me again?'

'My love, I am commanded by the Queen to attend upon her.' Despite his protestations there was a ring of pride in his voice which fanned the outrage consuming Gabriellen. It was the third time he had mentioned the Queen's command. Clearly he had found favour in Elizabeth's eyes. At that moment Gabriellen hated the Queen. It was cruel of Elizabeth to take Jack from her after the empty weeks of waiting. The older their sovereign became, the greater the number of handsome gallants she demanded surround her. Since the recent death of Robert, Earl of Leicester, Elizabeth's greatest love, nothing less than total devotion from her courtiers pleased the Queen. When she was pleased she

259

raised them high. Established favourites such as Raleigh and Essex vied to take Leicester's place. Did Jack aim that high? She gazed into his handsome face, seeing the confidence of a soldier of fortune.

Three months away from Jack had heightened her love for him. But she was no longer an impressionable young girl. The responsibilities she had assumed in those months had matured her. In her weeks with the troupe she had mixed with noblemen and characters from the Underworld. She had seen ambition gleam too often in others' eyes not to mistake it now in Jack's. But he loved her. He would never put ambition before herself. It was foolish to feel hurt and jealous because his duty bound him to the Queen. But she did.

Jack drew her behind a covered booth selling pewterware, but even here they were pushed and jostled by the crowd. There was nowhere within Smithfield to give them the privacy they craved.

'Would you have me ignore Her Majesty's command?' Jack coerced with a smile.

'Of course Her Majesty must be obeyed!' Anger crept into her voice.

Jack looked down at Gabriellen, surprised by the terseness of her tone. She had always been so adoring, so yielding. Now her slanted green eyes glowed with a feral light. The fire and passion burning in those lovely depths roused his desire. To come here, he had risked the Queen's displeasure. Only this morning Elizabeth had laughed with him, calling him her bold adventurer. That had drawn a scowl from Raleigh and earned him a venomous glare from the Earl of Essex. Jack knew the Queen was playing with him, as she did all her courtiers. That both Essex and Raleigh had later snubbed him had elated him further. It meant they saw him as a rival for Elizabeth's affections. Wealth and power were at last within his grasp – providing that for some weeks ahead the Queen learned nothing of his private life. None of this showed in his face as he took Gabriellen's hand and pulled her closer.

'I stole these precious moments away from Court because I could not bear another day without sight of you.' Jack looked over her head at the crowd and glowered. 'Now I've seen you, that is not enough.'

'Then stay!' she urged. They stood close. His grey eyes

were startlingly pale against the deep bronze of his face and
short dark hair. Love and yearning robbed her of reason.
She saw only his mouth poised above hers, tantalisingly
close. With the press of the crowd around them, it was
impossible to hold him as she longed to and lose herself in
the pleasure of his kiss.

'My love,' Jack said, his eyes smoky with promise, 'no
post at Court is worth the torment of wanting you and not
having you. But alas, I have duties there now, and greater
men than I have learned the folly of taking too lightly
those duties. A spell in the Tower was their punishment.
Regrettably . . .'

'You must attend the Queen?' she finished for him
angrily. He had lulled her into false security then tried to
frighten her by using the threat of the Tower as an excuse
to leave. 'Then go! Heaven forfend I should prevent you
from joining the line of courtiers pandering to an aging
woman's vanity.'

Tight-lipped with fury, she turned to leave. A jerk of his
arm pulled her hard against him, his eyes as stormy as her
own. 'Damnation, Gabriellen! Is that what you think?'

'Yes!'

Following hot upon her accusation was the shock that
she should think so ill of him. Yet she knew she was right.
Love and loyalty rose up to defend his actions, but honesty
won. A surge of the Angel temper engulfed her. Did he
think her a child – a fool to be tricked into compliance?
Rage and shattered ideals battled within her. Wrenching
her arm from his grasp, she turned on her heel, defiance
in her stride as she walked away.

'Gabriellen, stop!'

Many heads turned at the cool authority of his tone, but
to Jack's astonishment Gabriellen ignored his command.
Would the woman give him no peace? Didn't she know
what he risked by staying? No woman was worth losing all
he had striven for. Yet, seeing the proud set of her back
as she continued to walk away from him, he knew he could
not let her go. Damn her beguiling green eyes! he cursed
as he marched after her.

'Gabriellen!' He caught her shoulder and spun her round
to face him. Her eyes were bright with angry tears and
her face bleached of all colour. Though her chin tilted
obstinately, she did not pull away from him. Confident of

her love, he had thought her pliable to his demands. Now she outfaced him, her tempestuous nature at odds with his. She was more beautiful than he remembered. And that passionate nature, when not turned upon him in fury, had woven a web which had clung tenaciously to his mind throughout the long weeks at sea.

His lips curved, assured in the knowledge that his smile had melted many a woman's heart. 'Gabriellen, my love,' he said softly as he led her between two empty booths where the passage was deserted of people, 'how can you think I would wish to be anywhere without you at my side?'

Staring deep into her eyes, he saw the pain and uncertainty there. His smile broadened and he raised her chin with his hand. 'Those three months without you seemed like an eternity.' A glance over her shoulder showed him they were still alone and he bent his head towards her. Their lips touched. Briefly, her mouth quivered beneath his kiss, then to his surprise she pulled away.

She blushed as she looked around. 'Not here in public, Jack. Would you treat me as a common doxy?'

'There's no one to see us,' he laughed aside her protest. Her kiss had told him it was hurt pride which prompted her anger. 'Kiss me.'

'Not here.' Her voice remained infuriatingly cool.

The wench presumed to judge him – to test the measure of his love. Damn her, he would tolerate no jealous rages! A few months at Court would yield the answer to his dreams. Each day the Queen showed him greater favour. Gabriellen must be patient. Steel entered his grey eyes as he stared down at her. 'I left a sweet angel at Plymouth. In her place I return to a virago.' A pulse throbbed above his ruff, showing the control he was exercising upon his temper. 'Did I not come to the fair as arranged? At no little risk of arousing the Queen's displeasure. I risked it willingly for sight of you.'

'And now you cannot wait to return to your more august mistress!' Fists clenched against the silken folds of her gown, she stepped back, her anger turned against herself. His warm, masculine voice never failed to bring her senses alive. It took all her willpower to remain resolute against the hunger in his eyes. One part of her – that wild side which could never bow its head to reason – wanted to throw herself into his arms. Yet something borne within her anger held her back. The blood of Wildboar Tom ran hotly through her veins. No man, not even Jack, would ever use her. She loved him and had denied him nothing of that love. There was no need for Poggs or her father to warn her against Jack's faults, the least of which was his burning ambition. She could forgive him that. But never, never, would she take second place in his life to another woman. Even if that woman was the Queen of England.

When she lifted her eyes to meet his stare, they were green splinters of ice. 'Go to her. The Queen crooks her little finger and you must run. The choice is yours.'

Jack stared at her, his lips whitening. 'I'm damned if I'll be threatened by a firebrand.'

'And I'll not wait around while you dance attendance upon another.' The words burst out in bitter ire. Her pain and disappointment were too great to halt them. 'Your duty to the Queen is one thing. Paying court to her is different.'

She turned away. Choking off a sob, she pressed her knuckle against her trembling mouth as tears smarted in her eyes.

Jack breathed deeply and snaffled a curse at her obstinacy. He put a hand on her waist and spoke over her shoulder. 'My love, understandably you are upset. I had planned a loving reunion – not a few stolen moments like this.' He stripped off a jewelled glove and touched her cheek. Her face was white, freckles standing out across her nose, and her blazing eyes were like Esmond's in a murderous rage. 'Gabriellen, why must you make it so hard upon yourself? I love you. I'll come to you at the Bel Savage when I can. Tonight, if possible.'

The warmth of his breath caressed her neck. She turned to regard him. For a timeless moment she was unable to drag her eyes from his commanding stare, which was full of the sultry promise that had the power to turn her limbs to liquid. She swayed towards him, love overwhelming her anger. A flash of light from his hand caught her eye and her attention turned upon the huge diamond ring on his finger. It branded him a royal favourite.

'You have been well rewarded for your services,' she retorted, her anger returning. 'I have heard Her Majesty tolerates no rivals. As you have said, the Tower awaits those who take solace in another's arms. Would you condemn our love to sordid secrecy?'

'You exaggerate. Have you not my heart? What more do you want?'

Why did he not reassure her with talk of their future? Her whole being ached with love for him. His desire for her was there in the darkening of his eyes. It should be enough. Jack loved her – and yet . . . His manner was different. Why was he so evasive? 'I had expected to be your wife!' she countered. 'Or did I mistake your intentions? I trusted you, Jack.'

There was a tautness to his face which guarded his thoughts from her. Her hurt intensified. What did she know of Jack the man? Were his promises of love the dishonourable words of seduction? She stared into his eyes, striving to overcome her pain as she demanded softly, 'What am I to you, Jack?'

Impatience drew down his brows. 'Godswounds, Gabriellen! This is not the time or the place to discuss our future. I love you. Let it suffice for now.'

'No!' She could not believe he was acting this way. Not after the promises he had made her. His expression was cold. There was a hardness about his manner, unlike the Jack she remembered. He expected her unquestioning obedience without thought for her feelings. Her temper soared out of control. 'You are shamed to own you love a playwright's daughter. Go to your Queen! Let her heap you with riches, if that's so important to you.'

Her words caught him offguard. For a moment the carefully controlled visage of the courtier slipped. What she saw whipped her anger to a blistering fury. The grey eyes were fired with ambition, the tilt of his head arrogant. Her rage exploded, fed by disillusion. 'Leave me. Go to Elizabeth. Bow and toady to her whims to win her favour. What do I care? I never want to see you again.'

'If that's what you wish, so be it!' he retaliated fiercely. His boots grated against the stony ground, and before her astonished gaze he disappeared from sight.

'Jack!' she shouted, appalled at what she had done. Lifting her skirts she ran after him. 'Jack!'

Several men turned in her direction and grinned lasciviously. One shouted, 'Is it me you're calling, sweeting?' He guffawed, encouraged by his companions. 'Jack's me name. Jack the lad, that's me!'

Gabriellen ignored them as she frantically scanned the

crowd. Jack was far ahead, the white ostrich feather in his cap like a pennant flying inches above most men's heads, his broad shoulders and long stride cutting effortlessly through the press of the crowd. Gabriellen fought to part the merrymakers surrounding her. It was useless.

Shakily, she put a hand to her mouth as realisation of what she had done swamped her. How could she, after all those months of waiting, have railed and shouted at him like a shrew? Despair flooded over her as she told herself she had allowed her temper to drive away the man she loved.

Chapter Eighteen

Autumn was a temperamental season, but this mid-October morning Richmond Park basked in sunlight, its trees and plants laden with fruits, aglow in a profusion of colour. Mountain ash with its red clusters of berries and leaves turning a rich gold; the romantically named traveller's joy, mantled by its feathery-white seeds. Amongst scarlet rosehips, blackberries and elderberries, the pink breasts of bullfinches were joined by the blues, yellows and greens of finches and tits banqueting on the fruit. An occasional lizard sunned itself on a rock, scampering for cover among the buttercups, red campions and plum-coloured mallow as the Queen's party galloped by. Overhead, against a sketchy white-bearded sky, a darting, twittering cloud of swallows amassed in preparation for their long flight south.

The courtiers streamed behind their Sovereign who had set a furious pace. It was the first time she had been in the field since Leicester's death after weeks of bleak and unrelenting mourning at Court. In fact, at one time there had been doubts as to the Queen's sanity. On hearing the news of her favourite's death, Elizabeth had locked herself in her rooms for three days. Only her old friend and counsellor Lord Burghley had braved her wrath and finally taken an axe to the door. She had emerged pale and haggard, like a wooden effigy. In the day she attended to matters of state, retiring unattended to her rooms every evening. Now she rode as though putting a devil to rest.

Jack, along with many others, gave a relieved sigh when Elizabeth finally drew rein. The last weeks had been a turbulent time for him. He had only returned to Court three days ago, after urgent business had taken him to York for three weeks. His jaw clenched at the memory. The death of a business associate there had left him the beneficiary of a sizeable income. Welcome though the increase in his wealth had been, he had been glad to escape the constraints of York and return to London. The business was run by capable hands, as it had been during the three years of his partner's illness. He had no worries on that score. The income would be channelled into building a house on the land he had purchased by the river near Chelsea. He pushed the unpleasant memories of his stay in York to the back of his mind. However financially rewarding, his ties with that city marked a phase of his life he would rather forget; like his childhood in the fisherman's hut in Hastings and the years amongst the criminal underworld in Alsatia.

He surveyed the black-clad courtiers, still in mourning for Leicester. All, that was, except for the Earl of Essex. For all he was Leicester's stepson, he was dressed in silver satin embroidered with gold. As Jack watched, Essex edged his horse close to the Queen's side. Since Leicester's death Robert Devereux, Earl of Essex, had thrust himself forward at every opportunity, determined to supercede his step-father in all things. It was not enough that he held the post of Master of the Horse as Leicester had done in the past. He was heavily in debt, his lands mortgaged. He needed the Queen's favour.

Jack could understand ambition but he knew his own limitations. No man would ever rule Elizabeth. But Essex was the golden boy at Court. At just over twenty, he was tall, handsome, red-haired and flamboyant. He charmed everyone. And Elizabeth, ever hungry for adoration, banquetted her fill upon the young man's attention.

Jack liked Essex. Despite the disparity in their backgrounds, they had much in common. Occasionally in the past they had joined company in the whorehouses and gaming dens of London, notably Nell Lovegood's house.

The Queen's face shed its sadness as her gaze fell upon Essex. Those years in Alsatia had taught Jack to judge people well. He knew where his quickest route to success lay. Essex was swift to reward his friends. As the Queen's favourite, the rewards could be high indeed.

Jack shaded his eyes against the sun as the Queen released her hawk. It soared into the sky, then swooped down with the speed of a striking arrow, its talons locking into the back of a young rabbit. The courtiers dutifully cheered as they jostled for position closer to their Sovereign. The speed of Jack's chestnut gelding had kept him ahead of the rest and now, at her side, he watched her smile with tight-lipped satisfaction. When Elizabeth's brittle stare rested upon him, he felt his body burn with anticipation.

'A splendid kill, madam,' he said.

She looked at his empty wrist and raised an enquiring brow. 'You do not carry a hawk?'

To his ears her voice carried a flicker of contempt. His pleasure curdled. He sat rigid in the saddle, resenting even from the Queen any reminder of his lowly birth. 'My skill is with the sword and at the helm of a ship.' His forced smile did not reach his eyes and he saw her stare harden. It was not his way to cringe or fawn. The Queen often responded favourably to Essex's outspoken boldness. The risk was great. If he offended . . . inwardly he shuddered. Banishment would be the least he would face. Keeping his head held high, he continued, adding a touch of irony to his words which was daringly short of insolence, 'Falconry is a noble art, madam. When I hunt, I need no other but my own hand to bring my quarry down. Whether it be boar, stag or Spaniard.'

She did not reply. The compressed lines of her mouth warned him that disaster might at any moment crash around his head. It chilled his blood. The Queen's moods were uncertain, volatile and unpredictable. Had he gone too far? Boldly he faced her, though his stomach quaked. He would not back down. As he continued to hold her imperious stare, he knew he would rather sail headlong into an enemy fleet than again bear the agony of awaiting her displeasure. There was a flicker of amusement in the dark eyes, then a muscle twitched at the corner of her carmined mouth, followed by a bark of laughter.

'God's breath, you are a refreshing rascal, Stoneham.'

Jack relaxed. His gamble had paid off. Elizabeth had no liking for milksops, but it was a dangerous path to risk challenging her wit or majesty. A wrong word could turn her amusement to volcanic fury. Now, thank God, she was smiling.

'My bold adventurer, that chestnut of yours is a magnificent animal.' She ran a practised stare over the gelding's body. 'It has speed, stamina and grace. Tomorrow we shall hunt the stag. You must join us. I would see this prowess of which you boast.'

Behind her invitation was the sting of a scorpion, but

Jack had no misgivings as he bowed in acknowledgement. He knew himself the equal of any man in the field. Elizabeth would discover that his was no idle boast. Seeing her about to turn her attention upon another, he saw an opportunity to ingratiate himself further in her eyes.

'If the animal pleases Your Majesty – ' he was all humility, false though it was ' – Red Sun is yours.'

'A generous gift. Mayhap too generous for a sea captain.' Her oval face was stern and imposing. That sharp assessing stare impaled him, all humour stripped from her eyes. 'Unless you seek greater rewards for this generosity?'

Jack knew he had blundered. Fool! he cursed himself. That was a clumsy gesture and she has seen through it. He was quick to recover, his voice low and persuasive. 'When a man would willingly give his life for Your Majesty – ' He paused, allowing her time to remember his exploits in the defeat of the Armada. To his alarm, her eyes glinted like black ice – and he knew how treacherous that could be. He added quickly, 'Much as I would miss Red Sun, what worth is a gift if it is given without sacrifice?' He turned upon her the twisted smile which had softened every woman's heart he had met. 'I fear, though, I shall envy the horse for he will be favoured by the gentle touch of your hands and hear soft words of praise, which all here would die to achieve.'

'Stoneham, you are a rogue!' There was a wicked gleam in her eyes. Again he was walking over quicksand. 'You know how to flatter an old woman and make her feel young again.'

'It was not flattery.' Jack was astounded to find that he meant those words. Elizabeth had a presence which made him forget the wrinkles that time had carved beneath the thick mask of powder. 'You will never be old, madam. You are our sun, and the glory and beauty of that never diminishes.'

The sincerity of his tone pleased her. Playfully, if painfully, she rapped him on the forearm with her riding crop. 'Keep your horse, my bold adventurer. Horse and master suit each other well.'

Jack glowed from the warmth of the compliment. Elizabeth had been impressed by Red Sun. There was a way he could serve her and at the same time repay a debt to a friend. He owed Mark for saving Gabriellen's life. Elizabeth was passionately fond of horses. A recommendation would

269

stand them both in good stead. 'In truth, Red Sun is not the finest of his breed. Perhaps Your Majesty has heard of the Rowan strain?'

The courtiers fidgeted restlessly around them, jealous of the time and attention Jack had claimed from their mistress. Every antagonistic glower confirmed his growing favour with the Queen. It was a heady power, and one he was not so reckless as to allow to go to his head.

The royal stables were Elizabeth's pride. Her interest was again caught, eager to learn more. 'My Lord of Leicester mentioned the quality of this Rowan strain. He was not a man who judged horseflesh lightly.' Her eyes dulled with pain as she spoke of her dead favourite.

She turned to Essex, whose handsome face was strained with suppressed anger. Clearly he was furious at the attention the Queen had given Jack. He cursed himself for a fool. If he lost Essex's goodwill, he could lose everything. He needed Essex as a friend, not an enemy.

'What says my Master of the Horse?' Elizabeth queried.

'The Rowan strain are magnificent beasts. So much so that I had already resolved to approach Mr Rowan. Your Majesty has had more weighty matters to trouble you in recent weeks than the consideration of improving your stables.'

'Is that so?' A coating of frost touched her voice. 'I alone would be the judge of that.'

It was a warning to Essex not to presume. Jack saw Essex's hand move towards his sword hilt, the cords of his neck above his ruff showing his battle to contain his rage. Dear God, Jack thought with shock, did Essex not know the peril of showing his jealousy and ill-temper in the Queen's presence? Men had been banished – nay, sent to the Tower – for less. Since Leicester's death, Essex's rise at Court had been with the dazzling speed of a shooting star. It could burn itself out just as quickly. The moment was fraught with tension. Jack could feel the courtiers around them poised in anticipation of what must surely be the favourite's fall from grace. He touched his spur to Red Sun's side. The gelding reared, knocking into Essex's mount and earning Jack a peal of abuse from the nobleman who quickly brought his horse back under control.

'A spirited animal,' Elizabeth commented dryly. 'You guide a ship more ably than you hunt, Stoneham. But then, the thrills of a sea chase are often so much more rewarding.'

The reference to his privateering was unmistakable, a trade she publicly deplored whilst privately glorying in the share which filled her treasury's coffers. A snigger from behind Jack brought a flash of anger to his eyes. He quickly hid it, his manner and smile nonchalant when he answered Elizabeth. 'I was not born to the saddle but to the sea. It is there I would serve Your Majesty.'

'As indeed you have.' Elizabeth laughed wickedly, a barb in every word. 'By filling my coffers at the expense of the Spanish. Some would name you pirate!'

Jack felt a chill as cold as the North Sea seep into his veins. Pirates were summarily hung, or tied to posts set in the river bed to drown at high tide. 'What would Your Majesty name me?'

It was a daring challenge. A hush settled over the party as the courtiers awaited her reply. Nothing delighted them more than to witness a man's disgrace. Elizabeth cast a speculative look over them, her voice teasing but her eyes filled with contempt. 'You are, as is every man here, a soldier of fortune.'

Jack held her stare. He swallowed against the dryness of his throat, the ties of his ruff cutting into the back of his sweating neck like the sharpened blade of an axe. Elizabeth's expression was impassive. Then, unexpectedly, she said: 'Tonight, after the dancing, I plan a small card party in my anterooms. Be pleased to join us, Captain Stoneham.'

Without waiting for his reply, she turned to Essex, laughing as she kicked her mount into a canter. The spell of the Queen's intoxicating gaze was broken. It was as though a candle had been snuffed, leaving Jack in a darkened room. The invitation had earned him a curious glower from Essex. He knew then that the Queen was using him as a pawn to teach the favourite that he was not indispensable. No man was. Jack determined never to forget that. Greater men than he had failed and paid the price.

What was her hold over men? A magnetic personality coupled with the potency of supreme power? For Jack it certainly was not sexual. Though perhaps if she had been thirty years younger, it would have been different. Thank God, it was not. He thrust away that thought, as he would contact with a leper. Elizabeth was a dazzling prize, but not quite flesh and blood. Not that he believed her virginal

271

as she would have the world think her. The passion was there in her fierce indomitable spirit. England was her true lover. She'd not share that with any man. God knows, Leicester had been panting like a lapdog after her for nigh on thirty years. If she had shared her bed with him, she certainly had no intention of sharing her crown. But the fascination was there, captivating Jack as it did every man who served her. Her briefest word was capable of elating him or casting him into black despair. To be near Elizabeth was to be drawn dangerously near a dark, voracious flame.

In her fifty-fifth year she was no longer beautiful, but her carefully painted face was arresting. She was an enigma, a maze of complexities, ultimately feminine, capricious and prevaricating. But always below that bejewelled, frivolously dressed surface, was the iron-willed monarch with the heart and stomach of a King – as she had so proudly proclaimed during her speech to her troops at Tilbury. Jack did not doubt it. He would have added that she had the survival instincts of a lion, with teeth and claws to match.

The Queen's party again broke into a gallop, but Jack was too absorbed to take any pleasure from the hunt. He had not survived the rigours of an apprenticeship in the Underworld to meet an untimely end at Court. The fisherman's son had come a long way. He would go much farther. Tonight he would have won admittance to Elizabeth's inner sanctum.

A stab of regret clouded his moment of triumph. The Queen played cards until the early hours of the morning, and she had also as good as commanded him to attend the earlier dancing. Again there would be no time to visit the Bel Savage Inn. No time to make his peace with Gabriellen. An image of her mocked him, damn her. The triumph of his advancement at Court turned to bile in his throat. For a month he'd tried to forget the playwright's daughter. Within his grasp was the future he craved. He stared at the Queen riding ahead, Essex now a respectful pace or two behind her. Success at Court meant one walked a high and perilous tightrope. Danger had always excited him.

He urged Red Sun faster, until he was level with Essex. The Earl glowered across at him, having labelled him a rival to the Queen's affections. Jack smiled.

'We both have the interests of Her Majesty at heart, my lord. I would serve her best through you.'

Essex curled his proud lip back into a sneer. Jack held that assessing gaze, his own voice hard. 'I do not give my allegiance easily, my lord. We are both ambitious. What sense is there in working against each other? I would be your ally, not enemy. The Queen has expressed an interest in the Rowan horses. I happen to know that Mr Rowan is in London. Red Sun was one of Rowan's first season of foals. In his stable he has two year olds which make Red Sun look like a broken-down nag. What finer gift could you give Her Majesty to commemorate her Accession Day next month than such a horse?' Seeing the Earl's continued scepticism, Jack added: 'I recommend Rowan because he's a friend of mine. He once did me a service.'

Essex made no comment. After a long moment when Jack's heartbeat matched the pace of his gelding's drumming hooves, the Earl gave a slight nod.

'Get Rowan to bring some of his horses to Court. I will look at them.'

It was enough. From that moment Jack would serve Essex. Therein would lie his road to fortune. He fell back amongst the other riders, their dour looks proof of their jealousy that he had won the attention of both the Queen and her new favourite. It had been easier than he dared hope.

Again, without warning, a pair of fiery green eyes rose to his mind and mocked him. Devil take her for an enticing witch! He could not get Gabriellen out of his blood. He stilled a burst of laughter. Success had intoxicated him. He saw his dreams unfurling before him. Everything he desired would be his. *Everything*.

'So you're to leave me too, Mark?' said Gabriellen. They walked slowly through the riverside gardens, avoiding the noisy crowds who were leaving the bear-baiting pit. Mark led her to a stone seat and drew her down beside him. She looked at him accusingly. 'Did you bring me to The Rose to see the play as a farewell treat?' The pleasure of the afternoon withered. During the month since her quarrel with Jack when he had stormed away, Mark had become her confidant. She saw the Welshman only once a week, but it was to him that she poured out her worries over the troupe.

There was still no patron. Anthony Culpepper had

273

already joined another company. Last night Cesare and Umberto, their differences healed with his departure, had told her that they had received an offer from Lord Mincham's players. She had been bitterly disappointed that Lord Mincham had not acknowledged her letter, though Mark had told her that he was currently at his country estate, laid low with the ague.

How much longer could Esmond afford to keep the remainder of the troupe together? Robin was growing restless and Gabriellen suspected that he, too, had received another offer. Poggs alone had assured her that he had no intention of abandoning her father. His loyalty touched Gabriellen, but she was realistic. Without an income, Esmond would surely bankrupt himself before winter was out if he continued to support the players. Also, unless they left for Chichester within two weeks, the Sussex roads would become a quagmire, completely impassable until the first frost.

Could she bear to leave London? Daily she hoped Jack would seek her out. Had their love meant so little to him that one quarrel had destroyed it? If so, he had not loved her. And that she would not believe.

Mark took her hand, squeezing it through the thickness of their gloves. Somewhere near the riverbank a dog which had been continually howling began to yelp. Diverted, Mark frowned and glanced briefly towards the sound. He hated to see animals abused. His defence of Soulful the bear had proved that. It would not have surprised Gabriellen if he had gone to see what was wrong with the animal. Instead he turned back to her, his eyes filled with concern.

'I wanted to be sure that you were all right before I left. Are you returning to Chichester?'

'What choice have we? Father is again in debt. You can imagine the cost of supporting the players for so many unproductive weeks. That is why we had to move from the Bel Savage to cheaper rooms. It will be less expensive to live in Chichester. Not that we can travel until Nan is brought to bed, which cannot be long now. For her sake, I pray so. She's so large she cannot walk. I'm worried about her, and Father too. There's been no word from him for two weeks. According to Poggs, he disappears like this two or three times a year. But how could he do it now, when Nan needs him?'

'Esmond is a law unto himself,' Mark said with a frown.

Gabriellen hesitated. She needed to talk of her fears to someone. But was it fair to burden Mark, since he was leaving London? The howls and yelps from the dog continued and as they both looked towards the river, she could not help saying, 'What if Father has come to harm?'

Mark held her troubled stare. 'Esmond is safe. I made discreet enquiries about him. He was seen four nights ago.'

'Where?'

'He was seen, let that suffice.' Mark became absorbed in wiping some dust off the toe of his boot.

'I know Father's habits.' Gabriellen voiced her impatience. 'Do not patronise me with half-truths. I'm not so squirrel-witted that I would swoon should you mention he was in a gaming or bawdy house.'

'No, I do not expect you would.' He raised a brow in mock reproof. 'I was considering your sensibilities as a woman.'

'Sensibilities be damned!' She looked up at the cloud-mottled sky in exasperation. Drawing a deep breath, she controlled the urge to shake him. 'I'm sleepless with worry over him. My weeks on the road have shown me the disreputable side of his life. Was he at Nell Lovegood's establishment?'

'What do you know of such a place?'

He sounded so shocked, she could not contain a dimpled smile. 'Nan has mentioned it many times, especially when Esmond stays out until the early hours of the morning. I believe it is a favourite haunt of his.'

'It was at Nell Lovegood's that he was seen.'

The now frantic yelping of the dog claimed her attention. They both stood up.

'I'm sorry, Ellen,' said Mark. 'I must see what ails the dog. It's obviously in great pain.'

She was already walking ahead of him, unable to hear the sound of an animal in distress without helping. At the sight which greeted them at the riverbank, her blood boiled. A liver and white mongrel was tied to a stake driven into the river bed. Now, as the tide was rising, the terrified dog was swimming frantically round and round on its short rope to stop itself from drowning. As though that torture was not cruel enough, four youths were pelting the poor creature with stones, and its head and back were already bloody.

Mark yelled at the boys: 'Stop that, you damned hellions!'

Seeing his determined run towards them, they backed away and began to run along the muddy river's edge. Mark caught two and boxed their ears, but the mournful howls and yelps of the dog stopped him punishing them further, and he let them go.

'Get back, Ellen,' he commanded as he retraced his steps.

Gabriellen ignored him. Twice she had seen the dog's head disappear under the murky water. Holding her cumbersome skirts high she ran down to the river mud and plunged up to her ankles in oozing slime, immediately losing a shoe.

Mark overtook her, shouting over his shoulder, 'Go back to the bank, Ellen. You'll ruin your clothes.'

Retreating, she watched as he reached the struggling dog. Water flowed up to his thighs as he cut the rope with his dagger and lifted the trembling animal into his arms. As though sensing that Mark would not harm it, it burrowed against the warmth of his chest, pitiful whimpers testimony to its suffering. Seeing the blood which covered the dog's head, the scarlet stain darkening Mark's doublet, Gabriellen sat down on the grassy bank and tore a strip from her cotton petticoat. She handed it to Mark as he lowered himself beside her.

He took it wordlessly, his dark head bent over the whimpering dog. It lifted its muzzle. Sorrowful brown eyes regarded them through blood-matted lashes. In one place the skull was laid open to the bone.

'The poor creature,' Gabriellen said. 'Those despicable brutes! I'd like to get my hands on them. A good whipping is what they need.'

Mark finished binding the dog's head, the exhausted animal pressing closer to his chest. With a chuckle, he looked at Gabriellen. 'You're a bloodthirsty soul. And you've ruined your clothes.'

'In just cause! Sweet Jesu, I cannot stand to see needless suffering.'

The river mud had been icy and her sodden feet were numb with cold. It would take all Nan's skill to repair the damage to her gown. How dare Mark laugh at her! She regarded his dishevelled figure. There was little of the original colour left showing on his mud-streaked doublet and trunks. His hose and boots were unrecognisable. She wrinkled her nose. The stagnant stench of rotting garbage clung to his clothes. And he had the audacity to mock her state! For once she could think of nothing pertinent to say and resorted to a peevish: 'You should see yourself, Mark Rowan. There's even mud on your face. You look like a guttersnipe.'

He raised a dark brow, goading her to unreasonable fury. He grinned unabashed, eyes bright with merriment. 'Then we are a pair of guttersnipes. How are we going to get you back to the inn? Have you considered that?'

Gabriellen stared down at her billowing skirts. The hem of her gown and petticoats were encrusted with foul-smelling mud. A grubby pink toe peeked through the torn foot of her hose where she had lost her shoe. There was something ludicrous in the sight of that protruding toe. Suddenly the absurdity of their position and the appalling state of her attire struck her. Her shoulders began to shake and she bent forward, holding her face in her hands.

'Oh Lord, Ellen,' Mark said worriedly. 'You're not going into hysterics over your gown, are you?' Then, to his relief, she raised her face and he saw that she was laughing.

Mark stared at her as though her wits had addled. It was enough to send her into further convulsions. At last she managed to say, 'Look at us! I feel like a naughty child. Aunt Dotty was always scolding me for dirtying or tearing my clothes in just such an escapade.'

'You are an unusual woman. Have you no thought for your ruined clothes?'

She shrugged and stroked the dog's back. 'A contrasting border will put my gown to rights. I fear that this little mite will take longer to mend.'

The Welshman's broad grin encompassed the two of them. 'I just hope I can get you back to the inn without us both being arrested as vagabonds.' They pressed their heads together as their sense of the ridiculous overwhelmed them both. Between their bodies the dog whimpered softly. His pain sobered them, but tears of merriment remained in their eyes as Mark helped Gabriellen to her feet.

'What shall we do with the poor wretch?' she said, laying her hand upon the wet quivering body.

277

'There's a day or two before I leave for Wales. Hopefully by then he will be strong enough to travel.' Mark bent over the dog as it lifted its head to lick his cheek.

'What breed is he?' Gabriellen asked, suppressing the urge to take the forlorn animal in her arms. He was settled and comfortable in Mark's hold. 'From the looks of those long ears, he must be part spaniel.'

'He's not much more than a pup. Twelve weeks old at most. From the shape of his ribcage, I'd say there's alaunt or greyhound in his blood. I think I'll call him Hywel.'

Gabriellen frowned. 'Howl! That's rather unkind. Wouldn't you have howled if you were being stoned to death?'

'Not howl!' Mark tutted. 'Though I suppose it's too much to expect an Englishwoman to know any Welsh history. Hywel was a Welsh Prince. A friend of King Athelstan.'

'Then it's a good name. If my Welsh history is so bad,' she cast him a saucy look from beneath her lashes, 'it's because I've never had a handsome Welshman to instruct me before.'

Throughout the walk back over London Bridge and along Cheapside, they could not contain bouts of laughter at the number of disdainful stares directed at them. There was still an air of celebration in the streets after the defeat of the Armada. Sadly, though, the number of grey, starving faces, or limbless men begging in doorways and on church steps, had increased. Whilst Drake and captains like Jack were welcomed as heroes, these poor wretches – the common sailors wounded in battle – were forgotten and neglected.

As they turned into Ludgate, walking past the Bel Savage to a cheaper inn where the players now stayed, Gabriellen's thoughts were upon Mark's return to Wales. Her mood sobered. 'How is Jesmaine? Are you taking her with you?'

'She refuses to leave London.' Mark did not seem unduly concerned. 'Since she set herself up as an astrologer, people are flocking to her to have their horoscopes cast. I cannot blame her for not wanting to give up her newfound fame in order to shut herself away on a remote Welsh farm.'

'Surely if she loves you?'

He smiled wryly and shook his head, eyes for once solemn. 'Love is never that simple, is it?'

She looked away, unable to meet his sympathetic stare.

'I will return to London in the spring.' His voice brightened. 'And I have good news. The Earl of Essex has expressed a wish to inspect the best of my two year olds. Her Majesty passed comment upon Red Sun. Essex wished to purchase a mare for the Queen's Accession Day present. He was furious when I told him that the ideal mare, by far the most superior of all my stock, would not be for sale until the spring.' Mark laughed. 'Essex consigned me to the devil for an impertinent knave. He's not used to having his will thwarted. He demanded the mare immediately. I refused, saying that I would not surrender second best to the Queen.'

'That was your chance to win acclaim for the Rowan Strain.' Gabriellen was aghast. 'How could you throw it away?'

Mark grinned, his eyebrows arching into a dark curl which had fallen forward over his brow. 'I persuaded him to come round to my way of thinking.'

Gabriellen stared at him with astonishment which turned rapidly to admiration. 'The Earl of Essex is more proud than Lucifer and has a temper to match. And you persuaded him . . .' She stopped short and flung her arms round his shoulders with a delighted laugh. 'Oh, Mark, you always know how to chase my melancholy away. I shall miss you whilst you are in Wales.'

Hywel gave a protesting whimper and, contrite, she drew back to discover Mark looking at her with unusual solemnity. When he did not speak she averted her gaze to a dried-out holly bush which the light breeze was slapping against the wattle and daub wall of the inn. The bush was brown with age and almost devoid of its leaves and berries. Every inn, whether in town or country, had such a bush above its door. It denoted that the establishment was a tavern. They had reached the inn entrance and as Mark turned to go, he gasped. Looking guilty, he drew a sealed letter from inside his leather doublet.

'I almost forgot this, what with arriving at The Rose with barely time to spare before the play began. Then the distraction afterwards . . .' He shrugged and handed it to her with a grin. 'Jack was with Essex yesterday. He asked me to give you this.'

Gabriellen snatched off her glove and tore at the seal,

breaking a nail in her eagerness. It contained a single line. 'I shall come to you Thursday night. Jack.'

She closed her eyes and rested against the wall of the inn. Her relief was so great she could not be angry at the summary way he had dismissed his five-week absence.

The sand in the hourglass had swallowed another hour. Gabriellen rubbed the windowpane misted by her breath and stared out into the inn yard. The lighted flambeaux were burning low and in the road outside she heard the watch calling the midnight hour. Jack would not come now. She dragged herself away from the window and closed the shutter. Pulling at the ties of the narrow ruff at her wrist, she scowled at the coffer holding the untouched flagon of malmsey and platters of cold chicken with its now congealed cinnamon and wine sauce, game pies, and Jack's favourite dish, date slices with spiced wine. The candle stub had burnt to its last inch, the intimate glow which it gave out mocking her. She pulled the pearl-studded French cap from her head and tossed it onto the bed. The violence with which she tugged free the pins from her hair made her wince. Shaking her hair to her shoulders, she glared accusingly at the door. Was the ordeal of loving always this painful?

She turned towards the bed to struggle with the lacings at her back, a frustrating and almost impossible task. There was no one to help her. Agnes had retired hours ago. Above her head a bird or rat padded over the attic timbers. Outside the east wind banged a loose shutter and a sudden splatter of hail was gusted against the window pane. A miserable night, she thought, as she wriggled to free herself of the stubborn laces. Failing, she cursed long and roundly.

'Is that any way to greet your lover?' The soft voice came from the shadows by the door.

Whirling round, Gabriellen stared at Jack's tall figure silhouetted by the moonlight from the gallery. Then the door closed. Her anger forgotten, she launched herself into his open arms to receive his kiss, rough with hunger and desire.

'My love, my own sweet love,' he said gruffly against her ear, before his mouth again claimed hers, his hands impatient with the restricting layers of her clothing.

*

280

The first glow of dawn penetrated the room as Gabriellen started awake. She shook the fuzziness of sleep from her mind. What noise had disturbed her so brusquely? Her heart was hammering against her breastbone. Then it came again, the piercing scream prickling the hairs on her scalp.

'Christ's bones! Someone is being murdered!' Jack sat up.

Gabriellen swung her feet to the floor and reached for her night wrap. 'I think it's Nan. I must do what I can.' She thrust her feet into velvet slippers and hurried to the door. Opening it, she paused. 'Later we must speak, Jack.'

'I do not know when I can get away from Court.' In the dim light which kept his figure shadowed from her, the wariness in his voice was chillingly apparent. Nan screamed again. Gabriellen had no time to spare for him. Their night of love had changed nothing. 'That is for you to decide,' she said in a hard voice which did not sound like her own. 'Father intends to return to Chichester for the winter.'

She shut the door on his uncharitable oath and hurried to Nan's room, a few doors down the gallery. Agnes and Moll, the landlord's wife, were bent over the straining figure on the birthing stool.

'Gabby, you should not be here,' Agnes said over her shoulder. ''Tis not fitting, an unmarried . . .'

'Oh, enough of that nonsense,' Gabriellen interrupted impatiently. 'Has the midwife been sent for?'

'Aye, two hours past,' Agnes wailed. 'She's sobering up in the kitchen. Cupshot slut!'

'Surely we can get another?' Gabriellen was appalled that Nan must suffer the inefficiency of a drunken midwife.

'Bertha is the best there is hereabouts.' Moll sniffed and wiped her hands on the apron which covered her enormous girth. 'I've had ten and Bertha delivered them all. Five of them are still alive.'

She seemed proud that five of her children had survived. Gabriellen was shocked that five had died.

''Sides, after ten of them, I knows what to do.' Moll turned back to Nan who was slumped forward and groaning. 'It won't be long now. Head's coming.'

Gabriellen took Nan's hand as the next pain gripped her. She spoke soothingly, feeling useless and helpless.

'Has Esmond returned?' Nan asked between pains.

Gabriellen shook her head, angry that her father should

have so little thought for his mistress at this time. She knelt at Nan's side, ignoring the woman's nails digging into her forearms as yet another pain attacked her. Somehow she found the right words of comfort.

The sun was already over the stable roof before Laurence Angel was born. For a twin he was a lusty child, the power of his screams evidence of his sturdy constitution. His twin was not so eager to appear before an audience. The sun arced across the sky, followed by the moon. By dawn the next morning the birth room stank of sweat and blood, the air tense as Bertha and Moll still struggled to turn the breech birth. Nan no longer screamed. She was slipping into unconsciousness.

Esmond burst into the room.

'This is no place for a man,' Bertha shouted.

Gabriellen held out Laurence to him. 'You have a son, Father, but the other babe is in breech.'

An animal groan came from the bed and Esmond pushed past the midwife to look down at Nan's face, contorted with pain. 'Do something for her!' Esmond's eyes were wild. 'Damn me for a knave, I should have been here.'

'It must be the babe or the mother,' Bertha proclaimed. 'Else both will die.'

'Save the mother,' Esmond said, backing out of the door.

Gabriellen followed her father. There was nothing she could do for Nan, and from Esmond's stricken look he needed her.

'Save Nan,' she said, looking back at the women bent over the straining figure on the bed. 'I pray we are not too late even for that.'

Chapter Nineteen

Winter in Chichester was bleak and unrelenting. Nan spent her days propped on a day bed before the parlour fire, her recovery slow after Laurence's birth. She never complained but there was sadness in her eyes at the frequency with which Esmond stayed away from home. Her father's absences worried Gabriellen. He was drinking heavily and showed little interest in his writing. She alone knew that most of the latest play *Unholy Revenge* was written by herself without any help from him. It was based on Wildboar Tom's escapades. Where Esmond had seen the play as a bitter recrimination against his ancestor, Gabriellen had made it into a tragi-comedy.

As spring approached, Esmond became more belligerent, his moods unpredictable. The atmosphere in the house grew strained. It was a relief for Gabriellen when Jack sailed to Chichester and took her aboard *The Swift*. They had not seen each other for several weeks and were together for three days whilst he sailed back to Deptford to oversee the repairs of *The Bonaventure Elizabeth*. That Jack was prepared to risk the Queen's wrath to spend time with her proved the measure of his love. For that she could forgive his boundless ambition, and she no longer regarded the Queen as a rival. Yet he never mentioned marriage and she was too proud to raise the subject. Loving him so passionately, she bore the dishonour of being his mistress with fortitude. But should he ever betray her . . .

The thought set her mouth into a thin line. It was a subject she refused to contemplate. She trusted Jack. He would never betray her.

Assured of his love, she had returned to Chichester happier than she had been for months. Her arrival was met with uneasy glances from Poggs and Agnes. Before they could speak, Esmond swayed drunkenly into the room.

'My daughter,' he slurred, 'Stoneham's whore, has returned. I won't have you cheapening yourself this way. It's to end, do you hear me? Or else the knave must wed you.'

'As you wed Nan to spare her shame?' Gabriellen flared. She would not have her love for Jack debased, especially by Esmond who was no better himself. 'What's good enough for the father is good enough for the daughter.'

'Is it, by God!' Esmond snarled, cuffing her ears so hard she crashed back against the wall. 'Is this how Dorothy brought you up?'

Putting a hand to her ringing head, she glared at him, unrepentant and defiant. 'I love Jack. We cannot marry yet. He needs more time at Court to secure his future. He means to marry me, Father. I'll not give him up.'

The heat of her stare made him grow pale. He shook his head and sank down on to a chair. 'Can you not see that you demean yourself? I want better for you than a buccaneer. The man's an ambitious rogue.'

'You judge me too harshly, Father.' She swallowed her anger, needing to make him see reason. 'Jack loves me.'

He took her hand, becoming maudlin as he patted it. 'I should have warned you against such men.' He stood up and rubbed a hand across his eyes. 'You are still an innocent in many ways. I would not see you hurt.'

'Have faith in me. But I'll not have Jack spoken ill of.' When his lips turned down in censure, her resolution to remain calm faltered. 'Are you so pure and blameless that you can condemn another?' she accused. 'What of the hours that you're away from the house? Are you gambling again? How much money have we left?'

Esmond flushed. 'Devil take you for an unnatural wretch,' he stormed as he moved unsteadily from the room. 'I am the master here and answerable to no one. Especially a young chit of an ungrateful daughter.'

'That's not fair, Esmond,' Poggs defended Gabriellen.

He swung round at the door and glowered at the clown. 'Keep out of this, Poggs, or get out. Damn it, haven't I kept the lot of you for years?'

'Father! That's unjust.' Gabriellen ran after him. Poggs took her arm and stopped her.

'Let him go. It's the drink talking.'

'He should not speak to you that way.' Gabriellen shook

her head. 'You've known him longer than anyone.'

'And it is easy to forgive an old friend who is talking in his cups. He drinks to forget his worries. The creditors were around again today.'

'How much do we owe?'

Poggs sighed. 'You know Esmond, he won't say. But you're not to worry. Something will turn up. It always does. Esmond has never failed us.'

Mark quickened his pace through the warren of London streets. The evening mist crept up with the stealth of a thief, partially obscuring the two figures he was following. He had been observing their movements all winter. Tonight Sir John Garfield and Sir Henry Kettering had arranged a secret meeting in the cellar of a disused warehouse. Mark expected all the names he had learned from Prew's messenger to be present. Once the men were within, he intended to listen to their conversation. If they were guilty of treason, the guard were alerted and hiding in the alleys off Cheapside awaiting his summons.

Few lights thrust out their golden haloes to penetrate the grey haze. The last of the shops were being shuttered: mercers rolling up their velvets and silks; silversmiths locking away their precious plate; 'prentices swept and sluiced bloodied sawdust and debris from the slaughterhouses which were pounced on by scavaging dogs. Respectable citizens were safe behind barred doors. This was the time for the nocturnal miscreants to scuttle from their dens. The bankrupt or felon who feared arrest or recognition by the law during the day, now walked with jaunty step, fearless under cover of night. The muffled figure of a lawyer, doctor or clergyman hurried on its way. Men who during daylight hours appeared sober and sour-faced, turned hypocrite and degenerate as they slunk to sleazy taverns or trugging-houses, pickling their wits with cheap liquor and buying any vice for a penny. The street-bawds retreated into the noise and warmth of the stews; the cozeners and sneak-thieves, with pockets bulging, assembled in the lairs of their Upright Men, to be paid for their stolen wares.

Disguised as a ragged beggar Mark kept to the shadows as they approached a dilapidated warehouse near the river. Mark ducked into a dark alleyway as Kettering and a man Mark guessed was a Jesuit priest cast furtive glances around

285

them before disappearing into a roofless building. A few minutes later Garfield and two other men arrived, then four more. Mark nodded to his accomplice on the opposite side of the street, indicating that he would follow the conspirators inside. He was guided by the direction of their voices and silently hid himself behind a central pillar. The men were squatting on the floor around a single candlestick and the priest was just coming to the end of intoning a blessing. Ten minutes later Mark had all the information he needed. It was another plot against the Queen's life. One of the men was a glover by trade and they intended to poison the fabric of a pair of jewelled riding gauntlets sent with a petition to Her Majesty. Still undetected by the conspirators, he crept from the cellar. Outside he signalled his accomplice to fetch the guard and stood back to wait, ready to follow if any of the men should leave before the guard arrived.

He breathed on to his cupped hands to bring some warmth to their half-frozen joints, and settled into the shadows to wait. Mark cursed the tardiness of the guard as he scanned the street. From behind a high wooden fence an upstairs light reflected off a rising metal object. Mark watched as the hook on the end of a long pole rose up from the street to hover outside an opened dark window above a prosperous chandler's shop. There was another glint of metal before the hook was skilfully manoeuvred through the window. Moments later it was drawn out, a pearl-studded cap dangling like a landed trout from the point. The Angler, or Hooker, as this type of thief was named, was practised in his art. The long pole appeared a second time, but Mark returned his attention to the warehouse.

The mist was thickening and was icy in its penetration of his ragged garments. Suddenly he felt a tingling at the back of his neck which alerted him to impending danger. That sixth sense warned that he, the watcher, was also being observed.

Pressing back against the wooden wall of another warehouse, he surveyed his surroundings. The Angler had departed with his spoils and the street ahead and the dark alley looked deserted. Yet he knew someone was behind him. He could smell the rancid odour of an unwashed body which stood as still as himself, making no sound. From the other end of the street he heard the purposeful tread of the advancing guard. He winced at the heavy footsteps of the dozen men. They sounded like a legion of Roman soldiers on the rampage in the distorting atmosphere of the mist. Undoubtedly they would alert the men they came to arrest. There was a shout within the warehouse; at the same moment the guard broke through the door.

Several things happened at once. The guard burst in. A pistol was fired and shouts broke out. The stench of unwashed flesh was closer to Mark and he was about to turn and face whoever was creeping up on him when he heard running footsteps, the clatter of someone colliding with an empty barrel and cursing before running on. Mark leapt out of his hiding place and grabbed the fleeing conspirator.

Careful even now to disguise his Welsh accent, he shouted to the guard emerging from the warehouse: 'There's another over here.'

Mark rejoined his accomplice as they watched the guard march away. From the prisoners he had seen, he knew his work but partially done. Kettering, Garfield, the priest, the glover, and three others were captured. Another Catholic nobleman had escaped, together with an unknown man. Neither had Victor Prew been present. But the merchant was a wily intriguer and since the meeting in the churchyard with Templeton, and the interception of the letter from the fair, Mark had no other evidence that Prew was involved with the Catholics who would depose the Queen. He had only his gut instinct and still meant to unravel the truth.

'Damn you, Rowan!' The hunched figure in the alleyway spat on to the ground as his quarry escaped him. He resheathed his dagger and leaned on his long hooked pole as he hung back in the shadows. He'd been within three yards of stabbing the Welshman in the back when that damned guard appeared.

Cecil Gubbett jabbed a finger in the air in an obscene gesture in the direction Mark Rowan had taken. Despite the disguise, he had recognised the Welshman. And what was a stallion-man doing in this district? Those guards had not chanced upon the meeting in the warehouse. Rowan was behind their presence, he'd warrant. There was more to the Welshman than he'd thought. Gubbett rubbed his knobbly hands together. He might have missed his chance to get even with Rowan tonight, but his time would come. Rowan would pay dearly for banning him from the lucrative spoils to be had at the fairs. The hunchback grinned evilly. Next time Rowan ventured into the London night, he'd get more than he bargained for.

Late one night in April Esmond reeled into the house, rousing everyone from their beds.

'Get packed. We leave for London as soon as the city gates are opened in the morning.'

Gabriellen could only guess from what trouble her father was fleeing. Most likely mounting debts.

Once back in London, Esmond took the latest play to the Master of Revels office in the old converted priory of St John at Clerkenwell. After he obtained his licence for the play to be performed, he disappeared for two weeks. Now the last of the money he'd left for them had gone.

Gabriellen answered the knock on their door. To her dismay it was the landlord of the shabby rooms they rented.

'My father is not at home, Mr Hoggard.' She held her weight against the door when he tried to force it open.

Hoggard rubbed his stubbly jaw, which was infested with open sores, and leered through the crack. He licked his lips as he regarded Agnes's rump which swayed from side to side as she scrubbed the wooden floor.

'What do you want, Mr Hoggard?' Gabriellen demanded. Laurence had begun to cry and she was impatient to tend him.

'Angel owes two weeks' rent,' Hoggard said in ugly tones, his breath reeking of rotten teeth and onions. 'Pay up by tonight, or me lads will be round 'ere to throw yer out. An' they'll make bloody sure I ain't out of pocket for me pains.'

'You will have your rent, Mr Hoggard,' Gabriellen answered, and shut the door in his face.

'I better 'ad,' Hoggard shouted through the keyhole. 'Don't come the high-flown gentry mort with me. Pay up or you're out.'

Agnes sat back on her heels and wiped a tendril of hair from her cheek with a soapy hand. 'That one means what he says. He turned a widow and her four children out during that thunderstorm last week.'

'He'll not turn us out.' Gabriellen's hands were on her hips. 'I'd swear Father said he'd paid the rent until the end of the month.' She scowled at the door. 'Hoggard by name, pig by nature.'

Poggs took down his flute from the shelf above the hearth. 'Don't you fret yourself, Gabby. You'll have the rent by nightfall.'

'No, Poggs,' she said, touched by his loyalty. 'That villain is trying to cheat us. The rent was paid. I'll not have you playing in the streets – you're one of England's finest clowns. The best troupes have asked you to join them since our return. Why do you stay with us?'

Poggs grinned. 'I don't put a price on loyalty. Esmond made me what I am. A little humility now and again is good for us. Good Lord, Gabby, you'd not have me become as affected as Cornelius Hope, would you?' He kicked up his feet in an impromptu jig and danced out of the door.

'I wonder sometimes if Father realises the immense debt he owes to Poggs.' Gabriellen put a hand to her throat, easing the tight bud of emotion which had lodged there. Laurence gave another wail of complaint and Gabriellen lifted him from his cradle and held him against her shoulder. Looking across at Agnes, the thought that the clown and his wife would leave them was unbearable. Yet did not loyalty and friendship work two ways? In fairness she could not allow them to ignore the opportunities which were given to them.

'Poggs wastes his talent.' Gabriellen paced the room, patting the baby's back to soothe his cries. 'He should not have to perform on street corners. Speak to him, Agnes. By rights he should be appearing at The Rose or The Theatre.'

Agnes shook her head. 'He'll never desert Esmond. And do thee think I would be parted from thee?'

'Without you and Poggs these last months, I could never have managed,' Gabriellen said, moved by Agnes's loyalty.

'Thee would cope. That's thy way.' Agnes took the now sleeping baby from Gabriellen and laid him in the cradle. Straightening, she looked across at Nan who had fallen asleep over her sewing. 'It's good to see the colour back in her cheeks. When Larry was born I thought we'd lost her. Now she's almost back to normal and can give Esmond the kind of loving he needs, thee will see a change in thy father. In his way he cares for Nan. Her illness struck him hard.'

Outside in the corridor a slurred voice was raised in a

drunken song. Recognising the off-key rendering, Gabriel-len opened the door, her hands going to her hips again. 'Father, where have you been? Could you have not sent us word, so that we knew you were safe?' Her tirade faded as she saw that there were two men in the ill-lit passage. Esmond was leaning heavily upon his companion for support.

'No lecture, Gabby.' Esmond raised his head and squint-ed at her. His face was ruddy from the exertion of climbing the stairs. Before she could speak, he waved a finger at her. 'I hash juss cause for celebrashion.' He hiccoughed and continued with careful enunciation, 'My good friend here has solved all our problems.'

Gabriellen gave his companion a suspicious look. To her astonishment she met Jack's amused stare. She had been so angry at Esmond's absence that she had failed to recog-nise her lover. Irrepressible as ever, he winked at her over Esmond's grey hair. It was five weeks since his last visit to Chichester. Then he had stayed only two nights and left after an argument with Esmond.

'I'm delighted you two have resolved your differences,' she said with relief.

Her gaze sought Jack's as he came closer. Somehow she managed to restrain the impulse to run to his arms. Her hunger for his embrace was mirrored by the gleam in his eyes.

'Wine! Bring us wine, daughter! We have much to cele-brate.' Esmond waved a hand expansively. The grand ges-ture sent him reeling off balance. Jack grabbed his doublet to stop him from falling.

Esmond pulled himself free and controlled the slurring of his voice. His histrionics would have put Cornelius Hope to shame. 'Sweetest daughter, summon my loyal followers. I have an announcement. Thanks to the intercession of my dear friend, Captain Stoneham, our troupe will be reunited under a new patron – Lord Mincham. Of course, I had approached his lordship myself – my letter was most elo-quent on the subject of his patronage. But his lordship has been indisposed for some months. It seemed my letter, together with Stoneham's encouragement, has brought us a new patron.'

Gabriellen was too delighted at the news to correct Esmond that it was she and not him who had written to

Lord Mincham. Esmond had dismissed the man, his remarks contemptuous of the amateur status of his present players.

Esmond affected a regal pose, one hand on his hip, the other upraised as he elaborated. 'His lordship, dissatisfied with the incompetent performance of his players, dismissed most of them. I am their new manager. Poggs, Crofton and Flowerdew – if I can track that young rascal down – will all be employed. Cesare and Umberto have already been retained by Lord Mincham. Is that not wonderful news?'

'The best, Father.' Gabriellen smiled her pleasure. She leaned back against the door as Jack helped Esmond into the room. She followed them inside, unable to take her eyes off Jack's tall figure as he helped her father to a stool. Esmond swayed precariously before sitting down and pulling a fat purse from inside his doublet.

'This is just the beginning.' He jingled the coins in the purse. 'Mincham has agreed to build us our own playhouse, The Angel. What do you think of that, daughter? Tomorrow we move from this scurvy rathole to rooms more fitting our rising station.' He fell awkwardly from the stool and stared around him, his eyes large as he attempted to focus them. 'Where's the wine? Bring wine for our honoured guest, daughter. And where's that damned fellow Poggs? Not here! How can we celebrate if . . .' His voice trailed away as his head nodded down on to his chest. He had fallen asleep.

Jack heaved Esmond over his shoulder and turned to Gabriellen. 'He'd better sleep this off. Where's his bed?'

She showed him through to the adjoining room. Esmond was settled in the box-bed, which was built like a closet against the wall, and the hangings drawn across his snoring figure.

When Jack held out his arms, Gabriellen moved into them to receive his kiss. He did not release her until she was breathless, saying ruefully, 'I suspect it's too much to hope that we can find privacy here.'

'Do you think of nothing but fornication?' she scolded, but her sparkling eyes betrayed her own need for him after so long apart.

'Not after five weeks without you.' He nipped her ear far from gently, earning himself a playful slap on his chest. 'Is there nowhere we can be alone?'

'Nowhere.' At his answering grimace, she laughed softly. 'I sleep on a truckle bed behind a curtain in the parlour.'

'Then Lord Mincham's offer has not come a moment too soon.' His lips were against her hair and travelled lower to nuzzle her ear as he spoke. 'Now that the players' future is assured, you will have more freedom. I've taken rooms on London Bridge. They are close to the new playhouse and the house on Bankside which Esmond has rented. I want you to live there. It will make it easier for me to visit you.'

'No, Jack.' She drew a deep breath, all coquetry and softness vanishing as outrage consumed her. 'I'll not be set up like a concubine. Take those rooms, and whenever you are free of Court duties I will meet you there?'

A diabolical gleam entered his eyes. 'If it's marriage you seek, I'll not be blackmailed into it.'

She shoved him away from her. 'That's unjust! I did not mention marriage.' Her pride matched his. Tipping up her chin, she glared at him. 'I'm not so selfish I would have you lose all you've worked for by incurring the Queen's anger. But I warn you, I'll not be used. Neither will I be taken for granted. Until we are wed, I will live with my family.'

Jack took her shoulders and gave her a rough shake. 'Why must you be so stubborn? You say you love me. This is our chance to be together.'

'Upon terms I find impossible to accept.'

'You know I cannot marry you, Gabriellen. Not yet.' The admission was wrenched from him. As he turned his head away to look across the room, the jagged scar just above his beard showed white with tension. His body was rigid. Then, with a harsh expulsion of breath, he turned back to her. 'You don't know what you ask of me. I'll not lose you, my love. If the only way I can keep you is to marry you – then, damn you, I shall wed you. Though it must be done in secret. And upon your head be the consequences.'

'And have you resent me for the rest of your life for forcing your hand?' She shook her head. 'Until you are ready to accept me openly as your wife, we are best as we are.'

'I shall never understand you.'

The relief in his voice was so obvious, she retaliated with painful irony, 'I think, my love, that sometimes I understand you only too well.'

'Then you will know that now I have only one thing on my mind.' He laughed wickedly and began to kiss her in a way that made her forget everything but the taste of his lips and the strength of his arms around her. At last he pulled back. 'Have you any idea of the torture you put me through? For five weeks I've starved for you, my darling.'

'You are too impetuous. The day is young. How long do we have before you return to Court?'

'Five or six hours.'

She took down a cloak from a peg on the wall, her cheeks dimpled as she teased. 'There is more to love than fornication. We have so little time to talk. Edward Alleyn is playing his famous role of Tamburlaine at The Theatre. He's a wonderful actor. Mark took me to see him in *Dr Faustus*.' The disapproval in Jack's features prompted another suggestion. 'If you do not wish to see the play, could we not visit the Tabard Inn in Southwark? Mark said a magician performs there in the afternoons, but we never went before he returned to Wales.'

'You have seen much of Rowan, it would appear?' He looked at her oddly, his expression inscrutable.

'You know we are friends,' she defended hotly. 'And if you dare presume he is more than that . . .' She choked on the force of her anger. 'What kind of a woman do you take me for?'

'You are my woman, Gabriellen,' he stated with lethal calmness. 'I would kill anyone who became your lover.'

She stared into his ruthless face and her temper erupted. She should be pleased he felt so strongly. Instead she resented the way he would rule her. 'Until I am your wife, Jack Stoneham, you have no rights over me. If I so choose, I will take whom I please to my bed.'

The words were hurled at him without thought, their utter absurdity made nonsense of them. It was inconceivable to her that she would permit any man to make love to her other than Jack. To her horror his face had gone white beneath his tan. His fingers closed like manacles over her wrist as he pulled her roughly against him.

'Never say that, even in jest.'

For a moment it was as though she was looking into the face of a stranger. His grey eyes were harder than the ice they resembled.

Angrily, she sucked in her breath, her tone brittle with accusation. 'You must know there will never be anyone else?'

'Prove it!'

The tender gaze of the lover had fallen away and in his eyes blazed a cold unremitting light. For the first time she saw behind the masquerade of elegant courtier and adoring lover. She saw the real Jack Stoneham. A true Elizabethan. Ambition and power were his master. A man who was utterly selfish – an adventurer, a merciless and dangerous rogue. A man devoid of scruples and honour. Disliking the change in him, she pulled away.

With a harsh laugh, he pressed her against the wall. 'You have not thanked me for saving the troupe. Does not my persuading Lord Mincham to engage your father's players deserve some reward?'

His mouth ravaged hers. She resented his callous treatment. But even as her mind objected, her blood responded to the passion in his kiss. She glanced towards the bed, shocked that Jack should wish to make love to her in the same room where her father slept. Not that there was much privacy in the manner in which they lived. Often at night she had lain awake, aware that Esmond and Nan, or Poggs and Agnes, were making love with little more than a screen or a curtain between them.

Jack laughed against her ear, the sound almost drowned by her father's snores. 'Esmond is out cold. Pay him no mind.'

'No, Jack.'

'Yes, my love.'

He was incorrigible. He swept aside her protest, kissing her with such passion, she was caught in the vortex of his desire, falling victim to the barrage of his ardent kisses. After weeks of abstinence she wanted him with a need which threatened to overwhelm her. The touch of his hands forcing down into her bodice to seek her breasts left her gasping with longing, but decency prevailed. It was one thing to go with him to his rooms or his ship, quite another to allow him to make love to her when her father was in the same room – sound asleep or not.

'No, Jack.' She pushed against his chest. 'Not here.'

'Yes, here.' His hands slid beneath her skirts to caress her thighs. 'You are my woman. I'll prove it to you now.'

His face was dark with an ugly passion which was beyond reasoning with. At the demanding caress of his hands, her blood betrayed her. He took her with an almost brutal lack of courtesy, lifting her up so that her legs curled around his hips. As he thrust deep inside her, her fingers clawed against his shoulders for support. A last protest was captured by his mouth as he drove hungrily into her, insatiable in his savage need. She despised herself for her body's answering passion, but the flame once kindled would not be doused. Her response became as urgent as his. At last he shuddered and held her tight.

'I love you, Gabriellen. Don't ever speak of taking other lovers again.' He eased back from her and smiled, a wide impudent smile, which was without shame for his own actions or condemnation for hers. 'Was that not proof of my love?'

He adjusted his clothing and helped her smooth down the folds of her velvet gown. Her cheeks were burning from embarrassment at her wanton response to his inopportune lovemaking.

'You used me like a whore, Jack,' she accused. 'I did not deserve that.'

'Nonsense! I but proved you my woman,' he said fiercely. 'I'd have expected as much were you my wife.'

She looked at him. He was unrepentant. He did not realise how deeply he had shamed her, cheapened her love. Her eyes narrowed. 'Were I your wife, we would have been in the privacy of our own home. Not where anyone could walk in upon us.'

'You really are upset!' He was genuinely surprised. He smiled crookedly. At the sight of his chipped tooth which she always found so rakishly attractive, her anger mellowed. He kissed her tenderly, saying softly, 'I'm a man governed by my passions, but never doubt that I truly love you.' He held out his arm for her to take. 'Now, I believe you expressed a desire to visit the play?'

She bit back a retort, disgruntled that only now, when his appetite was appeased, was he prepared to gratify her wishes.

*

The move south of the river was not as favourable as Gabriellen had anticipated. The house itself was delightful, built on the outskirts of the Liberty of Old Parris Garden. Three storeys high, it stood in its own grounds enclosed by a high wall. It even had a rose garden. But it was the surroundings which disturbed Gabriellen. Barely a stone's throw away was Bankside, a district notorious for its brothels, cockpits and beargardens. It was also the haunt of cut-purses, whores, and all types of villains.

A month after their move Gabriellen waited whilst Poggs handed out the contents of a food basket to the prisoners within The Clink, whose hands were outstretched, their voices imploring through the metal grating. Twice a week she came with food, remembering how Poggs had told her that once Esmond would have died in prison had it not been for such charity shown to him. At all other times she avoided the prison, though the cries of the inmates could be heard in the nearby streets. There seemed to Gabriellen to be an air of evil in the Southwark streets which even the impressive structure of the Bishop of Winchester's Palace did nothing to alleviate.

She suppressed a shudder as they walked away. Few children played in these streets. By the age of seven they were skilled beggars and sneak-thieves, and a year or two later the girls joined their older sisters in the brothels. It was not a place she wished Laurence to be brought up in. Once Poggs rejoined her, she walked briskly away from the prison.

'This place gives me the shivers,' she whispered. 'So many faces reflect misery and degradation. Eyes seem to watch from every window. It's odd, but on several occasions I thought my purse was about to be stolen, then inexplicably the cut-purse disappeared. They must know I could never catch them in these twisting lanes.'

'You are the daughter of Esmond Angel. Your father has moved in many circles during his varied life. He's respected amongst the fraternity here. If any should dare to harm one of Esmond's household, they'd find themselves answerable to One-eyed Ned.' He cast a furtive glance over his shoulder before adding in a low voice, 'To cross One-eyed Ned is to court a dagger between the ribs.'

'Are you saying that Father is an acquaintance of that arch-villain?' she asked, shocked.

Poggs shrugged, tapped his freckled nose with his fore-finger and refused to say more.

Later that night Gabriellen challenged Esmond about Poggs's revelation. 'Father, what are your dealings with this cut-throat, One-eyed Ned?'

Esmond choked on his wine and took a moment to recover his breath. When he did, he was belligerent. ''Tis none of your affair. I know him. Let that suffice.'

'How can you consort with such villains?' she cried, so startled at the statement, she forgot her outrage that Esmond had set up home in this disreputable district.

'If you want respectability, go back to Chichester. Those pious citizens have no love for us. Their hostility was plain enough this winter. Were you not spat upon by Goodwife Baker for being Wildboar's kin? Believe me, you're safer here.'

'Safe! Living amongst prostitutes and thieves?' Her ire exploded into indignation.

'Watch your tongue, daughter,' Esmond bellowed. 'I've said we're safe here. One-eyed Ned is an Upright Man – what you would call a leader, in control of this Underworld community. His word is law in this district. Suffice to say he owes me. Speak ill of him at your peril outside these walls.'

'Father, can you not see that this One-eyed Ned is evil? Is it he who has led you into gambling and the bad company which – ?'

She stopped abruptly as Esmond advanced towards her, his face patched with red. 'The company you keep is little better. Stoneham is an arrant rogue. He'd put Wildboar himself to shame. It was through One-eyed Ned that I first met that coxcomb paramour of yours.'

'Jack would never – ' she began, but was halted by Esmond's bray of laughter.

'Love blinds you. There's much you do not know about Stoneham. I warrant he has a secret or two beneath his cap.'

That was all Esmond would say upon the subject and when Gabriellen tackled Jack he was similarly evasive about his dealings with One-eyed Ned.

A few days later, determined to learn more of this arch-villain, she questioned a beggar sitting in a doorway. The man was what Poggs had called a counterfeit crank – a pretended epileptic. As the crowds converged upon The Rose playhouse last week, he had thrown a fit, fooling her by his display. The realistic way he foamed at the mouth and rolled his eyes back until only the whites showed, his limbs twitching in a contorted frenzy, had roused her pity as it had many other bystanders'. She was about to throw him some pennies when Poggs stopped her and drew her aside. Once the crowd dispersed, the epileptic made a remarkable recovery and ran off, laughing.

Seeing the man hunched in a doorway, Gabriellen approached. When he began to roll his eyes as a prelude to his act, she forestalled him by saying sharply: 'I know you to be a counterfeit crank, you'll get nothing from me. Unless, that is, you answer my question. What do you know of One-eyed Ned?'

The man's face turned the colour of rancid tallow, spittle spraying from his toothless mouth as he scrambled to his feet. 'I knows nothing.' He ran off.

'That's not a question you ask around here.' A well-dressed gallant spoke from the shadows of a doorway.

Gabriellen glanced up and saw the sign of the Cardinal's hat painted above the door. The crude sign had nothing to do with piety. Agnes had told her with a giggle that the phallic-looking red mitre was used to depict the profession of the women within. Gabriellen pulled her cloak closer about her figure as the man stepped out of the brothel. The wide brim of his hat was pulled low over his face, shielding his features, except for the pointed beard on his chin. It was black with a reddish streak in its centre. Gabriellen took a step back.

'Come away, mistress,' Agnes urged, tugging at her arm.

'The daughter of Esmond Angel need fear nothing,' the cultured voice declared in a silky purr. 'Unless she pokes her pretty nose where it does not concern her. The man of whom you speak has spies everywhere. It would be a shame if that lovely face of yours was cut to serve as warning.'

'Is that how this One-eyed Ned holds sway over his brethren? By terror?' Gabriellen gave him a hard stare. She would not reveal to this stranger that his words had frightened her. 'A true man would hold their loyalty by respect.'

'The knife is something these people respect.' The cultured voice now sounded menacing.

'Men are easily impressed,' she replied, trying to be coldly dignified. There was something about this man's manner which made her uneasy. 'I think I have the information I seek.' She carefully lifted her velvet skirts aside and walked haughtily past him.

'The threats of One-eyed Ned do not impress you, Miss Angel?'

It was disconcerting that he knew her name. She turned to regard him. His clothes were impeccable: the gold lace and seed pearls sewn on to his doublet would keep a family in food for a year. 'No man who resorts to threats impresses me, sir.'

She saw his lips part in a smile. As he took a step towards her, she looked primly up at the sign over the brothel door. 'Neither do men who frequent such lowly establishments.'

She turned on her heel and walked on with her head held uncomfortably high. It was some moments later before it struck her that when he had stepped out of the shadows, he had been wearing an eye-patch.

As summer followed spring Gabriellen forgot the sinister references to One-eyed Ned. Work on the playhouse had commenced. The land had been cleared and the circular wooden building had begun to rise. *Unholy Revenge* was rehearsed and the players had taken it to several towns as far north as Oxford. Gabriellen missed the company of the actors. Nan, who had at last recovered from Laurence's birth, travelled with them. The baby however was left behind, together with Agnes to help Gabriellen look after him.

Two or three times a week Jack would send word to Gabriellen to meet him at his rooms on London Bridge. Though he never mentioned marriage, he was in all other respects the perfect lover. He insisted she dress in the finest silk gowns, and every week a new jewel or accessory was added to her collection. Yet nothing could ease her qualms of conscience. She hated the need for secrecy. It went against her forthright nature. On the rare occasions they went out in public together, they were both heavily masked. With every passing week the secrecy became more onerous to bear.

'It's just for a few more months, my darling,' Jack assured her. His kisses effectively silenced her misgivings.

It was not until he had left her that she realised again that nothing had advanced between them, and with each meeting she felt herself more securely ensconced in the role of his mistress.

Though Jack still evaded setting a date for their marriage, for the first time in a year Gabriellen felt that there was stability in her life. Once the playhouse was completed, the future of her family and the players would be assured.

Gabriellen was sitting on the parlour floor playing with Laurence when there was an angry battering upon the door. Laurence began to cry as the hammering continued. Gathering him into her arms, she went to investigate, her temper already simmering at the uncalled for rudeness of the knocking. Agnes was at the door before her.

'I demand to see Esmond Angel,' the shrill voice proclaimed from the doorway. 'If I do not, there'll be a warrant out for his arrest before nightfall.'

Gabriellen recognised Victor Prew's whine. Was her father again in debt to this officious toad? The man was angry enough to carry out his threat.

'Bring Mr Prew into the parlour, Agnes,' Gabriellen said above Laurence's howls. The baby showed every sign of inheriting the Angels' fiery temperament and her attention was on him as she stepped back to allow Prew to enter the room. She could not abide the merchant, but clearly he must be made to see reason. 'Please sit down, Mr Prew.'

She spent a moment soothing her half-brother until his cries subsided to a protesting hiccough. Handing Laurence to Agnes, Gabriellen said: 'Once he is settled, will you bring us some wine and biscuits?'

'This is not a social call,' Prew declared rudely. 'Where's your father? Fetch him at once, unless you wish to see him rotting in a debtor's gaol.'

Gabriellen's temper stirred. She fixed him with a fierce stare until his small eyes blinked.

'My father travels with the players. They are in Oxfordshire this week. I do not expect him to return to London for some weeks.'

'How convenient for him! Yet again he seeks to delay repaying his debt. He wriggled out of payment last time. He'll not do so again. I'll have my five hundred marks or see him swing for it. There's more than one crime the justices would like to hear of where Esmond Angel is concerned. Hanging crimes.'

'How dare you threaten my father? Get out!' She rounded on him, hands on hips, her eyes flashing dangerously. When he did not move she picked up a bronze candlestick, holding it with menacing intent above her head. 'Get out of my house, and take your foul lies with you. Go, before I forget I am a gentlewoman and beat you for the lying cur you are!'

A strange expression transformed Prew's narrow face. His eyes shone and his breathing was unsteady. 'I am leaving, Miss Angel. But I shall return. Indeed, I shall return.'

Chapter Twenty

Mark Rowan whistled Hywel to heel as he walked out of the stables towards the paddocks where his sister, Aphra, was training a young colt on a leading rein. The June morning was warm, although milky clouds obscured the tops of the surrounding hills. He breathed deeply of air that was cool and crisp. Like iced lemon-water, Mark thought. It carried the tang of freshness from the waterfall which plummeted down the hillside behind the house to feed the valley lake.

From the flint and thatch forge behind him came the ring of hammer upon iron. There Aphra's husband, Saul Bywood, was shoeing the eight horses Mark had selected to take to London. Those not bought by the Queen's Master of the Horse for Her Majesty's stables would be sold at auction in the capital.

Mark rested a booted foot on the lowest rung of the paddock fence, and regarded last year's foals grazing with their mothers. The lush pastures and emerald backdrop of the hills was the perfect setting for their bright chestnut coats. He moved on to a smaller enclosure, his approach greeted by a whinny. Cadwallader trotted to the gate to nuzzle his hand and take the proffered apple. Mark ran an experienced eye over the young stallion: the proud arch of his neck, the way he held his tail high, his sleek muscles and deep chest were all signs of his strength, stamina and superb breeding. The creamy white blaze from forelock to muzzle and the four white stockings above his hooves, were highly prized markings. Cadwallader had exceeded all expectations. Already the young stallion had successfully covered two of the Rowan mares. In the autumn the foals would be born and Mark was confident they would be the first of the improved Rowan strain. Within a decade Mark planned that the Rowan horses would be the finest of their kind.

He lifted his eyes to the dough-coloured sky and followed the path of an eagle as it soared towards its eyrie. He was at one with his surroundings – at peace and content. Most of the winter he had spent in London; he had been in Wales for only six weeks. Time enough to make him realise how much he missed his home, family, and the work they were doing here.

His sharp eyes caught the movement of a distant rider approaching along the valley. Intuition prickled within him. The summons had come, as he knew it must. He did not want to leave so soon, but Sir Francis Walsingham insisted he remain a spy. It seemed he had performed his duties too well. No one suspected the double life of the stallion-man who travelled so freely about the country.

Besides, there was still a matter unresolved from last year's investigations. Garfield and Kettering and their cronies might be in prison, but Victor Prew remained free. Although nothing had been proved against the merchant, Mark would stake his reputation that Prew was guilty. What disturbed him most was Prew's determination to maintain a hold over Esmond Angel. Why? Obviously the merchant saw the players as useful to him. Especially a troupe whose reputation could gain them the entrée to Court and the Queen. Did Prew plan to get close enough to Elizabeth to assassinate her? Clearly he must be kept under close observation. Also, the players must be protected from any implication of treason by association with Prew. So far Mark's warnings had been ignored by Esmond. When he returned to London, he hoped he would not find the playwright in even greater debt to the merchant.

With only a day or two left to him in Wales, Mark did not want to waste his time in worries about Gabriellen's father. Nor did he like admitting how much he had missed the teasing companionship of the playwright's daughter.

Giving Cadwallader a final pat, he turned his attention to another paddock where Glendower galloped back and forth along the edge of one fence. The stallion was restless. Strangely, Glendower seemed to enjoy the life on the road. The old reprobate! Mark grinned as he watched the horse rear up, pawing the air with his forelegs in open challenge to Cadwallader across the fields. The younger stallion answered with a loud neigh and began to parade up and down his own fence, displaying himself to the nearest mares.

A call from his sister drew Mark's attention. He turned to watch her walk towards him. Her dress, like the woman herself, was unconventional. She wore a simple russet gown which ended just above her mannish but practical boots. Her long stride was unhampered by a farthingale and her thick black hair was restrained by a plain white cap. It was the attire she always wore when working with the horses and it had scandalised many a chance visitor. Aphra was one of the most practical women Mark knew and he admired her for it. Although in her late twenties, and despite bearing six children, Aphra was slender, her pale skin smooth as a young maiden's.

'A rider comes, brother.' Aphra shielded her eyes against the watery sun trying to pierce through the clouds. 'He's ridden hard. He'll be Walsingham's messenger, look you. Come with orders from his master.'

'You have a fertile imagination!' Mark scoffed.

Aphra studied his set expression. Her brown eyes were unusually sombre. Mark was on his guard. He never spoke of his involvement with the Queen's Secretary of State.

'I know you lead two lives.' She spoke her thoughts aloud. 'So do not bother to deny it. There was something about your manner when I mentioned the fate of Anthony Babington and his followers.' She laughed, seeing his frown. 'Don't look so dour. I know you better than anyone. Why, it's proud I am of you. Any Catholic who would shackle us to Spain or Rome deserves to die.' Her soft melodic voice roughened with passion. 'I cannot forget the barbarous treatment of our father at Spanish hands. Would that I were a man.' Her eyes blazed with the fighting spirit of a rampaging Celt. 'I'd see them all meet a traitor's death.'

'There's bloodthirsty you are, sister dear.' Mark regarded her affectionately. 'You are a born romantic, Aphra. I'm but a humble stallion-man who tramps the highways – and you would make of me a Machiavelli.'

'I give you more credit,' she retaliated with disdain. 'He was an amoral opportunist. What you do is for the good of our state, not yourself.'

Mark hugged his sister. 'You are loyal, but misguided. And very like a firebrand I met in England.'

'That would be the estimable Gabriellen, I suppose.' Aphra looked sideways at him through her black lashes. 'You speak of her often. More so than the fortune-teller Jesmaine, whom you profess to be in love with.'

'Did I say I loved Jesmaine?'

Aphra met her brother's non-committal look with resignation. Actually Mark had not spoken of love. Sometimes she wondered if he would ever love again. Meredith's death had numbed his heart. He had loved her passionately and idealistically, as only a man of eighteen could. Being five years Mark's senior, there had been a time when Aphra had known his every mood and thought. Not so now. Each time he returned to Rowan Hall he was more withdrawn, giving less readily of himself. This last winter he had been more reticent than ever, though outwardly he was the same teasing, jovial brother he had always been.

'Isn't it time you gave thought to marriage?'

His rugged face tightened with annoyance at her question. He bent to fondle Hywel's long brown ears to evade her question. Picking up a stick which Hywel had dropped at his feet, Mark threw it. As the dog raced off, he thrust his thumbs into the dagger belt at his hip and leaned back against the fence.

There were screams of delight from the orchard where four of Aphra's children were playing. The two youngest were still confined to the nursery. Mark's stare concentrated on the house. The sight of it brought a familiar ache of pride and frustration to his chest. Pride for what it once had been. Frustration at the decaying splendour he could not afford to renovate. After four generations of Rowan occupation, its stone walls had mellowed to blend harmoniously with the landscape. The erratic construction of the five gables had been built around a quadrangle, with a dozen tall brick chimneys rising elegantly from the shingle-tiled roof. Ivy covered two of the gables and hid the holes in the roof in the west wing. The shutters were locked over the oriel window in the old hall. Sadly, that was a part of the house which was never used now. Nor could be, until the ancient hammer beams, damaged thirty years ago in a fire, were repaired. Another gable stared back at him, its unglazed windows also shuttered, the wall beneath them stained with moss from the broken guttering. His gaze moved from the house to the stables and barn. Newly restored and extended, they were a heartening sight. They had taken the profits of three years' work to build, and he did not begrudge a penny spent on them. He could live with damp and discomfort. The Rowan horses could not. He knew Aphra and Saul felt the same, but not everyone would.

'Time enough for marriage when the Hall is refurbished,' he stated flatly.

'You do not see Jesmaine as your future bride?'

'She would not be happy living in such isolation, splendid as it is. And I could not give this up for anyone.' His voice was gruff with emotion. 'Perhaps I shall never marry. You and Saul have given me nephews and nieces enough to inherit the estate.'

'You've bees in your head to think like that!' Aphra folded her arms and regarded him in the same manner she would one of her own wayward children. 'It's time you put Meredith's death behind you and considered the future. Look you, there's women aplenty who would jump at the chance of having the Hall as their home. Especially since its master is handsome, generous and kind.'

'Whoa, sister, you are biased!' He laughed, discounting her compliments. 'Like me, you love this place. You do not see the dilapidation. In fairness to you and Saul, the future mistress of Rowan Hall must be prepared to work as hard as the rest of us.'

He could now hear the sound of the rider approaching, but did not immediately turn his gaze from the house. In his mind, he did not see the partial ruin. He saw it as it would be in a decade or more, whole again, stately and dignified in this beautiful valley. It would be a home his children would be proud of. The thought rose unbidden. Children meant marriage and he was not ready for that step yet. He did not want a marriage of convenience. He wanted what had been within his grasp with Meredith. Love, and more than that, a soul-mate who shared his love of horses and his life here. He mentally shook himself, his thoughts cynical. Your Welsh blood makes of you a romantic loon, Emrys Marcus Llewelyn. Meredith, as much as you loved her, was never a soul-mate.

The work he did for Walsingham was too dangerous to

consider marriage as yet. He was content with Jesmaine, but she had been adamant that she would never live away from London. Also she had told him that she was barren, and despite his flippant remarks to Aphra, Mark wanted a child of his to inherit the estate.

The arrival of the rider had alerted Saul. He stood in the doorway of the forge, his shirt sleeves rolled up over his muscled forearms, his stocky body filling the portal as he wiped his hands on his leather apron. His skills as a farrier were invaluable to the stud farm. All three of them worked well together. Saul was an easy-going, dependable and amiable partner.

When the rider turned in Mark's direction, Saul retreated into the darkness of the forge. The sound of his hammer again rang out, soothing and rhythmical as a Latin chant.

'Mr Rowan,' called the rider as he halted before Mark.

He dragged his thoughts back to the present. At three and twenty he could afford to wait before he need take a wife. Until then, his alliance with Jesmaine suited him.

Recognising the badge on the sleeve of the rider as that of Walsingham, Mark bade him dismount and enter the house. With Hywel running ahead they entered the library and Mark held out his hand for the document giving him Walsingham's orders.

'So, Father, are you pleased with the playhouse?' Gabriellen raised her voice above the hammering of the workmen. 'The Angel will open to its public in a week.'

'The work has progressed better than I dared hope.' Esmond nodded with satisfaction as he surveyed the wooden circular building which rose three galleries high. He had returned with the players to the city yesterday and this was his first sight of the new playhouse.

His pride was immense. The theatre smelt of newcut timber and fresh thatch. Unfortunately, the August afternoon was overcast, the poor light distorting the outline of the structure to his impaired vision. He knew its layout, which followed that of the other London theatres. The design originated from the galleried yards of the larger inns. Except for a narrow roof over these galleries, the playhouse was open to the elements. Behind the stage was the tiring-house. The stage itself, jutting from one side into the middle of the yard, was also protected by a cover or 'heavens'. The tower was a storey higher than the rest of the building, and it was from here that a trumpet fanfare would announce the start of each play. Above the tower was a flagpole from which would fly the scarlet standard with its golden angel.

'How many will it hold?' he asked.

'Two thousand – possibly more,' Gabriellen replied. 'All the seating in the galleries has been cushioned. Whether the groundlings within this yard will stand, or have benches provided, will determine the audience capacity. However, there has been one alteration to the original design.' She paused, anxious that in this she had made the right decision. 'I was not happy that there were only two entrances each side of the yard. Such an arrangement was inconvenient for those wishing the comfort of the galleries. Our most prestigious customers would be forced to pay their entrance penny at the first door, push their way through the crowd, and then pay a further charge to gain admittance to the gallery. There is now a third entrance whereby the gallery-goers can enter separately, pay the extra money, and gain direct access to their seats.'

'The innovation is so simple it amazes me no one thought of it before. Each day you prove your worth more.' Esmond smiled fondly and put his arm around her shoulder. 'Your encouragement helped me finish *Unholy Revenge*. It has been a great success wherever we played.'

Gabriellen smothered a momentary pique. It was typical of him not to acknowledge that the play had been almost entirely her work. Its success was accolade enough. In this male province no credit would be given to a woman playwright, and certainly no self-respecting company would perform a play written by one. It was a prejudice she found hard to accept. In truth, she could not see why women should not act upon the stage. Her own performance of the enchantress had proved that, given the opportunity, a woman could win the acclaim of an audience as skilfully as any man.

Esmond clapped his hands, drawing the attention of the players who stood around surveying the playhouse. 'The builders are about to finish for the day. Since we have a few hours of daylight left, we shall rehearse. Samuel Lacey is still mistiming the last scene. By the way, where is he?'

The actors coughed and looked blankly back at Esmond.

Lacey, who had replaced Culpepper, was an accomplished enough actor, but he drank too much and was becoming unreliable.

Cesare stepped forward. 'Maestro, Lacey no here. He go to the Tabard Inn.'

'Thank you, Cesare.' Esmond dismissed the musician, before turning to Gabriellen. 'Lacey is becoming worse. The man's a sot. Yet who can I get to replace him?'

A door slammed by the stage and a hush settled over the players when a man strode into the theatre.

'I have heard nothing but praise for Lord Mincham's Men.' Anthony Culpepper's voice carried to everyone present. His long blond hair was swept back from his smooth face and had been curled so that it fell in waves to his shoulders. He was dressed in a tawny-orange doublet and hose, his shoes adorned with diamond buckles. He had prospered in his absence from the troupe or found himself a wealthy lover, Esmond accurately surmised.

Culpepper placed a jewelled, gloved hand on his hip, striking an affected pose which was meant to impress them. 'Word has it that your play *Unholy Revenge* has met with outstanding success,' he continued. 'Christopher Marlowe has, of course, declared it a trifling inconsequence. But that's Kit Marlowe for you! Obviously he sees Esmond as a rival or he would not have commented at all.' Culpepper flicked some imaginary dust from the sleeve of his doublet and looked down his Roman nose at the gathering. 'Yet you perform this masterpiece with an untalented ape in the leading role. Surely, Esmond, you could do better than that buffoon, Lacey?'

Gabriellen watched the reaction of the players. All who had been with the troupe under Lord Barpham's patronage looked wary. Cesare stared at the toe of his shoe whilst Umberto's expression was murderous. He made no secret of his hatred for Culpepper who had caused a rift between him and his lover.

'Good actors are not easy to find,' Esmond rapped back.

'Neither are good patrons,' Culpepper responded with acerbity. 'Mincham is wealthy enough, but with no great standing at Court. Though the Earl of Essex has voiced his intention of having you perform at a banquet he is planning at Essex House. It is also said he will attend the playhouse opening. Is that so?'

309

Esmond regarded Culpepper with contempt. 'Those who remained loyal to me have prospered. You lost no time in deserting us when Barpham was killed. Why should you interest yourself in us now? Unless your employment with the Lord Admiral's Men afforded you only secondary parts? Surely you had not expected to supplant the great Edward Alleyn's place in that company?'

Culpepper smiled. 'Such roles have kept me in the public eye. The playgoers adore me. I am hailed in the streets. However, I would not be averse to a change – should the right opportunity be offered.'

Gabriellen whispered to her father, 'Say you'll not consider it. He almost split the troupe last time. And now his self-importance has grown, he'll be as conceited as Hope.'

Esmond refused to meet her eye. He passed a hand over his chin as he considered the actor's proposition. The atmosphere within the playhouse was heavy with tension as the company awaited his verdict. The silence drew out as Esmond watched Culpepper. A sheen of sweat dampened the actor's brow. Beneath that silent scrutiny Culpepper abandoned his haughty pose. His twisting fingers betrayed his loss of control.

'I was wrong to leave the troupe as I did,' he burst out. 'The offer to join the Lord Admiral's players was too great. After so long away from the excitement of the play, I could not face returning to obscurity.'

'During your time with us you caused nothing but trouble and discord,' Esmond declared.

'I also filled every innyard and Guildhall where we played. Have you forgotten that?' Recovering his hauteur Culpepper strutted to and fro, preening his flaxen moustache and beard. 'And I never missed a performance or rehearsal. I did not come here to plead, Mr Angel, but to offer you my services. For this playhouse to win the audiences from The Rose which is close by, and also from The Theatre and The Curtain in Shoreditch, you must surpass every performance they put on. Lacey is not the man to achieve that. I am.'

Gabriellen saw her father look at Poggs who spread his hands in resignation. Esmond cleared his throat. 'Culpepper, there is a position within the troupe if you wish it. No one disputes your acting skills. But I warn you, I will tolerate no further disruption amongst my players. We

310

begin rehearsal immediately. My daughter will give you a copy of your lines.'

That rehearsal erupted into chaos. A leak was discovered in the tiring-house roof and the costumes were wet from the previous night's rain. The actors stumbled over their lines and tempers shortened. In her appointed role of book-holder, Gabriellen stood at the corner of the stage, her body soon aching with fatigue and tension. Disharmony governed every action. To ease the discord she gently encouraged the actors. Her words were wasted. The players remained antagonistic. Culpepper's reinstatement was resented. Robin was sullen. Umberto broke two strings on his lute, and each entrance of Culpepper on stage was greeted by a discordant twang from his instrument. Will Appleshot repeatedly farted in the middle of Culpepper's speeches, which sent the two young apprentice players into hysterical laughter.

'Dolts! Imbeciles!' Esmond raged, his patience at an end. 'I've never seen such incompetence. You shame me. You're a disgrace to our patron. A herd of braying asses has more talent than you.'

He continued to berate them. Throughout, Culpepper remained aloof, using a dagger point to pare his fingernails, insolent in his belief that he was not at fault. Poggs was cheerfully nonchalant, but to Gabriellen's dismay the rest of the company were ashen and visibly quaking in their boots, their glares virulently turned upon the leading actor. Culpepper had not been with them an hour and already the friendly relations within the troupe were deteriorating.

'God grant me the patience of Job,' Esmond ranted. 'We shall begin again – this time with a measure of talent. If I wanted a rabble of unpolished, inept strolling players, I could hire them off the street.'

In their eagerness to prove their worth, the rehearsal disintegrated into a total disaster. Lines were forgotten. Entrances missed. Robin tripped over the train of his gown and sprained his wrist in the fall. Poggs was catapulted up through the trap door with such violence that he lost his balance and dragged Will Appleshot and Francis Crofton to the floor with him.

Esmond exploded once again. 'Are you all cupshot? You are better suited to be inmates of Bedlam than to grace this playhouse.'

All the players began speaking at once as they converged on Esmond.

'Enough!' he bellowed. 'You will learn to deal comfortably with each other, or pay the price. From what I saw today, Culpepper was not at fault.'

'You take his side!' Robin wailed.

'Maestro,' Umberto implored, 'already the trouble it starts.'

'And you are adding to it,' Esmond roared. 'I have said, desist.' His voice rolled around the amphitheatre like a thunderclap. White-faced, the actors, including Culpepper, fell silent. 'That's better. If Culpepper causes trouble he will lose his place as our leading man and be given minor roles. Others who disobey me will find their wages cut. In this I will be obeyed.'

Suitably chastened, the players hung their heads and shuffled uncomfortably. Most knew to their peril that once roused, the infamous Angel temper was remorseless. For the first time Gabriellen saw some of the players look with hostility upon her father.

'Father, a word if you please? In the meantime, could not the players take a short rest?'

'Order must be rescued from this shambles.'

'It will be established the faster if you give them a few moments for their tempers to cool,' Gabriellen reasoned as she drew Esmond away. 'You are pushing them too hard.' She looked at him sternly, noting again the deep furrows which worry had carved into his brow. 'You push yourself even harder. The players have never failed you. They will not now. There's more than today's events troubling you, is there not?'

'Why should you think that?'

'Because I have come to know you well in the last year, Father. Are we in debt again?'

'Insolent chit! Have we not one of the wealthiest men in England as our patron?'

She was not fooled by his bluster. There was something shifty in the way he met her gaze. Her misgivings increased. She was certain that he was gambling again. How much had he lost during the two months on the road? Not that he would tell her if she asked.

'You have always drawn the best from your actors because they respect you,' she encouraged. 'Your ill-temper will not bully them into performing well.'

'You have taken on many responsibilities this last year, daughter.' The wide innocence in his eyes belied the guile behind his apparent capitulation. 'Save your shrewish tongue for others. Since you profess to know how to run this troupe better than I . . . then do so. I see Samuel Lacey has just arrived, and the damn' fool's brought an unwelcome visitor.' He spoke quickly and began to back away from her. 'Tell Lacey he can take my role in the play. You can pacify his choler at finding he's no longer our leading actor. I've business elsewhere.'

He was gone before she could bring him to task. An argument had broken out on the stage as Lacey began shouting at Culpepper.

It was then she saw Lacey's guest. So that was why her father had scuttled off. Victor Prew – she should have guessed! Her temper rose. Esmond had been quick to call her shrew, but was quicker still to leave her to deal with the unpleasant situations his debts brought upon him. Prew could wait. She gave the merchant a brief nod of acknowledgement, then turned her attention to placating the actors.

'Gentlemen,' she said in a firm voice which cut across Lacey's and Culpepper's shouting, 'my father has been called away upon urgent business. These arguments are childish and unworthy of you. Our first performance at The Angel must be our finest yet. Lord Mincham expects it. Our glory must reflect his glory. Our disgrace is his disgrace. It is the duty of every player to serve the company first and their own ambition second.'

She looked directly at Samuel Lacey. He had taken the news of his replacement badly, and who could blame him? She shot a baleful glare at Culpepper for his lack of tact. She would speak with him later. Now her concern was for Lacey. His stocky figure bristled with affront. His clean-shaven, square face was set into a disgruntled pout. Gabriellen sympathised with him. He had worked hard during his time with the players. He was an enthusiastic and competent actor, but lacked the spark of greatness which emanated from both Hope and Culpepper. Possibly that was why he drank so heavily. She could not forget that he had saved the troupe after Culpepper deserted them, and his skills were such that the company would be the poorer should he leave them. Unfortunately, she had never met a more touchy breed than actors when it came to affronted pride.

'Samuel, there have been some last-minute changes. We have been most fortunate that Mr Culpepper has joined our players. It does not alter your status with us. For some time my father has wished to devote more time to his playwriting. There is no actor more worthy than yourself to play my father's roles. It is a challenge I know you will rise to with dexterity and pride.'

Samuel Lacey clutched at the opportunity to salvage his self-esteem. 'I would be churlish to refuse. Esmond will be missed. His fertile pen created memorable roles for himself.' He removed his hat. His short brown hair grew into a peak low over his brow, giving his long narrow face an elfin look. He bowed gallantly. 'I am, as always, Lord Mincham's servant.'

Gabriellen smiled her appreciation, knowing it must have cost the actor dear. She opened the playbook and took her place on stage, her voice warm with encouragement. 'Let us begin with scene one. I have every confidence that after the opening of The Angel, the Lord Admiral's players had better start looking to their laurels. It will be Lord Mincham's Men who are the toast of London. To work, gentlemen.'

Culpepper did not move. Gabriellen looked askance at him. 'Have you a problem, Mr Culpepper?'

His nostrils flared as he regarded her with a look of horror and disgust. 'Surely Esmond is to oversee the play? I take no orders from a woman.'

'I am my father's advocate. The rehearsal will continue under my direction. I know my father's mind on this play. Take your place, Mr Culpepper, if you please.'

He preened his moustache. 'With respect, madam, I will not. I will wait until Esmond returns.'

Gabriellen controlled her anger at his prejudice and contempt. 'Very well.' She turned her back on him and beckoned to Samuel Lacey. 'Samuel, if you would be so kind as to resume the lead role? I shall speak my father's lines. The rehearsal will continue without Mr Culpepper.'

'You would take the lead from me,' Culpepper roared. 'This is infamous. You heard Angel. *I* am the lead.'

'But you have refused to act.' Gabriellen smiled sweetly

at him. 'We cannot afford to waste an entire afternoon. We open in a week. If you have not learnt your part by then, Mr Culpepper, then Samuel will have to take your place.'

'By heaven, this is outrageous!' Culpepper stormed.

'Then act, sir,' Gabriellen returned.

Culpepper snatched up his script, his expression mutinous.

Gabriellen addressed the players. 'We will break for half an hour while Mr Culpepper reads through his lines.'

She turned abstractedly to Victor Prew who continued to hover. If the merchant was chasing Esmond for an overdue debt, it would be foolish of her to antagonise him further. 'Mr Prew, did you wish to see my father or are you here as Samuel's guest? If so, please take a seat in the gallery and enjoy our rehearsal. I warn you, though, they are sometimes tempestuous.'

'I should enjoy that.' There was a brittle gleam in his small eyes which made Gabriellen uncomfortable. 'May I say how well you handled a delicate situation? My admiration for you grows with each meeting, Miss Angel.'

Gabriellen smiled thinly. Compliments from the merchant always made her uneasy. Excusing herself, she went to check what costume changes would be needed to accommodate the change of roles. Culpepper had withdrawn to a quiet corner to read the script and the tension in the playhouse began to ease. On her return from the tiring-room, she clapped her hands for the actors to begin.

This time the rehearsal progressed smoothly. Culpepper dominated the stage, his expertise banishing the resentment of the players. However unpleasant and disruptive Culpepper's habits were off-stage, he was a great actor.

The inevitable mistakes, Culpepper overcame with masterly skill. He held the continuity of the play together. By improvising when necessary, he guided the actors through each scene, and at times his stinging wit brought tears of laughter to Gabriellen's eyes.

As she watched, Gabriellen fell beneath the spell Culpepper wove. Though this was but a rehearsal, he spared himself nothing in his portrayal. He moved with the grace and regality of a prowling lion. His fair, handsome looks and swaggering figure were what an audience demanded of their male leads. He became Wildboar Tom, the wild, irrepressible rascal, unprincipled swashbuckler and lecher. He stalk-

315

ed the stage with such swaggering panache, he could not fail to have an audience cheering at his exploits. Even at his most villainous, Culpepper exuded an air of menace overlaid with black humour which could wring a macabre laugh from even the most sanctimonious spectator. Wildboar did not emerge from the play as an unsullied hero, but in Culpepper's hands he would be immortal as a loveable, if disreputable, blackguard.

If only Culpepper could be such a guiding force off-stage. It was there dissent would grow and fester. For better or worse, Culpepper was back. Trouble was bound to be brewing on the horizon.

As the last lines faded the sound of applause came from the lower gallery. Gabriellen had forgotten Victor Prew had been watching.

'Miss Angel, never have I enjoyed a play more.' Prew minced forward to claim her attention. 'A veritable masterpiece. And your stage direction – subtly given, of course, yet I saw how the players responded. Would that I could write prose which would be worthy praise to your accomplishments.'

'You are too kind, Mr Prew. I but prompt the players and make sure they do not miss their cue.'

'Dear lady, you do so much more. You are superbly gifted. May I presume to say you are an inspiration to us all?'

Gabriellen shook her head, but Prew caught the glimmer of annoyance in her eyes. Oh, she was incomparable, he thought with growing fervour. Such vivacity. What hidden radiance lay beneath her controlled composure! That strong will was like a flame beckoning him. He had no time for soft feminine wiles, but that strength and fury excited him.

Mark entered the labyrinth of squalid lanes and vermin-infested taverns of Alsatia. It was not a place he ventured into without qualms. Tonight, disguised as a bearded, one-eyed seaman, he lounged in a dark corner of a tavern watching his quarry. The taproom was ill lit by spluttering tallow candles, its grime-encrusted walls grey and uninviting. The rough wooden benches and trestles were battered and scarred from the nightly fights which broke out. The rushes on the stone-flagged floor were mildewed and stinking. A dog with ribs sticking through its coat pounced on a rat in a corner. With the rodent's feet dangling from between its fangs, the dog bolted for the outer door, followed by two snarling companions bent on stealing its trophy.

A fug of tobacco added to the air of decadence filling the interior. By the smoking fireplace a ragged beggar was singing a ribald song. In another corner a coney-catcher sat at a table alone, absently shuffling a pack of cards, whilst scanning the occupants of the room to assess a likely victim. The man paused and scratched his head. Picking a louse from its long greasy depths, he squashed it between his fingers.

A stream of shouted obscenities pierced the drone of voices as two harlots shrieked insults at each other. With dirt-streaked hands outstretched, they grabbed at each other's hair and fell against a table before rolling on to the floor. Several men cheered them on, shouting wagers as to the winner, whilst the women reduced each other's clothing to tatters.

Mark had never considered himself a prude and had spent many an enjoyable evening in the more prestigious brothels, such as Nell Lovegood's house. This place turned his stomach. It was permeated with corruption.

From across the murky room Victor Prew pushed past a drunken couple, who were intent on groping their way up the stairs. Mark watched as Prew accosted a tall, buxom whore. The prostitute gave him a grim caricature of a smile. She had clearly been in the trade for a dozen years or more, her hard face and eyes raddled by debauchery. After they had disappeared up the stairs, Mark settled down to stare into his tankard and wait.

The scraps of information he had gathered in the last weeks were slowly combining to form the details of another plot. All Mark's instincts told him Prew was involved. Yet despite the thoroughness of his investigations, he had failed to incriminate the merchant. This time Prew had taken pains not to be directly implicated. Mark suspected that the merchandise Prew imported from the Mediterranean was used as a cover for messages to be brought in from Spain and France. Even so, the watch he had put on the various ports used by Prew's agents had so far yielded nothing.

Mark grimaced at the bitterness of the ale as he continued

317

to scan the taproom for any sign that Prew was here to meet an accomplice. Each face was noted and discarded as a candidate. Mark had been in this work long enough to develop a sixth sense where such creatures were concerned. Though his gaze never left the taproom door, his mind travelled back over the past weeks. Two of his horses had been purchased by the Queen as hunters. On his visit to the royal stables, he had unexpectedly met Her Majesty inspecting a new foal.

A single circuit of the yard by the two geldings had been enough to earn her nod of approval. Expecting dismissal, he had been surprised when she beckoned him to bring to her the horse he was leading.

As her elegant hands caressed its neck she said quietly, 'Your name is known to me, Rowan, and not just as a horse-breeder. Walsingham speaks highly of you.' Her black eyes flickered over him and the grim lines of her thin lips softened. She held out a hand for him to kiss in homage.

He bowed over her fingers, his heart hammering with pride. 'I am yours to command, Gracious Majesty.'

'You are the protector of my life. Were it not for the need for secrecy in your work, I would richly reward you.'

'My service is an honour. England is great because of you. There can be no price a subject can place upon their duty to their beloved Sovereign.'

She gave a dry laugh. 'The Welsh in you compliments my aging bones. But I see honesty in your eyes. A rare commodity at Court. Would that all my subjects were not so avaricious in their servitude! I do not forget my debts, Rowan.'

With that she had left him and Mark acknowledged that he would spare himself no sacrifice, no hardship, to continue to serve Elizabeth Tudor.

The outer door of the taproom opened and the arrival of two sailors jerked him from his reverie. He drew back into the shadows, and studied one of them closer. The dim lighting made it difficult to see clearly, but he was certain that the man was the midshipman Prew had met in his Bristol warehouse some weeks ago. The two seamen headed straight for the stairs and the private rooms above. What better place than the anonymity of a trugging-house as lowly as this for a secret meeting of conspirators?

Mark followed, pausing to decline the invitation of a

scrawny adolescent prostitute who could not be older than twelve. At the top of the stairs Mark found several doors leading off the landing. There was no sign of the sailors. He moved along the passage to listen at the first door. The rhythmic grunts of lovemaking in its last throes sent him onwards to the next. A light showed through a panel of the ill-fitting door. Hearing a man's voice within, Mark put his eye to the crack. An aging pederast with a grotesque cod-piece like a thrusting bowsprit was being undressed by a painted catamite. Again, Mark moved on. Through a similar crack in the next door a man was enthusiastically dealing with two very imaginative and capable females.

'Landlord!' a voice bellowed. 'Landlord!' The sailor Mark had been following emerged from a door at the end of the landing. A wench joined him, wearing nothing but scarlet knee hose and garters, her pale body covered with bruises. 'Damn you, landlord!' the man shouted. 'Bring ale. Enough for four!'

There were sounds of giggling from within the room which told Mark the two sailors were engaged in matters far removed from treachery. His second sight of the sailor had shown Mark that this man had a deeper, receding hairline than the one he had mistaken him for.

Retracing his steps, Mark stood back into a doorway when the landlord lumbered down the narrow corridor carrying a tray of unappetising meat and two pitchers of ale. As Mark's back touched the door he heard the ill-fitting latch click open. From within he heard the whine of a whip. A movement of blood-flecked, pale flesh caught his attention. Prew's spindly body was bent over a stool while the woman brought the scourge down upon his naked back and buttocks. After each stroke the merchant grovelled at the whore's feet, begging for more.

The downpour which greeted Mark's arrival in the street was welcoming in its freshness. He lifted his face for the water to cascade over it, washing away the disgust he felt at the scene he had witnessed. Four figures stumbled from the tavern behind him, and, on his guard, he remained aware of them as they wended their way down the street. One was shorter than the others and walked with a curious hobbling gait.

Mark put his hand on the cudgel and dagger he carried

319

at his waist. Night was not a time to walk unprotected through the streets of Alsatia. A man could be murdered for the price of the clothes on his back.

The rain washed away the accumulated garbage in the narrow street and, in so doing, discharged its putrid smells to assault wayfarers. Rats foraged amongst the debris, and from a pile of rags in an upturned barrel came the snore of a vagabond. Mark guessed the hour to be past midnight, and quickened his stride. Drunken laughter and singing came from several brothels and taverns. He leaped over puddles reflecting the dim rushlight from an unshuttered window. He longed now for the warmth of Jesmaine's bed. Thoughts of her fragrant body and the pleasure she could evoke momentarily distracted him. In a mood of mellow anticipation, he turned the corner into a dark street. Before he had gone several paces, he heard a footfall behind him.

Swinging round, he crouched like a wrestler, his arms and the poniard extended. There were three of them, burly figures with massive shoulders and fists like anvils. They charged together, battering Mark against a wall. He overcame the pain and struck out with his dagger, slashing one opponent's arm whilst at the same time punching another man in the face.

Mark felt no fear. He was an accomplished wrestler, and his lean body was deceptive. His shoulders and arms were strong and muscular from long hours of cutting down trees and building fences during the winters in Wales. Briefly he managed to hold his own, but when his attackers all rushed him at once, he was no match for them. Their fists slammed into his face and chest without mercy, each punch weakening him.

Fighting on, Mark jabbed a fist into the fleshy jaw of an assailant. The force of the blow cracked his knuckles and they flared into a furnace of pain. It was a punch which would have felled an ox and it had broken his hand. The man went down, knocked out cold. Another leaped into the fray to take his place. As Mark's poniard come up in defence a heavy weight fell upon his back, knocking him off balance. At the same time his cloak was thrown over his head, blinding him. Stumbling, he struck out wildly. Whoever had leaped on to his back, jumped off, emitting a demoniacal shriek. Mark felt his dagger strike through to a bone. A man swore profanely. But before Mark could recover his balance, a knee was rammed into his groin. Excruciating pain burned like red-hot pincers through him, leaving him sweating and gasping.

A second kick toppled him to the ground. He tasted blood and spat out the filth of the gutter from his mouth. Boots thudded into his ribs and stomach. Unable to escape the ring of feet, he rolled into a ball, seeking to protect his head. His purse, containing a few copper coins, was taken from him as was the dagger. Also his warm cloak. That he was spared being stripped naked he owed only to the threadbare quality of his seaman's disguise. His ragged shirt and breeches were worthless. They continued to kick him, and through a swollen eye he saw a macabre figure jumping up and down with glee.

'You thought you'd rob Cecil Gubbett of his lawful earnings,' the hunchback screamed. 'I said I'd make you pay for that. Don't know what you're up to sniffing round 'ere. 'Appen I'm doing some cove a good turn. You've 'ad this coming a long time, Rowan. I ain't forgot Soulful and 'ow you 'ad me banished from the fairs last summer. Gubbett always repays a service done to 'im.'

The abuse faded in Mark's ears as blackness engulfed him. Sometime in the night the rain roused him to consciousness. He was lying in a pool of water, his hands and feet numb with cold. The instinct to survive made him try to rise. If he lay here all night, he would die. He levered himself on to his knees. The pain in his head and from his cracked ribs left him gasping, darkness rushing in to swamp him.

Chapter Twenty-One

Each night Gabriellen fell exhausted on to her pillow. Esmond had disappeared for four days and left her in charge. Daily she was in confrontation with Anthony Culpepper who refused to take orders from a woman. Yesterday, from sheer exasperation, she had slapped his insolent face.

'In my father's absence, I am his representative. If you don't like taking orders from a woman, you can leave and go to the devil!'

For several moments Culpepper blinked back at her, his high colour testimony to his astonished outrage. But he was shrewd enough to weigh the consequences before he reacted.

Surprisingly, Samuel Lacey intervened. The older actor had settled comfortably into Esmond's roles and was not now prepared to relinquish them to resume the responsibility of the lead. 'Miss Angel has only the welfare of the company at heart. Without her guidance we would not be ready to open tomorrow. Put your prejudices aside, man.'

At Lacey's championship, Gabriellen relaxed. She dimpled prettily and, though aware that Culpepper's preference was for men rather than women, plied him with the Angel charm. Since childhood she had realised that such persuasion could be as devastating as the infamous Angel rages. It worked and Culpepper had conceded to her authority.

The actor's tantrums were one of many problems to be dealt with. Costumes had to be altered to fit the new roles of Culpepper and Lacey. Any special effects required in the play had to be tested for safety, and often accidents occurred, disrupting the rehearsal for an entire morning. Twice that week Jack had sent word for Gabriellen to join him in his rooms. Those moments were too precious to miss. They were her relief from the strain of encouraging the players, ministering to minor injuries, chasing the builders to complete jobs left undone, and running the household.

In Jack's arms she could forget her worries about the troupe and her misgivings about her father. She could rest, feel protected, comforted and loved. But those magical hours were dearly paid for. More problems greeted her return to the house in Bankside. Laurence was teething and fretful. Any sign of an infant fever sent Nan and Agnes into a mindless panic. Here Gabriellen's knowledge of herbs served her well. She brewed infusions for the babe to ease his pain and insisted that both women drank camomile tisanes to calm their nerves. There were also a growing number of creditors to deal with. The butcher, apothecary and candlemaker were all threatening to have Esmond arrested for debt if their bills were not settled immediately.

Somehow Gabriellen coped. The costumes were finished. So was the building work on the theatre. Esmond returned. The creditors were paid. Gabriellen did not ask how. To her relief the opening of The Angel was a resounding success.

Lord Mincham basked in the praise lavished upon both the splendour of his theatre and the excellence of the play. Several noblemen attended as Lord Mincham's guests, the most prestigious of these the Earl of Essex and another favourite counsellor of the Queen, Sir Christopher Hatton. Both had professed their pleasure. Jack, who was now often in Essex's company, forwent the pleasures of the Court to stay and celebrate with the players.

Later that night in the rooms on London Bridge, Gabriellen lay beside him, for once unable to respond to his caresses.

'What's amiss?' Jack asked tersely. 'You've been distracted all evening. The day went well, did it not? Or is it that my attentions bore you?'

She chuckled, despite her worries. 'Jack, how can you think that? It's just . . .' She checked. Her foremost fear was groundless. She was allowing the darkness to exaggerate it. 'It's nothing. I'm being foolish. Our time together is always so short. Let's not waste it.'

She rolled across Jack and began to kiss him. But somehow her heart was not in making love and, sensing it, he pushed her away at arm's length.

'Are you still concerned at Mark's absence?'

His astuteness surprised her. The light from the bedside candle shone on his face. To her relief there was no sign of the resentment he sometimes showed at her friendship with the Welshman. 'We had arranged two visits this week, one to Westminster Abbey to see the tombs of our Kings and Queens, and yesterday to visit the book stalls in St Paul's. Both times he did not come. What worries me is that he sent no word.'

Jack looked affronted. 'I would take you to these sights if I could. It is not always easy. Should we be seen . . .' He shifted his gaze to look past her shoulder, his tone hardening. 'I thought you understood my position at Court?'

'I try to, but sometimes I wonder if you are ashamed that your mistress is a mere playwright's daughter?'

She saw the cold calculation shining in his eyes and quickly changed the subject. It was ground they had covered many times. 'That is not what troubles me at the moment,' she said firmly. 'Yesterday's excursion was important to me. Mark knew that. I wanted to buy a copy of *Holinshed's Chronicle* for Father's name day next week.' Jack frowned, oblivious of the significance of her disappointment. 'That chronicle tells the history of England's Kings and Queens,' she explained. 'Father lost his copy. It's a valuable aid to a playwright. Mark would not deliberately disappoint me.'

'Probably he received an offer for his horses which has to be dealt with. Several noblemen have expressed a wish to own a Rowan mare. Did Mark tell you that the Queen thought so highly of them that she purchased two geldings? Essex, not to be outdone, bought a mare for his own use.'

'Yes, and I am delighted at his success. But even if his work takes him away, he always sends word.' She was emphatic. 'He also promised to attend the opening of the playhouse today. I can't believe he would miss that. Something has happened to him.'

'Rowan can look after himself.' Jack no longer hid his irritation. 'Tomorrow my ships sail to Hull and I go on to York. It's been six months since I visited my business interests there.'

'You leave tomorrow?' The unexpected news momentarily cast all other thoughts from her mind. 'For how long?'

'Four months at least. From York I sail to the Spanish Main. I have Letters of Marque, and will return with my holds bulging with Spanish plunder.'

'I thought you wished to give up buccaneering?'

'So I do. But there's no quicker way to make your fortune. This is done in the name of the Queen.'

'Four months is a long time, Jack.' She was hurt that he announced his departure in such a careless manner. At times he could be thoughtless. She forced a bright smile and, determined not to show how it had upset her, leaned across to kiss him. 'Since your leaving is but a few hours away, let's not waste this night, my love.'

Jack grinned, the candlelight revealing his chipped tooth. She touched it with her finger. 'This tooth of yours gives you such a roguish air.' She kissed the edge of the scar which showed just above the clipped line of his beard. 'Are both of these mementoes from your buccaneering days?'

'Would you like them to be?'

She shrugged. 'Where did they come from?'

'Nowhere so romantic as the Spanish Main. The tooth was broken when I was seventeen and fleeing from three sailors who took exception to my winning a month's wages from them at cards. I tripped as I tried to lose them in a dark alley and broke it on a doorstep. They did not catch me, though. The scar came from a knife fight in a tavern.'

'Such a disreputable life.' She shook her head, looking at him in mock disapproval. 'You and Mark are so different. Yet you are close friends.'

'Your thoughts are on the Welshman again.'

There was a challenge in Jack's voice. It vexed her. How could he be jealous of her friendship with Mark? 'Oh, Jack,' she murmured. 'Is not my being here proof of my devotion?'

Her hair had grown almost long enough to cover her breasts, and fell forward like a shimmering veil. As she moved it caressed his chest. His grey eyes glinted for a moment, then burned with resurgent desire.

'Show me how much you will miss me when I sail,' he said provocatively, running his hands down her spine.

She was trembling, her body shamelessly undulating to

the pleasure of his caress. Rising on to her knees, Gabriellen straddled him and eased forward, resting her hands on his ribs. She stretched to kiss his throat, her breasts tingling as they pressed against the hair of his chest. Her hands slid upwards over his shoulders, admiring the firmness of their powerful strength. He moved against her and she felt the smooth hardness, the demanding rigidity, of his manhood against her thighs. At first their lovemaking was reminiscent of the sweet rapture of familiar sensations so often experienced when they lay together. She moved sensuously above him as his hands stroked slowly downward over the swell of her breasts and the curve of her hips. Soon, their needs brought a rougher urgency to their lovemaking. She sank down upon him, sheathing the hard heat of him within her. Jack gasped, pulling her head down to receive his kiss. When his lips circled each breast, his teeth gently teased the nipple. She moaned softly, a need unfurling and expanding deep inside as her movements increased in tempo.

With a twist of his body, Jack rolled and pulled her down on the mattress, rearing over her. The hypnotic caress of his mouth and tongue across her body set every sense and nerve ending aglow. Gabriellen responded, craving more from him, and receiving it. They soared onward until, breathless, she cried out: 'Jack! Oh Jack!'

As the last waves of fulfilment stilled, she gazed up at him. The grey pre-dawn light was full upon his face. He was grinning down at her. 'You seem insufferably self-satisfied,' she murmured lethargically.

'I wanted you to remember this night in the weeks we are apart.'

'How could I forget it?' She put her palm to his jaw and stroked his trimmed beard. 'But such memories will make our separation the harder to endure.'

His grin widened. 'I would seal my brand upon you, my sultry enchantress. You are mine, Gabriellen. Do not forget that whilst I am away.'

'Do you not trust me?' She sat up, her eyes taking on a feral glow as her indignation sparked.

A drowsy grunt was her reply as he turned on to his side, already sliding into sleep.

'Jack! I said, do you not trust me?'

'My dear, all women are whores at heart,' he mumbled.

Incensed, Gabriellen grabbed a pillow and swung it against his head. He turned in surprise. Before he could retaliate, she seized the advantage. Rolling on to her knees, she struck him furiously with the pillow, time and again. 'How dare you think I'd play you false? You name me whore, when it is you who refuse to have our union blessed by the church.'

He put up a hand to stave off her attack. 'Damnation, woman! I regard you as my wife in everything but name.'

'They are but words, Jack. Empty, meaningless words.'

The pace of her blows increased. Uncontrolled rage possessed her. That ungovernable demon which lurked within her, ready at any unguarded moment to rise up, did so now. It tore away any façade of gentility, to rip at her composure with the brutality of a tigress's claws. 'You are an arrant knave, Jack Stoneham. A despicable philanderer.'

'Gabriellen, have you taken leave of your senses?' Jack snarled as he sat up and failed to grab her wrist.

Her reply was a hard thump on his chest which burst the seam of the abused pillow. The goose feathers shot forth like a volley from a cannon. They stuck in her mouth, in her hair, and on the sheen of perspiration which dampened her body. In a shower of white feathers she continued to hit him, her scorn silenced by the need to spit tufts of plumage from her mouth.

Suddenly she saw the havoc she had created. Every piece of furniture in the room was covered in feathers, as was the black velvet doublet, trunk hose and cloak Jack had earlier discarded. Even their bodies were covered in the snowy down. They looked preposterous, as undignified as brawling children. But so comical. Her sense of humour doused her anger. Clutching the empty pillowcase to her breasts, she rocked backwards and forwards with laughter.

As abruptly as she had begun to laugh, she ceased. Jack had not joined in her amusement. He was looking at her as though her wits had addled.

'Good God, woman! That cursed temper of yours is the plague of my life. I'm glad you find your antics amusing. Look at my cloak and doublet. The white down will stick to it like molten wax. It will be unfit to wear again. Have you no sense of decorum?'

She looked at him with hurt incredulity. He had always encouraged her wildness and unpredictability. Her eyes dilated as she reached for her chemise and pulled it over her head. Standing up, she scrambled into her petticoats. When she addressed him, her voice was frosty. 'You knew I had a temper from the first moment we met. If you want a mouse-hearted mistress, then look elsewhere. Though I doubt such a meek-spirited creature would have sacrificed her reputation, as I have, on your account.'

She struggled into her gown. Knowing that she was dependent upon him to fasten the back lacings only served to enflame her anger. He had risen from the bed and in frigid silence was pulling on his shirt. That silence snapped what was left of her control. She rounded on him, her hands planted on her hips and her green eyes flashing fire. 'I am as I am. But I'm no whore. Nor shall I be treated or spoken to as one.'

His expression remained glacial. She turned her back on him and dressed, hearing his movements behind her. Still seething, she cried out without turning. 'Why all this pother, Jack? 'Tis only a suit of clothes. Are they more important than our love?'

There was no need to look at him to know he was tight-lipped with silent anger. He resented any criticism. Her temper continued to simmer as she pulled on her stockings and rammed her feet into her shoes. How could he be so heartless? Heaven forfend she should ruin his Jack-a-Dandy plumage! Clearly his clothes meant more to him than her feelings. That knowledge cut deep. Her emotions erupted with volcanic force, refusing to be contained. She whirled to face him, her breathing erratic. 'A murrain on you, Jack. Have you nothing to say?'

He was adjusting the narrow fluted ruffs at his wrists with terse jerking movements. When he lifted his head to regard her, there was a restrained ferocity in his handsome face, a ruthlessness, which would have frightened her had she not been too irate to recognise it.

'You are in the wrong, Gabriellen,' he drawled. 'When you're in this mood there's no reasoning with you.'

'Is there not?' She jabbed the words at him. His statement was so conceited that for a moment she eyed the other pillow and was sorely tempted to launch into a second attack. Restraint won. The violence of her fury began to take its toll and she started to tremble. Disconcerted, she said the first words which came into her head. 'At least I've still got a sense of humour. And I'm ruled by love, not ambition.'

'Get your cloak, Gabriellen.' His tone and expression were dark and forbidding.

Such a formidable countenance might strike terror into his seamen, might even impress his contemporaries at Court. It roused her past all caution. In the name of love she had cast aside honour and suffered the censure of her father. What she would not tolerate was Jack's lack of respect.

Her eyes widened mutinously. 'Is that all you can say? Dismiss me as though I were a common trollop!' Her fists clenched, stabbing the air in impotent fury. 'Damn you, Jack! You're a selfish bastard. I deserve better from you.'

Suddenly she was in his arms, her cheek laid against the silk of his shirt, her hands stilled against his chest. He touched her tousled hair. His voice was still harsh, as though drawn from him against his will. 'My love, I am all you say and more. Yet know this, firebrand and enchantress that you are . . .' His hold upon her tightened. 'You are my only love. My woman.'

It was typical of him that even now it was an order, not an appeal. He lifted her face with his fingers and his gaze, now tender and devoid of mockery, destroyed her anger. 'Am I so heartless, Gabriellen?'

Annoyed with herself that his slightest touch could mellow her rage, she looked into his face. The knave was smiling. Unapologetic, too assured, but heart-wrenchingly attractive. She could not stop the leaping of her pulses. Why did she love him so desperately? She could not bear him to set sail on a long voyage with bad feeling between them.

'You are all I have called you and more, Jack Stoneham. And, for my sins, I love you.'

Jack kissed her hair. 'And for my greater sins, I love you.'

He caressed her lips lightly with his own and then stepped back towards the bed, drawing her with him.

''Tis daylight,' she murmured, glancing towards the window.

'Then we still have two hours before I join my ship at the wharf.'

He swept the feather-strewn coverlet and sheet from the

bed. The growing ardour in his gaze coerced her to follow
him. There was no need for further words. Their priorities
might differ, but Jack desired her. Loved her. And her
love for him was absolute.

Jesmaine snapped her almanac shut. She pushed her hands
through her dark, unbound hair and hung her head as she
slowly massaged her temples. The zodiac chart she had cast
lay spread on the table before her. Still the danger was
there in Mark's ruling house. Pushing the chart aside she
dealt the cards into rows. Danger. Always danger. The
knave and the queen ever present and threatening. Lately
the ace of spades had begun to appear. The death card. Its
appearance frightened her. Dear God, hadn't Mark suffered
enough?

If only she could see wherein lay the danger. Though
her powers were great, that was always denied her. During
the year since she had set up these rooms in Bishopsgate
she had developed her skills to become an accomplished
scryer. But the crystal only showed her glimpses of what
Mark's future held. Sinister scenes of murder, betrayal,
and always danger.

Hearing a knock upon the outer door, Jesmaine stared
blankly in its direction. She had cancelled all her appoint-
ments this week and a notice had been nailed on the door
saying that she was not available for consultations. The
knock came again – loud, insistent and determined. She
picked up the cards and folded the chart before walking
through the parlour into the small square entrance hall.
Some of the exotic ornaments she had used in her fairground tent were displayed here, together with a brightly
cushioned settle should her customers be obliged to wait.

When she opened the door, surprise caught her
unawares. It was replaced instantly by anger, by the fierce
need of a woman to protect her mate. She barred the doorway, her eyes narrowing. Hostility stripped the sensuality
from her face.

'Is Mark Rowan here?'

'Why do you come? You're not welcome.'

'I came because I'm worried about Mark. Has something
happened to him?'

'He is safe enough now.' Jesmaine gave way to the
months of resentment at the close friendship Mark had

maintained with Gabriellen. She did not want this woman in her house. She wanted to protect Mark from the danger she felt this creature would bring him. At that moment Hywel began to bark, and with his paws slithering on the polished floorboards, thrust his way past Jesmaine.

Yelping with excitement, the dog circled Gabriellen, his tail wagging furiously. She bent to ruffle his ears. When she straightened, her stare was puzzled. 'Is Mark hurt in some way? Is that why you won't let me see him?' The question was quietly spoken, but carried the force of a command.

'Come here, Hywel!' Jesmaine ordered the dog inside and then began to close the door. She had almost given in to that cool authority.

Gabriellen put out a hand to stop the door shutting. 'Has Mark said he does not wish to see me?'

Jesmaine stared at the younger woman with loathing. She pushed a lank strand of hair from her eyes, hating to acknowledge that she must look an unkempt slut. A week ago when Mark had been brought home, she would have thrown herself at this woman in a violent fury, believing her the cause of his condition. After a week of worry she was now too exhausted. The nights of sleepless vigilance had taken all her energy. 'Mark can say nothing.' Her voice broke as the strain began to show. She controlled it and swept back her long ebony hair. 'I say you will not see him. I have seen in the stars that you bring danger to him.'

'But that's not possible.' Gabriellen voiced her shock. 'We are friends. I owe Mark my life. What has happened? Tell me.'

The green eyes regarding her were distraught with fear. Jesmaine felt a momentary compassion. She blamed Gabriellen for all that had befallen Mark, but the woman was clearly concerned. Jesmaine hesitated. Her first instincts remained to send this woman away, but Mark thought highly of Gabriellen. Perhaps something could be gained from this meeting? If she could persuade Gabriellen to have her horoscope cast, or even her palm read, there might be a way of saving Mark from the danger which hung over his life.

'You may see him.' Begrudgingly, Jesmaine opened the door for Gabriellen to enter. 'Perhaps it will make you realise the wisdom behind my words.'

331

Gabriellen had expected stronger resistance to her request. She was surprised when Jesmaine gave in so easily. But she was shocked by the lack of care in the fortune-teller's appearance. Her hair was straggly, her gold brocade gown carelessly laced and crumpled as though she had slept in it. Purple shadows of fatigue ringed Jesmaine's eyes. Her cheeks were sunken, and her full lips thinned with strain. How badly was Mark hurt?

Following Jesmaine, she absently noted the cleanliness of the rooms, the bright but tasteful colours which echoed her vivacious personality. As they walked through the parlour towards what she guessed was the bedchamber, Hywel ran ahead of them. He lay down at the side of the bed with his head upon his paws. Above Hywel's soft whimpering was the harsh labour of Mark's breathing. Jesmaine motioned Gabriellen to stay back and crossed to the bed. Pulling open the bed hangings, she bent over the mattress. When she straightened, she beckoned Gabriellen closer.

At the sight of Mark's battered face on the pillow she put a shaking hand to her mouth in horror. He had been brutishly beaten. Fever flamed his hollow, beard-stubbled cheeks. Several bruises and swollen cuts distorted his face into a macabre mask. His eyes were closed. Both his hands, which lay outside the scarlet and gold coverlet, were bandaged. Gabriellen looked down at him with growing alarm. He lay so still. Too still.

'Mark!'

There was no response.

'Mark! It's Ellen.' She touched his hot brow, her voice sharpening. 'Mark!'

'He does not hear you,' Jesmaine said from behind her. 'At least for the moment he is quiet.'

It was worse than Gabriellen feared. Without taking her eyes from him, she said in astonishment, 'And you think I am in some way responsible? Sweet Jesu, I care for Mark as I would a brother.' She stared down at the prostrate figure on the bed, unaware that tears were streaming down her cheeks. Mark had always been so strong, so capable. Yet she had seen the ague strip a powerful body to skeletal thinness. And together with the injuries he had sustained, it could very well prove fatal. Her lips quivered as she gazed helplessly down at the Welshman. Her voice choked on a sob. 'Oh, Mark.'

Jesmaine watched her narrowly. She was too tired for further recrimination. Gabriellen was so visibly upset that the fortune-teller relented towards her. 'This is a shock for you.'

'What does the physician say to Mark's chances?'

'I sent him away after he had applied his leeches. Fool that he was, he wanted to bleed him. As if Mark had not lost enough blood from his wounds! He may call himself a physician but he was no better than those "piss-prophets" who examine urine to make a diagnosis.'

Gabriellen nodded in agreement, but pressed her, 'Why are you so convinced that I am to blame for this?'

'I'm no charlatan,' Jesmaine returned with a flash of the old animosity. 'I know what is in the stars. It is written that you will bring harm to Mark.'

Gabriellen swayed at the harsh note of sincerity in Jesmaine's voice which frightened her. She covered her face with her hands and was surprised at their wetness from her tears. Lowering them, she drew a steadying breath and asked, 'How did it happen?'

'You truly care for him,' Jesmaine said softly. There was resignation and a rough kindness in her voice. 'That is something. Come, I will tell you.'

Jesmaine moved to the door and gestured for her to follow. As they entered the parlour Gabriellen asked, 'Should not Mark be watched? Is there nothing to be done?'

'All that can be done, has been done. If he should stir, Hywel will alert us.'

Jesmaine sat on a stool by the hearth, indicating that Gabriellen should take the wooden settle opposite her. 'The night Mark was attacked, he had told me not to wait up for him as he would be late home. After he left I began to feel uneasy. When he had not returned by midnight, I sensed he was in danger. The cards had shown this for some time, but not when it would happen. I consulted them again. It was there. Clear to see. The crystal showed me Mark lying in an alley. I acted at once. There's a water carrier who rents the rooms next door. I woke him. I was so upset that even though he believed my fears were groundless, he agreed to accompany me to search for Mark. It was Hywel who found him two hours later. It was almost dawn by then. Mark was lying in a gutter in the rain. He must have been set upon by thieves. Apart from two broken ribs, a broken hand and severe internal bruising, it must be obvious to you that he has the lung fever.' Tears rose to Jesmaine's eyes and she stood up to turn her back on Gabriellen. It was a moment before she spoke again. 'The fever is growing worse.'

Gabriellen looked through the door into the chamber beyond where a bandaged hand was visible as it lay upon the coverlet.

'Where was he found?'

'Carmelite Street.'

'But that's part of the area they call Alsatia! It's more notorious than Bankside. What was Mark doing there?'

'Since he cannot talk, I do not know.' The antagonism was back in Jesmaine's voice and directed against Gabriellen.

A movement from the bedchamber caught both women's attention. Mark's hands pushed at the covers as he began to twist and turn. Hywel sat up, looking from his master to Jesmaine who was already half-way across the parlour floor. Gabriellen was close behind her.

As they reached the bed Mark began to cough, long wrenching spasms which left him weakened and gasping. Jesmaine held his head in her arm and put a cup to his mouth, but the liquid dribbled back through bloodless lips. Unable to stand by and do nothing, Gabriellen took up a linen cloth from a bowl of cool water. Ringing it out, she placed it against Mark's burning brow. It was some minutes before the coughing subsided. Then his body began to shiver.

Jesmaine worked in silence, clearly too worn out to talk, or protest at Gabriellen's presence. She built up the fire. When Mark began to fling his limbs wildly about, she helped Jesmaine restrain him. As his fever rose he began to mumble in delirium. Gabriellen spoke softly to the patient, her soothing voice gradually calming his incoherent speech until after an hour he became still.

When Gabriellen made to draw away, she realised her hand had been gripping Mark's as she willed him to rest quieter. She withdrew it self-consciously and discovered Jesmaine's thoughtful stare upon her. The fortune-teller looked ready to drop from tiredness. Gabriellen came to her side, saying with concern, 'You're exhausted. Get some sleep or you'll be ill. I will see to Mark's needs.'

'It is for me to look after my man, not you.' Some of the old defiance was back in Jesmaine's tone, but her eyes were drained of energy.

'What are friends for if they cannot help in a time of need? Mark is mortally ill. Don't let your mistrust of me be the cause of his death.'

Suddenly Jesmaine's face crumpled and her body shook with sobs. Gabriellen put her arms around her. 'Rest now. I'll send word to my father that I'm here. We can take it in turns to tend Mark. I shall stay as long as you need me. Perhaps it will never be possible for us to be friends. But until Mark is well, for his sake, we can work together.'

Jesmaine raised her head, her tear-brimmed eyes filled with anguish. 'It would be churlish to refuse. Mark may respond to your voice. He has great affection for you.'

Gabriellen put her hand over Jesmaine's wrist. 'Don't be jealous of that. What Mark and I feel for each other is . . .' She paused, finding it difficult to put into words. 'It is an affinity which was forged when he saved my life. We have many interests in common and have the same sense of humour. He's like a brother, a mentor, a very special friend. Mark loves you. And I love only one man – Jack Stoneham. I will love Jack until I die.'

Jesmaine looked at her with something like pity. 'It is a rare love which lasts forever. It endures only when bestowed upon a man of impeccable honour. You're an idealist, Miss Angel. Love is not an ideal. Your bold sea captain is your first lover. No woman forgets the first man who steals her heart.' She paused, watching Gabriellen shrewdly before continuing with greater confidence: 'Unlike you, I have had many men. Perhaps no more than three of them have I really loved.'

She smiled and shook her head at Gabriellen's shocked expression. 'I know something of love. Time creates many tests. Absences can stretch trust to its limit and beyond. Lust, greed, jealousy, ambition and betrayal at sometime test love. Sometimes they are too terrible for any amount of love to sustain itself against them.'

'I do not believe that.'

'There are many things you do not want to believe. That does not mean they do not exist.' Jesmaine swayed. As she put a hand to her head, her body toppled sideways. Gabriellen caught her arm and stopped her from falling.

'Go and rest, Jesmaine. I will see to Mark's needs while you sleep.'

Esmond stared down at the document over which his quill was poised. He raised his head to study the man opposite him. The single eye regarded him like a hawk.

'You still retain a one-third interest in the establishment.' One-eyed Ned fingered the reddish streak in his beard, showing his impatience at Esmond's hesitation. 'It will bring you a goodly profit from the quarterly shareout. To maintain its reputation as the best trugging-house in the city, money will have to be spent on it. Now that Stoneham and myself are your partners, the place will flourish.'

'Unfortunately, you're right.' Esmond looked round at the fading wall hangings. The place was beginning to look tawdry and that would never do. 'My family have owned it for three generations. It does not deal with riffraff. The highest in the land come here for entertainment. That's where the profits lie, in keeping the gentry and nobility happy.'

'Nell Lovegood knows her business, as did her mother before her.' Ned crossed one leg over the other, the candle-light reflected in the abundance of semi-precious gems sewn on to his slashed doublet. There was a gleam of speculation in his eyes as he watched the auburn-haired, buxom madam of the house, moving amongst the customers. Nell's hearty laugh accompanied each risqué aside. When Ned turned back to watch Esmond who was still fidgeting with the quill, his patience ran out.

'Hell's bowels, man! It's a fair price Stoneham and I are offering. We're prepared to invest in the property, expand it. In a year your profits will triple. You'll be no worse off. It's still a goodly inheritance for your children.'

'Should anything happen to me, the money will be paid to Gabriellen?' Esmond leaned forward, staring hard at his companion. He knew that Ned, with his foppish appearance, was aping a class he could never attain. 'I have your word on that?'

'You have.' One-eyed Ned made a sign which in the unwritten law of the Underworld was a bond which could not in honour be broken.

Esmond sat back. 'My daughter need never know from what source this money is earned?'

336

Ned laughed, his saturnine, bearded face reddening with amusement. 'You old rogue and reprobate, Angel! The respectable life of a playwright and sharer in Lord Mincham's Men is softening you. Do you fear Miss Angel's censure? I've heard her temper is the match of yours, and she's a haughty wench. She'd not be so fond of walking along Bankside with her nose stuck in the air if she knew the source of the money which put those expensive clothes on her back! Your name is enough to strike fear and respect in many quarters of Bankside and Alsatia, yet you shrink from her learning the truth.'

'If you had a daughter, Ned, you would be the same.'

Ned laughed derisively. 'You talk as though she's spent her life in a nunnery. She's Stoneham's whore!'

Esmond's hand shot out, grabbing the front of Ned's saffron doublet. Both men leapt to their feet with Esmond still holding fast to Ned. Several heads turned in their direction.

'Insult my daughter and you insult me.' His voice carried the underlying violence and threat which twenty years ago had placed him as high in the Underworld hierarchy as his companion was now.

From across the table Ned's stare burned into him. Esmond recognised his danger but refused to back down. One-eyed Ned was an Upright Man. At a click of his fingers a dozen of his minions would throw Esmond into the street or river. Ned was ten years younger than Esmond, of muscular build with no spare flesh. Despite his eye-patch he was handsome enough to be a favourite with the ladies. Outwardly he dressed and, when he chose, acted and spoke like a nobleman. Beneath that sophisticated façade was a man who would show no mercy. It was said a score of men had died by his hand. Esmond held Ned's stare without fear. With a forced laugh, Ned raised his hands in supplication.

'Would I insult my good friend?'

Esmond relaxed, but though he sat down, did not pick up the quill. He studied Ned. They'd known each other for years, but Ned did not know the meaning of loyalty. How could he be certain that Ned would not swindle Gabriellen and Laurence out of their inheritance?

He reassured himself with the knowledge that Stoneham would never allow Ned to steal from Gabriellen. Not while

Stoneham and his daughter were lovers. He could wish that alliance more permanent. Stoneham would climb high. Perhaps he would not make such a bad husband for Gabriellen? In recent months Esmond had mellowed towards the captain's association with his daughter. He had even hinted that a marriage between them would seal this deal. Stoneham had shied away, declaring that at this stage it would ruin his advancement at Court. The rogue had been charming, devout in his love for Gabriellen. He had asked for Esmond's forbearance. In a year, two at the most, he would own a grand house and a rising fortune. Gabriellen would live the rest of her days in luxury as a grand lady.

One-eyed Ned sat back in his chair and studied Esmond's drawn face. Once there had not been a rogue or a coney-catcher to hold a candle to him. Most of the ruses to trick a cove of his money, which Ned had learnt as a youth, had been mastered after watching Esmond charm and trick his quarry out of sizeable fortunes. Esmond Angel's day was almost done. That he even considered Ned's and Stoneham's offer to buy shares in Nell Lovegood's establishment was proof that Esmond was in financial difficulty. How long would the money given to him today last? Within six months to a year, Ned could see Esmond irretrievably bound to the moneylenders.

The Upright Man looked round the large open room with its painted silk hangings and discreet alcoves. His gaze travelled up the carved oak staircase. Above them were four rooms set aside for gaming. Another dozen provided the customers with the services to satisfy all carnal tastes and pleasures.

His gaze returned to Esmond, his tone encouraging. 'Nell Lovegood's is unrivalled as a brothel and gaming house. Since Stoneham has bought the property next door the two will now be knocked into one. Our profits will increase. We have dealt well enough in other business ventures in the past. This shall be our greatest success yet.'

Still Esmond hesitated. He had taken little interest in the brothel for many years, though in his youth he had freely enjoyed the use of his inheritance. Sabine had changed that. She had encouraged his writing. Virtuous and gentle, she would have been shocked to learn the source of his income. As his thoughts rushed on, a guilt he had thought long buried unexpectedly made him feel ashamed. But compared

338

to the other secret he had kept for so long from Sabine, the income from the brothel was a trivial matter. He had always known the danger of Sabine's highly strung nature. But he had never guessed how catastrophic her horror would be at discovering his other secret.

'Sign it, Esmond.' Ned's impatient voice broke across Esmond's remorse. 'Do I need to remind you that if your debts are not paid, you will be arrested? Too many creditors are baying at your heels, not the least of whom is Prew.' An evil gleam brightened the single blue eye. 'Of course, I could have some of my boys silence Prew's threats for good.'

'There's much in my life I'm not proud of,' Esmond said, stiffly. 'Several men have ended their days on my sword. But I've never murdered anyone in cold-blood. Nor will I be a party to it. Prew is a leech that is slowly sucking me dry. But I'm still enough of a gentleman to honour my debts.'

Esmond signed with a flourish and thrust the quill and parchment across the table. He gestured for a pot-girl to bring him more brandy. Ned watched Esmond down several cups before the playwright picked one of the girls to accompany him to an upper room. Twice whilst crossing to the stairs he stumbled, against a table and then a chair. But though he had been drinking heavily, the playwright was far from cupshot. Ned had seen Esmond hold twice that amount before it affected his wits or balance. Now he was showing his age – losing his edge. In their game, that could lead to the gallows. Esmond was wise to change his ways.

Ned rolled his gold earring between his fingers, his sardonic face thoughtful. He suspected that Esmond's sight was failing him. That would explain the large sums lost at cards. Two years ago it was unheard of for him to lose a hand. Ned shrugged. Esmond's misfortune was his gain. Now he was a part-owner of Nell Lovegood's, his status in the hierarchy of the Underworld would rise. He would be its uncrowned king.

Whilst Jesmaine slept the clock round, Gabriellen brewed an infusion of herbs which she had learned from Aunt Dorothy. She was desperate for any means of lowering Mark's fever. For two days an uneasy companionship had existed between the two women. Gabriellen was fascinated by the instruments of Jesmaine's trade, but had refused to allow the fortune-teller to read her palm or cast her horoscope.

When she was helping Jesmaine tidy the rooms one morning, she saw inside a small chamber whose door had been hidden by a wall hanging. On a bench stood rows of strange-shaped glass vessels, some of which were attached to a wooden support with a candlestick underneath. Her eyes lit up. This was something she had not encountered before, and it intrigued her. 'What is this room used for?'

'It is there Mark experiments with alchemy,' Jesmaine said. 'Has he not spoken of it to you?' At Gabriellen's denial, Jesmaine looked pleased. 'I have some interest in it myself.'

'You mean Mark seeks the philosopher's stone from which it is said all metal will turn into gold?'

Jesmaine gave a slow smile. 'Mark would be horrified to hear you say that. It is true that alchemy is the study of transmutation. The whole universe is a living process. The seed into a plant. The egg into a chicken. Once metals are heated they become liquid. Wood when burnt becomes ash.' Seeing Gabriellen's interest, Jesmaine continued with a touch of pride: 'Many astrologers are alchemists. Some people would say that gives our profession the taint of necromancy. I disagree. We do not make spells or love-potions. I leave that to the charlatans.'

'Mark said you have many notable clients. That eminent clergy consult you as to the likelihood of receiving bishop-rics. Wealthy merchants upon the outcome of lawsuits. Not to mention the stream of courtiers who are eager to consult you. Am I right?'

'Many noblemen,' Jesmaine replied. 'They are always intriguing for power, or seeking to win a new paramour to their beds.'

'You also have many healing skills. You are an accomplished woman, Jesmaine.'

A slight sound from across the room was instantly detected by the two women. They ran into the bedchamber. From Mark's high colour it was obvious that he was approaching the crisis of the fever. For the next day and night both women went without sleep. It took their combined strength to hold Mark down when the fever rose to its pitch, their torment aggravated by the sweltering heat of a hot September day.

With sleeves rolled to her elbows, Gabriellen replaced a drying cloth upon Mark's hot brow with a cool one, whilst Jesmaine forced liquid between his lips. All night he called out in Welsh – sometimes angrily, sometimes with tender inflection. After a while the ramblings became incoherent mumbles. Finally, they stopped. There was an outbreak of cool perspiration covering Mark's face. His fever had broken.

The women sat slumped on either side of the bed, their heads bowed with tiredness. Mark's breathing was now slow and even. In the quietness of the room, Gabriellen heard the whisper of candle flames and the muffled whimpers from Hywel, his paws twitching in a dreaming sleep as he lay by the bed.

She disentangled her fingers from Mark's hand. She had been willing him to get better by seeking to transfer some of her strength into his body which was fighting for its life. As she moved away from the bed, there was a soft gasp from Jesmaine. Gabriellen turned and saw Mark's eyes flicker open. He was staring up at Jesmaine, a tender smile curving his lips. Gabriellen felt a rush of relief and breathed softly, 'Dear God, thank you for sparing him.'

She put her hand to her throat to ease the constriction caused by emotion. Mark turned his head towards her. His hair curled over his sweat-streaked brow.

'Looks like the score is even between us, Ellen.' His voice was cracked and pitched low.

'You gave us a scare, Mark. It is to Jesmaine that you owe your life. She spent a week at your bedside without sleep. I've been here but a few days to help her. Now I must go.'

She turned to Jesmaine. 'May I return tomorrow?'

The fortune-teller nodded, the wariness back in her eyes. 'I will shop for food on the way.'

'Thank you.' Jesmaine's voice had lost its friendliness.

Gabriellen smiled and bade Mark rest. As she stepped into the street, she felt desolate. Emptiness seeped coldly into the place that had been warm with cherished friendship a few moments ago. She could not forget Jesmaine's prophecy that somehow in the future her friendship with Mark would threaten his life.

Chapter Twenty-Two

It was a sultry July evening in 1590. Every window of the Great Hall of Greenwich Palace had been thrown open to catch what little air stirred the night. Rapturous applause greeted the end of Esmond Angel's latest comedy *The Widow went A-Wooing*. Few knew it had been written entirely by Gabriellen. Her Majesty, sitting on her high throne, was holding her sides, unable to contain her raucous laughter.

She beckoned Lord Mincham and Esmond forward. The peer strutted to the dais, his bald head gleaming like a golden sunrise beneath the light of a hundred candles. From where Gabriellen stood at the side of the stage, she watched her father bow to Her Majesty. Elizabeth leaned forward on her throne, her praise loud for all to hear. Esmond answered too softly for Gabriellen to catch his words. His wit provoked another burst of laughter from the Queen, causing Gabriellen to blink rapidly to dispel the tears of pride which blurred her vision. Her play was a success.

Esmond was receiving the acclaim but it was her words which had brought laughter to her Sovereign's lips, and even made the stalwart Queen wipe a surreptitious tear from her eye when the widow's ardent lover was killed. It was her genius which had made Her Majesty applaud with such fervour. From the conversation carrying to Gabriellen, every courtier present was laughing and enthusing over the merits of the play. The triumph made her light-headed and her whole body glowed with pride and happiness. She was a playwright and the Court admired her work. There could be no greater tribute to her skill.

At her side Anthony Culpepper snorted deprecatingly. 'It was my talent which brought the play to life. I am ignored, whilst Mincham enjoys Her Majesty's praise.'

'Without Lord Mincham's patronage, we would not exist,' Gabriellen maintained as she observed the pouting carmined mouth of the actor. She was too ecstatic to allow Culpepper's mood to spoil her elation. His egotism was worse than ever Cornelius Hope's had been. Culpepper became more insufferable by the day. At every rehearsal he set the other players against each other, but during a performance he held the audience enthralled. There was no doubt he was a superb actor. Women swooned to see him. His smooth classical features and blond flowing hair might give him the looks of a demi-god, but offstage he had the ethics of a sewer rat.

Unfortunately, success made Culpepper harder than ever to stomach. He was so impressed by his own importance, he regarded every other player as beneath him. He lorded it over them. Ridiculing and reviling them. Preying upon their insecurities to swell his own conceit. It took all Esmond's skill and Gabriellen's patience to keep the peace. It was impossible to dismiss him. Within a few weeks of joining the troupe, it was obvious that Culpepper had become Lord Mincham's lover. Towards Gabriellen, Culpepper showed open disdain and since he had become ensconced as the leading actor, refused to rehearse unless Esmond attended. He tolerated Gabriellen's presence at the playhouse only so long as she did not interfere. Had he known the play had been her work, he would have refused to perform.

Gabriellen never showed the pain or anger his attitude caused her. What use? It was a belief universal among all men that no woman had the wit or ability to write a play, and only a bawd would flaunt herself upon the stage. Philosophically, she accepted the prejudices heaped against her. But tonight nothing could take away the triumph that although Esmond received the acclaim, it was her wit every man and woman present at Court was truly honouring.

Moving away from the posturing Culpepper, Gabriellen's gaze roamed over the extravagantly clothed courtiers. The women all looked hot and uncomfortable. Their enormous ruffs, vast diaphanous hoods, volumes of trailing veils, all flowing over farthingales the size of cartwheels, made them look like an army of winged chariots in full charge. Despite the brilliant plumage vying for her attention, her gaze was drawn to Jack.

343

He stood close to the dais next to the Earl of Essex, dressed in black satin encrusted with an intricate leaf design of pearls. The red-haired earl was the darling of the Queen's court, but in Gabriellen's eyes Jack outshone him. There was not a man in the assembly who came close to him for looks, grace and commanding presence.

The heat of the Great Hall pressed down upon her and she felt close to swooning. The air was thick from the overpowering perfumes which failed to disguise the stench of sweating bodies. How the courtiers endured this over-crowding was beyond her understanding. A distance of more than forty feet separated Gabriellen from her lover, yet she could feel her skin burning from the sexual tension of being so close to him, yet so far away. In the six weeks since he had returned from the Caribbean, with his ships' holds crammed with Spanish plunder, she had seen him only four times. For the last two weeks he had been in York dealing with his business there. She had not seen him upon his return. Now her need to speak with him blotted out the splendour and excitement of the Court.

As a circle of beautiful ladies-in-waiting clustered around the Earl of Essex and his companions, jealousy stabbed at Gabriellen. Not once had Jack looked in her direction. She would not be so slighted. Could he be ashamed of her? Her eyes narrowed dangerously.

Damn his arrogance! Damn his high-flown ambition! She'd not tolerate being ignored. Throughout the two weeks since he had left for York, she had been anxious and worried by recent events. They were two weeks when, more than any other in their relationship, she had needed his reassurance and love. Now he ignored her, surrounded by simpering noblewomen. It emphasised the vast divide in their lifestyles and added to her uncertainties. Her chin lifted. The wildness inherited from Wildboar drove her now.

Devil take Jack's rules, she fumed. Why should they not occasionally be seen together in public? She needed to talk to him urgently and she meant to do just that.

As the Queen began to move out of the hall, Gabriellen hurried down the steps of the stage, heading through the press of courtiers towards Jack.

With one eye on the departure of the Queen, Jack was talking to a lady-in-waiting who made no secret of her interest in him. She extolled his bravery as a sea commander. Her voluptuous body leaned closer. From his superior height Jack was given a generous view of her upthrust breasts. With a sudden heating of his blood he remembered how eagerly she had served his needs last night. To escape the crush from the dancing he had taken a stroll in the palace grounds and had discovered her following him. Without preamble, he had tumbled her on the grass of the palace lawns.

Her name escaped him. There had been many such chance encounters. They meant nothing to him. Only Gabriellen had the power to draw him back time and again to her bed.

He became aware of courtiers parting to allow a woman to pass through. His attention rivetted upon the tall figure gliding through the press, the lady-in-waiting was forgotten.

A connoisseur of women, Jack never failed to marvel at the way Gabriellen moved, unconscious of the sensuality of her body. Her oyster silk gown was elegant but unremarkable amongst the jewel-studded extravagances of the ladies around her. Nevertheless, it added to the impact of her striking figure and countenance. Beside her other women paled into insignificance. Every man's head turned as she passed. None would forget the lure of those tumultuous green eyes, the seductive promise of high cheekbones and full lips which, though breaking every rule of established beauty, made Gabriellen the more memorable. Hers was a beauty which became more refined with every passing year.

For a moment he forgot the danger of discovery. Clearly Gabriellen had not. His attention won, she pointed towards the gardens and then passed him by without a second glance. Seeing that several courtiers had begun to follow her, Jack excused himself to Essex. Taking a circuitous route, he hurried through a string of anterooms which ran parallel with the corridor. Waiting in the doorway of a deserted scrivener's room, he saw Gabriellen turn the corner some distance ahead of her stalking admirers. Jack grabbed her wrist and pulled her into the tiny chamber, shutting the door firmly behind him.

'My heart,' he said, the words muffled as his lips crushed down upon hers.

It was some moments later before they broke breathlessly

345

apart, and to Gabriellen's delight his eyes sparkled with a possessive light. 'Every man in that Hall wanted you as you walked past. You cannot imagine the torment you put me through.'

'Did I?' There was a tightness to her voice which surprised him. It sounded very like the false sweetness she could assume before a storm of temper broke forth. 'From the way you were flirting with that lady-in-waiting, I'm surprised you even noticed me.'

'She's the wife of an influential member of the Privy Council,' Jack lied. 'I was merely being polite.'

He pulled her down on to a window seat and his hand slid under her gown to her knee. As it reached her inner thigh she clamped her fingers over it, the moonlight reflecting the feral glitter in her eyes. 'Jack, I will not be tumbled in the Queen's Palace like a serving maid. I have to talk to you. It's been two weeks since I've seen you.'

'Don't I know it, my angel!' He grinned lopsidedly at his play on words. 'Now you are here, why waste the privacy of the moment? My love, holding you is not enough. I want you!'

He kissed her throat, the inducement of his lips causing her neck to loll back and almost bringing her to submission. But the memory of a fortnight of anxiety remained, cooling her ardour. 'Jack, first we must talk.'

'Nay, sweeting. Later we will talk. I am starved from being so long without you. Relax. No one will come here.' As he spoke he kissed her lids, her brow, her cheeks, and ended by nuzzling her ear. 'Love me, Gabriellen.'

'I fear I have loved you too well.' Her voice broke.

He chuckled wickedly, his hand moving with assured insistence along her inner thigh. 'Your passion has always delighted me. Relax, my darling.'

She tore her lips from his and there was such pain and uncertainty in her lovely face, he eased back with a sigh.

'I'm with child, Jack.'

His flippant remark stuck in his throat. A chill plunged through him, shrivelling desire.

'Are you certain?'

'Yes.'

Gabriellen stared at him in an agony of doubting silence. He looked very pale. But, she had not thought he would be ecstatic at her news. It went contrary to his plans.

346

However, she had not expected him to look like a man who had just received a mortal blow. The thought was unpalatable. Leaping to her feet, her silk skirts billowed around her as she swung away to pace the room.

'It is a setback to your plans, Jack. But is thought of a child so terrible? We have been lovers for two years. Surely it was inevitable?'

'I had hoped to spare you,' he said, avoiding her gaze.

'Spare me!' She stared at him incredulously. 'I can think of nothing more wonderful than having your child. Surely, after all you have worked for, you want a son to inherit? I know you had not planned for us to marry for another year or so . . .'

'You do not understand.' He stood up, his expression blank. 'I should have told you before – I have a son. Three, to be precise, and a daughter.'

'I never realised you were a widower,' she began. Then the awesome hardness of his face stopped her. She backed away from him. 'Tell me that what I'm thinking isn't true.' Her voice rose in a desperate plea. 'Tell me, Jack!'

'I'm sorry, Gabriellen. I'm already married. I've been so for eight years. My family live in York.'

She shook her head, refusing to believe it. 'Do not jest, Jack.' The severity of his face told her this was no jest. At least he had the grace to look ashamed. The blood drained from her face. It felt as if it had seeped out of her body, leaving her frozen and trembling. She bowed her head and leant against the scrivener's desk for support.

Their love was a mockery. Jack had lied to her. Abused her trust. Deceived her. Betrayed her in the most callous manner. She felt sick and her stomach heaved at the horror of his treachery. Clamping a hand to her mouth, she controlled her nausea.

'Gabriellen, my love.' He took her arm.

She struck his hand away and swung round to face him. Her eyes glittered so savagely, he fell back a step. Quickly recovering his composure, he held out his hand again, his voice husky and cajoling. 'It changes nothing. I love you, Gabriellen, not my wife. I'll never abandon you. You and the child will want for nothing. We must be discreet. It would be disastrous enough should news of my marriage reach the Queen, but this scandal could destroy me.'

'Oh, for mercy's sake, Jack, spare me your hypocrisy!'

The contempt in her voice was too real to laugh aside. His throat went dry. He had always won her round. Suddenly she was no longer the frisky kitten to tease but an enraged tigress about to pounce, claws extended.

She flew at him, her hands pounding against his chest. 'My God, I trusted you. Foul, treacherous knave! You betrayed me!'

'I love you, Gabriellen.' He caught her wrists and forced her hands down to her sides. 'Damnation, woman, will you listen to me? I could not live without you. Would you have become my mistress had I told you I was married?'

'No.'

'Then how else was I to win you?' He smiled, confident he could charm her. 'I will not give you up, Gabriellen.'

She stood still and unyielding in his arms. 'You have destroyed all that I hold dear. I trusted you. You used me to satisfy your base desire, without thought of my dishonour. Get out of my sight. I hate you. I never want to set eyes on your treacherous face again.'

Her voice, harshened by the storm of invective, flayed him. Releasing her wrists, he tipped up her chin with his forefinger, his lips parting in his most disarming smile. 'You do not mean that, Gabriellen.'

'Don't I?' She swung up her fist with all her strength and hit him on the jaw. 'If I had a knife I would plunge it through your cold unfeeling heart. Everything between us has been a lie. You took me for a gullible fool, Jack. I shall never forgive you.'

'Gabriellen, listen to me. I love you.'

She turned her back on him. The sight of his distraught handsome face added to her torture. Imbecile that she was, she still loved him. But she would not give in. She could forgive him many things, but not such brutal betrayal. 'You only love yourself, Jack. You disgust me. If you touch me, I'll scream. I shall scream loud enough to bring the Palace guards.'

'Gabriellen!' His voice cracked in a hoarse entreaty.

She could hear his tense angry breathing behind her. 'Leave me, Jack. The sight of you sickens me.'

It cost every ounce of willpower she possessed to harden her heart against him.

As she stared unseeing at the rows of ledgers upon a shelf, there was a rush of cool air and the door slammed shut. She stood motionless where he had left her, gathering the force of her rage around her for protection. The room grew cold. The awesome silence closed in upon her, stripping her of courage, demoralising her, until she was defenceless against the cruel truth which threatened her sanity. Jack had deceived her from their very first meeting. Their love was a lie. He had never intended to wed her.

Her hand crept instinctively up to the emerald pendant. Her fingers closed around it with loathing. She jerked her hand, seeking to rip it from her neck. The chain held, cutting into her flesh. The pain was negligible compared to the laceration which tore her heart bare. She pulled again and the chain snapped. Raising her hand, she was about to hurl the pendant, the token of Jack's love, into the blackest corner of the room.

Her arm froze, her fingers stubbornly locked against the jewel. She could not throw it away. She pressed the pendant against her flat stomach, with its secret life. Love was no longer blind. It was barbarously revealed in all its agony. No words of hate, spoken in fury, could destroy its devouring flame. How she despised herself for her weakness.

Chapter Twenty-Three

Jack braced himself against the wheel of *The Golden Lady*, fighting for control as the ship plunged her way through the heavy swells of the English Channel. Rain hammered against his protective oilskin. The darkness was cleaved apart as forked lightning was accompanied by a cannonade of thunder. For the dozenth time, Jack wondered why the hell he was on this Godforsaken voyage. It was Gabriellen's fault. He would be dry and warm in London if the woman had been reasonable. Had not returned his last two letters to her unopened. His expletive was swallowed up by another crash of thunder.

A wave crashed over the deck, drenching him. As its white foam gushed over the hatches, a sailor cried out in terror as he lost his hold on the ratlines and was swept overboard.

Clenching his jaw, Jack needed all his strength to keep the ship into the wind or the vessel would capsize. Yet still he could not free his mind from thoughts of Gabriellen. He had been a fool not to tell her he was married. God knows, he had not expected her to act so irrationally. Hadn't he told her the child made no difference to his feelings for her? Of course he would stand by her. He loved her. But the damned woman had to take it into her head that he had abused her honour. Christ's entrails! She had wanted him as passionately as he had wanted her. Women! He would never understand them.

To his mind Gabriellen had a perverse way of showing the love she so ardently professed. He had risked his position at Court – everything he had worked for – should it be discovered Gabriellen was his mistress. The Queen was not known for her clemency towards philanderers. As the storm intensified, his thoughts matched it in violence.

He could feel the timbers of the ship shuddering as it

ploughed through the gigantic waves. For two days they had been fighting the storm and now his mood was as filthy as the weather. Devil take Gabriellen! No woman before had treated him so scurvily. But he could not get her out of his thoughts. To teach her a lesson he had come aboard his ship. Any one of his captains could have made this voyage, but his three weeks at sea would give her time to cool that temper of hers. He was prepared to forgive her for the harsh words she had spoken. Understandably, she had been upset. When he returned she would be so pleased to see him, it would be as though their quarrel had never been.

He peered into the lightening sky. The storm was passing. Seth Bridges climbed on to the poop deck, a goblet of mulled wine steaming in his hand.

'You've been on deck six hours, captain,' he said. 'Let Harry Dobson take over. You look all in.'

'Not until I've taken our bearings.' Jack drank the hot wine and handed the goblet back to Seth. It temporarily revived him.

'That were some storm.' Seth sounded ill at ease. 'Where do yer reckon we are? Not off the Spanish coast, are we?'

'I hope not.' Jack grinned wryly. 'I don't fancy being hanged for a pirate. I would guess we are somewhere off the coast of Poitou. Though that takes us too close to Spanish waters for my liking, especially since we became separated from *The Bonaventure Elizabeth* yesterday.'

The wind was dropping and the waves heaved less violently. Jack scanned the sky. Clouds obscured the stars, the mariner's night chart. In an hour it would be daylight. 'Bring me some of that game pie if there's any left,' he called after Seth as his servant moved to the stairs. 'I've a feeling it could be a long day.'

Jack consulted his compass and steered *The Golden Lady* northwards. The merchantman responded instantly to the wheel. There was not a vessel to match her, Jack thought with pride. She was the first ship he had owned and to his mind the best of his fleet. His hands tightened over the wheel as he became plagued by conflicting emotions. If it had not been for *The Lady* he would still be a bachelor. Not that his wife Elizabeth had stopped his roving ways. It was the ship he had come to love, not the woman who had brought it to him. It had set the path to his future.

Ambition had fired him. The fisherman's hut on Hastings beach was far behind him now. Until he had met Gabriellen, marriage had been no hardship. His visits to York were rare.

At sixteen Elizabeth had been a pretty but unremarkable conquest. The small merchant ship he was serving on had docked in York for two days. Two months later they had returned. Within the hour Elizabeth's irate father was aboard, demanding Jack marry his daughter. She was pregnant. Since the merchant was wealthy and Elizabeth his only heir, Jack readily agreed. *The Lady* had been her dowry. Jack was nineteen at the time and had thought his future assured. After eight years of marriage, Elizabeth's passion was undiminished. When Jack was away she channelled all her energies into running her father's business. As an importer of precious gems, she employed only the best cutters, selling the stones to jewellers in England and the continent. Although Elizabeth's beauty had hardened since their marriage, she was still attractive. Over the years Jack had developed a careless affection for her. Unfortunately, she had no sense of humour and her conversation, which centred on either the gem trade or their children, bored him.

Until his last visit, Jack had taken little interest in his infant children. He had been surprised to discover how tall and sturdy his second son, John, had grown. For the first time he saw John as a person not a child. At the age of six the boy was constantly into scrapes and mischief, and his mother despaired of his pert tongue. He was the image of Jack and a son to be proud of. When Jack had returned to London the previous week he had been satisfied with his life. Elizabeth made few demands upon him. Providing he spent Christmas and at least one other visit in York every year, she was content. She was astute enough to realise that with her husband rising so high in favour at Court, she could very soon become Lady Elizabeth Stoneham. It echoed Jack's own ambition.

Much as he loved Gabriellen, he was shrewd enough to know that a playwright's daughter could never bring him the fortune or fame he sought. Gabriellen was the ideal mistress. Should the Queen ever learn that he was married – in fact had been so for several years – surely it could not set Her Majesty too violently against him? The more he thought about it, the better he felt. He had not been proud of deceiving Gabriellen. He had done it to spare her feelings. Nothing need change. Once Gabriellen's temper had cooled, she would see reason. He would never give her up. And there was no cause why he should.

When the violence fell away from the wind, Jack nodded to Harry Dobson, who usually captained this ship, to take over at the helm.

'It'll take us two days to get back on course,' Dobson said as he peered up at the furled top gallants. He turned to Jack who was shouting for more sail now that the wind had dropped. 'No regrets, captain? Instead of fighting for your life against the elements, you could have spent the last two days being flattered and diverted at Court.'

Jack looked into Dobson's leathery face. His long hair and dun-coloured beard were stiff with drying spume. They had faced many such dangers together, and though Jack was not given to confidences, he favoured Dobson with a wry grin. 'Court life can be unbearably tedious. Live for the opportunity of today, that's my motto. I'm not one for regrets.'

He moved to the ship's rail. The sun climbed higher on the milky horizon and gradually his mood brightened. He felt exhilarated after pitting his seamanship and strength against the dangers of the elements. He thrived upon such risk. To emerge from near death unscathed, reaffirmed his belief that he was destined for greatness.

'Ship on starboard bow,' a shout came from the crow's nest.

Jack stared across the choppy sea. As *The Golden Lady* rose high on the crest of a wave, he saw the full-bellied sails of a galleon. A Spanish prize!

Already his luck had changed. 'Steer nor-west,' Jack commanded. 'Gunners to arms.'

'Two ships on starboard bow!' the lookout shouted. Then his voice became shrill with alarm. 'Four ships on starboard bow.'

Jack tensed. It was not a single galleon but a convoy. Capable though *The Lady* was with her extra guns supplied by Lord Barpham, she could never take on four Spanish ships and survive.

'Come about!' he yelled, knowing already it was too late. They would have been seen. As the ship turned to port, he saw that the largest of the galleons was gaining on them, her gunports open ready to attack. Captain Jack Stoneham was now the hunted not the hunter. And the Spanish had every cause to wish him at the bottom of the ocean.

'What ails thee, Miss Gabby?' Agnes hobbled into the orchard where Gabriellen sat on the grass surrounded by wooden horses and soldiers as she played with Laurence. 'I've never seen thee so downcast. Missing that rascal Jack, are thee?'

The face lifted to the servant was so distraught, Agnes sank down on to the grass beside her and took her mistress's hand. 'I know it's hard for thee when he's at sea. It's only been a few weeks. It won't be long before he's back.'

Gabriellen watched Laurence toddle over to a flower bed and pick the petals off a marigold. 'He's married, Agnes. And I'm with child.'

'Oh, my poor lamb.' Agnes put a hand reddened from scrubbing to her wide mouth. 'Does Esmond know?'

Gabriellen shook her head. 'I would rather he did not. Father has enough worries. Every day this month Prew has been pestering him. I think he owes the merchant a great deal of money. What use is there in adding to his problems?'

Agnes studied her mistress. There were dark shadows under her eyes and her lovely face was pinched and pale. Since the night of the court play she had lost all her vitality. That must have been when she had learned that Stoneham was married. After all his false promises, it was no wonder Gabby was so devastated. A pity that Mark Rowan was not in London. He would know how to cheer her. But the Welshman had taken his stallion to the Kent and Sussex Fairs and would not be back in London until September. That was another month away. It did not help her mistress's low spirits to have Victor Prew visiting so often. Agnes did not like the way the merchant found so many excuses to call.

There was a distant ringing of the doorbell from the house. Gabriellen sprang to her feet. 'I'll answer it, Agnes.' Her face lit up with expectancy as she ran towards the building.

The servant watched her go. Every time the doorbell rang it was the same. Despite Gabriellen's disillusion and anger, she was expecting Jack Stoneham to call. And, whether he was married or not, she still loved him. Agnes shook her head sadly. It would only lead to heartbreak and misery. Her young mistress loved that scoundrel too well to give him up. Not that Gabby would listen to advice she did not want to hear. She was too headstrong for her own good.

Inside the house Gabriellen paused to smooth the folds of her gown and pat a tendril of hair back into place under her French hood. When she opened the door, her disappointment could not be more bitter as she was greeted by Victor Prew.

'Good day, Mr Prew.' She managed a chill semblance of civility. Despite the merchant's pestering, Esmond insisted that Prew be treated with courtesy. Gabriellen suspected that her father hoped to defer the payments on his present loan. 'I regret my father is not at home. He is at The Angel. The players are rehearsing tomorrow's play.'

Victor Prew swept off his high domed hat and bowed to her, his pink scalp shining through his elaborately curled but sparse hair. 'It was not just your father I have come to see.' He smiled, his teeth yellow against his pallid face. 'It's almost dark. Esmond will be home soon, I'm sure. I have rather distressing news, I fear, which concerns you all.'

'You had better come into the parlour.' Gabriellen turned to Agnes who had followed her into the house and was holding Laurence in her arms. She nodded for her to accompany them.

As Victor Prew stepped over the threshold a sickly perfume of violets filled the corridor. She need not have feared that she would be alone with him. Nan was sitting on the window seat, her head bent over a nightgown she was stitching for Laurence. The seamstress looked up, her expression guarded as she saw their guest.

Prew bowed to her and raised her hand to his lips. 'Mistress Woodruff, how well you are looking. It is many weeks since I last saw you.'

'How nice to see you, Mr Prew,' Nan replied. 'I always seem to miss you on your visits.'

Gabriellen and Agnes looked at each other, knowing that the seamstress always made herself scarce whenever the merchant called. She had no time for Prew. She had once stated that being in the same room as him made her skin feel as if it was ready to break out in boils.

But Prew was right. Nan did look well. Since Easter her recovery had been remarkable. Her returning liveliness and gaiety had kept Esmond at home in the evenings. If anyone could curb her father's gambling Nan could, though her liking for wine encouraged Esmond's own excessive drinking. Better that than gambling. It was good to hear him laughing and relaxed. Esmond was more settled.

Gabriellen wished she could say the same for her own life. Pain gripped her breast. Jack's betrayal gave her no rest. Seeing that Agnes was watching her with concern, Gabriellen gestured for Mr Prew to sit down. Too restless herself to settle, she paced the parlour floor, her skirt swishing over the rushes and filling the room with the scent of rosemary and lavender which was sprinkled amongst them. She paid little attention to Prew's words.

After weeks of worry, she admitted that her love for Jack was as fierce as ever. She still had not forgiven him, but her anger had begun to cool. At first she had cursed and reviled him; now the acuteness of her loss savaged her sleepless nights. If only he had been honest with her. In her heart she knew that nothing could have denied their passion. Her blood was too hot to bow to convention. But that did not excuse his conduct. It was hard to forgive his lies. In the end it would be herself who would bear the shame. Surely if she loved Jack, even that should matter little? And she loved Jack more than she loved life itself.

Her hand rested upon her stomach. Until now few people knew she was Jack's mistress. They had always been discreet. In fact, most acquaintances slyly hinted at a courtship between her and Mark Rowan, as they were seen so often together. She hoped for Mark's sake that such unfounded gossip did not reach Jesmaine. Suddenly she became aware that Prew was talking about Jack. She turned to him absently. 'I'm sorry, Mr Prew. What was that you said?'

'Such dreadful news. I came to tell you as I know Captain Stoneham is an associate of Esmond's. I know he called here on occasion. A tragic loss. They say the Queen shut herself away for an hour and would see no one when she heard.'

'Heard what?' Gabriellen stared at the merchant with mounting alarm. His narrow face was grave, but there was an unpleasant light in his eyes. 'A privateer came upon the wreckage. The figurehead of *The Golden Lady* was found floating amongst other charred debris. The ship was sunk by the Spanish. The Queen's favourite pirate is dead.'

Having delivered his news, Victor Prew saw Gabriellen sway, her hand going to her head. There was not a shred of colour in her face. Overcome by his blunder, he stepped towards her. 'Miss Angel, this must be a terrible shock to you. How thoughtless of me to blurt out such tragic tidings.'

To his relief Gabriellen did not swoon and he guided her to the nearest seat. She sank down upon it in a daze.

'Mr Prew,' Nan admonished him from the window seat, 'you forget Miss Angel is a gentlewoman by birth. You have quite overset her.' The seamstress held out her arms to take Laurence from Agnes. 'See to Gabriellen. She was out in that hot sun too long. No wonder she looks so ill.'

'No. I am all right, Nan.' Gabriellen's voice seemed to come from a great distance. She stared fixedly ahead, her face devoid of all emotion.

Prew took her hand and chaffed it comfortingly. 'How appalling of me not to spare your sensibilities. I had not realised you knew Captain Stoneham well.'

The lame servant pushed him out of the way, her voice sharp. 'The captain has been a friend of the family for years.'

Gabriellen stood up, her eyes glazed. 'You are sure that Captain Stoneham is dead? He was not taken prisoner?'

'Little chance of that, unless the Spanish preferred to hang him in Madrid. Then they would have sent word to gloat. They could not resist letting the Queen know that her sea captains are not invincible against the might of Spain.'

Gabriellen struggled to regain control of her senses. She was numb. Too dazed to think straight, too stunned to feel grief, her mind settled upon inconsequentials. Clearly Prew did not know that Jack had been her lover. The man was a gossip. She did not want her name spread across London as Jack's mistress, especially now she was carrying his child. But even that scarcely registered. She just wanted to get Prew out of the house so that she could shut herself in her room. The years of Aunt Dorothy's training came to her aid.

'It was good of you to take the trouble to inform us,' she said. Her voice broke and before she summoned the strength to go on, she heard her father's voice shouting from the hall.

'Gabby . . . Nan, I'm home.' Esmond entered the parlour. Seeing their guest, his expression was far from welcoming. 'To what do we owe this pleasure, Prew? I thought our business was to be settled on Friday. Today is Tuesday.'

'Grave news, Esmond, I came at once,' Prew simpered. 'A private word in your study, if you please.'

When Esmond and Prew disappeared, Gabriellen fled to her room. Closing the door, she flung herself on to her bed and with an animal cry curled into a ball, hugging a pillow close to her stomach, her body shaking with violent sobs.

Agnes touched her shoulder and gathered her into her arms. 'Cry all thee want, my precious.'

The servant's heart went out to the young woman. Gently she took off the French hood Gabriellen was wearing and unpinned her hair. Gabriellen clung to her, sobbing. The sun had slid down over the rooftops and twilight filled the room before finally, exhausted, Gabriellen fell into a fitful doze. Agnes stared down at the ashen face. What would happen to the beautiful, wild creature? Gabriellen's secret was safe with her. But for how long? And how would Esmond take the news that his daughter was with child? Agnes shivered. The master's rages were fearsome to behold.

The mist swirled through the ruins of the abbey set in the heart of the Kent Weald. The broken walls were covered by brambles and ivy from nearly a half-century of neglect. Once this had been an imposing landmark where pilgrims had taken shelter on their journey to Thomas à Becket's tomb at Canterbury. Since the dissolution, Becket's tomb was gone and this once proud abbey was no more than a labyrinth of broken walls. Many of the stones had been carried away by the local inhabitants and used to build barns and cottages.

Mark Rowan crouched unseen behind a flint wall which had once been part of the Abbot's guest house. Inside the voices were clear, arguing heatedly, unaware that they were being overheard. The Irish priest Mark had followed here recited his master's orders.

'It cannot be long now before the Protestant bitch takes

up residence again at Nonsuch Palace. Our marksman will be hidden in a tree. I've seen him shoot a skylark from the sky. No one will suspect him. He is already working in the grounds. He will strike whilst that witch's daughter is practising her archery at the butts. He will have a horse in readiness to flee, and more posted at intervals to the coast.'

'Brother Patrick, the plan is simple,' a gruff voice broke in to dispute. 'Is it not too simple?'

'Simplicity is often the best,' the priest replied. 'Few know of this plot. That must remain so. You two will ensure that the marksman gets safely to France. The password is "Justice is done". Our church will rise again. New abbeys will replace this ruin. My uncle was Abbot here. He was slain at his altar by Henry's murdering soldiers.'

'Then give us your blessing, brother,' the gruff voice requested.

There was a shuffling as the two men went down on their knees and the priest spoke the Benediction over them. He ended by adding, 'Be in readiness for the marksman's arrival. Our agent in London will pay you well. We cannot fail.' The Irish brogue rose with fervour. 'Soon England will be free from its heresy. Go with God, my brothers.'

Mark drew back into the shadows at the sound of the men leaving the ruin. He had learned more than he had expected. It would be simple enough to have a watch put on the grounds of Nonsuch Palace when the Queen was in residence. As to the agent Brother Patrick had mentioned, Mark had no doubts of his identity. Twice last month the priest had met Victor Prew.

In the study downstairs in the house in Bankside, Esmond raised his head from his hands and regarded Prew. His first reaction was anger, his second caution. His debts to Prew now ran to nearly one thousand pounds. He could not believe they had mounted so heavily. Prew was serious in his threats to have him arrested. He stared hard at the merchant whose figure, even in the bright candlelight, was a hazy blur. The consequences of his failing sight had almost ruined him. His debts were mounting, but gambling had always been a way of life to him. Now he found he could not stop. His luck would change. It had never run against him for so long before.

He no longer trusted the cards, and turned instead to

the dice. There were several means to falsify their weight, but these too had let him down. He swore roundly beneath his breath. His failing sight was robbing him of his dignity. Even the acclaim he received as a playwright was not rightly his. It cut through his pride to admit that Gabriellen had written the last two plays without any help from him. Reaching for the brandy flagon, he filled his horn cup. He studied it and not the merchant when he spoke.

'I will consider what you say.'

Prew put a hand over Esmond's, preventing him from raising his cup to drink. 'Consider my proposal well. I'll return on Friday as agreed.' His voice was menacing. 'If the debt is not paid in full, you will find yourself rotting in prison. The alternative should be easy enough for you to arrange.'

Esmond sank his head into his hands as the merchant left. The thought of a debtor's prison filled him with dread. He would die there. Perhaps a fitting end, he thought cynically. But no Angel gave up without a fight. At five and forty, and even partially blind, he was not beaten yet. He had an idea for a brilliant play. If he kept off the drink, it could be his best yet.

The door opened and Nan came in. 'Has that objectionable man gone at last?' she said. 'He's not been threatening you again about the money we owe, I hope?' She wore a loose robe and her hair hung over her shoulders. Twisting her now slender body, she sat on his lap, her arms folded around his neck. 'The playhouse is doing well, is it not?'

She was looking down at him and though he could not see her face clearly, he knew she was smiling. 'Forget Prew, my love. Forget our debts. We have a good life here in Bankside.'

Then she moved against him, placing ardent kisses upon his face and chin, the heat of her body engulfing him like the steam from an oven. Her lack of inhibitions delighted him.

'Aw, Esmond, have you no kiss for your Nan?' She laughed and filled his cup with brandy. Taking a large gulp, she handed it to him. 'Come to bed. I've been waiting for you.'

He kissed her before pushing her away. 'I have to speak to Gabby. The death of Stoneham must have hit her hard.'

Nan kissed him, saying persuasively, 'Agnes is with Gabby. Leave her be.' She rubbed her body against his. 'Come, love your Nan. I'll make you forget your troubles. Don't I always?'

'I must speak with my daughter.' Reluctantly, he raised his hands to push his mistress away. She was naked beneath her robe. It fell open as she slid to the floor to sit between his knees, her hand slipping inside his codpiece, the insistent play of her fingers driving every other thought from his mind. Despair was washed away, replaced by desire as Nan's competent hands worked their spell upon him.

Esmond left the unpleasant interview with Gabriellen until the next morning. He had never expected it would be as bad as this. Still in her nightgown, her hair a tangled mess about her shoulders and her eyes red-raw with weeping, she stood with her head against the window pane. She looked for all the world as if he had just condemned her to the stake.

'I cannot believe you would ask this of me,' she said in a voice shaken with grief. All the vitality had fled from her. At another time she would have raged at the absurdity of his proposition. Now she stared back at him blank-eyed, a pale shadow of the virago he had expected to answer him.

'It is not just for myself I ask. Think of Laurence.'

'That's not fair, Father.'

Esmond winced. Even dazed with grief as she was, Gabriellen spoke the truth. He hardened himself. 'I would never survive prison. And what of your condition?' He played his winning card. Last night Nan had told him that she believed Gabriellen was with child. When he had entered the chamber a few moments ago, he had found his daughter retching into a basin. 'In a few months you will no longer be able to hide your shame.'

Her shoulders squared in proud defiance. 'I carry the child of the man I love. I am not ashamed. I had thought to return to Chichester and live quietly there.'

'They will condemn you more in Chichester than if you remain in London. Be sensible, Gabriellen. Here is a way out of your predicament. God's nightgown! In Chichester they will pillory you for a whore. You will be reviled for the rest of your life. Who will marry you once it is known

361

you have borne an illegitimate child?'

'I have no wish to marry. I will survive. I am not the first. What of Nan?'

'She is different.'

'You mean she is your whore, not your daughter?' Gabriellen returned with a flash of her old vigour.

Esmond curbed his anger. She was being deliberately stubborn. 'For all you were Jack's mistress, you are still an innocent in many ways. Not so Nan. Your Aunt Dorothy would shudder in her grave to hear your shameless talk. This is for your own good, Gabriellen. A chance for you to lead a respectable life.' He crossed to the door. Turning, he looked at her meaningfully. 'I will leave you to think on my words. Jack is dead. The fate of our family is in your hands. And if that does not move you, think of your child. Do you want its life blighted with the stigma of bastardy?'

He went out quickly, his last words echoing behind him.

As the door shut, Gabriellen sank to the floor, rocking herself backwards and forwards. There were no tears left to ease the aching rawness of her misery. Besides, crying was useless now. As Gabriellen thought of her father's proposal, anger flamed in her. The only man she would ever love was dead, and now her father expected her to marry that loathsome toad Victor Prew. What did she care for the life of luxury he had promised her? The very thought of his skinny, unattractive body made her feel sick. How dare that bleating weasel threaten her father with gaol if she did not agree!

She sat on the floor, staring at the wall. Her chaotic thoughts tumbled in confusion through her mind. Without Jack her life was nothing. Yet there was the child to consider. And Esmond. . . . Damn her father! He had laid many burdens on her shoulders and she had carried them without complaint. But not this! What he asked of her was too much.

Chapter Twenty-Four

It was three days before Gabriellen emerged from her room. Tonight she must give her father his answer before Prew arrived. She moved like a sleepwalker. Every waking moment brought the unbearable ache of her grief. An hour ago her father had reminded her of her duty to the family. The need had then come upon her to visit Jack's rooms on London Bridge for the last time.

She left her chamber and walked down the stairs. Laurence was crying in the garden, obviously unhappy at being ignored, whilst Nan and a laundry-maid, who came once a week, were laying the linen sheets on the grass to dry. From the attic bedchambers above, where the apprentice players slept, she heard Robin Flowerdew and Will Appleshot laughing together. Soon they would be leaving for the playhouse. Poggs and her father had already left. For them it was a normal day. Not so for herself. Once her decision was made, it would become a day which would change her whole life.

Her step faltered on the stair. She stood for a moment, clutching the rail, her body convulsed with loathing as once again she was faced with this dreadful choice she was being forced to make.

'Miss Gabby?' Agnes approached from the hallway below, carrying a tray of food. 'Thee must eat something.'

'I'm not hungry, Agnes. I'm going out.'

'Thee canna go alone.' The servant put down the tray on the floor, determination written on her face as she barred Gabriellen's passage at the foot of the stairs.

'I have to get out of the house, Agnes. I need to think.'

'As if thee be in any fit state to go out alone. Not even a cloak to protect thee. 'Tis overcast and likely to rain. Wait while I get the cloaks, my dear. I'll accompany thee.'

When Agnes disappeared from sight Gabriellen opened

the door and went into the street. She walked along it in a trance, looking straight ahead, seeing nothing of the pitiful beggars or hearing their pleas for alms. A young lad knocked against her shoulder. She did not notice that he had cut her purse and run off. An older footpad, seeing her as easy pickings, had his eye on the emerald pendant at her neck and was trailing her.

Agnes, puffing up from behind, guessed his intent, boxed his ears, and hissed fiercely that Gabriellen's father was a friend of One-eyed Ned. The footpad backed off at once and went in search of less dangerous game.

Watchful for other incidents, Agnes stayed several paces behind her mistress. Clearly, Gabriellen was locked into a world of despair and grief. The servant gave her mistress the privacy she needed.

Gabriellen merged with the flow of people approaching London Bridge. In the past she had taken care not to lift her gaze to the traitors' heads bleached white on the poles which lined the Bridge Gatehouse, but today she stared up at them. If Jack had not drowned at sea, but had been taken prisoner by the Spanish, such a grisly fate could befall his remains. A spasm of nausea gripped her and she hurried on, her eyes again blinded by tears. Halfway across the bridge, she stopped. There was a cart outside Jack's lodgings and a manservant was heaving a sea-chest into it. Jack's sea-chest. When he disappeared back inside the house, Gabriellen broke into a run. That was Jack's property. As she reached the first floor where Jack had his rooms, the man appeared carrying another trunk.

'Stop!' she commanded. 'Where are you going with that? It belongs to Captain Stoneham.'

The servant looked over his shoulder, and a woman's voice ordered the chest loaded on to the cart. Pushing roughly past Gabriellen, he went out into the street. It was like a fuse to an incendiary. She broke through her lethargy to act. She ran into the room, ready to attack anyone who dared to steal Jack's possessions. A short woman was standing by the fireplace, throwing the last of a bundle of letters into the fire. As the flames licked around them, Gabriellen recognised her own writing upon them. A sharp pain clutched at her heart. They were her love letters to Jack. How dare this woman, whom she presumed to be the landlady, burn them? A cry of pure fury burst from her.

364

'These rooms are paid for until Candlemas.' She made a dash to rescue the letters from the flames, but was too late. Shaking with outrage, she rounded on the woman, her hands on her hips as she scolded. 'How dare you throw Captain Stoneham's possessions into the street? Get out before I call the constable.'

The woman turned and the look she gave Gabriellen was filled with such loathing that it momentarily took her aback. 'You must be one of my husband's doxies.' Her mouth turned down with prim disgust. 'Those obscene letters, recalling in detail my husband's exploits as a lover, were yours, I presume? You were not the only one, you know. Jack did not know the meaning of fidelity, either to his wife or his mistresses.'

A confrontation with Jack's wife was the last thing Gabriellen had expected. It caught her temporarily offguard. She stood unmoving as the firelight flickered in a room devoid of Jack's belongings. Then she looked at the woman before her, and saw a plump, pretty woman about six years older than herself. A woman, Gabriellen told herself, who had the greater right to mourn Jack. Her anger cooled. She could understand this woman's hatred for her, but she did not return it. Rather, she felt kinship with her. The woman must feel as wretched as she did at Jack's death, although she noted that her manner showed very little grief, only a determination to collect all her husband's property.

'Until a few weeks ago I had no idea that Jack was married,' Gabriellen said without apology.

'Would it have made any difference?'

The shrill accusation in Elizabeth Stoneham's voice destroyed Gabriellen's compassion. Her anger began to rise. 'It did not make any difference to Jack, did it?'

The cold blue eyes watching her were malicious with jealousy. 'No. But it was to me he always came back. You see, I held the purse-strings. My father's wealth bought his grand Court clothes. My dowry was *The Golden Lady*. And what is a dashing sea captain without a ship? Nothing. Our marriage raised him from a penniless second-in-command to the owner of his own vessel.'

Such disloyalty from Jack's wife appalled Gabriellen. The woman was a shrew, petty-minded and grasping. It was small wonder he rarely visited York. The last of her sympathy for Jack's widow left her. 'You delude yourself, Mistress Stoneham. You were a stepping stone towards the mountain of Jack's ambition.' She could not stop herself defending her lover. 'He was too much of a man not to rise high.'

Her gaze scanned the room. On a coffer stood a pearl-handled fan and a silver-backed hair brush. They were presents to her from Jack. She picked them up. 'These are mine.'

When Elizabeth Stoneham made to snatch them from her, Gabriellen jerked her hand back. The older woman's face twisted with anger. 'Give them to me! As Jack's widow, everything in this room is mine. If you try and steal them, I shall call a constable and have you charged with theft.'

Gabriellen had already noted that several other expensive gifts Jack had bought her had been taken by his widow. To try and retrieve them would lead to an undignified scene, but she had no intention of relinquishing these, especially the brush. It was the last gift Jack had given her.

'The brush is undoubtedly mine.' Gabriellen plucked a tawny-blonde hair from its bristles to emphasise her point. Gripping the handle firmly, she held it out towards Elizabeth Stoneham. In other circumstances she would have spared Jack's wife, but the woman's avarice and spite deserved no mercy. The inscription on its back was clear to see.

Gabriellen.
My own true Angel. Keeper of my heart.
I love you. Jack.

'Harlot!' Elizabeth Stoneham screeched. 'Is that how Jack paid you for your services? With gifts instead of money. You were his concubine, nothing more. One among many. He was always generous after he got what he wanted.'

Nothing in Gabriellen's expression betrayed how deeply those words hurt her. It was not in her nature to allow any insult to go without retaliation. She stood very still, with the formality which came before the first thrust of a duel. Hers was to be a lunge straight at the heart without preliminaries. 'Only you, Mistress Stoneham, know how much Jack was in love with you on the day that you were married. As I have absolute faith in the depth of his love for me, on the day that he died.'

366

An outraged scream from Elizabeth Stoneham followed Gabriellen's exit from the room. When she was again in the street she looked up to the overhanging window of Jack's rooms. For a moment she thought she saw him standing there looking down at her – waiting for her. The image was so clear it shook her. Was it Jack's ghost? Or something more profound? During the days she had stayed with Jesmaine when Mark was ill, the fortune-teller had spoken of the subconscious mind which could pick up images. Jesmaine said that she had this gift. It was what made her so successful in her predictions for a person's future. Gabriellen felt a surge of hope. If what Jesmaine had said was true, could it be possible that Jack was still alive?

She looked up at the window, but only blank panes stared back at her. She shivered, and was surprised to discover that a warm cloak had been placed over her shoulders. Agnes stood silently at her side, her presence comforting.

Gabriellen said, 'I am going to Bishopsgate. I must speak with Jesmaine.'

Her footsteps no longer dragged as she continued across the bridge towards the city. For the first time in three days she had hope. She did not even notice that it had begun to rain.

Jesmaine betrayed no surprise at her visit. She had heard the rumours of Stoneham's death. Yet Gabriellen must know that Mark would not return to London until September.

'It is not Mark I have come to see,' Gabriellen said hollowly. She stood on the step, her wet uncovered hair dripping down on to her face. It was almost a year since Mark's illness and the women had not met in that time. It was the tragic look in Gabriellen's eyes which made the fortune-teller take pity on her.

'Come in. How may I help you?'

Gabriellen, with Agnes behind her, followed Jesmaine into the parlour.

'I have been told that Jack is dead, yet I have a strong feeling that it is not so. You have the gift to see many things hidden to others.'

When Gabriellen put out her hands, imploring and des-

367

perate in a last fragile hope, Jesmaine saw they were shaking. 'Tell me, Jesmaine, will the crystal show you if Jack is alive?'

'I can promise nothing.'

Jesmaine hedged around the truth. She had always seen Jack Stoneham as a threat to Mark's life. If he was dead, that danger was over. Yet if he was not . . . Better if she knew what the future held. The crystal had not shown all. Perhaps with Gabriellen present, she might learn more than she had before. She would do it for Mark. Motioning Gabriellen to sit at the table, Jesmaine closed the window shutters. She lit a single candle. 'There must be no distractions.'

She fetched the crystal ball, placed it on the table and sat down opposite Gabriellen. Holding her hands palm upwards each side of the crystal, she took Gabriellen's hands in hers, saying, 'Concentrate your thoughts upon Jack Stoneham.'

The younger woman's fingers were icy beneath Jesmaine's. She stared into Gabriellen's green eyes. They were without guile, the pupils dilated with shock and inner pain. Taking several even breaths, Jesmaine turned her attention to the crystal. Silently she recited an incantation which cleared her mind of everything but the task in hand. Her breathing slowed, her eyes became round and unblinking. Often it did not work. On those occasions she told her clients what they wanted to hear. It kept them happy and ensured they would return. This time she found herself willing it to work.

She sat a long time, her thoughts locked upon the repeated words of the incantation. An image appeared and was gone, elusive as a will-o'-the-wisp. She concentrated harder. Another image flickered before her eyes and was gone. Then, like several closed doors being opened to reveal adjoining rooms, scenes were disclosed to her. A wedding. A baby. The spectre of death. Men huddled in conspiracy. The gallows. Men fighting. The sky lit with a fearful orange glow. And always there was the dark shadow of danger.

The force which generated these images flowed from Gabriellen. Was it her future? Mark had not featured in them. That was heartening, but did not mean that he was safe from her influence. At this moment Gabriellen's thoughts were upon Jack Stoneham. Jesmaine focussed her thoughts upon the Welshman. His face appeared in the crystal. He was laughing. Then there was only the over-whelming sensation of fear. The figure of death appeared. But for whom did he beckon? That was not revealed.

Jesmaine now felt a will stronger than hers blocking her thoughts of Mark and the danger to him. Across the table from her, the green eyes above the crystal were bright and unblinking, compelling Jesmaine to channel her energies towards the sea or a distant shore. Jesmaine fought it.

The crystal showed a scene in the dark of night, the figures distorted. Then something happened which she had never experienced before. She felt a freezing, bone-aching cold enter her body. Unrelenting cramps tortured her limbs. She wanted to stretch but could not. She was bent, forced into an agonised posture. Before her horrified gaze the scene expanded. She was no longer a part of it, but a spectator.

A dark-haired man, wearing rags and covered in blood and filth, was suspended in an iron cage. The dim moonlit scene made it impossible to see the situation of the cage, and all Jesmaine's concentration was upon the figure who was crouched like an ape in the confined space. Was this the future Gabriellen would bring to Mark? Traitors were confined in such a way. But Mark was loyal to the Queen. Jesmaine's thoughts raced as she tried to see the prisoner more clearly. The man stirred and Jesmaine knew he was close to death, but still she could not see his features. She concentrated harder on the face and slowly the image began to clear.

Then the servant who had accompanied Gabriellen began to cough. The distraction shattered the image and the scene disappeared.

Jesmaine let out a cry. 'Get that woman out of here. I've lost it. Curse it! I've lost it.'

Agnes hurried outside, but as Jesmaine cleared her mind to reconjure the scene, she knew it was too late. There was a void. Just an empty feeling. An impending sense of betrayal. There had been no images to show that the sea captain was alive and Jesmaine was stricken at the danger she believed this woman would bring to Mark.

'Your captain is dead,' she said coldly. 'And if you care for Mark, you will stay out of his life. You bring him danger.'

★

Vengeance smouldered in Victor Prew's breast. Nothing had changed. Esmond Angel still saw himself as a man above him. Well, he was about to learn otherwise. He faced his adversary. If he could not have Gabriellen then he would break this man and take pleasure in doing it. He had spent a fortune on cultivating the actors. Too many of the plots of his Catholic friends had been thwarted. Had he been able to attend the Court when Angel's play was presented, he would have ensured that a fanatic, who would give his life for the cause they served, accompanied him. He would have plunged a dagger into the Protestant bitch's throat. At one time he had hoped Culpepper, a secret Catholic, would have taken on the role of assassin. Culpepper had been a disappointment. Having returned to the stage in the great roles created by Angel, the actor had become absorbed in his own glory and forgotten his vows to help his Catholic friends. Still Prew persisted in his schemes. As Gabriellen's husband he still could gain that position within the Court. But more than that, he wanted the woman herself.

'My daughter is not here.' Esmond's once stentorian voice was a thread of its former self. 'I told you on Tuesday, the decision is hers.'

'You think I am not good enough for her,' Prew shouted, spite lacing every word. 'My money was good enough though, wasn't it?'

He glared triumphantly at the playwright who sat hunched and despondent in a chair. So this family thought they could scorn him with impunity? He'd see them all rot in gaol first! That haughty bitch Gabriellen included, if she had refused his suit. His conceit at his own self-importance expanded. No one played him for a fool and escaped the consequences. It was a heady sensation to wield such power over a man like Angel. He revelled in it. Thrusting out his narrow chest in its thick bombast padding, he strutted to the window.

'All these months you thought you were leading me by the nose – denying me the shares I wanted in the players' company. I knew you were patronising me, but I waited. I've wanted Gabriellen for a long time. I thought for a while that there was an understanding between her and that Welshman, Rowan, but he's not been near her for months.' He crossed the floor to scowl at Esmond. The playwright kept his head averted, his fists clenching as he looked down

370

at them. Prew could not contain his satisfaction at having him beaten. 'If I don't get Gabriellen, you're a dead man. You'll not just be left to rot in prison for debt – you'll hang, Angel.'

Before Prew could guess his intent the older man was out of the chair, had grabbed him by the front of his doublet and pressed him up against the wall. 'Don't threaten me, Prew. My daughter needs a real man, not a runt. If you want her, you will have to win her. I'll not force her into marriage with vermin the likes of you.'

'Vermin, is it now?' Prew squeaked through the pressure being exerted upon his windpipe. His eyes rolled in terror and he began to sweat copiously. Angel was not the broken man he had believed. Not yet anyway. 'I've not wasted these last months. I've learnt a great deal about your early life. You've made enemies. Do you remember old Fossett?'

Finding himself abruptly released, Prew pulled down his doublet and straightened his ruff. Angel had gone pale, the hand he extended towards the wine flagon was unsteady – a sure sign that he had caught the playwright offguard. Of a certainty, Esmond would not have been expecting that line of attack. The actor would have believed those incidents long buried. Prew watched as Esmond filled a goblet and downed its contents. Once a man was down, Prew knew when to kick him.

'The Fossetts have a particular grudge against you,' he announced, taking vindictive pleasure in having Esmond at his mercy. 'They'll swear that you ran off with the takings. Also that in the process of the robbery, you killed one son.'

'That's all lies.' Esmond sounded old and frail, the threat clearly a shock to him. 'Tobias Fossett challenged me to a duel. There were witnesses.'

'All dead,' Prew smirked. 'It will be your word against theirs. The word of a respectable family against the grandson of Wildboar Angel.'

With satisfaction Prew watched Esmond's shoulders sag in despair. When he raised his head, his eyes were blank with defeat. Prew suppressed the desire to hug himself. He had won. Won! Expectantly, he waited for the playwright's words.

'Do what you will with me.' Esmond looked down his nose at him. There was a proud nobility in the way he held himself. 'I love my daughter too well to condemn her to a life of misery, just to save my worthless hide.'

'Then hang and be eternally damned, Angel.' Prew's voice broke on a croak of rage and he gulped for breath. Unfastening his doublet, he drew out a document. 'These are the papers for your arrest. The constable awaits outside.'

Shaking with frustration and fury, he stamped from the room to summon the constable. His foot caught against an unseen object, his humiliation complete as he pitched forward. As his face smashed against the linen-fold panelling, he heard the bone in his nose crack.

'Mr Prew, are you hurt?' There was a rustle of silk and the sweet fragrance of gillyflowers as Gabriellen knelt at his side. Her green eyes, even in the gloom of the passage, were unnaturally bright. Those who knew her better would have quaked at that look. Prew was dazzled.

Embarrassed at being caught at such a disadvantage, he scrambled to his feet. Drawing out his kerchief, he held it to his bleeding nose. After the defeat he had suffered at the hands of her father, he was mollified by her concern. Her sweet smile disarmed him.

Agnes, who had heard his threats as they entered the house, had seen the rage which had catapulted Gabriellen out of her grief. She hid a smile as her mistress bent solicitously over the merchant. Discreetly hidden behind a coffer was the walking stick which she had thrust out to trip Prew. If Agnes knew her mistress, the puny man was about to pay dearly for daring to threaten Esmond Angel.

Gabriellen smiled, but kept her gaze lowered so that Prew did not see the hostility blazing in her eyes. 'Your nose is bleeding. I must attend to it. I am mortified that such an accident should befall you in our house.' She spoke quickly, guiding him away from the front door, having already instructed Agnes to get rid of the constable outside. 'Surely you were not about to leave us? My father said you wished to speak with me, Mr Prew.'

She led him into the parlour. 'Please be seated. I'll fetch a bowl to cleanse your wound, and a pain-soothing posset to ease your discomfort.' The merchant's nose was fast distorting under a hideous black swelling. In view of the fate to which he would, without compunction, condemn her father, she felt no remorse for her drastic measures. 'I fear your nose is broken, Mr Prew. I cannot imagine how you could have tripped.'

She went into the kitchen and collected what she needed. Agnes came in, and nodded. 'The constable has gone.'

'Good. Now I leave it to you to make sure that Prew and I are not disturbed. He will pay dearly for the way he threatened Father. He will not learn how neatly he has been gulled until it is too late.'

'Oh, Miss Gabby, thee canna mean to wed him?'

She gave a bitter laugh. 'Why not? Do you think I can sit back and allow my father to be hanged?'

The maid looked at her gravely, her doubts dark in her eyes. Gabriellen clenched her hands into fists. How dare Prew threaten Esmond? The audacity of it – the sheer insolence of the mealy-mouthed rat, the self-righteous hypocrisy of the snivelling little man! And how self-sacrificing her father had been in his declaration of love for her. Those words had brought tears to her eyes. They had strengthened her resolve more than force could ever have done.

'You heard Jesmaine tell me Jack was dead.' Her voice was tight and she held out her hands in despair. 'What have I to live for now, except to help my child and my family? No sacrifice is too great to save them.'

A tear spilled on to her cheek and she brushed it angrily away. Every day for the rest of her life she would mourn Jack, but she would not cry for him again. Tears were a weakness she could not afford. A grim smile twisted her lips. 'Prew will not suspect anything. Within the hour, I shall have him down on his knees, begging me to marry him. But I tell you this, Agnes, I do not come cheaply. Before I agree, he will not only have cancelled my father's debts, but agreed upon an annual allowance to support him, Nan and Laurence. By marrying Prew, Jack's child will not be born a bastard.'

'But what will happen when he learns the truth, as one day he must?' Agnes put both hands to her cheeks in horror.

Gabriellen shrugged, her face bleak and uncompromising. The hatred she felt for Prew at this moment was all that sustained her. She had to have something to fight for. Jack was dead and Jesmaine had made it frighteningly clear that she was a danger to Mark. Just when she needed the advice and friendship of the Welshman, she was too shaken by Jesmaine's prophecy to risk contacting him – even if it was possible, since he was somewhere in Kent. She could not think rationally. Her father's life was at stake. That was all that mattered. 'I'll worry about that later. I've no intention of staying with him. I shall return to Chichester and bring up my child. By then my husband will have learnt his error in threatening an Angel.'

'Think carefully, I beg thee. 'Tis not right thee should barter thyself so.'

Gabriellen turned away to pick up the bowl and posset she had prepared. As she did so she sniffed, her hand making a quick, furtive gesture to wipe away a wayward tear. For her family's sake she must hide her abhorrence for the merchant. Her sacrifice would save them from ruin. Many women were forced into arranged marriages with men they did not love. Prew was a weakling. It would be a marriage upon her terms.

It had all been so easy. As Gabriellen had predicted, Prew had proposed to her that same day. The deed done, a numbness had settled over Gabriellen's emotions. Now, a month later, she stood in her bedchamber, dressed in her bridal finery and steeling herself for the ordeal ahead. The door opened and Esmond came in, his face haggard with guilt.

'Even now you do not have to make this sacrifice, my dear.'

'I thought we had said all there was to say on the matter? It's for the best. I'm doing it as much for my child as for you, Father, so do not blame yourself.'

'I still think you should wait until Rowan returns.' He used his last ploy to stop her. 'Word could be sent to Prew that you have fallen foul of a fever. The wedding will be deferred for another month.'

She shook her head. 'I would not involve Mark in our family problems. I know him. He would bankrupt himself to help free you of this debt. It's not fair to ask him. He has worked hard to build up his breeding mares and stables.'

'I do not talk of my debts, my dear. I talk of your future happiness. Rowan would make a good husband.'

'Mark loves Jesmaine. You talk nonsense, Father.'

'Rowan will never wed his fortune-teller. She would be an unsuitable wife for him. The woman he marries must have an empathy with the horses he cherishes so dearly.'

She raised an eyebrow, imitating Mark when he teased her. 'And you think because I have a love of animals, I will make Mark a suitable wife?' Her bantering tone dropped and she looked at him sombrely. 'I would never deceive Mark. Neither would I expect him to bring up Jack's child. I care for Mark too much to risk placing him in the danger Jesmaine foretold. It would be poor reward for his friendship.'

'Jesmaine could be allowing jealousy to colour her words,' Esmond prompted.

Gabriellen shook her head. 'I shall love only Jack. Have you ceased loving my mother since she died?'

Esmond took her into his arms and there were tears in his eyes. 'No, she is the only woman I have given my whole heart to. But she died whilst my love was at its height and untarnished by disillusion. Not so you. Before his death, Jack had callously betrayed you. Don't throw away a chance of happiness.'

'I am doing this for my child, and those whom I care for most.'

Her defiance humbled him and he hugged her close, then stepping back took a deep breath. 'I am proud of you, daughter. Very proud. I wish I could have done better by you.'

'You have given me what I value most – an education. You taught me not to feel inferior because I am a woman. You have shown me the wonder of creating a play and the joy of seeing it performed. And you gave me the chance to love Jack. I have no regrets.'

She kissed his cheek, his beard tickling her chin. 'Prew used threats and blackmail to win me as his bride. He will learn how hollow was his conquest. I am no man's plunder.'

'Do not underestimate him, my dear. He is a cruel, vengeful man when thwarted.' Then, seeing her pallor, he reassured her, 'But you can charm him. No doubt you will lead him by the nose in a merry dance.'

For a moment it seemed her control crumpled. She swayed and put a hand to her head. Esmond cursed his lack of tact and failing sight. She was an expert actress when the need arose. He had seen only her resilience, the bad light had hidden from him the grief and pain in her eyes. Misguided loyalty was pushing her into this. Bereavement had numbed her beyond rational thought. He had to stop her before it was too late. 'Don't do this, Gabby. Don't marry Prew. I'll go away. Adopt a disguise. Prew's spies and the law will never find me.'

'No.' The rawness of her pain burst through. 'Do you think I could bear to lose you as well? It is only a question of time before I leave Prew. He must suspect nothing yet. You need the earnings from the playhouse this autumn to tide you over the winter in Chichester. Prew refused to pay you an annuity because you would not sell him your shares in the theatre.'

'He wanted them too much. I never trust a man when desperation edges his voice. You have done what you can. You won a hard bargain from the merchant. He is a man who will want payment in full.'

The wedding party was crowded into the porch of the church. The guests remained solemn-faced throughout the service. Even when they stepped inside the church for the blessing, Gabriellen could not shake the numbness which had settled over her since Jack's death. Once outside, her arm was taken by Prew. Two diminutive women approached, both pinch-faced and nervous. One was in her fifties, the other about thirty.

'My dear mother, and sister Clemence,' Prew introduced them. The women moved forward simpering in unison and each gave Gabriellen a cold unemotional kiss on her cheek. A middle-aged man approached next, a merchant from his dress and a look of disapproval on his pompous face. Gabriellen guessed that the only pleasure he got from life was counting his money. 'This is Hugh Mottram, Clemence's husband.'

Gabriellen inclined her head in acknowledgement. They were a dour, uninspiring family after the colourful characters of the players. That they saw her as beneath them revived a dangerous demon within her. She despised pretentious arrogance. She would enjoy putting them in their place. The actress in her rose to the fore. Hugh Mottram was favoured by her dimpled smile.

'I had no idea Victor had so venerable a brother by

marriage. You must tell me all about yourself, Hugh.' She laughed and put a hand upon his arm. 'You do not mind if I call you Hugh? Such a distinguished name, for such a distinguished person.'

A flush of colour suffused the merchant's already ruddy cheeks and a salacious gleam came into his bulbous eyes. Both his wife and Mistress Prew exchanged shocked glances. Gabriellen summed the two women up as prudes, and Mottram as a man who was probably too fastidious to visit a brothel. She'd wager though he kept a mistress in better style than he kept his timid wife.

Esmond coughed and attempted light-heartedness. 'Well, Prew, are you not going to kiss your bride?'

A shocked gasp was uttered by Mistress Prew. 'Not here in the street!' She turned to her daughter, saying in a piercing whisper, 'What kind of a depraved family has Victor married into? I suppose one really cannot expect no better from common players.'

'One cannot expect *any* better, Mistress Prew,' Gabriellen corrected her, sarcastically mimicking her affected tones.

'Well, really! She even has the brazenness to admit it,' Mistress Prew answered with a disdainful sniff, Gabriellen's irony completely lost on her.

Poggs and Esmond were having difficulty restraining their laughter. But at Gabriellen's side Victor Prew stood very stiff and reproving. He had missed nothing.

'I trust, Esmond,' Prew stated primly, 'that you have no bawdry planned which will upset my mother. She is a gentlewoman by breeding.'

'Yes, one can always tell a first generation whose fortune has been made in trade,' Esmond said cuttingly. 'My family comes from a long line of mercenaries. If I were a braggart I could, without lie, claim that on my paternal side my lineage goes back to the time of King John, of infamous name, to a Baron Thomas D'Angell. A brigand who won his spurs by seizing a castle whose misguided allegiance still held to Richard the Lionheart. But it's not my way to preen or brag.' He slapped Prew on the back in affected bonhomie. 'In God's eyes we are all equal. Personally, though, I suspect that some are more equal than others.'

'You blaspheme, man.' Prew looked about to throw a seizure. 'I'll not have my mother and sister subjected to your heresy. Nor now, of course, my wife.'

Gabriellen, who had until now been enjoying the sparring between the two families, sobered. She was bound to this sanctimonious man. The awesomeness of what she had done struck her. Somehow she managed to suppress a shudder as she looked at the puny figure of her husband. What she saw in his face disgusted her. Pomposity, intolerance, and lurking just behind those small rodent eyes, something chilling which she could not as yet understand. What kind of man had she married? In her mind's eye she saw him as he would have been as a spoilt, opinionated child, the type who pulls the wings off butterflies. She carefully masked her loathing. She had deliberately not let her mind go past the wedding day. The ceremony which would free her father from his debts and the threat of the gallows. The depth of his unselfish love in allowing her to decide had given her the courage to continue with this travesty. Even now she refused to think beyond the wedding feast which Agnes and Nan had worked so hard to prepare.

There was little laughter and cheering to accompany the bridal couple to the house in Bankside for the wedding breakfast. Poggs had danced ahead of them playing his pipe until Mistress Prew had held her hand to her head and whined that such a racket quite shredded her poor nerves. Throughout the meal any attempt at ribaldry was quashed by horrified gasps from both Prew and his three guests. Even when Umberto played the lute and Cesare sang a romantic love song, it was met with tongues clicking in disapproval.

'These proceedings are undignified and unseemly,' Mistress Prew complained. 'Really, my dear Victor, I am at a loss to understand this hasty marriage. Such a family. So common. Of course I do not believe a word of what her father said about them having noble blood.'

Gabriellen drew a breath to retaliate when Prew interceded for her. 'What Esmond said is true, though I gather some of this noble blood came to them from the wrong side of the blanket.'

Gabriellen had taken enough. She stood up and clapped her hands. 'Poggs, take up your pipes and Umberto your tabour. The bride wishes to dance.'

'Oh, Victor, it is getting late.' Mistress Prew put one hand to her brow in a melodramatic gesture which was so poorly executed it caused a bout of sniggering from the apprentice players. Mistress Prew was too engrossed in her performance to notice, as she continued in a suitably weak voice: 'The noise of music and dancing will be too much for me. I think we should all leave.'

'My dear,' Prew turned to Gabriellen, 'have you everything ready to take to your new home?'

His expression betrayed his eagerness to be alone with her, and Gabriellen felt the first stab of panic. The thought of his hands upon her made her feel physically ill. That was something she would have to learn to endure. But not for a few hours yet. She smiled sweetly at him, her eyes round and innocent. 'I have, but we cannot go yet. Though if your mother is so overcome she must leave, it is regrettable. And, were we not all family, an appalling display of bad manners.'

It was obvious to Gabriellen that Mistress Prew was the type of woman who used frailty to get her own way. Such underhand tactics might work with her son. Gabriellen was made of sterner stuff. The Prew family were about to learn that she intended to be mistress of her own household.

Prew had the grace to blush, his colour deepening as Mistress Prew, with remarkable vigour for one who moments earlier had professed illness, moved to the door.

Gabriellen raised her voice so that it would carry to the departing woman. 'If your mother is ill, of course your sister and Mr Mottram must escort her home. We, however, shall remain. Why, we are barely through half of the banquet dishes which Nan and Agnes spent hours cooking. Not to mention that my father has taken the trouble to prepare a lavish entertainment to celebrate our wedding. I will not insult him by leaving early.'

Mistress Prew halted in mid-step and turned back. Her narrow face was frigid with censure. 'I have always been a martyr to poor health. A weak chest that leaves me with scarce the strength to rise from bed for days at a time.' A condescending smile played upon her lips. 'I'm sure I would not wish to insult your father, but such entertainments . . .' She left the sentence unfinished and wrinkled her nose, as though a bad smell had just wafted under it. 'My child, would they be seemly for a genteel matron like myself to witness?'

'I am not your child, Mistress Prew. And since our gracious Sovereign enjoyed the self-same entertainments not a month past, I would have thought they *were* suitable. I do not think my father planned a Roman orgy.'

'Gabriellen!' Victor Prew looked at her with outrage. 'I'll thank you not to talk to my mother in that manner.'

'Then thank your mother not to insult my family, sir. For someone who affects so many genteel airs, I would have thought the first she would have learnt was common courtesy.'

'I'm not staying here to be insulted by a playwright's daughter,' Mistress Prew shouted, at a volume which could only have come from very strong lungs. Had there been any question of her suffering from a headache, it would have left her crippled with agony.

Victor Prew hurried after his mother, but Gabriellen did not stop to watch. She turned away and with a fiery gleam in her eyes surveyed the players. 'Where is the music? Is there no one here who will dance with the bride on her wedding day?'

Poggs struck up a tune and Umberto picked up the lute from the window seat and followed Poggs into the garden. Cesare bowed to Gabriellen, his bearded face strained and unhappy. 'Too late, I think, come my words. This man Prew, he no is good. I say to Umberto I would marry you, for the sake of the babe you carry. He say, what you want with a poor musician like me? A man who would never be a man in your eyes.'

Gabriellen put a finger to his lips. 'No. Do not say that, Cesare. It takes a very special man to offer me what you have just done. I'm honoured you would even consider marrying me.' She smiled at him fondly. 'Now I see my husband has returned. Poggs is playing a reel.' She put out her arm for him to take. 'Let us dance. I know I should be in mourning for Jack and eschew all such pleasures, but I want to dance in his memory. In memory of the day I fell in love with him at Poggs's and Agnes's wedding. I want to dance for him.' Her voice broke. 'Dear God, Cesare, otherwise I do not think I can bear it.'

Chapter Twenty-Five

Gabriellen stared at the early morning rain running down the panes of her bedchamber window. At her side Prew stirred and she felt the mattress move as he left her. When the adjoining door which linked his bedchamber with hers closed, she flung back the covers and rose from her marriage bed. She staggered at the pain which accompanied every movement, and looked down at the tattered remains of her nightgown, flecked with blood and Prew's saliva. Her jaw set rigid against her agony, she tore off the offending garment and hurled it into a far corner of the room. She shuddered with abhorrence, her glare venomous as it fixed on the connecting door.

'Bastard!' she spat out in a low hoarse voice. 'Filthy, depraved bastard.'

Moving to the washbasin, she saturated a rough cloth in cold water and scrubbed at her sore body. She had never felt so defiled. Never again would she endure Prew's loathsome practices. Touching the bruises on her cheek and breasts, hatred gouged through her. The horror of the humiliation she had suffered at her husband's hands when he had discovered she was not a virgin, was a scar she would bear for life. Her flesh shrank on her bones at the memory. At first his fumbling attentions had been no more than a gross parody of the act of love. She had endured them with gritted teeth and frigid body whilst her mind locked upon her grief for Jack. The torpor was shattered by Prew's screech of rage.

'Harlot! Jezebel! Whore! You've come to me tainted. Bitch! Who was it?' His voice rose to a high-pitched scream. 'Tell me, who was it?'

She remained silent. Furious, he began to slap and punch her. She retaliated, instinctively kicking, biting and scratching to be free of him. Gabriellen pressed a shaking hand to her temple to blot out the repulsive memory. If she had to fight to her last breath she would not allow herself to be so humiliated again. Yet how was she to avoid it? She was too proud after a single night of marriage to return to her father's house. Besides, knowing Esmond's temper as she did, it was likely he would react with violence. She had not sacrificed so much for him to be arrested for attacking Prew.

Wincing at the stiffness in her limbs, Gabriellen reached for her petticoats and began to dress. For the moment she must bide her time and wait. At least now she knew the extent of Prew's depravity and was armed against it. She crossed the chamber to her clothes chest. From beneath the nightgowns and chemises, she took the dagger Mark had given her when they had travelled to Winchester. Sliding the blade from its enamelled sheath, she touched her thumb to its sharp edge with satisfaction. With a snap she plunged it back into its casing. She would keep it with her at all times. Even when she slept. Perhaps to threaten Prew would be enough? Insight told her that physically to fight her husband was not the way to stop a further attack. Had not her violent response to his abuse roused him to a greater frenzy?

In one so puny, she had been startled at Prew's strength. He had become seized in the grip of a lecherous insanity. It had terrified her – shocked and filled her with repugnance. The more she fought him and caused him physical pain, the more excited and aroused he became. To stop Prew she would have to remain indifferent to his taunts and attentions.

The chamber door opened and she spun round, her face blank of all expression as she regarded her husband. A smirk touched his thin lips as his gaze rested upon the bruises on her arms. Her hands clenched with disgust, but she was reassured by the feel of the dagger against her palm. Keeping her hand hidden in her petticoats, she turned away to pick up a black bodice which fastened at the front. She pulled it on to cover her breasts from his leering gaze, secreting the dagger in her cleavage when she fastened the garment.

'You'll wear bright colours as befits a new bride,' Prew shouted.

Not troubling to answer, Gabriellen reached for the black

382

satin overskirt. She intended to continue her mourning for Jack out of respect for his memory.

'I said, you will wear bright colours.'

Again she ignored him.

'You're my wife and you will obey me!'

'I shall wear what pleases me.'

She sat down in front of a Venetian looking glass and began to brush her hair. Not with the silver-backed brush Jack had bought her – that was safely hidden away – but with an ivory one she had used since a child.

'Strumpet! I am master in my own house. Do as I say!' Prew stormed at her. He could feel his blood growing hot in anticipation of her retaliation. To his annoyance she did not respond. He despised her for the way she had tricked him. But last night she had fought like an ancient warrior queen, exciting him more than any woman had before. This indifference left him unmoved. His lips curled back into a sneer. He had seen the fury she had unleashed upon Cornelius Hope when he had turned upon her father. That was the way to rouse her spirit. He chewed the end of his wispy moustache in anticipation. Only when she fought him, as she had last evening, was he capable of an erection. Or he could prove his supremacy over her by beating her into submission.

'I intend to visit Angel today. He'll not get away with this,' he announced. His small eyes hard and vindictive, he waited for her anger to erupt. She remained impassive, goading him further. 'My mother warned me a playwright's daughter would be no better than a whore. She was right. Now both you and your father shall pay for this deceit.'

'How did I deceive you?' Gabriellen answered, still with her back to him. 'Did you not go down on your knees and beg me to marry you? I told you I was unworthy – that I did not love you. You would not listen. You begged me to marry you!'

She was laughing at him. How dare she throw that in his face? She had led him on. Made him play the love-sick fool. Shaking with rage, he closed the gap between them. How dare she ignore him like this. He was her husband. Her master. Grabbing her hair, he wound it round his hand. With a vicious tug, he forced her head back. A vein throbbed into life upon her temple and tears of pain glistened in her green eyes, but she made no sound. He jerked harder. His breathing quickened at seeing her lips become bloodless as she bit into them to restrain a cry.

'You'll pay for gulling me, you bitch,' he gloated as he stared into her face. It was as expressionless as marble. His outrage soared. 'Who was your lover?'

Her lips twisted with contempt but she held her silence.

'Was it that Welshman? He was always sniffing at your door like a dog after a bitch on heat. Tired of you, did he? He's not been near all summer.'

The green eyes staring up at him were devoid of fire, denying him the pleasure he sought. With a curse Prew released her hair. She would not rise to his baiting. Still, there was another way.

'You and your father thought yourselves so clever,' he sneered. 'He unburdened himself of a daughter no decent man would touch. You were sold to clear his debts. Now you're my property. Last night was just a taste of what's to come. You may be the highest-priced whore in London, but you'll earn every penny of that debt. As for your father . . .'

He gave a harsh malignant laugh, rubbing his hands together as he contemplated his revenge. 'There's still the matter of Fossett left unsettled. That's a hanging offence. I'm off now to see that justice is done. Angel will be in prison before the day is out.'

Gabriellen swivelled round on the stool. He'd thought that would capture her interest. When she stood up, he could not contain his sardonic laughter. He was in command again. The feeling of power was intoxicating. Whatever his demands she must obey him. That was the law. Some of his antagonism that she had not come to him a virgin dissipated. How much better a woman of experience, one who would be grateful that he had saved her reputation. If she was accommodating to him, he would not act against her father. Esmond Angel was her weakness. Better to keep him free and have the threat of his imprisonment over her. That would keep her in his power.

Prew could not resist humbling her proud spirit further. 'Dear Mama will be dining with us. You will apologise to her for your rudeness yesterday. This house is larger than my sister's. Mama has often expressed a wish to be mistress again here. In the past her poor health needed the constant attention of my sister. I dismissed my housekeeper last week, since as my wife you will perform those duties. We shall have a special celebration meal for dear Mama tonight, then I shall ask her to come and live with us. It will be one of your duties to tend her in her sick bed.'

The hairbrush dug into Gabriellen's palm as she controlled her rising anger. A sharp pain from where he had pulled her hair stabbed like needles behind her eyes. The expression in his eyes was the most evil she had ever encountered. She was afraid, deeply afraid, but she dare not show it. The pressure of the dagger case hidden in her bodice reassured her. This time Prew would not overpower her. She must shrug off the lethargy which had settled over her since Jack's death. Prew was like a leech, growing strong upon the blood and suffering of his prey. Her husband was about to discover to his cost that she was no one's victim. She must be careful. Should she lose her temper, any advantage she would gain by intimidating Prew would be lost. She moved towards him, the actress in her concealing her hatred.

'You mistake the matter. Firstly, I will not be threatened. Especially by such a feeble apology for manhood as yourself.' She jabbed her finger into his chest and he took a startled step backwards. 'Secondly, neither will I tolerate my father being threatened.'

His mouth sagged open and he gulped like a landed fish. His face lost its high colour. Like all bullies when shown a will greater than theirs, his bravado crumbled. He took several more paces back, but was stopped by the bedpost. He sidestepped around it. Gabriellen pursued him and, still stabbing at him with her finger, delivered her ultimatum.

'Thirdly, should ever my father be so much as looked at twice by a constable of the watch, I will tell your precious mama what a perverted louse you are. And I have no intention of being a servant to your mother, who plays upon an imaginary illness to achieve her own ends. The day she moves into this house, I shall leave.'

Prew stumbled over a shoe in his haste to withdraw from the room. His face was covered in a sheen of perspiration. Gabriellen knew she could not back down. If she did their roles would become reversed. 'Do I make myself clear?'

Prew began to salivate. Suddenly she was alarmed that she'd gone too far. He was growing excited at her scolding. 'Very clear. But then, I see that Mama's presence sleeping in the next chamber could be a hindrance to our sport. For now she will stay with my sister.'

Her repugnance intensified. What type of man had she married? She remembered once laughing hilariously when Jack had told her that there were men who liked to be subjugated by women – to play the bonded slave to a warrior queen, the tortured sacrifice to a pagan priestess, or the whipping boy of a cruel princess. Now she nearly gagged on her rising nausea, her disgust was so acute. Was Prew such a deviant? She no longer found the stories of those bizarre sexual rituals amusing.

Prew must have sensed her alarm. He had paused at the door, his eyes glowing with a fanatical light. 'There is one matter I do insist upon, for the good of your soul. You will receive instruction in the Catholic faith.'

'I will do no such thing,' Gabriellen began.

Prew gave her a look which turned her blood to ice. A transformation came over him and he appeared to change in stature as he strode to a chest and took out a whip.

'As your husband, it is my duty to save your soul,' he cried, bringing down the whip upon her shoulders. 'You will recant your heresy.'

Her dagger was useless against the length of that vicious lash and he wielded it with the skill of long practice. The fourth blow, searing in its agony, brought Gabriellen to her knees. She bit her lip to stop herself crying out. There was no escaping the wicked lash as it descended with increasing ferocity. By the ninth blow she was prostrate on the floor, her fingers clawing at the polished floorboards as she tried to heave herself away from the demented figure standing over her. Terrified she could lose her child, she bore the beating in silence, knowing that to cry out would only inflame him further. But the beating had been enough to arouse him. When she was too weak to resist, he raped her.

It was early October before Mark Rowan returned to London. He had spent all summer following the Jesuit priest and gathering enough evidence to arrest his paymaster. So far the plan to assassinate the Queen had been frustrated by Her Majesty's own whims. She had gone on a late summer's progress, and upon her return had taken up residence at her favourite palace at Greenwich. Mark now had all the evidence he needed.

He had reached the capital just as the curfew was being sounded and duty had taken him to the ramshackle dwelling in Whitefriars which he kept for his secret activities. He changed into a fresh disguise. Throughout his relationship with Jesmaine he had taken pains not to involve her in his secret work, though he suspected that she knew he had a double identity and that his work was dangerous.

Tonight he was dressed as a palace servant, complete with the Tudor rose sewn on to his sleeve. His swarthy features and dark hair were disguised by a reddish beard, false bushy brows and a wig. By the time he was ready to leave, there was still no sign of Bartholomew Pudsey from whom he rented this room. That was a shame. He would have liked to have spoken to him before he left for the palace. Pudsey, in his role of pseudo-cripple begging by the West door of Westminster Abbey, missed nothing of what was going on in London. Several times Pudsey had given him valuable information about Jesuit priests hiding in the city.

During his walk to the river, Mark wondered how both Jesmaine and Gabriellen had fared during his absence. He had heard nothing from either of them. That did not unduly trouble him. The circumstances of his work made contact with them difficult. Gabriellen must be suffering at the rumours of Jack's death. Mark did not want to believe his friend was dead, but if he had not drowned and was now in the hands of the Inquisition, the Spanish would have announced that one of the Queen's most notorious sea captains was at their mercy. With each week which passed without news, it became more certain that Jack had died. Mark bowed his head in acceptance. Tomorrow he must go to Gabriellen and give her what comfort he could.

An evening mist was rising as he stepped into the wherry which would take him to Greenwich. He pulled the hood of his cloak over his nose and mouth to block out the noxious vapours. The river was a rubbish tip of decomposing debris. He stared back along the Thames. In the moonlight the four turrets of the Tower keep dominated the church spires rising behind it. To the north of that awesome prison were the rooms he shared with Jesmaine. His expression softened. She would be preparing to retire for the night, the rooms pleasantly warm and fragrantly sweet from the perfumed candles she always burned. Jesmaine was the perfect mistress, exciting and uninhibited. But the time would come when they would inevitably part. His life was in Wales, whereas Jesmaine was happily settled in London with an established clientele.

Upon his arrival at the palace he was searched by the guard to check that he carried no weapon. He gave the appropriate answers to their questions and was allowed to pass. Shown into the anteroom of the Secretary of State's chambers, he was told to wait. The servant informed him that Walsingham was in attendance upon the Queen.

An hour later he was admitted to the inner chamber. Lord Walsingham sat at his desk in the flickering candle-light, surrounded by letters and boxes, his seals and ink to hand, the chill air warmed by a glowing charcoal brazier. He was attired in sombre velvet and a plain piecrust ruff. At Mark's entrance he returned his quill to the inkwell and sanded the document he had just signed. Gesturing to him to sit in a chair opposite his desk, Walsingham subjected him to a cold scrutiny. Mark held it confidently, though he was aware that should he fail in his service to this man, that stare, without the flicker of an eyelid, could send him to rot in the Tower.

'That disguise is good, Rowan. But for the eyes I would have not recognised you.'

Mark relaxed as Walsingham continued, 'The gardener at Nonsuch has been arrested. He has confessed to being the marksman. He also named the priest and two other accomplices. The Jesuit seems to have gone to ground. Have you any idea where he may be?'

Mark sat forward. 'Two days ago he was at Eltham. Plans are being laid for another attempt on the Queen's life during her Accession Day parade next month.'

Walsingham tapped a finger upon his desk as he considered Mark's words. 'With each failure the Catholics grow more desperate. This Accession Day plot must bring into the open those of wealth and influence whom we have been seeking these last two years.'

'That is my belief also, my lord.' Mark held Walsing-ham's piercing stare for a moment before continuing in an urgent tone, 'Time is short. There is too much at stake for me to continue this work alone. Give me two men and I'll pursue the enquiries I've been making in the Capital. I promise you the conspirators' names before the month's end.'

'This priest does not suspect you? Or his accomplice in the city? You have been watching them a long time.'

'I take care never to use the same disguise twice.'

Walsingham nodded. He picked up his quill and drew several documents towards him. 'Two men will be sent to you. I expect all involved locked in the Tower before the month is out.'

When Mark Rowan left the chamber, an inner door opened and Elizabeth Tudor came in to pace the room with long manly strides. 'I heard it all. Still these damned Papists continue with their plotting! Have I been too lenient with them that they repay me with treachery?' She beat one fist into her open palm. 'Perhaps I should light the fires of Smithfield as vengefully as my sister did? Only I would rid England of all Papists and not heretics by those flames.'

'You have always ruled England wisely, madam. The people love you. Most of your Catholic nobles are loyal. And we have these fanatics under vigilant watch.'

'Thanks to Rowan and his like.' Elizabeth paced with such energy the papers on the desk began to stir and lift. Following a furious swish of her full skirts the documents wafted across the desk, forcing Walsingham to make an ungainly dive to save them from scattering on the floor. The Queen rounded on him as he sorted his disturbed papers back into their tidy piles. He stopped in mid movement as he caught the expression on her face. Her eyes appeared to burn with all the fires of hell.

'I was assured by my council that the death of Mary of Scots would bring an end to the Catholic plots. God knows I did not want Mary's death. She was my cousin – my sister Queen.' Elizabeth's fist slammed down on to the desk, upsetting the inkwell.

Walsingham saved his precious papers from the dark flow spreading across the surface. 'Rowan is the best there is,' he placated. 'Once these conspirators are brought to justice, you will live in peace.'

'Peace!' The strident voice reverberated off the panelled walls. 'What peace have I with Mary of Scotland's death upon my conscience? Already some within the council are insisting I name her son James my heir.' Her hands on her hips, she returned to her pacing. 'Do those fools think I want to be reminded of my barren state? That, married as I am solely to England, I shall have no child from this body? Damn them all!' She kicked a footstool out of the way, her fingers drumming upon her padded hips. 'Don't those fools know that by naming an heir, I sow the seeds of rebellion within my kingdom? Would that more of my so-called faithful councillors were as loyal as Rowan. Without the diligent work of my wily horse-breeder, I would be just another rotting carcass.'

Mark walked through the maze of corridors of the palace. Torches lit every passage, revealing the sleeping figures curled on the floor wherever they could find a space. For the most part they were servants, but one or two bore the ruddy faces of country gentlemen, merchants or lawyers who had come to London to petition the Queen. These unfortunates must be prepared to spend days, sometimes weeks, awaiting the chance to present their case to the Queen. Often their money gave out long before the Sovereign gave them audience. He stepped carefully over the sleeping forms. In his disguise as a servant it would be another three hours before he could leave the palace. Until then he would snatch what sleep he could. He found a vacant corner, and wrapping his plain woollen cloak around him, lay down on the worn flagstones. He had long ago learned to snatch sleep in the most uncomfortable places, but it was always the slumber of a man on guard.

A carefree whistling brought Mark instantly awake. From the stiffness in his shoulders he estimated he had slept for over an hour. He sat up and saw that the man's whistling came from the direction of the Queen's apartments. As the tall figure passed the end of the corridor, Mark recognised the Earl of Essex. He looked insufferably pleased with himself. His place as the Queen's favourite was assured, despite his frequent tantrums. There were times when for all Essex's manly strength and vigour, he acted like a spoilt child. If the Queen denied him a favour, or slighted him by showing greater favour to Raleigh, he retired to Essex House in a sulk. There he would remain in his room for days, feigning illness, until the Queen relented and sent word desiring his company. At each return to Court Essex became more arrogant, more convinced of his own importance to Her Majesty.

Mark shook his head. He liked the young nobleman well enough. When Essex chose to exert his charm, he had a way of inspiring loyalty and trust. But there was something which disturbed him about the Earl. Mark suspected that he saw himself as King. A dangerous path. A wise man would have learnt from the tribulations of his stepfather, Robert Dudley. The Queen had loved the Earl of Leicester for more than thirty years, yet she had denied him the crown matrimonial. Mark suspected that what Elizabeth felt for Leicester's stepson was the infatuation of an aging woman seeking to regain her youth. And Essex was no wily diplomat. He was impetuous and hot-headed. A dangerous combination when coupled with boundless ambition and sense of self-worth. It had led many men such as he to an untimely end upon the scaffold.

The London sky was fiery with a crimson dawn as Mark let himself into the house in Bishopsgate. At the sound of the latch clicking shut an excited yelp came from the parlour. Moments later a blur of white and brown launched itself into his outstretched arms. With a laugh Mark buried his head in the dog's coat to avoid the long pink tongue licking at his face. He put Hywel down and stroked his squirming back.

'You've grown fat, boy.' He rubbed the long ears affectionately. 'Too many sweetmeats and not enough exercise.'

An exotic perfume wafted into the hallway and Mark looked up to see Jesmaine standing in the parlour doorway. She rested one hand above her head on the frame, the other on her rounded hip. The scarlet of her robe stretched tight across her breasts and hips. Her black hair was tousled, falling to her thighs in abandoned disarray which set his pulses racing.

She moved into his arms, her mouth hungry against his. As she pressed against him, he could feel her nakedness beneath her silken robe. With a throaty laugh, Jesmaine drew away. Taking his hand, she led him towards the bedchamber. There was an erotic promise in her every movement. Her robe slipped down over one shoulder, revealing her smooth olive skin and the ruby crest of her uptilted breast.

Hywel let out a telling sigh and slunk off back to the hearth as his master disappeared into the adjoining room.

It was noon before Mark rose and broke his fast with bread, cheese and ale. 'That was some homecoming, my lovely.' He caught her hand and kissed her palm as she moved to clear his trencher. They smiled into each other's eyes and as Jesmaine turned away, he said, 'You must have heard that Stoneham is dead. I must visit Ellen today.'

'Your precious Ellen no longer needs you to protect her.' Mark gave her a look which warned Jesmaine he would tolerate none of her jealous scorn. She shrugged, hiding the hurt that after the passion of their reunion he should hurry to Gabriellen's side. Picking up the water jug and discovering it empty, Jesmaine clasped it to her chest. 'Gabriellen has done very well for herself whilst you were away. And spared little time in mourning her lover, for all she carries his child. A month ago she was married.'

She watched the doubt shadow his eyes and he stepped back as though riding a blow to the chin. 'To whom?'

'Some merchant, I believe. He took the daughter in payment for her father's debt. Well matched, that pair. Come spring, the merchant will be presented with a six-month child – Stoneham's bastard.'

'Was his name Prew?' Mark barked out in a voice he had never used to her before. It was gruff with fear.

'Yes – Prew. She does not need you.'

He stared at her narrowly in a way that chilled Jesmaine's blood. 'You know much of this matter. Is it common gossip?'

'No.' Jesmaine put down the jug, picked up the empty water pail in its stead and moved to the door. She hoped with the playwright's daughter married, Mark would forget her. 'Gabriellen came here seeking the truth of Stoneham's death. I have always known she was a danger to you. This time the crystal confirmed it. She is better out of your life, Mark. Now I must go to the conduit for water.'

'You will go nowhere until you have told me everything.' He barred her path. 'Precisely what did you see in the crystal? And what did you tell Ellen?'

For an instant Jesmaine contemplated lying. There was a look in Mark's eyes which frightened her. He looked capable of anything. Only last night the stars had portrayed that he was approaching a crossroads in his life. His horoscope had shown her that Mars, dark and dangerous, was in the ascendancy. It would be a time of conflict – a time when evil could triumph over good.

Chapter Twenty-Six

On the point of leaving to visit Gabriellen, Mark received
a message from Bartholomew Pudsey which took him off
in pursuit of the priest he had previously been trailing. His
work took him from London for several days, during which
time he intercepted a letter from the conspirators with
information which would hang them all. This was now in
Walsingham's hands. Early this morning the traitors should
have been arrested and Mark was free to seek out
Gabriellen.

He slowed his pace as he approached Prew's house. The
damp October wind blew the fallen leaves on to the rutted
paths. Hywel, who was sniffing in the gutter ahead, put a
rat into flight. The dog set off in pursuit until Mark's
command brought him back to heel. Mark looked above
the two rows of gabled houses to the narrow band of overcast sky between. Already the ground was becoming soft
from the autumn rain. He could not delay his return to
Wales much longer or the roads would be impassable.

The Vale of Clwyd seemed another world away from the
bustle of London life. Its peace and tranquillity beckoned.
Before he returned to his home he must speak with Gabriellen. No easy meeting this. His emotions were bewildering,
part rage at her marriage, part anxiety at how she fared.

He stepped over the rotting carcass of a squashed cat run
over by a cart. The walk from Bishopsgate had rubbed a
blister on his toe from wearing new leather thigh boots,
and the stiffness of his lace-pointed ruff chaffed his neck.
After the comfort of his old leather doublet, the close-fitting
green velvet felt constricting across his broad shoulders.

What would Gabriellen feel at the arrest of her husband?
Especially should she learn that he was responsible for it.
He was certain that she had no idea that Prew was a Cath-
olic, let alone bent upon murder. Or that, through the

394

cargo he imported from the Continent, Prew received instructions and money from King Philip of Spain. Mark suspected his interest in the players had been to gain access to Court, whereby an assassination attempt would be made on the Queen. Those schemes had been thwarted time and again by Esmond. The playwright had outfoxed the merchant. No doubt he had merely taken Prew for a sycophant eager to win the favour of nobles by associating with the players.

As King Philip's paymaster, Prew took pains to keep in the background of the plots. How aptly that suited his craven character! Others risked their lives, whilst he remained safe at home. Clearly King Philip had grown impatient at the lack of success. Expediency had drawn Prew out into the open before he found himself answerable to the Spanish King's wrath.

During the merchant's dealings with the players, he had obviously become enamoured of Ellen. A man of Prew's weakness would be drawn by her strength. Mark felt his gut tightening. He still could not come to terms with the knowledge that Ellen had wed such a man. The thought of the merchant laying his depraved hands upon her, filled him with a sick and unreasonable fury. From his investigations he had learned that Prew had spent little time at home lately. Three weeks had been taken up by the need to travel to Bristol to sort out a business complication. Apparently his agent there had been robbing him. The last ten days he had been at a Catholic manor in Kent, finalising the last details of the Accession Day Plot.

Mark pulled the doorbell and heard it ring inside the house. A sharp-faced, nervous maidservant answered, easing open the door to peer through a narrow crack.

'Can I be helping you, sir? Master's not at home.'

'I have come to call upon your mistress.'

The maidservant looked apprehensive. 'I don't know about that, sir. The mistress don't receive visitors.'

'Is she ill?' Mark asked with concern.

The maid shuffled her feet and took a moment to answer. 'No, Mistress Prew is not ill.' She peered shortsightedly at his velvet doublet and highly polished boots, and looked more at ease. 'Are you with Lord Mincham's Men?'

'I am not. Tell your mistress Mark Rowan would speak with her. I'm sure she will see me.'

'If you're not a player, then you had best come inside. The master gave strict instructions that upon no account were any of them to set foot in this house.' She stepped back and led Mark into the front parlour.

He looked round the room as he waited. Hywel lay obediently at his feet. Everything spoke of the merchant's wealth. There were a dozen pieces of silver plate and candlesticks on the dresser. A brightly coloured Persian carpet covered the table and two highbacked, carved chairs took pride of place each side of the hearth. Few houses outside a nobleman's manor possessed furniture of such richness and quality.

Hywel gave a soft whimper and sat up, his ears pricked as he looked towards the door. There was the sound of a light footfall and the rustle of silk, and then Gabriellen entered the room. She was dressed from head to toe in black, only a narrow white ruff at her throat and a row of pearls in her heart-shaped headdress relieving the starkness of her attire. There looked to be no difference in her slender figure, but her stiffened jet-sewn stomacher was tightly laced and falling to a low point as it did, would disguise any thickening of her waist. Had he not known, he would never have suspected her condition.

'Goodday, Mark. Your visit is a pleasant surprise.'

She spoke politely as though to a stranger. He frowned. For a woman of so honest a nature, why did she refuse to meet his eye? She paused to ruffle Hywel's ears then crossed to sit in the chair by the hearth. Something was very wrong.

'What made you do it?' It was the last question he had intended to ask, but now he was here he could not prevent himself from pursuing the matter. He stood gazing down at her. She looked pale and under a great deal of strain. 'How could you marry a fiend such as Prew?'

Her head came up, and her knuckles whitened over the chair arm. She did not answer. Refusing to meet his stare, she continued to fondle Hywel.

'Was it to get your father out of debt? Or because you carried Jack's child?' He felt his temper rising and fought to control it.

She glanced nervously at the door, her voice hoarse. 'Who told you about the child?'

'Jesmaine. She also said that she had warned you that our friendship placed my life in danger. Is that why you left me no word of this marriage?' He took her hand and was startled to find it was trembling. When he gave it a reassuring squeeze, he was annoyed that she still appeared wary, refusing to look him in the face. He reached for her other hand, and raised her with gentle insistence to her feet. Hywel, now ignored, put his head down on his paws and closed his eyes. 'Ellen, why did you marry Prew?'

Gabriellen swayed and Mark, thinking her about to swoon, caught her in his arms. The feel of her body pressed against his roused a fierce need to protect her. She looked so unhappy and vulnerable, it caught at his heart.

She took a deep breath and said shakily, 'You must have heard of Jack's death?'

At his nod, she groaned and pressed her brow against his shoulder. 'I loved him so much. We had a terrible argument. I told him I hated him, and sent him away. And now he's dead.'

'You must not blame yourself,' Mark soothed. 'Jack loved you. Every time he went to sea there was a risk. He knew that. It was part of his life.'

She inhaled a shuddering breath. 'Did you know Jack was married, Mark?'

'He was what!' It was an accusation, not a question. 'I had no idea. I knew there was much about Jack's life which he liked to keep secret, but I never suspected that. Sweet Jesu, Ellen! No wonder you quarrelled. I suppose you told him about the child?'

'Yes.' She gave a heart-wrenching sigh and buried her head against his neck as she clung to him in her sorrow. There was no coquetry or guile in the gesture, just the action of a friend seeking comfort. Yet his need to protect her was like no loyalty he had ever experienced before.

Leaning back, he wiped a tear from her cheek. It was then he noticed the livid bruise on the side of the brow she had kept averted from him.

'Did Prew do that?'

'It doesn't matter, Mark. I can handle him.'

His fingers dug into her shoulders as he gazed into her face, his stare piercing through the confusion and pain in her eyes. 'Why did you marry him? Why did you not come to me? I would have helped you. By all that's holy, if it was just because of the child, I would have married you!'

The statement shocked him, as much by its unpremeditated eruption as by the utter certainty that he meant what he said.

To his consternation, Gabriellen burst into tears. His arm went around her and he drew her head against his chest. He guessed they were tears too long held back, and she needed the release they would bring her. Told that Jack was dead and blackmailed into an abhorrent marriage, her life these past weeks must have been a living hell. He had seen how his level-headed and practical sister Aphra had become irrational and given to bouts of uncontrolled weeping during her pregnancies. In the present circumstances it was no wonder that even Gabriellen's valiant spirit had cracked.

Not for long. With remarkable speed the flood abated and she hiccoughed to a halt. He attempted to lighten the moment with a jest. 'I had not realised how cataclysmic a proposal of marriage could be. I'll go prepared with a bucket and sponge next time.'

'Fool!' she said huskily, her eyes overbright. She took a handkerchief from the black satin pocket suspended on a ribbon from her waist, and blew her nose.

The tears had not marred her face. Rather her beauty became ethereal. Her smile was wistful and she touched her long elegant fingers tentatively to his cheek. 'You are a good friend.'

He saw her eyes widen as her gaze noticed his finery. 'Such a dashing figure you cut, Mark. So handsome – so worthy. Everything a woman could want in a husband. It would be a great honour to have become your wife. But I care for you too much to force another man's child upon you. Marriage would be too great a sacrifice for you to pay in the name of that friendship.' The teasing light was suddenly doused in her green eyes, her voice growing sombre. 'Besides, Jesmaine told me I will bring danger to you.'

'I am used to danger. It is part of my life. Jesmaine has always been jealous of our friendship.' Mark frowned and took her hand, holding it close to his chest.

She looked down at their joined hands and ran her thumb over his brown fingers. 'Your friendship means everything to me. Just knowing you are there, gives me the strength I need to endure.'

He battled to keep his own complex emotions under

control. It was unlikely from her bruises that she could have come to care for Prew since their marriage.

'There's news which will disturb you, Ellen. You had better sit down.'

He waited until she was seated. Still holding her hand, he squatted at her side. For a moment he did not speak; she had already borne so much with fortitude. He could see close up that her face was transparently pale. Outside the window a cart rumbled past and behind the room's panelling a mouse scampered. Mark squeezed Gabriellen's hand, willing her to be strong. She responded with a wan smile.

'Do you care for Prew?' he found the need first to ask.

'No.' The accompanying shudder of revulsion told him much. 'I despise him. But he has evidence against Esmond which will put him in prison if I leave. And he is a Catholic . . . a fanatical one.' Another shudder gripped her body.

'It is worse than that,' Mark began slowly, trying to find the words to soften the blow he must deal her. 'Prew is known to be in the pay of Philip of Spain.' Her eyes widened with shock, but she said nothing so he went on, 'This morning he and several others involved in a plot against the Queen's life should have been arrested.'

Her hand clenched beneath his as the shock of his words registered. 'I knew he was capable of stooping low, but not to this.'

Mark had not thought it possible for her pallor to increase, but it did. Her mouth became a thin twisted line of hatred. She began to breathe in laboured gasps and he felt another shudder pass through her rigid body.

She cried out then in anguish, 'By God's son, I am worse than defiled! I am married to a traitor.'

'It will not reflect on you. There is no doubt of your innocence.'

She jumped up and paced the room, her quick, angry steps displacing the layer of rushes as her long skirts swept over them. Raising her fist, she thumped it against the oak lintel above the inglenook fireplace. For several moments she remained poised, her brow resting on her hand as she stared down at the unlit logs stacked in the grate. At last she faced him and said, 'But how do you know all this?'

He was relieved to see that the life was returning to her

eyes. 'I just know. Let that suffice.'

Gabriellen studied him. The light of battle had returned to her eyes and the colour had come back to her cheeks. A flash of the Ellen he knew so well showed through her torment as a teasing smile tilted her lips. 'I always suspected there was much about yourself you did not tell me. You're more than a horse-breeder, aren't you?'

Mark stood up. The admiration he saw in her eyes unsettled him. 'It will not be long before soldiers are sent to search the house for evidence against your husband.'

'I will not be here.' Her voice carried its old defiance. 'I've no intention of remaining in the house of a traitor. Will you take me away, Mark?'

'How long will it take to collect your clothes?'

'I want nothing that was bought with Prew's money. I have a few personal possessions in my room. I will take those.'

From the shadows of the alleyway opposite, the travel-stained figure of the merchant watched his wife and the Welshman leave. What he had seen confirmed his darkest suspicions. Such a tender reunion he had witnessed through the front parlour window. So it was Rowan who had been her lover. The way they had clung together proved it. Did they now think to play him for a cuckold? Those two would pay for making a fool of him. He did not have much time.

By a cat's whisker he had escaped Walsingham's guards. The others had all been taken. From an upstairs window of the manor, he had seen the riders galloping through the trees towards the house. He alone had reached the priest's hole cut into the stairwell in time to hide. He sat quaking with fear as he heard the stamp of the soldiers' boots over the house. An icy sweat broke out over him as he heard again their harsh, angry voices and the screams of the conspirators as they were dragged from the manor. They would talk. If his identity was not already known, it would be once the rack or the thumbscrews were applied. Only the need for money had made him return to London. In a secret hiding place behind a brick in the inglenook fireplace was a hoard of gold coins. He had to get out of the country. Soon Walsingham's spies would be watching for him at every port. He scuttled across the road and entered the house. Minutes later he was back in the street again, his doublet bulging and his legs buckled from the weight of the gold he carried. He turned towards Bankside.

He knew what direction Gabriellen had taken. She was returning to her father. What she did not know was that the players were at Lord Mincham's estate in Surrey. Lord Mincham's daughter was to be betrothed and there was to be a week of celebrations, the players providing the entertainment.

'I do not like the idea of leaving you unprotected in this house, Ellen,' Mark said as he lit a candle against the gathering dusk. In an hour he must make his final report to Walsingham's secretary. For Gabriellen's sake he must learn that Prew was safely locked in the Tower. 'I wish I could stay, but an urgent appointment . . .'

'Do not worry about me,' Gabriellen smiled. 'I am sure the others will return soon. They will not be late if Nan has taken Laurence with her. I expect Jesmaine is worrying about you. It is time you got back to her.'

He turned away so that she would not see his expression. 'I shall be returning to Wales soon. I cannot expect Saul and Aphra to manage the farm on their own through the winter.'

'Shall I see you again before you leave?'

The catch in her voice made him turn to study her. He nodded. 'Of course. My mind will rest easier if I know you are settled.'

'When Jack asked you to look after me, you certainly took your duty seriously,' she teased, but at the stiffening of his expression, fell silent.

The silence between them grew strained. She had never needed Mark's friendship more, but he was deliberately putting a distance between them. Why? She had not taken his offer of marriage seriously. It had been a chivalrous gesture, and she would treasure it. When he returned to Wales she would miss him desperately. Until now she had not realised how much she had come to rely upon his companionship, and the pleasure it brought her.

With a sinking feeling, it dawned on her that it could be a long time before she saw him again. A chill crept through her. 'I shall miss you, Mark. I wish you every success in Wales. Think of me sometimes.'

'As if I could forget you.' His voice was gruff and he

cleared his throat before adding, 'Look you, my meeting will not take more than two hours. I'll leave Hywel with you for company. I'll be back by eight o'clock. I shall stay with you until your father returns.'

Without the players, the house in Bankside was oppressively empty. Unable to settle, Gabriellen prowled the deserted rooms. It still did not seem possible that Prew had the courage to plot against the Queen's life. But then, since her marriage she had seen all that was unpleasant and fanatical in his nature. There was a side to him which was not quite sane.

There had been no repetition of that first humiliation she had suffered. Providing she showed no fear, and had agreed to take instruction from the priest who had twice visited the house, she had ruled him. Not that there had been occasion for him to attempt to force his attentions upon her. Complications in his business had kept him from home. Now she realised that during some of that time, he had been plotting to murder their Queen.

With him in the Tower she would be free to resume her own life. It solved the problem of her unborn child. She would live in Chichester this winter and her baby would be born there. When she returned to London, no one would be the wiser that she had not carried the child a full nine months after their marriage. She had little sympathy for her husband. If he was a traitor, he deserved whatever befell him.

The tight lacing of her gown was always more uncomfortable in the evenings. Free from the restraints of prying servants, there would be no fear of discovery. She could afford to relax. Going to her old room, she changed into a loose silk gown over which she wore an open robe of gold damask edged with sable. No longer restricted, the child moved within her. Gabriellen smiled and placed a hand over her rounded stomach. By her reckoning she was nearly five months now and the movements were very distinct. 'You will be a strong and lusty child, my precious. Like your brave father.'

Her throat convulsed as grief for Jack returned. Hywel gave a low growl, interrupting her thoughts. The dog's hackles rose as he stood for a moment, stiff-legged, his head on one side, listening. He let out a high-pitched bark and raced to the back of the house, barking ferociously. Who was out there? One of the players perhaps? They did not usually enter by the back gate. Suddenly nervous, she looked around the room and picked up a heavy brass poker and a lighted candle. Why had she so relaxed her vigilance as to leave her dagger upstairs? It was the first time she had been without it in weeks.

The dog's barking was rising to a crescendo. Cautiously, Gabriellen edged towards the back of the house which was in darkness. Hywel was in the passage which led to a cellar door. 'Here, boy,' she called. Knowing the dog's hunting instincts, she suspected he had heard a mouse. There could be no one in the cellar.

Still Hywel continued to growl and scratch at the cellar door with his paws. 'Hywel, it's only a mouse,' she said sternly. 'Leave it. Come here!'

Exasperated by the dog's persistence, she turned away to return to the light and warmth of the parlour. At that moment the cellar door crashed open and Hywel, snapping and snarling, disappeared from sight. There were two thuds, a yelp of pain, and the dog was silenced.

'Hywel!' Gabriellen called. At the lack of response her hand tightened around the poker. 'Who's there?'

Cruel laughter greeted her demand. Gabriellen screamed. The candle fell from her trembling fingers and the flame went out. How had Prew got into the house? Too late she remembered the broken lock on the outside cellar door. Esmond should have mended it long before she had left home. It was one of countless household tasks which so easily slipped his mind.

As the shadowy figure lurched towards her, Gabriellen backed away. The train of her loose gown and robe wrapped around her ankles, slowing her retreat. Prew was looming nearer. She could smell sweat and his sickly violet perfume. Her hand touched the parlour door. Once inside and the bolt thrown, she would be safe. Even as her fingers closed over the bolt, Prew hurled himself at the door.

'Oh no, you don't,' he shouted. 'Whore and heretic! You'll take what's coming to you!'

In the brighter candlelight of the parlour she saw he held a whip. He was breathing heavily and his mouth was twisted with cruelty. 'You thought to cuckold me, did you? We'll see if your paramour will find you so appealing when I've finished with you.' He raised the whip to strike her.

Instinctively, Gabriellen put her hand across her stomach. Prew saw the movement and froze. As the candle-light played over her figure, her flimsy gown accentuated the advanced state of her pregnancy. His eyes glinted insanely.

'God's holy passion! Did you think to foster upon me the Welshman's bastard? You'll pay for your harlotry!'

The whip came down across her shoulder, ripping through the fabric of her garments to lacerate her skin. Biting back a scream of pain, Gabriellen struck at him with the poker. She hit his arm but the momentum of her swing caught her off balance. Staggering sideways to recover her-self, her foot caught in the trailing hem of her robe, pitching her heavily against the corner of the oak dresser. Its sharp protrusion stabbed deep into her stomach like a knife.

She clung to the dresser for support whilst several lashes reduced her robe to rags. The fiery agony in her back made her catch her breath, but it was another, deeper, grinding pain which brought her to her knees. Wide-eyed, she stared unseeing at her tormentor as yet another pain bent her double. The poker fell from her fingers. Time and again the whip descended mercilessly on her back. Gabriellen hunched over, scarcely feeling the vicious blows, her terri-fied mind centred upon that other pain.

Prew had worked himself into a fever. The whip had torn his wife's clothing to shreds, and the sight of the blood he had raised on her pale flesh sent him into paroxysms of lust. He rubbed his throbbing crotch, his face covered with sweat. A cry of rage broke from his salivating lips as the doorbell sounded. At the same time Gabriellen screamed. Prew stared down at the contorted figure on the floor. He saw then that it was not the pain he had inflicted upon her which had made her writhe. Her back was arched and rigid, her hands clutching her distended stomach. The whore was miscarrying her bastard. Divine judgement. He sniffed and rubbed his sweating face on his sleeve. Left alone, she would probably die. What more fitting end for the way she had tricked him?

The frenzy which had gripped him ebbed. He had delayed here too long. He had his own life to save. The soldiers were bound to come here to check on his where-abouts. Had it been them at the door? At least the bell had stopped ringing. But Gabriellen's screams must have been heard. Prew felt the first pricklings of fear for his own safety.

He threw down the scourge and backed away from the groaning woman on the floor. There was no time to waste. He must flee. His life depended on leaving London at once. He started for the front door and stopped. Not that way. How could he have forgotten the pouch of gold hidden in the cellar?

A hoarse groan from Gabriellen carried to him as he sped down the stairs into the cellar. He paused a moment to savour her agony. 'Suffer, you adulterous bitch!'

Just as he reached out to pick up the money pouch, the outer cellar door was kicked open. Flattening himself against the wall, Prew held his breath so as not to betray his hiding place. From the brief glimpse he had of the intruder, he recognised Rowan. The Welshman stumbled against the money pouch and there was the chink of coins as it was kicked into some corner of the cellar. A plague on it! He'd have the devil's own job to find it now.

There was an angry curse in Welsh as the man saw his dog lying on the floor where Prew had clubbed him. Prew put his hand to the cudgel thrust into his waist band. The dog whined softly. As Rowan bent over it, Prew sprang forward, striking him over the head. Rowan slumped over his dog.

Where was his gold? Prew began to search. Above him there was a loud kicking on the door. A pox on Rowan! He must have called the Watch. Prew scrambled on the floor for the money pouch and found only two coins. A groan from Rowan warned him the man was beginning to stir. He must get away. There was no time to find his gold. Much as he hated leaving behind five hundred pounds, it was that or his life.

He ran out into the night. But as his breath burned deep into his lungs, he vowed that one day he would return. The Angel family still had much to answer for. He wasn't finished with them yet. That five hundred pounds would be added to the score, every penny of which would one day be paid in full measure, one way or another.

Mark swore as he staggered to his feet and put a hand to his head. What the hell had hit him? He heard the sound of someone running through the garden. There was a lingering scent of violets. Prew had been here. With luck the constables would get him. Hywel was on his feet, whimpering. What had happened here? Suddenly his head cleared. Ellen! He had heard her scream. Ignoring the hammers pounding in his skull, Mark raced up the stairs, shouting her name.

'Mark, help me!' The tortured cry came from the parlour.

One look at her twisted body told him everything. He paused only long enough to open the front door to the Watch who were still banging on it and shouted at them to fetch a midwife. Lifting Ellen's groaning figure he carried her to her chamber. Hours later he was still alone with her, wiping her sweating brow, speaking soft words of comfort as her body convulsed and her womb finally relinquished the lifeless form.

Chapter Twenty-Seven

On the night Gabriellen lost Jack's son something inside her snapped. It was as though her body and mind simply said: Enough. For two years she had been coping with other people's problems, trying to hold the players together and boost her father's spirits. Added to that was the crushing blow of Jack's deceit, quickly followed by the news of his death.

These she had faced and dealt with. Not so her miscarriage. The babe had meant so much to her. Through her son Jack would have lived on. From the moment she had known of the baby's existence she had loved it. The need to secure the child's future and to save her father had given her the strength to face an abhorrent marriage. Without the child her life had become a void, meaningless, without purpose.

Everyone was so kind, but it was through a hazy dreamworld that she accepted the presence of friends and of new acquaintances, who had been so generous and understanding. The house she was in now was an unfamiliar one, with people who were strangers and sometimes spoke an unintelligible language. At other times the beauty of their melodic voices pierced her torpor. She barely remembered the journey to Wales. She had wanted to escape London and Chichester and the memories of Jack. Aphra and Saul had welcomed her unreservedly. Mark had become her anchor.

In a trancelike state, she performed the rituals of everyday life. No conscious thought was needed to perform the household tasks. The long rides across a countryside more beautiful and majestic than her native Sussex were part of the dreamscape that brought peace and serenity. Though she took part in the daily routine, a part of her remained removed from it. It was a protective cocoon she had woven for herself. Safe inside it there was no pain – no memory. There were times when the edges would crack and the pain filter through, but with each day she was more able to bear it.

She was never alone. Often, surrounded by the noisy, boisterous children, who drew her into their games, Gabriellen would smile. But no matter how comical their antics, her spirit was too heavy to rise to laughter. In the quiet evening hours, when the whole family was assembled, she would close her eyes and listen to the rich voices of Mark and Saul singing. There were always songs, they were part of the Welsh household. Soft humming began as they sat mending the horses' tack, and soon Mark would take the lead and Saul and Aphra follow. She could listen to Mark's baritone voice for hours, his cheerful company blanketing her grief.

She lost track of the passage of time. The valley shed its red and gold autumn mantle, the trees now stark and skeletal against the green hills.

The nights were the worst. The lacerations on her back had healed, leaving a few pink scars which would eventually fade. But the nightmares did not lessen. Each night they chased each other through her sleep. Often she would awake bathed in perspiration, her screams rousing either Mark or Aphra who came to comfort her. One morning she awoke shivering. Another restless night had made the covers slip from the bed. She sat up to drag them back over her, and caught sight of the pristine brightness at the window. Wrapping the covers around her, she went to the mullioned alcove and looked out.

It had snowed in the night. Everywhere was covered in a thick layer, the trees and fences capped with a four-inch icing. A door opened below and the excited whoops of the children drifted to her. They ran, skipped and rolled in the snow. Then, screaming with delight, they began to hurl snowballs at each other. As she watched, Mark and Saul emerged from a barn, each pulling a wooden sled on which rested several sheaves of hay. The children shouted with delight as they followed their uncle and father to the farthest pasture. Diverted, Gabriellen watched the procession. The hay was spread over the snow for the horses to eat. The sleds now empty, the party set out towards a low hill. At its crest the children piled on to the sleds and hurtled down the slope.

Suddenly Gabriellen felt her lethargy slide from her. With a shock she realised that it was nearly Christmas and that she had been staying with Mark's family in Wales for nearly two months. Grieving for Jack and her lost child would not bring them back. It was time to resume her life.

She saw Aphra emerge from the house. Like the men she was dressed in thick knee breeches and high boots. Over these she wore a hip-length jerkin made out of sheepskin, and on her head was a coney fur hood. Protected against the cold, Aphra began to tramp through the thick snow towards a paddock. With the coming of the snow the workload of the farm had doubled. The hours would be long and hard. Here was her chance to repay the kindness shown her. Gabriellen reached for her clothes, eager to be a part of the team which must all pull together to survive the winter in this remote valley.

When everyone came into the house at midday to eat, they found a hot meal waiting for them and Gabriellen demanded a set of clothes that would be as practical as Aphra's so that she could help outside.

Mark threw back his head, laughing at the transformation in her. He swung her round in his arms and grinned across at Aphra and Saul. 'Did I not tell you she was a rare woman?'

'Put me down, Mark.' Gabriellen blushed and beat against his chest. 'Your sister will think me a hoyden.' She turned to Aphra, her tone apologetic. 'You have shown me nothing but kindness since I arrived. So far I have done little to repay your hospitality.'

'You were Mark's guest.' Aphra's dark eyes sparkled with pleasure. 'You have been through a terrible ordeal. Such things take time to recover from. I am glad Mark brought you here. There is no better place to dispel melancholy.' She smiled. 'But then, I am naturally prejudiced.'

Gabriellen returned the warmth of her smile. 'Everything I have seen – the beautiful valley and this old, dignified house which is always filled with laughter – makes me envy you. Mark has always been a good friend. I am again in his debt. This time he saved not only my life, but my sanity.'

Aphra gave her a strange knowing look which puzzled Gabriellen. Then, seeing her confusion, Aphra laughed and said, 'I shall fetch the clothes for you at once. I'm not one to reject a willing helper.'

The bizarre outfit she fashioned was warm and comfortable. Since the afternoon sky remained swollen with snow clouds, it was decided that as many of the horses as possible should be brought under cover. Even the older children took part in herding the mares and foals into the barns. As Gabriellen emerged from a barn, a snowball hit her on the side of the head. Gasping with surprise, she looked round to see Mark grinning at her.

'Attack an unarmed woman, would you!' she challenged. A surge of devilry broke through the last of her apathy. She scooped up a handful of snow and fashioned it into a missile. 'Is that how the Welsh wage war, by ambushing the unwitting?' She rallied. 'We English fight head on.' She let fly the snowball. To her vexation, Mark ducked and it whizzed harmlessly over his head.

'Pathetic,' he jeered. His second snowball landed on her neck. 'I never knew a woman who could throw straight.'

'Ow!' she yelped, as a piece of the snow found its way under her collar, leaving a freezing trail as it melted against her warm skin. Her spirit roused, she gathered another handful of snow. 'You'll pay for that, Mark Rowan. This is war!'

Hywel was joined by several of the farm dogs, their excited barking soon drawing the attention of the rest of the family as Gabriellen and Mark hurled snowballs at each other. Seeing Aphra emerge from the barn, Gabriellen called out: 'Mark says women can't throw. Help me prove him wrong, Aphra.' Her next shot caught him on the ear.

'You seem to be coping on your own.' Aphra laughed and was joined by Saul. The couple stood with their arms round each other as they watched the fight become something more than a test of aim. The children took sides, making snowballs faster than Gabriellen could throw them. Her fur hood had fallen back, there was snow in her hair and her face was pink from exertion. When she caught Mark on the nose, she jumped up and down, as delighted as a child.

'That does it,' he shouted. 'I was only playing before.

You want a battle, madam, you shall have one.'

The barrage of his blows thudding against her coat beat Gabriellen back until, laughing helplessly, she collapsed on to the snow. 'Mercy! I surrender.' She held her sides, laughing so much she could hardly breathe. 'Mercy!'

Mark pulled her to her feet, his face as red as her own from the cold but his eyes ablaze with pleasure. 'It's good to hear you laughing again, Ellen. I was beginning to fear you had forgotten how.'

He had deliberately goaded her. The childish fun of the snowball fight had shown her that life went on and that her grieving was behind her. Not forgotten, never that, but bearable.

Nocturnal London held no threat or fear for Esmond Angel. When two rank-smelling forms rose up out of the filth of the gutter, daggers gleaming menacingly in the moonlight, he spoke the password of the Underworld and went unmolested. He strode on purposefully, aware of but ignoring the presence of invisible creatures who shuffled like vermin in the darkest shadows. From the alehouses and ordinaries seeped raucous voices, salacious whispers, and the persuasive drone of tricksters dunning their victims. Every so often a female voice would call down to him from the open window of a brothel or a tavern door would open. Its spear of light, hazy with tobacco smoke, showed carousers sprawled at tables with naked girls on their knees, oblivious to the nip or foist who relieved them of their valuables. These lowly pursuits were a far cry from the pleasures offered at Nell Lovegood's which Esmond had just left. But a summons from One-eyed Ned was not something it was prudent to ignore.

Esmond strolled with confidence through the dark unlit labyrinth of intertwined lanes and alleys. His failing sight was no disadvantage in this warren he had once known as home. To safeguard himself from tripping over an unseen object in his path, he had taken to carrying a carved walking stick which also doubled as a weapon.

A tall figure materialised menacingly before him. 'Take pity, good master! I am a poor blind man,' the beggar wailed.

'Not so blind that you'd miss the chance to cut my purse.'

411

Esmond drew his sword and prodded the belly of the scarecrow-thin figure. The man shuffled backwards with an oath.

'Mercy, I did not recognise you, Angel.'

Esmond regarded the bow-legged, bald-headed man whom he had forced to step into the light from an unshuttered window. It was not a sight which inspired confidence. The snub nose and large protruding eyes were familiar, as were the stick-thin wrists and bony ankles projecting from his ragged clothes.

'Trout-face Carfax, you old villain,' Esmond chortled. 'Still up to your tricks?'

Trout-face visibly relaxed. 'I thought yer'd gone respectable on us, Angel. Wot yer doin' in these parts?'

'Same as you, paying my respects to One-eyed Ned.'

Trout-face walked at Esmond's side. He was a clapperdudgeon – a beggar born – easily recognised by his long patched cloak and the wooden dish he carried at his girdle.

'I heard tell you and One-eyed Ned were partners in more than one venture,' the beggar commented.

Esmond coughed into his hand. 'Ned is first and last his own man. The playhouse is my life now.'

'Aye, if you say so, Angel,' Trout-face sniggered. 'You always 'ad more than one card up your sleeve, as I remember.'

They had reached the barn One-eyed Ned used for his weekly gatherings. Once inside, the noise of three hundred drunken revelling criminals and bawds was deafening. Trout-face Carfax slunk off to join his cronies. Esmond saw him join a group of pseudo-cripples, some of whom were rubbing ratsbane into the raw flesh of their sores to make them fester and weep.

A young boy was crying as his father peeled off a grimy bandage, the tender flesh raw as the skin was ripped from it. Esmond shuddered with distaste. He despised the practice of mutilating the young. A week earlier a mixture of crowsfoot, spearwort and salt would have been rubbed into the boy's already lacerated skin. The treatment was painful but in some ways he was more fortunate than the children whose limbs were cold-heartedly broken and distorted, the better to wring pity from people when the beggars called for alms. They were the lowest of the ranks within the Underworld and Esmond had little to do with them.

412

He raised his hand in greeting to several acquaintances and crossed to where a group of young boys were wrestling by two devices each hung with hawk's bells. Clapping his hands, he stopped their scuffling. 'Young scamps, to work! Show me how well I trained you last week.'

He positioned several weighted purses and kerchiefs in the various pockets suspended from the belled device, then leaned back against the wall to watch the nimble foists at work. Four boys sidled past the contraption and came to stand before Esmond, their dirty, pinched faces beaming with pride. Each held out a purse or kerchief. The fifth was not so deft. The tinkling of bells as he bungled cutting a purse was met with derisive jeers.

'Practise longer, young Jeb. We'll make a Judicial Nipper of you yet,' Esmond encouraged.

He turned his attention to the line of men and women filing past One-eyed Ned at the far end of the barn. The Upright Man was seated in a highbacked chair of throne-like proportions on a raised dais. As he watched he saw purses, jewellery, silverware, and expensive clothing placed on various piles before One-eyed Ned who called to the scrivener the price of their worth, which the man recorded, then handed the thief his cut of the takings. The most valuable goods would be shipped to the continent for sale; others, Esmond knew, would be fenced, some even sold back to their owners for a reward.

A young bawd caught Esmond's attention. She was blonde and beautiful, her eyes bold, and there was a confident sway to her hips as she mounted the dais. She held out a gold watch, a roll of lace and a bulging leather purse. There was a cheer from the crowd as she held her booty high for all to see.

'Have I not done well, my lover?' she addressed One-eyed Ned.

He shot out a hand and grabbed the woman's unbraided hair, with a vicious jerk bringing her to her knees. His handsome aristocratic features twisted into a cold mask.

'Where's the rest of it, Beth? You were seen lifting a gold chain from a cove in St Paul's Walk.'

'There were nothing else. Would I cheat you, Ned?'

The wench screamed as he pulled harder on her hair. 'You're one of the best, Beth, but you've got above yourself.'

A dagger flashed in the light of the oil cressets as Ned laid the blade along her cheek. 'Time you learned I won't be cheated by anyone.' He grinned, his teeth flashing evilly above his red-streaked beard. 'But your face is your fortune, Beth. This time I'll not spoil it.'

The wench's breasts heaved as she fought against her terror. Ned moved swiftly to spread her left hand on the table before him. Then the blade slashed downwards. Beth screamed and fell into a faint. With a disdainful flick of his wrist Ned swept the two dismembered fingers on to the floor. They were seized on by his black bull mastiff and eaten. Ned placed a beringed hand on the dog's head. As far as Esmond could remember the dog was the only creature to whom Ned had ever shown any real affection.

Beth groaned and opened her eyes. Blood dripped from her mutilated hand on to her skirts.

Ned scowled at her. 'Next time it will be the whole hand.'

As she swayed to her feet, he gripped her right wrist. Her eyes were round as trenchers in her terror.

'Get your hand tended, then come to my rooms tonight. You were a fool to think that because you are my woman, you could escape my judgement.'

Esmond swallowed down his nausea. Justice in the Underworld was swift and arbitrary. If Ned showed a moment's weakness he would lose control of the rabble he ruled. The Underworld was not a place for faint-hearts or the squeamish.

Esmond moved to the dais. He did not take his place in the queue. He was one of the honoured few who could approach the Upright Man direct. One-eyed Ned smiled as he saw Esmond's approach. He waved aside the grovelling minions who served him with the reverence due to a king.

Ned nodded towards the pickpockets who were again wrestling each other. 'The young lads learn quickly under your tutelage, Esmond.' His smile broadened. 'You have just returned from entertaining the guests at Sir Richard Fleetwood's house in the Strand. Tell me the layout of the house and how our men may best gain an entry.'

Esmond gave him the details without a qualm. He insisted that at least a month passed before any house he had played at was robbed. And for the information he gave, he received a quarter of the profit. Since the episode with

Prew he had vowed never again to fall into the hands of the moneylenders. For a time he had tried to give up gambling, but it was in his blood. He had once more succumbed to the temptation offered by roguery. It was the life he knew best and had once excelled in. Respectability was all very well, but it did not always pay the bills.

This winter he had paid off all his creditors and at last he was amassing the money which would support his family in the years ahead. The playhouse was bringing in a profit, but in recent weeks the attendances had been dropping. He needed a new play to recapture the audiences. And for that he needed Gabriellen. He was too proud to recall her from Wales. She had suffered enough because of him, let her have her convalescence in peace. But he must provide for his family. With his eyesight failing, he must live by the wits which had never yet betrayed him – and to the devil with the consequences.

That winter was like nothing Gabriellen had experienced before. Even in a blizzard, the horses had to be fed and watered. Whatever Aphra did, Gabriellen was prepared to match her. The work was hard, and the cold bit through to the bone. So much so that often Gabriellen's fingers were swollen and painful. But there was always laughter in the house. For two months the valley was cut off, yet not once did Gabriellen feel isolated or deprived.

Often she caught Aphra and Saul watching Mark and herself when they were together, their glances more speculative during the evenings when she would play the spinnet and Mark would sing. It was those looks which left her vaguely discomfited. Aphra had more than once hinted at a romance between Mark and herself. Gabriellen strongly denied it. She still loved Jack. Her sorrow at his death had mellowed the earlier pain of his betrayal. If only he were able to walk through that door now, she knew she would forgive him everything. But Jack was dead. In eight months there had been no word. Each day found her more and more in Mark's company, and often it was she who sought him out. She was drawn to him, finding solace from her pain in his presence.

She looked across at Mark as he sat with Hywel at his feet whilst he told a story to Aphra's children.

'Bedtime,' he said as he finished.

'Just a little longer, Uncle,' Owen, the eldest of them, pleaded. 'Please tell us another story.'

Mark looked over the children's heads to where Gabriellen sat at work over a spinning wheel. 'No more stories.'

The children groaned in unison.

'But shall we show Gabriellen the tricks Hywel can do?' He winked at her.

'Yes,' they chorused, so loudly that Hywel began to bark.

Gabriellen stopped her spinning. 'I would like to see his tricks,' she said to humour the children, and waited for the usual begging or playing dead that most dogs were taught.

Mark stood up. 'Hywel must go into the yard for this. You and the children can watch from the door where it's warmer.'

They all moved to the courtyard door as Mark took the dog outside. He ordered Hywel to sit. The dog sat very straight, his tail wagging as he looked up expectantly at his master.

'Hywel, salute Queen Elizabeth,' Mark commanded.

The dog leapt into the air, gave a backward somersault and landed on all fours, then sat and raised a paw to his eye.

Gabriellen clapped with delight at the trick.

Mark held up a hand, looking very serious as he commanded: 'Hywel, salute the King of Spain.'

Hywel growled, and lifting his back leg, urinated.

The children fell about laughing and Gabriellen joined in their irreverent mirth.

So passed many such days of easy laughter during that winter. There had been several blizzards and by the end of February provisions were running low. Deer tracks had been found around the hay sheaves in the far paddock and Aphra suggested that Mark take Gabriellen on a day's hunting. It had not snowed for days. Mark carried a bow slung across his shoulders, and the sturdy Welsh ponies they rode were sure-footed upon the whitened ground. The deer trail took them far along the valley, until finally their quarry became visible ahead. By the time they had singled out a buck and Mark had killed it, the sky had turned an ominous dun colour.

Coin-sized snowflakes began to fall as Mark tied the buck on to his horse. He looked across at Gabriellen. 'We have come further from the farm than I intended. Snow like this will become treacherous long before we reach the safety of Rowan Hall. We had better make for the woodcutter's hut in Badger's Wood. Saul keeps all the huts on the estate stocked with provisions for just such an emergency.'

Gabriellen felt a twinge of misgiving. Did this mean she would spend the night alone with Mark? She pushed her unease aside. What choice was there? She knew the danger of travelling in a snowstorm. They could fall into a drift and freeze to death.

The horses were bedded down in the stable next to the woodcutter's hut, and they ran into the larger building. As Gabriellen stamped the snow from her boots, Mark lit the fire to warm and cheer the tiny cabin. Outside the wind accompanying the snow rose to gale proportions.

Gabriellen stirred, then came awake abruptly at the unexpected heat of another body curled against her own. She edged away but found herself trapped by a strong arm, her body pinned to the palliasse laid near the still glowing fire. Close to her ear she could hear the sound of Mark's rhythmic breathing. He was still asleep. For a moment she was tempted to stay where she was. They were both fully clothed, but the warmth of his body burned through to her flesh.

She remembered with a blush how he had comforted her in the night when she had woken from a nightmare. In her dream she had once again been subjected to Prew's rape. Mark had taken her into his arms and kissed her, speaking softly to calm her trembling until finally she had fallen asleep.

The temptation to snuggle down and enjoy the protection of Mark's strength was almost overpowering. She resisted. He had been the perfect friend and gentleman, making no attempt to press his attentions upon her. Throughout the evening as they ate and laughed companionably, he had watched her closely. Unspoken, Jack's memory was between them. Her gaze would lower from Mark's and he would continue their conversation. Any awkwardness over the sleeping accommodation was soon overcome. There were two palliasses stuffed with sweet hay and herbs. In the cramped confines of the hut these were been placed before the log fire. Turning their backs on each other, they had slept.

Lifting Mark's arm, she rolled away from his sleeping form. She rose and stretched her arms to ease the stiffness from her body. The interior of the hut was lit only by the intimate glow of the log fire. It must be morning. She opened the wooden shutter over the single window to look out. For a moment she stared blankly at the frosty mass over the panes. Then with a start she remembered there was no glass in this window. She touched the compacted ice. It was solid. Snow had blown against the hut in a drift.

'Mark!' she called as she hurried to the door. There was no budging it. 'Mark, we're trapped!'

She swung round to find him sitting up watching her. He ran a hand through the tumble of blue-black curls which capped his head and raised one eyebrow. There was no surprise in his expression. She looked round the tiny hut, suddenly nervous. There was a pile of logs in one corner and on a shelf a ham, fresh vegetables, and the jar of pickled herrings from which they had eaten last night. Now she saw that in addition to these provisions, two rabbits hung from a hook in a corner and a large loaf of bread was behind the ham. There was enough food for over a week if need be. So there was no danger. Or was there . . . ?

How was it that amongst these stores laid in against a chance blizzard or rainstorm, there was fresh meat and a loaf? And why was Mark smiling! Damn him, the knave was grinning. Her hands rested on her hips as she regarded him with dawning suspicion. 'You planned this!'

'Very carefully.'

He was unrepentant. 'You came to Wales to recover from a frightful ordeal. Your nightmares are proof that the past haunts you still. Until you can put those memories behind you, you will never be truly whole again.'

'Are you saying I should forget Jack?' Her voice rose in attack. 'That is impossible. I love him. I will always love him.'

'Jack is dead. I refer to the horrors to which Prew subjected you. He has mentally scarred you.'

'He is no longer part of my life. He's fled England, and good riddance.' Gabriellen fed her indignation until she began to shake with anger. 'This is infamous, Mark. God knows how long we will be trapped here. Of all people, I thought I could trust you.' She hurled each word at him in deliberate challenge. 'You are supposed to be my friend.'

His expression did not change. 'What we have goes beyond common friendship. Let me exorcise your nightmares, Ellen.'

He stood up and crossed to her. Still defensive, Gabriellen backed away. Mark halted, his voice low and persuasive. 'Do you want to spend the rest of your life reliving the terrors of your husband's perversions?'

At her horrified gasp, he took her in his arms. 'I know what Prew was capable of. He was an animal. You are young and healthy. Do you want his sick mind to leave you maimed for life? I'm not asking for your love, Ellen. And I would do nothing to harm you, or to force you against your will. But I know you better than you are prepared to know yourself. There is an affinity between us few couples attain.' His hands moved to stroke her hair in a featherlight caress. 'I want you, Ellen. We each have our own allotted time and place. Nothing can discredit the love you had for Jack, but Prew destroyed something in you. Would you let him emerge the victor? Ellen – my dear, valiant Ellen, let this be our time and place.'

He took her face in his hands, his dark eyes tender, but commanding her to submit to him. That unspoken demand caused her heart to arrest its beating. The only peace she had known since she had learned of Jack's death had been in Mark's company. When he had held her so tenderly last night she had felt her fears stilled, and his arms had become a haven which made her pain recede and diminish. She looked at him now through fresh eyes. With his black hair ruffled from sleep and falling over his brow, the angular planes of his face were softened and ruggedly handsome. Though of average height, he carried no spare flesh and his body was broad-shouldered and muscular. But it was the tenderness in his expression, the prepossessing confidence of his lips parting in a smiling challenge, which made his masculinity impossible to ignore.

'And what of Jesmaine?' she asked, seeking to delay what was fast becoming inevitable.

'I do not love her,' he said simply.

'And we are not in love.'

'But we have need of each other. What we have is more abiding than love, which can be transient and fleeting.'

As he spoke his fingers played across the nape of her neck in a light but insistent caress. His lips drew nearer, but he did not kiss her. Instead his gaze fixed upon her face took on such a compelling significance it brought a tightness to her chest. The touch of his hands, sensually circling her neck, was bringing a glow to her blood. She was held spellbound. For the first time in months she felt her senses stir and begin to come alive. But how could he look at her that way? She had told him of Prew's rape. How could he look at her with other than disgust? Still there was only tenderness in his eyes, and inexorable promise.

'Let this be our time, Ellen.'

It was not a plea, it was a command. His eyes were dark with burning desire, to which he would never give way unless she consented. 'Ellen, for once in your life, think of yourself. Your needs. All that has happened to you in the last months is because you put others first.'

His lips were against her ear as he spoke, sparking a yearning deep within her to feel clean and unsullied again. After the degradation Prew had forced on her, she had felt dirtied and defiled. There was reverence in Mark's touch and the sybaritic persuasion of his voice. His was a healthy desire for a beautiful woman, and beneath that adoring veneration she weakened. His arms became her sanctuary.

'Oh, Mark, cast out the memory of what I endured.' It was a plea from the depths of her heart.

'My lovely, I will do that and more, I promise.'

He kissed her then, gently at first, but as her lips warmed and parted beneath his, the pressure deepened, fulfilling the need of her quickening pulses. With a soft moan she surrendered. There was a moment as Mark touched her breast when the horror of Prew's depravity returned and her skin turned to ice and her body became frigid. Mark stilled his caresses, kissing her with lingering tenderness until she again relaxed and her body became pliant and willing beneath his experienced touch.

'Relax, my darling,' he breathed against her throat. 'We have all the time you need. No one will disturb us.'

She abandoned herself to his skill. The scars of Prew's abuse were healed by Mark's caresses. There could be no comparison to the love she had known with Jack. Mark was different. How could one compare the consuming blaze of the sun to the sybaritic light of the moon? Or the heat of a devouring heath fire to the lure of the flame from a home-guiding beacon? Enfolded in his arms, abandoned to

420

the thrill of his kisses, her body came alive again. She felt clean, untarnished and reborn. After months when every day had seemed more empty than the last, she felt again the singing of her blood, a piquancy in all her senses.

Mark drew the pins from her hair so that it tumbled down to her waist. He ran his fingers through it, then lifting the tresses, buried his face in the shining curls.

'It was an act of sacrilege when I sheared you of this glory.'

'Nay,' she answered softly, taking his hand and kissing the calloused palm before placing it on her breast, 'you saved my life.'

He smiled crookedly, his free hand caressing the nape of her neck, luxuriating, arousing. 'It was my pleasure.'

With slow veneration Mark undressed her in the warmth of the firelight, until she stood unashamedly naked. 'You are more beautiful than I remember,' he said as he gazed at her flawless body with its high uptilted breasts, a waist a man could span with his hands, and long shapely legs.

'I should hope so,' she answered with a low provocative laugh. 'I was ravaged by fever and must have looked an absolute fright.'

'Never that. Even then you were incomparable.'

'Oh, Mark. Don't make me out to be something special. I'm not. Just love me. At this moment I desperately need to be held and loved. I know it's wanton and wicked, but I want to be whole again.'

Mark saw the yearning in her eyes, the vulnerability and the passion, smouldering, awaiting his rekindling. This would be a time forever encapsulated in their memories. It must be unequivocal, a mystical harmony, the like of which they would attain with no other lover.

'Forget about guilt, Ellen. This is not wanton. It is inevitable. It is not wicked. It is right. So very right.'

It was his last coherent thought for her hands were boldly divesting him of his clothing, her fingers caressing his burning flesh. Their gazes never leaving each other, they sank down on to the soft palliasse. Mark took her hand and kissed each fingertip in turn. Gabriellen gasped softly. Her heart began to pound, its beat quickening to drive her blood in an ecstatic millrace around her body. Where Mark's lips touched her skin it tingled deliciously, the sensation sweeping through her entire body to her toes. She ran her thumbs slowly through the fine dark hairs on his forearms as she looked at his body. He was so magnificently male, his muscles clearly defined and no spare flesh to mar his lithe beauty. Her breathing quickened at seeing his desire revealed so unmistakably. Then her gaze was again drawn to his. For each of them it was a time of exploration and slow discovery. Of delights to be savoured, equally giving and taking pleasure in each other. Every touch of infinite tenderness was like the very first touch of a lover, heightening their senses to an awareness never before experienced. Each responded to the other's sensuality, their bodies moving slowly and sinuously, communicating the growing fervour which became a frenzy of passion.

A sweet delirium gripped Gabriellen as Mark's tongue tasted every curve and hollow of her body. His lips roamed over her breasts and taut ribcage, down across the flatness of her stomach, and his warm breath blew across the soft curls of her womanhood. She moaned her pleasure, her body avid as her hips rose, her fingers guiding him to plunge deep inside her.

Mark paused, the exquisite moment of oneness enshrined, cherished. Then he was enfolded by her arms, her legs, her warm pulsing body, until neither could bear it any longer and the increasing rhythm of their bodies was matched in demanding unison. Their deep kiss captured simultaneous moans of pleasure. Their movements stilled, their ragged breathing subsided into exhausted silence. Mark stirred. Raising himself on to his elbow, he stared tenderly into Gabriellen's eyes.

'Say nothing,' she said languidly, placing a finger to his swollen lips. 'It was perfect.'

She rolled him on to his back and kissed him until she was breathless. Resting her head on his chest, she sighed with satisfaction. Mark shifted his weight, and lifting the mane of her tawny-gold hair, kissed her neck. Her breath caught on a soft gasp and he ran his hands over the sleek lines of her back in a way that made her purr like a contented lioness. When his lips travelled down her spine, she no longer purred but moaned and moved rhythmically with pleasure. His response was immediate, but their discovery of each other was just beginning, his need to bring her to the highest peak of pleasure, to a joy never before dreamed of, greater than the urge to seek his own fulfilment.

When the storm of their passion had passed, he cushioned her in his arms, and as he gazed into her eyes, saw his own reflection mirrored in their lustrous depths. A strange constriction settled around his chest. It had not been part of his plan to find himself in love with Ellen. And certainly not while she remained so firmly in love with Jack. It was a moment which could only be dispatched with levity.

At the soft rumble of laughter echoing in Mark's chest, Gabriellen raised her head to regard him. He held a widgeon's wing feather in his hand and began to stroke it down her spine. It tickled, and with a gasp she wriggled to snatch it from him. With a flick of his body he rolled her on to her back and proceeded to stroke the feather over her breasts and stomach. Helpless with laughter, she tried to snatch the feather from him. They rolled across the room, her writhing body as he continued to tickle her provoking the inevitable consequences. Only when she was straddled above him did he allow her to capture the feather. As she bent forward to snatch it from him, her green eyes sparkled with devilment.

'Tickle me, would you?' she teased. 'How shall I repay you?'

Mark chuckled, and parting her hair, wound it into a rope around his neck. His lips against her ear, he taunted, 'I'm sure you will think of something.'

Their laughter mingled, becoming husky with returning passion. It became the pattern of their days while the snow held them prisoner. Nine carefree, ecstatic days before a grinning rescue party from Rowan Hall decided that by now their food supplies would be almost gone, and came to dig them out.

The library of Rowan Hall was speckled by the sunlight which filtered through the ivy surrounding its mullioned window. Gabriellen sat on the window seat with Hywel curled in her lap. She laid aside her book. The printed words refused to hold her attention for she preferred to watch Mark as he sketched. A tangle of dark curls had fallen over his brow, and as he worked, he caught his lower lip between his teeth. His brown hands holding the charcoal stick moved quickly over the paper. At that moment Mark lifted his gaze and, meeting hers, he smiled. It was as

423

tangible as a caress, his eyes lighting with tenderness and the affectionate humour only lovers can share.

During the last month since they had become lovers, Gabriellen had discovered that drawing was one of the many pastimes Mark excelled in. He was a skilled artist and had painted several miniatures of his family. The library contained scores of sketches of the Rowan horses, pets, and of the house itself. This morning he showed her his drawings of the Hall as it would be when fully renovated. When he asked her opinion, she was deeply flattered. Each of the damaged rooms, like the Old Baron's Hall, was drawn in detail. She had exclaimed with delight to see that he intended to restore the hammerbeamed roof to its former splendour.

He laughed at her enthusiasm. 'Some would say I am taking a step back in time. You do not think I would be better served modernising the old hall into a two-storey structure?'

'Nay, Mark.' She was emphatic. 'It would rob the place of its dignity. The Baron's Hall is modest in size. If this beautiful house were mine, I'd restore it exactly to its ancient grandeur. But then, I'm a dreamer with a love of history. Your books on astronomy and mathematics show you to be a man of forward vision.'

Now, as Mark sketched, they sat in companionable silence. The library contained over a hundred books, many rare and beautifully illuminated. They were a treasure trove Gabriellen never tired of dipping into. This afternoon a log fire crackled in the grate, dispelling the chill of the March wind.

By an unspoken agreement within the family, they were not interrupted during their sojourns in the library. Much as Gabriellen adored Aphra's children, these hours of privacy with Mark were special to her. They were almost as special as the nights when he shared her bed.

In the last month she had come to know a peace and contentment she had never before experienced. It was not that she never thought of Jack. She did, daily, whenever she was on her own. Yet the moment Mark walked into a room, he alone occupied her thoughts and emotions. Deliberately, she refused to analyse her feelings. Her heart still ached with the emptiness of loving Jack and knowing she would never again be held in his arms. Her grief had not dimmed, nor her love. But Mark had become very special to her, otherwise she would not have taken him as her lover. But her feelings confused her. Loving Jack, how could she be so infatuated with Mark? It was somehow disloyal to them both.

'You're frowning, Ellen,' Mark broke through her thoughts. 'You were thinking of Jack, weren't you?'

Her heart twisted at the gruffness in his voice. They had always been honest with each other and she would not lie to him. 'Yes. But I was also thinking of you.'

He sat back in his chair and rolled the charcoal between his fingers, his long lashes effectively shielding the expression in his eyes. There was a slight tightening about his jaw. Was Mark falling in love with her? The thought brought elation and fear. To acknowledge it would be to profane her love for Jack.

Mark looked so handsome, a rush of affection swamped her control. Pushing Hywel off her lap, she stood up and smoothed the folds of her sapphire velvet gown which in country fashion was unencumbered by a farthingale. Drawn by his presence, she crossed the room to put her arms around his neck and kiss his cheek. From over his shoulder she saw the charcoal sketch of herself.

'Why, you have made me look beautiful,' she said in mock rebuke. 'You are a flatterer, Mark.'

'There is no flattery. I have drawn what I see.'

She touched his cleanshaven cheek with her fingertips, her heart aching with the depth of her affection. 'Oh, Mark.'

The words were inadequate to cover the confusion of her emotions. He answered by capturing her hand and squeezing it. There were often times when their understanding of each other was conveyed without need of words.

They kissed and Mark drew Gabriellen on to his lap. She gazed deep into his eyes, troubled lest she had wounded him by her admission that her thoughts had been on Jack. His dark eyes looked down at her with their usual tenderness, though always at such times she sensed, rather than saw, a restraint in him. Even in their most intimate moments they spoke no words of love, made no demands upon each other for the future.

'I have begun to think about writing another play,' she announced.

425

Mark smiled. 'I'm glad to hear it. It is a good sign that you are putting the bad memories behind you.' He looked at her through lowered lashes which guarded the expression in his eyes. 'I suppose soon you will be wanting to return to London and the players?'

'I have been a guest here for so long, I fear I shall overstay my welcome.'

'You could never do that, Ellen.'

There was a catch in his voice beneath the warmth which told Gabriellen that he had fallen in love with her. She was not yet ready for another commitment. She regarded him seriously. 'I must return to London soon. Father will have need of me. But I shall never forget my time here.' Her voice unexpectedly broke and a rush of affection for him brought a lump to her throat as she rested her head against his chest.

'Kiss me, Mark.' She locked her hands behind his neck to draw his head down. The moment his lips claimed hers, the guilt and uncertainty fled. The past was forgotten, the future vanished; there was only the present, and this euphoria she had never thought it possible to achieve.

When at last Mark drew back, Gabriellen laughed breathlessly. 'I would call myself a playwright, yet I cannot put into words what I feel at this moment.'

'No words are needed between us, Ellen. There is just the music in our hearts.'

'Only the Welsh could define it so, Emrys Marcus Llewelyn,' she smiled, unable to resist teasing his Welshness. 'But you are right. It is a beautiful, celestial music.'

He raised a mocking brow. 'Celestial as in divine, but not holy. There is nothing saintly about my thoughts. Nor yours, from the sparkle in your lovely eyes.'

Gabriellen laughed, kissing him in a way which proved how correctly he had gauged her thoughts. She clung to him, her face glowing with happiness. A movement from the window caught her attention. As one they both looked towards it.

With the thaw, spring had touched the valley with its verdant rebirth. The trees paraded their new leaves, the gorse on the hills was garlanded with bright yellow flowers. Closer to the house the grounds undulated with the bobbing heads of hundreds of daffodils and crocuses which tesselated the lawns. Gabriellen scarcely noted the beauty of the valley, seeing only the two distant specks of oncoming riders.

'It seems you have visitors,' she said, irritated that the intimacy of their afternoon would be disturbed.

Mark grinned at her wickedly. 'Time enough for another kiss before we must greet them. Anyone arriving at this late hour is bound to stay the night.'

'You are incorrigible,' she whispered against his lips as she eagerly complied.

The both knew it took a rider twenty minutes to ride the length of the valley. There were several streams to ford upon the way.

The kiss led to caresses, the caresses igniting a hunger that only consummation could appease. Its enjoyment was heightened by the spontaneity of their lovemaking.

When they finally rose and adjusted their garments they smiled tenderly at each other. On hearing the riders clatter into the courtyard, Gabriellen patted a loose strand of tawny-gold hair back beneath her headdress. To her dismay her hands were still shaking from the storm of sensations Mark had aroused in her.

When moments later Mark and Gabriellen entered the courtyard, the riders' backs were to them as they dismounted.There was something about the set of the taller one's shoulders which brought her hand to her throat. The blood drained from her face. Mark looked at her sharply. For an instant her legs buckled, threatening to betray her. She grasped Mark's arm for support. With her body still glowing from the pleasure of his lovemaking, she stared, shamed, into the face of Jack Stoneham.

Chapter Twenty-Eight

'Gabriellen! Mark!' The ghostly apparition laughed. 'Well, have you nothing to say?'

Gabriellen's heart seemed to explode into a thousand fragments, then rejoin to beat painfully an erratic rhythm. Disbelief, joy and a sobering edge of mortification were the emotions uppermost in her mind. How could she face Jack straight from giving herself so ardently to Mark? She had prayed for the day she would be reunited with Jack. Lived it in her imagination in a dozen variations. But never like this. Yet a stubborn part of her mind refused to feel ashamed of her affair with Mark. Her hand closed tighter over his arm, needing to draw from his strength. He squeezed it, reassuring her, before disengaging her hold and standing back.

Jack frowned, his voice harsh as he stared at Gabriellen who had turned white as a snowdrop. 'What greeting is this?'

Mark recovered his composure first. 'We had no idea you were alive, let alone returned to our shores.' Giving Gabriellen a gentle push, he propelled her forward. 'You have stunned us all. Especially Ellen.'

'She does look as if she's seen the devil incarnate.' Jack put his head on one side and regarded her ruefully. 'Then, we parted upon bad terms. Perhaps she has not forgiven me?'

It was only when he smiled, revealing his broken tooth, that Gabriellen believed this was not a bizarre dream. She shook off her stupor and guilt. Jack was alive! And here she was, behaving like a witless moon-calf.

'Jack! Oh, Jack, I thought I was dreaming.' She was laughing and crying with happiness as she ran into his arms.

He swung her round and round, laughing and kissing

428

her at the same time. He groaned against her ear, 'Now I know I am alive. These last months I've yearned to hold you.'

The joy Mark saw in Gabriellen's face was like a hammer blow to his heart. Moments earlier she had cried out with passion as he held her. Now the adoration in her gaze was for another. He had not expected to feel such desolation, such a perplexity of relief that his friend lived – and impotent anger. He glanced away from the couple to take a grip upon his emotions. Encountering Saul's gaze, he saw the depth of understanding and sympathy in his eyes. Aphra was looking positively hostile at the sight of the entwined lovers. And Gabriellen as she turned to face him, her cheeks scorched by a fierce heat and her green eyes beseeching, was obviously stricken with guilt. She was silently asking his forgiveness. What was there for him to forgive? This last month would be indelibly engraved on his memory.

He hoped no one was aware how forced was his smile. Conscious of Gabriellen's anguish, he stepped forward and clapped Jack on the shoulder. 'I might have known no Spaniard was a match for you. For a while there, my friend, you had us all worried.' He turned briefly to Jack's companion. 'It's good to see you, too, Seth.'

The manservant's pock-marked face split into a grin.

'Tis thanks to the cap'n we escaped the Spanish prison.'

'Seth exaggerates.' Jack beamed at his servant. 'But a Spanish prison makes you value your life, loyalty and friends.' He embraced Mark. Keeping one arm about the Welshman's shoulders, he put the other about Gabriellen. 'You have proved your friendship, Rowan. Esmond told me everything. I could murder that lecher Prew! How like the cur to flee to safety abroad. If ever he returns to England, he'll pay with his life for what he did to Gabriellen. Bringing her here was the best cure she could have. For that I thank you.'

'There is no need for thanks,' Mark replied with quiet dignity. 'I did it for Ellen.'

Gabriellen looked into his emotionless face with increasing distress. Her body still tingled from his lovemaking, yet Mark sounded as remote and unruffled as though they were strangers. Was it so easy for men to cast aside their emotions? No, the tightness remained about Mark's jaw. He was right, of course. How could any of them get through this day if they gave way to a sense of betrayal? They had both believed Jack was dead. Now he had returned, everything would change. Her love for him was as fierce as ever and her joy that he was alive made her forgive him for the way he had played her false.

But as she gazed at Mark she knew that she would never forget this winter. He had given her back her sanity.

Suddenly Aphra spoke out. 'It is many years since you visited us, captain. Come, we are all standing here like strangers. It is a time for rejoicing.'

To Gabriellen's relief, Aphra made light of the situation. Whether she approved of it, was another matter. Taking her cue from her brother, she said, 'We all feared for your safety. When did you arrive in England?'

'That's the Aphra I remember,' Jack answered with a laugh. 'Always full of questions.'

Saul went with Seth to stable the horses as the others walked through to the parlour. Immediately, Aphra disappeared to bring refreshments, and tactfully Mark excused himself.

As soon as they were alone, Jack pulled her into his arms. 'My love, I've hungered for this moment. The thought of you kept me alive. The thought of us together.'

His lips plundered hers, ravaging their tenderness still swollen from Mark's kisses. The passion in his kiss could not fail to stir her hot blood, but the unexpectedness of his arrival had struck like an avalanche at her emotions. She was still too stunned to think straight.

'I still can't believe you are alive. I'm so happy . . .' To her consternation, she burst into tears.

'My love.' Jack gathered her close. 'You've suffered no less than I. But have you forgiven me?'

She lifted her head to gaze up at him. 'How could I not? I thought I would go mad with grief, especially after I lost our child.'

'I'll never forsake you again, my love.' His voice was gruff with emotion. 'My life is nothing without you, Gabriellen.'

His handsome face was thinner and paler from the long months shut away from the sun. The neatly trimmed beard showed the first strands of grey and the lines at the corners of his eyes and mouth were deeper than before his imprisonment. The evidence of his suffering squeezed at her heart.

Self-reproach for her own faithlessness magnified within her. She had found forgetfulness of her sorrows and happiness here in Wales, whilst he had suffered in a Spanish prison.

Her conflicting emotions were so fierce she began to tremble. Jack mistook it for passion. He pulled her against him. Through the velvet of his unpadded doublet she felt the outline of his ribs where a year ago there had been hard muscle. His ordeal must have been terrible, whilst she had fallen like a strumpet into his best friend's arms. She tried to block out the memory of Mark's kisses and failed miserably. Suddenly she could not meet his gaze, and tearing herself out of his hold, hugged her arms about her body as she wrenched out: 'I'm sorry, Jack.'

She could not look at him to see how he had gauged her apology.

'Whatever has passed these last months, I am as much to blame. You were married to a perverted monster. But he can no longer hurt you.'

From his tone she could not tell whether he was deliberately closing his mind to the possibility that she had been Mark's mistress, and choosing instead the safer ground. It was not like Jack to evade such an issue. She forced herself to hold his gaze and was surprised by the anguish she saw on his face.

He smiled lopsidedly. 'I will try and be patient, but certes, it's been so long, my love.'

He held out his hand to her and she took it, allowing him to draw her close. His kiss was restrained, though it conveyed his passion and pent-up desire. She eased back from him, knowing that she could never allow Jack to make love to her in Mark's house. 'Please, Jack, not here. Someone may come in.'

'Not for a while.' He chuckled wickedly. 'Rowan is nothing if not discreet. He will know we want to be alone.'

The mention of Mark was like a spear plunging through Gabriellen. What must he be feeling? This last month with him had been something very special. She had not expected it to end so abruptly.

Jack was oblivious of her reluctance. 'When do you think we can retire for the night?' he declared ardently. 'Do you think it will scandalise them if I whisk you away now? I want you, Gabriellen.'

431

'Would you shame me before my friends?'

'Good God, woman! We've been apart for months.' Jack gave her a challenging look which drained the colour from her face.

She put a shaking hand to her head. 'Please, Jack, try and understand. My marriage was an abomination.' She turned away, unable to face his white-lipped anger. 'We have both suffered, all because of a stupid quarrel. I love you, Jack, but I'm no longer young and impressionable. Once we leave here we can begin a new life.'

'This is a poor welcome from one who professes to love me.'

'Fornication is not the beginning and end of love, Jack,' she declared indignantly. 'What of respect? Consideration? It is a poor kind of love, if you cannot spare my feelings for just one night. Tomorrow we can leave here.'

'Tomorrow I must go to York.' His disappointment was savage. 'I have to save what I can from a disastrous business contract my wife entered into. I have only ten days before I must return to Court. My enemies lost no time in gloating that my grieving widow had acquired a new business partner and future husband. The man's a fortune-hunter. I'll be lucky if I discover one-quarter of my income still intact.'

At the mention of his wife, Gabriellen went cold. She drew a deep breath. Jealousy was not an emotion she was used to feeling. She did not question her love for Jack, but she realised that in the last year she had changed. It was impossible for her not to have done over the last months. He, however, expected everything to be the same. How could it be? From the beginning their emotions had been governed by physical attraction. An attraction so searing it had overpowered everything else. They could never marry, since both Prew and Elizabeth Stoneham still lived, but if she was to be his mistress, it would not be the one-sided affair of the past.

'Let's not quarrel, Jack.'

'Then you'll not be so cruel as to deny me?'

The certainty behind his lopsided smile annoyed her. Her eyes slanted with warning. 'Only for this one night.'

The annoyance hardening his face increased her vexation. Had she always been so gullible to his persuasion? She knew she had. Love had blinded her to his faults. She did not love him less, but maturity had tempered her wildness.

432

Never again would she allow another to take control of her life. Loving Jack, she saw no shame in being his mistress, but it would now be upon equal terms.

It was obvious that he did not understand her reasons. At the same time she was aware of the blow his pride had suffered from his wife's behaviour. His pallor and thinness were proof of his temporary vulnerability. Any sign of weakness was so unlike him that she wanted to spare him further pain. His audacity was part of the attraction which had captured her heart. Her mood mellowed as she realised that despite his anger at what was happening in York, he had come to her first.

'Do you doubt that I love you?'

'No. You are alive. I am overjoyed. There will be many nights of love.'

'Then forget convention, Gabriellen. Our friends will understand.' He took her face in his hands. 'My love, I've yearned for this night for months. No amount of torture the Inquisitors inflicted could break me. And why? Because the image of you was carved in my mind. I had wronged you. I prayed for the chance to make amends. My wife means nothing to me. You are the only woman I will ever love.'

As she saw the ardour darken his eyes, she almost faltered.

'Our former relations were based upon a lie. The lie that you were free to wed me.' She countered his attraction with cold reason. 'Now neither of us is free to marry, though to me you were always my husband – in thought and deed, if not in name. But I will not sleep with you in this house.'

'The Gabriellen I left behind would not have been so cruel,' he jibed. The resolute glitter in her eyes warned him that no amount of persuasion would change her mind.

'That Gabriellen was a naive child,' she warned. But her joy at his return was too great to allow dissension to mar their reunion. A dimple appeared beside her mouth as she smiled. 'Now I am a woman, and worldly-wise enough to place more importance upon your love than upon vows bartered and paid for, our bodies sold in marriage for the sake of the respectability demanded by the church.'

He took her again in his embrace. 'You must know I can deny you nothing.' He swore softly to himself as he cocked his head towards the door, where the sound of rattling pewterware warned of Aphra's approach. His kiss was swift and predatory.

At a tentative knock upon the door they broke apart. Aphra entered, followed by the rest of the family.

Their entrance brought a change in Gabriellen which Jack understood with painful clarity. Had her stay here been innocent she would have seated herself upon the settle so that he could sit next to her. Instead she moved away to sit on a stool by the fire. A flush stained her cheeks and she avoided everyone's curious gaze.

'Jack, how did you escape the Spanish?' Aphra claimed his attention. 'Did they welcome you as a hero at Court?'

He took a moment to regain control of himself. From the moment Esmond had told him that Gabriellen was in Wales, he had suspected that she and Rowan would become lovers. Jealousy burned in him. For a moment he was tempted to call Rowan out and settle the matter. But Gabriellen had shown that she still loved him. He conquered his rage and jealousy, though they remained simmering just beneath the surface. They had believed him dead, and it was not as though he was entirely innocent. Had he not managed to seduce his gaoler's wife, he would still be mouldering in a Spanish fortress.

He turned to answer Aphra, nothing of his inner fury showing on his face. 'My reception was gratifying,' he replied with a modest inclination of the head. Then a devilish gleam brightened his eyes. 'Though I think Her Majesty was disappointed that the Spanish galleon I stole did not have its holds filled with booty. For myself, I was too desperate to be choosy.' He laughed. 'She's a fine ship. I intend to rename her *The Angel*.'

Mark saw Gabriellen's blush turn fiery. Did she regret their affair? He could not read her face which was turned towards the fire. Unconsciously his hand bunched into a fist as he turned his attention to Jack who was watching Gabriellen with a thoughtful frown.

'A very fitting name for your ship,' Mark said to break the tension in the room.

As he watched Gabriellen he saw a change come over her, her earlier guilt sloughed from her like an unwanted skin. The face she turned upon Jack was radiant with love, as she asked, 'Where were you a prisoner? How did you escape?'

Jack relaxed at the evidence of Gabriellen's love for him, clear for all to see. 'My ship was overrun by the Spanish, and sunk. Myself and several of my crew were taken prisoner by Rodriguez D'Almeira. By diabolical misfortune he happened to be the cousin of Don Carlos D'Almeira, a powerful grandee and advisor to King Philip. Don Carlos has a long-standing grudge against me. *The Bonaventure Elizabeth*, the first Spanish ship I captured, was owned by Don Carlos. It was also carrying several chests of silver and gold plate, part of the Grandee's personal fortune. Don Rodriguez saw my capture as a way of gaining favour with his influential cousin. I was to be made an example of. Whilst I awaited Don Carlos's arrival from Madrid, I was strung up in a cage over the walls of D'Almeira's fortress on the coast.'

A gasp from Gabriellen halted Jack. 'I'm sorry, my love, I had no wish to upset you.'

'Jesmaine saw the cage. She told me of it. But she thought . . .' Gabriellen broke off. 'She did not realise it was you. She told me you were dead.'

'It would take more than deprivation and punishment to kill me off,' Jack blustered. 'And of course they made sure I had just enough food and water to stay alive. But after six weeks I was close to death. Don Carlos had been kept in Madrid with a broken leg and I was taken from the cage to a prison tower. I was kept alive so that Don Carlos could inflict his vengeance upon me, and on my men. Knowing that his arrival was imminent, I became desperate. Eventually, I managed to escape and also free my men from the dungeons, though two died from their treatment there.'

'You make it sound simple, but it could not have been,' Gabriellen queried. 'You're too modest, Jack. How did you come to escape?'

He paced the parlour. He was not about to reveal that he had seduced D'Almeira's wife to get free. 'As luck would have it, one of the guards had no love for his master,' he told them. 'Don Rodriguez hanged his father for stealing bread so that his family would not starve. I had managed to keep hidden the diamond ring given me by our Queen. It proved bribe enough for him to drug the garrison's wine and allow myself and my men to escape. Fortunately another of D'Almeira's galleons was anchored in the bay, the men ashore enjoying the entertainments of the town.

We swam out and climbed aboard. It was the season of storms which probably saved us from being recaptured by the fleet D'Almeira sent after us. Several times we were hard put to outrun them. A final storm near wrecked us off the Normandy coast and it took a month to repair the masts. After that it was a short sail across the Channel.' His teeth flashed as he smiled, sardonically. 'Just off Lizard Head we were met by an English patrol. We narrowly escaped being blown out of the water in their zeal to sink a Spanish prize. My duty took me first to Court to report to Her Majesty. It was three weeks before I could leave, but in the meantime I had visited Esmond and learned that Gabriellen was here.'

'Why did not you send us word?' she choked out. 'You must have known how we suffered, believing you dead.'

'If I had known how long the delay would be, I would have done so. I had thought that after reporting to the Queen I would be able to seek you out within a day or two. I wanted to surprise you.'

'Well, you certainly did that,' Aphra observed.

Whilst Jack had been speaking, it had grown dark. When Aphra rose to prepare the evening meal, Gabriellen went with her. 'Stay, Ellen. You will want to be with Jack,' Aphra insisted.

She shook her head. 'I will help you. A room must also be prepared for your guest.'

There were no awkward questions from Aphra, and for that Gabriellen was grateful. The older woman gently squeezed her shoulder, saying, 'You will be leaving us now. I have come to think of us as friends, Ellen.'

'I shall never forget your kindness, Aphra.'

Two hours later the meal over, and the tension in the house was obvious. Mark was unusually quiet. Jack looked tired and brooding. Gabriellen found the strain unendurable. How could she go on pretending that Mark was merely a friend?

Aphra, seeing her pallor, came to her aid. 'Ellen, you look tired. I am sure Jack will forgive you if you retire early.' She turned a radiant smile on Jack, explaining, 'We were worried about Ellen's health when she came here. It would be awful if too much excitement brought about a relapse.'

Gabriellen stood up. 'There is no risk of that.' Her gaze

436

did not quite hold Jack's as she went on, 'This has been a momentous day. If you will excuse me . . .' She did not wait for their reply, so great was her need to be on her own.

In the parlour Aphra also made her excuses and left the men to their ale. Saul stood up, saying, 'I'll make a last check on the horses and then I too will retire. It's good to know that the Spanish are no match for our sea captains. Your escape was bravely done.' He put up a hand to stop Mark who rose to help him on his rounds of the stables. 'You stay here, Mark. You two will have much to discuss.'

That was an understatement, Mark thought caustically. Yet what could be said? It was not for him to dictate Ellen's future. She must decide. He would do nothing to jeopardise her happiness. As to his own guilt, that he had betrayed Jack's friendship by his affair with Gabriellen . . . ? He shrugged it aside. He knew Jack well enough to know when his friend was evading certain incidents in a story.

'As so infamous an enemy of Spain, Jack, your escape was little short of miraculous.' Mark poured two tankards of ale and passed one to him. They had been drinking steadily all evening. 'How fortunate you found a guard who bore a grudge against your captor. Or was there more to it than that? Were you merely sparing the sensibilities of the women?'

Jack winked. 'There was no bribed guard, just the wife of my gaoler.'

'I take it she became your mistress and helped you escape?'

'Something like that.' The gleam in Jack's eyes confirmed Mark's suspicions. He had been unfaithful to Ellen.

Jack stood up to pace the room. There was a slight stiffness to his once fluid grace, a barely perceptible droop of those proud shoulders, which betrayed how much the long ride from London had taken its toll upon his strength. It would be some months before he made a full recovery.

'The woman was as much a prisoner as I. She hated her brutish husband,' he elaborated. 'She was a willing mistress and saw my escape as a means of winning her own freedom. She agreed to help me if I took her with me.'

He stuck his thumbs into the sword belt at his waist, and continued. 'She wanted to leave Spain and enjoy the freedom of a more liberated city such as Paris. She had enough jewels to set herself up and I stayed with her long enough to see her settled. I owed her that much. She already had her eye on a French count to be her protector when I left.'

'And your use for her was at an end?' Mark said with unusual asperity.

Jack grinned. 'We used each other, and mutually benefitted from the arrangement.'

Mark stood up, turning his back. He wanted to smash the conceit from Jack's face. With each word he spoke, Mark felt the years of friendship sliding away. The widening rift between them could never be breached. But he could not forget that Jack had once saved his life.

Mark clenched his fist, restraining his need to punch that arrogant jaw for the way he had first deceived Gabriellen by not telling her of his marriage. But Jack was still recovering from imprisonment. He'd not strike a weakened man.

Jack watched Mark with piercing concentration. 'I had not expected to find Gabriellen so changed. Her new maturity is dignified, although uncomfortable to accept. I should not have kept my marriage a secret from her.'

Mark checked his anger. 'Ellen deserved better than the way you treated her.'

The air was charged with an unspoken threat. Mark stood with legs apart, expecting Jack to retaliate. To his surprise, Jack lowered his gaze.

'Gabriellen was never like my other women.' The bluster was gone from Jack's voice. 'I always feared losing her. I'd not risk that now. I could not live without her. I never thought I'd say that about any woman.'

Mark downed the contents of his goblet. 'Then be sure you do not fail her,' he warned. 'If you use her as callously as you did the Spanish woman, you will have me to answer to.'

Jack's lips compressed. 'How quickly you defend her! It was not just friendship which made you bring her here?'

'Gabriellen needed a friend,' Mark answered gruffly. 'Prew was a pervert. She lost the child because he had taken a whip to her. And despite her resilience, she has not escaped without mental scars.'

'So the knight errant in you came to the rescue?'

Mark regarded Jack with a forthrightness which stopped

438

just short of challenge. 'You asked me once to look after her.'

Jack paced the parlour. 'I've been away nine months. Gabriellen and I parted in anger. Nine months is a long time.' He stood by the fireplace, one hand resting on his sword hilt. He swung about to face Mark, his stare accusing. 'To be truthful, her welcome was not the one I envisaged.'

'What the hell did you expect? The loss of the child hit her hard. Your arrival was like a bolt from the blue. Why did you not send word?'

'I thought to surprise you.' Jack's expression hardened. 'I succeeded, it would seem. I saw the glances Gabriellen gave you. Very revealing they were. Do you love her?'

Mark did not deign to answer.

A stain of angry colour spread over Jack's face. They stood across the room from each other, their silence a duel of nerves. Jack fingered his beard as he studied Mark. Something in the Welshman's eyes warned him that the unspoken question on his lips was better left that way. He had fought Mark in sword practice enough times to know that they were evenly matched. A duel might prove who was the better swordsman, but it would never prove which was the master of Gabriellen's heart. Jack concealed his jealous fury.

'So it would seem we are no longer friends but rivals?'

'If you were not still weak from your imprisonment,' Mark threatened, 'I'd thrash you for the misery you've caused Ellen.'

'So you do love her?' Jack blazed. 'Yet I have the prior claim. Gabriellen has always regarded me as her husband in all but name.'

He saw no more than the blur of Mark's fist before it slammed into his face. Pain closed his right eye, the impact of the blow knocking him back against the table. The months in prison had slowed his reflexes, he thought grimly, as he shook his head to clear his dazed senses. What he saw in Mark's eyes stopped him coming up to retaliate. He held up his hands, indicating he'd had enough.

Mark stood with legs braced and fists ready. Jack studied him, one eye already blackening. 'Tomorrow I leave. Would that Gabriellen could come with me. I shall return

439

within the week. That will be the last you will see of her.'

'You think you can stop me?' Mark bristled.

Jack gave a harsh laugh devoid of humour. 'No, but I know Gabriellen. Whatever ghost she sought to lay in Wales, it was not mine. She loves me. In her eyes I, and not Prew, am her husband. That is why she will not see you again.'

Esmond had not meant to stay the night at Nell Lovegood's, but drink and amiable company had coerced him. Now in the grey glimmering of dawn his conscience troubled him. He'd been away from Nan and the players for four days and had become more deeply embroiled in One-eyed Ned's nefarious schemes. It pained him to realise he was sliding back into the old life. Opening a shutter, he put up a hand to shield his aching eyes from the first rays of the sun. The gauzy haze of dawn touched the narrow fetid lanes with golden fingers. A fool's paradise, a faery world of make believe.

He scowled. What was he doing here? Seeking his lost youth, an inner voice jeered. He resented the fact that his debts had made it necessary to take One-eyed Ned as his partner in this place. Pride had urged him to prove to the younger Upright Man that he had not lost his skill – that he was still the man he once had been.

A false, foolish pride. His life was with the players now. They needed him. But he could not rid himself of the knowledge that he was failing them, as his sight was failing him. Where was the new play? Unstarted. Where was the fellowship and loyalty which had once existed within the troupe? Slowly disintegrating with their fall in popularity.

He laid his brow against the window pane. He missed his daughter. Gabriellen was the one who inspired him to better things. It was her he truly wanted to impress, not One-eyed Ned. She'd be returning soon. He did not want her to find the troupe so despondent. A start must be made today. New costumes for the players would lift their spirits, and he would begin work on a play.

The brightening rays now showed the ragged vagabonds scurrying to their dens. A window was flung open opposite. A blowsy woman in a large lacy nightcap flung out the nightslops on to a hapless beggar passing below. The colourful abuse hurled back at the matron made Esmond grin as he collected his cloak and let himself out into the street.

He walked with care through the miry runnels whilst the church bells called the citizens to prayer. Around him maidservants hurried to market, colliers carried sacks of coal, and water-carriers bent low under the weight of their yokes and casks. The 'prentices were unbarring shutters in the shops of merchants and craftsmen. Already the hawkers and chimney sweeps raised their voices above the din of lathes and hammers turning out barrels, candlesticks, pots and pans.

Coming out of Fleet Street, he took a short cut through St Paul's churchyard. His good humour faded as he recognised the voice of the man preaching at the cross. The sermon brought an angry flush to his face as the young Lord Barpham condemned all plays and actors.

'Do they not indulge in bawdry and induce whoredom?' Barpham expounded. 'Do they not make a mockery of the cuckold, revere unchastity and infidelity? They are the devil's instrument. The playhouses are the cess-pits of our civilisation. They encourage wanton kissing and every profanity. As for the actors, they are rogues of the highest order, their antics scratching the itching humours of scab-bed minds.'

'Nay, my lord.' Esmond lifted his stentorian voice to flay the orator. 'A player is the embodiment of all we are capable of attaining. By his actions he fortifies moral precepts with examples, for what we see him perform we believe truly achievable. He is the inspiration for us to follow the quest of our heroes; to emulate the greatness of our ancestors.'

Lord Barpham flung out an accusing arm, spittle spraying from his mouth as he shouted: 'So speaks an unworthy sinner. Amongst his troupe are lechers and sodomites. He would teach us deception and hypocrisy. Teach us to steal, deflower honest wives, and condone buggery. No profanity is too great. This degenerate would incite us to riot, treachery, and even glorify murder.'

Esmond elbowed his way through the crowd, his face red with fury. Standing with legs apart, one hand on his hip, he shook a fist at the man in the pulpit. 'Where in our plays is it seen that justice does not prevail? Is not the lecher always disgraced, the villain apprehended? We portray parasites and scoundrels so that men may be aware of them, and avoid their foul practices.' Esmond flung out an arm in dramatic appeal to his audience. 'Does not a worthy actor bring joy to the hearts of the people, inspire them with hope?'

Lord Barpham thumped the pulpit with his hand. 'There speaks the devil. By his own words he would make of a common vagrant a god. Blasphemer! Acolyte of Satan!'

A puritan close to Esmond took up the chant. 'Disciple of Beelzebub.'

A red mist formed in Esmond's brain. There was nothing he despised more than bigotry and Lord Barpham was the worst of his kind. Unable to vent his rage on Barpham, he rounded on the puritan near to him. Slamming his fist into the screeching mouth, he dislodged several teeth and knocked him to the ground. A hand tweaked at his doublet as he bent over the fallen man to deliver a second blow, and a voice hissed a warning.

'Run, man. They've called the Watch.'

Esmond whirled to stare into Trout-face Carfax's bulging eyes. The beggar yelled out: 'Clubs! Clubs!'

Within moments the 'prentices rallied to the battlecry. The crowd scattered at the sound of the dreaded call to arms. From all sides came the cry as the numbers of the unruly apprentices swelled, striking blows indiscriminately in their eagerness for a fight – the cause was irrelevant.

Under cover of the confusion, Trout-face grabbed Esmond's arm. 'This way.'

He stumbled blindly through the churchyard, aware of the angry shouts of the Watch close behind. His eyes betrayed him as he stumbled into obstacles and was eventually tripped up by a scavaging dog. As he rose to his feet, four hands clamped down on his arms.

'Sir, we arrest you in the Queen's Majesty's name for grievous assault, and charge you to obey us.'

Protest was useless. Esmond was disarmed and taken to The Counter prison in Wood Street. Esmond knew enough of prisons to know that there were three types of accommodation in this one, providing one had the money to pay for it. Paupers were immediately consigned to The Hole, a brutal squalid quarter, overcrowded and rife with disease. More often than not prisoners died of fever or starvation here long before they came to trial or were released.

Esmond had no intention of mouldering away. He patted his purse, knowing he had the choice of the Knight's Ward where conditions were tolerable, though less comfortable than if he paid for the privilege of lodging in the Master's Side.

Held under restraint whilst his name was registered in the prison black book and his choice of lodging made, he paid the first in a constant stream of demands for bribes. Then he was led towards the first doorway leading to the Master's Side. He was about to pay the turnkey a shilling to pass through when he was distracted by the scufflings and groans of another prisoner being hauled in. A cursory glance over his shoulder showed him Trout-face being dragged in by his heels. The beggar's head was battered and bleeding from being knocked against stones and he was barely conscious. As Esmond watched, a prison sergeant ran a hand over Trout-face's bony figure, and finding only a few pennies, ordered him sent to The Hole.

'Give him a place in the Knight's Ward,' Esmond offered, feeling guilty that in trying to save him, Trout-face had been arrested. He handed over enough coins to keep Trout-face in relative comfort for a week or two. But at the rate the prison garnish, as the bribes were called, was leeched out of a prisoner, it might give him no more than a day or two's reprieve from The Hole. After that he must rely on the charity of the citizens of London.

Esmond was taken through several doors. At each the turnkey demanded anything from a shilling to a half-crown for the privilege of passing through. Finally he was brought to the hall on the Master's Side. Esmond cynically noted a tapestry depicting the story of the Prodigal Son. Here, under threat of having his hat, cloak and other garments forcibly stripped from him, he had to part with a further two shillings to remain unmolested. Only then was he shoved into a narrow cobweb-hung room with a mildewed straw pallet, dirty sheets, and a candle-stub to light his privileged abode.

As the door clanged shut behind him, Esmond sank down on to the inhospitable pallet and rested his head in his hands. It could be weeks, if not months, before he was either brought to trial or released. How long would his money last before he must take the ignoble path through the Knight's Ward to end his days in The Hole? To be poor in prison, he mused with bitter cynicism, was to be buried without being dead.

A sleepless night for Gabriellen brought with it a return of her resolution, and the morning found her in confrontation with Jack. From the bruising around his eye, it was obvious that he and Mark had been fighting. Mark had been attending the birth of a foal when she came downstairs that morning, and as yet she had not spoken to him. When questioned, Jack had refused to give her a straight account of their quarrel. From the fierceness of his gaze, it was obviously not a subject he was prepared to discuss. Had he guessed that Mark had been her lover? Strangely, he did not pursue the matter.

'We have been given a second chance, my love.' He gazed down into Gabriellen's upturned face. 'I will buy a house for you on the river so that I can come to you whenever I am free from my duties at Court.'

It was the assumption that she would give up everything to become his concubine which placed them at odds. Also, after her initial joy at his return, she found she could not entirely wipe out the memory of the pain of his betrayal. She needed to test the strength of his declared love.

'I will not be set up as a courtesan. I shall continue to live with the players and we will see each other as before. This time there will be no lies or deceit. And no more secrecy. You have a duty to your wife, but the ties of our love must be those of trust and fidelity. Those are my terms.'

'The devil they are, madam!' His grey eyes glinted dangerously as his hands gripped her shoulders. 'Certes! You speak of love, then in the same breath make such demands . . .'

Gabriellen cut him short, refusing to be diverted. 'What of you, Jack? Did you not speak of love, yet without hesitation discard my honour and reputation? If your ambition is greater than your love for me, then you are not worthy of my love.'

'I love you, Gabriellen. What must I say to convince you? Do you think that whilst in prison I did not regret the manner of our parting? Christ, woman, would you be

444

more cruel than the rack?' The desire in his eyes almost destroyed her will to resist.

She lowered her gaze. The last year had taught her much. She might have flouted the dictates of convention, but no man would ever again use her to his own ends. Not even Jack. 'I will be your mistress, but I've also a duty to my father. I shall return to Bankside. You have your life at sea and Court – mine is with the players. We will meet whenever possible.'

'I will not be dictated to by a woman. By God, you sound so much like a wife – jealous and petty and . . .'

'And you sound like a spoilt child!' She could not believe that they could be arguing so heatedly. 'Nothing worthwhile in this life is without its price. We will be together whenever you are in London. I will not be shut away from my family and friends while I await your visits. You are ambitious, Jack, and I will never stand in your way, for you are destined for greatness. But what life would I have shut away in isolation? Like my father, playwrighting is in my blood. And I'm good, Jack, although my name can never be put to the work. It was my play the Queen applauded. Mine, Jack, not Father's. I don't expect you to give up the sea, yet you demand a similar sacrifice from me.'

His fingers dug into her shoulders as he glared down at her. She held his gaze without blinking. The determination shining brightly in her eyes was proving to be more than a match for his. She saw conflicting emotions pass across his face: anger; desire; frustration; pain; eventually love and reluctant admiration.

'Don't you realise that you are the only woman I want?' The admission was torn from him with a groan. 'You mean more to me than fame or fortune. During my imprisonment I did not fear death or regret the loss of all I had striven to achieve. What are wealth and power to a man if he be denied the love of the only woman he cares for? You are my reason for living, Gabriellen. Not power, not ambition – you.'

'I would not be so cruel as to deny you your destiny, my love. In that, I would never constrain you.'

He kissed her with a tenderness which proved his love beyond doubt. The magic of his touch had lost none of its

445

potency. Ensnared once more, she abandoned herself to its sweetness. Taking her face in his hands, he smiled down at her. 'I shall return within the week. Until then, I shall count the hours until I can hold you once more in my arms.'

His farewell kiss before the entire family was deliberately long, a provocative reminder to Mark of his prior claim.

Gabriellen watched him ride away until he was no more than a dot on the horizon. She was the last to leave the courtyard. Suddenly she could not face the curiosity of her friends. Especially Mark. Now she felt the sick realisation that she had betrayed not only Jack but also her dearest friend. Whilst she was delighted that Jack had proved his love by agreeing to her conditions, she was at a loss to explain the sadness she felt at leaving Wales.

What she needed was a long ride to clear her mind and allow her to think. Saddling Sable, she rode out into the yard. Mark was leading Cadwallader to service one of the mares tied to the mating post. When he handed the stallion's reins to a groom and moved towards her, she shook her head.

'I don't want to talk, Mark. I need some time on my own.'

His jaw tightened. 'Remember, there is always a place for you here, Ellen.'

He stood back to let her pass. She rode for an hour, until she felt Sable's stride beginning to flag. There was a lake ahead. Throwing herself on the bank beside it, she propped herself up on one elbow to stare across its shimmering surface. The hills around lay in purple shadow and a breeze stirred the rushes. She lay so still, trying to fathom her confusion, that a foraging heron waded a few feet in front of her, unaware of her presence.

A long time later she sat up, dropping her head down upon her drawn-up knees. She loved Jack and for him must sacrifice her friendship with Mark. The choice should have been easy, but it was not. Mark held a very special place in her heart. No longer could she define it as brotherly. He had saved both her life and her sanity: debts which could never be repaid, but which had formed an indissoluble bond between them.

It was long past noon when she remounted. She knew that when she left Wales, she would probably never see

446

Mark again. That would leave an empty void in her life which once had been filled with warmth and comradeship. Downhearted, she paid little heed to her route, but felt no surprise to discover the woodcutter's hut ahead. As she had known he would be, Glendower was cropping at the hay rick in the stable. Inside the hut she found Mark crouching by the fire, stirring a pot of stewed rabbit he was heating up.

'I had a feeling you would come here,' he said simply. 'From your expression, you have decided to go with Jack, haven't you?'

'I made that decision three years ago, Mark.'

'And nothing has changed?'

'Much has changed. How could it not? Yet shameless as it sounds, I do not regret our affair. This woodman's hut will always be my Eden. I shall never forget what happened here.'

'Will you tell Jack? He has his suspicions.'

She looked him squarely in the eye. 'If Jack asks, I will tell him. There was much about his escape he did not tell me. Knowing him, I would guess there was a woman involved.' She saw by Mark's raised eyebrow that she had guessed right. 'I would rather not know the details. If it gave him his freedom, I accept it as a necessary infidelity. From the first moment I saw him, I fell under Jack's spell. Yet, without abiding affection, I could never give so much of myself to a man as I gave to you.' She swallowed hard, her throat constricting as she tried to put her feelings into words. 'Always with you, Mark, I felt such . . . such completeness in everything we did together.'

No longer able to meet the intensity of his gaze, she stared at a point above his shoulder. 'From Jack's black eye, it is obvious you and he fought last night. Our affair has made it impossible for us to go back to the easy friendship we once shared. I shall never forget you, Mark.'

'Then I wish you happiness, Ellen.'

His rugged face blurred through the tears she could no longer contain. 'Goodbye, Emrys Llewelyn. I knew a peace here in Wales I had not dreamed was possible.'

He moved swiftly to stand very close to her. 'Christ's blood, woman, I'll not let you go!'

He reached for her but she sprang back. 'You must, Mark.' Her voice cracked and she ran from the hut.

447

Mark was at the door in pursuit of her. As he reached the stable, she rode out mounted on Sable. The look on her face stopped him in his tracks. Anguish warred with obstinacy, desolation battled with stubbornness. He who knew her so well saw the end of their intimacy written in her beautiful sad face. He rammed his fist against the stable door. Glendower shied at the fright it gave him. Mark stood rigid, unaware of the pain shooting up his hand and arm.

He would not return to the house until Ellen left. The taverns of Llangollen beckoned. He'd go there. God alone knew how much he needed to drink himself into oblivion.

Without Mark, the atmosphere of Rowan Hall changed. There was accusation in Aphra's eyes which accentuated Gabriellen's own sense of loss. Before Jack came back for her, she took the pouch of gold coins Prew had left on the cellar floor in London and laid it on Mark's desk with a note.

Dear Emrys Llewelyn, my trusted friend,
I want nothing that was my husband's. Please take this and use it. The debt I owe you for my life and sanity is beyond price. Rebuild the Baron's Hall. Let me in this way be a part of your dream, Mark. As I can never be a part of your life.
*   Love, Ellen*

Chapter Twenty-Nine

On Gabriellen's return to Bankside she was devastated to learn that no word had been heard of Esmond for six weeks. Refusing to believe that one night he had become the victim of a cut-throat and been left to die in the gutter, she plunged into a search for him which eventually led her to The Counter in Wood Street.

'Two months you've been here!' She gazed around the filthy cell, her voice harsh with indignation. 'It's outrageous. Why didn't you let the players know where you were? They would have helped. Poggs and Nan have been at their wits' end with worry. As have I since I returned. Jack learned your whereabouts from a man called Edward Dawkins, else we would never have found you.'

'You shouldn't have brought her, Stoneham,' Esmond groaned.

'Had I not, Gabriellen would have come alone,' Jack replied. 'I'd not risk that.'

There was a moment's strained silence. An icy east wind whined through the unglazed window, shredding the festoons of cobwebs and carrying with it the stench of the midden in the yard below. Esmond stood in the darkest corner of the dingy cell, his figure obscured by shadows. When he spoke, his voice was shaky with anger and despair. 'Do you think I wanted anyone to witness my shame?'

'Then your pride could have killed you.' Gabriellen was appalled, both at the squalor of the gaol and her father's stubbornness. 'Surely you know that with the exception of Culpepper, the players would follow you to hell and back in their loyalty?'

'That's why I sent no word. It was better this way. I should have known you would not let matters rest.' When he stepped forward into the feeble light from the small window, his pallor and thinness shocked her. Esmond had aged considerably this winter.

Anguish at his plight almost swamped her resolve. He would despise her pity, and in his present mood only respond to firmness. 'Why did you not send for a lawyer?' She put her hands on her hips, exasperated at his obstinacy. 'Could not Lord Mincham have settled the matter of assault? Why did you not send him word?'

'Keep your voice down, Gabby.' Esmond glanced anxiously towards the door. 'Our patron would not approve of my bringing disrepute to his players, and I've reasons why I don't want my name brought before a court. When my money ran out, an associate sent in enough to keep me in comfort. He owed me that much.'

Bitterness swept through Esmond. One-eyed Ned would willingly pay the garnish. With him a prisoner, and believing Stoneham dead, Ned had likely taken all the profits of Nell Lovegood's for himself. 'I could not risk being brought to trial,' he explained. Then, uncomfortable under Gabriellen's candid stare, he ran a finger under his limp ruff. 'Prew was right when he said that I could be hanged for my crimes. Once in court, who knows what evidence they could drag up against me? Not that I murdered anyone as he claimed . . . that was an accident. But I daren't take the risk of being tried. Not when bribery can serve as well to get me out of here.'

He turned away and putting a hand on the wall, bowed his head against it. 'You should not have come, Gabby. I'd rather you'd been spared seeing me like this.'

Gabriellen hid her shock at her father's confession. She knew his life had been far from exemplary, but she was only just beginning to realise how involved he had been with the Underworld. Never one to condemn those whom she loved, whatever their failings, she put her hand on his shoulder. 'I love you dearly, Father. I could not leave you to suffer alone. Tell me what must be done. Jack said you've spent most of your savings already in bribes to stay in the Master's Side, yet swine are kept in better comfort.'

Esmond rested one dirt-smeared hand on hers and rubbed the other across his brow as though it pained him. His hair was tangled with straw, and his ruff and shirt were grey with grime. There were holes in his brown hose, and in his worn and filthy russet doublet and breeches he could have been mistaken for a vagabond.

'Believe me, this is luxury compared to the other quarters offered here,' he commented sourly. 'Trout-face, who was arrested with me, only lasted a week in The Hole. The cold killed him, and he was a hardened beggar used to a rough life.'

He turned to face Jack Stoneham. 'Our business venture has prospered. There's money enough there to furnish me with the bribes I need to be free of this place, and to compensate you for the losses you sustained in York. I'll leave you to deal with collecting the funds from our partner.'

'We'll soon have you out of here, Esmond,' Jack vowed.

Esmond sniffed and looked away as tears of emotion welled in his eyes. Clearing his throat, he said tautly: 'Promise me you will not come again, Gabby? This is no place for a lady.'

She smiled wanly. 'It is no place for a gentleman either. Is respectability such an onerous yoke, Father?'

He answered her smile with a return of good humour. 'It sits more comfortably than a noose, daughter. When I get out, I promise you, I shall change my ways.'

A bout of coughing wracked his emaciated figure and droplets of sweat broke out on his brow as he fought for breath. He waved Gabriellen aside as she moved towards him. 'Stay back. 'Tis nothing.'

When the coughing halted he crossed to a rickety table and picked up a sheaf of papers. 'Look, I've already started a new play. It's different from anything I've ever done. The characters are all animals. It parodies the vices of usury and the Underworld. The hero will appear as a lion; the usurer into whose clutches he falls, a vulture; the heroine a unicorn; the gaoler a crow; and other members of the fraternity – cats, magpies, ravens and rats, ruled over by an eagle. I have named it *The Miscreant's Tale*. Take these notes and see what you would make of it. I owe the players a new play to be performed as soon as I am released.'

'It's a fine state of affairs when our manager absents himself for weeks at a time.' Anthony Culpepper tossed back his fair hair to address the assembled players in scathing tones.

A heavy downpour had brought a halt to rehearsal on the open stage and the players were crowded into the tiring-house. Surrounded by props and costumes, they studied their copied parts as Agnes handed round horn cups of mulled wine.

Culpepper ungraciously waved aside the cup offered to him, his handsome features distorted by a sneer. 'The costumes are but half completed . . . only one of the four special stage effects works properly . . . As for the three 'prentice boys . . .' He glowered at the culprits jostling each other and sniggering in a corner. 'They're incompetent jackanapes who grow more unruly by the day. And those musicians! Damned Italians, always moody and temperamental. Twice last week they drowned my most eloquent speeches by making the devil's own racket upon tabour and lute.'

Gabriellen put down her quill and set aside the papers containing a carefully drawn plot of the play. She had scrupulously studied every scene; inserted details of the actors involved, noting their entrances and exits and changes of costumes, plus any musical accompaniment required or special effects. A second copy of this was nailed up in the tiring-house for the actors to memorise, but throughout rehearsals she prompted and cued the players to ensure the smooth running of the play. Since Esmond's retirement from the stage this had been his responsibility, but in his absence there was no one else to perform the task. Gabriellen marshalled the performance with expertise. Her hard work was appreciated by all the actors except Culpepper.

At the insult to the Florentine cousins, she saw Cesare, the more volatile of the two, start forward, his hand gripping his long thin dagger. 'I cut out his lying tongue! He take back his words or I prick him good.'

Gabriellen hastily intervened. 'In those circumstances, Mr Culpepper, you were deliberately trying to cut both Samuel's and Robin's speeches. Something you would not have dared do had my father been present.'

Culpepper ignored Gabriellen's words, refusing as he always did to acknowledge her presence at the playhouse. In the meantime Umberto had restrained Cesare, and speaking loudly in Italian led him back to their stools. Culpepper caressed his beard as he rested one foot gracefully on a wooden coffer which held stage props. His manner arrogant, he addressed Poggs as the most senior player. 'And where, pray, is the estimable maestro who neglects us so?'

He mimicked Cesare's accent further to emphasise his contempt.

Gabriellen glared at the leading actor, her patience precariously thin. 'With respect, Mr Culpepper, you know Father was called to Chichester on a matter of business. Unfortunately, he contracted a severe chill there. He has sent us written instructions for the play's performance. I expect his return this weekend. The opening has been billed for next week and my father will take the part of the fox who is the narrator of the story.'

'Did someone speak?' Culpepper raised his fair brows in surprise as he glanced at each of the players. He shrugged. 'It must have been a mouse that squeaked.'

Gabriellen stood up, her eyes glittering as her temper erupted. She twisted her fingers together, struggling to master the fury which threatened to choke her.

Poggs came to her defence. 'Damn your insolence, man! We all know how hard Gabriellen has worked to keep up the morale of this troupe. Without her, there would be no new play. She's spent nights copying out each of our parts and has been tireless in helping Nan with the costumes. Also she has been our bookholder, prompting those in need.'

'I need no help from any wench,' Culpepper raged. 'It's an affront, and degrading, that a woman presumes to interfere.'

'She alone knows Esmond's mind on this play,' Poggs scowled. 'Gabriellen is his mouthpiece.'

'We should all be grateful to her,' Samuel Lacey added. 'It's not as though she's running the troupe, is it? There was no one else to replace Esmond, and to be honest, I think she has done very well . . . for a woman.'

Poggs looked anxiously at Gabriellen to judge her reaction. Clearly she was furious. Her face was devoid of colour and her eyes were large and shining with a light that threatened to make a rampaging tigress look like a playful kitten in comparison. Something in his worried look must have penetrated her anger. Folding her arms across her breast, she turned away to inspect the row of costumes awaiting final fittings. Poggs gave a silent whistle of relief that a further scene had been averted. It would not be the first time that after a confrontation with Gabriellen, Culpepper had stormed out. He would sulk for days, even feigning illness and refusing to perform, until he was placated by the offer of an additional soliloquy in the current play.

'The rain has stopped,' Poggs announced with relief. 'We waste time on pointless bickering. Esmond has worked hard on this play, even from his sickbed. You show scant gratitude by your disloyalty, Culpepper. Shall we proceed with the rehearsal, gentlemen?'

He ushered the players back on stage. As he passed Gabriellen's angry figure, he winked encouragement at her. Apart from Nan, who had a right to know the truth, Poggs was the only one to whom she had confided her father's true fate. Without the clown's intercession and understanding, her temperament would have clashed disastrously with Culpepper's tantrums and histrionics.

Gabriellen took up the prompt book and held it out to Poggs who hovered by the door. 'Today it would be better if you took over my duties.'

'Don't take Culpepper's prejudice badly. Acting is a male domain, and players such as he will jealously guard it.' He grinned. 'No man likes to admit that a woman could be his equal – Culpepper least of all.'

'Yet we have a Queen on the throne. I dare any man to refute that she is not the equal of her father.'

'She'd have his head off if he did,' Poggs quipped. 'But I take your meaning. In a more tolerant age, you would make both a great playwright and a player.'

An impatient shout from Culpepper took him hurrying on to the stage. Gabriellen left the playhouse, her fast stride working off her anger at the injustice against her sex. What use to rail against it? Better to channel that frustration into proving to herself that she was as good a playwright as her father. Was not her work performed in Esmond's name? She laughed with grim humour. Culpepper was so proud of the new plays which had gained him the notice of the public, the pompous man would have an apoplexy if he knew he owed his success to her.

Since the success of her play *A Widow Went A-Wooing* at Court, Esmond had fallen back on his old habits of gambling and drinking, leaving her to produce the plays for the troupe. *The Miscreant's Tale* had been worked upon out of boredom and now that Gabriellen had returned, he had left her to finish it.

Apart from the disagreements within the troupe, Gabriellen had been faced with problems arising from both hers and Jack's return to London. They meant she had seen little of him in recent weeks. He had spent a month in York, trying to save what he could from the ruins of the business there. Once Elizabeth Stoneham's partner had learned Jack was alive, he fled the country, taking all the money and gems he could lay hands on. It had almost bankrupted Jack to save the business. Whilst amassing the money to free Esmond, he had also spent a great deal of his time at Court. Only by gaining the Queen's favour would he recover his finances.

On their arrival in London, Jack had tried to persuade Gabriellen to take a house in Lambeth where he could visit her. She had resolved that she would be ruled by her head and not her heart. Knowing that within a few months he would return to the sea to recoup his fortune, she refused. Besides, it was obvious that her father needed her steadying influence. Also a few short weeks in the company of the players had brought an excitement back to her blood. Despite the arguments and tribulations, she enjoyed her life with the players too much to live in isolation as Jack's concubine.

The house in Bankside was large enough to accommodate them all. Gabriellen had her own suite of rooms on the second floor and Jack visited her there often, his presence accepted without comment by the players who shared the house.

The Miscreant's Tale opened at The Angel and immediately proved the most successful play in London. After three weeks, when the audience still filled the playhouse to capacity, Esmond celebrated with a lavish banquet for the players. Success was a bond which smoothed over past disagreements. Even Culpepper mellowed, his mood affable as he basked in the roar of applause which followed his exits from the stage.

The flow of malmsey wine had brought a flush to the players' faces. Their voices grew louder as they effusively praised each other, or repeated the words of acclaim delivered by an eminent member of the audience. They were boisterous in their excitement, flamboyant in their mannerisms and volatile in temperament. They were unlike any other group of people, larger than life and twice as preposterous in their self-importance. But an hour in their company set Gabriellen's pulses racing and she was proud to be a part of their world.

At the end of the meal, Umberto and Cesare took up their instruments. Poggs jumped to his feet and began to kick up his heels in a jig as he danced around the table, his voice raised in a popular song. When the others joined in the singing, Jack drew Gabriellen away from the revellers to a quieter place on a window seat overlooking the garden.

'My time at Court has finally been rewarded. Her Majesty has granted me Letters of Marque. I sail for the Spanish Main as soon as my ships are provisioned.'

'We have had so little time together.' She could not hide her disappointment. The brevity of their reconciliation meant that, though their passion for each other was as fierce as ever, occasionally an underlying tension marred their quieter moments. By mutual agreement neither spoke of her sojourn in Wales.

'Will you miss me?' Jack grinned, revealing his chipped tooth, his manner showing his confidence. 'You've become so involved with the players these last weeks, I begin to wonder.'

She moved into the circle of his arms and kissed him. 'Of course I'll miss you. But after your months of imprisonment, I suspect the prospect of piracy on the Spanish Main is a strong lure. Not to mention your hunger for fame. How can I, a mere woman, compete with that?'

'You name me pirate?' A wicked gleam brightened his grey eyes. 'Madam, I am a respectable privateer. As a pirate I could be hanged for robbery on the Spanish Main. But as a privateer with the Queen's Letters of Marque, I destroy the ships of the enemy of our country – my plunder becomes the prize of war. Were I pirate indeed, I would take you captive to be my slave during the long months at sea.' He took her face in his hands and stared down at her. 'Would that such a dream were possible. Were it not for the danger, I would have you at my side.'

'Is there any chance you will return before Christmas?'

'In fairness, I can make no promises.'

'A pity.' She leaned back in his arms and held his stare with unwavering candour. 'I am with child. It is due in December. I know you resented my last pregnancy, but I want children, Jack.'

'Last time I acted like an ass. I had wished to spare you from public censure.' His gaze assessed her troubled stare. There was a tautness in the set of his bearded jaw. 'December, you say?'

She nodded, seeing in his eyes the unspoken question. A question to which she did not know the answer. Was the father of this child Jack, or Mark?

'It seems our reunion was a fruitful one.' The look in his eyes changed to one of fierce pride. 'I will return to England for the birth of my son. In my heart you are my true wife, not Elizabeth. Never doubt that, my darling.'

Gabriellen wound her arms around his neck and pulled his head down to meet her lips. Whatever Jack's reservations, pride made him accept the child as his own. It made her love for him stronger than ever. By his unquestioning acceptance, he healed the breach of his past infidelities. Jack had his responsibilities towards his own family in York, but he had vowed that he and Elizabeth were estranged. He had sworn Gabriellen was the only woman he loved – the only woman he wanted. And she believed him.

Throughout the summer and autumn Gabriellen devoted her time to the players. The weeks in prison had undermined Esmond's robust health. He was given to bouts of ague, the fever and its resultant shaking keeping him to his bed for several days. When he recovered he would disappear for three or four days and return looking pale and red-eyed from his excesses.

Gabriellen confronted him after one of these jaunts. 'Why do you ruin your health this way? You neglect the players and your writing. You are failing not only Lord Mincham but people who are your friends.'

'God's nightgown! I built the troupe to what it is.' He winced at the loudness of his own voice and rubbed a hand across his throbbing temples.

'Is it because your sight is getting worse?' Gabriellen said softly, and put a hand on his arm. 'Drink will not solve the problem.'

'It makes me forget I will soon be blind, a useless burden to everyone.'

The fear in his eyes wrenched at her heart.

'Never useless, Father. Never a burden to those who love you. You can still dictate your plays to me. Your writing is a genius the people love you for.'

'Your talent is greater than mine,' Esmond said without rancour or jealousy. 'You write the plays. Let me enjoy my pleasures while I still can. You'd not begrudge me that?'

It was a plea she could not ignore. The father she believed invincible had shown her his vulnerability. His failing sight had not cooled the wildness in his blood. There was still a rogue within Esmond Angel who could not be tamed. Neither would she wish to be the one to cage that spirit. It had made him what he was.

'I cannot run the troupe without your help.' She changed tactics. 'A servant came from Lord Mincham today. His lordship would attend the playhouse in three days with a party of friends to see *The Miscreant's Tale*.'

Esmond threw up his hands in exasperation. 'Have I not problems enough? Does Lord Mincham think I can perform miracles? The *Tale* has not been performed for weeks. We will need to rehearse it every day, whilst still performing *Unholy Revenge*. Then there are the stage props. Last time it took Crofton two days to get them working properly. And what of the playbills already posted for *The Enchantress* which we were to perform next week? They'll have to be changed.' He rubbed his chin. 'What printer will print new ones at such short notice? Then there's . . .'

'Father, we have always coped before.' Gabriellen laid a hand on his arm. Before his illness Esmond had taken such changes in his stride. She went to an ironbound chest and, taking a key from the chatelaine about her waist, unlocked it. Carefully moving aside several sheaves of papers, she took out a leatherbound prompt book and the copied parts of *The Miscreant's Tale*. Handing them to Esmond, she said, 'Rehearsal can start today. I will see to the playbills. Then check with Nan that the costumes are ready. If I remember correctly, the magpie's head was damaged when Lacey trod on it and has not yet been repaired. I shall meet you at The Angel in an hour.'

Esmond left the house, his expression less harassed.

'Was that Lord Mincham's servant I saw earlier?' Agnes said, bending her tall figure under the low lintel of the door as she limped into the parlour. She was carrying the struggling Laurence and put him down on the floor to crawl about.

'Yes, he is coming to watch the *Tale* on Friday. Father

458

was worried we could not be ready in time. He's gone to The Angel.'

'Esmond's back, is he? That will put poor Nan's mind at rest. But I suppose it's thee who has organised things to run smoothly as usual?' Agnes sped after Laurence who was crawling into the hall and heading towards the open door of the cellar. She turned him around before he could topple down the steep steps. 'If I take my eyes off the rascal, he's heading for mischief.' She cut short her laughter and regarded Gabriellen's rounding stomach. 'In another month, thee'll not be able to dash about so. Thee looks tired. Thee take on too much for the troupe. Not that all of them appreciate it.'

Gabriellen's expression became dreamy. 'I wouldn't change it, Agnes. I feel alive when I'm with the players – that my life has some purpose. What I would not give to be an actor!'

'That's not possible,' Agnes warned.

'I accept that. Though it sticks in my throat to have to admit it.'

'Don't thee let such nonsense upset thee. Thee's twice the playwright Esmond ever was. Sometimes I think it would be worth the uproar just to let that conceited popinjay Culpepper know his greatest lines came from a woman's pen.'

Gabriellen looked stricken. 'How many know that I wrote them? It's supposed to be a secret.'

'Now don't thee go fretting thyself. Poggs guessed, of course. From the first he spotted the talent thee brought to Esmond's scenes. But no one else suspects.' Agnes laughed. 'Vanity and pride would not permit certain of the players to consider a woman capable of such genius.'

There was a wail from Laurence as he tried to pull himself to his feet by holding on to the half-empty coal basket by the fire. It toppled over and he fell down amid a scatter of sea-coal. By the time Agnes reached him he was sucking on a piece, and his long yellow skirts were black with dust, as was his face.

Agnes held him at arm's length and Laurence screamed in protest. 'This one will grow up to be forever in trouble. Everything is an adventure to him.'

Gabriellen laughed as Agnes took Laurence into the kitchen to wash him. Her own child kicked within her, and her hand rested against the movement. Apart from her worry over Esmond's health, life was good. The Angel playhouse was flourishing, and with it the fortunes of the actors. Jack was back in favour at Court. She had heard from Esmond that Mark was in London, and that since winning the Queen's patronage his horses were sought by the highest nobles in the land. Esmond had told her that he had met Mark in Gracechurch Street in the company of the fortune-teller. She had been hurt that he made no attempt to see her. Did he regard her defection from Wales as betrayal? After the tenderness they had shared, it must have seemed that way.

Gabriellen arrived at The Angel at noon the next day to find the rehearsal in disorder.

'No! No! No!' Esmond shouted to the sullen-looking actors on the stage. 'Do it again. Lacey, you are supposed to be a raven – stick out your neck and strut like one as you select your victim.' He rounded on Umberto who was dressed in doublet and hose of black and white for his role as the magpie. 'Umberto, you are a foist intent on stealing a gold chain or watch, anything that glitters. But you must get your timing right. Start the scene from where the raven drops a key in front of the badger who has just come to the city. This is supposed to be a comic piece. Poggs, are you ready?'

Gabriellen sat next to her father as the scene began. The clown removed the grey and black mummer's mask from his head. 'We'll have them falling off their seats with laughter.'

Lacey strutted forward into the badger's path, dropped a key and bent to pick it up as Umberto sidled up behind them. When Poggs was unable to go forward or retreat, Umberto pretended to recognise the raven as an enemy.

'Knave! I know you for a rogue,' he shouted. 'You shall pay for your villainy.'

The raven ran away, collecting several purses from the characters he jostled in the crowd.

Gabriellen found herself caught up in the excitement of the scene as she watched the antics on stage. Umberto was off, dashing after the raven and knocking Poggs to the floor. In the confusion the magpie managed to steal the badger's timepiece. Emitting a scream of rage Poggs, the badger, leapt up. The three actors chased each other around the stage, joined by the 'prentices dressed as a squirrel, mole and rabbit, who had discovered their purses stolen. Gabriellen laughed out loud to see the birds hopping and flapping their wings whilst Poggs gave little jumps as he shuffled about in a hilarious manner. Finally, the raven and magpie, thinking they had escaped the irate badger, were caught by Culpepper.

Dressed in a magnificent tawny velvet doublet and breeches glittering with topazes and agates, Culpepper dominated the stage. The jewels had been a gift from Lord Mincham. Not for Culpepper a lion mask to cover his face. He had declared his audience must see him. He wore a fox-fur cap, and an impressive collar of the same, decorating a gold velvet cloak to give the impression of a mane. The costume was majestic enough to satisfy even his vanity.

Culpepper held up his hand for the rehearsal to stop. He struck a haughty pose, his eyes malevolent and his expression mutinous. 'It will not do, Esmond. At this point the play needs more drama. The paltry few lines you give me are inadequate.' He strode to the front of the stage and turned to where seats would be put on the platform for Lord Mincham and his guests. Taking up various stances, he extemporised a new speech on the wickedness of the Underworld. When Culpepper drew his sword, clearly intending to add another fight sequence to extend his part further, Esmond cut him short.

'The play remains as it is.'

'Our patron wants a spectacle to impress his guests!' exclaimed Culpepper. 'It is long since we have been invited to Court. Nothing should be stinted in our quest towards that goal. The rough and tumble comedy of the last scene should be enhanced by a soliloquy of a higher wit, which would appeal to Her Majesty. Our triumph is Lord Mincham's triumph. His lordship is displeased that another Court performance has been denied us.'

'There is not time for another speech to be written,' Esmond retorted.

'It would grieve me to inform his lordship that you no longer have his interests at heart.'

'That is blackmail, sir!' Gabriellen could no longer control her outburst. This was another ruse by Culpepper to dominate even the minor scenes in the play.

461

For the first time in weeks he whirled around to address her directly. The loathing and disgust in his eyes struck her with the force of a slap.

'The wench dares slander me! What does the ignorant creature know of our craft? We are artists beyond the understanding of any woman. Get her out of here. Her presence discredits our standing.'

'God's nightgown!' Esmond bellowed. 'My daughter stays. She's done as much for this company as any man.'

'She interferes in matters of which she knows nothing. I'll work with no woman. Either she leaves, or I do.'

'Then go, and be damned!' Esmond raged.

'No, Father!' Gabriellen intervened. 'Culpepper knows that without him, his lordship will withdraw his patronage. It is I who must leave.'

'Then I go too,' Poggs defended.

'We too no stay,' Cesare and Umberto said in unison.

'You must!' Gabriellen implored, though her heart swelled with pride at their loyalty. 'I'll not be the cause of the troupe's disbandment.'

'And I will not have my authority undermined,' Esmond shouted. Perspiration glistened on his brow as he glared at Culpepper. 'Especially by an actor who thinks he can lord it over us.' He shrugged off the tiredness of recent weeks, again the firebrand who could reduce most men to quivering submission. He bore down on Culpepper. 'Mark well, my conceited fellow, that you left us once before. You soon came back to eat humble pie. With the Admiral's players you will never take the lead. What other companies come close to us as rivals? How long will Mincham remain infatuated with a man who is no longer the toast of the city?'

Culpepper smirked. 'For longer than this troupe will exist.'

Poggs was holding back Cesare who was spoiling for a fight with Culpepper.

'Gabriellen, she work hard,' the Italian shouted. 'She no deserve you treat her this way. Our troupe is no large. She do many jobs. Save us much trouble . . . and much money.'

'Aye!' The assembled troupe chorused their agreement.

'Then let her take up a needle and help Nan,' Culpepper sneered. 'Or she could sweep the auditorium after each performance. Tasks befitting a woman.'

'My daughter is our scrivener and knows the plays as

462

well as I. It would take months to train a bookholder to replace her. I cannot do everything myself. Not when you want three new plays a year. Do you think I have money to throw away on employing unnecessary people?'

'If the wench stays . . .' Culpepper paused to preen his moustache. 'Then surely, Esmond, you will have the time to add the scene I suggested to the play?' He capitulated only in as much as he could use this chance to force Esmond to expand his part.

Esmond glared imperiously at him. 'You will be given fifteen lines, no more. But in fairness to Lacey, he shall have another ten – providing this rehearsal is so polished I can leave early enough to produce them for you this evening. You will have but one day to rehearse them before the performance. Be sure you do not let me down.'

'Just ensure Mistress Prew keeps her peace and knows her place,' Culpepper warned.

'My daughter prefers to be known as Mistress Angel,' Esmond corrected. 'And I will have her treated with respect.'

Esmond turned to Gabriellen and said in an undertone, 'I trust you can come up with the promised lines, my dear, else Culpepper will carry out his threat?'

Gabriellen sighed. To be able to dismiss Culpepper was a dream she knew could never be realised. The leading actor remained Lord Mincham's lover. With the power that gave him, he was only prepared to tolerate Esmond's superiority whilst her father continued to create the roles which were winning Culpepper the reputation of a rival to Edward Alleyn.

She sat next to Esmond throughout the rehearsal, whispering to him any defects in an actor's presentation which his poor sight had failed to detect.

During their walk home, he said solemnly, 'I had not realised how difficult Culpepper makes your work with the troupe. You are my eyes, Gabby. My inspiration. There would be no troupe without you. You were right to berate me this morning. By my absences I am failing those who look to me both as employer and friend. I will mend my ways.'

'I'll not fail you, Father. Or those who need me.' His words made worthwhile the effort it had cost her to swallow her pride and be pleasant to Culpepper.

The lines were produced and Lord Mincham was delighted with the performance. Six weeks later the troupe was summoned to perform at Court for the yearly celebration of the Queen's accession to the throne. Gabriellen, as a woman, was excluded from the performance at Whitehall.

'No one deserves more than you to be there, Gabby,' Esmond said as he prepared to leave for Court.

Her father's praise was accolade enough. She patted her rounded stomach. 'I am eight months gone with child. My figure would be an affront to our barren Queen.' A bright smile hid her disappointment.

The Miscreant's Tale was highly acclaimed by Queen Elizabeth, and the troupe talked of nothing else for weeks. It frustrated Gabriellen that though she had become the driving force behind every production, she would never achieve any credit for her work. Unwilling to forsake her life with the players, she mastered her disappointment and philosophically accepted that her achievements must remain a secret.

In the first week of December, Jack returned to England. A month later Ambrose was born. His cap of tawny hair was all Gabriellen's, as were his green eyes as they changed from their baby darkness. If Jack had any reservations about the child's parentage he did not show them and accepted him readily as his own.

Summer of 1592 brought the plague to London. The playhouses were closed and the players forced once more to take to the road to make a living. Lord Mincham's Men were no exception. Culpepper deserted them to spend the plague months in luxury with Lord Mincham on his estate in Derbyshire. The players decided to journey west for the St James's Day Fair at Bristol. Since Jack was once more at sea, Gabriellen went with them.

Without their leading actor, Robin Flowerdew abandoned his dresses to take the lead. Will Appleshot, confident now after four years as an apprentice with the troupe, took the female parts. Though Gabriellen hungered to be a part of the play, she agreed with her father that it would be courting danger. Instead she was given the task of adapting the plays to fit the special skills of the younger actors.

No longer having to endure Culpepper's barbed tongue, the apprentices became daily more confident and accomplished. It was a carefree season for the company, albeit short-lived.

Winter brought no respite from the plague and they took up residence in Chichester. Those who wished visited relatives and the troupe was disbanded until the spring. For any who wished to remain there was always room in the Angels' household. To Gabriellen's delight, Jack on his return to England took a month away from Court to visit them. The following spring, with the playhouses still closed, the troupe again travelled the country, and Jack continued to gain fame and fortune from his exploits at sea.

The players were not so fortunate. Each month the takings grew less. Fear of plague kept people away – a fear that was brought home to the players one September evening at dusk as they approached a large Berkshire village.

The bridge across the river leading to the village was blocked with people. Many held pitchforks and scythes, others carried flaming torches.

'Get back!' A blacksmith in his leather apron, his shirt sleeves rolled back over huge muscled arms, stood squarely in front of the first wagon. 'You're not welcome here.'

Esmond stood up and passed the reins to Gabriellen who was seated beside him. 'Good sir, we are Lord Mincham's players, come to entertain you at your annual fair.'

'There'll be no fair here this year. Get you gone!' The blacksmith brandished a weighty hammer menacingly. 'It's vagabonds and the likes of you who would bring the plague to our village.'

Esmond smiled and spread his arms as though to encompass the whole of the crowd within his reassurance. 'We have not been within fifty miles of a plague victim in months. Our play is a comedy. It will cheer you in these sorry times.'

'It will take us to our graves.' The blacksmith stood his ground.

An angry murmuring broke out behind him as a puritan preacher pushed his way through the crowd. ''Tis the judgement of the Almighty that those who indulge in lewdness and idolatry shall be cast into the pit of Satan. Repent, sinners!'

Esmond drew himself up, his hand placed imperiously

over his heart in a pose he favoured when he played King Arthur. 'We are honest, law-abiding players. We have been fêted by our most august Majesty. Stand aside and allow us to pass. The playbills have been posted and a play there shall be.'

The blacksmith drew back his lips, showing pointed black teeth. 'The first man to try and cross this bridge ends up in the river.'

'Hold tight, Gabby,' Esmond ordered. 'No ruffian will stop me performing once a play has been billed.'

'Father, perhaps you should reconsider?' She turned a worried face towards him. She was nearly eight months pregnant with her second child and the crowd had the look of a mob bent upon murder. 'These are no ruffians, but well-dressed, respectable members of the village. Clearly they fear the plague. They are desperate people.'

'Lily-livered cowards, more like,' he snorted in disgust.

The villagers' angry voices became louder as they moved forward. The orange flames of the torches threw their frightened faces into relief. Their eyes were staring and malevolent, their hatred awesome in the gathering darkness.

She peered around the covered side of the wagon and gestured to Lacey, who was driving the other wagon, to swing around. Turning back to Esmond, she reasoned, 'Father, this is no time to argue. We can make camp on the rise we passed a mile back.'

Even as she spoke a young man who was unarmed picked up a stone and hurled it at them, shouting, 'Get out of here. You're not wanted.'

'Piss off!'

'Plague carriers!'

'Vagabonds! Rogues!'

Other began to chant abuse and throw stones. The first attack acted as a spur. Amidst gruesome shouts they charged, the metal scythes and pitchforks glinting evilly in the torchlight.

Gabriellen bit back a scream. Their horses began to prance, catching the aura of fear and menace from the villagers. Esmond flicked the whip across their backs and started to turn the wagon around. A hail of stones clattered off its side and a sharp flint cut Gabriellen's hand. The frightened horses were difficult to control and Esmond hauled on the reins as the wagon lurched precariously over the uneven ground at the side of the road. There was a clatter of dislodged pans and a thud of falling furniture in the sleeping quarters inside. At the first jolt which jarred her body, Gabriellen gripped the wagon's sides, terror overtaking her for the safety of her unborn child. She could feel the perspiration break out along her spine and her rapid heartbeat was stifling. She had miscarried one child. Dear God, let it not happen again.

The mob surrounded them, screaming abuse. The scene on the road became a macabre nightmare as Esmond turned the wagon away from the crowd. It careened from side to side dangerously as he struggled to stop the horses from bolting. Twice Gabriellen was roughly jolted, her body bumping down hard as it contacted the wooden seat. The sound of the shouting gradually grew fainter as the three wagons sped away. The ordeal was harrowing and was to become the first of several such instances as fear of the plague spread through England.

That night Gabriellen went into premature labour. At dawn her daughter Jacquetta was born, tiny but perfect, and with a surprisingly lusty wail for an infant born before its time.

During the next year there was little money taken at performances. Had it not been for the money sent from London by Esmond's business associate, they would have starved. There had been no word of Prew since he had fled England and all his property had been confiscated by the crown. That had not troubled Gabriellen. She wanted no reminders of her life with the merchant, refusing even to bear his name. Both her children had been recorded in the Parish registers and baptised with the surname Angel. Throughout the difficult days, Esmond refused to allow the troupe to be disbanded. Somehow there was always just enough money to keep them together.

For three years the plague raged. When eventually Lord Mincham's Men returned to London in the spring of 1595, they were almost destitute.

Chapter Thirty

Finances, or the lack of them, were a constant worry to Gabriellen in the following months. Lord Mincham had been generous, but three years' closure and neglect had taken its toll of the playhouse. Most of the thatch had been lost in a storm, and house martins had colonised the upper gallery.

The most horrific experience of their return was at Bankside. They arrived at the rented house to discover it had been looted of all their possessions. The discovery of five skeletons in an upper room made Gabriellen flee to the garden to be sick. Three of the skeletons were of children – plague victims. Their remains were burned but Nan, Agnes and the apprentices refused to live in the house again, and another property was found closer to the river.

Once the playhouse reopened, the players' fortunes turned. After three years of fear of the plague, the citizens of London were eager for diversion. Every performance played to capacity audiences and slowly their coffers began to refill.

Best of all was Esmond's improved health. Fortunately the blindness which he had for so long feared had been slow in overtaking his sight. More heartening still was that he had kept free of debt since Gabriellen's marriage to Prew. She knew her father blamed himself for the horrors of that ordeal. It was a part of her life she chose to forget. There had been no word of Prew, except that he was suspected of living on the Continent. Occasionally she awoke, sweating and shaking, from a nightmare where he was back in England. It was her greatest fear. Her husband was too evil and vindictive not to want vengeance upon her family.

Deliberately, she turned her thoughts from him. There were other matters which worried her and were more pressing. Jack showed no signs of curbing his own extravagance.

He had started to build a house on the land he owned near Chelsea, proclaiming himself to the world a man of status and a favoured courtier. In the meantime, when not at Court or sea, he stayed with Gabriellen at Bankside, spending a fortune on the fine clothes needed for Court. The support of his family in York further drained his resources, not that Gabriellen begrudged his children anything. She had fallen in love with Jack because he was so like her father. Alas, he was often too like Esmond for her peace of mind.

Jack laughed her fears aside, confident that the means were always at hand to recoup their losses. Walsingham, Christopher Hatton, even Drake were dead. Raleigh was in disgrace – first consigned to the Tower for marrying Bess Throckmorton, the Queen's maid-of-honour, and then shunned after a voyage to colonise Guiana resulted in failure. The way was open for a wily diplomat or a bold adventurer to aim high.

Not that anyone could topple Jack's friend the Earl of Essex from the Queen's favour. And for that, Gabriellen was grateful. It was selfish, she knew, but the greater the popularity Jack achieved at Court, the less she saw of him. Ambition ruled him. To that end he allowed nothing to stand in his way. He did not even see that it had begun to erode their love. Gabriellen suppressed her sighs. She had known Jack's faults when she left Wales with him.

England was still at war with Spain though engagements were sporadic. When the creditors became too pressing, Jack obtained Letters of Marque. These ventures were profitable to both the Queen and him, and kept him in favour at Court. Gabriellen saw only the danger to his life, but her pleas for him to give up the sea were in vain. He thrived on the glory it brought him. He never returned to England without his holds being full of Spanish treasure. People now recognised him and shouted his name in the streets. But Her Majesty was too astute openly to bestow rank or position upon a man the Spanish regarded as a pirate.

It was rank and position he coveted most.

In early March he had sailed with his three ships to patrol the Atlantic and engage any Spanish galleon separated from its convoy. By ill fate, during Jack's voyage Calais came under threat from the Spanish fleet. At Easter Essex sailed with one hundred and twenty ships to attack them. Calais was saved and the English pursued the retreating Spanish. On 20 June the entire Spanish fleet was destroyed at Cadiz and the city taken. Later Jack learned that Essex had knighted sixty-eight of his followers. Jack returned from the Atlantic a month later, the Spanish treasure ship he had captured a poor recompense for the lost opportunity of the knighthood he desired.

'By God's Holy Passion!' he had raved on his return to Bankside. 'What devil's misadventure put me on the other side of the world when Essex sailed into battle? Christ's nails, I should have been there!'

'The Spanish ship brought you £10,000 and you think yourself ill-used?' Gabriellen responded hotly, hurt that after three months at sea, their reunion was spoilt by his surly mood.

'I expected more support from you.' Jack stormed out in a rage. It was their first quarrel since leaving Wales, and though they quickly made up, Jack's attitude had shown her the cracks appearing in their relationship.

Upon Essex's return, the Earl had become the darling of the people and Jack spent more time than ever at Court or Essex House.

Gabriellen picked up a quill to work out her frustration in a new play. For an hour the parchment remained blank before her staring eyes. Inspiration failed her. Esmond was so busy running the troupe and rehearsals that he relied on her to write most of the plays, his praise of her accomplishments lavish. Every morning she still attended the rehearsals to be his eyes, but Culpepper remained antagonistic if he suspected any direction came from her.

She had proved she could write successful plays but it was no longer enough. A part of her remained unfulfilled. Jack was not there often enough to share her successes. She sighed. Jack was simply not there often enough . . . Their passion was as fierce as ever, but he was allowing his ambition to take precedence and Gabriellen found this increasingly hard to bear. Twice a year he visited York to see his children and ensure his gem business remained secure.

Fool! she upbraided herself. Be grateful for what you have. A man who loves you and has given you two wonderful children. Who has become estranged from his family because of you. It was her latest pregnancy which was making her feel melancholy.

Jack laughed aside her fears that they were growing apart. 'I fell in love with your impetuousness, your lack of convention. But you were a young woman then. This obsession you have with the players is not natural. You are a matron of five and twenty with two children, and bearing another. You tax yourself with the troupe's problems and wear yourself out with this foolish writing of plays.'

In a moment of loneliness and discontent, she found her mind returning to her stay in Wales. Jack had never understood her as Mark had. She missed her friend. There was no one to tease her in the way that he had, or to debate points of history or philosophy as they had done in Wales. But that time had been a midwinter madness, a time stolen from their real lives. The disloyalty of her straying thoughts made her bow her head.

She had heard from Mark only once since she had left Wales. He had sent a groom with a gift last New Year, a mare sired by Cadwallader and named Ceridwen after the Welsh goddess of poetic inspiration. All the accompanying note had said was:

> The Baron's Hall is completed. Accept Ceridwen in memory of a dream.

The ambiguity of those words had stayed with her. The note had been burned before Jack returned and the arrival of Ceridwen explained as repayment of a loan. Jack had not questioned it, as he had never questioned her about her stay in Wales. For her part she tried not to dwell on it. But there were times when memory resurrected the pain of their parting, and she would yearn for word or sight of Mark. When she walked the streets of London she found herself searching the crowds, knowing that it was a dark curly head she sought, the sound of a lilting Welsh voice she pined to hear. Whether by design or deliberation, she never saw him.

She shook her head to clear her wayward thoughts. It was Jack's lengthening absences which were making her restless and discontent, but she was wrong to blame his ambition. She had always known how it drove him. It was her heavy body which made her feel both restless and

471

unattractive. Once the child was born in a few weeks, she would feel different. Had not Jack promised that in another year, two at the most, he would give up the sea? It had given him the fame he craved, and once his house at Chelsea was finished, there would not be such a drain on his fortune. Though his popularity grew, he still craved the knighthood which eluded him. Nor had he won a permanent position at Court. The Queen took pleasure in his company and valued his success as a privateer too much to give him a secure post which would allow him to leave the sea. There was also his partnership with her father which both men were infuriatingly evasive about. Knowing both had past links with the Underworld, she hoped the venture was legal.

She dragged her mind back to the new play which was refusing to take shape. Earlier she had finished copying up Esmond's dictation but this was her own play, her fifth written without Esmond's help, but which of course was accredited to her father's name.

Uninspired, she went out into the garden. It was late summer, over a year since their return to London. She dabbed at her neck with a handkerchief dampened with rosewater. Her gown had a high standing collar instead of a ruff and its neck was cut low, but the heat was still overwhelming. She sat on a stone bench under a willow tree and held out her hands as Jacquetta got up from playing ball with Agnes and toddled towards her.

Ambrose and Laurence were quarrelling. Moments earlier they had been chasing each other across the garden with wooden swords, playing at pirates. Laurence, at eight, was a lively blond-haired boy, always into mischief. Ambrose spurred him on, forever at his side, no matter the danger or recklessness of their games. Now Ambrose was bending over a wall, shouting at Barnaby the cat. There was a blur of black and white as Barnaby ran up a tree, his white face glaring down through the leaves. When Ambrose straightened, Gabriellen saw he had a bird in his hand. Holding it carefully, he ran to her.

'Mama, it's a young owl with a broken wing. Say I can keep it and make it well?' His green eyes shone with excitement. 'Bodkin won't be any trouble.'

Gabriellen summoned the maid to take Jacquetta into the house and stood up, putting her hands to the small of her back to ease its aching. In the next week or two she would be brought to childbed.

She smiled at Ambrose. 'So he has a name already? Bodkin. It suits him.' She laughed at the eagerness in Ambrose's face and studied the owl. 'It is old enough to survive away from its mother. But you must feed it and care for it yourself.'

She touched a curl of her son's corn-gold hair. He never could resist helping an injured animal. His colouring was hers, but he had a way of smiling which tugged at her heart.

When the boys ran off, Agnes seated herself at Gabriellen's side. 'Thee look tired. Thee spend too long shut in Esmond's study, writing. Was that a messenger from thy captain who arrived earlier? Is there to be another place at dinner, or is he still at Court?'

Gabriellen leaned her head back and allowed the sun to play over her face. She sighed. 'Jack is with the Earl of Essex at his house in Wanstead. The Earl has quarrelled with the Queen and retired from Court in one of his famous sulks.' She laughed softly. 'Essex is very sure of his hold over the Queen. No other man at Court dares to speak his mind as he does. Always after a period, when her Majesty's moods are said to be at their worst, she forgives him and orders him back to her side. One day, surely, he will go too far.'

'Meanwhile the captain could have no more influential friend at Court,' said Agnes.

That was where the trouble lay. 'Jack wants power. The Queen may deny Essex nothing for himself, but she refuses to give his friends the posts he seeks for them. It is almost as though she fears he will gain too much power.' She smiled, lightening the mood. 'I expect Jack to return in a few days. Did you know that his son John, who stayed with us last winter, is now a page in the Earl's household? Apparently he's well liked by Essex, and Jack is convinced John will rise high.'

'With his father's charm,' Agnes responded, 'how can he fail?'

Gabriellen hid her misgivings. She had met Essex several times when he had visited The Angel. He was charming, courteous, and had won the hearts of all the players. Yet there was something about his friendliness which made

Gabriellen uneasy. It was the look in his eyes which was disturbing. It was as yet just a spark, but it heralded an instability which could ignite the torch of insanity, should that proud will be thwarted.

'Essex! Essex! God bless the Earl of Essex!'

Mark Rowan rode through the chanting crowds surrounding the Earl's house at Wanstead. Since Cadiz, Essex was undoubtedly the darling of the people, the only favourite of the Queen to ride so high in popular acclaim. Leicester had been too devious and aloof; Raleigh too clever and arrogant, so that at one time he was the most hated man in England. Essex was young, dashing, the epitome of chivalry. He courted the people, and for his pains they adored him. A perilous combination.

Mark felt a touch of unease for the young Earl. He had worked for Walsingham too long not to know the frisson of encroaching danger when he came across it. Throughout her reign, Elizabeth Tudor alone had roused her people's cheers. Vain to a fault, her jealousy was not a demon to rouse. She would tolerate no rival, Mark was certain. How long before she saw Essex's popularity as a threat?

The cheering crowds upset the young gelding Mark was leading. Halting Glendower, who had quietened in his advanced years, Mark shortened the gelding's rein and spoke softly to the horse. This was the second of Cadwallader's sons the Earl had added to his stables. The gelding was still skittish as they approached the stableyard and the head groom came out to greet them. Several falconers, with hooded hawks on their wrists, awaited the arrival of the Earl's hunting party. Within moments he and his companions appeared. Among the joking, boisterous men, Mark noticed Jack Stoneham.

At the same moment the gelding reared, frightened by the noise. Leaping to the ground, Mark pulled on the leading rein to bring the horse down on all fours. Snorting, the gelding was brought under control, a muscle flickering along his chestnut back as his agitation remained. He arched his neck and tail, displaying the perfection of his sleek body.

'So this is the gelding, Rowan?' Essex, magnificent in a jewelled doublet worthy of a king, walked round the horse. He nodded with satisfaction. 'A worthy animal. Those mar-

'kings and colouring will make him stand out in a crowd.'

'He is a fine animal and has the stamina to match, my lord,' Mark replied, adding ambiguously, 'He's fast enough to keep you at the head of the hunt.'

Essex tossed back his red hair, his eyes narrowing, suspicious of affront. Mark was no fawning purveyor of horseflesh seeking to ingratiate himself with the nobility. The Welshman returned his stare, with openness and respect. Essex liked that in a man. He smiled, subjecting Mark to the effortless charm which had won the hearts of so many Englishmen. 'Today the horse will rest. Tomorrow I shall put him to the test in the hunt. You will join us, I hope, Rowan?'

'I would be honoured, my lord.'

The Earl moved away and as Mark prepared to remount Glendower, Jack came to his side. They studied each other, assessing, guarded. Then Jack smiled. 'It's been a long time, Mark. We were friends for many years. I'd not like what happened in Wales to come between us.'

'How is Ellen?' It was deliberate provocation, but Jack's smile did not waver. 'She's well. And so involved with the players you would think she was their manager, not Esmond.'

'If any woman could carve herself a place in a man's world, it would be Ellen.' Mark ran his hand down Glendower's nose, needing a moment away from Jack's stare to control his emotions. The letter she had written thanking him for Ceridwen had been brief. The birth of her children now bound her irrevocably to Stoneham.

Jack hesitated, then with a steely glitter in his eye, suggested: 'Tomorrow Essex has invited you to hunt. Afterwards, why not join us for a meal with the players?'

'That cannot be,' he answered quickly – too quickly. Much as Mark wanted to see Ellen, it was better he did not. For five years they had gone their separate ways. 'My stay in London is short. I have much to do before I return to Wales.'

'It is not like you to ignore old friends. If I return without you, Gabriellen will bombard me with questions. She speaks of Aphra with great affection. And there are the children.' Jack saw Mark's expression tighten and pursued his advantage ruthlessly. 'Our eldest, Ambrose, is into one scrape after another. Gabriellen despairs he has inherited the wildness of Wildboar Tom. But for all that, he's a clever lad, quick-witted and always full of questions.'

'Ambrose is an uncommon name.'

There was a strange light in Mark's eyes which Jack met with defiance. 'Gabriellen chose it. When he's eight, Essex has agreed to take him as a page in his household. With his sharp wits, he'll soon find favour at Court. Though the scamp has no thought in his head but to be a great sea captain. It's in the blood, I suppose.'

Mark did not miss the challenge in those words. 'How old is he?'

'Four,' Jack said summarily, his attention taken by a tall dark-haired page who was approaching. He beckoned to the lad. The likeness between the two was unmistakable. Jack put a hand on the boy's shoulder. 'This is John, my second eldest by Elizabeth.'

Mark looked at the page. He was the image of Jack, tall for his age, with clear grey eyes which sparkled with a hunger to experience everything life had to offer. That same light had burned brightly in Jack's eyes when Mark had first met him. It did not escape his attention that a dairy maid hovered by the buttery door, watching John. Already women noticed the youth. He would be another adventurer. 'He is a fine lad, Jack. You must be proud of him.'

'York was no place for the lad. His mother would have ruined the boy. You like it here, do you not, John?'

'I do indeed, Papa. His lordship has promised that the next time he sets sail, he will take me with him.'

A shadow darkened Jack's face. 'God willing, I shall be in England also to sail with him. Go about your duties, John. I will speak with you later.' He watched the boy as he disappeared into the kitchens. 'I admit he's my favourite. He fears nothing. Talks have begun for his marriage to the heiress of Sir William Trenault. A goodly match. I've been fortunate in my children. But what of you, Mark? Surely by now you've snapped up some wealthy heiress?'

'No. I have been too busy with the restoration of the house. Jesmaine would never settle in Wales. She came to stay for six months whilst the plague was at its height, but she has little love of horses and isolation.'

'You still see the fortune-teller?'

'When I'm in London.'

'Do you continue to serve Walsingham?'

476

Mark nodded. Jack was the only man he trusted with the secret of his double life. 'How can I desert the service of Her Majesty whilst her enemies continue to plot against her?'

'After the hunt tomorrow, come to The Angel with me. One of Gabriellen's plays is being performed – under Esmond's name of course.'

To refuse would appear churlish and whatever Mark's misgivings, he did want to see Gabriellen again.

The next day Mark witnessed the full extent of Essex's popularity. Everywhere the Earl appeared people ran to cheer him. It was like a royal progress. But though the people might proclaim him the hero of Cadiz, Her Majesty did not. She had been furious that King Philip's treasure ships, which had been anchored in Cadiz harbour, had been burnt and sunk, rather than fallen into English hands. 12,000,000 ducats had been lost to the English crown and Elizabeth, ever aware of the stupendous cost of war, had fumed at the depletion of her coffers. Stung by what she saw as the Queen's injustice, Essex had been equally scathing in his reply. Their quarrel had been swift and violent.

For weeks the Earl paced the corridors of his home, his moods erratic. Only when he ventured abroad and the people showed their love for him did he shrug off his melancholy. During the hunt, he had been delighted at the stamina of his new gelding. The chase had raised his spirits.

'Who will wager that Gloriana will be dancing upon my arm before the week is out?' he declared exuberantly. 'She will not deny herself my company.'

Upon their return to Wanstead, the Queen's messenger was awaiting them.

'Do you not fear that Essex will one day go too far?' Mark asked Jack as they rode towards Bankside.

'The Queen loves him. Look how she summoned him back to Court.'

'Has it not occurred to you that she may fear his popularity?' Mark said gravely. 'Better to have your enemy playing the lapdog at your feet, than poised with a knife at your back. How long before someone plays upon Essex's conceit – suggests he could be king?'

Jack saw that Mark was serious and frowned. 'Such talk is treason. Essex is no fool. The Queen is besotted by him.'

'Elizabeth Tudor is besotted by her own Majesty. She is sixty-six and will not even name a successor,' Mark reasoned. 'Why do you think that is?'

'Because she wants to keep Jamie Stuart of Scotland sweating on his inheritance,' said Jack. 'She'll play this like she played the marriage field. She thrives on keeping everyone guessing. That way she is fawned upon for her favour. That's what comes of having a woman on the throne.'

'She is a diplomat first – a woman second. Never forget that, Jack,' Mark warned. 'To name her successor would be to set up an opposing faction. Insurrection would challenge her authority. Essex is the balm to her advancing age. She uses him as she does the red wigs, the vast panniered gowns and wired veils which frame her figure. Beneath the glittering façade, the powder and paint which show a youthful face to the world, there is a wrinkled, ageing woman whose heart is of stone. Without compunction she will see Essex lose his head before she allows the crown to be put in peril.' Mark regarded Jack, his voice troubled. 'If Essex falls, his followers will go with him.'

'Your years in Walsingham's pay have made you sceptical.' Jack dismissed his words. 'Essex is harmless. Ambitious, I grant you. He needs to be, for his lands are mortgaged so heavily he's constantly in debt.'

They dismounted in the vicinity of The Angel and paid a waiting lad sixpence to look after their horses during the performance.

'And mind you look to their welfare,' Jack warned. 'I don't want to return to learn a prigger of prancers has made off with them. I'm a friend of One-eyed Ned, so guard them well if you value the skin on your back.'

'Yer 'orse be safe wi' me, Cap'n Stoneham,' the boy returned, his grimy face glowing with admiration. 'Yer ain't looking fer a cabin boy when next yer sail, is yer, cap'n?'

'Nay, lad. But give it a year or two and you'll be strong enough to sail with me.'

Jack turned away, laughing. 'There's scarce a week goes by when some lad does not want to join my crew.'

'It's a tribute to your reputation. You have become a hero, Jack,' Mark said with sincerity as they entered the playhouse.

He took his place on the lower gallery by the side of the

stage and from habit began to scan the crowd filling the playhouse. The wooden benches in the pit were already full, the occupants noisy as they shouted to make themselves heard above the clamour. An occasional fight broke out; ribald comments followed in the wake of hawkers of wine, nuts, apples and beer, constantly on sale throughout the afternoon. In the galleries there were more women present than in the years before the plague, but they were usually masked or veiled. He was disappointed that there was no sign of Gabriellen. He had expected her to be in the audience.

The trumpet sounded to announce the start of the play. As Esmond appeared as the Prologue, there was a disturbance in the gallery opposite Mark which caught his attention. A large man, masked and cloaked, elbowed his way to the front bench and sat down, staring with rigid intent at the stage. His stance was one of pure malevolence and from Mark's sharp eyes even the mask did not hide the fleshy features of Cornelius Hope. The intensity of the hatred which the actor levelled upon Esmond Angel disturbed him. Hope was no longer so popular as an actor. He remembered Gabriellen's account of his leaving the troupe and his vow of vengeance.

The play progressed to the cheers and accolades of the crowd, Cornelius Hope alone remaining aloof from the general acclaim. He looked apoplectic. In the intervening years, as Esmond's popularity rose and Hope's fell, his hatred had festered. Esmond must be warned, though Mark suspected that he would laugh that warning aside.

The play over, Mark conquered the turbulent emotions which the prospect of a reunion with Gabriellen roused in him. Nothing showed in his face but amiability as he chatted easily to Jack while entering the stableyard of the Angel household.

Giving the horses into the care of a stable-lad, Jack asked: 'Where's Mistress Gabriellen?'

'In the garden, captain.'

'This way,' he indicated with a sweep of his hand, and led Mark across the lawns which led down to the river.

When they stepped through a brick arch into the walled garden, Jack stood back. He studied Mark closely. There was a rigidity to the Welshman's jaw which was singularly revealing. Gabriellen was sitting on a wooden bench with her back to them. Jack was annoyed that she was simply dressed. She wore no farthingale beneath her lilac gown. She was not even wearing a headdress, though he admitted that her unbraided hair, turned to pale gold by the late afternoon sunlight as it waved down her back, was a charming sight. Laurence and Ambrose were sitting at her feet as she read to them. Ambrose, always too full of energy to sit still for long, was the first to see them.

'Papa!' He gave a delighted shriek and was on his feet, running towards him. Jack swung him up into the air, but his gaze remained upon Mark who was looking at the spot where Gabriellen sat. Jack's line of vision took in both figures. What he saw did not amuse him.

The cry from Ambrose had brought Gabriellen to her feet and she turned to greet him. When she saw their visitor, the book fell from her hands on to the grass. Mark had paled visibly. There was no mistaking the pain in his eyes as he saw the advanced state of Gabriellen's pregnancy. So he still loved her? Jack felt the old jealousy stir, though it was tempered by the grim certainty that Mark must be aching inside. No man could bear to look upon the woman he loved and see her carrying another's child. He should know. He had suffered that agony himself, not knowing whether Gabriellen carried his or Mark's child. Upon Ambrose's birth he had convinced himself that the boy was his son. Now let the Welshman suffer.

Lowering the boy to the ground, Jack saw Gabriellen quickly recover her composure, but her hands crossed in front of her as though she would hide her condition. Then, with an embarrassed laugh, she shook her head and came to greet them.

'Mark! What a surprise.' Pleasure made her eyes sparkle in a way Jack had not seen them do in months.

'You are looking radiant, Ellen.' Mark took her hand and raised it to his lips.

It was a circumspect enough greeting, but it sent a white-hot rage through Jack. He controlled it with difficulty. He'd been a fool to bring Mark here. Friendship could not survive their rivalry over a woman they both loved.

After those first brief moments of shock, Gabriellen took a grip on her emotions. 'So formal a greeting, Mark? After five years.' She laughed, and rising on tiptoe, lightly pressed a kiss on his cheek as she had so often done in the past.

Mark tensed at the touch and smell of her. Five years had not diminished his love for her. He curbed the need to take her into his arms, his voice even as he observed, 'The oldest boy must be Laurence. He has the look of Esmond about him.'

He nodded to Ambrose whom Jack had lifted on to his shoulders. 'And who may this young rascal be?'

'Rascal is right,' Gabriellen laughed, though her gaze dropped from Mark's as she added, 'My son Ambrose.'

'Your son indeed, Ellen, with that tawny mane and mischievous green eyes. A very English name.'

Her head came up, holding his gaze levelly. The silent question darkened his eyes to ebony. Her brow lifted, copying the mannerism he used to taunt her, especially about their nationalities. 'Yes, very English.'

There was no need for words. Mark knew, as Jack did not, that Ambrose was the English equivalent of Emrys. Was the boy *his* son? The colouring gave nothing away.

The strain of the next hours drained Gabriellen of energy. Jack never left her and Mark alone. The usual boisterous meal with the players over, the three of them withdrew to a small parlour to talk in more privacy. Throughout she could feel Jack watching them. The actress in her took command. She laughed, jested and questioned Mark about his family, his home and his horses. Jack said little, his expression masked as he sat back in his chair, twisting a large sapphire ring which had been given him by the Queen.

When Mark praised Gabriellen's latest plays which he had seen performed by Lord Mincham's Men at Chester earlier that summer, Jack cut across his remarks.

'Can you not reason with her about this playwriting nonsense? Esmond of course encourages her, but it is no light matter. The mob will turn on her should they learn they have been duped. Is that not so, Mark?'

'I write for my own amusement,' Gabriellen said softly, but the defiance was plain in her voice.

Jack turned an accusing stare upon Mark. 'You've always encouraged her in this unwomanly obsession she has to write. Tell her I speak the truth.'

'Ellen is a gifted storyteller. We Welsh appreciate that.' He looked across the table at her and smiled. 'Yet Jack is right. England is not ready to accept such talent from a woman's hand. One day it will happen – not too far in the future we must hope. Until then the world will be a sadder place without her plays.'

The tension between the three friends intensified. To relieve it, Gabriellen moved over to the virginals and began to play. Quite unwittingly she found herself playing the tunes Mark had sung in Wales. Aware that some devil of Jack's own summoning had made him bring Mark here at this time, she tried to soothe the discomfort Mark must be feeling. She played the tune to a song they had composed together during an afternoon when they had been housebound by a blizzard. At the opening chords Mark stood up and came to stand by her shoulder. He sang with such poignancy, his rich voice alone enough to thrill, let alone the memories it evoked. After they had composed the song they had made love in the library before the roaring fire.

During the song Jack had risen from his chair and crossed the room to lean on the edge of a desk, alternately watching them and rolling a pair of dice on the table. With each verse his expression became more thunderous. Regretting her indiscretion, Gabriellen's fingers jarred upon the notes. She stood up quickly, alarmed to find that she was shaking.

Jack was looking at her oddly. 'What ails you?'

She saw Mark put out a hand to steady her and moved out of his reach. His hand fell to his side. Too many memories had been evoked. These men, one friend, one lover, were both special to her. She did not want to hurt either of them. But she knew it was already too late for that. The knowledge tore at her conscience. 'Please forgive me.' Her voice was unsteady. 'I am weary and would retire.'

Before she had undressed Jack came into their bedchamber. 'What was that scene all about? As if I did not know.'

All evening she had tried to act as though everything was normal. She knew that Jack had wanted Mark to see her in her present condition, and was feminine enough to resent it. What better brand could a man put upon a woman than to parade her heavy with his child? Her swollen body made her ungainly; even her high cheekbones had disappeared as pregnancy had fleshed out her face and arms. She was pale and her hair had lost its lustre. Her restraint broke. A violent trembling seized her. Her emotions were torn asunder and she could find no peace. What devious form did Jack's love take that he must torment her like this?

She whirled round on him, her cheeks flushed with anger. This was not the powder keg temper of her youth which she had learned to govern over the years. Now she turned upon him with the chilling dignity of insight and lost ideals. 'The scene was of your making. You provided the setting. What did you expect from it? Or was it just to salve your pride?'

'Guilt makes you defensive. I know your tactics, Gabriellen.' Jack advanced on her, his fingers digging into her shoulders as he pulled her against him.

'Rather it is shame which makes me angry. Not at what I have done. I am ashamed that you forget the debt I owe Mark. Ashamed that for all the wrong reasons you brought him here. You played the wronged lover. Hypocrite! How innocent are you, Jack?'

A muscle twitched in his cheek as she went on. 'I suspect there was a woman involved in your escape from Spain. And what of your visits to York? You told me you were estranged from your wife, and I believed you. Have I ever questioned you further? Yet you brought Mark here not in friendship, but to flaunt your ascendancy over him. To prove how very much your woman I am. Such conduct is unworthy of you.' She turned away, anger leaving her drained of energy. 'Leave me, Jack. The hour is early. You have a guest to entertain.'

'He's left. Gone back to his beloved Jesmaine. He's leaving for Wales at the end of the week and asked me to say his goodbyes for him.'

'You brought him here, then allow him to go without a farewell? That was despicable.'

'Would you rather he had stayed and we had duelled?' His grey eyes bored into hers. 'Don't be so naive. It would have come to that. Mark and I both knew it. You're mine, Gabriellen. I'll not give you up. I'll kill Rowan if he tries to take you from me.'

'There is no question of that, Jack.'

'I'm glad to hear it, else he would be a dead man.'

Despite her ungainly bulk she launched herself at him, striking his chest with her fists. 'Mark saved my sanity in Wales. I'm carrying our third child, Jack. What further proof do you need of my love?'

He caught her wrists and held her away from him. 'But

you refuse to live with me. I built the house at Chelsea for you, Gabriellen.'

'At Chelsea I would be just your housekeeper. Here I am needed by many. That does not mean I love you less.'

'Does it not? I saw the way you looked at Rowan, and he you . . . the man is in love with you.'

'You are being absurd. Jealousy does not suit you, Jack.'

'Absurd, am I!' The scar above his beard was white from anger. 'Stay here with your precious players. I'm off to where my company is better appreciated.'

He marched from the room, slamming the door as he left.

Gabriellen stared at the closed portal in disbelief. Then, hurt and disillusioned by Jack's callousness, she flung herself down on the bed and wept.

A week later Sabine was born. Esmond sent word to Jack at Court. It was another week before, pale and contrite, he visited Gabriellen.

The subject of Mark's visit and their quarrel was never raised, but it lay between them.

Chapter Thirty-One

Over the next two years Jack witnessed the popularity of the Earl of Essex rise and wane in the royal favour. Foolhardy pride and arrogance were his downfall. His boldness and daring provided his anchor at Court, and he was appointed Earl Marshal of England. But his outspokenness in Council, persistently contradicting the Queen, came to a head when they were discussing the appointment of a new Lord Deputy for Ireland. In a fit of rage Essex turned his back upon Elizabeth, the grossest of all insults. In retaliation she boxed his ears before the councillors, screaming at him, 'Go and be hanged.'

With a loud oath Essex rounded on her, his sword drawn, shouting, 'This is an outrage. I would not have borne such an insult from your father's hand.'

Whilst he was forcibly restrained by the Lord Admiral, the Queen regarded him in deathly silence. A sword drawn in anger against the Sovereign was treason. The Council waited for Elizabeth to order his arrest. The guards were not called and Essex wrenched himself from the Lord Admiral's hold. He left the Council in a demented rage, storming from the palace to fuel his sense of injustice at Wanstead.

As the long months of impasse continued, Jack along with all of Essex's friends urged him to apologise to the Queen. Stubbornly, he refused.

'By God's son, I'm no lapdog like Leicester to run back to her with my tail between my legs,' Essex railed. 'I will not grovel to her. I'm the only man at Court to stand up to Elizabeth. She respects that.'

'Are you sure she does not resent it, my lord?' Jack pursued. 'Insults were hurled on both sides, but she is the Queen. It's been months, not merely weeks this time, and no word from Court. My friend, forget your pride. Go to Court.'

'Never!' Essex thumped the card table they were sitting at. With an oath he dashed the cards to the floor and stood up to pace the room. 'If you value my friendship, Stoneham, consider that an end to the matter.'

At that peremptory tone Jack felt his own temper rise. He controlled it. When Essex affected this chill arrogance, he assumed all the dignity of his Earldom. There was no reasoning with him at such times.

The rift between the Queen and the Earl Marshal of England was healed only when disaster struck her forces in Ireland. Two thousand English soldiers were routed at Blackwater by the rebel Earl of Tyrone's army. Ulster lay unguarded to the rebel forces and was laid waste in reprisals against the English. Upon hearing the news, Essex returned to Court with all speed, bound by his duty as Earl Marshal to offer his services to the Crown. He returned with the post of Lord Deputy of Ireland – the least sought after in England. Ireland was not only the graveyard of thousands of English soldiers, but that of lost reputations. Many worthy men had failed there and lost their lives, Walter Devereux, Essex's father, among them.

Jack sailed to Ireland with Essex in March 1599. For six months he was part of that inglorious venture, burning and pillaging. He saw, disheartened, that as many men died from dysentery, malaria and from the malignant humours of stinking, mist-shrouded bogs, as from battle wounds. Even his robust health suffered, but he finally won his coveted knighthood. Expressly against the Queen's orders, Essex knighted many of his followers. Sir Jack Stoneham . . . it sounded good to his ears.

The campaign failed, as had others before it. Robbed of victory, Essex negotiated a truce with Tyrone – against the Queen's explicit command.

It was the beginning of his downfall and that of any man rash enough to follow him blindly.

Gabriellen was at the playhouse which was eerily quiet after the audience had departed for the day. There was the creak of a floorboard and a fierce 'Shush' from a group of apprentices as they crept past the rows of costumes in the tiring-house, intent on avoiding her vigilant eye.

'Where are you three off to?' Gabriellen emerged from the far side of the costumes to cut off their retreat. In her hand were three brooms. 'The galleries have yet to be swept.'

She grinned to herself as they went off muttering, but by the time they reached the stage she could hear their laughter and the thud of wooden sticks as they enacted a mock battle with the broom handles. She turned to Nan as they hung up the last of the costumes, having checked them for damage. 'You'd better let out these straining seams,' she said, holding out a red doublet worn by Will Appleshot. 'Since Will discovered the joys of the ale-pot, his waist is thickening.'

Nan laughed. 'Regular rakehell, that young man has become. By the way, have you seen the King's crown? When the scene finished Lacey must have left it on the balcony at the rear of the stage again.'

'I'll fetch it.' Gabriellen climbed the stairs to collect it. As she picked up the brass crown there was a disturbance from the entrance to the pit.

The youngest apprentice stopped his sweeping to lean over the upper gallery and shout: 'Look, it's Cap'n Stoneham, returned from Ireland.'

Gabriellen held on to the balcony rail, her heart beating faster. Had Jack returned? She waited expectantly for his figure to emerge from the shadows. There was no mistaking that confident stride. She paused upon seeing his travel-stained appearance. He was pulling off his riding gloves, his face splashed with mud and haggard with fatigue. Panic set her heart drumming. What save some dire catastrophe had brought him here at such a punishing pace? Then he turned, sensing her presence, and looked up. When their gazes met, her alarm faded. He stood unmoving, watching her with veneration as she came slowly down the stairs leading on to the stage. Then with impatient step he covered the space between them and she descended into his arms.

'My love, my darling heart.' He held her close. ''Tis good to be back. To breathe wholesome air and hold you again.'

There was a chorus of whistles from the apprentices in the galleries and with a smile Gabriellen drew Jack into the privacy of the tiring-house. Nan had tactfully disappeared. Once they were alone Gabriellen wrapped her arms around him, unmindful after six months of parting that he smelt of horses and sweat. To her surprise she felt him trembling. His eyes closed against his weariness. He was near exhaustion.

'Whatever is wrong, Jack? Come back to the house. I'll give Nan the keys. She can lock up here.'

Within moments she was back with him and they made the short journey to the riverbank house. 'You look as though you've been riding all night,' she said anxiously as he rested an arm heavily upon her shoulders. 'Is Seth Bridges not with you?'

'Still not embarked from Ireland. Essex took a fit to see the Queen.' Jack's step slowed as his energy fast drained from him.

In the parlour Cesare looked up from restringing his guitar. '*Buon giorno, Capitano*. Eh, Umberto, the capitano, he return,' he called to his cousin who appeared in the doorway of the next room. Poggs was with him.

'Back from the wars, Stoneham.' The clown grinned. 'What news?'

Umberto put a hand on Poggs's shoulder. '*Silenzio*, Poggs! The capitano look dead to his feet. He rest now, talk later. *Si*?'

Jack nodded gratefully.

Agnes bustled in carrying a tray containing a flagon of brandy and some cold meats. 'I'll put these in your room, Miss Gabby. The cap'n looks like he's not slept in days.'

Jack's exhaustion showed in the willing way he allowed himself to be led to the stairs.

Poggs called after them, 'Good to have you back safely, cap'n.'

As they mounted the stairs he put an arm around Gabriellen's shoulders and leaned heavily upon her, his voice slurring with the effort it cost him to speak. 'It's good to be back. But there's trouble ahead.' He paused on the landing to kiss her. '*Certes*, I missed you, Gabriellen.'

He swayed and they laughed together at his weakness. 'Something serious has happened to make you push yourself so hard,' she said as they entered the chamber and Jack sank down on to the bed. He ran a hand through his windswept hair. 'Serious indeed. Essex had heard his enemies were speaking against him at Court. Ireland was a débâcle. Summoning a few of his friends, the Earl sailed

488

for home. He forced us to ride, sparing neither man nor beast, for a day and a night until we reached Nonsuch Palace. We did not even stop for food.'

Gabriellen pressed a goblet of brandy into his hand and he drank a large draught whilst she pulled off his boots. The drink revived him and with a grin he pulled her into his arms. But his embrace was too weary and troubled for passion.

'I waited for him in an ante-chamber at Nonsuch in case Elizabeth refused to see him.' Jack's hold upon her waist tightened as though he needed the reassurance of holding her to obliterate the dread which hounded him. 'Essex was like one deranged. He did not even stop to wash or change his clothes. Pushing aside the guards, he rushed through the presence chamber, the privy chamber, and in desperation burst unannounced into her rooms. I had a glimpse of Elizabeth seated at her dressing table as her women prepared her for the day.' He wiped a sleeve across his gaunt face, his grey eyes grim. 'For a moment I thought that reckless deed would see him sent to the Tower. Without her wig and paint, she looked so – so incredibly old, a wrinkled, balding crone. Before the door closed I saw him fling himself on his knees, entreating her to listen to his reasons for leaving his post.'

Gabriellen sat on the edge of the bed and took Jack's hand as he lay back. 'And did she forgive him?' she asked, appalled, her fears all for him, not the brash and foolhardy Essex.

'Apparently so. He's to attend her later today. He was jaunty enough when I left, bragging of her kindness to him.'

Gabriellen stared into Jack's tired face. 'She will not forgive him for seeing her without her finery. Her vanity is too great. And did he not desert his command against her orders? I pray her wrath will escape you.'

His eyes were drooping with tiredness as he murmured, 'Have you no kiss for me? No kiss for Sir Jack Stoneham?'

'Oh, Jack, I am delighted that you received your knighthood!' She kissed him ardently. His lips parted in brief response, then his hands slackened about her waist and his even breathing told her he was asleep. She smiled down at him and touched his bearded jaw. The months of deprivation had fined the flesh from his cheeks. Heartrendingly, he looked as he had when first she had met him. How fierce her love for him had been all those years ago – like a blazing comet. Eleven years. How quickly they had flown. Like all comets her love had a long and searing tail, which still burned undimmed at moments such as this.

Loosening Jack's doublet and removing his swordbelt from his waist, she stood over his sleeping form. She could not shake the fear from her mind that Essex had over-reached himself. Not only had he disobeyed the Queen's commands, but he had dared to burst in upon her, exposing the disabilities of her sixty-six years. How could that young hot-head have hidden his disgust in time? No, the Queen would never forgive him. Gabriellen shivered in the chill morning light. By God's Holy Mercy, let Jack be spared.

She went to the window, her body cold, not from the river mist which lay over the gardens, but from dread. If Essex fell from favour, it would touch any who had befriended him.

Jack slept the clock around. It was late in the afternoon when Esmond returned to the house, his expression troubled from the rumours which were spreading through the capital. Essex was under guard in his own lodging, to await a summons before the Council Chamber in disgrace. The charges were disobedience, contemptuous disregard of his duty by instigation of an ignoble truce, and desertion of his command.

The next morning when Jack returned to Court, the guard crossed their halberds, barring his admittance. He was escorted to an ante-chamber. After he had endured three hours of anxious pacing, a clerk appeared. On the orders of the Council Jack was dismissed from Court for the duration of the Queen's pleasure.

On hearing the news on his return to Bankside, fear clutched at Gabriellen's heart. What would happen next?

Esmond surveyed the wooden circle of The Angel play-house with satisfaction. It was good to be back in London. The months on the road had been profitable but he was getting too old for the wandering life. He rubbed his thick-ening girth, content with his present circumstances. The last years had been good to him financially. The players were a close-knit band and even Culpepper had mellowed. His role as Lord Mincham's lover assured him of a superior

490

status within the company. Only occasionally now did he ridicule his companions to feed his own self-importance. Esmond enjoyed a moment of complacency. Even his home life was settled. Nan remained his helpmeet and bedfellow. And young Laurence . . . He smiled at thoughts of his son. The boy was his delight. A sturdy lad, full of devilment, and a true Angel. Fate seemed at last to have smiled on him, Esmond decided.

The only shadow on the horizon was his eyesight. He had been spared blindness for longer than he had expected. Unfortunately, this last year his sight had noticeably deteriorated.

This winter in London would further augment his coffers. The citizens were hungry for plays and Lord Mincham's Men would not disappoint them. With Richard Greene dying in 1592 of a surfeit of Rhenish wine and pickled herrings, so it was said, and Christopher Marlowe killed last year in a tavern fight, the name Angel was proclaimed as that of London's leading playwright. A glorious accolade, Esmond was proud to admit, even though it was the genius of his daughter's pen which brought it such renown. Of course there were rivals emerging to take Kit Marlowe's place, his old friend Will Shakespeare for one. Having seen his *Henry VI* performed, Esmond had been one of the first to announce to its creator that it was a masterpiece. He had no doubt Shakespeare's would be a name to be remembered.

Today the players began rehearsal for Gabriellen's latest play, *The Impudent Rascal*. It was based on the most amusing and outrageous exploits which Esmond and Jack had related to her about their life in the Underworld.

Poggs ambled over carrying his copied out part, his freckled face split by a broad grin. 'This play must be our best yet.' He nodded towards the tiring-house where loud bursts of laughter could be heard from the other players. 'Do you hear them, Esmond? Not one of them has complained that their lines are too few. It's the wittiest and the sauciest play Gabby has written.' He laughed again. 'There's not one of them suspects its true writer. They believe you to be a genius, Esmond.'

Beneath the pride, there was a flicker of sadness in the playwright's eyes. 'By God's nightgown, I wish I'd written the piece! I'm proud of Gabriellen. 'Tis a mortal shame she's denied acclaim for her work.'

'Lord Mincham would be horrified,' said Poggs. 'And the same crowd who cheer this play believing it written by a man, would pillory her for a wanton or worse. Especially if it becomes common gossip that she is Stoneham's mistress. They'd like as not have her stripped and flogged through the town. It's unjust, hypocritical, downright absurd . . .' The clown began to work himself into a fury.

Esmond put a hand on his shoulder. 'I feel as you do. Gabriellen has a brilliant talent. It's a crime it cannot be acknowledged. Still, at least this way she can see her work performed. And she knows the praise is hers by rights.' He spread his arms wide to take in the playhouse. 'I've much to thank Gabriellen for.'

Poggs nodded. 'You're very close with your emotions, Esmond. It's about time you showed Gabby how much you appreciate her hard work.'

Esmond was taken aback. 'What the devil do you mean by that? I've nothing but love and admiration for her. After the play's opening I shall hold a banquet in her honour,' he responded, piqued that Poggs should criticise him. 'Now to work, my friend. Summon the players. The rehearsal will begin.'

The final rehearsal over, Esmond dismissed the players. As their voices receded, he looked up at the sky through the open roof. Even with his impaired vision he could appreciate the glorious scarlet sunset, heralding a fine day for tomorrow's performance. The shadows around him lengthened as he continued to stare upwards and slowly turned around to take in the entire circle of the playhouse. He visualised the scarlet flag overhead with its golden angel, unable to see it in the darkening gloom, and felt a glow of satisfaction.

Life had never seemed better than at that moment. Lord Mincham was a generous patron. Nell Lovegood's establishment thrived and had become one of the most popular bordellos in the capital. Esmond's coffers had never been so full. Given a successful year in London, he could afford to support his family even when he became blind. One more year was all he wanted. With the income from Nell Lovegood's, they could all live comfortably in Chichester.

He turned towards the entrance to the tiring-house where

a glimmer of light was visible. Where was Nan? Would she never finish her sewing? She worked too hard. Esmond smiled. He was very fond of the seamstress. He did not love her as he had loved Gabriellen's mother, but Nan was a great comfort in his middle age. He grinned to himself. It was even several months since he had been unfaithful to her, and it was a jolt to discover how important the woman had become to his happiness. Age had mellowed the rogue in him.

He chuckled. Why, he was almost respectable. And not before time! he could almost hear his sister Dorothy chide him. The memory of her momentarily saddened him, but he shrugged off his gloomy thoughts. Life was good to him now. Even his encroaching blindness he had come to accept with resignation. Though he had neglected his writing in recent years, he had several ideas for future plays, and Gabriellen was always willing to copy down his dictation. He was revered wherever he went, and knew that when his sight failed, there would always be a friend willing to escort him to Nell Lovegood's or a tavern for an evening of convivial entertainment and drinking.

There was no doubt in his mind that tomorrow the play would be a resounding success. Following that would be the banquet. He smiled, knowing how pleased Gabriellen would be at the surprise. Poggs had been right. He could not remember when he had last told his daughter that he loved her. It was remiss of him. Without Gabriellen he would be nothing. She had given him back his self-respect, saved him from debt and imprisonment. He touched the parchment inside his doublet. He had struggled painfully for two days with a poem he intended to dedicate to her. At the banquet tomorrow she would know the depth of his admiration and respect.

The darkness was almost total. Where was Nan? He called her name. There was no answer. He was standing in the centre of the playhouse, where the groundlings watched the performance. The open space was cluttered with carpentry trestles and wood. In the morning Francis Crofton would rig up the scaffolding to hold the special effects which were the highlight of the final act. Aware that he could stumble over them, Esmond picked up a torch from its sconce on the wall. Lighting it from his tinder box, he held it high and made his way to the tiring-room. The seamstress would sit up all night working on the costumes if he did not stop her.

He lifted the curtain by the side of the stage, and paused. There was no sign of Nan amongst the rails of costumes.

'Nan! It's late. What are you doing, woman?'

'A moment, Esmond.' Her voice came to him from the far side of the room. He lifted the torch the better to throw its light over a greater distance. Noticing the dim flickering of a candle, he moved impatiently towards it.

That the torch had touched against the gauze of one of Robin Flowerdew's long veils was hidden from his blurred sight. A snake of flame ran up the material towards the other costumes and licked at the curtain of the tiring-room itself.

Esmond found Nan sitting on a stool in an alcove behind the back of the stage. Her back was to him as she sat hunched over a cloak, sewing seed pearls on to it. He put his arm about her waist and stooped to kiss her cheek.

'Leave that, my dear. The players have gone home. If we do not leave now, Larry will be abed. I know how much you like to spend an hour with him in the evening.'

'But the cloak will not be ready in time,' she wailed.

'Bring it with you.' He kissed her brow. Unexpectedly he was overcome with the warmth of the emotion he felt for his mistress. 'You're a good woman. You've given me a fine son in Larry. Would that I could have married you and spared him the stigma of bastardy.'

'We both knew that was not possible.' Nan laid her cheek against his hand resting on her shoulder. 'What better family could Larry have than the players? They all adore him.'

Esmond sighed. 'I've been happy with you, Nan. I'd have married you if I could.'

'I know you would, my darling. I've no regrets.'

She reached up her hand to slide it about his neck and draw his head down for a kiss. Taking the cloak from her, Esmond pulled her to her feet. For a moment she looked into his face. Then her mouth opened in a choked cry of horror.

At the same time Esmond became aware of the smell of smoke and the crackle of flames. Whirling around, he saw the orange brightness at the other end of the room. Nan began to scream. A solid barricade of flame trapped them.

494

Its great tentacles reached out to speed along the wooden walls, devouring the costumes and the tinder-dry roof thatch in its voracious hunger. They were doomed. The only way out was through that advancing wall of flame.

'Don't let me burn,' Nan screamed. 'Dear God, don't let the flames get me!' She put her hands to her face, her voice a shriek of terror. 'Don't let me burn, I beg you, Esmond. Spare me! Sweet Jesu, spare me!'

She clung to him, hysterical and weeping. The inferno roared in his ears. His body was drenched in a stinging sweat. Esmond drew her head against his shoulder. Already the heat was singeing his hair.

'Christ have mercy on us!' The cry was torn from his lips as he unsheathed his dagger. The thickening smoke smarted in his eyes and clawed at his throat. With a quick upward thrust, he plunged the blade through Nan's ribs into her heart. Her weight sagged in his arms. It was a poor reward for her love and loyalty, but at least he had spared her the horror of being burnt alive.

Holding her tight, he buried his face in her hair. He felt the poem he had written to Gabriellen scratch against his chest. His daughter would never know how much he loved her.

He screamed as the first of the flames touched his back. 'Christ in His compassion, have mercy . . .'

Esmond fell to the floor, Nan still locked in his arms, as they were engulfed by the flames.

Chapter Thirty-Two

The tiny church of St Ethelburga in Bishopsgate was filled to overflowing for the funeral service. Even when the double coffin was borne outside into the London churchyard, Gabriellen was aware of the press of the crowd. She had not realised how popular and respected her father had become.

Upon going through his papers, Gabriellen had discovered that her mother had been buried at St Ethelburga's and it was with her that Esmond wished to be laid to rest. This had presented a dilemma. Horrifically, the fire had fused the two bodies together. It was a cruel twist of fate that even in death Esmond could not share Sabine's grave. Those entwined bodies locked in death would have desecrated the memory of his earlier love. By way of compromise he and Nan were laid to rest beside the grave of Sabine Angel. In the circumstances, Gabriellen believed that her mother would not be affronted. She prayed so. It had been hard to know what to do for the best.

Even the weather was irreverently unsuitable for the solemn occasion. It was a hot September day without a cloud in the sky. Yet somehow it was in the brightness of sunshine that Gabriellen knew her father would have wanted to be buried.

While the priest's voice intoned a final prayer, Gabriellen looked at the assembled mourners. Lord Mincham stood to one side of his players, all of whom were unashamedly weeping. To her surprise and gratification, no less than ten courtiers were present. Every acting troupe in London was represented. Amongst their number were the most famous of their players and playwrights, including Edward Alleyn, the leading actor from The Admiral's Men, Richard Burbage, and Esmond's friend William Shakespeare of the more recently formed Lord Chamberlain's Men. Despite her grief, Gabriellen was proud at this imposing tribute to her

496

father. It would have meant much to Esmond to have known himself so respected amongst his peers.

Amid the blur of people, she recognised the familiar faces of many regular playgoers to The Angel, and finally a more disreputable gathering from Bankside, the coney-catchers, cut-purses, beggars, even the pimps and their whores. He had been friends with beggars and nobles. There had always been dark corners to his life – some, she reflected wryly, would no doubt be better left undiscovered. It did not alter her love for him. He had been a man of many parts: actor, playwright, philanderer, gambler, and very likely rogue. Clearly he would be missed by many.

As the coffin was lowered into the ground, she leaned heavily upon Jack's arm, unable to prevent her tears. He supported and comforted her, his own eyes filled with a watery brightness. The service over, he drew her aside as the mourners filed past to pay their last respects. All present were invited to the funeral banquet at the house in Bankside. As far as Gabriellen could determine Esmond had left no will, but since there was only herself and Laurence to inherit, she would not bar her illegitimate half-brother from his share of their father's estate.

The courtiers were the first to leave and she curtsied as Lord Mincham approached.

'My condolences, Mistress Angel,' his lordship said. His bald head was shiny from the heat. He dabbed at it with a scented kerchief which he fluttered as he spoke. 'A tragic loss. There'll never be another playwright quite like Esmond.'

Gabriellen bowed her head in acknowledgement. Since the last five plays performed in Esmond's name had been written by herself, she alone knew the grim humour behind his words.

Lord Mincham touched the kerchief to his sweeping russet moustache and the small beard which covered his pointed chin. 'The playhouse will be rebuilt and dedicated in memory of him. It will keep the name Angel.'

'That is very generous of you, my lord. Before his death my father dictated to me two more plays. Once these are properly copied, I will submit them to you for your approval.'

'Two new plays!' Lord Mincham's owlish eyes became rounder, his excitement obvious by the renewed waving of his kerchief. 'My dear Culpepper will be delighted. He says that Esmond is master of the blend of tragedy and the risqué. Of course, *The Impudent Rascal* has still to be presented to the public. When it was performed last week at Mincham House, my guests praised it most highly. I shall ensure it is performed at The Rose in the next few weeks. Another play like *The Rascal*, and I shall be deemed the greatest patron of the stage.' He looked at Gabriellen sharply. 'These new plays are the equal of Esmond's past successes, I trust?'

'They are, my lord,' she replied coolly. The plays were as yet unwritten. Their conception had been a desperate need to retain the link with her father after his death. They would be her best plays ever, a tribute to Esmond. However, she resented the note of rapacity she detected in Lord Mincham's voice. His lordship might be landed and wealthy, but he was sly and ineffectual, which was why he had been overlooked for a Court appointment. His patronage of the players was his only way of winning notice there.

'These plays will be a memorial to my father,' she insisted. 'When they are first performed it must be for an occasion worthy of his memory.'

'I could not agree more. I shall look forward to reading them,' Lord Mincham declared, his gaze becoming fawning as it fell upon Anthony Culpepper. The actor was glowering at Gabriellen for claiming his lordship's attention for so long.

Each of the players came forward to stand by the grave. Poggs was too overcome to speak. His figure hunched in misery, he hurried away.

Cesare took hold of Gabriellen's hands, his black eyes bright with tears of grief. 'The maestro, he was the best. He give Umberto and me work when to England we come. He good friend. I miss him. We all miss the maestro.'

Gabriellen nodded. 'He will live on in our hearts and through his plays.'

'*Si.*' His voice cracked. Umberto stepped forward to place his arms about Cesare's shoulders and lead him away.

'So many people loved Father.' She looked up at Jack. He smiled back at her, and then his hand was taken by a tall dark-haired man wearing a black eye-patch. There was a broad red streak in his black beard. The man carried himself with the air of a nobleman, but there was a look in his single blue eye which was too calculating to be trustworthy.

'May I introduce Edward Dawkin, my dear?' Jack said, his manner unusually guarded. 'He was an acquaintance of Esmond's.'

'I was his business partner,' Edward Dawkin said as he bowed over her hand. 'Your father's interests were diverse. Be assured that each quarter day a full account of his profits will be sent to you.'

'What business interests were these, Mr Dawkin?' she asked. From the sternness of Jack's face, she surmised that he, too, had dealings with this man – a connection he did not wish known. She had not lived in Southwark for so long not to recognise the notorious One-eyed Ned, leader of the Underworld of criminals. What business could her father, or Jack, have with him?

'At Esmond's request, I cannot divulge the nature of our partnership.'

Gabriellen regarded him haughtily. 'My father was many things. I am aware there is much from his youth he would keep secret from me. Apparently he was respected by the Underworld. I do not condemn my father for his way of life, but if this money is illegally gained, I want no part of it.'

'It is honestly gotten,' One-eyed Ned grinned. 'To uphold your father's wishes, I can say no more. When your brother Laurence becomes of age, the one-third partnership passes to him. Until then you receive the income to support him.' He took a document from his doublet and handed it to her. 'This is the signed agreement between Esmond and myself. It makes me his executor upon his death in respect of this income. Your father's share cannot be sold. Rather, when Laurence inherits, he can buy out myself and my partner if he so wishes. Esmond was firm upon this. The business had been in his family for three generations.'

Gabriellen looked at Jack who had remained silent throughout the interchange. 'In this you can trust Mr Dawkin,' he said. 'This document is more binding than anything a lawyer could devise.' His lips twisted at her puzzlement. 'Honour among thieves, don't they say?'

'They do indeed, Captain Stoneham,' One-eyed Ned responded.

Gabriellen put a hand to her head. She was too deep in

grief to pay full attention to these new developments. 'My father made no will. But if this document is legal, and I presume that it is, his intentions are very clear. However, I cannot discuss it further now.'

One-eyed Ned placed his hand over his heart and bowed to her. 'I would not have mentioned the matter at such a time, but our paths are unlikely to cross in the future. No more need be said upon the matter.' With that he blended into the dispersing mourners and disappeared from sight.

'What an extraordinary turn of events,' Gabriellen said dazedly. 'I doubt I will ever know every side of my father's character.'

A smell of exotic perfume wafted to her on the breeze, accompanied by a rustling of silk. She saw Jack's eyes widen with surprise as he stared over her shoulder. Gabriellen turned, startled to see Jesmaine standing a few feet from her. The fortune-teller was dressed in a scarlet skirt and sapphire bodice but had draped a long black lace veil over her head and shoulders. She clutched the edges of this together as though wishing to hide behind it. Gabriellen moved towards her.

'Thank you for coming to pay your respects to my father.'

'I did not know him well, but our paths crossed often during my years on the road. Nan I knew better. She came to me several times – often when your father had been missing for some days and she was worried for his safety. At her last visit I saw the fire and her death. I tried to warn her but she did not listen. She loved Esmond.'

'You saw the fire? Why did you not warn us?' Gabriellen's voice rose. 'They could have been saved.'

Jesmaine stared at her with saddened eyes. 'I did not know when it would happen or where, only that it would. I saw the fire as I see many things which are written in the stars,' she persisted. 'But these flames will rise again if you do not take steps to avoid them. The lives of both you and Captain Stoneham are at risk from them. Also Mark. The planets tell me he is being drawn back to you.' Her eyes glazed, she seemed to be staring through Gabriellen. Her voice dropped to a low note that was barely audible. 'There is anger all around you.' She stepped back from Gabriellen. 'If you have any regard for Mark, stay out of his life, I beg you.' She pointed an accusing finger at Jack. 'You, too, will not be spared. Whilst ambition remains your master, it will destroy all you seek to achieve.'

'The woman is mad!' Jack started forward, but Gabriellen stepped in front of him to bar his way.

'Let her go, Jack. She loves Mark and naturally fears for him.' She stared hard into his face. 'Jesmaine is gifted. She does see the future. She saw you were a prisoner in Spain.'

'A lucky guess. The woman must know Rowan still loves you.' He gave Gabriellen a hard look, but seeing the strain on her face from her father's death, his manner softened.

'Superstitious prattle, the lot of Jesmaine's talk! The fire was an accident. I'm my own master, and can control my own destiny. Jesmaine is jealous. Though she's right in one respect – if Rowan still loves you, I'd fight him to the death to keep you. You're my woman, Gabriellen, remember that.'

The words sounded uncomfortably like a threat. She disengaged herself from his grasp in readiness for retaliation when her attention was caught by the figure of a tall, thin, middle-aged woman bearing down upon them. This formidable matron was accompanied by three very tall and equally thin men, all in their fifties. Any departing mourner who blocked their passage was rudely shoved aside as this quartet stormed the grave.

The newcomers were strangers to Gabriellen. Their behaviour provoked her. It was overbearing and unfitting for the occasion. When they deliberately ignored her, her anger surfaced. In the most offensive manner, they pushed the grave digger out of the way as he began to fill in the grave.

Gabriellen addressed them coldly. 'Your pardon, good people. Is it Nan Woodruff you would pay your respects to? Or Esmond Angel?'

The woman's deep-set colourless eyes glowed with venom. Her thin, hard face seemed prematurely wrinkled. Closer to, it was likely she was younger than Gabriellen had thought. But those eyes! Gabriellen suppressed an inner shudder at their hostile scrutiny. Why, they could rival the Medusa's, turning all they stared upon to ice instead of stone. With an effort, Gabriellen controlled her temper. Despite their appalling conduct they were here to honour the dead.

Sniffing with disapproval, the woman turned away. She then spat into the grave. The three men followed suit.

'You fiends!' Gabriellen started forward, outraged at the sacrilege to her father's remains.

Jack put a restraining hand on her shoulder, urging gently, 'They're some sort of religious fanatics. Don't let them upset you.' His face set with fury, he rapped out: 'Get you gone before I forcibly remove you. A deed I would relish, were it not out of keeping with the solemnity of this day.'

'The fine coxcomb defends his strumpet well,' the woman shrilled. 'Like father, like daughter. How fitting the profligate was buried with both his concubines.'

'I think you had better leave,' Gabriellen ordered.

'Aye, you're that unholy villain's daughter. You've the same way of holding your head when angry. But don't you go ordering me to leave. I've every right to be here.' She folded her hands over her waist in pious righteousness. 'I am Charity Angel, though I prefer to be known by my maiden name of Fossett. I am that blackguard's wife.'

'That is not possible!' Gabriellen retaliated heatedly. 'My father had but one wife – my mother. She lies there in the next grave.'

A dry laugh greeted her words. 'Your mother was his paramour! I was his wife. His *true* wife. His first wife. Very likely he went through a mock marriage with that conniving French bitch. How else could he get her into his bed? She was not so accommodating as the others. I doubt he ever told her that their marriage was bigamous. Unless she found out, and that was why she drowned herself? He'd been married to me for five years before they met.'

Gabriellen began to shake as anger overtook her. This demented creature might be Charity by name, but she had not a speck of charity in her nature. Gabriellen had heard enough of her iniquitous lies. 'May the Lord forgive you for your wickedness. Such lies . . . evil lies!'

''Tis the truth.' The oldest of the three men spoke. 'We were witnesses.'

'The devil you say!' Jack intervened. 'I've known Angel for many years. He never mentioned any wife but Sabine.'

'He had more than a marriage to keep hidden,' the shortest of the three declared. 'He had the death of our brother and father on his conscience.'

Through the depths of her anger, the name Fossett nagged at Gabriellen's mind. She had heard it before. Could

502

there be some truth in what they said? No, impossible. But memory tugged with alarming clarity. Had not Prew threatened Esmond with the name of Fossett?

'This is not a matter to be resolved over my father's grave.'

'You're very haughty for an upstart bastard,' Charity Angel sneered.

The statement doused the fire within Gabriellen. Her head reeled as it dawned on her that Esmond's marriage to this woman made her illegitimate.

Jack took charge. 'I don't know what malicious ploy brought you here. Clearly it was not reverence for the man we have just buried.'

'We came to make sure we were not cheated of our rights,' the widow screeched. 'Esmond was my husband. All of his property and money reverts to me. There is a house in Chichester which should fetch a goodly sum. It is little enough to comfort me in my old age after the years of misery that man subjected me to.'

'Aye, and property in London as well, if my memory serves me aright.' The oldest man's eyes were hard with avarice.

'There is no property in London,' Jack lied, knowing they could never trace Esmond's interest in the brothel. 'As to this conjectured marriage, it is a scurvy trick to steal this woman's inheritance. And poorly done.'

'My marriage lines are proof of the deed,' the woman said smugly. 'No court in the land will dispute them.'

'When were you married?' Gabriellen demanded. 'Why should my father have kept it a secret? It makes no sense.'

'Because he was a murderer and a bigamist. Not to mention a fortune-hunter. My father took him in as a clerk. He repaid him by ravishing me, knowing that once I was dishonoured my father would have no choice but to arrange our marriage. I brought Esmond a rich dowry, which he'd whored and gambled away inside a year. There were always women. When he took up with that French harlot and set up home with her, it was too humiliating to be borne. My brother Tobias challenged him to a duel.' Bitterness twisted her hard face into an ugly mask. 'That swine ran my brother through! On hearing the news my father suffered a seizure. He lay paralysed in his bed for eight years before the Good Lord released him in death.'

'And all this happened without Esmond's being brought to justice?' Jack challenged. 'Do you honestly expect us to swallow that?'

'The reason he was not dragged before the courts was that I did not want my good name ruined. They would have hanged him – a quick death with little suffering. I'd have had to live with the shame of the trial – be the butt of gossip and ridicule. But that blackguard continued to suffer! While he was married to me, he could not marry the whore he loved. Any children he spawned were by-blows. That was my revenge. That's why I spit upon his grave.'

Gabriellen covered her ears with her hands, wanting to shut out the words. 'No! You lie! Father would never . . . He loved Sabine. He'd not . . .' Tears choked in her throat. 'Tell them, Jack.'

Above his beard his scar was white with his anger, but the rigid set of his face told her that he believed Esmond capable of all they accused. Had her father lied to seduce Sabine as Jack had lied to her? It explained why Esmond had never married Nan to make Laurence legitimate. She lowered her clenched fists, her eyes filled with loathing as she regarded the Fossett family. Whatever the circumstances of this harridan's marriage to her father – and she did not believe Esmond entirely to blame – she would not give up the house in Chichester without a court battle. It had been her home for so many years. Uncle Ezekiel had always meant her to have it.

Whatever it took, this woman would not set foot in that house. She would fight them, and by so doing clear her father's name of Tobias Fossett's murder.

On a moonless night in November 1600, a French fishing smack anchored off the Kent coast to await a signal from the beach. In the distance a few lights were visible from the unshuttered tavern windows of the town of Rye. The white-haired and bearded figure wrapped in a concealing cloak stared at the land from the prow of the vessel, his thin lips turned down with bitterness. Ten years was a long time to linger upon thoughts of revenge. Each year the malignant tumour of hatred spread within him, fed by years of poverty, of being reduced to begging on the streets of a foreign land. For ten years, as he struggled to survive and gradually build a new life for himself, he had cursed the name of Angel.

Revenge was costly and must be planned with care, especially when every single insult and injury he had suffered in the intervening years must be paid for in full. He had heard of Esmond Angel's death amongst the gossip which filtered through to him from England. A fitting end. He could not have planned it better himself. Now payment was due from that devil's daughter. How sweet would be the reckoning!

A light flashed from the shore and shortly thereafter three rowing boats drew alongside the fishing smack. The illicit cargo of silks and spices was unloaded along with the passenger.

At the touch of his boat's prow against the shingle, the passenger leaped ashore. He stumbled, going down on his knees. As his fingers clutched hold of the pebbles, he lifted one high and kissed it. His exile was over. His white hair, long beard and thickened figure would make him unrecognisable to those who had known him before. The hour of his revenge was close at hand. Victor Prew tossed back his head and laughed, the harsh cackle of insanity drawing anxious glances from the smugglers.

In December the network of spies Mark had set up learned of a new threat to the Queen's life. For some weeks Jesmaine had been acting strangely and now, as he prepared to leave her to answer Walsingham's summons, he saw how thin she had become.

'Must you go out tonight, Mark?' She put out a pleading hand to stop him.

'You know I must.'

She shook her head, her eyes wide with anxiety. 'But there is danger. I sense it.'

He smiled indulgently. 'There is always danger in this work. I shall take especial care.'

She threw herself into his arms. 'I love you, Mark. Never forget that. Never forget the warnings I have given you.'

He kissed her tenderly and found she was shaking. 'I'm afraid. Tonight something terrible will happen, I know it.'

'Jesmaine, my darling, you worry too much. I can take care of myself.' Her panic undermined his resolve and he felt a strong compulsion to stay with her. Tonight she

seemed strangely vulnerable. 'I will return as soon as I can.'
He patted the sword and dagger at his side. 'I am armed.
I know the secret words to get me safely through the Under-
world districts. Stop worrying.'

He kissed her again and left quickly, pausing only to pat
Hywel who wagged his tail as Mark collected his cloak from
its hook. 'No walk for you tonight, old boy.' Some of
Jesmaine's unease had transferred itself to him. 'Stay on
guard.'

An hour later Mark stood at Walsingham's side in the
torture chamber of the Tower. The room reeked of sweat,
fear, blood and scorched flesh. Shadows thrown up by the
torches danced on the walls with demonic disrespect for
the suffering within the room. The scratch of a quill on
parchment from the clerk perched on a stool across the
room died away. The only sound now was the harsh
laboured breathing of the figure stretched on the rack.

'I'm innocent. I know nothing,' the tormented voice
wailed.

How often had these walls echoed to that denial? Mark
knew that this man was as guilty as hell. Even so, this was
the side of his work he detested, and after so many years
had never fully come to terms with. But if a man would
not voluntarily talk to disclose the Queen's enemies, torture
soon loosened his tongue. The figure stretched on the rack
was more stubborn than most. He was not much more than
twenty, and from the fine clothes which had been stripped
from him, had been something of a fop. He was brave to
hold out for so long against the pain. Mark looked at the
prisoner whose stretched torso glistened with sweat. Blood
congealed on his sunken cheeks where he had bitten his
tongue through. His narrow beard was flecked with pink
froth, the handsome face contorted in a permanent mask
of agony. Earlier they had pulled out his nails and his flesh
was blistered from the hot irons. At a nod from Walsingham
the torturer turned the rack another notch. The figure
jerked rigid, a hideous scream raising the hairs on Mark's
body.

'Tell us the name of your paymaster and the torture will
stop,' Walsingham demanded, his deep-set eyes dispassion-
ate. 'His name, damn you!'

The man slumped unconscious.

'Revive him,' Walsingham snapped. His long bony face

showed merely impatience that he was being delayed from other duties by the man's stubbornness.

A dousing with icy water roused a groan from the prisoner. As Walsingham nodded to the torturer to recommence, Mark stepped forward. His stomach would stand no more.

'Look you, man, you suffer in vain.' His accent was more pronounced as he hid his distaste and injected compassion into its lilting tone. 'Two others were taken this night. They have already spoken out. Would you die unshriven? For you will die if you do not speak. The rack is just the beginning. Next they will blind you, then castrate you. You'll be talking fast enough by then, but it will be too late – you'll be a living corpse. Spare yourself, man. You're just a pawn. It's the paymaster we want.'

The figure remained silent. Walsingham gave an impatient gesture towards the brazier and the torturer stepped forward holding a device of red-hot iron with two glowing circles set the space of two eyeballs apart.

'Look well, man,' Mark said, hating the suffering but knowing it must be done if Elizabeth Tudor was to remain safe on her throne. 'This is Purgatory on earth. It will be the last sight you ever see.'

The man's eyes were almost starting from his head as the iron pressed closer. 'God rot you! I'll speak.' The prisoner's voice cracked with terror. 'Mother of God, I can't take any more. Not for the likes of that lunatic.'

The torturer stepped back into the shadows and Walsingham, pressing a nosegay to his face, leaned forward. 'Who is the paymaster?'

'The man's known only by the name of Whitebeard.'

'That's of no use to us,' Walsingham snarled.

'It's all he knows,' Mark affirmed. 'It's a start.'

'Where can I find Whitebeard?'

The tortured figure grimaced as he forced the words through his cracked and bloodied lips. 'In hell . . . where the mad bastard belongs . . .'

Mark was dismissed, but the questioning continued. He could hear the prisoner's screams as he left the torture chamber. He breathed easier as he left the forbidding precincts of the Tower. Whitebeard would be found, but experience warned Mark that this was likely to be a long and difficult assignment. Tomorrow he would leave London and begin his search. He could be away for months. He quickened his step to return to Jesmaine, eager to drown in her perfumed sensuality and cast from his mind the gory images of the torture chamber.

Jesmaine could not sleep. The feeling of danger persisted. She paced back and forth across the chamber, her restless steps accompanied by sympathetic whimpering from Hywel. To reassure herself, she picked up the cards and dealt them in ritual order upon the table. The coloured figures jumbled before her tired eyes. Danger was everywhere, but remained elusive. She learned nothing more. The last card she turned over was the card of death. With a strangled sob, she cast it to the floor. What good to know that Mark faced death if she could not see its form?

Breathing in hard short gasps, she uncovered the crystal. Through blurred eyes she stared into it, but panic robbed her mind of the familiar chant which brought on her visions. Sobbing wildly, she sank her head forward on to her hands. A cold nose thrust itself against her elbow as Hywel fretted at her obvious distress.

She jumped at an impatient knocking outside. Hywel growled and ran barking to the outer door.

'Who's there?' she demanded.

'Open up, mistress,' a gruff voice she did not recognise answered. 'I've word of Mr Rowan. He's hurt. Hurt bad.'

Her fingers trembled as she drew back the bolt. The door was pushed hard, sending her reeling back into the room as four burly men burst in. Through the blur of tears blinding her eyes she stared at them. One grabbed her throat and pushed her up against the wall. She needed no second sight to determine their intent. Too late she realised the premonition of danger had been for herself, not Mark. The cruel expressions temporarily paralysed her with fear. Hywel snarled and leaped at a smaller figure hidden behind them.

Her mind registered the lust on the men's faces. She saw Hywel hurl himself at the white-haired and bearded smaller man. She saw a club raised, knocking the courageous dog to the floor and beating him until he was dead. Then her stare was fixed on the men advancing towards her. She had never known such animal panic. Always with men she had used their lust to her advantage. Her lovers had been numerous but she had ruled them, governing and channelling their passion. This was primeval rape, beyond reasoning, beyond her control. She was gripped by terror.

Rough hands seized her, hauled her to the floor, stripped the clothes from her struggling figure. Each man held a spreadeagled limb as the white-bearded man stood over her. He dropped his breeches and hose, the foulness of his manhood rising at the jerking movements of his hands. With a savage grunt he threw himself down upon her. The harder she struggled, the greater the man's excitement. He was a devil, grunting names and obscenities, laughing as he used her as the instrument of his vengeance upon Mark and Gabriellen.

Tonight he defiled her as he believed Mark had defiled his wife. But his sick mind went past that. When eventually he achieved his disgusting and obscene release, the man Jesmaine recognised as Victor Prew rolled aside. She was fallen upon by the others, crazed by their lust. All her adult life she had gloried in her sensuality and passion, enjoying sex. This was a mindless screaming horror, watched by Prew who urged his creatures on to every form of base depravity.

Fetid breath assailed her proud mouth, lust-craved faces pressed against her frozen cheeks. She was powerless, her womanhood degraded, as time and again they brutally had their will of her. Her flesh was theirs. She was debased, an object of shame. Unbearable pain lanced through her as she began to haemorrhage, engulfing her in excruciating torment. Mercifully she sank into unconsciousness and was spared the knowledge of the final indignities which brought an end to her life.

Chapter Thirty-Three

The news of Jesmaine's death was the gossip of London. Gabriellen heard it whilst shopping at the market stalls in Cheapside. The gruesome details of the attack lost nothing in the telling and, appalled, she ran to the astrologer's house to offer her condolences to Mark. The house was shuttered. Her frantic banging on the door brought a cackle from a woman opposite. She sat by an open window carding wool before spinning it into yarn, her face a huge circle of quivering flesh.

'Ain't no one there,' the woman shouted. ''Er lover's gone. Stayed long enough ter rouse the constables, then scarpered. Funeral's this afternoon, if you knew 'er. I wouldn't wish 'er end on any woman, but she were a necromancer. Them as 'ave dealings with the devil . . . I could tell you stories about 'er which would make yer 'air stand on end.'

Gabriellen rounded on the gossip. 'She was a gifted scryer, and a more generous Christian than you will ever be.'

Two hours later Gabriellen attended the funeral. Besides the priest there was only one figure at the graveside, his dark head bowed in grief. Out of respect for his mourning she stayed back, close enough to hear the priest's droning words. After the priest left Mark remained where he was, twisting a feathered cap in his hands. She saw a shudder grip his figure and when he turned to find her watching him, there was the glitter of tears on his cheeks.

Wordlessly she held out her hands to him and he gripped them hard as he mastered his emotions. 'It's my fault she's dead,' he said hollowly. 'It was done as a warning to me. When I find the bastards, they'll pay.'

'Don't torture yourself so, Mark,' she said.

The look in his dark eyes was that of a man who sought

death. It frightened her. 'Don't do anything rash. These men will be found and will pay for their crimes. Jesmaine loved you. Remember the good times.'

'I did not love her,' he said brokenly. 'And she deserved better from me. As God is my witness, her death will be avenged.'

He lifted her hand to his lips, his voice harsh. 'Goodbye, Ellen.'

His tone alarmed her. 'No, Mark, not goodbye.' Impulse made her throw her arms around him and hold him close. 'Aphra told me you have long worked to protect the Queen's life. That work is important, Mark. Promise me you will take care.'

For a long moment he stared into her fearful eyes. Then he nodded and walked away.

A month later Gabriellen summoned Lord Mincham's Men to the house in Bankside, after sending the copied parts of her latest play *Boudicca* to the senior players. There was a buzz of excitement as she walked into the parlour. Culpepper was conspicuous by his absence.

'It is a masterpiece,' announced Samuel Lacey as he hugged his script close to his chest.

'Esmond outshone himself with this one.' Will Appleshot affected a pose reminiscent of the absent Culpepper. 'As the Iceni Queen, I shall at last be acknowledged as the equal of Flowerdew in the female roles.'

Gabriellen stared round the gathering and noticing that Robin also was absent, was prompted to state: 'But, Will, surely Robin will take the lead?'

Will Appleshot eyed her with open contempt. 'Culpepper sacked him. I am now the female lead.' In recent years she had noticed the mincing manner of the young player becoming more exaggerated and effeminate. In the last year Culpepper had taken an interest in Will and the boy had become his willing acolyte. Now, as he regarded her, he conveyed all the disdain for her of the man he worshipped. Suspicion grew within her that Will had become Culpepper's lover.

There was dislike for all womankind in the youth's arrogant stare. 'And by what right, mistress, do you think you can summon us like common lackeys?'

'That's enough, Appleshot.' Poggs pushed the actor

down on to a stool. 'If you had but the sense to see it, you would realise that it has been Mistress Gabby's hard work which has kept this troupe together these last years.'

'Culpepper is now our manager,' Will sneered. 'And I for one will not tolerate a woman interfering in the running of the troupe.'

'Who said Culpepper is the manager?' Poggs rounded on Will like a snapping terrier.

'Who else but Lord Mincham?'

'I no work for Culpepper.' Umberto stood up and looked pointedly at his cousin.

'I too no work for him.' Cesare went to Umberto's side. 'Culpepper, he destroy what the maestro make of us. Who agree?'

Samuel Lacey shifted uncomfortably on his seat. 'Can't say I like the thought of Culpepper in charge. He's only interested in his own importance.'

'Then those who do not wish to serve me, can leave,' Culpepper expounded from the doorway.

There was an outbreak of angry muttering.

'Gentlemen!' Gabriellen shouted above the din, seeking to bring order. 'Gentlemen, have you forgotten why we are here? In two weeks, on Twelfth Night, the play *Boudicca* is to be staged before the Queen at Court. It is a tribute to my father and you are squabbling like starlings. Esmond would turn in his grave if he saw how his troupe was behaving.'

'May I remind you, Mistress Angel, this is no longer your father's troupe.' Culpepper preened his fair moustache with a pomposity which made Gabriellen itch to strike the sneer from his face.

'But it is Esmond Angel's play,' she heatedly reminded him. 'Poggs knows much of Father's mind on its production. I suggest that for this performance, he guides you all.'

'Just as long as you keep your interfering nose out of the rehearsals,' Culpepper flung back. 'Were it not for the esteem in which we held Esmond, your presence would never have been tolerated at the playhouse. Esmond was a genius.' He raised the script he was holding. 'This proves he was truly the "maestro", as the musicians named him. If you want to help, we need a seamstress.'

Gabriellen bit back her rejoinder. The prejudice against

512

her sex was no longer disguised. She had written the play, but Culpepper was determined that she would have nothing to do with its performance. How she would have loved to throw in his face the knowledge that it was her work he was praising. It would do no good. He probably would not even believe her. If he did, she knew without doubt, he would never perform in it. And he was spiteful enough to make sure that the news leaked abroad, and her father's name would then be held to ridicule, as would those of friends who had been loyal to the troupe. She could not allow that.

Later that evening she railed at Jack about Culpepper's prejudice.

'My love, you have always known it was so,' he said, drawing her down on to his lap. 'You have done your best for the players and they have rejected you. And this play, from what I have seen of it, could be dangerous. There are parts which sound perilously close to treason.'

'That's not true, Jack,' she defended her work, knowing he had never approved of her playwriting.

'Gabriellen, I know what I read.' His expression was serious. 'You write of rebellion. Such words can be twisted. They could land you in the Tower.'

She shook her head. 'The play is about the life of Boudicca, Queen of the Iceni, and her triumph over the Roman legions who would enslave her people. The reference to Boudicca's undefeated spirit is a direct tribute to our own Queen. Has she not triumphed over the might of Rome and Spain who would have made Catholics of us all?'

'Nevertheless, it borders upon sedition,' Jack answered with growing heat. 'It's time you put this playwriting nonsense behind you now Esmond is dead. The players no longer need you. Have I not been patient these last years? I've a grand house in Chelsea which stands empty because you refuse to live with me there. Come with me.'

'How can I sit back and allow all my father worked for to be destroyed?'

'Certes, but you're a stubborn jade! The players will never accept you as their manager. After the court performance, Cesare and Umberto have threatened to leave. Poggs also is dissatisfied. And he's not getting any younger. There would be a place for him and Agnes if you wish it.'

'I shall think on it, Jack. First we must get the play

513

ready for the performance at Court. Poggs knows I wrote it, and he's willing to give my directions to the players. Also, this afternoon I received an invitation from Lord Mincham to join his party at Court to see the play. He meant it as a tribute to Father.'

Jack's expression changed to one of calculation. 'I shall, of course, accompany you to Court. It is my chance to regain the Queen's favour. I will summon the tailor and dressmaker. You will need a new gown, and I a jewelled doublet and hose.'

It was Gabriellen's turn to be concerned. 'Why is your return to favour so important, Jack? Has not the business in York prospered this last year? You've spent time enough there. Do not your ships expand your trade with the continent?'

'Would you make of me a merchant?' he snapped. 'Without the Queen's favour there are no Letters of Marque. No rich prizes to be won.'

It was the same story – his ambition was relentless. She left his lap to stand with arms folded, glaring down at him as she accused: 'I thought when we met you wished to end your seafaring life?'

'Then I had not tasted the fame such a life can bring. Since Drake's death, it is I the Spanish fear most. Once Her Majesty saw me as her foremost captain. Yet now I am ignored.'

'Because of the company you keep. Essex is in disgrace.'

'I will not desert a friend when he has need of me.' Jack stood up to pace the room. It was an old and familiar argument. And one in which he refused to listen to reason.

'Essex is going his own way to the devil. Must you join him?' The words of Jesmaine's prophecy at Esmond's graveside rang through her mind. In desperation she threw herself against him, her hands gripping his velvet sleeves as she pleaded, 'It is madness to follow Essex. The Queen will destroy him. For a year he has remained confined, his letters to Elizabeth ignored. She has even refused to renew his lease on the duties of new wine, his only source of income. She has abandoned him, Jack. And he, incautious fool, cried aloud in his folly, that her "mind is as crooked as her carcass". Another nail in his coffin. In his megalomania he will bring you to ruin, as he will those other malcontents who flock to his house.'

514

'You talk like a woman, Gabriellen,' he scoffed. 'I thought you would understand.'

She heard the pain in his voice and faltered. His pride was at stake. The pride of a man who had come from nothing to greatness, whose courage and dash were a legend and who feared no mortal. What Jack feared was insignificance. The Queen could plummet him back to obscurity upon a whim. To prevent that, he would take whatever measures he thought necessary.

Her throat worked convulsively. Why must he pursue danger so recklessly? Her silent question was answered by the excitement glittering in his eyes. His calling of adventurer was stronger in his blood than his love for her. It was that will to triumph, to achieve greatness, which had won her love in the first place. He had not changed. Love alone would never mellow his ambition. But that ambition was all for himself. That she sought to win the acknowledgement she deserved for her plays, he regarded as unimportant. He wanted her to live quietly at Chelsea, a servant to attend to his comforts. Could he not see that his ambition was destroying her love for him? It was driving them apart, making of them strangers. Their passion for each other was undiminished but Gabriellen yearned for something more from their relationship. Jack had never accepted her as his equal and that rankled.

Fear for him pushed discontent aside. She still loved him and she feared ambition would bring his downfall. Her hand slid up to caress his cheek. 'I understand too well, my darling. You have been scorned by the Queen and it hurts you. But it is to her your loyalty must lie. Essex is her vassal. Where is your gallantry and chivalry? Would you follow in the footsteps of his rash pride and countenance open rebellion?'

'It has not come to that – yet.'

'But it will, Jack.' Her voice broke, her green eyes flashing defiance. 'I fear it will. Then what?'

The steel was back in his eyes as he looked down at her. 'Then we must pray Her Majesty does not forget her loyal sea captain as she has chosen to forget her Earl Marshal.'

Christmas was not a time of revelry for Mark. A week after Jesmaine's death he had overheard a drunken lout bragging of the rape. The man died by Mark's hand an hour later, after he had revealed the name of his accomplices. Three more had met their end by his dagger, but their leader still eluded him: a man known as Whitebeard, King Philip's paymaster. From the description and other information Mark had been gathering, it was Victor Prew returned in all his vengeance.

Mark's foraging through the Underworld haunts had shown him that the traitor and murderer had fled from London. There was something twisted in Whitebeard's character which made any who referred to him name him lunatic. Terrified that Prew would next turn his wrath against Gabriellen, Mark put a dozen men on his trail. Clearly Prew had not expected a manhunt after Jesmaine's death. It put him to flight. Mark had finally discovered his trail and it not a day old. It took him to Rye and then on to the slums of Rome and the Vatican itself. There Prew eluded him. In the disguise of a pilgrim Mark found he could not flush Prew from the safety of the Pope's see. The glorious art treasures of Rome which Mark had long yearned to visit gave him little pleasure.

After a month he abandoned his search and returned to London. By chance he learned of another conspiracy which Walsingham must act against at once. His years as an agent had taught him the need for patience. Prew was a fanatical Catholic, and bent upon revenge. He would return to England, and when he did . . . God have pity on him, for Mark knew he would not.

Gabriellen attended the play at the palace. It had been her last work and she knew it to be her finest. It likened Elizabeth Tudor, who had triumphed over the might of Spain, to the fabled Queen of the Iceni who had courageously taken on the strength of the Roman Army, though Gabriellen took care in her writing that the similarities ended there. The Iceni Queen had finally been defeated and had taken poison to escape her enemy's wrath. The play was the story of a queen's resilience and bravery, of fearlessly encountering the odds stacked against her. A woman greater than any man of her time because she controlled them – as Elizabeth did.

From the side of the stage, Gabriellen clasped her hands together to control her excitement as she watched the final act. The audience was enthralled. Until this last scene the

Queen had several times nodded her approval at Boudicca's triumphs. A glance at Her Majesty now showed Elizabeth leaning forward on her throne, her face waxen beneath the heavy makeup. As Boudicca fell to the ground, the poison bottle in her hand, tears glistened in Gabriellen's eyes that so brave a woman and queen had been defeated in life, if not in death. Culpepper, as the Roman Governor, stood over Boudicca's corpse gloating. A tense silence fell upon the audience as Samuel Lacey, playing Boudicca's second in command, strode to the front of the stage to deliver the short epilogue.

' "Here lies an indomitable queen," ' Lacey expounded. ' "Her last address to her army was: 'Win the battle or perish. That is what I, a woman, intend to do. Let the men live in slavery if they wish.' " ' He whirled around and flung an accusing arm towards Culpepper. ' "She is dead, but her spirit lives on. The spirit of a free Britain. In time who will remember the name of Suetonius Paulinus, the Governor of Britain, who triumphed this day? It will be the name of Boudicca which will become a legend and fill our people's hearts with pride." '

Samuel Lacey gave the best performance of his life and as his ringing voice faded, silence fell over the hall. Only the rustle of silks was audible as the courtiers shifted to look towards their Queen. Silence hung like a pall over the hall. It expanded, grew to an ominous chill. The actors looked askance at each other, whilst Gabriellen stared at the dais, puzzled.

Elizabeth sat rigid upon her throne, a white hand drumming upon its arm. Not a courtier stirred; all eyes were upon the Queen awaiting her response. What could be wrong? It was a great dramatic play. Surely Her Majesty had not found it wanting? Suddenly the awesome truth struck Gabriellen. Her eyes widened in alarm. It had offended. But how? She closed her eyes against a rush of fear and nausea, her breathing shallow and painful. There was a scraping of chairs. Her eyes opened to see the courtiers rising, following the Queen's example. Elizabeth stood glaring at the stage, until with an imperious flick of her fan she turned on her heel and left the hall without a word. Gabriellen froze as with much embarrassed coughing and shuffling, the Court followed.

'Why is she offended?' Gabriellen spun round to face

Jack. 'Is it not obvious that the play glorifies the fortitude of our Queen?'

'God's soul,' Culpepper groaned, his lips quivering with fear, 'I deliver my best oratory ever and the Queen walks out. A plague on it! 'Tis infamous. We are undone.'

The actors crowded together, all talking at once, their expressions ranging from red-faced humiliation to white-faced shock.

Gabriellen's gaze was fixed upon Lord Mincham across the room. He was speaking with great agitation to Lord Robert Cecil, who had succeeded his father as the Queen's Chief Minister. She saw Mincham's hand fly to his mouth in horror as he violently shook his head. The short, hunchbacked figure of Cecil looked sourly towards the players. Worried by this, Gabriellen moved towards them. Lord Mincham saw her approach, his relief obvious.

'My dear, will you explain to his lordship that when your father wrote the play, it was to honour Elizabeth?' Mincham dabbed at his bald, sweating pate, his russet moustache wilting as his discomposure intensified.

'I am at a loss that there is any misunderstanding,' she said in passionate defence of her work. 'The play is an accolade to Elizabeth's greatness. Throughout her reign she has triumphed over her enemies. It is clear in the script that any reference to Her Majesty is in praise of her valour, of her ability to rouse the people's love . . . That if called upon, all England will die for her.'

Cecil regarded her impassioned face with frosty contempt. 'Were the words performed today those written by your father?'

'It was his play.' Gabriellen felt her throat go dry. Here was a new threat. She must not let her temper betray her secret. The lies concerning her work never came easily. Now they stuck in her throat. What was Cecil hinting at? Something terrible, from his blank expression. 'It was written from devotion, as a tribute to our Queen,' she insisted. 'I do not understand why it has met with so icy a reception.'

'It shows a Queen crushed and fallen,' Cecil declared in a scathing voice. 'To many, it will be seen as provocation to rebellion.'

'That is absurd!' Gabriellen shook her head vehemently.

518

She took a grip of her rising fear. Cecil was a dangerous man to provoke. There was no disputing that he had the Queen's interests at heart, but there was an inhuman quality about him which repelled Gabriellen. It was the coldness in his eyes, like a viper's. The lack of humour in his ascetic face. She drew a steadying breath and held that pitiless stare. 'The play was a tribute to Her Majesty's greatness, I swear it. I know what was in my father's mind when he wrote it – reverence and respect for Her Majesty.'

'It has subversive undertones,' Cecil returned stiffly. He turned on the trembling figure of Lord Mincham. 'I shall investigate your motives for staging this play.'

Mincham blanched, his slack mouth gaping open as he vainly fought to find the words to exonerate himself.

'Lord Mincham is innocent of any crime,' Gabriellen rose to the man's defence. 'The play was passed by the Master of the Revels. It was specially chosen last month to be performed here, to celebrate Her Majesty's long reign.'

'Unfortunately it was performed on the very day that the Privy Council learned that certain of Her Majesty's subjects are in secret negotiation with James Stuart of Scotland,' Cecil announced, taking no pains to hide his hostility. 'What does that suggest to you?'

'It suggests, my Lord Chief Minister, that you are jumping at ghosts,' Gabriellen retaliated, knowing that in this, attack was her only form of defence. 'My father was a loyal subject of Her Majesty. He would never insult her, or incite dissent against her rule.'

'Perhaps the speeches were tampered with?' Lord Cecil insinuated slyly.

Gabriellen lost her temper. 'It was performed as it was written.'

'You are very sure of that, Mistress Angel – and rather too defensive,' Cecil countered. 'What are you hiding?'

Gabriellen drew herself up to her full height and glared down at the short, hunchbacked figure. At that moment she was too outraged by his insinuations to be afraid. 'I should know every word which was written. My father dictated the play to me. It is not common knowledge, but he was going blind. He could no longer see to write. The copied parts for all the actors are in my own handwriting. No one is more horrified than myself that this play should

519

have offended Her Majesty. If I could have an audience with her? Just a few moments of her time to exonerate my father's name . . .'

'That will not be possible,' Cecil said incisively. He looked past Gabriellen to where Jack stood in angry silence. The Chief Minister's lip curled into a sneer and his contemptuous stare swept over Lord Mincham. 'The responsibility of a patron to his players is to ensure they do not incite rebellion. Perhaps you should reconsider your patronage, Lord Mincham? This play is tainted with sedition. Henceforth it is banned. And any who perform it will be implicated as being party to open rebellion.'

'But that was farthest from my – my father's mind,' Gabriellen outfaced the condemnation in Cecil's hard eyes. Inwardly she was beginning to shake, but the hands clenched into fists at her sides showed the willpower exerted to hide her fright of him. The slightest weakness and he would be merciless. 'If I could but explain to Her Majesty?'

The implacable face was set against her. 'It is not the Queen's habit to grant audience to the paramours of her sea captains. Especially one who has borne three children out of wedlock. Lord Mincham was again remiss in permitting your presence here, Mistress Angel. Your conduct with Sir Jack Stoneham is an affront and an insult to Her Majesty's virgin state. Be thankful the writer of that play is already in God's hands, or he would now be on his way to the Tower.'

He turned his back on her and left. Gabriellen put a hand to her face, unable to control the trembling which seized her.

Jack took her in his arms. 'Don't let Cecil's words upset you. It's a good play.' He lowered his voice to a whisper. 'Better than anything Esmond could have written.'

She pulled back in his embrace to stare up at him, distraught. 'It is not just my father's reputation and this play which are in contention. You heard Cecil's words. He would see the troupe disbanded. I had not realised it is common knowledge that I am your mistress, or that it could so harm your future. This must inevitably rebound upon you. Oh, Jack, I'm so sorry. It's all my fault. I've ruined your chances at Court. I've ruined your life.'

'Did I not say Elizabeth has turned tyrant?' He held her tight, forcing her to look into his eyes. 'You're not to blame. We are ruled by a despot. A shrivelled spinster who is jealous of others who have found love and happiness. I see now that was my crime. As she has banished others before me in her insane jealousy against lovers, she would emasculate all men. Any who came close to her she eventually destroyed. But what she forgets is that she is old. The tigress's claws are worn away and her teeth loosening. Old men may still tremble in their hose at her rages, but there is a new generation now. We will not cringe like mice, awaiting her demise. We must act to secure our future.' He gave a twisted smile. 'As your play says, my darling: ' "Let the men live in slavery if they wish." I wish not.'

Gabriellen clutched hold of his sleeve. 'That is the voice of madness! My words were never meant to incite. What have I done? I must leave the players lest my friends suffer for my folly. I will not be the cause of your downfall. Would that I still had the house in Chichester where you could visit me in safety – but that wretched legal wrangle is no nearer conclusion.'

'There will be no more talk of your leaving.' He gave her a slight shake and looked over her head to the players, sullenly leaving the stage. 'This is not the place to talk.'

'I'm afraid, Jack.'

He smiled. 'That does not sound like the Gabriellen I admire and love. These events have unsettled you. In the morning you'll feel differently. Knowing you, you will feel anger at the injustice done here this night.'

She shook her head, her heart pounding with fear. His handsome face became a blur as her eyes misted with tears. 'I doubt it. My play has brought danger to my friends. Worse, it has earned you the Queen's censure. It could mean the Tower. I'll not be the cause of your ruin. Forget me, Jack. Make your peace with the Queen.'

'I will not give you up.' The passion in his voice sent a thrill through her, but at the same time heightened her fears for him. 'You are my life, Gabriellen.'

'Then give up this madness in seeking out Essex, I beg you. The Queen is old. How much longer can she live? Five years? For once in your life, Jack, err on the side of caution.'

To her dismay, she realised he was not listening. What he wanted in this world, he took. He was thirty-seven, at the height of his powers, with absolute confidence that he was master of his own destiny. It was that arrogance which had won her love. Now that same arrogance filled her with dread.

'Essex is no friend to you if he plants the seeds of insurrection,' she reasoned. 'You have risen high, Jack. Why risk it all now? If you will not think of yourself, think of the children. They idolise you. Would you see their ideals crumble to dust? If you love me, think of me. How could I live, knowing I was the cause of your death?'

'Death is for failures.' The look in his eyes warned her he would not be turned from his course. 'We shall succeed. When have I ever failed?'

There was no arguing with that supreme confidence. It had carried him from the poverty and humbleness of a fisherman's hut to being recognised in the street and hailed as a hero, the most revered and feared English captain on the Spanish Main. Even his business in York had never been more profitable. Why must his ambition remain insatiable?

There was silence in the room, except for the crackle of the fire. It was midday but several candles were burning to combat the gloom. Outside, fog pressed against the window panes, obscuring light, while the sound of church bells was muffled by the heavy air. It was into this sombre atmosphere that Gabriellen entered. All the players assembled in the parlour stood up. Only Culpepper and Will Appleshot were absent. But then she had not expected them to be present.

'I shall miss you all,' she said, and needed to clear her throat before continuing. 'Though I shall not be so far away at Willowbank in Chelsea. A visit will always be welcome from any of you.'

'We shall miss you too, Mistress Gabriellen,' Samuel Lacey said kindly. 'The troupe will not be the same without your encouragement.'

She smiled fondly. 'Be loyal to your patron, and try and be tolerant of Culpepper's managership. It is in his own interests to do what is best for the troupe. I'm sorry that so few of you will be remaining together, but I wish you all every success.'

She crossed to Umberto who was gripping the beribboned neck of his guitar, his knuckles white. Today the two Florentines were leaving the troupe. From the wide cuff of her sleeve, she took out a large pearl drop earring which had been one of her father's favourites and held it out to the musician. 'Father would have liked you to have this as a keepsake.'

'I no need a gift to remember the maestro by. This I shall treasure.' His long brown fingers closed over the pearl and his head bowed.

'Good fortune be with you, my friend.' She kissed his cheek before turning to Cesare.

He was dressed with his usual flamboyance in a kingfisher green and purple slashed doublet and hose. But the vivacity had gone from his dark eyes and face. His once black hair was now badger-grey and retreating at the temples, though his trimmed beard was still dark. His swarthy skin was sallow and scored with the lines of advancing age; she had never noticed until now.

'Thirteen years we have been together, Cesare. It is a long time. And you were with my father for many years before I joined the troupe.' She pressed into his hand a gold and ivory manicure set decorated with amethysts which Esmond had always carried with him.

Cesare blinked rapidly against the encroaching tears. 'I no worthy of this. It is too much.'

Gabriellen covered his hand with her own. 'It is little enough to show for your friendship and loyalty over the years. I understand you are returning to Florence to be reunited with your families? I wish you well and happiness.'

'*Grazie*. You too be happy.' He pressed her fingers to his lips. 'Last year in a tavern I talked to a sailor. He come from Florence. He tell me my father is dead. Time for me to go home now. Make peace with Mama.'

Gabriellen blinked aside her own tears and turned gratefully to Poggs and Agnes who were joining her at Willowbank. In the last year Poggs had been suffering from pains in his chest, and his joints had begun to stiffen, making it painful for him to dance. They had agreed to come and help with the house and children. Not as common servants, for their friendship went too deep for that, but as paid helpers and companions.

Gabriellen paused in the doorway for a last look back at

the troupe. 'Good fortune to you all. May Lord Mincham's Men continue to be the pride of London.'

Victor Prew threw his wooden spoon into the greasy bowl of potage. He had been back in London a week and the cold damp weather made his bones ache. Two more failed attempts on Elizabeth Tudor's life had earned him dismissal from both Rome and King Philip's payroll.

Adopting a disguise, he had left his rooms in Rome minutes before the guards had come to arrest him. This time he had fled with a fortune in jewels he had amassed over the years. The Queen of England might be too well protected to fall victim to his plans, not so his other enemies. He had wealth aplenty to pursue his own vendetta against them.

The back street ordinary was as obnoxious as the food it served. On a vacant table opposite them a rat nibbled at a piecrust. The food was inedible. Prew pushed it aside, concealing his disgust when his companion picked up his bowl to gulp down the food as though he had not eaten in a week. Sitting back on his stool, the man wiped his mouth with his sleeve. His small eyes were almost hidden under thick brown brows.

'Now we've eaten,' the man known only as the Woodman grunted, 'who, and where? And what'll you pay?'

His words were as graceless as his manners, Prew thought with an inward sneer. Not that he would say so aloud. The Woodman was too handy with that damned axe of his. What else could one expect from a paid assassin? 'The man's name is Rowan. He's a horse-breeder in Wales. You get twenty marks now and another forty when he's dead.'

'Forty marks now and eighty when he's dead,' the Woodman demanded. His small yellow eyes glittered with menace. 'If you don't pay up when the job's done . . .' He drew his finger across his throat. 'You'll not see another week out, I promise.'

Prew felt the sweat begin to run down his face. 'I'll want proof of Rowan's death.'

The Woodman laughed. 'You can have his head. He'll not be needing it.' He reached out to fondle the long-handled axe resting by the side of the table.

Prew nodded. He had waited a long time for his revenge. He would not be cheated. Rowan's head would be a fine trophy to give that whore Gabriellen in remembrance of her lover – just before she too was killed.

Chapter Thirty-Four

Not even the pain of parting from the players was allowed to spoil their arrival at Willowbank, and by the time they approached the final bend in the river the fog had begun to lift.

Jack stood in the prow of the wherry rowed by four oarsmen as they approached the landing stage of his house just past the village of Chelsea on the Thames. The stiffening breeze ruffled his dark hair beneath his jewelled cap. Immense pride was apparent in his tanned face. At last he was to take up proper residence in the grand house which proclaimed him to the world a man of substance. Through the thinning fog Gabriellen saw the group of willows at the river's edge from which the house had taken its name. Beyond rose the tall redbrick chimneys of her new home.

Jacquetta and Sabine were asleep in her arms, whilst Ambrose leaned over the wherry's side as he stood next to Jack.

'Is that the house I can see through the trees, Papa?' he demanded, green eyes screwed up against the strengthening sunlight. Jack rumpled the boy's fair hair and then made a snatch to catch him as Ambrose overbalanced.

'How many times must I tell you? You treat a river with respect.' He gave the boy a slight shake to emphasise his words. 'As soon as it gets warmer I must teach you to swim. In the meantime, stay away from the river.'

Ambrose wriggled from Jack's clutches, his green eyes idolising the man towering over him. 'Papa, how can I be a famous sea captain like you, and kill the Spanish, if I have to stay away from the river? When will you take me to sea?'

Jack laid a hand on the boy's shoulder. 'Time enough for that.' His voice deepened with pride as he turned to Gabriellen, but sensitive as always where Jack and Ambrose were concerned, she heard too the note of defiance in his voice. 'My son has no fear. At his age I too could not wait to join my father at sea. Even though he was just a fisherman.'

'Our son is the most fortunate of boys. You are the hero of so many.'

As the men lifted their oars and the wherry bumped against the landing steps, Gabriellen gazed at the impressive house. The house which by rights should belong to Jack's wife. She crushed down any guilt. Since Jack's return from Spain, Elizabeth Stoneham had made it obvious she was content to live apart from her husband.

Jack leaped ashore. First he guided Ambrose to safety before the boy in his excitement tried to jump without aid, then he took Sabine in one arm and steadied Gabriellen with the other as she stepped ashore. Agnes and Poggs helped Jacquetta who was awake now and impatient to explore her new surroundings.

Handing the still sleeping Sabine to Agnes, Jack put his arm around Gabriellen's waist. His voice rich with pride, he announced: 'Behold your new home.'

They stood in the gardens which stretched down to the river. The lawns were vast and well tended. The double bayfronted redbrick house had a façade of a dozen windows and was built around an inner courtyard with a fountain. It was imposing, as befitted the home of a knight of the realm, and with thirty rooms overlarge for Gabriellen's taste. Every brick was a monument to the rank and status the courtier Sir Jack Stoneham had achieved. It was also a monument to his self-importance.

Throughout January 1601 Gabriellen saw little of Jack. He spent most of his days and a good many nights at Essex House. She had expected that by her move to Willowbank, Jack would have become more settled. Instead it drove him on to greater ambition. Fear for his safety was as acute as her disappointment.

A domestic life at Willowbank was choking her. She could no longer seek respite in her writing. Inspiration had gone and the empty void in her life seemed to be widening as her restlessness grew. She hated what she felt was disloyalty to Jack, but since he had become bent upon insurrection, the rift between them had increased. They hardly spoke without arguing. Nothing Gabriellen said could stop his pursuit of rebellion. He was not the only malcontent; other noblemen gathered around the volatile Earl of Essex, who raved of the wrongs done him by their Sovereign.

Each week Jack became more remote. Long hours of his visits to Willowbank were spent shut in his study. He was obsessed. The Queen had forgotten her sea captain and Jack would not forgive her that.

In the middle of the month Gabriellen awoke before dawn. Rolling on to her side to put an arm around Jack, she found he was not in bed. She started, the fear which was now with her constantly making her sit up and pull aside the bedhangings to scan the dark room. The wind moaned down the chimney and under the door of the chamber. Its draught rustled the rushes and stirred the tapestry, so that the pale figures on it seemed to move with a stealthy life. Jack stood by the window. He was wearing a fur-lined robe and one hand moodily fingered his bearded chin as he stared through the frost-coated panes towards the river and London.

'Come back to bed,' she urged softly. 'It's freezing, and there's another hour before dawn.'

'Go to sleep.' His voice was abstracted. 'I'll go down to my study. I'll not disturb you there.'

'How can I sleep when you are like this?' She got out of bed, shivering as the cold bit into her warm flesh, and pulled on a robe over her nakedness. Going to his side, she put her arm around his waist. He did not respond and she could feel the tension in his body.

'Go back to bed. You will get cold.' The bleakness of his tone smote her.

'Don't shut me out, Jack. We are becoming strangers. This obsession with Essex is destroying everything that was good between us. We never talk now, because you refuse to discuss your actions.'

'I do what must be done.'

He was patronising her. The flaring of her eyes must have warned him of her anger. He touched her hair.

'I need your understanding in this – not your censure,' he insisted. 'I must protect my interests. The Queen would reduce me to a pauper. I'll not stand by and allow that to happen. You and the children will not suffer because I was too weak to stand up to a tyrant.'

Despite her fears, she did understand his frustration and humiliation. It did not make joining Essex's faction right: 'No one could accuse you of weakness, Jack. Sometimes it takes a greater courage to ride a blow to one's pride. You could lose everything by open revolt.'

'I could also reach heights even I had not envisaged, should we succeed.'

Talk like that terrified her. She did not believe that Essex would win. True, the people adored him, but the Queen had held their hearts for forty years. 'I wish I had your faith, Jack. We have so much, why risk it? Be content with what you have achieved. Ambition will destroy you.'

He put her from him, his eyes and voice icy. 'Would you make me a milksop? A man is master in his own home and of his own destiny.'

'Only a fool will not listen to reason,' she returned, her rising temper driving away the chill of the night.

'If you think me a fool, madam, we have nothing more to say to each other.'

He strode to the door.

'It is your pride that makes a fool of you,' she hurled at him. 'Go to Essex. Listen to those miscreants. But tell me this – which one of them cares whether you live or die? They feed their own jealousy and resentment because they are all in some way failures. Not so you, Jack. You were not born with a title and fortune. What you have, you have won for yourself. That I have always admired and respected.' He halted by the door, his expression hidden from her. She moved to his side and put her hands upon his chest. 'I'll not pander to your vanity by speaking only what you wish to hear. I speak the truth to save you.' Taking his hands, she sank to the floor at his feet. 'Give up this madness. It is you who are important. Not lands. Not fortune.'

'Don't beg, Gabriellen.' His voice thickened with tenderness. Stooping, he lifted her in his arms. 'All my life I have fought for what I wanted. I cannot stop now.' He kissed her. 'What I do, I do for you.'

'No, Jack. This you do for yourself.'

The sadness she felt was in her voice. She had accepted his self-centred ambition years ago. It had made him great. She had accepted the pain of his marriage. That had been before he met her. His love and fidelity were her mainstay.

Whilst she had them, she would forgive him much and stand by him through fame or misfortune.

Her lips met his as he carried her to the bed. In his arms, their recent conflicts faded. Yet honesty made her wonder if the very desperation of their lovemaking was an effort to reclaim the magic of the past. Rational thought fled as he kissed her with a thoroughness which drove the cold from her body, kindling her responses until her whole being was aflame. Entwined in each other's arms, gentleness ended and desire took its place, banishing doubts in the mindless, harmonious meeting of bodies. Lips and hands sought the familiar curves and hollows of flesh freely offered; limbs interlaced and parted; sighs of pleasure were muffled by ardent kisses. She felt the heat and hardness of his body as he covered her, and through half-closed lids saw his eyes stark with the hunger of his desire. He moved against her. Whispered words of love mingled with soft moans of ecstasy, their conflict forgotten, banished by the rapture of their passion.

It was only in the bright light of day, when Jack had ridden away, that Gabriellen's unease returned. Nothing she had said or done had changed anything.

Gabriellen sat in the nursery at the top of the house as the children worked at their studies. Jacquetta sat over her horn-book, copying the letters, and having finished his work, Ambrose was busy drawing Bodkin who perched on the windowsill watching him. Twelve-year-old Laurence was chewing the end of a quill, his face screwed into a scowl as he puzzled over the sums Gabriellen had set him. She looked at him worriedly. He had nimble enough wits when it came to getting into mischief, but writing and arithmetic were a struggle for him. Too often he allowed his concentration to wander. Ambrose, at nine, was far ahead of him in his studies. Not that he was innocent of devilry, but Ambrose also had a serious and considerate side to his nature. Laurence had that streak of wildness which Gabriellen had dreaded would appear in him. He was all Esmond, with none of Nan Woodruff's calming restraint.

Suddenly Bodkin fluttered up into the air and flew round the room before landing on Ambrose's shoulder. Where he had perched was an inky pellet. Laurence was grinning.

'If you are not going to do your work, Larry,' Gabriellen said sternly, 'go and see if Poggs needs help. He's setting up the archery butts for your afternoon practice.'

Laurence leaped from his stool to run from the room, almost colliding with Poggs who was entering. 'I'll saddle the horses,' Laurence shouted back as he disappeared from sight. 'You promised we could ride after lessons.' His tousled head reappeared round the door and he grinned. 'I'll saddle Ceridwen too. You'll join us, won't you, dear sister? Do say you will.'

'Mama, please say yes.' Ambrose added his excited voice to Laurence's. 'Then we can ride as far as Fox's Wood.'

'Tell Laurence we will ride in an hour, so not to saddle the horses just yet.'

Gabriellen looked at Poggs who was rubbing his swollen knuckles, a sign he was disturbed. 'Cornelius Hope is below.'

'What can he want? I doubt it's a courtesy call. He's not been near the troupe for years. From what I hear, only the minor companies will employ him now.' She looked at Agnes who was stacking wooden bricks for Sabine to knock down.

'It bodes no good,' Agnes answered. 'Thee take care, Gabby.'

'I'd rather not see him alone, Poggs,' she said, remembering with a shudder Hope's attack on her at the tavern. 'Ask a maid to bring us wine and saffron cakes, then join me if you will.'

'Hope is up to no good,' Poggs grunted. 'If he's here, it's because he wants something.'

Gabriellen and Poggs entered the winter parlour to discover Hope standing before the fire, warming his buttocks.

'My dear Gabriellen!' Hope beamed at her. 'It is good to see you looking so well, considering the blow you must have been dealt by the Queen's dislike of the play.'

'I have put it behind me,' she answered coolly.

The actor was looking too pleased with himself for her peace of mind. Yet his dyed hair looked like straw, and his fleshy jowls rested on his deep ruff. The years had obviously not treated him kindly.

Gabriellen continued warily, 'Lord Mincham fortunately did not withdraw his patronage from the troupe, though he abandoned his idea of rebuilding The Angel. And he

531

'refuses to allow his men to perform any of Esmond's plays.'

'Foolish in the extreme to deny the public the pleasure of his masterpieces.' Hope smiled, his expression as sly as it was falsely affable. 'Especially his later plays.'

'Other companies have been more understanding,' she answered. Since Esmond's death, Gabriellen had kept all the bound plays in a chest. Any company wishing to perform one had to apply to her for permission. On payment of a fee, they would be loaned a copy on condition it was returned at the end of the performance. She allowed only the most reputable companies to put on Esmond's plays. In this way, she hoped to avoid their being copied and used without payment to her family. It was common practice for companies to steal others' plays, and several times she had heard of new dramas which were replicas of her work.

'My father was a great playwright,' she continued stiffly. 'It is a tribute to him that the Lord Chamberlain's or the Admiral's Men wish to perform his plays.'

'Would they be so eager were they to know their true authorship?'

A maid entered with a tray of refreshments and Gabriellen waited until she left before replying. Whilst pouring wine, she was aware of Poggs's stiff figure by the window. The pause had given her time to regain her composure. She knew what Hope was hinting at, but she was ready for him. Holding out a goblet, she said smoothly, 'I have no idea to what you refer, Mr Hope. But I will not have ill spoken of my father.'

Hope gave a cruel laugh. 'You always were high-stomached for a woman! You know what I mean. Those last plays were never written by Esmond. I knew his work well. Oh, the later works were brilliant, don't get me wrong, but Esmond did not write them.' He smirked. 'We both know who did.'

Poggs darted forward. 'What the devil do you mean by that? Esmond wrote those plays. Now get out of this house, before I call the servants to throw you out.'

'Hold your tongue, little man,' Hope ordered. 'Your vehemence proves me right. Have me thrown from this house at your peril.'

'Gentlemen!' Gabriellen raised her voice to make herself heard. 'I think Mr Hope had better explain his accusations.'

'You'll not dupe me with your haughty manner, Mistress

Angel. *You* wrote those plays. By Christ, that such brilliance should come from a woman's pen is infamous! Were the truth to become public knowledge, some would even say the devil had a hand in it. At first I was mortified that I had prostituted my talent by performing such work. Then, in truth, I had to admit the plays were good. 'Twould be a pity should they all be destroyed and you persecuted for having written them. Do you think you would be spared the Tower should Her Majesty learn that the playwright of *Boudicca* is alive?'

'I deny this absurdity, of course.' Gabriellen held her head high as she challenged him. Her palms had broken out into a sweat and she gripped them together to control the fright his words had given her.

'You can deny it all you will but the plays are written in your hand. Is that not proof enough?'

'I copied them out because my father was going blind.'

'This is news to me!' Cornelius feigned ignorance. 'As I am sure it will be to Culpepper. If Esmond had a disability, he hid it well. Then, pride can make a man do that. But who will believe you when every actor who worked with Esmond knew nothing of his failing sight?'

'I knew,' Poggs intervened.

Cornelius eyed the retired clown belligerently. 'Your loyalty to Esmond was renowned. And to his daughter. You would say anything to defend them.' Cornelius spread his hands wide, his florid face assuming a hurt expression. 'But what need for these harsh words? Your secret could be safe with me, my dear. With a little inducement, of course. I but want a play from you – a lost play of Esmond Angel's found in an old chest. The part you will write specifically for me will be the finest you have ever written. That is the price of my silence.'

'I will not be blackmailed!' Gabriellen advanced on him and Hope retreated several steps across the room. 'I cannot write this play because I did not write the others.'

'That's a lie!' he shouted. 'I give you one more chance to agree to my demands. Otherwise . . .'

'Get out of this house, Hope.' Gabriellen flung out her arm, indicating the door. 'I deny everything you have said. Those plays were written by Esmond Angel.'

Hope gathered up his gloves from the table and stamped to the door. 'You had your chance. I will not allow the theatre to be held up to mockery. You will be exposed, madam, for the base wanton creature that you are. You'll not be so proud then, I warrant.'

When he had left, Gabriellen sank down on to a chair.

Poggs put a hand on her shoulder, his voice strained with fear. 'Why do you not write the play? He means what he says.'

'Had I agreed to his terms, he would not stop at one play. Can't you see that once written, that very play would be proof that I am the playwright? Hope is guessing. Robin Flowerdew, Francis Crofton and Samuel Lacey will attest to Father's failing sight. Cesare and Umberto would, too, if they were in England.'

'The musicians are in Italy, and Crofton has gone to live with his sister in Scotland after a quarrel with Culpepper. Flowerdew is still smarting from his dismissal. Like most actors, he's only interested in himself. He will not take sides. Hope has not forgotten the trouncing you gave him at Taunton. I fear he means to make trouble.'

'It is his word against mine.' Gabriellen laughed bitterly. 'And I have the prejudice of the theatre on my side. What playwright or actor could admit that a woman could write to rival Marlowe, Shakespeare, or my father?'

'But Hope can cause trouble.' Poggs shook his grizzled head. 'You must take care. I fear that Hope seeks your ruin. Word must be sent to Sir Jack at once.'

'No, Poggs. Jack has worries enough without this,' she insisted. 'I must change into my riding habit. I promised the boys I would ride with them.'

'Is that wise in the circumstances?' Poggs tried to dissuade her.

'Even if Hope means to discredit me, it will take time. I expect he will start with the Master of Revels.'

As soon as Gabriellen had ridden out, Poggs sent word to Essex House. He knew Hope would strike without delay and Gabriellen was vulnerable here.

The angry voices rose in cadence at Essex House, Jack's foremost among them. 'If if is agreed that a play will be staged as a warning to the Queen that her tyranny will not be tolerated, then let it be Shakespeare's *Richard II*, not Angel's *Boudicca*.'

His arguments were echoed by Sir Christopher Blount

and Sir Gilli Meyricke, both of whom had been close friends of Essex for years.

The young Earl of Southampton leaned across the table, incensed that his idea was being challenged. 'But Elizabeth has already shown her displeasure at the play *Boudicca*. She has declared it seditious. Does it not show a queen vanquished?'

Jack thumped the table. He did not want Gabriellen's work involved. 'For that reason the players will not perform it. It has been banned. Stage *Richard II*. Does it not show the Peasants' Revolt?'

'Stoneham is right,' said Sir Christopher Blount.

Sir Gilli Meyricke added his voice. 'The warning in that play is clear. Do you not agree, Robin?'

A fanatical glow touched Essex's face. 'Much as I prefer *Boudicca* as it shows a proud queen brought to heel and broken, the people will not see it as such. They cannot miss the message in *Richard II*. That despot was overthrown by Henry IV. Yet I do not seek her downfall, merely to rescue the Queen from her evil advisers and effect a change of government,' he expounded. 'Yet let us not forgot, my friends, if our terms are not acceptable to Elizabeth, her death is inevitable, leaving the way clear for a grateful James VI of Scotland. Henry IV was generous to his followers. James will be no less so.'

Shouts of approval greeted his words. Jack sat back in his chair, studying his companions. Essex's reasons for revolt were easy to understand. Were they not an exaggerated replica of his own? Southampton he knew to be deeply in debt and young enough to have been caught beneath Essex's spell. But what of the others? Blount and Meyricke were old friends – equally rash and hot-tempered as their leader. He scanned the faces of his companions. Most were noblemen in financial difficulties who had been overlooked at Court. Failures. Gabriellen's word for them came back to haunt him. Had he too failed? Was that why he was here? No, he would not acknowledge failure. It was the Queen's ingratitude which spurred his rebellion. His eyes narrowed as yet another argument broke out. They were like starving dogs squabbling over a bone, each wanting the meatiest pickings for himself.

They were a strange assortment of malcontents. Some, obviously mercenaries, had ridden in from Wales and Scotland. There were even several Puritans who harangued the populace with doctrines sanctifying the deposition of monarchs. For a moment he felt disgust. Was Gabriellen right? Which of these men was truly his friend? None, if truth be known. They were too interested in themselves to spare a thought for others. As he would not spare a thought for them should they fall in this insurrection. Perhaps it was madness, but the seeds had taken root. He was confident of their success. He sat forward to voice an opinion then saw Seth Bridges signalling to him from the door.

'There's fear at the house that the mistress is in danger. Poggs thinks you should return.'

'What danger?' Jack saw from the pallor of Seth's pock-marked face that he thought the matter serious.

'She was threatened by an actor who called at the house. Cornelius Hope, his name was. He tried to blackmail her. When she refused him, he turned nasty. Poggs is convinced Hope will stir up trouble. There's some score going way back he wants to settle with the mistress. Out of spite, he could rouse the villagers against her.'

'I'll come at once.'

Jack returned to the table and waited for Essex to finish speaking. 'It is agreed then. Next week *Richard II* will be put on at The Globe.'

Jack made his excuses to Essex. The Earl eyed him warily. 'Whatever these private reasons are, be sure you return the day the play is performed. London will be roused and we must strike without delay.'

'I will be with you,' Jack vowed.

The Welsh valley had been free of snow for some weeks but the ground was hard with frost. Mark pulled the last of the hay bales from the cart and tossed it into the pasture. Taking up a pitchfork he spread hay over the frozen ground for the horses to eat. The young fillies were nervous today. Mark walked round the fence studying the ground. From a head count none of the horses was missing. There never had been a horse stolen from his land, but he'd not take any chances. At the far end of the fence he saw a large footprint which did not belong to himself or Saul. Someone had been here, and up to no good this close to the horses.

A pity Saul had taken Aphra to market that morning, but it could not be helped. Two men were better than one on such ventures. Horse theft was a hanging offence. The man could be armed and dangerous. Mark had worked for Walsingham too long to have qualms about such matters. As a precaution he returned to the house and primed his two German wheel-lock pistols, pulling up the striking pin to prevent their accidental firing. Fixing the holsters to his saddle, he rode out to search for the intruder's trail.

From his hiding place in the edge of the trees, the Woodman saw Rowan approaching. He had spent four days surveying the farm and surrounding land. His trap was carefully laid. Saul Bywood and his wife had ridden out earlier that day which lessened any complications. Mark Rowan was riding to his death.

Mark saw the trip rope leap up out of its covering of leaves a second before it caught Glendower across the knees and brought the stallion down. Kicking his feet out of the stirrups, he rolled free of the horse. He came up into a crouch with the dexterity of an accomplished wrestler as a shadow loomed over him. His first fear was for Glendower who had not struggled to his feet. Then he saw the heavy-set figure outlined against the grey sky, thick arms raised high, a glint of watery sunlight catching the edge of the lethal axe. Instinctively, Mark dived to one side. The axe jarred into the ground inches from his shoulder. Springing to his feet, he reached for the pistol holster on Glendower's back. The stallion still lay on his side, his head craning upwards as he tried to rise and failed. Glendower had broken his leg.

The pistol was free and in Mark's hand. The axe swung down a second time. He ducked and charged his assailant, his head butting the man's stomach. They both fell, rolled, and came on to their feet at the same time. Seeing the blade about to be swiped towards his chest, Mark leaped back. The bite of cold air hit his ribcage where the axe's edge cut through his sheepskin jerkin and leather doublet to the flesh. A peppering of sweat covered his skin. That had been too close. His opponent was some four inches taller than him and at least five stone heavier. As his attacker gathered himself for a second swing, Mark's thumb repositioned the striking hammer of the pistol. This was no ordinary horse-thief, the thought flashed through his mind. He knew the type. The brittle dispassion in the man's eye was that of a paid killer.

Further thoughts fled as the axe swooped down towards him. He side-stepped and, bringing up the pistol, fired.

'Judas's beard!' he swore. His hand must have been shaking for he had aimed at the attacker's heart and now saw that blood was soaking through the shoulder of the man's buff leather jerkin. The impact from the bullet at such close range knocked the axeman off-balance, his weapon hanging loose in one hand. Seeing him about to recover, Mark landed a punch in his stomach and as the man bent forward, put all his weight behind a second swing, ramming it to the jaw. That sent his attacker's huge frame crashing to the ground. He fell awkwardly. His eyes bulged with shock as he lay unmoving. Drawing his dagger, Mark put his knee on the man's chest and the blade to his throat.

'Who paid you?' he demanded, pressing the dagger harder against the flesh.

The Woodman did not answer or move. But the horror in his bloodshot eyes told its own story. The man had fallen on his axe and had broken his back. He was paralysed from the neck down. He would not speak. Why should he? He wanted only to die.

Mark stood up and sheathed his dagger. He felt no pity. 'Scum that you are, I've a good mind to leave you to be eaten by the wild pigs and kites.' He turned to walk away.

'You can't leave me,' a hoarse croak implored.

'Why not?' he ground out. 'Your back's broken. You won't be going anywhere. I'll send word to the Sheriff there's a felon on my land. He should arrive by tomorrow morning. Better start to pray that by then the kites have left you your eyes and the pigs your hands and feet. The Sheriff can save you for the hangman's rope. Justice is done either way.'

'Bastard!'

'You want mercy, tell me who paid you to kill me.'

'Go to hell.'

Mark turned his back and left him. He went to Glendower and knelt at the stallion's head. The horse raised his muzzle, his velvety brown eyes glazed with pain. Grimmouthed, Mark reached for the second pistol. His eyes misted as he put the barrel to Glendower's head. His hand shook and he hardened himself to what must be done. He pulled the trigger. The horse quivered and lay still.

Pain clamped tight Mark's throat, spearing down to his

chest. He bowed over the chestnut neck. He had lost a loyal and faithful friend. For eighteen years, since the very moment of Glendower's birth, they had been together. Wiping a hand across the dampness on his cheek, he stroked the white blaze on the stallion's muzzle in a last farewell.

He stood up slowly and hearing a restless hoof stamping in the nearby undergrowth, discovered the assassin's horse. He mounted, and as he rode past Glendower, paused to look down at the noble stallion. He did not spare a second glance for the Woodman who cried out as he passed.

Within the hour he was back in the wood, driving a wagon, with two grooms accompanying him. Taking out spades, they began to dig. As Mark worked he could hear the snorting of the wild pigs which had begun to snuffle closer. The Woodman began to shout for mercy. Ignoring his cries, Mark occasionally shooed the swine away and for the next hour worked off his anger at Glendower's unnecessary death by digging a grave in the hard earth. Shovelling some lime into the hole, Mark nodded to the grooms to help him roll Glendower into it. By the time they had finished, the Woodman was ready to tell Mark all he needed to know.

Only then did he heave the Woodman into the wagon and take him to the house for Aphra to tend on her return. The Sheriff had already been summoned. Tomorrow Mark would leave Wales for London. If Prew had returned to England and was behind this, then Gabriellen's life also was in danger.

Chapter Thirty-Five

The ride to Fox's Wood exhilarated Gabriellen. Toby Gordon, the groom who accompanied her and the two boys, was a young man of twenty. He had lost a hand during the Irish campaign and Jack had given him work. Despite his handicap Toby was a cheerful man who loved horses and children and always had a dozen tales to tell of his life at sea. He had been one of the few crewmen to survive the sinking of *The Golden Lady* and their subsequent escape from Spain. He was devoted to Jack, and Laurence and Ambrose obeyed him as they did no other servant.

Toby rode just ahead with the boys who were insisting on jumping an uprooted tree. Gabriellen lagged behind, smiling fondly at the antics of her brother and son. The weather was mild for the last day of January, but there was a promise of rain in the dismal grey sky. She ran a hand over Ceridwen's chestnut neck. The mare was a link with Mark she cherished, and as always when she rode her, Gabriellen's thoughts would return to her stay in Wales. An image of Mark's haggard appearance as she had last seen him at Jesmaine's graveside haunted her. She had heard nothing from the Welshman since then. How had he fared? She felt the heaviness of guilt that their friendship had ended. There were still times when she missed his banter and teasing. She should not have allowed him to grieve alone after Jesmaine's death. He had needed her friendship then, as she had needed his in Wales.

Her gaze was drawn to Ambrose whose pony jumped the tree with ease whilst Laurence's shied away from it.

'Come on, cabbage-head,' Ambrose taunted. 'Don't sit there like a basket of turnips. You have to encourage the mare over the jump, not lose your temper and try and force it.'

An expression crossed Ambrose's face which sent a jolt

through Gabriellen's breast. In that moment, he looked like Mark. Secretly, she believed him to be Mark's child, but since he bore her colouring she could never be entirely certain.

There was a whoop of joy as Laurence's pony jumped the tree. Gabriellen smiled at the boys as the first spots of rain fell.

'Last one home's a scaredy-titmouse,' Ambrose yelled as he dug in his heels to urge his pony to a gallop.

'Ambrose, come back here!' Gabriellen ordered. 'The village is ahead. How many times must I tell you? It's too dangerous to ride fast through the street. Someone may be hurt.'

He slowed his pace and allowed the others to catch him up. He whipped off his hat and struck Laurence across the sleeve with it. 'Once through the village, I'll race you.'

'I wager my dagger against your new longbow that I beat you,' Laurence answered, sounding so like Esmond that Gabriellen felt her eyes fill with tears.

'There will be no wagering,' she responded as they approached the village.

Forced to bend her head against the slashing rain, she was unaware that the few villagers caught in the rain had stopped to stare at her.

'There she is – Stoneham's harlot!' a man shouted.

Shocked, Gabriellen looked over her shoulder at the three rough-looking men, probably farm labourers. Their coarse vulgar faces were flushed with drink and they were obviously looking for sport.

'Lewd Jezebel!' another voice from across the street joined in. Four men who from their sombre garb were Puritans began to walk across the road to block the road. 'Sister of Babylon! Daughter of Gomorrah!'

Fury raged within her at their accusations. Her first instinct was to stay and answer them. The pious condemnation in their faces warned her of the folly of that. It frightened her, as much for the children's safety as her own. Ahead, Toby and the boys glanced over their shoulders as they cantered on, their faces white with fear. Kicking Ceridwen into a gallop, she shouted: 'Ride hard. Stop for nothing.'

One of the farm labourers, faster than the others, made a grab at Ceridwen's bridle. His fingers touched it. At the same moment the mare veered, startled by his abrupt movement, and his hands snatched at air. Gabriellen felt her skirts grabbed, the heavy velvet jerking her against the high back of the saddle. A cry rose to her throat as she clung to the pommel, terrified that she would be pulled to the ground. Then the stitching at her waist tore, the gown and her petticoat ripping to leave a strip waving like a pennant in the labourer's fist. The flapping material further frightened the excited mare. With Gabriellen's hands loose on the reins Ceridwen pranced sideways, backing into a garden fence, then began to circle. Several precious moments were lost before Gabriellen regained control and turned the mare once more towards Willowbank.

Her kicking to urge the mare forward had exposed Gabriellen's thigh. The sight of her bare flesh stirred the labourers' lust.

'Stop her!' a man behind her yelled. 'We'll give the whore something to put in her plays.'

Their jeering faded as they saved their breath to pursue her along the road, their hands outstretched to pull her from the saddle. Their words confirmed that Hope was behind this. A glance showed Gabriellen that Toby and the boys had passed the Puritans but her way was blocked as these men spread across the street, determined to stop her flight.

She lowered her head as Ceridwen charged towards them. They gave no sign of stepping aside. Had she the courage to run a man down? Gabriellen gritted her teeth and braced herself. She had to. Her thoughts ran like quicksilver through her mind, while the events around her seemed to be happening at a frighteningly slow pace.

'Stop her! Drag her to the ground!' a ruffian wheezed breathlessly as he continued to run alongside.

'The pen of a corrupt and evil wanton will not flourish in this land,' a Puritan proclaimed. 'Come, good people of this hamlet, rid yourselves of the devil's handmaiden in your midst.'

'Mama! Mama!' she could hear Ambrose screaming.

Dimly she was aware of faces appearing at windows, of doors opening hesitantly as figures peered out. If those farm labourers caught her, they would take pleasure in stripping her naked. And very likely those damned Puritans would look on, saying it was the Lord's judgement.

Or were they Puritans? She was almost upon them. She could see their unkempt hair, the shadow of neglected beards. Suddenly the truth came to her. They were strolling players, men sent by Hope to stir up public feeling against her. So far the downpour had kept the villagers from joining in the pursuit. Ceridwen had outstripped the running labourer and Gabriellen heard the man's shout as he skidded on the wet muddy road and fell headlong into a puddle. The pseudo-Puritans blocked the road ahead.

Gripping her riding whip in her hand, Gabriellen bore down upon them. At the last moment the one directly in Ceridwen's path jumped aside. Another forgot his religious fanatic's role and leered at her naked legs as he tried to grab the bridle. He succeeded, hauling on the mare's head with all his strength to slow her careering pace.

'Well done, man. She's ours now!' a jubilant voice shouted.

Scalding fear choked Gabriellen's scream. She raised her whip, striking the man who still clung to the bridle across the face. Blood from his gashed cheek spurted across her knee and splashed her torn petticoat. He fell back to the ground, clutching his face with his hands. She was free. There was a sickening crunch as Ceridwen's back hoof came down on her attacker's shin, crushing the bone.

Open road lay ahead. She was safe. Thank God she had escaped! She was passing the last cottage when a sharp pain in her back rocked her forward in the saddle. Another blow hit the side of her head. They were stoning her! She cried out when two more stones struck her head and back. The blows had dazed her and she was reeling in the saddle. Another like that and she would be knocked to the ground.

The next stone fell harmlessly on the track a few feet behind her. She dared not slacken her pace. Willowbank was just ahead. Toby had opened the tall iron gates. The moment she was through them, he slammed them shut.

'Get into the house, mistress,' he shouted. 'I'll rouse the servants.'

Gabriellen was shaking so violently that as she leaped from the saddle, her legs gave way and she fell to her knees in the flagstoned courtyard. Laurence's and Ambrose's screams had alerted the household. As she tried to stand, Agnes was at her side, lifting her to her feet.

'Shutter and bar the windows,' Gabriellen managed to

gasp. 'Hope has raised the village against me.'

A deafening boom of thunder resounded overhead, its violence making Gabriellen start. As its rumbling faded, the torrential rain drummed in her ears and stung her face.

'While this storm holds, thee will be safe.' Agnes drew her inside the house. 'Seth left two hours ago to fetch Sir Jack. Poggs suspected Hope would lose no time. The cap'n will be here soon.' She shook her head as she regarded Gabriellen's bedraggled and dripping figure. 'Look at thee. There's blood in thy hair and thee be drenched to the skin.' Tears filled the servant's eyes as she helped Gabriellen off with her cloak. 'A pox on Hope! If I see that swine, I swear I'll not be responsible for my actions.'

'Mama!' Ambrose threw himself against Gabriellen's skirts. 'I wanted to come back and save you. Toby stopped me. Why were those men so hateful to you?'

'It seems I have made an enemy,' she said, stroking his hair. 'You were very brave. I'm proud of you. Papa will be here soon. Go with Poggs and put on dry clothes. The danger is past.'

'Don't thee believe that!' Agnes whispered in a voice which would not reach the boys who were chasing each other up the stairs to their rooms, their fears quietened. 'Hope means to do thee harm. It would be wise if thee left Willowbank.'

'I will not be hounded from my home by Hope's malicious rumours,' Gabriellen declared. 'I shall insist my father wrote the plays and prefer charges against Hope for defamation of character.'

'Fine words.' Agnes wrung her hands as she followed Gabriellen to the stairs. 'That all takes time. Hope has worked his mischief already. We'll have a mob at the door once the storm dies away. There's many who revile thee for thy position here. Would rise against thee, seeing thee as evil and corrupt. Even the women will support them. Thee be the mistress who has usurped the wife's place in this house.'

Gabriellen leaned heavily on the newel post. 'Few know of Jack's marriage.'

'Hope will make it his business to spread gossip.' Agnes dabbed at a tear on her cheek. 'I'm sorry, Gabby. Thee dunna deserve this. But I've seen what a mob can do. Did they not once turn upon me? Thee must go from here.

544

Think of the children. What if the mob fire the house?'

'It would not come to that. Jack is a hero of the people.'

Agnes eyed her sadly. 'Are thee prepared to take that risk?'

'I don't want to leave Willowbank, Jack.' Gabriellen faced her lover and slapped his hand away as he pulled her cloak over her shoulders and began to fasten it.

'So you have been saying for the last hour. But leave you will. I'll not have your life endangered.'

'If I run away, I may as well proclaim my guilt. Cornelius Hope will have won.'

She tried to undo the ties and this time Jack smacked her hand away. Taking her shoulder, he gave her a rough shake.

'Gabriellen, the rain has almost stopped. The barge I hired to take you and the children to safety is ready. Will you stop arguing and get yourself aboard?' He began to propel her out of the house.

She turned to ask Poggs to help her. He was holding Jacquetta's hand and Agnes carried Sabine. Both of them refused to meet her stare. At a nod from Jack they hurried to the landing stage. With undignified haste, Gabriellen was made to follow.

'I will not run away, Jack.' She finally wrenched her arm from his iron grip. Her face set with determination, she sat down on the topmost of the stone landing steps, heedless of the wet seeping into her billowing velvet skirts. 'Hope will not drive me from my home.'

'Your sentiments are commendable.' Jack's voice softened though it still had a thread of steel running through it. 'They are also foolhardy. If those ruffians are still in the village, they could break into the house. It is more than your honour which will be lost – it will be your life.' He put his hands on his hips and stared down at her, his lips twisting with bleak humour. 'I had forgotten what a stubborn wench you can be.'

So saying, he bent and hoisted her over his shoulder. 'It comes to something when I have to abduct my own woman.'

With an oath on his breath, he stepped on to the barge. 'Cast off,' he commanded the rowers. 'Row as you have never rowed before.'

A chorus of giggles from Ambrose, Laurence and Jacquetta greeted his buccaneering manner. The children's amusement stung Gabriellen into striking her fists against his broad back. 'Damn you, put me down! I'll not be treated like a child, nor bullied into submission.'

He placed her under the barge's small protective awning, his expression grim as he stood back to look towards the house.

'Of all the mean and underhand tricks . . .' Her tirade ended in a gasp as she saw what held his attention. A score of men armed with cudgels were running up the drive from the direction of the village. The six remaining servants from the house, together with another dozen men who had sailed with Jack and had been recruited that afternoon in a London tavern by Seth Bridges, stood in defence of the house.

'Did you really want to stay and argue the rights and wrongs of Hope's accusations with them?' Jack commented as he sat beside her and took her in his arms.

She shook her head. 'I have brought more trouble upon you.' She looked into his serious face and touched his jaw with her fingers. 'Why do you bother with me? If I had written that stupid play for Hope, none of this would have been necessary. Indeed, if I had never written any play, it would be the better for us all!'

Jack kissed her brow. 'For all your stubbornness, those men did frighten you. You're safe now. So are the children.'

Neither of them paid any attention to the white-bearded figure in the wherry moving towards Willowbank. Its occupant watched with interest. The barge passed him by and as he drew level with Stoneham's house, Victor Prew saw the angry scene and a fight break out between a small mob and the servants. He ordered the wherry to turn around and keep Stoneham's barge in sight. Events had happened here he was not aware of. He would make it his business to find out about them. As he intended to find out everything about his wife before exacting retribution upon her.

It was fast growing dark and moths were attracted to the prow lanthorns of the Stoneham barge, the rising mist luminous as it cast a halo around the lights. They sped past the Palace at Whitehall where the sound of music and revelry drifted to them, and on down the river past Essex House where the music was louder, the carousers more boisterous in this rival Court. When they approached the city limits, out of the gossamer mist appeared tall ships at anchor, their masts lost in the darkness, their painted figureheads ghostly spectres beneath the thrusting bowsprits.

From the comfort of Jack's embrace, Gabriellen roused herself to ask, 'Where are you taking us?'

'To the one person I know who will safeguard you from the Queen's soldiers – should it come to that – and from public spite. It is the last place Hope, or anyone else, will think to look for you. I'm placing you under Edward Dawkin's protection.'

'But he's One-eyed Ned – a villain!' Jack put a finger to her lips to stop her protest.

'He is a friend. I need to know you are safe in the days ahead. Tomorrow I must return to Essex House.'

After the fright of the afternoon his words ignited her anger. 'Is pandering to Essex more important than the safety of our children? What sort of impression will One-eyed Ned make on Ambrose? And Laurence is so like Esmond, I shudder to think of the effect this will have on him. Such people are the very company I should make sure he avoids.'

'Perhaps you would prefer that I packed you and the children off to Wales for Rowan to dote over?'

'Just what do you mean by that?'

Their gazes locked in a clash of wills, Gabriellen's as bright and incensed as Jack's. The barge was heading for Bankside. The tide was ebbing and they came aground several paces from the weed-coated steps near the bearpit. Gabriellen found herself staring at the empty skyline where once the Angel had stood. Close by that site now was The Globe where the plays of her father's friend Will Shakespeare were acclaimed.

Jack grimaced as he saw the oozing mud he would have to walk across. 'Stay there, Gabriellen. I'll carry the children ashore, then come back for you to save spoiling your gown.'

'I may have been driven from my home by a band of hired ruffians, but I do not fear a little mud.' She stood up, lifted her skirts above her ankles and jumped down. Her expression was defiant as she met Jack's exasperated glare.

'Stubborn jade,' he muttered as he hoisted Ambrose to

his shoulders and lifted Sabine into his arms.

Gabriellen lost a shoe in her rebellious trek across the river mud. It brought back a rush of memories of that other occasion, almost at this very spot, when she and Mark had rescued Hywel. The contrast between their laughter and companionship at that time and Jack's bleak censure now added to her wretchedness. It was all very well acting and dressing as befitted a gentlewoman, but through her veins ran the wild blood of an outlaw. Jack might reap the benefits of her lack of convention, but he would never understand how little position or material possessions meant to her. Mark had understood.

Fortunately Poggs noticed the lost shoe and retrieved it for her. When Gabriellen stood on the bank she held on to his shoulder to put it back on her muddy foot.

'Look at you,' Jack tutted with disgust. 'You look like a guttersnipe.'

'Then I shall be at home with the company you are about to thrust me into,' she replied with equal sarcasm.

Having released Ambrose and given Sabine back into Agnes's care, Jack grabbed Gabriellen's arm and pulled her out of earshot of the servants. 'I can take just so much of your obstinacy, Gabriellen. Remember, Edwin Dawkin is my friend. He was also a friend of Esmond's. One day you will have more than the sanctuary he will offer you this night to be grateful to him for!'

They walked in angry silence through the dark streets. A few menacing forms detached themselves from the shadows. At a curt word from Jack, they slunk away and left them unmolested. That Jack obviously knew the password and appeared at ease amongst these arch-villains pricked her interest. She knew, of course, he had spent some time living on his wits in the streets of London, but it was a subject he refused to discuss.

Off the main street, in an alleyway, a large house stood separate from its neighbours. Lights shone in every window. A fiddler was playing in one part of the building, and viol and pipes in another. As they passed an open window on the second floor, there was a burst of drunken laughter. An object sailed through the window to land at Gabriellen's feet. She looked down at it with surprise, then had difficulty controlling her amusement as her sense of the ridiculous overcame her outrage. An exaggeratedly large and elaborately decorated codpiece lay on the point of her shoe. She kicked it off and subjected Jack to an arch look.

A groan escaped him. 'I'm sorry, Gabriellen. It would appear Ned is throwing a banquet. He will have some of the girls there to entertain his friends.'

She had never seen Jack embarrassed before and could not resist taunting him in return for the undignified way he had taken her aboard the barge. 'An entertainment which you seem overly familiar with. As, no doubt, was my father.'

At his shocked expression her good humour triumphed. 'Oh, Jack, I had not taken you for a monk before you met me. If it was not that this is such a deplorable place to bring the children, I would find the episode diverting.'

She dimpled mischievously. 'Of course, I have never been inside a bordello. But I must confess to a curiosity to know what they are like.'

'That does it!' Jack pulled her away from the open door. 'I'll find an inn for you to stay at.'

As he put a hand on Gabriellen's arm to lead her away, a voice from an upper window shouted: 'Stoneham! Is that you?'

Jack stood in the light cast by an open window on the first floor. A dark head appeared at the aperture.

'It is you! I thought I recognised your voice. What are you doing dithering outside? Not at all like you. Oh, your pardon.' One-eyed Ned had just seen Gabriellen. 'That looks like Mistress Angel with you. And, God's spleen – children too. Stay there. I'll be down.'

A bare-breasted woman sauntered out of the house. She stood in the doorway, the light behind her showing the outline of her hips and legs through the single petticoat she wore. Her yellow hair hung loose and matted about her shoulders, the heavy paint on her eyes and lips smeared, making a gross caricature of what once must have been a pretty woman. Though her face looked middle-aged, Gabriellen guessed from the firmness of her breasts she had probably not yet reached twenty. One-eyed Ned emerged from the door and pushed the woman back inside with a none too gentle slap on her behind. Ned wore a purple and silver doublet which was open to the waist to reveal a white silk shirt, and his shoes had diamond buckles. In fact, despite the apparent debauchery within the house, he looked as he had every time she had seen him – like a misplaced courtier.

'Good though it is to see you, Edward,' Jack began, 'it was a mistake for us to come here.'

One-eyed Ned surveyed their group with his single eye, his expression sobering. 'You are in trouble, my friend. Bring your family and servants through to the back of the house. It is quieter there. I shall send my guests on to Nell Lovegood's – they will be amply entertained there.' He turned to Gabriellen and bowed with courtly elegance. 'I regret, Mistress Angel, that you have witnessed this salacious celebration.'

'Do not turn your friends from your door on my account, Mr Dawkin. We planned to take rooms at an inn.'

'I'll not hear of it. You are Esmond Angel's daughter. If you are in trouble there is no safer place than under Edward Dawkin's roof.'

With some misgivings Gabriellen allowed Jack to escort her to the back of the house. One-eyed Ned went ahead of them to ensure that any open doors, whose occupants' antics might offend her, were firmly shut before she passed them by.

It was the beginning of the two most bizarre and perilous weeks of Gabriellen's life.

There were no more banquets given by Edward Dawkin while Gabriellen was a guest in his house. She was surprised how respectably her host could live when he chose. At odd hours of the day or evening he disappeared on business, but during her stay he was there more often than Jack.

According to Jack, events at Essex House were moving fast. This Saturday *Richard II* would be performed at The Globe. To Gabriellen's annoyance Jack had forbidden her attendance. She had been equally surprised when, in contradiction of Jack's wishes, One-eyed Ned, or Edward as he insisted she call him, offered to escort her. Tactfully, she declined, aware that if the play was meant to incite the people of London, there could well be trouble in the streets.

At first she had been uneasy in the Upright Man's company, his reputation as both arch-rogue and rake making her wary. However, he was their host, and out of politeness his company could not be avoided. As the days passed she began to relax in his presence, for to her he was always

550

courteous and charming. During the long hours when Jack was away, Edward frequently joined her in the parlour. Often he would speak with affection of her father. Gabriellen was surprised by the respect in which Edward held his memory.

'There will never be another Esmond Angel,' he said one evening as the serving maid cleared the plates from the table.

They had dined alone, Poggs and Agnes eating with the servants of the household, and Jack away at Essex House. Edward refilled the gold goblets with wine. He lived in luxury. His tableware was of gold and silver, as were the candlesticks which lit the intimate parlour. On the walls were the finest tapestries Gabriellen had seen. They were all stolen property, of course, brought to Edward to disperse by the gangs of thieves he ruled.

He raised his goblet in salute to her. 'There will never be another woman like Gabriellen Angel. Jack shamelessly neglects you.'

She shook her head, denying both statements, and smiled. 'I understand the ambition which drives him.' Her smile became wistful. 'Ambition is a mistress I can live with.'

Edward sat forward. Making a steeple of his fingers, he pressed them to his chin. His blue eye regarded her solemnly. 'You are an exceptional woman. You have many of Esmond's qualities, but I have discovered none of his weaknesses.'

Gabriellen laughed. 'I have many flaws. Jack will tell you that. I am stubborn, hot-headed, and despite my matronly years, at times something of a hoyden.'

Edward stood up and came to stand directly behind her chair. 'You are also a fascinating coquette,' he said, resting his hand on her shoulder.

Immediately she tensed, her eyes dangerously bright as she looked over her shoulder at him. 'You are too worldly a man, Mr Dawkin, to mistake the light-hearted bantering of a guest and her host for anything other than that. Whatever my faults, I hold loyalty and honour in high regard.'

The hand was removed from her shoulder and Edward returned to his seat. There was a glitter in his single eye which disturbed Gabriellen as he said, 'Jack is a most fortunate man.'

As he made no further advances, Gabriellen began to relax. She had to admit that she had enjoyed his company these last two weeks, and she was too sensible to take offence at his overture upon her virtue. His reputation had led her to expect no less. That he had taken her rebuff with gentlemanly acceptance provoked her curiosity about him.

At all times his manners towards her were as impeccable as his dress. These private rooms in his house, though furnished and adorned with stolen goods, were a tribute to his good taste. Nothing was cheap. His conversation proved him to be well educated – much more so than Jack. The charm he exerted was effortless. But she had lived long enough in Bankside to know that he ruled the Underworld as much from general fear of the retribution he could wield, as from respect.

Gabriellen sipped her wine and studied him over the rim of her goblet. What could have led such a man to take up this life? He was certainly an enigma. Jack had told her very little about him. Edward was forty-three, apparently, but for all his wild and disreputable living, could pass for a man several years younger. He was of average height and his figure still as slender as a man's half his age. There was little grey in his black hair and the red streak in his beard was probably hereditary. He was a distinguished and handsome man. She doubted Edward Dawkin received many refusals of his favours.

'You knew my father for many years, Edward. How did you meet him?'

'Over a game of primero at Nell Lovegood's.'

Gabriellen frowned. 'That is a tavern?'

Edward put his head on one side, his lips twisting into a grin. 'A different kind of establishment altogether. It is the most prestigious of its kind in London.'

Aware of exactly the kind of place to which he referred, she nodded and changed the subject. 'Delicacy precludes my enquiring more of that meeting. However, may I ask if, like my father, you were born a gentleman? Everything about your manner and this house suggests it.'

'Men have died for enquiring too closely into my past.'

Affronted, Gabriellen stood up. 'I do not repay an indebtedness, Mr Dawkin, by repeating gossip. I did not wish to pry. I asked out of interest. I should not have presumed.'

She moved to the door, but he was there before her.

'Your pardon. Please, sit down. Old habits die hard. It was your father who some twenty years ago told me to trust no one and keep my own counsel.'

'He certainly followed his own advice!'

She allowed herself to be led back to her seat.

'You sound bitter.'

'Did I not have the right to know that his marriage to my mother was bigamous? That I was base-born. It would have been easier to bear hearing it from him, rather than from that harridan who was his wife.' Her eyes misted and to combat the painful memory she drank down the contents of her goblet. 'I would not have loved him less.'

Edward refilled her wine cup. Picking up his own, he considered it before saying, 'I hated my father when I learned I was his by-blow. Esmond knew how I felt. He loved you too well to risk your feeling as I did.'

Gabriellen remained silent during this revelation. She rested her elbow on the table and propped her chin on her knuckles, wondering if Edward would say more. After another pause, he looked at her steadily. 'The first time I saw my father I was four. I lived with my grandparents in a farm cottage on the estate. My mother had died when I was born. I was my grandparents' shame, but they were too religious to turn me out. They clothed and fed me, and for the most part ignored me. One morning my father rode up from the manor to claim me. After fifteen years of marriage his wife was barren. He wanted an heir and I was his flesh and blood.'

He shrugged and tossed back his wine, refilling his goblet before he continued. Gabriellen sat very still, aware that this was a story few had heard.

'It was a different world at the manor,' Edward went on. 'For years my father treated me in every way as his legitimate son. Indeed, I was led to believe that I was. His wife's indifference did not trouble me, I was used to that. My clothes were the finest money could buy. I had a string of scholars to educate me, fencing and riding masters – everything a young gentleman should learn was taught to me. At seventeen I fell in love with the youngest of a neighbour's seven daughters. We were betrothed.'

He paused and drank from his goblet, his handsome face tight with suppressed anger. 'A month later my stepmother died. Four months after that, my father caused a scandal by marrying his young housekeeper. She was only five years older than myself, and until that time had acted the part of a pious and respectable widow.'

Edward laughed sardonically. 'She should have been on the stage! Six months after the wedding, my half-brother was born. She lost no time in spreading the news that I was a by-blow and that it was her son who was the legitimate heir. My betrothal was renounced, the woman I loved packed off to an aunt in Devon where a more suitable match was made for her. Within the next four years a further three boys filled the nursery. My father's second wife hated me, and from the first months of her marriage did everything to turn him against me. No lie was too great to defame my character. Father was besotted and believed her. He turned against me, but his conscience kept me by his side. Until that shrew made the basest accusation of all. Weeping hysterically, she declared that when Father was away from the house one morning, I tried to rape her. I was twenty and innocent of that charge. Without even a hearing, I was turned penniless from the house.'

He fingered the stem of his goblet, then with a shake of his head lounged back in his chair, hooking one arm over its carved back. 'Now why did I tell you all that? You are a good listener. A deceptive, seductive listener, to draw a man to indiscretion.'

The cruel injustice of his story moved her to compassion. 'You told me in confidence. I would not break it, even to Jack.'

With lightning speed he took her hand and raised it to his lips. 'You would keep a secret from Jack?'

She gently extracted her hand and stood up, disconcerted by the ardour in his voice. 'I have never broken a confidence. Since this does not affect Jack, I shall not begin now.' She moved to the door but again he was there before her.

'Always it is Jack – Jack!' he said savagely. 'He is a worthless rogue. Why do you stay with him?'

'I think this conversation has gone far enough, Mr Dawkin,' she said stiffly. She knew he was a dangerous man to cross. Her throat dried as she combated rising fear.

He gripped her arm, his fingers bruising her flesh as he growled, 'Your fidelity is wasted on Stoneham. I want you, Gabriellen. Jack will not return tonight. Come to my room.'

'I most certainly will not!' She tried to pull her arm free and instead found herself pressed against the length of his body. 'Let me go, Mr Dawkin.'

'Not without a kiss.' He pushed her against the wall, his mouth hot as it covered hers.

'No!' she cried, twisting her head away. He gripped her jaw, forcing her to endure his kiss. As he pulled away she brought up her hand to slap him. 'How dare you!' she seethed.

To her mounting fury, he caught her hand before it met its target. Twisting her arm behind her back, he subjected her once more to his ravaging kiss. When he released her, she was shaking with outrage.

'I knew I was not wrong,' he said hoarsely. 'Your trembling tells me that you want me.'

'You mistake the matter, sir,' she spat out, barely resisting the urge to wipe her mouth on her sleeve to rid it of the taste of him. 'Touch me again and Jack will learn of your infamy. You offered us your protection. When Jack returns we shall leave here.'

'You forget, I rule in Bankside.' His single eye glinted cruelly. 'Stoneham roams unmolested upon my orders. That can be changed. But if you were to show your gratitude . . .' He smiled in a way that made her blood run cold.

'There's no need to put on your haughty airs with me. You are your father's daughter. Do you not receive the profits from his business here in London? Perhaps it is time you learned where that money comes from.'

Gabriellen strained back from him but he held her tight. 'Until your brother reaches twenty-one, you are part owner of Nell Lovegood's most worthy establishment.'

She fought a wave of incredulity and nausea. 'A bordello? That cannot be!'

'It can – and is! Until a few years ago Esmond was the sole owner. It has been in your family for generations,' he rapped out, clearly enjoying her discomfiture and dismay. 'Lack of funds forced Esmond to sell a share in it to me, and to one other. Jack is that partner. And if ever a man enjoyed sampling the merchandise of his business more than Jack Stoneham, I have yet to meet such a one.'

'How can you speak such lies?' she raged. 'You who call Jack your friend.'

'Partner, dear lady. Partner – not friend.' Edward laughed at the horror on her face. 'But let this not spoil our pleasure. I admire your spirit, but your morals are no better than your father's. You are Stoneham's whore. I ask only a single night of your company. Why such misplaced morality? I would have thought a woman with your pride would want to pay Jack back for his countless peccadillos with the girls at Nell's and the women at Court.'

'You lie!'

'Such loyalty. Such trust,' Ned mocked. 'Why not ask Jack?'

'He loves me. I would not insult him by questioning his fidelity.'

'Then, madam, you are a fool. Possibly Jack does love you. He's certainly kept you in style over the years. These other women, he uses for a fleeting pleasure. They mean nothing to him – but they are as necessary to him as breathing.'

'I will not listen to you.' Gabriellen rose above the pain his words caused, to hurl her contempt in his face. 'Only the basest knave would malign a man to get his woman into bed.'

One-eyed Ned shrugged, though his hold upon her arms remained tight. 'Forget I spoke. Allow your love to blind you. You'd not be the first. Jack still manages to keep Elizabeth Stoneham sweet whilst he rakes in a small fortune every year from her father's business.' He bent his head, again, seeking to capture her lips as he murmured, 'You will not deny me, Gabriellen. No one does.'

Furious, she resorted to the trick Esmond had taught her as a girl. She scraped the sole of her shoe down the length of his shin, at the same time angrily defending her lover. 'Now I know you are lying! Jack saved that business and rescued Elizabeth from bankruptcy to help support his children in York, but he is estranged from his wife.'

With a snort of pain, One-eyed Ned thrust her away from him and rubbed his shin. His look was venomous as he glared at her. 'You bitch!' His lip curled with fury. 'No one does that to Edward Dawkin and gets away with it. Out of respect for your father, I'll not give you the thrashing you deserve. But you will hear the truth, and I hope it burns in your gut like the pox. So Jack is estranged from his wife, is he? I suppose out of the kindness of his heart he visits York two or three times a year? Just to support the children, is it? It's a task he must relish . . . from the rate his family expands. Is it six or seven little Stonehams now? Not forgetting the one his wife expects come April. Or did it slip his mind to mention the new additions to his brood? No wonder he has thrown in his lot with Essex! With such a large family in York, and another three bastards at Willowbank to support, he must be desperate for money.'

He stood back from the door to allow her to pass, but did not trouble to open it for her. As her hand rested on the latch, he threw his parting shot.

'No one refuses me, madam. I want you out of my house by tomorrow. I suggest you go to Nell Lovegood's. After all, you own it! Be fitting for you to mix with your fellow whores there. Consider the partnership I made with your father at an end. I have other interests on which to expend my time. Tell Jack I want the money for my share by the end of the week. He knows the price of refusing to meet my terms.'

'Which is?'

'Death, madam. You forget, my word is law. No one can escape my judgement.'

'Or your spite,' she bristled, too angry to consider how dangerous were her words. 'Your pride is wounded that I refused your favours! Call yourself a man? You act like a spoilt child. You revile Jack because you are jealous of him. You both served your apprenticeship in the London gutters. Jack rose above that to be a great man – a hero of the people. While for all your fine clothes and rich trappings, you still wallow in the gutter's filth and degradation.'

'Be thankful you are Esmond's daughter, or you would perish for your insults.' Ned put a hand to her throat, his thumbs pressing it menacingly. 'I was your father's acolyte. He taught me weakness was a luxury an Upright Man could not afford. I rule here because I have permitted no one to get the better of me. Jack is a mere pawn at Court, while I am King of Bankside.' He shoved her away from him, his tone ominous. 'A king has many powers, not least of life and death. I could have given you a night of pleasure. Instead you have lost my protection. In the days ahead you will have cause to rue your high-handedness. There's a man in London asking after you: shortish, stout, white-haired and bearded.'

'I know of no such man,' she said frostily.

'Do you not, Mistress Angel?' One-eyed Ned preened his beard. 'Or should I say, Mistress Prew? 'Tis your husband. There is already word out that he has paid an assassin to deal with another lover of yours in Wales.'

He laughed maliciously. 'By tomorrow you will begin to learn what it means to have denied Edward Dawkin.'

Gabriellen reeled away from him. She was horrified not only at the threat to Jack, but to Mark also. Had Prew sent a man to kill him? How could she discover the truth? There was danger all around her.

Everything was packed by the time Jack returned the next morning. He had come back to change his clothes and his mood was excited. Today *Richard II* was to be performed. Tomorrow would see the Queen's reaction. The rebels at Essex House were ready to rouse the people of London if the need arose.

'You cannot leave here, Gabriellen,' he said tersely. 'It is the safest place.'

'Have you heard a word I've said?' She rounded on him as he fastened his clean doublet. From his expression he clearly had not. 'Edward Dawkin made it very clear last evening that if I did not spend the night with him, we must leave. He also wants the money for his share in Nell Lovegood's.'

'You know about that?' Jack looked shocked. 'He was sworn to secrecy.'

'I heard a great deal more than my father's infamy last night. Ned had few kind words to spare for you. He said I was a fool to deny him, when you are so free with your favours.'

She had expected Jack to laugh her last comment aside. Instead he refused to hold her stare and turned away to rummage in a chest for a fresh ruff.

'It is absurd, is it not?' she pursued.

'Quite absurd, my dear. You did right not to heed him.'

There was something in his tone which struck a false note. If Jack was innocent of these accusations, he would be furious with Ned.

'Look at me, Jack.' She waited until he complied and saw that his expression was guarded. Could there be some truth in Ned's words? No, Jack would never betray her so falsely. Or would he? Why did he look so defensive? Her fists clenched as humiliation overran her. 'Ned spoke of your visits to York. Of your family . . . your growing family. Two more than when I came back to you from Wales, and another on the way.'

'And you believed him?'

She was beginning to find that she did. 'Your infidelity did not stop at Elizabeth. How many others? The girls at Nell Lovegood's? Ladies-in-waiting at Court?'

'Not now, Gabriellen,' he snapped irritably. 'I must find you lodgings, and I have to return to Essex House. Later, I will deal with Dawkin and his lies.'

'Are they lies, Jack? You have not denied them.'

'To do so would but give them substance. It says little for your loyalty that you listened without defending my name.'

Something in his tone aroused the suspicion that he was lying. Her faith was shaken. 'I defended it, Jack. Which is why I learned so much from Ned. You abused my love and trust once before. That time I forgave you. If you have done so again, then you have made a mockery of our love.'

The look he gave her was glacial. 'This is neither the time nor the place for this absurd discussion. Get your cloak. I will fetch the children.'

She ignored his command. Placing her hands on her hips, she faced him. 'Is Elizabeth with child?'

Without answering, he picked up her cloak and took hold of her arm. 'We must leave here, Gabriellen.'

She braced herself when he would have led her to the door. Her voice as leaden as her heart, she said, 'For us there is less time than you think. I am going nowhere until you answer my question. Is Elizabeth with child?'

'God's breath, Gabriellen,' he snarled, his patience at an end, 'she *is* my wife.'

The sound of her slap was like a pistol shot. Her palm stung as she stood back and watched Jack's cheek turn scarlet. 'Then go to your wife. You have killed my love and I want none of you.'

'You do not mean that, Gabriellen. You're just angry.'

'Justifiably so.' She swallowed against the pain grinding

at her heart. 'This is the ultimate betrayal.' She turned away, her head bowed as she fought to overcome her agony and disillusion.

'You are the only woman I have loved. Yes, damn you, I admit I lapsed occasionally,' he arrogantly declared. He took her shoulders and turned her to face him. 'I am a man. I'm only human. It's you I love and revere above all others.'

She jerked away from him, his touch repelling her. Did he still think her so young and gullible? 'You love only yourself. You have taken all I had to give, and left me ashes in return. I am empty. You have not even left me my self-respect. I shall send Poggs to collect my belongings from Willowbank.'

'Certes, woman, you are a stubborn jade! This talk of leaving is nonsense. You love me.' He gave her a shake, his face haggard. 'What must I do to prove my love?'

His words left her cold. 'Fidelity was the price I asked of you in Wales. You betrayed that vow. You will find solace enough in your peccadillos, or with your wife.'

'Gabriellen, sweetheart.' His voice was at its most persuasive. 'I love you.' He smiled in a way which had disarmed her so often.

It failed to move her. 'I do not make idle threats or promises. Ever since I have known you, you have lied and deceived me.' Anger broke through her misery. Why had she not seen his faults sooner? Jack was so like her father. When had Esmond ever been faithful to one woman? She was furious with herself for not having realised how deep ran Jack's selfishness. 'Our life together is over. I would rather live alone with dignity than be hidden away at Willowbank like a prize favourite in your growing harem.'

'You are distraught, my darling. I will never give you up. Never! Do you hear me.'

Her head tilted proudly and her green eyes blazed with resolve as she faced him. 'But it is I who have given you up. Once a rogue, always a rogue, Jack. How little you know me if you thought I would take second place to another woman.' She snatched her cloak from him. 'There is only one thing I ask of you – take the children and myself away from here. Somewhere safe where Victor Prew will not find me. He is back in England and searching for me.' There was no self-pity in her voice, only defiance. 'It would seem all my ghosts return to haunt me.'

'I will take you away from here, for clearly you cannot stay,' Jack said harshly. 'But this is not an end to the matter, Gabriellen. God knows you pick your timing! With Essex about to make his move, I am committed to him.' Again his smile failed to coerce her, the whiteness of the scar above his beard showing her the control he was exerting upon his temper. 'Once your anger has cooled, you will feel differently.'

She turned her back on his excuses. In one thing at least he was right. This was not the place to quarrel. 'I am ready to leave.'

He put a hand on her arm to detain her, his voice gruff. 'What we have is special. Never doubt it, my love.'

'It is not special enough that I am prepared to share it with every whore in London.' She pulled her cloak on. 'Perhaps I should go to Nell Lovegood's. It would be an appropriate residence, do you not agree?'

'You will not go near the place,' Jack snarled. 'I will settle this matter with Ned.'

'There is no need. I would sell the wretched place if I could, but Esmond was most specific it was to remain Laurence's inheritance. I have jewels enough to sell which will buy One-eyed Ned's share.'

'There's no reasoning with you when you are in this obstinate mood.' He marched out of the room.

A half hour later the family, together with Poggs and Agnes, were settled in a small but respectable inn near the remnants of abbey walls which were known as Convent Garden. The accommodation was cramped but only temporary and far enough away from One-eyed Ned to make Gabriellen feel easier.

'The rooms are paid for for two weeks,' Jack said. 'As soon as I can, I will return.'

He stooped to kiss her goodbye and she turned her head so that his mouth brushed her cheek. 'You must accept that it is over between us,' she said firmly. 'I will send Poggs to pay Ned. The income from Nell Lovegood's will be put aside to buy out your share as soon as possible. I would have returned to Chichester except no decision has yet been made on my uncle's house. I shall live quietly in the country somewhere. I have the income from Esmond's plays which are still proving popular. Of course, I shall not stop you from seeing the children whenever you wish.'

'You will not escape me, Gabriellen. I will be back.'

He pulled her into his arms and kissed her with all the passion which only a week ago would have left her swooning with desire. There was not even a flicker of response. She was immune to his charm, the beguilement of years finally obliterated by his betrayal.

Chapter Thirty-Six

In the late afternoon of Saturday 7 February the name of Essex hung like a storm cloud in the descending dusk, an undercurrent of tension pulsating throughout the London streets.

Three days ago Mark had returned to London and begun his hunt for Prew. From One-eyed Ned he had learned that Prew was hiding in Alsatia, but in the last two days had not returned to that particular lair. Mark did not believe that Prew had left the district, every instinct tuned by long years of spying sensed the evil of his presence lurking in the shadows.

Victor Prew spat in the gutter as he ducked into a dark doorway in the alleyway opposite Rowan's rooms. The ten angels Ned Dawkin had demanded for information Prew would find interesting had been worth it. He shook his head and gibbered beneath his breath. Rowan lived. A pox on the Woodman for failing. That had been money wasted.

It was growing late. Rowan would not be going far tonight. Now he knew where the Welshman was staying, he would make further plans. He might not be able to deliver Gabriellen her lover's head, but Rowan's presence here was an opportunity too good to be missed. Already a plan was forming in his mind. He licked his lips, muttering to himself as he slunk away into the shadows.

Later that night Mark sat in a nearby tavern. Fear for Gabriellen's life had brought him to London, but the rumours spreading through the streets tonight were of treason against the Queen. His first duty was to Elizabeth and he trusted that Jack had taken Gabriellen far from the city to safety. But if he was still involved with Essex's madcap schemes, Gabriellen would be doubly at risk.

On his arrival in London Mark had stopped at Willow-bank to warn Gabriellen that her husband was in England. He had been disturbed to find the place deserted except for a few servants. They had told him that Jack and Gabriellen had left for the city some days ago, after a mob had turned against the mistress. The next day soldiers had arrived to question Gabriellen about her father's plays.

This new development sent a chill of fear through Mark. Had someone discovered that she had written those works? The servants at Willowbank had no idea where Jack and Gabriellen were staying, or would not tell him if they did. They had, however, revealed that Gabriellen had ordered a Cornelius Hope from the house after an argument. Tomorrow at dawn Mark would start his search for her. He did not like the sound of these fresh developments. Both Hope and Prew were vindictive men. Gabriellen was in serious trouble.

He learned that she had until a few days ago been in Southwark, apparently under Ned's protection. It had disturbed Mark when Ned professed to know nothing of her whereabouts now. From the malicious glitter in his eye Mark had guessed that something had happened during Gabriellen's stay which had earned her Ned's displeasure.

Mark's attention was dragged back to events within the taproom. The atmosphere was tense with an undercurrent of excitement. Essex's name was mentioned frequently. Rumours were spreading like spoors on the wind. Mark wasted no time in gleaning what information he could. Tongues were loosened by ale and by the fervour roused from those who had seen the performance of Shakespeare's play *Richard II* that day. The Peasants' Revolt depicted therein had proved the people had a voice and that it could topple the mighty.

By the time the men in the taproom began to fall asleep over their ale, Mark had learned that the Privy Council had today ordered the Earl of Essex to present himself at Court to answer for his conduct. Arguments broke out as to whether the Earl had been wise to ignore the summons.

'It will mean the Tower for sure,' the innkeeper declared.

'No,' a young merchant countered. 'Good Queen Bess loves Essex. She'll forgive him. She always has.'

'Not this time,' a fat pedlar replied as he put his covered tray of wares on a table. ''Tis said he has secretly negotiated with James of Scotland, and that the Earl of Mar is to march into England with an army. What do you make of that?'

'I grant that Essex is an ambitious hot-head,' said the innkeeper, 'but he'd not go so far as treason.'

'Happen he has no choice.' The pedlar regarded his companions seriously. 'I just heard a messenger from the Earl calling all those loyal to him to attend the service at Paul's Cross tomorrow morning. 'Tis my opinion Essex is about to make his stand.'

Loud shouting broke out at this announcement, rousing several occupants from sleep to join in the argument. Mark, who had kept his own counsel throughout, had heard enough. The citizens of London were incensed. Essex was still their hero. They believed in him.

'The Council must be curbed.' The pedlar stood on a table to enforce his words. 'This summons was the work of Cecil. Who among you trusts that misshapen snake? And Raleigh is behind it too. He has no love for Essex.'

Mark stood up to make his way to his room as a chorus of abuse for Raleigh, whom they despised for his arrogance, filled the room. He paused by the doorway as the man on the table made himself heard above the noise. Mark watched him raise his tankard. He suspected that he was in the pay of Essex to rouse the people.

'Citizens, a toast!' the pedlar cried. 'The hero of Cadiz! A man wronged by his peers! Good health and long life to Robert Devereux, Earl of Essex.'

'To Essex!'

In unison they rose to drink.

'Are you for him, men?' the pedlar urged.

'Aye,' they chorused. 'God bless Essex!'

A candlemaker waved his tankard in the air, slopping ale down the front of his tallow-stained jerkin. 'A pox on the Council. I'm for Essex.'

'So am I,' several others raised the cry.

Their loyalty pledged, they vowed to support the Earl when called by him. Or would they? Mark wondered. Surely once sober the good citizens of London would not desert the Queen whom they had loved for forty years? He prayed he was not wrong in his judgement. He had little sympathy for Essex, whose plight was of his own making. He should have learned from his stepfather, the Earl of

Leicester. Elizabeth Tudor could be sweetened by soft words and adoration, but she could not be bested. To make a stand against her was to earn her enmity.

An insurrection was a last desperate ploy by Essex to regain favour. Did the arrogant fool not realise that he would be sealing his own death warrant, should a single blow be struck for him against the Sovereign? Elizabeth would not share the love of her people. She would not be dictated to. Neither would the daughter of Henry VIII forget an insult. In the last year, governed by his insane rages, Essex had been indiscreet in his condemnation of the Queen's heartlessness and tyranny.

Since Essex had refused to obey the Privy Council's summons, orders would be given for his arrest. He would have no choice but to flee the country or make a stand. Essex would not run, not without a fight. From the pedlar's words, tomorrow would bring rebellion to London.

Jack was with Essex the next morning when the Privy Council's delegation arrived at Essex House. Today, 8 February, the conspirators were confident they would overthrow the Council and replace them with men from their own faction. No harm would come to the Queen providing she agreed to their terms.

Despite the freezing cold, since dawn messengers had been sent to the capital to summon the supporters of the Earl. Already three hundred were assembled outside the gates of his residence. When the Keeper of the Privy Seal, Lord Egerton, and other officers of the crown arrived, they were jostled and abused by the massed crowd at the main gates. Eventually they were forced to gain admittance through a side entrance.

'Away with them!' the mob shouted when Essex came out to parley with Egerton. 'They betray you! You lose time.'

Jack agreed with the mob. 'My Lord, we must leave now. Surprise is our best stratagem of attack.'

'Lock them up!' the mob chanted.

'In the Queen's name,' Egerton pompously declared, 'I demand to know the meaning of this tumultuous gathering.'

'Kill them!' the crowd menaced.

Essex treated the nervous, white-faced man with his usual

566

gallantry. 'We can talk more privately in the house. This way, gentlemen.'

Egerton, who had feared his task would be a much harder one, took courage from the Earl's compliance. He paused to shout above the noise of the crowd who were still clamouring for his blood: 'Lay down your arms!'

He was greeted with abuse. Shaken, he summoned as much dignity as he could to lead the members of his delegation into the house. Before any of them had time to realise what was happening, they had all been taken prisoner.

Essex turned to his friends. 'Now we march on London.' He strode through the house, his laughter sounding close to insanity.

'Surely it is to Whitehall we ride?' the Earl of Southampton corrected.

'No, my messengers have roused the city,' Essex arrogantly declared. 'We ride to Cheapside. At St Paul's Cross the people are gathered to hear the Sunday sermon. Once our plans are known the Lord Mayor, sheriffs, the citizens and 'prentices will join us.'

Essex rode like a madman at the head of his party. Jack, in common with all his companions, had caught the Earl's excitement. It stayed with him until they approached the city. When he saw how few people were in the streets, and hardly any raising more than a half-hearted wave, or feeble cheer for Essex, his elation turned to doubt. Had they misjudged the populace? Where were the numbers promised?

They pounded down Fleet Street. Essex shouted the agreed ruse to bring the people to his side. 'To arms, good people! England is sold to the Spanish by Cecil and Raleigh. They will give the crown to the Infanta. Citizens of London, arm for England and the Queen!'

Their rallying cry fell upon deaf ears. The streets were unusually deserted. Men looked away and hurried to their homes. Housewives gathered up their offspring, cuffing any who hung back as they were shooed into the safety of their homes. Doors were banged shut and windows slammed.

Jack looked round and saw alarm on Christopher Blount's and Gilli Meyricke's faces. Even the Earl of Southampton looked subdued. Essex alone remained undaunted. He wheeled his horse in a circle, waving his sword wildly as he shouted: 'For the Queen! For the Queen!'

Jack felt a cold sweat break out on his body. Where were the people who had vowed to support Essex? He turned in his saddle. His throat dried upon discovering that many of the followers who had come with them from Essex House had slunk away into side streets. With satisfaction he noted that Seth Bridges remained with the dwindling band. For that loyalty Jack vowed to reward his manservant.

'We are betrayed!' he said to Christopher Blount.

Gilli Meyricke looked about the street in disbelief. 'We cannot fail!' His voice was thick with fear. ''Tis the scaffold if we do. Lord Egerton has seen our faces. We must go on.'

No one had envisaged failure. Jack's mind raced. The moment they had imprisoned Lord Egerton they had been committed to this course.

'Perhaps all is not lost,' he reasoned. 'The call was for the people to meet at St Paul's Cross. That must be why the streets are empty.'

'Yes,' Southampton agreed, but his face was pale and he was visibly shaken. 'That is where we will raise our army.'

Relief showed too quickly upon the men's faces to reassure Jack. They were clutching at straws and knew it. At that moment a trumpet blast carried faintly to them. Then another, closer, just inside the city walls.

'Those are the Queen's heralds,' Blount said, his face greying as the words of a proclamation reached them. It announced a royal pardon to any who deserted Essex's cause.

Meyricke shouted to Essex: 'London is being warned not to heed the Earl's cry to arms.'

'Because they fear us!' Essex shouted in triumph.

The Earl of Southampton rode level with Essex, his eyes wide with alarm. 'We are betrayed. Our plans are known.'

A voice from behind Jack screamed, 'We are undone! Seek audience with the Queen. Reason with her.'

'No!' Essex was firm, but Jack saw the sheen of fear which glistened on the Earl's face. His eyes were wild. Essex knew that this time there would be no mercy. Rash and opinionated, he refused to back down. Raising his sword, he spurred his horse forward.

Jack followed. He would not abandon Essex whilst there was still a chance of success. Fortunes were not made with faint hearts. What use to him was a royal pardon if he was plunged into obscurity? Disgrace faced him anyway, now that Egerton knew that he had ridden with Essex.

They advanced on Ludgate Hill where the streets were barricaded against them with chains and carts. Essex waved his sword aloft and ordered a charge.

The Queen's men swarmed around them. Jack remained at the Earl's side in the thick of the fighting. Several shots rang out. Fortunately for Essex, Jack noticed, one missed his head by inches but put a hole through his hat. Jack received a cut to his swordarm which was more inconvenient than serious as it bled profusely. He caught a glimpse of Seth as the servant cracked open a man's head with his cudgel. In the short skirmish several people were killed or maimed.

Loss of blood was making Jack light-headed and his arm ached as if the devil had sunk his teeth into it. It was soon obvious that the day was lost. Everywhere Jack looked, he saw the Earl's supporters deserting, until only a few staunch friends remained. The rebellion was over, inglorious by its very brevity.

'My Lord Essex, save yourself,' Jack urged when the outcome became inevitable. 'You, too, Southampton.'

'For the love of God, heed him, Robin!' Southampton screamed.

Essex cast him a tormented stare and nodded, knowing himself defeated. They began to fight their way to the river, fleeing down back streets as soon as they could escape the Queen's soldiers. At Queenhythe the Earl took a boat to Essex House. Jack, aware that his own neck was in danger, departed for Willowbank. First he allowed Seth to bind his arm. Fortunately the servant had survived without a scratch.

'Go to Deptford, Seth,' he ordered. '*The Swift* is at anchor awaiting repairs to her topgallant. Round up the crew. Under cover of darkness sail her up river to Blackfriars. I want her ready to sail on the night tide. We'll take on provisions in the morning at Rye. At least enough to get us to La Rochelle where we can take on more.'

'You take care, cap'n,' Seth warned. 'Willowbank is the first place they'll look for you.'

'I need only a half-hour there to get the strong box. Then I shall collect Gabriellen and the children. I intend to make a new life for myself in the West Indies, or bide there at least until I have sunk enough Spanish ships to satisfy Elizabeth's lust for gold and won myself a pardon.'

Six hours of searching had brought Mark no closer to finding Gabriellen. Another approach to One-eyed Ned had found the Upright Man singularly unco-operative, except for suggesting he try Nell Lovegood's. Two days ago Gabriellen had purchased his share of the property.

At the brothel he had learned nothing. Nell was unusually surly. It was the first she had heard that the ownership had passed to a woman instead of Esmond's son, especially as Jack had been in two nights ago and assured her Mistress Angel was the trustee of the business until her brother came of age. Each Monday, Mistress Angel's agent, a man called Poggs, would collect two-thirds of the weekly profits to be taken to a goldsmith for deposit. That surprised Mark. Why were not all the profits collected by Jack?

It would be two days before Poggs next came. He could not wait until then to find Gabriellen. If Poggs and Agnes were with her, they were a distinctive enough couple for someone to have noticed. His next call was on Bartholomew Pudsey, the pseudo-cripple who begged at the entrance of Westminster Abbey. He would spread the word through the Underworld to look out for these servants. Any information was to be sent to Mark at the conduit at Cheapside, where he would be at two, four and six o'clock, if necessary, until news reached him.

All morning he had heard the proclamations by the Queen's heralds. The unusually quiet streets made his search harder. Even most of the beggars had gone to ground. As he was leaving Cheapside at a quarter after two that afternoon, with no information as to Gabriellen's whereabouts, he saw Cornelius Hope. The actor was sauntering down Queen Street, a doxy on each arm. As they were about to enter an inn, no doubt seeking a private room, Mark drew his dagger and touched its point to Hope's ribs.

'Tell the women to leave,' he said in the actor's ear, 'I want to speak to you.'

Cornelius looked over his shoulder into Mark's cold and unyielding expression. The colour left his face. 'Good ladies,' he blustered, 'a moment if you please. I am unavoidably detained.'

'You promised us both a shilling for our time,' one wench shrilled. 'We ain't goin' nowhere wi'out our shilling. Or I'll tell our pimp you're a man who don' pay yer debts. Last time that 'appened, the bloke was gelded afore our pimp threw 'im in the Thames.'

'I shall be but a moment, dear ladies,' Cornelius wheedled.

Mark pressed the dagger harder, so that the point split the velvet doublet and pricked the actor's back. 'Give them their shilling. But don't try any rash moves.' He exerted more pressure with the knife.

Hope fumbled in the pouch at his waist, and producing two shillings handed them to the women. 'Wait inside, dear ladies. Don't go.'

The wench who had spoken winked at Mark. 'Thanks, mister. He ain't much of a lover-boy that one. Our pimp got 'imself killed in a fight last week. He worked a dozen girls if yer interested. Yer seem right 'andy with that knife.'

Mark smiled gallantly at the women. 'I must decline your offer. My home is not in London but Wales.'

'A pity that.' She eyed him boldly, thrusting out her ample breasts which were covered only by flimsy gauze above a low-cut bodice. 'Any time yer in Bread Street, ask fer Bethnal Kate. I'll give yer a night to remember, Welshman.'

Mark pushed Cornelius into the next alleyway. Doubling Hope's arm behind his back, he shoved him up against the wall.

'I hear you've been threatening Mistress Angel,' Mark said, jerking Hope's arm higher with each word. 'I don't take kindly to it when my friends are threatened. So what's this about?'

'Nothing, I swear it. A misunderstanding, dear man,' Hope wheezed through his pain.

'No misunderstanding. You were trying to blackmail Gabriellen, spreading rumours which were not true. You sent the soldiers to Willowbank. Why?'

'Because the woman is a traitor.' Hope mastered his fear and recovered some of his self-possession. 'She is using her father's name to spread sedition. The Queen was outraged by it.'

'You mean she refused to write a play for you?' Mark guessed the truth. 'I know you, Hope. You could not give a piss about what was written, unless it could benefit you.'

'She should answer for her crimes. Doubly so, since she is a woman. A whore who spreads . . .'

A grunt of pain cut off his words as Mark spun him round and smashed his fist into his fat paunch. He followed with a jab to Hope's eye which slammed the actor's head back against the wall. A third punch landed with a sickening crunch on Hope's nose.

'Not my face, I beg you, not my face!' Hope screamed.

Mark brought up the dagger and laid it against the actor's fleshy cheek. 'No troupe of players would hire an actor with a face so scarred it would turn the groundlings away in horror.' He allowed the blade to draw a thread of blood along the length of Hope's cheek.

'Spare me!' he whined, eyes rolling with fear. 'Sweet Jesu, spare me!'

'As you would have spared Gabriellen? I have friends who believe the only way to cure a blackmailer is to cut out his tongue.'

Hope whimpered, a dark stain spreading over his blue breeches as terror emptied his bladder. 'She's innocent,' he groaned. 'I'll swear to anyone who asks, Esmond Angel wrote those plays.'

'Then remember it well. Should one word of these rumours reach my friends, no matter where you are, within a day you will be lighter of a tongue.'

'I swear. Dear God, I swear,' Hope blubbered.

Mark withdrew the knife and watched the blood trickle down from Hope's jaw. The scar would not be deep, but it would remain long enough to serve as a powerful warning. 'Stay away from Gabriellen. And, remember, I do not make idle threats.'

Satisfied that Hope had been taught a lesson he would not forget in a hurry, and that Gabriellen was now safe from the actor's threats, Mark continued his search.

He was halfway along Queen Street when he caught the first sounds of fighting and saw some of the wounded as Essex's followers now deserted in droves. Through a turning he saw a group of horsemen gallop past on a parallel street. Their faces were blurs, but he could not mistake Red Sun as he sped past carrying Jack. There was no sign of pursuit and Mark ran down the side-street to follow the riders as they headed towards the river. They were not in sight as he came out on to the wider street, but a shout drew him on to Queenhythe.

He arrived there in time to see Essex being ferried towards Essex House and Jack stepping into another boat as his servant Seth Bridges cantered into Thames Street on Red Sun. Mark put two fingers to his lips and whistled shrilly in the way he used to call the horses in Wales. Would the gelding remember the call? Red Sun checked his pace, lifting his head in the direction of the whistle. Mark ran at full speed to catch up.

'Seth!' he shouted. 'Wait!'

The servant slapped his legs against Red Sun's sides and though Mark whistled a second time, it was a call from too far back in Red Sun's past for him to obey it now. As he watched the horse and rider disappear down Thames Street, Mark snatched off his battered velvet cap and slammed it down on the ground with impotent fury. He picked it up and trudged wearily back up the hill towards Cheapside. He had come so close to finding Gabriellen. Seth would have known where she was. It was nearly four o'clock. Would there be news for him at the conduit? He could not rid himself of the feeling that time was running out for Gabriellen.

Chapter Thirty-Seven

It was seven o'clock when Mark arrived back at the inn that evening. He still had no idea of Gabriellen's whereabouts. It left him with a sick feeling in his gut. He could not put out of his mind the presentiment that she was in danger.

As far as he knew Jack had escaped capture. All day rumours of the repercussions of Essex's rising had been circulating in the capital. Essex had returned to his home expecting to use the Lord Keeper as a hostage. Someone had released the prisoners in his absence, and Essex House was now surrounded by the Queen's men. As yet the Earl had refused to surrender.

When Mark entered the taproom, the landlord manoeuvred his massive bulk through the tables towards him.

'There you are, Mr Rowan. A messenger left word for you earlier.' The landlord rubbed his thick neck. 'Important, the lad said it was. A Mistress Angel has need of you. She's at the fourth house in a row of six houses and cottages in the lane between Lincoln's Inn Fields and Convent Garden. You can't miss it, so the lad says. The house is old, its roof bowed with age and the garden long neglected.'

'What time was the message brought?' Mark asked.

'About two hours ago, sir.'

Mark had saddled up and ridden out before he realised the oddness of Gabriellen's message. He had been looking for her, but how did she know he was in London? Any of Bartholomew Pudsey's messengers would have left a message at the conduit as arranged. Something was not right about this. But since it was the only lead he had as to Gabriellen's whereabouts, he would go there.

Once outside the city limits he looked up at the moon, grateful for its light. An amber ring surrounded its sphere and the heavy frost on the grassy track scrunched beneath his gelding's hooves.

Victor Prew hugged his arms about his body and stamped his feet to keep warm. Where the hell was Rowan? He'd have sworn he'd come running at that summons supposedly sent by Gabriellen. What had delayed him? Prew scowled at the house where candlelight filtered through the cracks in the shutters. He had been here since four this afternoon, needing time to prepare. Everything was now ready. Once it had grown dark, he and his accomplice had worked silently and quickly. Damn Rowan for the delay.

Prew wiped his sweating palms on his trunk-hose and glanced at his companion. The man sat motionless on a broken butter churn, like a ghoulish statue. Prew had been assured that he was the best of his kind, but this man they called 'Midden', on account of his smell, repelled him. Another fifty marks this was costing him, but it would be worth it.

Prew rubbed his hands in anticipation of Rowan's arrival. Revenge was close at hand. He felt no compassion for the servants or children who would die as well. Too often Poggs had used Prew as the butt of a joke. Poggs's wife was no better. He'd seen the pitying glances she had given Gabriellen on their wedding day. As for the children – bastards all of them, their existence ridiculing him for a cuckold. Good riddance to the lot of them. The only regret he had was that Gabriellen would not suffer hours of agony as he had planned. This way was a little too quick, but it was also effective. After the failure of the Woodman to kill Rowan, he could not afford to take chances. This way could not fail.

But where the hell was Rowan?

At the sound of a covered wagon and horses approaching from the lane, Prew drew back behind the trunk of an ancient oak tree on the edge of the overgrown orchard.

'Hell's bowels, what's this?' he muttered when it stopped in front of the house. The bright moonlight revealed Stoneham's tall figure as he leaped down from the driver's seat. Three other men climbed out of the wagon and all of them moved towards the house.

Prew began to twitch with frustration. This was not

meant to happen. Indeed it was not! What was Stoneham doing here? His investigations had told Prew that Gabriellen and Stoneham had parted after a quarrel. She had moved to this house last week. It was far enough from its neighbours to have given him the idea for his plan. Now Stoneham was complicating matters.

A trickle of saliva ran down Prew's chin. He could feel his revenge slipping away from him. Stoneham had been involved with Essex. If he was here, it was because he had escaped arrest. Suddenly Prew knew Stoneham had come for Gabriellen.

'No! You shan't have her!' His mutterings grew more wild.

The way Stoneham barged into the house with his companions and the shouting which followed sent Prew into a rage. One man emerged carrying a young crying child and put it into the wagon. Another followed.

Prew began to spit and froth at the mouth. No, they couldn't leave. They must die. Die! He turned to Midden. 'We must act now. Go and do your work.'

As his accomplice moved away, Prew edged from tree to tree to see what was happening within the house. Rowan must have slipped his trap, but Gabriellen would die. And her paramour Stoneham. He began to laugh softly as he saw Midden climb through the cellar window they had earlier prised open.

The Angel wench would die together with her brood. That devil Stoneham too! Fire and brimstone were the reward for their devilry. Fire and brimstone to herald their entrance into everlasting Purgatory.

The loud banging on the door made Gabriellen jump so violently that she stabbed herself with her sewing needle. Putting aside the doublet she was mending for Ambrose, she stood up.

'God 'a Mercy,' Agnes screamed. 'Is it the soldiers come for thee, mistress? Where can thee hide?'

'It cannot be the soldiers to question me about Father's plays,' Gabriellen answered. 'No one knows I'm here. Go and see who it is, Poggs. But take the pistol from that coffer.'

'Gabriellen, open the door.' At the sound of Jack's voice she felt a rush of relief. Rumours had reached her of the revolt. Thank God he was safe, was her first thought.

She was shocked by his appearance as he burst into the parlour. His clothes were covered in dust and splashed with blood. An improvised bandage was tied about his arm, and his face was grey with fatigue.

'Get your things together. *The Swift* awaits the tide at Blackfriars. Agnes, see to the children. There's no time to lose.'

'Agnes, stay where you are!' Gabriellen countermanded. Her eyes snapped with fury as she turned on Jack. 'I am not going anywhere with you. I made that clear two weeks ago. It's over between us.'

'I've no time to waste arguing, Gabriellen. You don't mean that. We'll start a new life in the West Indies. There'll be no more women, I promise. It's you I want. You I love.'

She shook her head. 'You made that promise once before, and broke it. I won't be one in a long line of your conquests. You'll never change. Your deceit destroyed my love. Go, Jack, while you can. I will not be party to your capture, but I am not coming with you.'

'I'm not leaving without you.' He went to the door and shouted to his men: 'The children are upstairs. Get them.'

'No, Jack.' Outraged, Gabriellen ran to the door, but he held her back. 'You can't do this,' she shouted, struggling in a frenzy to be free.

Horrified, she saw a sailor appear at the stairhead carrying Jacquetta who was beginning to cry.

'Put them in the wagon,' Jack ordered.

'Damn you, Jack!' she fumed. 'You've played some mean tricks in your time, but this is infamous.' She struck at him with her fists.

'I'm not leaving without you.'

He grabbed her arm and pulled her into the passage. Desperate to escape, she struck his wound with her fist and he released her with an oath.

'God's teeth, Gabriellen, you damned firebrand! This is no time for your obstinacy. If you won't come for me, you'll come for the children.'

He looked up at his men on the landing. One carried the sleeping Sabine. Toby Gordon was struggling with an outraged Ambrose, who was hooked under his arm and trying to kick the groom's shins. Behind them Laurence was screaming at the sailors to stop.

'Toby!' Gabriellen pleaded. 'You can't take my children.'

The groom from Willowbank looked shame-faced, but his first loyalty would always be to Jack. He ordered Ambrose to be quiet and began to carry him to the top of the stairs.

'What's happening?' Laurence demanded, pushing past Toby to stare at his sister who was still struggling with Jack. 'What are you doing here, Stoneham? You're not welcome. You've ruined Gabriellen's life with your lies. We don't want any part of you.'

'Stop that sailor taking Sabine!' Gabriellen shouted at her brother. 'Jack's stealing the children.'

She began to sob with anger and fury. 'How dare you do this to me, Jack? I deserve more from you for my years of loyalty. My life is here. So is the children's. Do you think by forcing me to go with you, I will love you again? I will hate you for it. I came to you of my own free will and earned dishonour for my love. I'm not your wife for you to order at will. I'm not even your chattel. I will stay.'

'You are coming with me.'

'Leave my sister alone!' Laurence's shout ended in a cry of pain when the sailor holding Sabine clouted him so hard, he was sent tumbling down the stairs.

Laurence lay groaning. Gabriellen ran to his side, her eyes large with contempt as she glared at Jack. 'Have you lost all decency? Go, Jack. I don't want you. I don't love you.'

'But I want you, Gabriellen,' he said in a tone she had never heard before. It was all pirate, mercenary, and without consideration for any will but his own.

Mark saw the coach blocking the lane. Then he heard the raised voices. Already made suspicious by the message, he tied his horse to a fence post. Keeping to the shadows of the overhanging trees, he edged forward to investigate. When he saw a man run out of the house with a child in his arms and put it in the wagon, he curbed his impulse to challenge him. Wasn't that Jack's voice within the house? Gabriellen's was raised in anger. He studied the scene. The front door was open and he could see other men and what looked like fighting taking place inside.

His years of working as Walsingham's spy had taught him caution. It was useless to rush headlong into that affray.

If he entered from the back of the house, surprise would serve him better. He skirted the high wall by the orchard which ran along the side of the house. On a level with the vegetable garden he hauled himself up on to the wall. Pausing a moment at the top, he surveyed the garden to get his bearings.

A movement caught his eye. A man had emerged from the orchard and was moving furtively around to the back of the house. Mark was about to follow him when he heard a low muttering voice close by. He scanned the orchard and saw a figure making strange jerking movements and rubbing his hands together. Some years ago Mark had had to question an inmate of St Bartholomew's Hospital in London where the insane were held. This man showed the same symptoms as several of those deranged patients who had been shackled to their beds.

Mark dropped silently from the wall. The man about to enter the house was probably the greater danger, but there was something about the other's movements which made him hesitate. When a second man came out of the house carrying another child, the figure grew more agitated. For a moment his contorted movements brought him into the moonlight. As the man's face turned towards the coach, Mark saw it clearly. The white beard and hair and fleshed-out face were unfamiliar to him. Then a gesture tugged at his memory. It was Victor Prew.

No longer hesitating, Mark attacked him. Gabriellen had Jack to protect her in the house from Prew's accomplice. Coming up behind the merchant, Mark put an arm across his throat and yanked Prew's arm behind his back before the man was even aware of his presence. Within the house the argument was growing more heated. Gabriellen sounded hysterical.

In no mood for prevarication, Mark put more pressure on Prew's arm and demanded, 'What were you up to? Tell me!'

Prew rolled his eyes and grunted, but refused to talk. Mark had a nasty feeling he had made the wrong decision. He should have tackled Prew's accomplice. 'What is your man doing in the house?' he pursued.

'He's sending them to hell!' Prew wheezed.

Out of patience, and worried at the events happening in the house, Mark dragged him across the garden to the front door. As they neared the building Prew began to struggle and gibber with fear. The scene in the house could have been lifted straight from Bedlam as Mark shoved Prew into their midst.

'Rowan!'

'Mark!'

'I found this vermin skulking in the garden,' he said. 'And up to no good. You did not by chance send me a message to come here, did you, Ellen?'

'No.'

Mark had only a fleeting glimpse of her beautiful face, upon which surprise had momentarily replaced anger.

'Plague on you, Rowan!' Jack shouted, reclaiming Mark's attention. 'What the devil are you doing here? I've matters to discuss with Gabriellen which are not your concern.'

Prew began to twitch and salivate uncontrollably in Mark's grasp, and unintelligible groans came from his slobbering lips. 'More to the point, what was Prew doing here? He tried to have me killed in Wales. His accomplice is at the back of the house.'

'Fire and brimstone!' Prew rolled his eyes, his efforts to be free growing more frantic. 'Let me go. Must get out.'

His deranged words sent fear through Mark. He shook Prew until he heard the man's teeth rattle. 'Is he setting fire to the cellar?'

Prew was terrified beyond hearing. 'Fire and brimstone. Heretics and devil's brood. You'll burn in hell.'

'What is the fool prattling about?' Jack demanded tersely.

A quick survey showed Mark that all the younger children were in the coach. Laurence sat on the floor rubbing his head. Jack had a firm grip upon Gabriellen's arm, and from the rip in the sleeve of her gown, she had been putting up a struggle. His temper rose at Jack's treatment of her, but it was Prew's presence here which alarmed him. That and his demented ravings.

'Where's the cellar door?' he asked Gabriellen.

'At the end of the kitchen opposite the garden door. But why?'

'I have a feeling Prew's accomplice may be firing the house,' Mark said as he shoved Prew towards Jack. 'Hold him!'

Prew thrust out his hands to claw at Jack's face to escape. It was then that Mark saw the dark stains on his hands.

'Get out!' he ordered as he bolted towards the cellar. 'That's gunpowder.'

Jack released Gabriellen and caught Prew. Scowling, he watched Mark run along the passage and enter the kitchen.

'Outside, Gabriellen,' Jack commanded, having seen Prew's hands for himself. 'No arguments. Rowan's right. The house could go up at any moment.'

'Mark, come back!' she screamed.

He opened the cellar door and smelt smoke. He also heard the hiss of gunpowder and saw a yellow flame snaking along the floor. At the same instant a window banged shut and he saw Prew's accomplice drop from sight.

In the hall Jack snapped at Gabriellen: 'Mark can look after himself. Save yourself, woman. And your brother.'

Gabriellen yanked Laurence to his feet and fled outside, followed by Poggs and Agnes.

'Yes, must get out,' Prew blubbered.

Jack gave him a vicious shake. Gabriellen had told him of the horror of her wedding night. Prew was an animal who deserved to die for what he had done. 'Blow us up, would you? You're not going anywhere, whoreson!' Jack raged. He kicked Prew hard on the buttocks and sent the merchant sprawling into the parlour. He saw Prew lying on the floor as he slammed and locked the door.

'No! You can't leave me here!' Prew screamed as he threw his body against the door. 'Bastard! Let me out!'

Jack ignored the cries, his concern only for his family. Ahead he saw Gabriellen trip and scream at Laurence to run on. Jack caught up with her and grabbed her arm, roughly hauling her to her feet and dragging her forward.

'Run,' he shouted to Poggs and Agnes. 'Get behind the wagon before we're all blown to hell.'

At the same moment Mark yelled his own warning, not knowing whether the others were still in the house or not. 'The fuse is lit! Get out! Save yourselves!'

He dashed to the back door, knowing he would never reach the front of the house. The rapid way the fuse had been burning made him doubt he would actually reach safety. Wrenching the garden door open, he raced through the overgrown weeds. He was halfway across the garden when he heard the bang. The blast hit him like a hammer blow and he felt himself lifted into the air.

The explosion knocked Gabriellen to the ground and she

felt its vibrations echo through the earth. The horses neighed with fear. Lifting her head, she saw Jack catch their bridles to stop them from bolting. A rain of debris splattered her as she heaved herself to her knees. Her toe caught in the ripped hem of her gown as she tried to rise, the cold air nipping her flesh where her sleeve hung from her shoulder. She put a grimy hand to her face to push back her loose hair as she stared at the house which had collapsed in upon itself. The ancient thatch was aflame, scattered sparks already taking hold of what was left of its standing timbers. Other small fires were springing up from the rubble.

She reeled forward, her gaze frantic as she scanned the garden. 'Mark!' she screamed. 'Mark!'

There was no answer.

Jack was at her side. 'You cannot stay here. It is as well the children were already in the wagon.' He spoke as though the explosion had been an inconvenience, nothing more. His face was streaked with sweat and dirt, his doublet and hose torn in several places. There was a fierce glint in his eyes, no trace of remorse at what had happened. Gabriellen had heard Prew's shout for help and guessed that Jack had trapped him in the house. She was a widow. Free. But that no longer mattered.

In a state of shock, she veered away from Jack. This was a side of his character she had not known existed. It appalled her. She saw the children by the wagon. Thank God they were safe, together with the servants. But where was Mark?

She stumbled towards the house like a sleep-walker. 'Mark! Oh, Mark, you can't be dead!'

'Stay back, Gabriellen.' Jack caught her to him. 'It's too dangerous.'

She wrenched herself away, her mind fixed upon what had befallen Mark. 'I must find him.'

'He's dead.' Jack gripped her shoulders and shook her. 'Look, the fire is beginning to draw a crowd. It lights up the sky like a beacon. The explosion will have been heard for miles. I can't stay here – I'll be arrested. I have to go. Come, Gabriellen, our life is together.'

'I can't leave Mark. He could be injured.' She strained away from Jack, but he continued to hold her. 'Don't you care? He was your friend.'

'And, it seems, your lover.'

'But for him we would all be dead in that house.' She looked into his angry face and wondered how once she could have loved him so passionately. How blinkered that love had made her. 'How can you be so selfish?'

Voices from the gathering crowd grew louder.

'Love makes me selfish,' Jack answered fiercely. 'You are coming with me, Gabriellen.'

'No, Jack.' She stood her ground, refusing to move. It was useless arguing with him in this mood. She had to make him see reason. Only then would she be able to search for Mark. 'What we once had was good, but that time has gone. Don't let us part as enemies. Please, let my children go. Whenever you return to England you will always be welcome to see them. I shall ensure that the money from Nell Lovegood's is kept safe for you.'

'What is left for you here?' Jack raged. 'Rowan is dead.'

'You don't know that! This is the danger Jesmaine prophesied to Mark. I am responsible. You must leave or you will be captured. Go, before the constable arrives. I no longer love you, but I still care enough not to see you destroyed.'

He put out a hand and let it fall to his side.

'My life is nothing without you, Gabriellen.'

'I'm sorry, Jack.' Her hand went to her throat, and feeling the familiar touch of the emerald pendant, she pulled it over her head. 'Take this back. You made a mockery of its inscription with your women. Love conquers everything – except betrayal. You will find solace with other paramours, and in the New World you will make a second fortune. I wanted a part of you that was not yours to give, nor ever will be to any one woman.' She rose up on tiptoe and kissed his mouth. 'Go with God, Jack. Be happy.'

He reeled away. Short of kidnapping Gabriellen he knew he had lost her. He could not believe she no longer loved him. In their long years together she had denied him nothing. He had but to smile or cajole and she would be held to his will. A caress would rouse her to splendid passion. He now saw his error. Her unique fire and spirit would be roused as quickly in jealousy and anger. She had warned him. But then, had she not always forgiven him in the past?

A look into her eyes, blazing with condemnation, told

him it would never be so again. Driven by selfish ambition and arrogance he had ignored the danger signs. By destroying her trust he had killed her love. He would never forget her. Never find a woman to match her spirit. He would never love another. The only thing he valued above all his achievements, Gabriellen's love, he had wantonly annihilated.

Curtly, he ordered the children to be taken out of the wagon. The vehicle would be too slow to push through the crowd. He turned back to Gabriellen, too proud to allow his pain at losing her to show. 'I give you my share in Nell's place. You will need the profits to support the children. I'll never forget you, Gabriellen.'

'Nor I you, Jack. We had many happy times together.'

He nodded, his expression inscrutable. Without a word he walked towards Mark's horse, standing in the lane. Moments later the sound of its hoofbeats faded into the distance.

There was no time to succumb to the emptiness inside her. Her fears now were for Mark.

Calling his name, she skirted the rubble to go to the back of the building. The house was on fire from end to end and the heat from the flames scorched her skin. At the rear it was spreading to the out-buildings and advancing slowly over the long, damp grass and overgrown bushes.

'Mark!' Her voice rose to a sob.

A low groan was just audible above the roar of the flames. She whirled and ran towards the sound. Almost hidden in the grass was Mark's sprawled body. His clothes were ripped and tattered, his skin in places blackened from the explosion. She lifted his wrist and felt for his pulse. Her hands were trembling so much she could not feel it.

'No, Mark, no! You can't be dead,' she gasped. Half fainting with panic, she put her fingers to the pulse point at his neck. Just perceptible was the flickering beat. He was alive, praise God, but he must be moved. The flames were perilously close. Within moments they would both be consumed.

'Poggs! Help me!' she screamed.

Lifting Mark's arms she began to haul his body slowly, backbreakingly, across the tangled garden. Several times her feet tripped over bramble runners and roots.

Poggs appeared and took Mark's feet and they carried

him further from the fire. Gabriellen sank down on the grass and put his head on her lap. 'He needs a physician, Poggs. Send one of the villagers to get the best there is.'

'We'd better get him into the wagon first,' Poggs advised. 'This frost could kill him. I'll send Agnes with the children to the Green Dragon Inn along the road. There's enough people here to help her.'

A messenger was despatched for the physician. The journey to the inn, a few hundred yards away, was a nightmare. The wagon was surrounded by people clamouring to know what had happened. The children were crying, though Agnes was doing her best to calm them. Through it all, Gabriellen held Mark's hand and willed him to live.

Chapter Thirty-Eight

The soft candlelight threw its glow over the motionless figure on the bed. Mark had been laid on his stomach since his back was covered in dozens of cuts and abrasions from the force of the blast. These had been left open to the air to heal, and treated with a soothing balm which glistened on his naked torso exposed above the sheet. They were not deep but would be painful when he awoke and moved. Mercifully, he had not suffered any broken bones or apparent internal bleeding. His head was turned towards Gabriellen on the pillow and several blue-black locks of hair curled around his face, softening the rugged features.

As she stared down at him, her eyes misted with anguish at his suffering. All she could think of was the danger she had brought to him. Again when she had needed him, he had not failed her. She smiled wryly. It was becoming a habit.

Inadvertently her hand tightened over his, and she felt an answering squeeze. His eyes were open, bright and clear of concussion.

'You gave me a terrible scare,' she said shakily.

'To awake and find you with me must mean I am in heaven. Am I not with an Angel?' He tried to roll onto his back and grimaced.

'Stay still,' she urged, 'and talk not of heaven. Were it not for you, we would all be dead.'

He bit his lip against his pain, and ignoring her words rolled on to his back. Taking both her hands, he drew her forward to lean over him. 'Your children – are they also safe?'

She nodded, too overcome to speak. Even now he thought of others and not himself.

'And what of Jack?'

Unable to meet his gaze, she stared down at their linked

586

hands. 'Unharmed by the explosion. His ship awaited him at Blackfriars. He's bound for the West Indies.'

'And you chose not to go with him?'

The husky expectancy in his voice made her look up. Seeing the anticipation in his eyes, her heart twisted. Mark still loved her. Incredibly, after the betrayal and the danger she had placed him in, he still loved her . . .

'It is over between Jack and myself,' she said, unable to hold his searching gaze. 'The dispute over Ezekiel's house has gone on long enough. If it means I must petition the Queen to get a decision, I will do so. I intend to live in Chichester with my children.'

'All men are not as Jack,' Mark said softly.

She shook her head, her stricken look beseeching him to say no more. 'I know. I would not have loved him had he been as other men.' Her gaze dropped to her hands again. She was unable to look at Mark as she explained, 'That was the folly of my infatuation. My obsession blinded me. I should have realised he would never change. I could not accept his other women.'

'Where will you live in the meantime? Why not come to Wales?'

She could feel the intensity of his stare willing her to look up at him. She did so and the fierce light in his eyes made her heart contract, though she found herself strangely unable to answer.

'I'm not asking for a commitment, Ellen. Where better than Wales for the children to forget the horrors of this night?'

The effort of conversation drained his strength and his eyes closed briefly as he mastered his weakness. 'My head aches as if the devil dances on it.'

Gabriellen mixed several drops of the potion left by the physician into some wine. 'Drink this. It will ease the pain.' Her voice cracked with emotion. She put a shaking hand to his swarthy cheek and felt the beginnings of stubble there. 'My dear Mark, I've so missed your friendship.'

'Then you will come to Wales?'

Her gaze lowered and she fidgeted with the corner of the sheet on the bed. His hand lifted her chin so that she met his gaze. His lips were white from the pain of his injuries, but that stare was indefatigable. 'Say yes.'

'We will talk about it when you are stronger.' She could

587

not deny that the temptation to visit Wales was great. It had been a sanctuary for her once before. 'Now you must rest,' she said firmly. 'There may be internal bleeding. The physician said it was too early to tell.'

'I have a headache and a few scratches. I'm not dying, Ellen,' he said tersely.

That sable stare held her transfixed. His tone determined, he continued: 'I've waited nearly a decade for you to realise that Jack was not the man for you.'

Though Mark's injuries were not life threatening it was obvious that they were serious enough to keep him abed for a day or two. Gabriellen refused to leave his bedside, but because she could still be under suspicion of writing the play *Boudicca* it was agreed that Poggs and Agnes would take the children to the farm of a friend of Mark's at Epsom. It was a precautionary measure. The explosion would have caused much speculation, her whereabouts might be traced by someone recognising a child or servant, and she could be arrested. A substantial payment to the landlord ensured his silence.

On the third morning she awoke, lying fully dressed on the bed at Mark's side. She smiled dreamily on seeing him resting on his elbow, looking down at her. The pain and pallor had gone from his face and he was staring at her with amused speculation. She made to sit up, but he put a hand on her shoulder, gently holding her down.

'Now, my dear Ellen, I want an answer to my question. Are you coming with me to Wales?'

'How can I say yes? I'm a fugitive. I want my father's name and my own cleared of deliberately inciting rebellion by my play. Also my children's future must be secured by winning the court case against Charity Angel.'

'It shall be done,' Mark reassured. 'But it can be done from Wales.'

'No, Mark. If your name is linked with mine at this time, you are in danger yourself of being implicated in treason.'

'That is not likely.' He smiled confidently as he put his hands on her shoulders. 'I will be at your side throughout any proceedings.'

When she shook her head in fearful denial, the intensity of his gaze shredded her composure.

'Last time I let you go because you still believed yourself in love with Jack,' he said with quiet insistence. 'Our time was not then. It is now. From the moment you ceased to be Jack's woman, you became mine. Nothing will take you from me.' He took her face in his hands, turning it to the light. He looked intently into her eyes, his voice adamant. 'Nothing. Ellen, I love you. I want you to be my wife. I'm not leaving for Wales without you.' He rolled her on to her back, and coiling her long hair into a rope, wound it about his neck to bind them close.

He kissed her into silence. She was unprepared for the effect on her senses. To the wild rhythm of her heart, the ecstatic singing of her blood, she was consumed by desire of a magnitude she had not believed possible. Consciousness became an ethereal thread as her mind was overpowered by emotion. Fleetingly, she felt herself back in the Welsh hut, reliving the ecstasy of those ten carefree days. Nothing had equalled it since.

Her body welcomed his, driven by the compulsion of his kisses. The heat of his fullness deep within her roused her to an unparalleled craving. It continued with building intensity, carrying her to an exalted pitch until the pulsing moment of unsurpassed release.

'Ellen, when will you admit that this is our destiny?' Mark said as he smiled down at her satiated figure.

She lay supine. Drained of energy by a sensual paralysis, she had not the strength to protest.

'Before we leave London,' he continued, 'I will go to Court to resolve these matters which trouble you.'

He feathered kisses along her neck, then looked deep into her eyes. 'It is February now. I have a mind for an Easter wedding.'

Throughout the next six weeks, Mark was often at Court. Jack, it seemed, had escaped on his ship and for that he was grateful. His friend would make a name for himself as a pirate, Mark was certain. Jack was a survivor.

During the first two weeks after Essex's arrest, Mark realised any petition on Gabriellen's behalf would be met with refusal. The suspicion of playwrighting alone would be enough to earn her the Queen's anger. Elizabeth was a woman in torment during the days of Essex's trial. No one was spared her irascible moods and bouts of ill temper.

Mark had never seen her look so old and haggard, or her proud carriage drag so wearily through the palace corridors. There was grimness and desolation in her eyes. On Shrove Tuesday Essex was found guilty of treason. He would die the following day. The Earl of Southampton, because of his youth, was given life imprisonment.

Essex died bravely. His rank spared him from being hanged, drawn and quartered as befitted a traitor, and he met his death by the axe – albeit took three blows to sever his head. Less fortunate still were Sir Christopher Blount and Sir Gilli Meyricke. A month after Essex mounted the scaffold, they faced the grisly horrors of a traitor's death.

It was late March before Mark was granted an audience with the Queen. It was short, and did not produce the result he had hoped for. Experienced though he was at diplomacy, there was no seeing behind the emotionless mask with which Elizabeth hid her feelings from the world. That self-containment had deepened since the death of Essex, her moods becoming more unpredictable by the day. Mark was ordered to present himself at the same hour the next day. Gabriellen was to join him to answer to the Queen for the charges of playwrighting and inciting rebellion. Upon the outcome of these charges Elizabeth would make her judgement on the court case against Charity Angel.

On Mark's return to their rooms, he found Gabriellen resigned to the meeting.

'It is my chance to clear my father's name. The play was meant as a tribute to Elizabeth, not to incite revolt.'

Suddenly Mark was seized with fear for her. 'Forget this madness, Ellen. Come with me tonight to Wales. There I will ensure that you are safe.'

The anguish in his voice unnerved her. Would she lose everything she held dear by her obstinate desire to clear her father's name? How would the Queen review her confession that she had written the play, together with several others? Her work had been acclaimed by the greatest actors of the day and was loved by the people. It was a triumph any woman would relish. Would Elizabeth see it as a woman breaking through the barriers into a man's world, something she herself had done to bring England to greatness? Or would the Virgin Queen judge her skill to be unfeminine, her unorthodox life wanton and therefore suspect?

'You, Mark, who fear nothing for yourself – fear for me.'

Gabriellen moved into his arms, needing the reassurance of his love. Tomorrow night she could be a prisoner in the Tower. But she was not ashamed of the plays she had written. She would not run away from the Queen's anger. She would face it with dignity and pride. Her belief in herself was her only weapon against prejudice and hypocrisy.

Each day and night with Mark was making it harder to bear the thought of their parting. Yet why should the Queen take pity on her? Elizabeth Tudor was not known for her compassion towards lovers.

Gabriellen twisted the long rope of pearls which hung level with her waist as she waited in the Presence Chamber. The afternoon sun lit the long room through its many windows, dust motes hovering like insects along the shafts. The windows were shut against the chill air and the press of bodies was becoming oppressive. Everyone was restless, shuffling their papers and shifting their feet to stir up the dust and squash the dried herbs strewn amongst the rushes on the floor. The crushed scent of rosemary and violets mingled with the exotic perfumes worn by the courtiers and the fusty smell of perspiration. The drone of voices rose and fell around her like bees hovering around their hive. Whenever the inner door opened all voices hushed with expectancy as the court official announced the next supplicant. When the door closed behind the petitioner, those still waiting resumed their anguished chatter. The tension within the chamber was like a living animal, growing with each passing hour and the fear that another day would pass without admittance.

Mark and Gabriellen had been here for three hours. Not long by the standards of many but to her strained nerves it felt like three lifetimes. So much was at stake. She had rehearsed her speech a dozen times, but now her memory failed her. She turned panic-filled eyes upon Mark, who answered her with a compassionate smile.

'It will not be long now. Keep calm. You must not lose your temper. Elizabeth will try and intimidate you. You are her match only if you keep a level head.'

'I'm not afraid. It's the waiting I cannot bear. Patience is not one of my virtues.'

'Or mine neither.' He put his hand into the pouch hanging from his waist. Quickly withdrawing it, he took her hand and slipped a ring on to her third finger. At her gasp, he held her hand firmly. 'It is time we were betrothed.' The love in his eyes was so profound, it stilled her trepidation and replaced her fears by a feeling of confidence and warmth. 'This ring is the talisman of our future. It will bring you luck.'

'I need no ring,' she said softly. 'You are my good luck, Mark. You always were.' She touched the large square sapphire flanked by diamonds, her eyes growing misty as she looked up at him yet beyond, seeing the void her life would be without him. Her voice cracked. 'How blind I've been over the years. There has always been a bond between us, an affinity of body and mind. I love you, Mark. Whatever the Queen's judgement, she cannot take that away from us.'

He squeezed her hand, his face alight with pleasure, but as he was about to speak a harsh voice cut across his words.

'Mistress Angel, Her Majesty will see you now.' The court official had come upon them unexpectedly, his blank expression callously indifferent to the ordeal which faced them.

Mark raised her hand to his lips, the warmth of his kiss sustaining her, as he said, 'We must not keep the Queen waiting, my dear.'

He held out his arm for her to take. As she placed her hand upon the ruff of his wrist, she saw the sapphire on her finger glinting in the sunlight. It seemed to wink its assurance that all would be well. Her fluttering heartbeat calmed and she relaxed as Mark led her into the adjoining chamber.

She had expected the Queen to be sitting upon her throne beneath the canopy of state. Instead Elizabeth stood by the window with her back to them, looking out into the palace gardens. Gabriellen saw the wide expanse of black satin skirts and the diaphanous veil shaped like angels' wings about her shoulders over a vast lace pointed ruff. Every article of the Queen's clothing was exaggerated to the point of absurdity, and the weight of those huge padded sleeves and skirts must be immense. Gabriellen sank into a curtsey with a swish of silk. Still the Queen appeared not to notice their presence. Unable to rise without Her Majesty's permission, Gabriellen froze in that position, her legs beginning to tremble from the strain. Mark gave a discreet cough.

Elizabeth spun round to face them. With an imperious gesture of her hand, she indicated that Gabriellen should rise. The sunlight struck the Queen's face, which shocked Gabriellen with its ravaged appearance beneath the thick white powder. Her bright red wig accentuated the hard lines which were carved into those indomitable features. Two thin lines were painted upon her plucked brows, and her pale, almost lashless eyes were as heavily lidded as those of a bird of prey. All beauty was stripped from that harsh uncompromising face which was as grotesque as a gargoyle. Gabriellen was too accomplished an actress to allow any of her shock to show on her face. She stood erect, head proudly held high as Elizabeth's black eyes subjected her to a pitiless stare.

'It has been brought to my attention that you and not Esmond Angel wrote that seditious play *Boudicca*. That this was not the first time you duped the good people of England by using your father's name to cover your indecent and questionable activities.'

Gabriellen felt the colour drain from her face at the accusation. She drew a deep breath to conduct her heated defence. 'Men such as Marlowe, Shakespeare and my father are hailed as geniuses for their wit and skill in creating plays. Is a woman's capability, then, less than a man's?'

The Queen drummed on the windowsill with her long elegant fingers. Her carmined lips were thin with censure, but she did not interrupt. Emboldened, Gabriellen went on: 'I helped with many of my father's later plays. His sight was failing and he dictated them to me. It seemed so natural to suggest plots and characters, that gradually I found I was doing more and more. I can assure Your Majesty that the play *Boudicca* was meant as a tribute to your supremacy. No monarch has done more to bring England to greatness. I have nothing but admiration for the way you have kept the power of France and Spain at bay. Boudicca was a queen who would not bow to the legions of Rome. The play was a tribute to her valiant spirit, her unquenchable courage. I never meant for her death to be interpreted as weakness. She is one of the greatest heroines of our country. As the play says, it is she who is remembered, not the Roman Governor who finally defeated her.'

'So shall Essex be remembered, do you think?' Elizabeth surprised her by asking.

'Essex could not raise the army he needed,' Gabriellen said with sincerity. 'The people loved you more than him. There were no riots or recriminations at his death. His revolt was pitiful and pathetic. It will never take more than a line or two in the history books. The exploits of Your Majesty will fill volumes.'

'You have an agile tongue.' Elizabeth tapped her fan against a pannier of her gown. 'What then of your involvement with Jack Stoneham? He was party to Essex's schemes. Why should I believe this play was not seditious?'

Gabriellen resented the allusion. Her knuckles showed white as she balled her fists and fought to control her anger. 'There is not a line in my play which does not praise Boudicca. The Romans were our conquerors. They made slaves of the Britons. Boudicca would free her people. As you, Ma'am, have freed us from the yoke of Rome.'

A light flashed in those cold unremitting eyes, but there was no softening of the blank expression which masked Elizabeth's thoughts.

The Queen looked at Mark and then back to Gabriellen. 'You are accompanied by Mr Rowan, a much respected servant of ours. What of your paramour? Where is Jack Stoneham?'

Gabriellen felt the danger closing in. The Queen was linking her with Jack who had shown himself a traitor. What mercy could she expect? Pride made her lift her chin a fraction higher. 'Sir Jack Stoneham is no longer my protector, nor has he been for some time. We parted before Essex's rebellion. I saw him once afterwards. The night of the revolt, to be exact. He bitterly regretted his misalliance and planned to take ship, to serve Your Majesty as best he could against the Spanish.'

'You mean he has turned pirate!' Elizabeth snorted with disgust. 'If he sets foot in England, it will be to dangle at the end of a rope.'

Mark saw Gabriellen's shaking hands clutch at her pearls. Her eyes blazed, but to his relief she was managing to control her temper. He stepped forward. 'Your Majesty, Captain Stoneham's crimes are not the issue here. Mistress Angel has no further connection with him. Indeed, she has graciously agreed to become my wife.'

The Queen's eyes narrowed dangerously. 'You'll get scant pleasure from her if she is charged with treason.'

'I have faith in Your Majesty's justice,' he replied deferentially. 'Mistress Angel's crime was to write a play which she believed honoured you. It was her misfortune that it was staged on the very day you learned of Essex's intrigue with King James of Scotland. Mistress Angel took up her father's pen to help support the troupe who had become a family to her. Esmond Angel was proud to stage her work under his name. I have known Mistress Angel for many years. There is no greater patriot, or woman, who holds you in higher esteem.'

'Mr Rowan, that is enough.' Elizabeth fixed a withering glare upon him. 'You are enamoured of this creature and would say anything to save her.'

Elizabeth paced from the window to the throne, her steps purposeful as a man's. Gabriellen felt her heart sink. It was impossible not to be awed by her presence. This was the daughter of Henry VIII, a woman who would sell her soul to save England. It was in the tilt of her head and the proud bearing of her carriage. Elizabeth was England. Its law. Its sovereignty.

Mark faced the Queen when she sat down, but there was no humility in his lilting voice when he spoke. 'I have always been your loyal and devoted servant. It was my duty to rout your enemies and defuse their plots. Do you doubt my loyalty? I have nothing but contempt for those who serve you ill. I could never give my name to a woman if I believed she was a traitor.'

The Queen sat forward on her throne, her lips pursed with censure at his presumption. 'There have been several occasions when your diligence has ensured my safety, if not my life. Are you calling in the debt, Rowan?'

He stepped forward and knelt at the Queen's feet. 'There is no debt. Nor would I presume to ask anything of Your Majesty that is not by justice required. Mistress Angel is innocent of the charges, I would stake my life upon it.'

'Such passion does not please us, Rowan.' Elizabeth put out a hand and touched the curls on his head. 'Especially when it is directed towards another.' Her lips twisted into a grim smile as she removed her hand. 'Your loyalty, however, deserves some reward. I am sickened by so much

595

death. Take this woman away. Marry her. Confine her in Wales and let there be no more plays written.'

Mark bowed low, but as he straightened prompted: 'There is also the question of the house in Chichester. Property legally Mistress Angel's, but which another is laying claim to.'

The Queen's painted eyebrows shot up. 'Is not Mistress Angel base-born? She has no rights to her father's estate, whereas Charity Angel was his legal wife. I cannot countenance immorality amongst my people. Adultery is a sin. Bastards cannot inherit.'

Gabriellen flushed hotly and Mark seeing her angry colour, held up a hand to stay her outburst. He intervened quickly. 'If it please Your Majesty to reconsider the matter, the property originally belonged to Mistress Angel's uncle. He and his wife were childless and brought Mistress Angel up as their own daughter. Mr Otley's will states that the house was to pass to Esmond, to be held in trust until Gabriellen married. Mistress Charity Angel has never been to Chichester or met Mr Otley. It would be in breach of a dying man's wishes should a stranger inherit his house while a woman he thought of as a daughter for twelve years is put aside.'

'Is not Mistress Angel to live in Wales?' Elizabeth leaned back upon her throne, her tone harsh and imperious as she rapped out: 'What ties will she then have with a house in Sussex?'

Mark cast about in his mind to answer the Queen, realising that her argument was uncomfortably logical. 'It was the wish of Mr Otley that she inherit.' He paused and then went on, 'The ties of memory and affection for the only home she has known, and an aunt and uncle she dearly loved.'

'Christ's bones! Spare me the sentimentality.' Elizabeth held up her hands in a terse commanding gesture. 'The next I know, the Celt in you will be breaking into song.'

Gabriellen closed her eyes at the sarcasm and bowed her head in despair. Without warning the Queen's mood had veered. It was said she was jealous of all lovers. For the space of several heartbeats the only sound in the Presence Chamber was the drumming of the Queen's fingers on the arm of her throne. At any moment Gabriellen was certain the guards would be called and they would both be arrested.

The threat of the Tower loomed frighteningly close. Taking a quivering breath, she opened her eyes, words in defence of Mark forming in her mind. They vanished as she saw that he was smiling. Had shock robbed him of his wits?

Gabriellen looked at the Queen. The masked expression revealed nothing. Yet there was a glimmer in her eye which had not been there earlier.

Elizabeth gave a laugh, dry and crackling as autumn leaves. 'Your loyalty would be poorly rewarded if I refused you. Away with you, Rowan, and take your betrothed from my sight. Speak with Cecil as to this house. In truth, you put a small enough price upon saving my life.'

By mid-afternoon the next day Gabriellen and Mark arrived at the farm in Epsom. As they approached a large duck pond, they were met by shouts from Ambrose and Laurence. Exchanging an apprehensive glance with Mark, Gabriellen veered towards the water, suspicious that mischief was afoot. Sure enough, Laurence was standing at the pond's edge shouting at Ambrose who was waist high in the water, in pursuit of a duck with a broken wing.

'Ambrose, get out of there!' Gabriellen called.

'But the duck, Mama!' her son protested. 'His wing's broken. A fox will get him if he can't fly away. I can mend it and look after him until it's healed.'

'Not if you're in bed with lung fever, child,' she said sternly. 'That water must be near freezing at this time of year.' She turned an angry glare upon Laurence. 'You're old enough to have more sense. You should have stopped him, not encouraged him.'

'Stop him!' Laurence said in mock horror, his expression so like Esmond's that Gabriellen felt a painful tug around her heart. 'I wagered his share of the cinnamon cakes Agnes is baking against mine that he couldn't reach the duck.'

With a theatrical groan she turned to Mark. 'Do you realise just what trials you are inflicting upon yourself by taking on this Angelic brood?'

She could see Ambrose's lips chattering but he was within reach of the duck and with a last lunge caught it in his arms. There was an indignant quacking and both boy and duck were submerged under the water.

Gabriellen screamed. Mark leapt to the ground and ran into the pond to haul Ambrose out of the water, still clinging to the duck. He was grinning with triumph, unafraid and unrepentant, his face covered with mud and weed.

Mark waded ashore and deposited Ambrose at his mother's side. 'You've more hair than wit, boy, to put a duck's life above your own.' He took the duck from Ambrose's arms and examined the broken wing.

'Take off those clothes,' Gabriellen said, removing her cloak when she saw Ambrose's lips turn blue with cold. 'You will take a fever.'

He put a fist to his mouth to stop it from trembling. His eyes were overbright, but at nine he thought himself no longer a child and refused to cry. He pulled off his clothes and Mark threw him his cloak to use as a towel. The boy's teeth chattered in the March wind as he peeled off the muddy and weed-speckled hose.

'Laurence, take hold of the duck,' Mark ordered. 'And don't let it go. It could have cost Ambrose his life.'

Mark knelt at the boy's side, wrapping the cloak about the naked shivering form. 'It was foolhardy what you did, but commendable. Though don't let on to your mother that I said so.' As Mark spoke he continued to dry the boy. He lifted the first foot and his hand checked.

Gabriellen, seeing the movement, put out a protesting hand to forestall any comment. She knew what Mark had seen. Ambrose was extremely sensitive about the abnormality of his toes. She checked her words as Mark continued to stare down. He was too considerate a man to make a chance remark which would wound another. He resumed drying Ambrose's feet without speaking, but the look he threw back at her over his shoulder was one of wonderment.

'Run back to the house, lad,' he said finally. 'The exercise will warm you. Agnes will give you a hot drink.'

As Ambrose sped off, Mark took Gabriellen into his arms. 'The smallest toe on Ambrose's foot is the same length as the fourth one. It is an oddity many of my family possess. He's my son. Why did you not tell me?'

She stared deep into his eyes. 'I was never sure. He was born exactly nine months after I left Wales. Jack accepted him as his own. It was better that way. But in her heart a mother knows the father of her child. Why else do you think I called him Ambrose? Oh, Emrys Llewelyn, how can you ever forgive me?' Taking his hand she laid it against her waist, her dimple appearing as she smiled. 'And there's every indication that Ambrose is not the only child of mine you've sired. This little one will not be denied his Welsh birthright. Will he be named Llewelyn or Marcus after your father?'

'I become twice a father in one day.' Mark grinned his delight. 'You realise that Aphra will never let me forget this? For years she has nagged me to settle down.'

'And such a family you have inherited. There is Jacquetta and Sabine – also Laurence.'

'There is room enough for them all at Rowan Hall. I have no grudge against Jack's children.' His expression became serious. 'Will you miss London? Rowan Hall is remote.'

'I loved my time in Wales. Your home is a place of peace and contentment.'

'What of your life and the links you have with the players? That excitement was once important to you.'

She shook her head and took both his hands in hers. 'I shall never write again. It's you I want, Mark, not adventure.'

He kissed her with the sweetness which she would know for the rest of her days. When he drew back, he said softly: 'But you shall continue to write. Do not the Welsh love to weave tales? Even if it's just for the enjoyment of our children and grandchildren, your stories must be told. It is the legacy you give our children. There is no greater gift.'

More Historical Fiction from Headline:

The powerful novel of Ireland in the Elizabethan age

The Pirate Queen

DIANA NORMAN
author of Daughter of Lîr

When Elizabeth the First learns of the hereditary treasure of the O'Flaherty clan chieftains, she immediately lays claim to it; she is, after all, Queen of England and Ireland. But the key to the treasure lies in finding the missing grandchild of the pirate queen, Grace O'Malley.

Streetwise, light-fingered, Barbary Clampett, whose survival has been filched out of other people's pockets, is wrenched from the stews of London to be groomed as the long-lost heir. But Barbary has a secret...and the woman who eventually goes to Ireland on the Queen's treasure hunt has allegiance only to herself.

Caught up in the massacres, cruelty and beauty of Ireland, however, she is allowed no neutrality. Besides, she falls in love and becomes drawn into the last great rebellion led by Hugh O'Neill, Earl of Tyrone, and the realisation that the piracy of the indomitable Grace O'Malley is outweighed by the piracy of England's Queen Elizabeth...

THE PIRATE QUEEN is the powerful story of a woman and a country fighting for the freedom that is rightfully theirs, set against the vivid and colourful background of the Elizabethan age.

'A spirited and at times highly amusing account of a ghastly episode in Irish history, told from the female point of view' *The Times*

'Very powerful. Opens fresh windows on to "known" history. Filled with delectable, unforgettable characters, humorous, and sinewy (sometimes bawdy) prose. Strongly recommended' *Good Book Guide*

Also by Diana Norman from Headline
DAUGHTER OF LÎR -'Rich and entertaining' *The Times*
THE MORNING GIFT

FICTION/HISTORICAL   0 7472 3825 1

More Compelling Fiction from Headline:

GWEN KIRKWOOD

FAIRLYDEN

A family saga of life on the land in 19th-century Scotland

Matthew Cameron's death ends the Camerons' three-life lease of the fertile farmstead of Nethertannoch. But Sandy Logan is determined to secure the tenancy in his name so that he can keep his promise to the dying Matthew - that he will love and protect his daughter, the beautiful and vulnerable Mattie, who has been deaf since childhood.

But the laird has other plans. Events explode into violence and Sandy is forced to flee with Mattie. They find refuge in the rundown farm of Fairlyden, which is owned by Daniel Munro. Daniel, crippled by rheumatism, does not welcome strangers, but something about the pair of fugitives touches his heart and he lets them stay.

Slowly they bring the farm to prosperity; Mattie with her hens and her sure touch with the cows, and Sandy with his strength and knowledge of horse breeding. But Daniel is the illegitimate son of the late Earl of Strathtod and Fairlyden belongs to him only for his lifetime; without heirs it will return to the estate of the present Earl, who has always hated Daniel. So Daniel comes up with a scheme to thwart his half-brother - a scheme that includes Mattie, and will have far-reaching consequences down the years.

FICTION/SAGA   0 7472 3692 5

A selection of bestsellers from Headline

FICTION

STUDPOKER	John Francome	£4.99 □
DANGEROUS LADY	Martina Cole	£4.99 □
TIME OFF FROM GOOD BEHAVIOUR	Susan Sussman	£4.99 □
THE KEY TO MIDNIGHT	Dean Koontz	£4.99 □
LEGAL TENDER	Richard Smitten	£5.99 □
BLESSINGS AND SORROWS	Christine Thomas	£4.99 □
VAGABONDS	Josephine Cox	£4.99 □
DAUGHTER OF TINTAGEL	Fay Sampson	£5.99 □
HAPPY ENDINGS	Sally Quinn	£5.99 □
BLOOD GAMES	Richard Laymon	£4.99 □
EXCEPTIONAL CLEARANCE	William J Caunitz	£4.99 □
QUILLER BAMBOO	Adam Hall	£4.99 □

NON-FICTION

RICHARD BRANSON: The Inside Story	Mick Brown	£6.99 □
PLAYFAIR FOOTBALL ANNUAL 1992-93	Jack Rollin	£3.99 □
DEBRETT'S ETIQUETTE & MODERN MANNERS	Elsie Burch Donald	£7.99 □
PLAYFIELD NON-LEAGUE FOOTBALL ANNUAL 1992-93	Bruce Smith	£3.99 □

SCIENCE FICTION AND FANTASY

THE CINEVERSE CYCLE OMNIBUS	Craig Shaw Gardner	£5.99 □
BURYING THE SHADOW	Storm Constantine	£4.99 □
THE LOST PRINCE	Bridget Wood	£5.99 □
KING OF THE DEAD	R A MacAvoy	£4.50 □
THE ULTIMATE WEREWOLF	Byron Preiss	£4.99 □

All Headline books are available at your local bookshop or newsagent, or can be ordered direct from the publisher. Just tick the titles you want and fill in the form below. Prices and availability subject to change without notice.

Headline Book Publishing PLC, Cash Sales Department, PO Box 11, Falmouth, Cornwall, TR10 9EN, England.

Please enclose a cheque or postal order to the value of the cover price and allow the following for postage and packing:
UK & BFPO: £1.00 for the first book, 50p for the second book and 30p for each additional book ordered up to a maximum charge of £3.00.
OVERSEAS & EIRE: £2.00 for the first book, £1.00 for the second book and 50p for each additional book.

Name ....

Address ....

....